# About the Author

Born in Paris in 1947, Christian Jacq first visited Egypt when he was seventeen, went on to study Egyptology and archaeology at the Sorbonne, and is now one of the world's leading Egyptologists. He is the author of the internationally bestselling RAMSES and THE MYSTERIES OF OSIRIS series, and several other novels on Ancient Egypt. Christian Jacq lives in Switzerland.

ALSO BY CHRISTIAN JACQ

*The Ramses Series*
Volume 1: The Son of the Light
Volume 2: The Temple of a Million Years
Volume 3: The Battle of Kadesh
Volume 4: The Lady of Abu Simbel
Volume 5: Under the Western Acacia

*The Stone of Light Series*
Volume 1: Nefer the Silent
Volume 2: The Wise Woman
Volume 3: Paneb the Ardent
Volume 4: The Place of Truth

*The Queen of Freedom Trilogy*
Volume 1: The Empire of Darkness
Volume 2: The War of the Crowns
Volume 3: The Flaming Sword

*The Judge of Egypt Trilogy*
Volume 1: Beneath the Pyramid
Volume 2: Secrets of the Desert
Volume 3: Shadow of the Sphinx

*The Mysteries of Osiris Series*
Volume 1: The Tree of Life
Volume 2: The Conspiracy of Evil
Volume 3: The Way of Fire
Volume 4: The Great Secret

*The Vengeance of the Gods Series*
Volume 1: Manhunt
Volume 2: The Divine Worshipper

The Black Pharaoh
The Tutankhamun Affair
For the Love of Philae
Champollion the Egyptian
Master Hiram & King Solomon
The Living Wisdom of Ancient Egypt

*About the Translator*
Sue Dyson is a prolific author of both fiction and non-fiction, including
over thirty novels both contemporary and historical. She has also
translated a wide variety of French fiction.

# The Queen of Freedom Trilogy

*The Empire of Darkness*
*The War of the Crowns*
*The Flaming Sword*

## CHRISTIAN JACQ

*Translated by Sue Dyson*

**POCKET BOOKS**

London · New York · Sydney · Toronto
A CBS COMPANY

The Queen of Freedom Trilogy first published in Great Britain by Pocket Books, 2008
An imprint of Simon & Schuster UK Ltd

A CBS COMPANY

Copyright © XO Editions, 2008
English translation copyright © Sue Dyson, 2008

*The Empire of Darkness* first published in France by XO Editions under the title
*L'Empire des Ténèbres*, 2001
First published in Great Britain by Simon & Schuster UK Ltd, 2002
Copyright © XO Editions, 2001
English translation copyright © Sue Dyson, 2002

*The War of the Crowns* first published in France by XO Editions
under the title *La Guerre des Couronnes*, 2002
First published in Great Britain by Simon & Schuster UK Ltd, 2003
Copyright © XO Editions, 2002
English translation copyright © Sue Dyson, 2002

*The Flaming Sword* first published in France by XO Editions under the title
*L'Épée Flamboyante*, 2002
First published in Great Britain by Simon & Schuster UK Ltd, 2003
Copyright © XO Editions, 2002
English translation copyright © Sue Dyson, 2002

1 3 5 7 9 10 8 6 4 2

Simon & Schuster UK Ltd
1st Floor
222 Gray's Inn Road
London WC1X 8HB

www.simonsays.co.uk

Simon & Schuster Australia
Sydney

A CIP catalogue record for this book is available from the British Library

ISBN 978-1-84739-367-8

Typest by Ellipsis Books Limited, Glasgow
Printed and bound in Great Britain by CPI Cox & Wyman, Reading, RG1 8EX

# The Empire of Darkness

# AHHOTEP, QUEEN FREEDOM

Around 1690 BC, Egypt was under Hyksos domination. But one young Theban princess refused to bear the invader's yoke any longer. Her name was Ahhotep. With very little chance of victory, she set about awakening her fellow Egyptians' consciences. Her Egyptian name, *Ahhotep*, is made up of two words: *Ah*, the moon-god, who is sometimes aggressive and fearsome, and *Hotep*, which means 'peace', 'fullness', 'completion'. The name Ahhotep is therefore a positive programme for a reign; it can be translated as 'The Moon is Full' – in other words may heavenly power come at the end of darkness – or as 'War and Peace'.

Three men, three Thebans, three pharaohs mark the life of Ahhotep: her husband, Seqen-en-Ra, and their two sons, Kames and Ahmose. From the very start, the queen made great sacrifices to invest all her energies in the campaign of reconquest, vital to reunite the Two Lands of Upper and Lower Egypt.

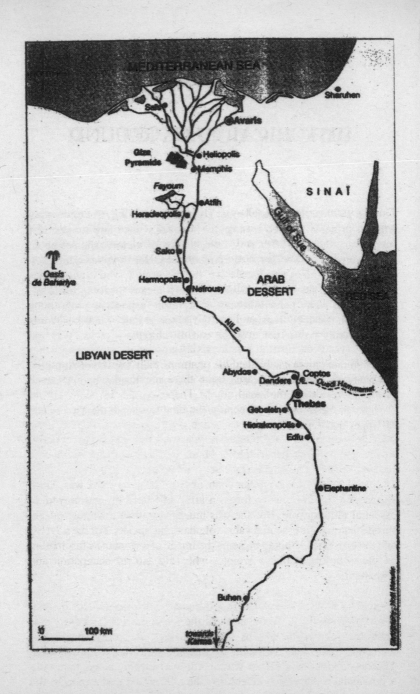

# HISTORICAL BACKGROUND

During its magnificent 3,000-year history, ancient Egypt experienced troubled periods. One of these marked the end of the Middle Kingdom, an era of peace, harmony and stability which began about 2060 BC.

Danger came from the north-east, in the eighteenth century BC, in the form of the Hyksos invasion.

Who were these Hyksos, called in Egyptian 'Hekau Khasut', 'Princes of Foreign Lands?' The debate continues, but it is certain that among them were Canaanites, Anatolians, Cyprians, Asians, Caucasians and others. This was the first invasion to strike Egypt.

The Hyksos occupation was long (lasting over a century) and very harsh. The invaders established the centre of their military and trading empire in the Delta, at Avaris. Soon there remained only one small island of resistance: the small city of Thebes.

Teti the Small became queen on the death of her husband, the last pharaoh to reign at Thebes before the occupation. She needed great courage to maintain a semblance of independence in her province. But salvation came from her daughter, Ahhotep, who was under the moon's protection and determined to resist.

Was Ahhotep the Egyptian Joan of Arc? In a way she was, since she incited the Thebans to form an army of liberation and played an essential military role. But she was much more than a warrior queen, for she restored the essential values of pharaonic society. For the novelist and the historian, Ahhotep presents the image of a woman as fascinating as she is unforgettable; a woman who said 'no' to occupation and barbarism.

Around 1730 BC, Thebes was the last small island in which Egyptian civilization survived. To the north of the town, the whole country was under the yoke of the Hyksos and their leader, the tyrant Apophis. To the south, there were the Nubians, allies of the Hyksos. Thebes – the Theban province was called Waset, '(divine) Power' – was then only a provincial town which celebrated the cult of the god Amon in the temple at Karnak (it was very modest compared to the immense temple-city that tourists visit today). As yet there was only one temple, built by Senusret I (XIIth dynasty). This temple no longer exists, for the pharaohs of the New Kingdom re-used the ancient blocks of stone as symbolic foundations for their own monuments. But digs have enabled archaeologists to find the separate parts of a shrine called 'the white temple of Senusret I', which has been reconstructed and shows the beauty of buildings of the time.

It was the horse, an animal hitherto unknown in Egypt, that gave the Hyksos their military superiority. Its role was a vital one: harnessed in pairs to a chariot, horses could carry four soldiers into battle, one driving the vehicle, the other three using bows or throwing bronze-headed spears. The Egyptians in turn adopted this 'weapon', as was seen many generations later at the battle of Kadesh, won by Ramses II.

The battle fought by Queen Ahhotep with her husband, Pharaoh Seqen, against the Hyksos was a ruthless one. The most moving testimony that has come down to us is the disfigured mummy of the young Seqen, known as Seqen-en-Ra, 'Valiant One of the Divine Light', whose face and head carry terrible wounds. The embalmers did not remove these signs, as they wished to preserve the memory of the fierce battle in which the heroic king was killed. At Ahhotep's side, he was the first pharaoh to resist the Hyksos occupation, because he wanted to see Egypt free again and reunified.

## KEY DATES

Ancient era (dynasties I and II) *c*. 3150–2690 BC

Old Kingdom (dynasties III–VI) *c*. 2690–2180 BC
The time of the great pyramids. The most famous pharaohs are Sneferu, Djoser and Khufu.

First intermediate period (dynasties IX–XI) *c*. 2180–2060 BC

Middle Kingdom (dynasties XI–XII) *c*. 2060–1785 BC Rule of the Amenemhat and Senusret dynasties.

Second intermediate period (dynasties XIII–XVII) *c*. 1785–1570 BC
Hyksos invasion and occupation.

New Kingdom (dynasties XVII–XX) *c*. 1570–1070 BC Among the most famous pharaohs are Hatshepsut, Akhenaton, Seti I and Ramses II.

Third intermediate period (dynasties XXI–XXV) *c*. 1070–672 BC

Low Era (dynasties XXV–XXX) 762–332 BC

Greco-Roman period 332 BC–AD 395
This includes Alexander the Great's conquest and the rule of the Ptolemies (including Cleopatra), then that of the Roman emperors.

Thebes, the last free place on Egyptian soil, 1690 BC

# 1

Ahhotep had not moved for more than half an hour. When she saw the last guard walk past the main gate of the palace, the beautiful brown-haired girl took advantage of the few minutes before the guard was relieved, and scurried into a thicket of tamarisks, where she hid until nightfall.

Ahhotep was the eighteen-year-old daughter of Queen Teti the Small, and she bore a strange name which could be translated as 'The Moon is Full', 'The Moon Has Been Appeased', or even as 'War and Peace' for, according to the sages, the moon was a warrior-god embodying the mystery of death and resurrection.

War ... It was the only way to rid the land of the Hyksos who controlled it all – with the exception of Thebes, the sacred city of the god Amon. Thanks to his protection, the Temple of Karnak and the town nearby had been spared by the barbarians, but for how much longer?

The Hyksos had flooded in through the Delta, forty years before, like a mighty swarm of locusts. Asians, Arabs, Canaanites, Syrians, Scythians, Minoans, Cyprians, Persians, Anatolians and yet more races, all armed to the teeth. They used strange four-legged creatures called horses, which had large heads and were bigger and faster than donkeys. The horses drew wheeled vehicles which moved incredibly swiftly, and which had enabled the attackers to massacre Pharaoh's soldiers.

Ahhotep cursed the softness and cowardice of the feeble Theban army. True, it could not hope to measure up to the large, powerful forces of occupation, with their terrifying new weapons; but failure to act would result in annihilation. When Apophis, the Hyksos's supreme commander, eventually decided to raze Thebes to the ground, the Egyptian soldiers would run away, and the population would be massacred, with the exception of pretty women, who would be used by the brutish soldiers for their pleasure, and sturdy children, who would be sent into slavery. The last free men on Egyptian soil would bow their heads, incapable of doing anything.

What was left of the wondrous realm of the pyramid-builders? A province caught between the occupying power in the North and its Nubian allies in the South, a temple built by Senusret I and left abandoned, and a palace which now looked anything but royal.

Without Teti the Small's resolution, even the House of the Queen would have been destroyed, and the Thebans, like all other Egyptians, would have become servants of the Hyksos. But, trapped in her isolation, Teti was beginning to weaken, and the supporters of Theban independence saw their numbers fall every day.

If there was only one rebel left, that person would be Ahhotep. The young girl had no fear of battle, suffering or death. Even with a dagger at her throat, she would still refuse to submit to the Hyksos yoke.

The courtiers mocked her as mad, regarding her as amusing rather than dangerous. They were wrong. Today was the start of the war for freedom. With an eighteen-year-old rebel as its only soldier, and a well-sharpened flint knife as its only weapon.

The guard had been changed, and Thebes was asleep. It was a long time since any banquets had been held or music played in the reception hall, with its faded paintings. And there was no longer a pharaoh to take his seat upon a desperately empty throne.

Ahhotep wanted to forget this heart-rending sight, and she ran towards the landing-stage. At the quay lay a half-derelict cargo-barge, once used to transport blocks of stone from the quarries, which the Hyksos had closed down, and a few small sailing-boats.

Among them was one small boat in good condition. This was the means of transport Ahhotep planned to use to leave the Theban enclave. She jumped nimbly down into the boat and seized the oars. As she was heading north, the current would be in her favour.

No one travelled on the river at night, for there were many dangers: hippopotamus, crocodiles, whirlpools . . . but Ahhotep had no choice. 'And when we have no choice,' she often declared loudly, 'we are free.'

Determinedly, the princess began to row.

Since no one could tell her precisely where the free area ended and Hyksos-occupied territory began, she would find out for herself. The queen's frightened advisers assumed that the Hyksos had made great progress since Apophis's seizure of power – and Apophis's reputation for cruelty exceeded his predecessors'. They were urging Teti to leave Thebes without delay.

But where could she live in safety?

As far as Ahhotep was concerned, the only refuge was in attack. The first skirmish would take place on the demarcation line and, if necessary, the princess herself would command the tattered remnants of the Egyptian army.

In the past forty years, thousands of her compatriots had been massacred. The Hyksos believed they could act with complete impunity and continue their reign of terror over the Two Lands of Upper and Lower Egypt. Ahhotep would soon show them that they were very wrong.

Never had an Egyptian princess, accustomed to the luxury of court, been forced to wield heavy oars like this, at the risk of spoiling her hands. But the survival of the country was at stake, and the pretty brunette thought only of the goal she must attain.

The boat bumped hard against something and almost capsized, but by great good luck it righted itself. Ahhotep glimpsed a dark form moving away, its powerful tail thrashing in water. She had disturbed a crocodile.

Refusing to be afraid, Ahhotep rowed on. Thanks to her excellent eyesight and the light of the full moon, she avoided the wreckage of a boat and a grassy islet where pelicans were sleeping. On the banks the peasants' houses stood abandoned. Fearing that the invaders were coming, the people had taken refuge in Thebes.

Not far away, she saw smoke.

Ahhotep slowed her pace, steered the boat towards the bank and hid it in a papyrus thicket, disturbing a cloud of sleeping egrets. Fearing that their cries might give her away, she waited some time before moving. When she eventually climbed up the sloping bank, she found herself in an abandoned field.

Was the smoke coming from a burning farm or from a Hyksos camp? Whichever the case, the enemy was very close.

'Well, well, little girl,' barked an aggressive voice, 'what are you doing here?'

Without a moment's hesitation, Ahhotep swing round and, brandishing her flint knife in her right hand, hurled herself at the enemy.

## 2

'Kill it,' ordered Apophis.

The young donkey saw its death approaching. Its large, soft eyes were filled with incomprehension. Why kill me? it thought. Since the age of six-months, it had constantly carried loads so heavy that they had hollowed its back. It had guided its companions in misfortune along every track and had never once lost its way. It had always obeyed orders without hesitation. But its owner, a merchant from the Arabian peninsula who had been in the Hyksos's service, had just died of a blood clot, and it was the invaders' custom to sacrifice a caravan-leader's best donkeys and throw their remains into a makeshift grave.

Indifferent to the slaughter, Apophis climbed slowly up the steps leading to his fortified palace. It stood at the heart of the citadel that dominated his capital, Avaris, which had been built in a fertile area of the north-eastern Delta.

Apophis, supreme commander of the Hyksos, was a tall fifty-year-old with a prominent nose, flaccid cheeks, a potbelly and thick legs. His manner was icy and his voice harsh, and the mere sight of him was enough to inspire fear. People forgot his ugliness and spoke of his unfathomable gaze, which could catch a man unawares and enter his soul like the blade of a dagger. It was impossible to know what he was thinking, this man who had terrorized Egypt for twenty years.

Whenever he thought of the Hyksos invasion, Apophis felt a surge of pride. Had it not put an end to thirteen centuries of Egyptian independence? Chariots and horses, then unknown to the pharaoh's army, had caused panic and made the conquest easy and swift, all the more so since many collaborators, like the Canaanites, had been happy to resort to treachery in order to win the conquerors' favour.

Although well paid, Pharaoh's hired mercenaries had turned their weapons against the Egyptian footsoldiers, who had thus been attacked

from within as well as without. And there were too few forts in the
Delta to stem the flood of invaders.

'A fine journey, my lord,' exclaimed Khamudi, Apophis's most
trusted henchman, bowing low.

Khamudi had a moon face, jet-black hair plastered to his round
head, slightly slanting eyes, plump hands and feet, and a heavy frame;
he looked much older than his thirty years. He hid his aggressive nature
beneath a feigned unctuousness, but everyone knew he would not
hesitate to kill anyone who got in his way.

'I trust you have put a stop to those regrettable incidents?'

'Oh yes, my lord,' confirmed Khamudi with a broad smile. 'No
more peasants will dare rebel, you can be certain of that.'

Apophis never smiled. The only time his face brightened was when
he witnessed the death-throes of an adversary who had been insane
enough to oppose Hyksos domination.

In this instance, a small village close to the new capital had recently
protested against the unbearable burden of taxation. Khamudi had
immediately unleashed his dogs of war, Cyprian pirates whom the
Hyksos had recruited from Egyptian prisons. Despite orders, they had
not spared even the children. When they left, nothing remained of the
village they had attacked.

'What about the harvests?' asked Apophis.

Khamudi's face fell. 'According to first reports, they aren't very good.'

Cold anger filled Apophis's eyes. 'Do you mean they'll be worse
than last year's?'

'I fear so, my lord.'

'The peasants are mocking us.'

'I'll have a few villages burnt. Then they'll realize that—'

'No,' interrupted Apophis. 'It's pointless killing slaves whose labour
may be useful. We must find another solution.'

'Believe me, they're frightened.'

'Perhaps too frightened.'

Khamudi was dismayed.

Apophis began climbing again; Khamudi followed, keeping one
step behind his master.

'Fear is a good counsellor,' Apophis went on, 'but dread can paralyse.
And we must have more wheat and barley to feed our officials and
our soldiers.'

'None of them will consent to work in the fields.'

'I don't need to be reminded of that.'

Khamudi bit his lip. A lover of food, good wines and voluptuous
women, he sometimes had a tendency to talk too much.

'We have conquered Egypt,' Apophis reminded him, 'and that

miserable Theban enclave, populated by cowards and old men, is certainly not going to pose a threat to us.'

'I was about to suggest that you destroy it without delay.'

'That would be a mistake, my friend, a grave mistake.'

'I don't understand.'

Soldiers armed with spears bowed as the two men passed by. Heading along a low-ceilinged, narrow passageway lit by torches, they reached a small room which had been constructed at the very centre of the fortress. Apophis was certain that no one would overhear them here.

He sat down on a low, plain chair made of sycamore wood. Khamudi remained standing.

Apophis said, 'Not all our allies are reliable. I am counting on you, my efficient and devoted friend, to put our own house in order.'

'Have no fear, my lord.'

'Use any means you like – yes, you heard me correctly: any. Whatever the circumstances, I shall approve and support your actions. The only thing that matters to me is the result. I do not wish to hear even one more dissenting voice in the Hyksos coalition.'

Khamudi almost drooled with delight. Those who had dared criticize him, even in their thoughts, had just been condemned to death.

'We still have a great deal of work to do to erase the remaining traces of the pharaoh's former regime,' Apophis continued. 'We must show the people of Egypt that the Hyksos revolution is all-powerful, and can never be reversed.'

'Then Thebes must die.'

'Of course, but first it must unwittingly serve my ends. The key to total victory is collaboration. Traitors helped us invade Egypt, and other traitors will help us to bring her to heel. Let us allow the last rebels to believe that Thebes represents a real hope, while insinuating a worm into the fruit.'

'The peasants . . .'

'If they harbour hopes of liberation, however distant, they will work with renewed ardour, little knowing that not one ear of corn will reach the rebels. And you, my friend, must demonstrate your skill in the art of lying and disinformation. Organize false networks of opponents, and then arrest a few members so that no doubts remain, and whip up the yokels' fervour.'

'My lord, I shall be obliged to kill a few of our own officers.'

'Concentrate on the Canaanites – they're a little too noisy for my taste.'

'As you wish, my lord.'

'Khamudi' – Apophis's tone made his henchman shiver – 'you're the only person who knows my real intentions. Make sure you don't forget that.'

'It is an immense privilege, and I shall prove myself worthy of it, my lord.'

## 3

Teti the Small was beside herself with worry, for there was no denying the facts: Ahhotep had vanished without trace. The headstrong girl was neither in her bedchamber nor in the library, where she spent hours reading stories written during the glorious Middle Kingdom period. Nor yet was she in the garden, where she loved to play with her enormous dog, Laughter, a half-wild creature which obeyed no one but her. In her absence, the guards had tethered the huge animal to the trunk of a sycamore tree.

'But, Qaris, you must know where she has gone.'

Qaris, the queen's steward, was the very soul of politeness, a plump, round-cheeked fellow who kept calm in all circumstances. He had taken on the difficult, if not impossible, task of maintaining some semblance of comfort in the royal palace at Thebes, which seemed destined for rapid decay.

'Alas, Majesty, I do not.'

'I am sure she has confided in you and you do not wish to betray her.'

'Truly I know nothing, Majesty. The guards have been informed.'

'The guards! A band of cowards who will die of fear before the Hyksos even arrive.'

Qaris could not deny this. He said, 'I have also alerted the army.'

Teti sighed. 'Does it still exist?'

'Majesty . . .'

'Attend to lunch, Qaris. Let us continue to pretend to live like a royal court.'

Shoulders bowed, the steward went off to attend to his duties. He had long since given up trying to comfort the queen with fine words he did not believe himself.

Teti was tired. She went to the throne chamber, which had been hastily created forty years earlier, when the court had fled the Memphis region and taken refuge in the small insignificant town of Thebes, 'the Iunu of the South.'

On the death of her husband, a pharaoh who had lacked true power, Teti had chosen not to be crowned as his successor. What was the use of bestowing inflated titles upon herself? That would only have attracted the anger of the Hyksos, who at present were too busy bleeding the country dry to crush wretched little Thebes beneath their heel.

The queen's strategy had worked. The invaders had forgotten the sacred city of Amon, convinced that it was peopled only by harmless old priests celebrating outmoded cults. And that was indeed the message Teti wished to send to the new capital, Avaris, in the hope that the Hyksos would leave the last free Egyptians to die in peace.

What else could she have done? The Theban army was nothing but an incompetent, ill-armed rabble. The soldiers' training amounted to grotesque parades which no longer even entertained the children. Experienced officers had given up hope, and limited themselves to maintaining the fabric of their barracks.

When the Hyksos eventually attacked, as they must surely do, both soldiers and guards would lay down their arms and try to pass as civilians in order to escape the ensuing massacre. And the most senior general, an old man in failing health, would be incapable of maintaining even a semblance of discipline among his troops.

From time to time, Teti convened the ghostly relic of a council, at which people spoke without laughing of a 'Theban kingdom'. For in theory Thebes still governed a few ruined provinces, each of which retained a governor and a scribe whose task was to proclaim the pharaoh's decrees. But no one believed in this masquerade any more. At the first sign of a threat from the Hyksos, all the governors would declare that they did not support Thebes in any way and that its queen was a dissident who should be severely punished.

Teti was surrounded by people who were insignificant, incompetent or corrupt. She had not even appointed a tjaty, since he would not have had the power to do anything. The only official posts remaining were those of the ministers for agriculture and finance, which were held by elderly courtiers who provided their dispirited staff with directionless leadership.

Loyalty had disappeared, and people thought only of themselves. By some miracle, the Thebans had agreed to retain the royal family, albeit in greatly reduced form, as if they were reluctant to forget the past. Thanks to Qaris's tireless efforts, Teti, Ahhotep and those close to them did not go hungry, even if the food put before them would have seemed pitiful to the monarchs of glorious ages gone by. Each day, the queen wept. Shut up in her paltry palace, which seemed more and more like a prison, she lived on memories and dreams, in which the future had no place.

Teti bowed before the empty throne, which no pharaoh would ever occupy again. Horus, the falcon of heaven, had flown away, never to return to the Earth from his celestial paradise. The happiness of the Two Lands, symbolized by the union of the plants of North and South, was no more than a mirage.

Although the queen hid her despair behind a mask of carefully applied face-paint – and it was scarce now – she had already thought several times of killing herself. What use was a queen without a crown, helpless in the face of a barbarian revolution?

The only thing that gave her the courage to go on living was gazing up at the stars. In them shone the immortal souls of reborn kings, who trod the path of righteousness for all time, beyond the reach of doubts and despair. And so Teti carried on her obscure existence as the last Queen of Egypt.

Qaris's discreet cough broke into her thoughts. 'Majesty,' he said. 'What is it?'

His voice unsteady, he said, 'The guards are asking to speak to you.'

'Can you not deal with it?'

'Their commander will speak only to you.'

'Very well. Show him into the audience chamber.'

Qaris's gaze was fixed on the empty throne. 'Majesty, were you thinking of . . . ?'

Teti smiled sadly. 'Of course not.'

'If we only had a pharaoh again . . .'

'Banish that thought from your mind, Qaris.'

Slowly, the queen closed the door of the throne chamber. From now on it would be left to its silence.

'If you wish, Majesty, I will have the floors cleaned and try to brighten up the paintings,' suggested Qaris.

'That will not be necessary.'

The queen went to her bedchamber to check her appearance in a bronze mirror, and put on a fine gold crown which other Great Royal Wives had worn before her. (Her last woman of the bedchamber had tried to steal it, but Teti had done no more than dismiss her.) The queen of the Theban enclave must continue to look like a queen. Fortunately, she still had a few dresses worthy of her rank and she took great care of them, for presenting a truly regal appearance was the one thing that sill made an impression on the forces of law and persuaded them that a governing authority still existed, however limited it might be.

Today, she chose a pink linen gown and golden sandals. As she put them on, for a moment the queen imagined that her province was a real country and that she was going to address a real representative of the law.

*

Surprised by the queen's noble bearing, the guard commander was silent for a few seconds. Then he bowed low and said, 'Majesty.'

'What is it, Commander?'

'It is a serious matter, Majesty, very serious.'

'Does it concern the safety of Thebes?'

'I fear so. Your daughter . . .'

The queen paled. 'Have you found her?'

'Not I personally. It was a border guard.'

'Is she . . . alive?'

'Oh yes, Majesty – no one could be more so! As for the guard, the princess wounded him in the arm with her knife.'

'Her knife? Are you mad?'

'The report is quite clear, Majesty. Princess Ahhotep tried to kill the guard who arrested her. She was so wild that he had to call for reinforcements to control her.'

Teti was struck by a terrible thought. 'Was she . . . harmed?'

'No, Majesty, for she identified herself immediately. At first the guards did not believe her, but her vehemence shook them. They were afraid of making a mistake, so they decided to tie her up and bring her to me.'

'Then this ridiculous matter is now closed.'

The commander met her eye. 'I fear not, Majesty.'

'What do you mean?'

'We cannot consider this incident a simple altercation.'

'Why not?'

'Because it is clear that the princess was leaving Theban territory to join the Hyksos.'

'How dare you!'

'The guards and I accuse Princess Ahhotep of treason. Given her rank an emergency court must be convened as a matter of urgency.'

'Do you realize that—'

'She will be condemned to death,' said the commander with relish. 'What could be more appropriate? If we do not make an example of her, there will be chaos.'

Teti swayed. 'No, it's impossible. You must be mistaken.'

'Facts are facts, Majesty.'

'I wish to see my daughter.'

'The interrogation was carried out properly, Majesty, I assure you.'

'Has Ahhotep confessed?'

'We will have her confession soon.'

Teti the Small drew herself up to her full height. 'I am the Queen of Thebes, and I demand to see my daughter immediately.'

# 4

The contrast between the two women was striking. Teti the Small was like a precious statuette, so slender she looked as though she might break; Ahhotep was tall, majestic, her hair hanging loose, her green eyes flashing with anger. They were equally beautiful, but had nothing else in common save the fact that they were both members of the royal family.

And the fact that they were being watched with cruel amusement by the guard commander and his four men, who held the princess bound and gagged. Teti knew she was embarking upon a decisive battle. If she lost, those who favoured collaboration with the Hyksos would strip her of her few remaining powers and deliver up the city of Amon to the invader.

'Release my daughter!' ordered the queen.

'She is dangerous, Majesty,' said the commander. 'We cannot take any risks.'

'I gave you an order,' she reminded him coldly.

The officer hesitated. He could sweep away this frail, defenceless creature with one swipe of his hand, and seize the palace's last few riches. But to take power that way would provoke hostility from both soldiers and priests, and no one would emerge victorious from the ensuing conflict.

'Let us be cautious, Majesty, and just remove the gag.'

Two guards untied the strip of coarse linen.

'Are you hurt, Ahhotep?' her mother asked.

'Only by these idiots' stupidity. It took five of them to overcome me – what fighters!'

'They accuse you of trying to escape and of treason.'

Everyone was expecting an explosion of anger, but the young woman remained strangely calm. She stared at each of the guards in turn, and each took a step backwards.

'Who,' said Ahhotep, 'dares tell such a lie?'

'You cannot deny that you were trying to escape,' said the commander defensively.

'Are these men really border guards?'

'Yes, my lady.'

'I was arrested at Mount of the Quails, was I not?'

'Indeed, but—'

'Is the border really that close to Thebes?'

'Of course not!'

'Then kindly explain why your guards were there, and why they had lit a fire.'

One of the men could not hold his tongue. 'We were there on our commander's orders – we're not responsible for anything.'

'And what were those orders?' asked Ahhotep angrily.

'Say nothing, you fools!' hissed the commander.

'You looted and burned a farm, didn't you? Instead of doing your duty and guarding the forward positions, you took advantage of your uniforms to rob unfortunate people who had taken refuge in the free area.'

The guards huddled together; their commander unsheathed his short-sword.

'Surely you aren't afraid of two women,' sneered Ahhotep.

There was no answer.

'You are the one who is guilty of treason,' she went on, 'and the queen demands that you bow down before her.'

Teti the Small gazed disdainfully at the accused man. 'Put up your sword and prostrate yourself before me.'

He burst out laughing. 'You are nothing now, Majesty, and your daughter's hands are bound. You should thank me for offering you a quick death.'

A menacing growl drew everyone's attention. Wheeling round, the ruffian saw Ahhotep's huge dog. Laughter. He raised his sword, but the attack was so swift that he had no time to use it. The dog sank its teeth into its victim's arm, and the man roared with pain.

'Untie me,' ordered Ahhotep, and the guards hastily obeyed.

Ahhotep stroked her dog, which looked up at her with gentleness and a satisfied expression, as if extremely proud of its latest exploit.

'How did that creature manage to get free?' whined the wounded man.

'A court shall indeed be convened urgently,' the princess informed him, 'but it will sit in judgement on you, a traitor who dared raise his hand against his queen and threaten her with death.'

The commander sobbed, 'You must forgive me. I didn't wish Her Majesty any harm.'

'A coward as well as a traitor,' said Ahhotep with contempt. 'Guards, throw this vermin in prison.'

Only too glad to be let off so lightly, the guards did not need to be told twice.

Tongue lolling out, Laughter stood up on his hind legs and put his enormous front paws on the princess's shoulders.

'So you were tied up and yet managed to free yourself, did you?'

The dog was incurably honest, and Ahhotep saw in his eyes that he had had some vital help.

'I shall solve this problem,' she promised.

'Ahhotep,' whispered Teti.

Seeing that her mother was on the point of collapse, the princess hurried to her and helped her to a chair

'So much violence,' said Teti, 'even here, in my palace. I no longer have the strength to bear such horrors.'

'Of course you have. You ought to rejoice.'

'Rejoice? Why?'

'Because the commander made such a huge mistake. That useless creature has at last shown you just what he's capable of. Replace him as soon as possible.'

Teti began to see her daughter in a fresh light. Although Ahhotep was already a woman, and a very attractive one at that, up to now the queen had regarded her as an undisciplined child, who thought only of escaping into her own imagination so as to forget her country's death-agonies.

'Ahhotep, I'm so tired.'

'Majesty, you have neither the right nor the time to be tired. It is only because of you that Egypt survives. If you give up, the enemy will have defeated us without even fighting.'

How sweet it would be to close my eyes for ever, thought the queen. But she knew her daughter was right. Aloud, she said, 'Do you really think we have a chance of defeating an enemy like the Hyksos?'

'Yes, if we really want to.'

Teti gazed at her thoughtfully for a moment, then said, 'Why did you venture so far from the place?'

'To find out the precise location of the border of what we dare to call 'the Theban kingdom'. But I failed, so I shall have to try again.'

'It's too dangerous.'

'But it's vital, Majesty. We cannot organize resistance if we don't know the enemy's positions.'

Teti took off her crown and laid it on her knees. 'The situation is desperate, Ahhotep. We have neither a pharaoh nor an army, and our only chance of survival is to persuade the Hyksos that Thebes is just a small town populated by harmless old men who spend their time praying to dead gods.'

'That will do excellently,' declared the princess. 'As long as the invaders regard us as utterly negligible, they won't attack us.'

'But we *are* negligible,' Teti sighed. 'May the sky-goddess permit us to die here, on our own land, in the illusion of freedom.'

'No.'

The queen stared at her daughter in astonishment.

'I will not accept as inevitable an outcome that is nothing of the kind,' Ahhotep continued passionately. 'If Amon has preserved Thebes's independence, it must surely be because he has a mission for his city. If we hide ourselves away, quaking with fear, we shall close our ears and no longer hear his voice.'

'Not a single man will have the courage to fight the Hyksos,' said Teti.

'Then the women shall do it.'

'Have you taken leave of your senses?'

'Mother, you are the earthly representative of Ma'at, are you not?'

The queen smiled faintly. Ma'at, goddess of harmony, righteousness and justice; Ma'at, depicted as a woman crowned with the rectrix, the feather that enabled birds to steer their flight; Ma'at, the foundation upon which the pharaohs had built both their civilization and the statues of the reborn, whose mouths, eyes and ears were opened by the priests.

'Even Thebes is no longer fit to welcome Ma'at,' lamented Teti.

'Of course it is, for you are the queen and Ma'at is made flesh in the office you fulfil.'

'That is nothing but a dream now, Ahhotep, a distant dream which has almost faded away.'

'Ma'at is nourished not by dreams but by reality,' said Ahhotep firmly. 'That is why we must reconquer our land and give it back to her.' She knelt before the queen. 'Majesty, I have taken up arms. All I have is a flint knife, but that is not such a bad start. If handled well, it is very effective.'

'Ahhotep! Surely you aren't thinking of fighting?'

'I have just done so, Majesty, and I shall do so again.'

'You're a young woman, not a soldier.'

'And where are they, those valiant soldiers of ours? If no one jolts them out of their stupor, they will sleep on for ever. It is our task to awaken them.'

Teti closed her eyes. 'It is insane, my dear daughter. You must forget these mad thoughts.'

The princess got to her feet. 'They are my only reason for living.'

'Is your determination really so strong?'

'It is as strong as granite.'

The queen sighed again. 'In that case, I shall help you with every last shred of my strength.'

## 5

Ten peasants were trudging slowly through the marshes, not far from the Hyksos's new capital. They were long-haired and unshaven, and dressed only in kilts made from reeds. They led four fat oxen towards a small island where juicy galengales grew.

Their leader, a man with a big, bushy moustache, growled to a straggler, 'Faster.'

'Haven't you had enough of playing the slave-master?'

'Take a look around you,' advised a third fellow, who had plastered himself with mud to guard against mosquitoes. 'It's a beautiful day, with a clear sky and a light northerly breeze. Why are you so bad-tempered?'

'Because the Hyksos have taken my land,' replied Moustache.

'Yes, but a man can get used to anything in time. Looking after oxen isn't so bad.'

'If you aren't free, everything is bad.'

Moustache thought of the hours he had spent irrigating his land, looking after his tools, sowing, harvesting, arguing with scribes at the Finance secretariat to get his taxes lowered – all that toil wasted. And then there was the struggle against nature, which could be generous one moment and merciless the next. He bemoaned his lot constantly, and dreaded what the future might hold in store for him.

Not content with having ruined him, the Hyksos had forced him to become leader of this miserable band of ox-herds, who habitually grazed their charges in an area which was often flooded. Quarrels were frequent, and the atmosphere oppressive.

'We're going to have grilled fish to eat,' announced a plump-cheeked fellow, licking his lips. 'I caught it before dawn, and we're not going to tell the officer.'

Each morning and evening, Hyksos soldiers counted the oxen. In exchange for their toil, the herdsmen were allowed just one spelt flatcake, some onions and – once a week – some dried fish, which was often inedible.

'If they see the smoke, they'll beat us,' said another man worriedly.

Plump-Cheeks shook his head. 'We're too deep into the marshes for them to spot it.'

Everyone's mouth watered at the thought of the feast.

'Watch out, all of you! There's someone on the little island.'

A strange, turbaned man with a large black beard was sitting on a papyrus mat, roasting a fish.

'He's an odd-looking fellow,' said Moustache.

'I bet he's an evil marsh-spirit. Let's get out of here.'

'No, let's go and take over his fire,' advised Plump-Cheeks. 'He won't stand a chance against all of us.'

As the oxen and herdsmen approached, the stranger stood up slowly and turned to face them.

'I tell you, we should run away,' said one of the ox-herds. 'He's not human,' and in panic he turned to flee.

But the stranger pulled out a slingshot and began to brandish it, whirling it round his head at an incredible speed. A stone flew out of it and struck the man on the back of the neck. He instantly collapsed into the murky water and would have drowned if Moustache hadn't dragged him out by the hair.

'Come here, friends,' said the stranger. 'You have nothing to fear.'

The ox-herds, scared to death as they were, found this difficult to believe. But Plump-Cheeks decided to obey, and his comrades followed suit.

'Don't forget your oxen,' their host reminded them with an ironic smile.

One of the animals was tired; it bellowed and refused to go any further. However, a few blows on its back with a stick soon changed its mind.

One by one, the peasants clambered up on to the little island. The Oxen shook themselves and were at last able to graze.

'Who is your leader?' asked the bearded man.

'He is,' replied Plump-Cheeks, pointing at Moustache. 'And who are you?'

'You may call me "Afghan".'

The peasants exchanged looks. None of them knew the word.

'What's an Afghan?' asked Plump-Cheeks.

The stranger reached into the pocket of his brown tunic and took out a blue stone. When he held it out to them, the ox-herds saw that it contained flecks of what looked like gold. The marvel dazzled them.

'That must be worth a fortune,' breathed Plump-Cheeks. 'It looks like lapis-lazuli.'

'There is nothing more beautiful,' agreed the Afghan. 'Where have you seen a stone like this before?'

'My cousin was a priest of Ptah. When he died, his colleagues gave him a heart-scarab made from lapis-lazuli, and I was allowed to admire it before it was placed on the mummy. How could I forget something so gorgeous?'

'Lapiz-lazuli comes from my country, Afghanistan. When a pharaoh ruled Egypt, my countrymen delivered it to him in large quantities, in exchange for gold. Only temples were allowed to work it. Today, everything has changed. The Hyksos invaders aren't interested in rites of symbols – or in buying lapis-lazuli, either. They would simply take it, as they take everything else. Because of them, Afghanistan has lost its main source of wealth.'

'So you're an enemy of the Hyksos, are you?'

'I'm the enemy of anyone who impoverishes me. My family owns the main seam of lapis-lazuli. They used to live on a splendid estate, had many servants and owned so many head of livestock that they had lost count of them. Since the loss of the trade with Egypt, they have been living in poverty. Last year my mother died of despair, and I have sworn to take revenge on those responsible for her death.'

'You mean . . . the Hyksos?'

'They have ruined me and condemned my people to poverty. I belong to a race of warriors, who do not tolerate such insults.'

'You'd do better to go home while you can,' advised Plump-Cheeks. 'Pharaoh's army has been wiped out, and there is no longer any opposition at all to the invaders.'

'Aren't you forgetting Thebes?' protested Moustache.

'Thebes?' Plump-Cheeks shook his head. 'That's just a mirage.'

'But isn't it the sacred city of Amon?' asked the Afghan.

'Yes, it is,' said Moustache. 'But nowadays it houses only a queen with no power at all and a few old priests who spend all their time praying – but that's only what people say.'

'You mean it's not true?'

'I hope not,' said Moustache fervently.

'Is there any organized resistance to the Hyksos?' asked the Afghan.

'If there was,' cut in Plump-Cheeks, 'we'd know about it. Why are you so interested, anyway, stranger?'

'You still don't understand, Egyptian. I want to sell my lapis-lazuli, become rich again and restore my tribe's fortunes. That is my only goal, and I shall devote my entire life to it, whatever the risks may be. If the Hyksos had been honest businessmen, I would have come to an understanding with them. But they will never sign a trading-agreement, for they're nothing but lawless predators. There's only one solution: to drive them out and support the return of the pharaohs – a pharaoh would never alter the rules of the game to suit himself.'

Plump-Cheeks burst out laughing. 'You're the funniest man I've ever met, Afghan. I bet nobody gets bored in your country.'

'My father delivered lapis-lazuli to Thebes – and was paid handsomely, I may say. He told me that Amon isn't the only god of the region, that he has an ally, Montu, represented by a bull strong enough to destroy any enemy.'

'The gods have left the Two Lands,' said Moustache sadly.

'Why shouldn't they come back?'

'Because soon there'll be no one left to welcome them.'

'Not even the Prince of Thebes?'

'It's a queen, not a prince, who rules the city, and no one knows if she's still alive.'

'Then the rebellion shall have its birth here,' said the Afghan, 'right here in this marsh.'

'And who's going to start it?' asked Plump-Cheeks worriedly.

'Those of you who agree to help me.'

'But . . . You're completely mad!'

'Any enemy can be beaten – especially if he thinks he's invincible. Just one little wasp causes great pain to the giant it stings, doesn't it?'

Moustache was intrigued. 'What's your plan?'

'To create a swarm of wasps. But sit yourselves down and let's smoke a plant from my country which relaxes the mind and makes one see things more clearly.'

Abandoning the overcooked fish to Plump-Cheeks – who guzzled it down in one mouthful, much to the dismay of his comrades the Afghan brought out and lit some little rolls of hashish, which he handed out to the peasants.

'Inhale slowly, and then let the smoke emerge from your nostrils and mouth. Little by little, you will forget your fear.'

At first they all coughed, but they soon got used to it.

'This isn't a marsh, it's a peaceful garden,' declared Plump-Cheeks.

Several of the other ox-herds agreed. Only Moustache seemed to have reservations.

'Smoking this plant doesn't just open the doors to dreams,' said the Afghan. 'It has another quality which will be very useful to us.'

'What quality?' asked Plump-Cheeks, whose pupils had dilated.

'It compels traitors to betray themselves.'

'Really? How does it do that?'

'They lose control, sweat profusely, stammer inconsistent explanations and eventually confess. Confess that they have been spying on their comrades for the Hyksos – as you have, for example.'

'What? Me?' stammered Plump-Cheeks. 'You're saying . . . you're just saying anything that comes into your head.'

'I saw you yesterday with a Hyksos officer,' said the Afghan. 'You took me for a beggar, so you weren't wary of me. You promised him you'd denounce the ox-herds as rebels, one by one, in return for a reward.'

Looks of hatred were turned on Plump-Cheeks.

'No, that's not true, comrades – at least, not completely. You don't understand. I lied to the officer, of course, I'd never betray you and—'

Vengeful hands seized him by the hair and plunged him face down into the marsh. He struggled for a few moments, then his corpse sank down into the mud.

'Now,' declared the Afghan, 'we can talk safely about the future. All of us here present shall become rebels. In doing so we'll be risking arrest, torture and death. But if we win we shall become very rich men.'

## 6

As Queen Teti and Princess Ahhotep left the palace, protected by Laughter, a young man stepped into their path.

'I'm the one who did it,' he declared proudly.

To Ahhotep's surprise, Laughter did not bare his teeth.

'My names is Seqen, Princess, and it was I who freed your dog so that he could come to your aid. Seeing him tied up made me realize you were in danger. So I did what I could.'

Seqen was clearly very nervous, and delivered his speech in a great hurry. He was a rather thin young fellow, scarcely older than Ahhotep, and his only obvious assets were his piercing eyes, which drew attention away from an unattractive face and an oversized forehead.

'Well done,' said Ahhotep. 'You saved Her Majesty's life.'

'And yours, too, Princess.'

'But you should bow before the Queen of Egypt.'

The young man did so, rather awkwardly.

'Stand up straight,' ordered Teti. 'I have not see you at the palace before, my boy. Where do you live?'

'On the southern outskirts of the city. I came here from the country to learn how to fight.'

'Have you been accepted into the army?' asked Ahhotep eagerly.

'Unfortunately not. It seems I'm not strong enough. So I have found work as a gardener's assistant. The gardener works me hard, and that pleases me a lot because soon I'll have the strong muscles I need.'

'How did you know Laughter is my dog?'

'The gardener told me,' said Seqen. 'He advised me to go home and forget that I had seen the guards' commander tie it to a tree.'

The dog placed an enormous front paw on Seqen's chest and almost knocked him over. It seems that Laughter's memory was not short.

Ahhotep said, 'I don't suppose your lodgings are very pleasant.'

'I am not unhappy, Princess. The widow who rents a room to me is a charming old lady, and I love listening to her talk about the happy times.'

'If her Majesty consents, from now on you shall live in a house belonging to the palace, and you will take charge of the poultry, the cats, the stewards' donkeys and, of course, my dog.'

Seqen looked thunderstruck. 'Princess, I . . .'

'Agreed,' said Teti.

'You are to begin immediately,' said Ahhotep. 'Laughter needs a long walk.'

Still in a state of shock, the young man scarcely felt the dog's thick pink tongue gently licking his hand.

'Laughter does not like being on a leash,' added the princess, 'but take one anyway, in case he meets someone unpleasant. He is rather demonstrative, and he is not used to hiding his feelings.'

For the moment, Ahhotep was in the queen's good graces. Not only had Teti not sent her away, but she had even listened to her daughter's plans for reforming the Theban government and making preparations for the reconquest of Egypt. How right, the princess thought, she had been to embark upon this adventure. By the sheer power of her own belief, she would awaken sleeping forces and give Teti back her will for victory.

'Where shall we begin, Majesty?' she asked.

'With the most important thing of all.'

'Are we going to appoint a commander-in-chief at last?'

'No, I'm talking about something vital,' said Teti.

'What could be more important today than a good leader and a good army?'

'Today, just as it was yesterday and will be tomorrow, the most important thing is the temple. If you persist in this insane struggle, you must enter its heart. But it is not without danger.'

'I am ready to take any risk.'

'The ancient pharaohs built dwellings for the gods and knew how to converse with them. Compared to those giants, we are less than dwarves.'

Ahhotep was undaunted, even though she could tell that the ordeal the queen was evoking would be formidable.

'Giving up would not be cowardice,' said Teti.

'How should I prepare myself?'

'In a different age, you would have had leisure to converse with wise men. But today time is short.'

Ahhotep had never heard her mother speak with such authority.

'I shall follow where you lead, Majesty.'

Ever since the golden age of the great pyramids, the Theban site had been held sacred; but not until the rule of Senusret I did Karnak become a temple worthy of that name,* although it was still much less imposing than the buildings at Iunu, Memphis or Elephantine.

The Hyksos invasion had interrupted building work on the temple. Since Pharaoh no longer ruled, the construction sites had been closed; like other shrines, however magnificent, modest Karnak was sinking into a deathly sleep.

In fact, according to the sages' teachings every building was to be regarded as a living being, in a perpetual state of growth; therefore each king must continue and augment the work of his predecessors, and no temple could ever be considered finished.

But the craftsmen's tools no longer made the stones ring, and not a single stone-cutter was at work. The only people living at Karnak were four 'Servants of God', four ritualists and ten 'Pure Priests', whose job was to carry out basic tasks; all were so old and so uninterested in the outside world that they had not ventured beyond the wall of sun-baked brick for several years.

Teti halted before the temple's main door, which was made of Phoenician cedar-wood. 'It is so long since it was opened to bring out the god's statue,' she said sorrowfully. 'And so long since a pharaoh celebrated the dawn ritual to awaken the divine energy. Yet Amon is still present, because a few of the faithful still worship him.'

'What danger could possibly threaten me in a place of peace and meditation like this?' asked Ahhotep in surprise.

'Do you know the name of the goddess who is the Wife of Amon?'

'Yes, Mut, the universal mother.'

'Her name also means "death",' revealed the queen, 'so she is represented as a terrifying, raging lioness. Her statue contains all the forces of destruction that we have failed to dispel since the invasion.'

'Why don't we use them against the Hyksos?'

'Because they would destroy everything in their path, Thebes included.'

'And yet it is Mut whom I must confront?'

'Only if you wish it, Ahhotep. No other power can make it possible for you to fight an enemy whom you have no chance of defeating. Alas, this power is too violent to be mastered.'

So, thought Ahhotep, that was why her mother had brought her to the temple: to make her see how foolish her plans were. Aloud, she said, 'You wanted to teach me a lesson, didn't you?'

---

* It was pharaohs of the Middle Kingdom, the Montuhoteps, who founded Karnak or, more likely, developed an ancient shrine erected on the site. Amenemhat I (1991–1962 BC) built a temple there, then Senusret I (1962–1928 BC) created remarkable monuments which we shall recall. The celebrated and magnificent 'white temple' still exists, rebuilt using stone blocks found in the third pylon at Karnak.

'Surely you are intelligent enough to realize that your rebellion will lead only to bloody failure?'

Ahhotep stared at the temple wall for a long time. 'Are you forbidding me to confront Mut?'

Teti stood very still. 'So my warnings were in vain.'

'I want to fight, Majesty. And if a goddess can help me I must not refuse her help.'

'You are mad, child! Mut will destroy you.'

'It would be a fine fate to die by a goddess's hand.'

Resignedly, the queen led Ahhotep to a little door guarded by a Pure Priest, and told him, 'Take the princess to Mut.'

'Majesty, surely you are not serious?'

'Obey.'

'But you know that—'

'Such is the will of Princess Ahhotep, and no one will make her change her mind.'

Visibly shaken, the Pure Priest took off the princess's shoes, then washed her hands and feet with water from the sacred lake. When he had finished, he said, 'I must tell the High Priest. Wait for me here.'

The thought of exploring the interior of the Karnak temple delighted Ahhotep, though the fear of facing Mut was strong within her breast.

'Farewell, my daughter,' said Teti sadly. 'At least you will not know the humiliation of the final wave of Hyksos invasion as it submerges Thebes.'

'Do you really think I have no chance?'

'Farewell, Ahhotep. May eternity treat you gently,' and she kissed her daughter tenderly.

As the queen was leaving, an old man who walked with a stick appeared. He came slowly over to Ahhotep and asked her, 'Are you the princess who dares defy the goddess with eyes of flame?'

'I am not defying her,' said Ahhotep. 'I wish to beg for her strength.'

'Have you lost your mind?'

'Quite the reverse. This is the only rational way of enabling Thebes to regain its dignity and courage.'

'You have both – but you lack self-awareness.'

'Are priests always so talkative?'

The old man gripped the head of his stick. 'As you wish, Princess. Face the bloodthirsty lioness, since that is your decision. But, before you do, behold the sun for the last time.'

## 7

For a moment, Ahhotep was simply a frightened girl, daunted by the thought of losing her life in an insane venture. But as soon as she saw the old priest's ironic smile she forgot her fears.

She said, 'The sacred songs say that the sun will rise every morning for the just, don't they?'

'Would you claim to be among the just, Princess?' asked the priest.

'Yes, because my only wish is to free my country from the Hyksos.'

'Then follow me.' Leaning heavily on his stick, the Servant of God led her past a magnificent limestone shrine whose breathtakingly perfect carvings were dedicated to the regeneration festival of Senusret I. There Pharaoh communed with the gods, who gave him the vital power to transform the One into many and thus create the provinces of Egypt, at once diverse and indivisible.

'I would like to stop here for a few moments,' said Ahhotep.

'There is no time.'

With regret, Ahhotep followed the priest to a formal garden in front of the main Karnak temple, which was formed from two porticoes built by Senusret I. One had square pillars; the other had pillars supporting colossal statues of Osiris, his arms folded across his chest and holding the sceptres of resurrection.

Here, before the Hyksos invasion, the king had acted as 'Master of the Accomplishment of Rites', and at dawn each day he had awoken the Hidden God, Amon, who was one with Ra, the primeval creative Light.

'Gaze upon the eternal East which is present upon this earth, Princess, the isle of the flame where, without human involvement, Ma'at continues to vanquish injustice, evil and chaos.'

'Then all is not lost,' breathed Ahhotep.

'No pharaoh has been crowned since the Two Lands became prisoners of darkness. That is why this temple works alone, as though we no longer existed. No one, today, knows how to master the magic of the gods.'

'Why does no one try?'

'Because Mut has erected insurmountable barriers. Owing to our cowardice and incompetence, she who was our mother has become our death.'

'And you accept this defeat without protest?'

'We are only ritualists, Princess; we cannot alter destiny. If you dare enter this shrine, you will not come out again. The fire of Mut's anger will consume you, and all that will remain of you will be ashes.'

Ahhotep was fascinated by the noble statues of Osiris, proof of the triumph of life over death. The divine power itself had guided the sculptor's hands.

The young woman walked towards the central gateway of pink granite.

'Go no further, Princess,' implored the priest.

'My mother has bidden me farewell. Since I am already dead in her eyes, I have nothing left to fear.'

When Ahhotep entered the temple, the old man turned and went back to his official house, beside the sacred lake. To see youth and beauty sacrificed like this caused him anguish, but he could do nothing to save her.

Silence. True silence, without a whisper, without a breath.

Ahhotep had stepped into an unknown universe where limestone and granite reigned. She was encouraged to continue on her way by wall-carvings depicting the coronation of Pharaoh, whose name was written on the tree of life. True, the offertory tables were empty, but the food engraved in the stone continued to feed the invisible power. And the golden ship, on its plinth, sailed into realms inaccessible to humankind.

Yes, this temple was intensely alive, beyond misfortune and baseness. It exuded power in its own right, the power of its enclosed world, and Ahhotep had the feeling that she was an intruder whom it would reject quickly and with great violence.

But she did not turn and run away. Perhaps her very presence had broken the spell condemning Thebes to immobility.

Ahhotep walked through another granite gateway and into a pillared hall partially open to the sky. A diffuse, almost unreal light shone there, conducive to meditation. The place was so peaceful that she no longer wished to leave. Surely, she thought, true happiness was to be found here, at the heart of these living stones. All she had to do was sit down, forget outside reality and allow time to annihilate itself.

The first trap!

Ahhotep leapt to her feet, furious with herself for being so lethargic.

An old sage, in the evening of his life, might have the right to savour a moment like this, but she most certainly did not.

Forcing herself to be alert, the princess pushed open the door of the roofed temple, which lay in darkness. Instinctively aware of stepping into another world whose laws were unknown to her, she halted on the threshold and bowed before the Invisible One.

'My father Amon,' she prayed, 'I know you have not abandoned us. But why does your voice not ring out?'

The only answer was silence. But it was not the silence of the dumb, for Ahhotep sensed a presence like that of a landscape which spoke to the soul, using words only a loving heart could hear. The shrine was becoming accustomed to her; it was not driving her away.

At that moment, the princess hesitated.

She did not know the words of power that would permit her to open the doors of the three inner shrines and see the gods embodied in their statues. If she did not conduct the proper rituals, would she profane the temple?

Opening these final doors might unleash a destructive fire which would ravage Thebes more viciously than any invasion. But turning back seemed an even more unforgivable form of defeat and, besides, it would mean she would never know if the gods' powers would have consented to become her allies.

Ahhotep thought hard. The central shrine must be reserved for Amon, who would remain veiled in mystery until his city was victorious; so one of the other doors must be Mut's. She chose the one to the right of the Hidden God. She broke the seal and drew the bolt slowly across.

Then she hesitated. The legends told of formidable guardians with the faces of crocodiles or snakes, who cut off the heads of the curious with a single slash of their knives. But, she told herself, they were no crueller than the Hyksos – and at least she would die at the heart of an intact temple, in a place which had not been violated.

Ahhotep pushed open the door of the shrine.

In terror, she saw the lioness about to spring on her and devour her. But the great beast, whose eyes were carved with incredible realism, merely glared at her ferociously.

'I come in peace, O Mut,' she prayed. 'Grant me your strength, so that Thebes may at last fight against the empire of darkness.'

Falling from a skylight in the roof-slabs above, a ray of light lit up the granite statue, which was taller than the princess. On Mut's robe were five-pointed stars, drawn inside a circle. The goddess held a gold sceptre, whose head was that of the god Set, while the other end was shaped like a fork.

It was the *Was*, the sceptre of power that had given the Theban province its name of Waset, 'the Powerful'. Ahhotep gazed in awe at the sacred emblem of Amon's city, which only the gods had the skill to wield.

'Mut, will you permit me to use this sceptre?'

The lioness's eyes grew red.

'I will make good use of it, I swear.'

But the moment she tried to take the *Was* from Mut's hand, a terrible sensation of burning made her let go. And the lioness's mouth opened wide to devour the helpless girl.


'You must eat at least something, Majesty,' urged Qaris.

'My daughter has gone to her death, and you wish me to eat!'

'Perhaps the goddess will have taken pity on her youth and beauty.'

'Do you really think the flame of Mut feels that kind of emotion?'

The steward hung his head. Ahhotep had been the last smile of a dying royal court. Without her, Teti the Small would soon lay down her crown, and the supporters of the Hyksos would at last offer up Thebes to the invaders.

Since he could not help the queen, Qaris withdrew. As he was leaving the queen's apartments, he bumped into Seqen, with Laughter beside him.

'A priest from Karnak wishes to see Her Majesty,' said Seqen.

'I shall inform her.'

Teti received the grim-faced old priest immediately.

'Quickly, speak!' she ordered.

'The gods are the gods, Majesty, and no one can transgress their laws.'

'My daughter . . . ?'

'Did she not know how dangerous her insane actions were?'

The queen almost collapsed in tears, but forced herself to remain composed and dignified, as her office demanded.

'No matter what state her corpse is in, I want to see it. And I shall conduct the funeral ceremonies myself.'

## 8

Apophis was justly proud of Avaris,* the capital of the Hyksos Empire. It was by far the largest city not only in Egypt but in all the neighbouring lands, too. Dominated by an impregnable citadel, the mere sight of which was enough to deter would-be attackers, it occupied a strategic position as the north-eastern gateway to the Delta. It was built on the eastern bank of the 'waters of Ra', at the junction of the roads and waterways that gave access to the eastern end of the ocean, and to Syria, Canaan and Lower Egypt. To the north, an opening in the vast drainage system created by the ancients at the heart of a succession of lakes made it possible to join the Path of Horus, which led to Sinai.

Controlling Avaris meant ruling the world.

As soon as the Hyksos arrived, the town's foreign inhabitants had given them enthusiastic support. And the new masters of the land had given the monuments and the Egyptian quarter as pasture to the sand-travellers, sworn enemies of pharaonic power.

The new principal temple was dedicated to Set, god of thunder and lightning, the expression of absolute, invincible power. Concluding that violence was the best policy, the Hyksos had wiped out a thousand-year-old civilization. It was from Set's unfettered power that Apophis drew the ability to vanquish any enemy.

From the heights of the citadel, he gazed down upon the streets, which were laid out at right-angles. This rigid arrangement made it easier to keep watch on the various groups of houses, the least ugly of which were reserved for high-ranking soldiers.

The river port of Avaris, the largest in Egypt, was home to both warships and merchant craft, whose incessant to-ing and fro-ing had turned the bustling city into the trading centre of the Hyksos Empire.

In Apophis's eyes, nothing was more beautiful than the formidable citadel, whose buttressed walls were nearly twenty cubits thick at their

---

*In Egyptian *Hut-Waret,* 'the Castle of the Sloping Land' or 'the Royal Foundation of the District'; the city covered more than 250 hectares.

base. He loved to climb to the top of the watchtower that guarded the northern approach to the fortress, and gaze out over his domain. He, who had risen from nothing, an Asian of no family or fortune, had become the master of Egypt, and his sphere of influence was growing by the day.

A small smile lit up his ugly face when his eyes rested on the tree-filled garden in the inner courtyard, sheltered by the fortifications. It had been a whim of his wife, an Egyptian woman from the Delta, a willing supporter of the Hyksos and one who loathed her fellow Egyptians.

Soon, Apophis would receive foreign envoys from the four corners of the empire. They would prostrate themselves before him, acknowledging his supremacy and his dazzling success. This happy event would be accompanied by a spectacular announcement, which would raise him to the summit of fame.

As luck would have it, the night was pitch black and the port of Avaris lay cloaked in darkness. Clouds hid the waxing moon and, if he were not to get lost, a man needed a good knowledge of the area where the grain silos stood.

The Hunchback had been born there, and he knew every nook and cranny of the district. Goods had once been freely exchanged there – without the knowledge of the tax-collectors. The pharaohs' rule had been bad enough, but Hyksos rule was turning out to be downright disastrous. It bled workers dry, reducing them to utter poverty.

A talented trader, the Hunchback had set up a secret market which the Hyksos knew nothing about. Nor did they know that his fabrics, sandals and ointments were destined – albeit in inadequate quantities – for the last free city in Egypt: Thebes.

Although his mother was Syrian, the Hunchback adored Egypt and hated the invaders, a set of drunkards who brought the common people closer to destruction each day, and who thought of nothing but strengthening their dictatorship. Living in Avaris was becoming a nightmare.

So when a man from Edfu, a town in Upper Egypt which was loyal to the Theban cause, had contacted the Hunchback to try and deliver grain to the resistance, the Hunchback had responded with enthusiasm. The first consignment was due to leave tonight, on an old boat which, according to its documentation, was carrying pots. The crew were trust-worthy, apart from a Canaanite oarsman who would be killed during the journey.

It was many long years since the Hunchback had been so elated. At last, a few Egyptians were showing their heads above the parapet.

They were a pitiful minority, it was true, but their first success would undoubtedly bring in other recruits.

The Hunchback's first task was to open the doors of several adjoining silos, remove some of the grain and send it to Thebes, which was desperately short of supplies. And then he must repeat the process as often as possible.

An owl hooted. Or, to be precise, someone imitated the bird's cry. The Hunchback hooted in reply, stressing the high notes.

The other person responded, accentuating the low notes.

The Hunchback and his contact made their way towards each other.

'Have you got the right keys?' asked the man from Edfu.

'Yes, I have, and all the transport documents are in order. The boat will have no difficulty passing through the military blockades and the great customs post at Khmun.'

'The crew are ready to load the grain. We mustn't waste a moment.'

The two men set off down an alleyway which led to the quayside.

'I don't understand,' exclaimed the Edfu man when they got there. 'The boat's there, right enough, but where are the sailors?'

'Perhaps they've stayed on board,' suggested the Hunchback.

'But my instructions were clear.'

A man appeared on the gangplank, and walked slowly down it. It was the Canaanite sailor.

'Greetings, friends,' he said. 'It's rather late to be wandering around here, don't you think? Tell me, Hunchback, what's that bunch of keys for?'

The Hunchback froze in silent fear.

'It wouldn't by any chance be for opening silos, would it? That's a serious crime, you know. And your friend there, might he be that man from Edfu who's trying to rally poor madmen to the Theban cause? Oh yes, no doubt you're wondering about the crew. They've all been arrested and will be executed at dawn in front of the citadel.'

The Hunchback and his ally tried to run, but fifty Hyksos soldiers barred their way.

An officer put wooden shackles on them, then spat in their faces.

'You halfwits!' exclaimed the Canaanite. 'Did you really think for one moment that you'd escape Apophis's watchful eye?'

'Others will take our place,' retorted the Hunchback.

'Don't fool yourself, cripple. We've identified every single terrorist in your network. By the time the sun is high in the sky, not one of them will be left alive.'

The Canaanite took great pleasure in slitting the throat of the man from Edfu, a cunning troublemaker who had eluded him for three years.

'Kill me too, you coward,' demanded the Hunchback.

The sailor was about to oblige when the soldiers parted to make way for Khamudi.

'My lord,' said the Canaanite, 'what a pleasant surprise. As you can see, my plan has proved a total success.'

'Arrest this traitor,' ordered Khamudi.

'My lord . . . But why?'

'Because you are an accomplice of these rebels.'

'I mingled with them to unmask them,' protested the Canaanite, 'but I followed my instructions to the letter.'

'You became friendly with these people and trafficked with them,' said Khamudi. 'That's why you stabbed the Edfu man – he was about to denounce you.'

'No, my lord, there's been a mistake.'

'Are you daring to tell me I'm wrong?'

'Oh no, my lord. I only meant that—'

'By insulting mc, you simply make things worse for yourself,' said Khamudi.

'I swear to you that I'm faithful to our great king, Apophis, that I obeyed my orders, that I—'

'Take him away.'

Ignoring the sailor's cries, the soldiers bound his arms and dragged him away, kicking him as they went.

'What a wonderful night,' remarked Khamudi, running a hand through his black hair, which shone with linseed oil. 'I've had an excellent dinner, and for dessert I'm going to exterminate the pro-Theban rebels. Aren't you pleased, Hunchback?'

'That Canaanite vermin was right. You're very much mistaken.'

Khamudi slapped him. 'Don't be insolent.'

'We shall never stop fighting you.'

'The rebels have been beaten once and for all, and now the people know that they must either collaborate with us or die.'

'And now everyone will know that you infiltrate spies into our networks, and the people will distrust one another. Soon you'll be both blind and deaf.'

Khamudi could happily have smashed the Hunchback's skull there and then, but the man's determination deserved better. 'Do you really believe that?'

'The breath of Amon will sweep the Hyksos away.'

'You have fought in vain and you will die in vain. But before you do you will tell me the names of your accomplices. The palace has some remarkable experts in torture. I strongly advise you to talk before I hand you over to them.'

## 9

'Majesty, your daughter is alive,' said the palace doctor in astonishment. 'The voice of her heart is deep and regular. I can find no signs at all of serious illness.'

'Alive?' asked Teti, equally astonished. 'Then why does she lie so still?'

'I cannot explain it.'

'There must be a treatment which will wake her.'

'I shall consult the ancient treaties, Majesty.'

'Hurry!'

Ahhotep was stretched out on her bed, her eyes wide open and staring. A ritualist from Karnak had found her lying on the threshold of Mut's shrine, and the priests had carried her body to the guard-post outside the palace.

Teti was not fully reassured by the doctor's amazing diagnosis. If Ahhotep did not emerge from this horrible oblivion, could she really be said to be alive?

A loud thud made her start. There came another, then another, like the sound of a battering-ram hitting the bedchamber door. The queen opened it, and scarcely had time to move out of the way before Laughter rushed in, lay down at the foot of the bed and began to growl. Now no one could go near the princess.

In the paved area between the citadel and the road to the Temple of Set stood several hundred soldiers in serried ranks. Their breastplates and spears glinted in the sunshine, proud symbols of Hyksos power. The soldiers held back the crowd, who were avid for the spectacle the heralds had promised. A large part of the population of Avaris had gathered there to witness the execution of the last few rebels.

Cheering erupted as Apophis appeared, dressed in a dark-red tunic and followed by the faithful Khamudi. Although the master of the empire was taciturn by nature and had little taste for festivities, he did not mind occasionally being the object of popular adoration.

Given his great plans, this ceremony was highly opportune: no Egyptian would be left in any doubt that supreme power was being exercised with extreme thoroughness.

He turned to Khamudi and asked, 'How many Canaanites did you arrest?'

'Four. They were a good source of information, and enabled us to identify about a hundred rebels.'

'Won't they talk at the moment of death?'

'No risk of that, my lord: I've had their tongues cut out.'

Apophis approved of such efficiency. Khamudi knew how to use his initiative without impinging on his master's absolute power.

'Did the Hunchback talk?'

'Half an hour of torture was all it took.'

'Anything interesting?'

'Nothing we didn't already know, only confirmation of a few names.'

'So all resistance has at last been eradicated,' said Apophis.

'There are no more organized groups of rebels, either in Avaris or in the Delta. There may be a few isolated individuals who'll try to re-group, but informers and the measures I've taken will enable us to destroy them.'

The headsmen had finished sharpening their axes, and were waiting for Apophis to address the crowd.

Like Khamudi, Apophis hated the sun and the heat, which made his legs swell up, whereas Khamudi suffered from palpitations. So the master of the empire's speech was extremely short.

'People of Avaris, these infamous criminals tried to undermine Hyksos rule. They are about to be executed before your eyes, and the same fate awaits anyone who follows their miserable example. Obey me, and you will have nothing to fear.'

At a signal from the officers, the crowd raised another cheer for Apophis, who withdrew while the headsmen raised their axes.

The Hunchback was the first to be beheaded. He died roaring the name 'Thebes!'

The executioners gathered up the heads and corpses, ready for throwing to the vultures. No Egyptian had a right to mummification, however perfunctory.

The Afghan and his little band had watched the slaughter with mounting horror.

Moustache was on the verge of tears. 'You see?' he said. 'The Hyksos are more ferocious than monsters of the desert. No one will ever defeat them.'

'Don't let yourself give way to despair,' urged the Afghan. 'They have the upper hand for the moment, but they must inevitably have weak points.'

'But you saw—'

'Watching that hideous spectacle was necessary. We must harden ourselves, and be aware at all times of the perils that lie in wait for us.'

'I'm not a warrior,' said Moustache miserably.

'But I am – and you will become one. I want to get rich, and you want to avenge your people and drive out the invaders. Our interests converge. That's what matters.'

Showing no emotion, the employees of the Temple of Set washed down the bloodied flagstones with bucketfuls of water.

From the doctor's dejected expression, Teti knew straight away that he had not found a remedy.

'I am sorry, Majesty,' he said, 'but the princess's case is beyond my skill.'

'Have you consulted the priests at Karnak?'

'They are quite clear: your daughter acted very imprudently.'

'Is there no incantation against the fate Mut has dispensed?'

'None that I know of.'

'If Ahhotep does not eat,' said Teti despairingly, 'she will die.'

'The princess's constitution is exceptionally strong.'

'There must be a magician somewhere who can break through this trance.'

'Perhaps so, but beware of charlatans, Majesty. The fact is that, with all our learning, we cannot cure the princess.'

'Get out of here!'

Affronted, the doctor bowed stiffly and left.

Laughter still stood guard, refusing all food. Even the queen could not go near Ahhotep.

Qaris came in and bowed. 'Your bedchamber is prepared for the night, Majesty,' he said.

'I shall stay here.'

'Majesty, you must rest.'

'Ahhotep might need me.'

'Am I to bring you a bed?'

'A chair with arms will suffice.'

'Majesty . . .' The steward looked distraught.

'What is it, Qaris?'

'There are rumours being spread by sailors . . . It seems that appalling things have been happening in Avaris. But perhaps you would rather not know?'

'Tell me.'

## 10

Whenever despair filled her heart, Teti the Small put on her face-paint. If her daughter died, she would have no further reason to continue a fight which was doomed to failure before it began – Qaris's revelations had proved that.

Forcing herself to recall the rare moments of happiness she had known, the queen reached into an oval basket and took out a wooden comb, an alabaster needle for untangling hair, a face-paint applicator and a mother-of-pearl shell, in which she mixed unguents. She had almost exhausted her reserves of the luxurious cosmetics that had once taken the temple laboratories forty days to manufacture.

Teti's favourite ointment was based on crushed galenite. It cleansed her skin and protected it from the sun, while accentuating her delicate features; it also repelled insects. In happier days, skilled experts would have painted her face, arranged her hair, and tended her hands and feet. Today Teti's own fingers smoothed red ochre over her lips.

The door burst open and Qaris said breathlessly, 'Majesty, come quickly!'

'Qaris, how dare you—'

'Forgive my intrusion, but the princess—'

Teti leapt to her feet. 'Ahhotep? No, Ahhotep mustn't die, not so young!'

Qaris beamed at her. 'The princess has woken up, Majesty.'

The queen was rooted to the spot. 'Don't lie to me, Qaris. That would be too cruel.'

'Come and see, Majesty, I beg you.'

Feeling as though she were sleepwalking, Teti the Small followed her steward.

Ahhotep was sitting naked on her bed – Qaris hastily averted his eyes – stroking Laughter's head while he licked his paws assiduously. 'Where is the goddess's sceptre?' she asked, in a strange voice.

'Ahhotep . . . You're alive!'

The princess looked at her mother in astonishment. 'Of course

I'm alive. You, on the other hand, look nearly dead with exhaustion.'

'Mut . . .'

'She was harsh with me, but I was able to touch the *Was*.'

'According to the priests at Karnak,' said Qaris slowly, 'the goddess has taken back her possession, Princess. It is truly a wonder that you emerged from such a deep trance.'

'We need the *Was* in order to fight, I'm sure of it.' Ahhotep got to her feet.

Teti covered her daughter's magnificent nakedness with a linen tunic and gave her water to drink. 'Don't you feel dizzy?' she asked.

'I feel perfectly well, Mother. If Mut's flame didn't burn me to death, if it showed me the path to true power, that must surely be because I am to be entrusted with a mission.'

'Don't be so eager to fight,' said Teti.

'Why not?'

'Because there's no room left for hope.'

Ahhotep took the queen by the shoulders. 'I want to know everything.'

'Are you really sure?'

'I've risked my life and I'll risk it again. Don't keep anything more from me.'

Teti sighed. 'As you wish. Qaris, you may speak.'

'Why Qaris? Why can't you tell me yourself?'

'Because I entrusted him with gathering information from our last supporters in the occupied lands.'

Ahhotep was astounded. 'You, Qaris? You took on such dangerous work?'

'I am wholly at the service of the queen and our country,' declared the steward proudly.

'Then you, like me, must believe victory is still possible.'

Sadness filled Qaris's eyes.

'Speak honestly,' said Teti.

'The words of the sages have fled,' lamented the steward, 'and the gods no longer recognize Egypt. The ships of day and night no longer sail; the sun's course has been disturbed, and in the end it will leave us for ever. Ma'at no longer rules the Two Lands, every province is desolate, and evil has imposed its tyranny everywhere.'

'These are nothing but gloomy words,' protested Ahhotep. 'The only thing that matters is the facts.'

'The traditional way of life no longer functions, Princess. Supplies of food no longer reach the temples, and even when they do, redistribution cannot be guaranteed any more. Those who produce food and all the other things we need are now earning nothing. The only ones who are making any money are the middle-men, who are in the pay of the Hyksos. The weaving-workshops are closed, linen robes are no longer made, we have no wigs or even sandals. Uncleanliness is no longer outlawed, so washermen refuse to play their trade; moreover, bakers refuse to bake bread and brewers to make beer. The thief has become rich, injustice is triumphant.'

'This distress is only temporary – and we still have Thebes.'

'But our city stands alone and isolated, Princess.'

'How can you be certain of that?'

'I shall show you.'

The steward led the queen and her daughter to a small, sparsely furnished room next to his bedchamber. He drew back a curtain to reveal a wooden model laid out on a low table.

'It's amazing!' exclaimed Ahhotep. 'That lotus flower is the Delta, Lower Egypt . . . and that waving stalk, that's the Nile Valley, Upper Egypt. And right down there, south of Swenet, is Nubia.'

'You can see every province, with its capital and its temples,' observed Teti. 'The surveyors and map-makers have done well. Thanks to our informants, we have been able to follow the enemy's progress.'

'Thebes is still free,' said Ahhotep. 'That's what matters.'

'Thebes is only a tiny island of freedom,' Qaris corrected her. 'The Hyksos control all the Northern provinces, they occupy Memphis, the country's main trading-centre, and they have set up a guard-post at Khmun to control trade.'

'Has the sacred city of Abydos fallen into their hands?'

'That is likely, Princess. Even more worryingly, Kebet, two days' march north of Thebes, is no safer, while at Per-Hathor, a day's march to the south, the Hyksos have built a new fortress.'

'In other words,' said Ahhotep, 'we are surrounded. But haven't we a loyal ally, Edfu, further south?'

'The governor, Emheb, is indeed loyal, but is he still alive? As for Elephantine, the capital of the first province of Upper Egypt and the border town with Nubia, she labours under the enemy yoke.'

'The Nubians are whole-hearted allies of the Hyksos,' added Teti, 'and the Hyksos are constantly expanding their empire. We no longer receive gold from Nubia or pines from Phoenicia. We cannot organize trading expeditions or go to the quarries, for the Hyksos control all means of communication.'

'Is there not one single province loyal to Thebes?' asked Ahhotep.

'They have been broken down into small principalities,' explained Qaris, 'and each local ruler has to obey a Hyksos officer who commands a local force. Apophis has succeeded in spinning a spider's web from which no town or city can escape.'

'Thebes is doomed,' concluded the queen. 'She will suffocate to death – unless Apophis decides to crush her beneath his heel.'

'But we can still grow and distribute our own food, can't we?'

'The management of food supplies has become so deplorable that we shall soon go hungry, and no one seems able to halt the decline,' said Teti.

'Up till now I have held out a desperate hope,' confessed Qaris. 'But our last group of secret supporters has just been wiped out, and we can no longer gather the information we need. We are deaf and blind: how can we possibly fight?'

'This is the end,' said Teti, and her steward agreed with a nod.

Ahhotep walked slowly round the model, studying it closely. 'It is the end of our inactivity,' she declared. 'It is because we haven't tried to do anything that we're in danger of being wiped out.'

'But the reality, Princess—'

'We don't know what the reality is, Qaris – at least, not completely. Our information is fragmentary, and I can't believe that not one single group of supporters has survived. Some of them must have, and we must make contact with them. But, above all, we must have the *Was*.'

## 11

Teti went pale. 'Ahhotep! Surely you wouldn't dare confront Mut again?'

'I have no choice, Mother.'

'She will never agree to give you her sceptre! This time her fire will utterly destroy you, you can be sure of that.'

'Death is better than cowardice.'

'There might perhaps be another solution,' suggested Qaris.

Ahhotep's face lit up. 'What do you have in mind?'

'We always say that only gods can wield the *Was*, but in fact there is one exception: the blind soothsayer who re-establishes the correct location of the boundary stones between fields after each annual flood. Because he acts as the interpreter of divine righteousness and therefore cannot show favour to anyone, he has the right to wield a staff shaped like the *Was*. But whether it has the same powers . . .'

'Where can I find this man?'

'I do not know, Princess. He has not carried out his duties for several years, which is why there are now so many lawsuits. Today, the strong abuse the weak, and falsehood triumphs.'

'Stop lamenting, Qaris! Which secretariat employs him?'

'The land registry.'

'We shall go there at once.'

The land registry, which stood not far from the temple at Karnak, was a sorry sight. Most of its whitewashed mud-brick buildings looked on the point of falling down. There was no sign of anyone at work, only wild dogs which ran away when Ahhotep and Qaris approached.

'Is there anybody here?' shouted Qaris.

A gust of wind was the only answer, a gust so powerful that two branches of an old tamarisk broke with an ominous cracking which made him jump.

'We ought to leave, Princess.'

'But . . . who is dealing with the registration of land?'

'No one, as you can see. Complaints pile up, but nothing is done about them.'

'Why doesn't the minister for agriculture do something?'

'He's like everyone else. All he thinks of is safeguarding his last few privileges.'

Ahhotep clenched her fists. 'He must be thrown into prison immediately.'

'First he would have to be tried,' objected Qaris, 'and proved incompetent. But he would bribe the jurors, so even that would not be enough.'

Suddenly the wild dogs began to bark, and formed a menacing circle round them. When Qaris tried to break the circle, one of the dogs bared its teeth and he had to back away.

'If they attack,' he said nervously, 'how can we defend ourselves?'

'For now they are content, as long as we show them respect,' said Ahhotep. 'Whatever we do, we mustn't move.'

An old man emerged from the main registry building and walked very slowly towards the intruders. He had sparse hair and a bony face, and wore a long kilt which had once been costly and impressive. In his right hand, he held a gnarled staff.

'Who are you?' he asked sternly.

'I am Princess Ahhotep, and my companion is Steward Qaris.'

'Ahhotep? Queen Teti's daughter?'

'The very same. And who are you?'

'I am the keeper of the dogs that guard the registry, to prevent thieves stealing documents.'

'Are you daring to call us thieves?' demanded Ahhotep.

'Go back to your palace, Princess. There's nothing here but old scrolls and tablets.'

'And yet you risk your life to protect them.'

The man smiled sadly. 'My life has lost all meaning, Princess, since I can no longer carry out my craft.'

Ahhotep scrutinized the old man closely. 'You . . . you're blind!'

'Yes, from birth.'

'Are you also a soothsayer?'

'Indeed I am, the last blind soothsayer in Thebes. For many years, I restored to their rightful places the boundary stones the flood had moved. But in those days justice reigned. Today there is no place for me.'

Ahhotep walked between two dogs, which merely whimpered, and touched the blind man's hands. 'Have you still got the staff known as "Fearsome", which only you can wield?'

'It is my most precious possession.'

'Will you entrust it to me?'

'I cannot see you, Princess, but I know that you are beautiful, very beautiful. Why should you risk destroying yourself?'

'Because I want to set Egypt free.'

'To set Egypt free? Wait here.'

Without hesitation, the blind man turned, walked quickly to a wooden hut roofed with papyrus stems, and went inside. When he emerged a few minutes later, he was holding a strange wooden sceptre-like staff; at the sight of it the dogs ran off.

'Let us sit down on the bench over there,' said the soothsayer.

Ahhotep gazed in fascination at the staff.

The old man explained. 'The head of this sacred staff is that of Set, with eyes of fire. It is he who sees the correct path, removes obstacles from it and strikes down falsehood. But the god charges a high price for his services. Any man vain enough to think he could master Set's power would be destroyed by the heavens' wrath. No one may use the gods for his own gain, especially not Set, for he dominates the powers of heaven and earth.'

'I need him,' declared Ahhotep. 'With his sceptre to guide it, my army will be victorious.'

'Set's will is unpredictable, Princess. He has become accustomed to my hand, not yours.'

'I am prepared to take that risk.'

'My lady, that is madness!'

'The only madness is to grovel before the invader.'

The soothsayer got to his feet, and Ahhotep followed suit.

'Turn round, Princess.'

The old man bound her eyes with a strip of linen, took her hands and led her to a fallow field.

'The owner of this field died a month ago,' he said. 'The flood carried away the boundary stones, and his heirs are tearing each other to pieces. I had not meant to intervene, because my skills have not been registered by a palace official. But today things are different, since you are ready to attempt the adventure and Steward Qaris's testimony will carry official status. But are you absolutely sure you want to do this?'

'Don't, Princess,' begged Qaris. 'The Staff of Set is filled with an energy which may well destroy you.'

Ahhotep shook her head. 'The blindfold will protect me from attack. Give me the staff, soothsayer.'

'If it permits you to hold it, Princess, be guided by it.'

Ahhotep did not falter, but took a firm grip of the staff. It was so burning hot that she let out a cry of pain. But she did not let go – and suddenly she saw a night sky, in which one star shone more brightly than the others. She went towards it, and it dimmed.

Three more times, the same thing happened. And each time, she followed the star. All at once the sky and the burning disappeared, and the blindfold fell away.

'The telling of the land has been carried out according to the laws of heaven,' declared the old man. 'The boundaries of this field have once again been properly established. Let Princess Ahhotep keep the Staff of Set and do the same for all Egypt.'

# 12

The sky was dark above the Temple of Set at Avaris. Serried ranks of clouds had drifted in from the north, threatening the Hyksos capital with a storm.

The city's principal temple was very different from the majestic Egyptian ones. It was built of brick rather than stone, and dedicated to the god of thunder and to Hadad, the Syrian storm-god. Before the temple stood a rectangular altar, surrounded by oak-trees and by ditches full of the whitened bones of sacrificed animals.

It was here that ten conspirators had agreed to meet. The most eminent of them was no less a person than the commander of Apophis's personal bodyguard. After long and careful discussion, he had succeeded in bringing together a Canaanite general, officers from Anatolia, and the lady Aberia, daughter of a Cyprian father and a Greek mother, who had been ordered by the tyrant to force prosperous Egyptian women into slavery.

All held important positions and had become rich by serving Egypt's new master unquestioningly. But in the months since Khamudi had risen to become Apophis's confidant, the situation had changed. The leading lights of the court were losing their influence, and Khamudi was doing everything he could to strengthen his power. True, he had proved his efficiency by destroying the last group of rebels; but there were whispers that he had taken advantage of the occasion to eliminate those loyal supporters of Apophis whom he thought too ambitious.

And so the commander of the bodyguard had asked himself a troubling question: 'Whose turn will it be next?'

The question had eventually aroused a few people's interest. They all feared that Apophis and Khamudi were preparing to seek out and destroy allies they considered burdensome, who would be replaced by men who had risen from nothing and who were willing to carry out even the vilest tasks. Hence this secret meeting.

The Anatolian officer in charge of training archers made sure that the area was secure. At night, the priests of Set slept in huts far from the temple, watched by guards controlled by one of the conspirators. There really was no better or safer place in which to draw up their plan of action.

'Shall we go into the temple?' suggested the Canaanite general.

'No, let's avoid the gaze of Set,' advised the Asian. 'Let's sit near that altar over there, in the shelter of the trees.'

The conspirators formed a circle.

'I now have reliable information,' said the general. 'Our agents who infiltrated a group of rebels have all been executed by Khamudi, on Apophis's orders.'

The lady Aberia, a statuesque woman with notably long, powerful hands, looked frightened. 'How could that happen?'

'I don't know. But I do know that several courtiers have died suddenly in recent weeks and that they have been replaced by men loyal to Khamudi. They're Libyans and Cyprian and Anatolian pirates – in other words, men who will kill without a moment's hesitation. And I repeat: these are facts, not rumours.'

A worried silence fell.

'Are we to be their next target?' wondered Aberia, still looking alarmed.

'I think so,' replied the general. 'None of us is close to Khamudi, and that is an unpardonable mistake on our part.'

'Why don't we kill him?' suggested an officer.

'It would only bring down Apophis's vengeance upon us.'

'Then we'll just have to kill them both.'

'Surely not,' objected one of his colleagues. 'We should simply tell our leader about Khamudi's plot. That will be enough.'

The general smiled grimly. 'You're forgetting that Khamudi is carrying out Apophis's orders. The truth is that we are all condemned to death.'

'Apophis is beyond our reach.'

'I remind you that I'm the commander of his personal bodyguard,' cut in the Asian. 'Khamudi dislikes me, but Apophis still trusts me.'

'What do you suggest?' asked the general.

'I'll take care of Apophis, and you must deal with Khamudi. The others can deal with the ordinary guards – they'll bow to the will of whoever is strongest. We must act quickly and as one. Our coordination must be perfect and leave nothing to chance.'

'But . . . but supposing we fail?' stammered an officer.

'Unless we do something, we'll simply be slaughtered. It's vital that we take the initiative.'

'Who is to succeed Apophis?' asked Aberia.

The question was met with consternation. The Asian and the general exchanged suspicious looks.

'We have time to wait and see,' suggested another officer.

'That is exactly what we do not have!' snapped the general. 'Improvisation would be fatal. We must choose our leader now, the man who is to replace the tyrant.'

'The more risks each person takes,' said the Asian, 'the greater the reward should be. As commander of Apophis's bodyguard, and the man who will have to kill him, am I not facing the greatest danger of all?'

'No one will deny you your moment of glory,' said the general, 'but ruling the Hyksos Empire will require other qualities, starting with the ability to control the army.'

Several officers nodded their agreement.

'Only the Canaanite soldiers will obey you,' objected the Asian, 'and they're in the minority. Wouldn't the hero who killed Apophis be the best man to unite all factions?'

'Why does it have to be one of you two?' protested an Anatolian officer. 'Our mountain warriors are unequalled, and our troops won't trust anyone but a fellow Anatolian.'

'Why not choose a pirate?' exclaimed the general furiously. 'If we lose our heads before we've even started this delicate operation, we're guaranteed to fail. If we each do what we are good at, we have a chance of succeeding.'

'You're right,' agreed the Asian, 'and the most important thing is for us to remain united.'

An Anatolian officer gave a sudden start. 'I heard something.'

The conspirators froze.

'Go and see,' ordered the general, sliding his dagger out of its sheath.

The officer seemed to be gone for an eternity. Even the Canaanite general found it difficult to breathe.

At last the man returned. 'Nothing to report, sir.'

Everyone breathed a sigh of relief.

'If we cannot reach agreement,' the general went on, 'we might as well give up here and now.'

'That's out of the question,' replied the Asian. 'Things have gone too far, and we must not hesitate now. I shall kill Apophis, the Anatolian officers will take care of Khamudi, and the general will take command of the Hyksos army. Afterwards, we shall call a meeting of senior courtiers and officers and choose our leader.'

'Very well,' nodded the Canaanite, and the other conspirators followed suit.

The moon appeared between two clouds, illuminating Aberia's statuesque figure as she stood up and went over to the general.

'I congratulate you,' she said. 'You persuaded us to embark on this mad adventure, and you've managed to settle our disagreements. For that you deserve a reward.' She laid her hands on his shoulders.

For a moment he thought she was going to kiss him. But, to his horrified surprise, her powerful fingers fastened tightly round his neck.

'Die, you mangy cur!' she hissed.

He fought to escape from this she-devil, but he fought in vain: she was inexorably strangling him.

Sword in hand, the Asian rushed at Aberia, but a volley of arrows plunged into his back, while twenty Cyprian pirates came rushing out of the shadows and fell upon the other conspirators, stabbing them to death with their daggers. The Anatolians fought valiantly, but were overcome by sheer force of numbers.

At the moment when the Canaanite general died, Khamudi appeared, wearing a satisfied smile. 'This is work well done,' he said. 'The plot has been nipped in the bud.'

Aberia spat on the general's corpse, and rubbed her hands. 'Our great king should be well pleased. And I must say, I found it most pleasurable myself.'

## 13

Apophis stood high on the walls of the citadel, gazing down at the port of Avaris, where sailors were swarming about, unloading a host of boats. The storehouses were bursting with wine, oils, precious woods, bronze and all sorts of other wares, which had turned the Hyksos capital into an exceedingly wealthy city where everything could be bought and sold. Business was booming and people thought only of getting rich, though they always remembered to bow the knee before their new master.

The old pharaonic way, based on redistribution and unity, had been abolished. Soon every province in Egypt would see jars imported from Cyprus, recognizable by their black, polished surface decorated with white incisions. In order to ensure they were imported in large numbers – which would bring him a handsome profit – Apophis had closed the traditional potters' workshops and given the craftsmen to his officers as slaves.

Khamudi came up to him and bowed. 'My lord, it is almost time. Here are the two things you asked for.' He handed Apophis a dagger and a flask.

The dagger had been made by a Mycenaean craftsman. It had a gold handle inlaid with silver lotus flowers, and a triangular bronze blade with a sharp point. The flask had two small handles and was made of blue porcelain. Its surface bore a map of Egypt. The miniaturist had done his work with exceptional skill, even managing to show the location of each province's capital city.

'The dagger makes me invulnerable,' said Apophis. 'It has powers which no enemy can destroy. Remember that, Khamudi, and make sure everyone knows. As for the flask, do you want to know what I'm going to do with it?'

Khamudi was nervous. 'Perhaps there's no need for me to know, my lord.'

'Are you not my faithful servant, the man who will never betray me? Watch.'

With his fingertips, Apophis touched the word 'Avaris' on the flask's surface, and it began to emit a disturbing reddish light.

Khamudi recoiled in terror.

'Don't be afraid, my friend. As you see, all I have to do is lift my finger to control each part of this country exactly as I wish – a country which thought it was protected by the gods. Not one cubit of the land of the pharaohs shall escape me.'

'Not even Thebes?'

Apophis smiled. 'Thebes's madness amuses me, and it's useful, too – for the moment. I know everything that happens there, and not one of its pathetic plans will come to fruition.'

Khamudi saw that the Hyksos emperor was not like other tyrants. Not only did he have a large, powerful army, but he also had supernatural powers, which even the finest warriors had no chance of defeating.

'Today is as important as the day we invaded Egypt,' declared Apophis, his voice icy with menace. 'The Egyptians will at last realize that I am their king and that they must submit to me and abandon hope of regaining their freedom, which they have lost for ever. Eventually, like all slaves, they will come to worship me. Let us begin by receiving the homage of our vassals.'

Dressed in a long red robe and a belt decorated with geometrical motifs, Apophis walked slowly into the pillared reception hall, which was crowded with envoys from every country of the Hyksos Empire.

They were all watched closely by Khamudi's men, and if anyone had tried to lift a hand against the emperor he would have been struck down instantly.

Apophis sat down on his throne, a modest chair made from pinewood. Through his ostentatious simplicity and austerity, he was building up a reputation as a careful administrator of the public good.

The procession of envoys began immediately. One after the other, they laid their countries' riches at Apophis's feet. There were soon heaps of precious stones, pots of priceless ointments, archers' wrist-protectors, breastplates, daggers . . . But Apophis showed not a glimmer of interest, such was his impatience to see the gifts from the Minoan envoy. The Great Island had signed a treaty of alliance with the Hyksos, but what did that signify? Only the splendour of its gifts would show whether its word was good.

The envoy approached, followed by ten of his countrymen, each of whom had the black hair and straight nose characteristic of their race. Two of them bore a low-cut embroidered kilt decorated with braid; there were diamonds stitched into the embroidery.

The envoy bowed. 'May our sovereign receive the homage of Minoa. She recognizes him as emperor of the most vast empire the world has ever known. May Apophis govern it with greatness.'

The other Minoans presented gold ingots and rings, swords, and silver goblets and vases, some of which were in the shape of the heads of lions or bulls. Admiring murmurs ran through the assembled throng. These were truly magnificent gifts.

'I accept this homage,' said Apophis. 'Henceforth, Minoa shall have nothing to fear from the Hyksos army. Let tributes be brought to me regularly, and I shall be the best possible defender of my Minoan vassals.'

The pharaohs had kept for use at court only one-tenth of the tributes paid to them, and had put the remainder back in the trading cycle. Apophis did exactly the opposite, in order to enrich those who administered his government and thus to ensure their devotion to him. Of course, this was among the most closely guarded of all state secrets, and Khamudi constantly praised his master's generosity and unshakeable determination to ensure that even the humblest folk were free from want.

At the moment, Apophis was thinking not of the profits his position brought him but of the immense empire he had come to possess. He ruled Egypt, Nubia, Canaan, Phoenicia, Syria, Cyprus, the Cyclades, Minoa, Anatolia and part of Asia. In all these regions egg-shaped jars in the Canaanite style were found. Their presence marked the Hyksos's control of all aspects of trade: they were a sign that Apophis held power and would not tolerate any dissent.

'I shall govern without Ma'at, the goddess of the vanquished,' he announced, 'and I shall impose everywhere the power of Set, which I alone can control. The Hyksos have struck down the Egyptians and I, Apophis, am the new pharaoh, the founder of a line which will eclipse all those that have gone before. My coronation names shall be "Beloved of Set", "Great is the Power of Ra", and "Great is His Heroic Victory", for even the sun answers to my desires. Thus I shall become King of Upper and Lower Egypt, and each time my name is written or spoken it shall be followed by the triple vow of "Life, blossoming, unity".'*

Taking care not to raise his eyes to his lord, Khamudi presented him with an amulet in the shape of a looped cross. Apophis hooked the ankh on to a gold chain and placed it round his neck.

'This lapis-lazuli amulet reveals the secrets of heaven and earth to me,' declared the emperor, 'and confers upon me the right of life and death over my subjects.'

A stunned silence fell. No one would ever have dreamt that Apophis

---

* 'Ankh, udja, seneb', often translated by the approximation 'Life, health, strength'.

would proclaim himself Pharaoh, adopting the traditional names and titles and thus inflicting a death-blow on Egypt's soul. They all realized they were in the presence of a ruthless warlord, determined first to pillage the ancient culture and then to wipe it out. By all accounts it was better to submit than to arouse his anger, particularly since the Hyksos army was steadily gathering strength, in both men and weaponry. This was the dawn of a new era, one in which strength – whether military or financial – would have the upper hand. And, since Apophis was its absolute master, all that anyone could do was obey him.

Only the old Nubian envoy dared to voice a reservation. 'To be a true pharaoh, Majesty, it is not enough to choose coronation names. It is also necessary to have them recognized by the gods, by inscribing them upon the Tree of Knowledge, at Iunu.'

Khamudi would gladly have ripped out the insolent man's tongue, but the Nubians were easily provoked and for the time being it was in Apophis's interest to treat them with respect.

The emperor remained calm. 'You are right, my friend. That is indeed the custom.'

'But, Majesty, are you planning to follow the custom?'

'My reign shall begin dazzlingly and shall eclipse those which have gone before, because the gods protect me. My first task tomorrow will be to go to Iunu, where my name shall be rendered immortal.'

## 14

Now that the treacherous commander was dead, Khamudi himself commanded Pharaoh Apophis's impressive personal bodyguard. Well protected in his canopied chariot, the sovereign could not be hit by an arrow or by stones thrown by rebels.

At the entrance to the ancient and sacred city of Iunu, the Hyksos had herded several hundred Egyptian peasants together, and forced them to cheer the king. Those who did not shout loudly enough would be sent to the copper mines of Sinai.

It was here, in the city of the all-creating sun, that Egyptian spirituality had taken form. It was here that sages had written the texts engraved inside the pyramids at Saqqara, to ensure the resurrection and continual evolution of the royal soul.

Apophis had not had the library at Iunu destroyed, for he planned to profit from the knowledge of the vanquished race in order to dominate them more completely and to extend his conquests further each day. The Egyptians were too bound up in their search for wisdom and social harmony, and had forgotten the most important thing: that only strength could give victory.

On the flagstones before the main temple in Iunu, alone in the sun, stood the High Priest. His head was shaven, he wore a panther-skin decorated with dozens of gold stars, and in his right hand he held a consecration sceptre.

'What do we know of this insolent man?' Apophis asked Khamudi, stepping down from his chariot.

'He is a scholar, attached to the ancient beliefs and regarded by his fellow priests as the guardian of tradition.'

'Tell him to bow before his king.'

Khamudi passed on the order, but the old priest remained as unbending as a statue from the age of the pyramid-builders.

Fighting to contain his fury, Apophis stepped forward. 'Do you not know the punishment you are risking?'

'I bow only before a pharaoh,' replied the High Priest.

'Well I am one! And I have in fact come to inscribe my coronation names on the Tree of Knowledge.'

'If you are what you claim to be, that is indeed your duty. Follow me.'

'I and my men will accompany you,' cut in Khamudi.

'That is out of the question,' replied the High Priest. 'Only Pharaoh may approach the sacred tree.'

'How dare you!'

'Enough, Khamudi. I, Apophis, am willing to conform to tradition.'

'It's too dangerous, my lord.'

'The High Priest of Iunu knows that, if anyone were to kill me, all the temples would be razed to the ground and the priests executed.'

The old man nodded.

'I shall follow you, High Priest.'

Apophis felt no emotion as he entered the magnificent shrine that had greeted every pharaoh since the uniting of the Two Lands. Then suddenly, for a few moments, the calm atmosphere of the place, where Ma'at was still worshipped, made him slightly nervous. To banish the feeling, he avoided looking at the carved panels and the columns of hieroglyphs which, even in the absence of human presence, celebrated the sacred rites and declared the presence of the powers of the Creator.

The High Priest entered a vast open-air courtyard, in the centre of which stood a giant persea tree with lance-shaped leaves.

'This tree was planted at the beginning of the reign of Pharaoh Djoser, the creator of the step pyramid,' explained the High Priest, 'and its longevity defies time. On the leaves of one of its main branches are written the names of the pharaohs whose reigns have been approved by the gods.'

'That's enough talk. Give me something to write my name with.'

'The rite specifically states that you must wear the ancient headdress, place a gold uraeus on your forehead, wear a short kilt, prostrate yourself and—'

'Stop this nonsense, old man! The Hyksos emperor does not submit to outdated rituals. Just give me something to write my name with on the leaves.'

'For the Stem of Millions of Years to continue to grow, you must use the brush of the god Thoth. Do you accept?'

Apophis shrugged.

The High Priest began to walk away.

'Where are you going?'

'To fetch the brush from the temple treasury.'

'Do not try to trick me.'

Apophis wished he had some protection. In the High Priest's place, he would have organized an ambush. But the devotees of the old cults disapproved of crime. They continued to cower in their unreal world, deluded by the illusion of Ma'at.

The old man soon returned, carrying an acacia-wood box. In it were a scribe's materials: a palette with holes for ink, cakes of red and black ink, pots of water, and a brush.

'Dilute the cake of black ink with a little water, dip in your brush and write.'

'Those are menial tasks. Do them yourself.'

'I can prepare the brush, but you must wield it.'

Apophis seized it and tried to write one of his names, 'Beloved of Set', on a broad, long leaf. But nothing showed on the leaf.

'Your ink is of poor quality,' he snarled.

'I guarantee that it is not.'

'Dilute the red.'

The High Priest did so, but the result was the same.

'Are you mocking me, old man?'

'You must face the truth: the Tree of Knowledge refuses to receive your names, for the gods will not admit you to the line of pharaohs.'

'Go and fetch some new cakes of ink immediately.'

'As you wish.'

When the High Priest returned, Apophis saw that the new cake of black ink had never been used.

'Never insult me with inferior things again, old man. As this day is a glorious one for the Hyksos, I shall forgive your ill will, but you will get no further mercy from me.'

His new attempt at writing on the tree's leaves ended in another failure.

'The ink is not responsible,' said the High Priest. 'You are not a pharaoh and you never will be.'

Apophis regarded him with icy hatred. 'You are putting a curse on me. Your sceptre – that's what it is.' He tore it from the old man's hands and broke it in two. 'See what I have done with your pitiful magic,' he sneered. 'Now the tree will accept me.'

But the brush slid across the leaf, leaving not a mark. Apophis flung the brush down and ground it beneath his heel.

'Who is permitted to enter this courtyard and read the names of the pharaohs?' he demanded.

'Only the High Priest of Iunu.'

'Will you place my name in the temple records?'

'That is impossible.'

'Do you not value your life, old man?'

'It is better to die in righteousness than to live in falsehood.'

'You are the only witness to the tree's refusal – so you must die.'

Apophis unsheathed his dagger and plunged it into the heart of the High Priest, who made no attempt to defend himself.

'I was beginning to get anxious, my lord,' said Khamudi. 'Did all go well?'

'Extremely well. My names are written for all eternity upon the Tree of Knowledge, and in much larger letters than my predecessors'. The gods bowed down before me, and we have no more to fear from Egyptian spells. Festivities are to be held, so that the common people may acclaim their new pharaoh.'

'I shall see to it at once. Anything else, my lord?'

'Have all the priests in this temple killed, close its doors and ensure that no one enters. That will ensure that my coronation names remain beyond the reach of human eyes.'

## 15

Ahhotep put on a peasant-woman's clothing and tied up her dark hair in a green band, the colour of which matched her eyes. It was decorated with small lotus blossoms, and had been given to her by her mother when she had her first blood.

Once satisfied with her humble appearance, she set off for the landing-stage.

Seqen intercepted her there. 'Princess . . .'

'What is it?'

'If you are going on a journey, it would be better to avoid the Nile – it is angry at the moment. The best thing would be to take the country roads. I can provide the finest bearer in all the region to carry what you need.'

He pointed to a handsome grey donkey with a white muzzle and belly. Its nostrils flared wide, its ears were huge, and lively intelligence shone in its eyes.

'Long-Ears is a giant among donkeys. He weighs more than five men, can carry an immense load without tiring, and will live to forty. He can work out the best route to take, and always knows if danger is near. I have filled his two panniers with mats, blankets, sandals, bread, dried fish, onions and water-skins.'

'Are you lending me your donkey?'

Seqen looked embarrassed. 'He will obey no one but me, Princess.'

'I am going to Kebet, and then to Per-Hathor. It will be dangerous.'

'My lady, I told you that I want to fight the Hyksos and I haven't changed my mind – in fact, I'm more determined than ever. We will pass for a couple of peasants and we shall be a lot less noticeable than a young woman travelling alone. And if we meet trouble, I shall defend you.'

How on earth could this thin, shy boy manage that? wondered Ahhotep. But his suggestion of posing as a married couple made sense.

'Laughter will guard Queen Teti while we are away,' added Seqen.

'With him to protect her, she will have nothing to fear.'

'In that case,' said Ahhotep, 'let's start at once.'

Long-Ears listened intently, and halted in his tracks.

Some distance away on the right bank of the Nile, where the river described a broad westerly curve, lay the town of Kebet. It was under the protection of Min, the god who ensured the fertility of nature and protected those who ventured into the desert.

Kebet lay seven days' march from the Red Sea, the gateway to east Africa and the Arabian peninsula. It was Egypt's principal centre for buying and selling minerals: quartz, jasper, emeralds, obsidian, breccia and porphyry were all to be found there, as were malachite, herbs and spices, resins and even ivory.

'Why has Long-Ears stopped?' asked Ahhotep.

Seqen stroked the donkey's head, but it did not move. 'There's danger close by,' he said. 'We must take another path.'

'But I need to know if Kebet is in Hyksos hands.'

'Then wait for me here.'

'Aren't we supposed to be behaving like a married couple?' asked Ahhotep.

'I shall talk to Long-Ears.'

After a long discussion, the donkey agreed to move forwards, but only very slowly.

As they rounded a thicket of tamarisks, they were confronted by a dozen armed Egyptian soldiers.

'This is Kebet guard-post,' declared their officer. 'Anyone who wants to travel north to trade must pay a fee: men, women, children and even their donkeys. Only the emperor's soldiers go free.'

'We only want to go into the town,' said Seqen, very humbly.

'Why?'

'To exchange mats for vegetables.'

'If you are planning to avoid paying the fee by going through the town, you can forget it. My colleagues are stationed at every exit. And they charge the same fee.'

'Yes, sir. Please, which is the right road for Kebet?'

'Go back the way you came and take the first path on your right. It will lead you to the main road, which ends at the town's main gate.'

Without undue haste, the peasant couple walked away, much to the disappointment of the officer, who would gladly have subjected the pretty brown-haired girl to a strict search.

Ahhotep had expected a city bustling with traders and mineral-hunters, a place with lively markets where people discussed business and caravans passed through on their way to the desert. But Kebet was almost empty and virtually all its famous inns were shut. In the narrow streets, the few passers-by walked quickly and refused to be drawn into conversation.

Here and there Ahhotep and Seqen saw small groups of Egyptian soldiers; but not a single Hyksos.

'I have a bad feeling about this place, Princess. We should leave at once.'

'We haven't found out anything yet. There must be at least one inn or ale-house open.'

On the north side of Kebet stood the great Temple of Min and Isis, surrounded by a wall of baked earthen brick, but this district was as dead as the others. Although the side doors of the temple were open, neither priests nor craftsmen entered or emerged.

'Over there,' said Ahhotep. 'A merchant delivering jars.'

The place was indeed an 'ale-house', and a rather sordid one at that, with dirty walls and smoke-blackened ceiling. In a corner, two very unalluring girls were tattooing lizards on their thighs.

A small, fat man with bad breath stepped in front of the pair. 'What do you want?'

'Some beers,' replied Seqen.

'Can you pay?'

'We'll give you a new mat.'

'Show me it.'

Seqen took it out of one of the panniers, all the time stroking Long-Ears, who did not like the innkeeper.

'It looks like a good-quality item, friend. And so does your donkey: a magnificent animal. You're not selling it, are you?'

'No. He's too useful.'

'A pity. And you're not looking for work for this pretty young girl, I suppose? I'd have some for her – and I can swear that the three of us would make a fortune. If her body's as good as her face, she'll have the best customers in Kebet.'

'We just want some beer to drink.'

'As you wish. But think about it.'

The pair sat down near the door. The prostitutes cast envious glances at Ahhotep, while the little fat man filled two cups with a murky liquid.

'I didn't know Kebet was such a quiet town,' said the princess with a smile.

'Everything's changed a lot. There used to be so many folk in here you couldn't hear yourself speak. Caravans left, caravans arrived – you didn't even have time to take a day off. But that was in the good old days, when people made a comfortable living. Now times are bad.

There are only three ale-houses left and fewer and fewer customers
... Where have you two come from?'

'From the countryside near Thebes.'

The innkeeper almost choked. 'Whatever you do, don't say the
name "Thebes",' he whispered urgently. 'There are Hyksos spies
everywhere.'

'Who's the mayor of this town?' asked Ahhotep.

'Lord Titi.'

'Is he in the pay of the Hyksos?'

The fat man scowled. 'Who might you be, asking questions like
that? I don't know anything, and I shan't tell you anything. You're
Theban rebels, aren't you? Get out of my ale-house, right now! There
have never been any rebels in my place and there never will be, and
you can shout that as loud as you like. Go on, get out!'

A loud braying made Seqen start. 'Long-Ears!'

As the young man leapt towards the door, someone hit him in the
stomach with a stick. He doubled up, gasping for breath; Ahhotep ran
to him and knelt down to help him.

A dozen angry soldiers came barging in.

'Whose is this donkey?' demanded one of them.

'Ours,' replied the princess.

'He's just broken an officer's arm. Follow me to the guard-post.'

The innkeeper pushed Ahhotep out of the way and bowed low
before the soldier. 'These two are Theban rebels – they threatened me
and they want to kill Lord Titi.'

Ahhotep and Seqen got to their feet.

'A fine prize,' said the soldier with a fierce smile. 'We'll take you
to the palace.'

The innkeeper grabbed the sleeve of the soldier's tunic. 'What about
my reward?'

The soldier knocked him out with a blow of his club. 'You overcharge
for your filthy beer, you son of a pig.'

## 16

'Two Theban rebels, here in my fine town? That's very interesting.' Titi, the mayor of Kebet, was a bearded man, with a round paunch and an aggressive voice. He spent much of his time cursing the soldiers, guards and servants who lived at the former royal palace, which had been transformed into a barracks.

Hands clasped behind his back, he walked slowly round his prisoners, who had been shackled by the soldiers.

'Who are you really?'

'Only peasants, my lord,' replied Seqen.

'You may be, but she most certainly is not. With such a flawless face and well-cared-for hands, she's a girl of very good family.'

'I'll tell you,' said Ahhotep, 'but only if I can be alone with you, and on condition that my companion comes to no harm.'

'Interesting: a rebel who imposes conditions . . . very interesting. You amuse me, my little one. Leave, all of you, and throw that fellow into prison.'

The interrogation room was a sinister place. It had wooden beds stained with dried blood, and whips hung on the peeling walls. But Ahhotep overcame her fear. She had not stood face to face with Mut only to end up tortured in a place like this, and she had had enough of being a prisoner in her own country.

'Take these shackles off at once.'

Titi rubbed his chin. 'And why should I obey you, young lady?'

'Because I am Princess Ahhotep, daughter of Queen Teti the Small, your sovereign.'

Titi stared at the magnificent young woman in stunned silence. 'If you really are who you claim to be, describe the palace at Thebes and write out for me the beginning of *The Tale of Sinuhe*, which your tutor must have made you read.'

'Set me free, and I will.'

'First I must search you.'

'If you dare touch me, you will regret it.'

Impressed by her regal bearing, Titi heeded the warning. 'Then describe the palace to me.'

Ahhotep did so.

'What is the queen's steward's name?'

'Qaris.'

Titi removed her wooden shackles, then handed her a scrap of papyrus and a brush.

Swiftly and accurately, Ahhotep drew the hieroglyphs that formed the beginning of the famous *Sinuhe*. The adventure story told of the flight of an eminent man who feared he would be wrongly accused of taking part in a plot against his king.

'Let's go somewhere more pleasant,' proposed Titi when she had finished.

'Set my companion free at once.'

'My men will release him from the cell and give him something to eat.'

The former royal palace at Kebet was in a dilapidated state. It had been a long time since a pharaoh had stayed in the town, and the majority of its apartments lay empty and neglected.

The mayor confined himself to a small two-pillared audience chamber, an office and a bedchamber whose windows gave on to the courtyard where the soldiers of his personal guard were quartered. The furnishings dated from the happy and prosperous days of the great pharaoh Amenemhat III, and were quite magnificent: seats and armchairs of sober design, elegant low tables, and delicate lampstands.

'I am overwhelmed to meet our last princess,' declared Titi, pouring cool beer into two cups. 'To tell the truth, I had heard your name spoken, but I wondered if you really existed. Forgive me for the deplorable quality of this beer, but the best brewers in the town have been requisitioned by the emperor.'

'Is Kebet occupied by the Hyksos?'

'They confine themselves to tours of inspection, because I managed to convince them that I am a loyal ally. But they aren't stupid enough to trust me completely, so they organize their own expeditions into the desert and give me no rights at all over the minerals they collect. I fear that Kebet, like most of the important cities in the land, may soon become a garrison town. The markets are dying and the people have barely enough to eat. Thanks to my good relations with the empire, I can still obtain sufficient grain, but for how much longer?'

'Have you created a network of rebels?'

'It would be impossible, Princess. There are spies everywhere – even in this palace. Last month, ten peasants suspected of being Theban sympathizers were beheaded. This barbarous behaviour has sown fear everywhere, and nobody wants to be a hero any more. All I can do is feign friendship with the Hyksos, so as to spare the people more suffering. Last year, I did manage to celebrate the great Festival of Min, but I had to do it secretly, inside the temple with a few priests who knew how to hold their tongues. For those few short hours, we felt renewed hope that in the distant future we might see our traditions flower again; but our hope was swiftly dispelled. Each day, the occupation grows harsher.'

'For that very reason, we must not stand idly by any longer,' declared Ahhotep.

'What are you planning to do, Princess?'

'Thebes will raise her head and the other cities will follow.'

'Thebes? But what military does she command?'

'They seem pitiful because our troops have no spirit of unity. But that will change, Lord Titi – I guarantee it. I am convinced that there are plenty of brave men and that all they need is to be given the will to fight.'

'Is that the queen's intention?'

'I shall persuade her.'

Titi shook his head. 'That is an audacious plan, Princess – I might even call it madness. The puny Theban forces will be wiped out by the Hyksos army.'

'I am not thinking of a frontal attack. First, we must spread the news that Thebes has not given up the fight; then resistance will grow. Will you help me?'

'I repeat: this is madness. But who could resist your enthusiasm? Listening to you, I feel as if I am growing young again.'

Ahhotep's smile would have won over even the most sceptical of men.

'Go on letting the Hyksos think you are their ally,' she advised, 'and meanwhile surround yourself with men who are ready to give their lives to save Egypt.'

'That won't be easy.'

'Until the tyrant falls, nothing will be easy. But we must go forward, whatever the cost. Can you not try to rally the villages around Kebet to our cause?'

'It would be extremely dangerous.'

'When I come back, we shall gather our supporters in the temple and prepare to advance northwards.'

'May the gods hear you, Princess.' Titi frowned worriedly. 'If you and your servant walked freely out of the palace,' he went on, 'a Hyksos spy would be bound to alert his masters. So I must have you expelled from the town by my soldiers, like undesirable persons. But, Princess, come back soon!'

There were four of them, tall, unshaven fellows, armed with short-swords, and they surrounded Ahhotep and Seqen, who were followed by Long-Ears. As they passed by, the inhabitants of Kebet shut their doors. A woman and her child ran away in terror.

'Where are you taking us?' asked Seqen.

'To the southern gate of the city. There will definitely be no Hyksos lookouts there. We'll set you on the right road for Thebes and you'll get home in peace – as long as you don't run into trouble.'

His three companions split their sides laughing.

'It's a good job we're with you, because this area isn't very safe. With all these cowardly Egyptians intent on robbing travellers.'

Seqen bristled. 'What did you just say?'

'Didn't you hear me properly, friend?'

'Where are you from, soldier?'

The soldier smiled sarcastically. 'Just like my comrades, from a barracks in Avaris, where we were told that the only good Egyptians were dead Egyptians.'

Lowering his head, Long-Ears butted a Hyksos soldier and hit him full in the back. Then, timing his attack carefully, he kicked one of the others and stove in his chest. Caught off guard, the other two swung round towards the donkey, giving Seqen enough time to seize a dagger and slit the throat of the loose-tongued man.

The last soldier tried to run away, but Seqen sprang at him. Despite being much the lighter man, he wrestled the soldier to the ground, face down, and drove the dagger-blade into the back of his neck.

## 17

Seqen got to his feet, looking perfectly calm.

Ahhotep flung her arms round his neck. 'You behaved like a true hero!'

'Without Long-Ears, we wouldn't have stood a chance.'

The princess stepped back and looked at him in an entirely new light. 'This is your first victory.'

'I was so furious at that rat Titi that I hadn't time to be afraid. He betrayed us to the Hyksos. Let's go back and kill him.'

'But suppose he's innocent?'

'You can't deny the facts, Princess.'

'I thought he seemed sincere, and determined to follow the plan we've formed. He might have been betrayed by some of his own men who he thought were loyal. The Hyksos have infiltrated everywhere, and Titi himself told me Kebet is full of spies.'

Seqen was shaken. 'Then you don't think he organized this ambush?'

'Perhaps not.'

'All the same, you're not sure.'

'I can't afford to be naïve.' Ahhotep gazed thoughtfully down at the four corpses. 'This is an extraordinary moment: we've won our first battle against the Hyksos. The soldiers took us for easy prey – lambs to be slaughtered – but they're the ones lying there, dead. May their god-cursed emperor make the same mistake!'

'So far,' Seqen reminded her, 'our army consists of precisely one princess, one donkey and one novice fighter.'

Ahhotep laid her hands gently on his shoulders. 'Don't you believe that the gods' magic has just changed sides? We aren't submitting any more, we're fighting – and we're winning.'

A strange feeling of anxiety washed over Seqen. 'Princess, I . . .'

'You're shivering, aren't you? Don't worry, it's reaction after the fighting. It will pass.'

'Princess, I wanted to say—'

'Let's not leave these bodies in plain sight. We'll drag them into the reeds on the riverbank. The vultures, crocodiles and rats will make short work of them.'

Walking behind Long-Ears, the pair travelled to the east of Thebes, where the desert met the fields, then took a diagonal route towards the river, in the hope of borrowing a boat to take them to Per-Hathor, a day's journey to the south.

Ahhotep was astonished to see how few peasants were at work. Most of the fields seemed to have been abandoned, and there was no sign of the flute-players whose music had once accompanied farming work. Evidently the farmers had lost the will to work and now did only the bare minimum.

The travellers encountered no soldiers or guards. The Theban region had been left to its own devices, without any protection. When the Hyksos eventually decided to attack the city of Amon, they would meet not the slightest resistance.

Dismayed and angry, Ahhotep now realized the full gravity of the situation. Waset, the last free province in Egypt, had bent the knee, defeated, even as it waited for the invaders to pour in.

Long-Ears decided to leave a path which was too exposed, and forced his way through some papyrus thickets. He halted a few paces from the river, in a place well screened by foliage.

Ahhotep and Seqen soon saw the reason for his caution: a Hyksos warship was sailing down the middle of the Nile. At the bow and stern were several soldiers, keeping a close watch on the banks. So the Hyksos could sail towards the Great South and Nubia without fear of opposition, while Thebes looked on helplessly.

'Let's take one of the desert paths,' said Seqen. 'On the river we'd be spotted straight away.'

The carob-tree was taller than five men, with dense foliage which provided the two Thebans and the donkey with an ideal shelter from which to observe the Hyksos fortress of Per-Hathor.

Ahhotep and Seqen lay on their bellies, side by side, astounded by what they saw. They had never imagined that such a monstrosity existed, so close to Thebes. Thick walls of brick, a walkway round the battlements, square towers, ditches for defence: these were just some of the features of the most formidable fortifications Egypt had ever seen. Moreover, in front of them a troop of Asian spear-throwers were practising.

'And this is only Per-Hathor,' whispered Seqen. 'Just think what Avaris must be like, Princess.'

'At least we know what we are up against.'

'This fortress is impregnable. And there must be many others like it, right across the country.'

'We'll destroy them one by one.'

Two Asian soldiers stopped training and looked towards the carob-tree.

'They've seen us,' murmured Seqen.

Ahhotep shook her head. 'The leaves hide us completely. But don't move, whatever you do.'

The two Hyksos headed towards the tree.

'If we run away,' said Seqen, 'they'll strike us down from behind. And if we stay here, they'll kill us anyway.'

'You take the taller one, I'll deal with the other.'

'The sound of fighting will attract their comrades – we have no chance. But I'll defend you to the last, as I promised, because – because I love you.'

An orange-yellow butterfly with a black head spotted with white alighted on Ahhotep's forehead.

The Asians were no more than ten paces away.

Ahhotep took Seqen's hand tenderly, and suddenly he was transported into a dream-world. He forgot the imminent danger, and closed his eyes to savour a moment he had not dared hope for.

After exchanging a few words, the two Hyksos soldiers turned back.

'This butterfly is called the monarch,' said Ahhotep. 'The birds don't attack or eat it. By settling on me, it made me invisible.'

Since they had just escaped from great danger, the two young people followed the tradition of kissing each other four times on the back of the hand. They stayed lying close together until sundown, when the Hyksos soldiers withdrew inside the fortress.

Ahhotep smiled and asked, 'Do you know what you said, Seqen?'

Displaying a degree of courage he would never have believed he had, the young man took her hand again. 'What I feel for you is like all the suns that have ever existed. A feeling that is at once uplifting, like the life-giving dawn sun, scorching hot like the noonday sun, and gentle like the evening sun. I fell in love with you the moment I saw you.'

'Love,' sighed Ahhotep. 'Is it still possible to love while Egypt is suffering a thousand deaths?'

'Without love, will we have the strength to fight to the death? I shall fight for my country, but also for you.'

His words brought Ahhotep back to present reality. 'We must leave here,' she said.

They went carefully in the darkness, all their senses fully alert in case they met a Hyksos patrol or Egyptian peasants who might think they were being threatened and attack without finding out who the strangers were. They also had to be wary of snakes.

Long-Ears seemed to understand the need for caution, for his hooves struck the ground so delicately that they made no sound. Several times, he halted and sniffed the air.

His nerves stretched to breaking point, Seqen felt capable of killing giants in order to save the princess's life. And he swore to himself that, if he reached Thebes safely, he would train with such intensity and dedication that he would become the finest soldier in Egypt.

At last, the outskirts of the city of Amon came in sight.

Despite his fears, Seqen wished that the journey could have lasted for ever. Bathed in moonlight, Ahhotep was as beautiful as a goddess. He had lived with her, close to her, and she would never again grant him such a privilege. How insane he had been, he, a man of the common people, to reveal his feelings like that to a princess! Shocked by his impertinence, she would send him away.

When they reached the palace, the guards hailed her.

'Feed Long-Ears, then go and rest,' she told Seqen. 'I need time to think.'

# 18

The Afghan and his right-hand man, Moustache, threw the bunches of grapes into the vat then climbed in to tread them. The juice began to flow out through a hole in the side and a wine-maker, who was a member of their rebel band, collected it in an earthenware jar.

The members of the little group had left Avaris, where the guards were so omnipresent that they could no longer meet without risking denunciation and arrest. The Afghan had, however, left a few informants in each district, people whom he would contact – at irregular intervals, so as not to attract the attention of the Hyksos.

In Avaris, under the iron fist of Khamudi's henchmen, almost all Egyptians had been reduced to slavery and despair. But there were still a few who were determined to fight to the end.

In the Delta countryside, the invaders' cruelty was no less severe; but the peasants had proved more difficult to control than the town-dwellers. The Afghan had been surprised by their refusal to accept tyranny and their unshakeable resolve to free themselves from it. Unfortunately, though, they were not soldiers and would form only a pitiful army compared to the Hyksos regiments.

As the Afghan often told his fellow rebels, the only sensible strategy was patience, backed by unfailing vigilance. Little by little they must win over the village headmen, and the small landowners; sound out each person who wanted to join the rebels, to see if they had the required qualities and ensure that they were not Hyksos spies trying to infiltrate the group. For his part, the Afghan preferred a small, reliable, close-knit band to a larger number of supporters who would be difficult to control and easy to detect.

The main priority was to kill as many Hyksos informants as possible, so that the emperor would gradually lose his eyes and ears.

Moustache paused in his grape-treading and wiped his brow. 'This will be good wine,' he predicted. 'But almost all of it will go to the Hyksos or be sold to foreign countries. We Egyptians are forced to toil like this, forced to produce more food each day, and yet we are dying of hunger.'

'Don't complain, my friend,' said the Afghan.

'Apophis has just had himself crowned pharaoh, and he's more powerful than ever. His empire is getting bigger and bigger, and his army's getting stronger and stronger.'

'Yes, that's true.'

'How can you keep on being so firm and resolute?'

'If I want to regain my fortune and re-establish normal trade between my country and Egypt, the only solution is to defeat the Hyksos. And I'm more stubborn than a disobedient donkey.'

'Deep down, you know we have no chance, don't you?'

'That's a question I don't ask myself – and you shouldn't, either. Has our man arrived with the sacks yet?'

'Yes, just now.'

'A promising recruit, don't you think?'

'Very. He owns three boats, two hundred cows and a palm-grove, and he controls more than a hundred and fifty peasants, all unquestioningly loyal to him. He offers us a safe haven and a forge where we can make weapons.'

The Afghan and Moustache left the pressing-room and went to clean themselves up – the Egyptian could not resist drinking some grape juice while his companion was washing. Then they went to a room containing a large vat which would receive the juice produced when the pulped grapes were put in sacks and pressed, using a technique handed down from one generation to the next.

The would-be rebel was waiting for them there. He was about sixty, with white hair and an air of authority. He asked, 'Are you the Afghan?'

'I am indeed.'

'And you, a foreigner, have become the leader of Egyptian rebels.'

'Does that displease you?'

'I bitterly regret the fact that none of us has the courage to do it. Do you know what you're risking?'

'There's nothing worse than poverty and dishonour. In my country I was a rich and respected man, but because of the Hyksos I have lost everything. They're going to pay dearly for that.'

'Aren't you exaggerating a bit?'

'It's plain to see that you don't know Afghans. No one has ever beaten them and no one ever will. However, we must go on with our work. This place seems peaceful enough, but I'm suspicious.'

Moustache fixed a sack of pulped grapes to either end of two poles.

'What happens next?' asked the Afghan.

'We lay our poles across each other, to form a cross, and then turn them above the vat.

'They must be kept well apart,' said the newcomer. 'It's a long time since I enjoyed this kind of exercise. Don't we look like three perfect wine-makers?'

Nimbly, he climbed on to the poles, which the other two were holding, and pushed them apart, bracing his feet and maintaining his balance by gripping one of them. 'Now turn them,' he said. 'The sacks will be pressed and will filter the juice.'

Although clumsy at first, the Afghan soon matched his companion's pace.

'And what about you?' he asked the recruit. 'Are you fully aware of the risks you're running? You are an eminent citizen, the Hyksos tolerate you, and yet you plan to throw yourself into an adventure which offers you far more chance of losing everything than of winning.'

'Up to now, I've collaborated. But I've had enough. In the end I realized that the occupation is going to bring Egypt to utter ruin and that, like everyone else, I'll eventually be ground beneath the Hyksos heel. Careful, don't turn too quickly! I almost lost my balance.'

'Can you really count on your peasants?'

'Their families have served mine for several generations, and they all hate the Hyksos. The Egyptians aren't warriors, I admit, but their appalling suffering will give them the strength they yet lack.'

'And what about your forge?' said the Afghan. 'Can we use it at any time?'

'We'll have to be careful. The Hyksos guards who inspect my lands use the forge to repair their weapons, but we'll still manage to make our own.'

'Have you got the metal we'll need?'

'Some – just a small stock.'

'How did you get it?'

The recruit hesitated.

'If we don't tell each other everything and trust each other completely,' said the Afghan, 'it isn't worth continuing. I'm willing to give you command of the rebels, but you must prove yourself worthy of it.'

Now the poles were turning at a regular pace, and the juice was flowing freely.

'I had a contact in Avaris,' said the recruit, 'a cousin who worked in the great forge there, and who managed to steal a little copper. But there was an unexpected search, and he was arrested.'

'How are we going to get more, then?' asked Moustache anxiously.

'We'll find a way,' promised his fellow countryman. 'For example, we can falsify Hyksos delivery notes.'

The Afghan cut in abruptly. 'Is it true that you were visited recently by a senior official?'

'Yes, but how do you know that?'

'When you are preparing to recruit someone new, you watch him carefully. It's a matter of our safety.'

'Of course. I understand.'

'What I don't understand,' said the Afghan, 'is why you had a conversation with Khamudi, Apophis's right-hand man.'

'It's very simple,' protested the Egyptian. 'Khamudi visited all the forges in the area, because he keeps a strict check on the production of weapons.'

'That isn't true. The only one he visited was yours, and he spent a long time talking to you.'

The Afghan suddenly let go of his pole, and the landowner fell heavily to the ground.

'My neck!' he moaned. 'It hurts, it really hurts. Why did you do that?'

'Because you're a traitor.'

'I'm not, I swear I'm not. You're making a mistake.'

'Oh no I'm not,' retorted the Afghan, picking up his pole and setting one end down on the man's throat. 'You were very careful not to reveal your friendship with Khamudi. And he ordered you to infiltrate my group, because you're one of the Hyksos's most loyal collaborators. You were a bit too clever for your own good, you scum. Your leader may think we're stupid, but he's wrong.'

'I swear that—'

'A traitor's oath is worth nothing – except this.' The Afghan rammed the pole with all his strength into the Hyksos spy's throat, crushing his laurynx; he died in a few seconds.

'He was too good a candidate to be true,' said the Afghan. 'Still, at least our security system worked. We must improve it still further.'

## 19

Seqen felt something huge and wet on his face as he slept beside Long-Ears. 'Oh, Laughter, it's you.'

The dog stopped licking him and tried to sit down on the young man's belly, but Seqen, fearful of being crushed under the weight, rolled aside and stood up.

The sun was already high in the sky. Seqen felt lost. He didn't know whether to go up to the palace or leave the city to escape the royal family's anger. If he begged Ahhotep for forgiveness, she might perhaps grant it, but why humiliate himself like that? However insane it might be, there was nothing discreditable about his love. And he was not the kind of man to run away like a coward.

'Come on, Laughter,' he said. 'We're going to see your mistress.'

The princess was wearing a long, pale-green dress, her face was almost bare of face-paint. She was reading sacred songs composed by the sages to the glory of the royal crowns, which were regarded as living beings that radiated fire capable of vanquishing the forces of darkness.

His face sombre, Seqen bowed low. 'Princess, I have brought Laughter back to you,' he said. 'Have I your permission to remain in Thebes?'

Ahhotep did not lift her eyes from her papyrus. 'Have your feelings changed?'

'My feelings . . .'

'Has your long sleep made you forget your absurd declaration?'

'No, of course not.'

'You should have thought deeply and realized that you have fallen victim to a mirage.'

'You're no mirage, Princess. You're the woman I love.'

'Are you quite sure of that?'

'On the life of Pharaoh, I swear it.'

'There is no Pharaoh any more.'

'Those who live for ever in the sky bear witness to my sincerity.'

Ahhotep laid the papyrus on a low table and looked the young man straight in the eye. 'Last night I couldn't sleep, because I couldn't stop thinking about you,' she confessed. 'I missed you.'

Seqen's heart raced. 'But . . .'

'It is possible that I love you. But marriage is something much more serious. Have you ever lain with a girl?'

Seqen blushed. 'No, I haven't.'

'And I have never lain with a man. Can you offer the proper marriage-gifts to a princess – that is to say, beds, chairs, storage chests, boxes for jewellery and face-paint, bracelets and rings, precious vases and luxurious fabrics which on her death will become her winding-sheet?'

Seqen was devastated. 'You know I cannot.'

'Never mind, I shall do without. My mother will protest, but I'll win her round. Now, let us be quite clear about what I require from my future husband. He must be neither greedy nor vain; nor must he be stupid, dishonest, or mean-spirited. He must not cosset himself and he must not be deaf to the voices of the gods.'

'I promise to do my best, but I don't know if—'

'You promise, that's what matters. Now let us deal with the most important matter of all. I want to have two sons as quickly as possible. The struggle against the Hyksos will be a long one, and I shall bring them up in the love of their country and the will to set it free. If you and I die, they will carry on our fight.'

Seqen smiled. 'I accept all your conditions.'

Their lips were almost touching.

'I'm not like other women, Seqen, and I am forbidden to become like them. Even if we're happy together, our life will be stormy.'

'You've already taught me not to be like other men. To live with you, I am willing to make any sacrifice at all.'

They shared their first kiss, at first hesitant then fevered.

Seqen's trembling hands slipped the gown from Ahhotep's perfect body, dared to touch her perfumed skin and ventured a first caress which made her whole being quiver. She, the conqueror and the fighter, abandoned herself to the arms of her lover as he discovered how to express his passion. And they gave themselves to each other, forgetting everything except their desire.

Although she was not feeling very well, Teti the Small received her daughter, with only Qaris in attendance.

'You have never looked so radiant, Ahhotep. Can it be that you bring good news from your expedition?'

'Unfortunately, Majesty, no. A seemingly impregnable fortress has been built at Per-Hathor, Hyksos boats travel up and down the Nile unhindered, and the Waset countryside has no military protection at all.'

'Did you reach Kebet?' asked Qaris.

'I met the mayor of the town, Lord Titi.'

'Titi?'

'Yes, that's right. I thought he was a strange man, somewhat disillusioned with the Hyksos. I hope I have given him back his taste for battle.'

'He is one of our most loyal allies,' said Qaris, 'but his network of rebels has been destroyed, and he himself escaped death only by claiming to be the emperor's loyal vassal.'

'Do you think he'd give orders for me to be killed by soldiers in the Hyksos's pay?'

'Oh no, Princess! He'd never do that.'

'Kebet will soon be a dead town,' predicted Ahhotep, 'and the Hyksos will probably build a fortress there, as fearsome as the one at Per Hathor. Titi's only remaining forces are a small personal bodyguard, and he can't even celebrate the Festival of Min except in great secrecy.'

Qaris was appalled. 'It's just as I thought: we're encircled. I'm sure the Theban enclave will soon fall.'

'I'm sure it won't,' retorted Ahhotep. 'We must win the people's hearts, organize resistance and loosen the Hyksos stranglehold little by little.'

'I have had news from Avaris,' said Qaris. 'Apophis has just proclaimed himself pharaoh, and his coronation names have been written on the Tree of Knowledge at Iunu.'

'How could he dare?' stammered Teti, her heart almost breaking.

'Before long, Majesty, we shall have to recognize his sovereignty and offer him allegiance. After all, Thebes, like the rest of the Two Lands, belongs to the King of Upper and Lower Egypt.'

The queen was on the verge of tears. 'Leave me, both of you.'

But Ahhotep took her arm and said, 'Come with me, Mother, I'm going to prove to you that there's still hope.'

She led her to her bedchamber and flung open the door.

Seqen, who was stretched out on the bed, gazing heavenwards, was so surprised that he only just had time to cover himself up.

'Ahhotep!' exclaimed Teti. 'Surely this doesn't mean that . . . ?'

'Yes, it does, Mother. Seqen and I have made love for the first time. From now on, we shall live together under the same roof, and we're therefore husband and wife. My husband himself will tell you how, with the aid of his donkey, he killed four Hyksos soldiers who wanted to kill us. We have won our first victory, Majesty!'

'Ahhotep, you . . .'

'Seqen doesn't belong to a great family, but what does that matter? Egyptian princesses marry the men they love, whatever their origin. He has no money, so he can't offer me a dowry, but that doesn't matter, either. We're living in a time of war. Our souls and our bodies are in harmony, and we're resolved to fight to the death. That's what matters, isn't it?'

Teti felt breathless. 'And do you want children?'

'We're going to have two sons, and they'll be as brave in war as their father.'

'Good, good.'

'Will you give us your blessing, Mother?'

'Well . . .'

Ahhotep threw her arms round her mother and kissed her on both cheeks.

## 20

In rage, the lady Tany hurled at the wall the mirror given her by her husband, the emperor. She hoped it would break, but the impact left the magnificent copper disc unharmed, so she stamped on it instead.

Born in the Delta, near Avaris, Tany had had the good fortune to catch the eye of Apophis, whose ugliness fascinated her. But she could not bear anyone to allude to her own ugliness, or mock her in the corridors of the palace. Small and fat, she had tried everything – slimming potions, beauty products, applications of mud – but the only result had been a succession of failures, each worse than the last. It was hardly surprising, because Tany loved oily food, rich sauces and cakes, all of which she refused to give up, and treated the palace doctors like charlatans.

Her mighty husband was too preoccupied with power to have much time for women. The cold blood that flowed in his veins did not arouse him to the games of love and if, from time to time, he violated some young Egyptian noblewoman who had been reduced to slavery, it was only to show that he exercised absolute power over his subjects.

Tany was of modest origins. She took great pleasure in humiliating the great ladies who were now her servants and whom, had it not been for the Hyksos invasions, she would have served. She never missed an opportunity to make them suffer or show them that they were lower than the dust. None could disobey her, still less dissent, for at one word from the emperor's wife the rebel would be first whipped, then beheaded. Not a week went by without the lady Tany taking great pleasure in watching such executions.

There was only one shadow on the horizon: the arrival at the palace of Khamudi's wife, Yima, an opulent blonde who constantly flirted and bobbed her head like a goose, especially when the emperor was around. But that pest of a woman knew her husband would not tolerate even the smallest misdemeanour: Khamudi had strangled his previous wife with his own hands when he caught her in the arms of a lover.

The lady Tany – Apophis had refused to bestow on her the titles of Empress or Queen of Egypt – liked Khamudi. He was brutal, ambitious and ruthless, with a calculating mind and a real gift for lying. In short, he had all the qualities necessary to become an important Hyksos dignitary. Of course, he would never remotely equal his master, Apophis, and it was in his own interest to remain second-in-command. If not, Tany herself would put an end to his brilliant career.

Angrily, she ordered one of her serving-maids to retrieve the mirror, and snapped at another, an Egyptian whose family had once been one of the richest in Sais, 'Paint my face properly.'

Though the girl was skilful, and did her very best to make Tany look less ugly and less masculine, the result was disastrous: the poor girl only made things worse.

'You're trying to mock me!' screeched Tany.

She lashed out with the mirror, and the servant collapsed, blood pouring from her head.

'Get rid of that creature,' she ordered the others, who were stupefied with horror, 'and wash my face. I must go and see the emperor.'

'Be quick and brief,' Apophis told his wife. 'The Great Council is awaiting me.'

'I don't involve myself in politics, but I have an interesting piece of information.'

'Then stop mumbling and speak clearly.'

'One of my serving-women confessed under torture that the Egyptians are still giving each other gifts without declaring them to the tax-collectors. I've drawn up a list of the guilty parties.'

'You've done well, Tany.'

The emperor left his office, took his seat in his travelling-chair and, under the watchful eyes of his bodyguards, was carried by slaves to the Temple of Set. Here, where the storm-god's protection was strongest, he would address his senior officials, announcing new directives which they must enforce without fail.

Thanks to his wife, he knew that the old Egyptian ways remained alive and that it would take more time to wipe them out. The richer a man is, the more he gives: so said the pharaohs, who had applied the rule to everyone, even themselves. Generosity was a social obligation and profit must not be a man's goal. A great man who lacked generosity destroyed his reputation, left the domain of Ma'at and became irredeemably mediocre, doomed to lose all he had thought he had gained.

The quality of what was produced was considered more important than its price at market, and it was the job of temples to check it, at the same time ensuring the proper circulation of offerings so that one of the most important aims of the pharaonic state might be accomplished: social cohesion, linked to the well-being of each individual.

Traditionally, all Egyptians, so long as they had the necessary skills, had been free to make what they needed themselves, and could gain a small profit through the system of barter, which extended to services. For example, a scribe who wanted to have a house built could write letters for the stone-cutter in return for a certain number of hours of the latter's work.

In this way, in the Two Lands every individual was at once a debtor and creditor to several other people. The pharaoh kept watch over the reciprocity of gifts and the proper circulation of generosity. He who received must give, even if the quantity were very small, and even if there were a delay. And the king, who had received so much from the gods, must give his people spiritual and material prosperity.

Apophis detested this law of Ma'at, this solidarity linking earthly beings with those in the world beyond. The Hyksos had realized that it was an obstacle to the full exercise of power and the accumulation of wealth by the ruling elite.

On the pavement before the Temple of Set, Khamudi greeted his master. 'My lord, all the necessary measures have been taken to ensure your safety.'

A heavy silence reigned inside the building. Not one general, provincial governor or head of a government secretariat was missing. They waited anxiously to learn what fate the emperor had in store for them. Apophis took time to enjoy the fear he inspired, before revealing his decisions.

'The Law of Ma'at is abolished once and for all,' he announced. 'Therefore we no longer need a tjaty or magistrates. Justice will be handed down by myself and my ministers, the most important of whom shall bear the title of High Treasurer of Lower Egypt. This vital role I entrust to my faithful Khamudi, who will also be my spokesman. He will write out my decrees on papyrus and ensure they are sent to all parts of the empire, so that none may be ignorant of them.'

Khamudi smiled broadly. He had officially become the second most important person in the state and was already imagining the fabulous profits he would make through controlling the papyrus industry. Sending out his master's decrees in written form would be an exhilarating task. Tomorrow, all the empire's subjects would think as they were told to think, and no one would have the right to speak a word in opposition.

'We have all shown too much forbearance to the people we have vanquished,' went on the emperor, 'and this softness must stop. The new law is simple: they collaborate, or else they will be condemned to slavery or to forced labour in the mines. As for rich landowners, craftsmen and merchants, they must declare to the High Treasurer everything they own – and I mean everything, including the smallest household object or scrap of fabric. We shall then tax them on their fortunes, and those who have lied will be severely punished. Khamudi's men will carry out frequent, detailed checks. Of course, the members of the ruling tribe will not have to pay this tax.'

All the dignitaries gave a sigh of relief.

'Furthermore, I do not wish the word "freedom" to be spoken ever again in my empire,' decreed Apophis. 'Laws will be enacted regulating all social and individual behaviour, and everyone must conform to the new code, whose guarantors you will be. I require detailed reports on every person exercising any responsibility, so that I can be informed without delay about anyone whose loyalty is suspect. So long as you obey me blindly, you, the senior officials of the Hyksos Empire, will be rich and powerful.'

A Canaanite asked to speak. 'Majesty, may we increase taxes in all the provinces?'

'Indeed, that is essential. I fix them at one-fifth of all income.'

'Forgive me, Majesty, but is that not enormously high?'

'We shall go much further, believe me. And the people will pay, under threat of reprisals. Know also that every ship will owe one-tenth of its cargo to the palace: that is the price of the right to sail upon the Nile or our canals.'

Khamudi was positively drooling.

'No more questions?'

'Yes, Majesty,' said a Syrian general. 'What about the rebel movement?'

'It has been almost wiped out. True, a few madmen still survive, but the necessary measures have been taken.'

'Why not raze Thebes to the ground?'

'Thebes is under control,' said Apophis. 'I am using it as bait to attract the last of the rebels and leave the Egyptians a false glimmer of hope. The desperate slave is less productive than the one who believes in a future, however far-off. I may add that large-scale immigration and forced marriages will fundamentally alter the population. In a few decades, the old civilization will have been extinguished and Egypt will be Hyksos for ever.'

# 21

The High Priest of Karnak could not sleep, so he decided to get up, leave his little house beside the sacred lake, and take a walk through Amon's domain.

How he would have loved to see great building-works undertaken, to see the temple grow and become more beautiful. But Thebes had been bled dry, and there was no longer a pharaoh. Karnak was lapsing into a deathlike slumber.

It was a beautiful evening. The fourteenth day of the rising moon, the left eye of Horus, was drawing to an end; once again, Set had tried in vain to cut it into pieces. Thoth, the god of knowledge, had caught his eye in his net in the ocean of energy, so that it could shine again and make minerals and plants blossom. Made whole again, the moon was the very image of life-giving vigour and the symbol of a happy Egypt, complete with all its provinces.

The High Priest rubbed his eyes. It must be a mirage. Yet he was wide awake and there was nothing wrong with his eyes. To be on the safe side, he gazed up at the full moon for several long minutes.

Then, sure of what he had seen, he headed for the palace as fast as his old legs could carry him.

'Forgive me for waking you, Steward, but this is very important,' said the High Priest.

'I was not sleeping,' said Qaris.

'Her Majesty must be told.'

'She is very tired, and she needs rest.'

'Look at the moon – look at it closely!'

From the palace window, Qaris looked out. Scarcely able to believe what he had seen, he ran to the queen's bed-chamber and woke her as gently as he could.

'What is happening, Qaris?' she asked sleepily.

'Something absolutely extraordinary, Majesty. The High Priest and I have both witnessed it, but only you can decide if our eyes are deceiving us. All you need do is look at the full moon.'

In her turn, Teti the Small gazed up at the sky's message. Awestruck, she whispered, 'Ahhotep . . . It's Ahhotep's face.'

She threw on a robe, and she and Qaris joined the High Priest.

'The oracle has spoken, Majesty,' said the High Priest. 'The princess herself must also see it, and then we shall know how to interpret it.'

'Laughter is guarding her rooms,' Qaris reminded him. 'He will not let anyone in.'

'This is too important . . . I shall take the risk, stay behind me.'

As soon as the High Priest approached, the huge dog opened its eyes and raised its heavy head, which was resting on a comfortable cushion.

'The heavens have spoken,' said the old man, 'and your mistress must hear their voice.'

Laughter gave a whine, of a kind the princess recognized immediately. Kissing Seqen lovingly on the forehead, she put on a tunic and opened the door of her bedchamber.

'High Priest! What are you doing here?'

'You must look at the full moon, Princess.'

She obeyed and said, 'It is splendid. The eye is full again, and the sun of night is driving away the darkness.'

'Do you see nothing else?'

'Is it not the sign of hope, which must inspire us to carry on the struggle?'

Teti and Qaris appeared.

'Look more carefully,' urged the queen.

'But what am I supposed to see?'

'The oracle has spoken,' repeated the High Priest, 'and we now know the will of the heavens. It is for you to draw the consequences from it.'


'I refuse,' said Ahhotep firmly. 'You are the rightful queen and you must remain so.'

'Three of us saw your face in the full moon,' said Teti, 'and you yourself did not recognize it. The manifestation of such an extraordinary sign leaves no room for doubt: your role is to embody its regenerative power upon earth. The time has come for me to step down, Ahhotep; I feel old and tired. Only a young queen, endowed with the magic of this office, can perhaps restore to Thebes the vigour it has lost.'

'But I don't want to take your place, Mother.'

'That is not what this is about. The Invisible has been made visible, the High Priest has authenticated the oracle. Would you rebel against the word of heaven, the dwelling-place of the souls of the pharaohs you revere?'

'I want to consult Mut.'

Mut, the eye of the Divine Light, wearer of the double crown, wife of the Divine Principle, nourished by Ma'at, at once female and male, appeared to Ahhotep in the place of silence.

Ahhotep dared gaze upon the statue, which was dimly lit by a ray of light passing through a small opening in the ceiling of the shrine.

'You have permitted me to touch your sceptre and you have made me taste your power. Thanks to you, I have fought my first battles, and I feel ready to continue the fight, whatever the dangers. But the sun of night demands yet more: that I become Queen of Egypt. I do not want that burden – it seems too heavy for my shoulders. But to defy the oracle and refuse the will of the gods would increase Thebes's suffering still further, and the rebels would lose all hope. At this moment I am lost, and I need you to show me the way. I beg you to answer this question: must I accept the full moon's decision?'

The lioness's eyes grew red and her smile broadened. And the granite head nodded, three times.

From the palace terrace, Teti and Ahhotep gazed out at the west bank of Thebes, where the sun would soon set to confront the trial of death and prepare for its resurrection. Already risen, the moon shone with unusual brilliance.

Teti smiled gently at her daughter. 'What is a Queen of Egypt? She is the beautiful Lady of the Two Lands, full of grace and the sweetness of love which appeases the god. She is imbued with magic, she sings the rites with a loving voice, she shakes the sistra with pure hands. She is the enchantress who fills the palace with her perfume and her dew, and speaks only words of meaning. She alone can see Horus and Set at peace; she alone knows the secrets of the eternal conflict between two celestial brothers. Everyone lives for the queen's words, for she has the power to reconcile opposites and bring about the reign of Ma'at and Hathor, righteousness and love.'

'Those are impossible goals, Mother.'

'And yet they are those the sages entrusted to the Queen of Egypt in the time of the pyramids. Many of those who preceded me succeeded in fulfilling them; I failed. You, who are about to succeed me, must never lose sight of them. The higher one climbs, the greater are one's duties. You will stand at the very summit, and will have neither rest nor any excuse for failure.'

Ahhotep was afraid; filled with a fear deeper and more intense than any she had ever felt before. She would rather have faced a band of Hyksos soldiers than this small, fragile woman whose greatness had just been revealed to her.

'The House of the Queen is dying,' Teti went on. 'You must rebuild it, surround yourself with skilful, loyal people, lead without causing conflict, bring prosperity to whatever you touch. I wish that the heavens were not so ruthless in burdening you with such a heavy office at a time when our country seems on the point of death. You are our last chance, Ahhotep.'

Suddenly, the beautiful young woman wished she could become a child again, prolong her adolescence, enjoy her beauty, savour the pleasures of life before the murderous darkness covered Thebes.

Teti read her daughter's thoughts. 'Too late,' she said. 'The oracle has spoken, you have Mut's agreement, and your fate has been written in the stone of her statue. Only one thing can prevent you fulfilling it.'

'What thing, Mother?'

'Failure to survive your initiation.'

## 22

As Princess Ahhotep approached the sacred lake of Karnak, thousands of swallows danced in the blue sky. Among them were the souls of the reborn, who had come from the other side of life to hail the initiation of a Queen of Egypt.

The young woman was so deep in contemplation that each ritual word engraved itself upon her heart, and the High Priest was so moved that he stammered. Never had he imagined that the gods would decide to entrust such a perilous office to such a wild creature. But the depths he glimpsed in Ahhotep's eyes proved to him that they had chosen wisely.

'Make your offering, Princess,' he said.

Ahhotep knelt facing the east, where the sun had just fought a victorious battle in the isle of flame. Her lips uttered the ancient dawn prayer, a hymn to the miracle of life, which had once again overcome death and the dragon of darkness.

'Let the purification be carried out.'

Two chantresses of Amon took off Ahhotep's white robe. Naked, she walked slowly down the steps into the peaceful waters of the sacred lake, the earthly image of the celestial *Nun*, the ocean of energy where all forms of life were born.

'Evil and destruction depart from you,' intoned a ritualist. 'As the divine water purifies you, so you become a daughter of the Light and of the stars.'

Ahhotep would have liked time to stop in its tracks. She felt protected, sheltered from all danger, in perfect communion with the unseen power that was bringing her to rebirth.

'Your limbs have been purified in the field of offerings,' continued the ritualist. 'None of them is lacking or at fault. Your being has been made young again, your soul can soar in the sky. Now you must enter the hall of Ma'at, where your heart shall be acknowledged as righteous.'

Regretfully, and wondering anxiously how she could be sure she had never violated the law of Ma'at, she climbed out of the sacred lake. When the sun had dried her skin, the chantresses of Amon dressed her in a tunic of immaculately white ancient linen.

Unhesitatingly she followed the ritualist to the entrance to a shrine. He opened the door. On one wall was a depiction of the god Osiris, the supreme judge. Facing the princess was the queen, holding in her right hand a golden ostrich plume, symbol of heaven's justice.

Ahhotep sensed that she was addressing not her mother but the earthly representative of the goddess of righteousness.

'You who judge me, you know my heart,' she declared. 'I have never sought to do evil and I have only one desire: to liberate Egypt and her people so that Ma'at may direct our course once more.'

'Are you ready, Ahhotep, to confront injustice, violence, hatred, falsehood and ingratitude without filling the vase of your heart with them?'

'I am.'

'Do you know that on the day of judgment your heart will be weighed and that it must be as light as an ostrich plume?'

'I do.'

'May the stone of Ma'at be the plinth on which you build your reign. Feed on Ma'at, live through her and with her. Earth and heaven will not push you away, the gods will fashion your king. Go towards the light, Ahhotep.'

Although the stages of the ritual were carried out slowly, the princess had the feeling that her initiation was taking place at almost breakneck pace. She crossed the star-strewn heavens, descended into the depths where Ptah, the divine craftsman, fashioned her limbs, climbed into the ship of Osiris, saw Ra at his rising and Atum at his dusk, drank the water of the flood and the milk of the celestial cow.

After she had been dressed in the ceremonial robe woven by the goddess Tayt, Ahhotep was perfumed and adorned with a great collar and bracelets.

'You have crossed space like the wind,' said the High Priest, 'and you have become one with the light on the horizon. May Horus, protector of royalty, and Thoth, master of knowledge, give you life as a queen.'

Ahhotep was summoned to stand on an offertory table. Two priests, one wearing the mask of a falcon and the other that of an ibis, raised vases above her head. Two rays emerged and bathed the young woman in an eerie light. Her heart swelled, and she saw into the far distance, like a bird of prey.

Priestesses covered her head with a headdress woven in imitation of a vulture's pelt, symbol of the heavenly mother; on top of this they placed the traditional crown of the queens of Egypt, in the shape of two tall feathers.

Teti the Small handed her a floral sceptre with a flexible shaft, the sign of female power.

Qaris had organized a modest banquet in one of the temple courtyards, away from prying eyes.

'Forgive the lack of elaborate ceremony, Majesty,' he said to Ahhotep, 'but your coronation must remain secret for as long as possible. In the palace there are too many curious ears. If the Hyksos were to find out that Thebes has chosen a young queen to govern her, their reaction might well be violent.'

'I also regret this secret coronation,' added Teti the Small. 'But we are rebels, and it had to be like this.'

The High Priest approached Ahhotep, carrying a bow and four arrows. 'We are in a place of peace, Majesty, but our land is occupied and henceforth you alone will represent the hope of freedom. In presenting you with these weapons, I beg you to embody the goddess of the city of Thebes, so that she may at last take up the struggle again.'

Ahhotep had never handled the large bow. Yet the faith within her enabled her to know instantly what to do. She shot the first arrow north, the second south, the third east, and the fourth west.

'May you have conquered all four directions, Majesty,' said the High Priest. 'They know who you are and what you wish. May the space crossed by the moon, your protector, inspire all that you do.'

Accompanied by Laughter, Seqen was permitted to sit beside his wife. The few guests sensed the gravity of the moment, and it robbed them of their appetite for the dishes prepared by the High Priest's cook. Only the dog did justice to the roast pigeons and the Nile perch.

'Seqen, is everything as usual at the palace?' asked Teti.

'Yes, all is calm. Rumour has it that you and your daughter are praying to Amon, begging him to protect the town from the fury of the Hykos.'

One of the High Priest's assistants brought a jar of wine. 'Here is a fine vintage dating from the year before the invasion,' he said. 'It still has the taste of freedom. But before it is drunk, I would like to sing you an ancient poem, accompanying myself on the harp.'

His voice was cracked, but the words were very clear.

'When a form takes flesh, it is condemned to die. The spirits of life will make your name live, and you will have a fine place in the West. But the river never ceases to flow, and each man must go at his appointed time. The tombs of the nobles have vanished; their walls have crumbled to dust as though they had never existed. Have one happy day, Queen of Egypt: rejoice in this moment. Follow your heart throughout your life, perfume your skin and wear lotus garlands at your throat; forget sadness while those you love are seated by your side. Remember this happiness until the moment when you step into the land of eternal silence.'

Everyone was plunged into gloom by these sombre words, which removed all gaiety from these poor festivities. Nevertheless, the wine was poured, and Seqen hoped that it would dispel the atmosphere of melancholy.

Laughter leapt up on his hind legs and, with one swipe of his paw, knocked away Ahhotep's cup as she put it to her lips. Then he turned towards the harpist, growling.

Ignoring him, the harpist ostentatiously drained his own cup.

Ahhotep stood up. 'You poisoned the wine, didn't you?'

'Yes, Majesty.'

'Are you in the service of the Hyksos?'

'No, Majesty, but I believe your enterprise to be utter folly, which will bring only misfortune and destruction. For that reason, I wanted us to die together, at the end of this banquet, in order to spare the country any more sufferings. But your dog decided otherwise . . .'

The harpist's lips turned white, he gasped for breath, his eyes bulged and his head fell to one side.

Ahhotep gazed up at the sky. 'Look at the moon. Its name, Ah, is masculine because the spirit that lives there is the god of battle. From now on, the silver disc in its ship shall be our rallying sign.'

On the palm of her left hand, the new queen drew what was both the beginning of her name and the programme for her reign.

## 23

Easily recognizable by his curly hair and by the mushroom-shaped headdress wound around his pointed head, Jannas the Asian was not displeased to be returning to Avaris on his flagship. As supreme commander of the Hyksos war-fleet, he maintained a discipline among his Anatolian pirates, Phoenicians and Cyprians at the point of a knife: these were men whose reputation for boldness and cruelty stood unchallenged.

Anyone who met Jannas for the first time would not have been afraid; quite the reverse. He was of average height, rather sickly in appearance, and moved and spoke slowly, giving the impression of a peaceable man in whom you could confide.

But those who had been taken in by that impression were all dead. Jannas had an aggressive nature which was all the more formidable because it found expression only in battle, and he was regarded as the greatest of all Hyksos heroes. He had triumphed in all four corners of the empire and had climbed to the highest rank in the army before being given command of the fleet by Apophis, who was obsessed with constantly improving his warships. Jannas knew every sailor, inspected every vessel himself, insisted on daily manoeuvres and punished ferociously even the slightest infringement of discipline.

Convinced that the empire would continue to grow because it was based on the army, the only worthy yardstick, Jannas was utterly loyal to Apophis. It was Apophis, after all, who had transformed the capital into a gigantic barracks where life was good.

The commander rarely rested, for he was ready to move at a moment's notice, wherever his informants indicated an attempt at sedition, however feeble. The mere sight of the Hyksos war-fleet was enough to put out the dwindling flames of rebellion. With the submission of Minoa, Apophis had achieved a decisive victory, a prelude to other conquests – which Jannas would spearhead.

Barring unexpected incidents, the commander planned to spend a week enjoying the quiet life of his official residence, and take the opportunity to enjoy regular massages. But he grew bored easily, and made sure to visit the port every single day; as he was doing now.

'My lord,' said a Cyprian captain as soon as Jannas stepped on to the quayside, 'something strange is going on.'

'Where?'

'In our disused warehouse. We've heard high-pitched cries, as if someone was torturing women. I have set men on guard all round it, and we await your orders.'

'Probably rebels who have taken Hyksos prisoners and are torturing them,' assumed Jannas, who was delighted by the thought of arresting them himself and making them pay for their crimes on the spot.

As they neared the warehouse, they caught the smell of burning flesh.

'Force the door,' ordered Jannas.

Ten soldiers ran at it with a beam and stove it in at the first attempt. The sight that met Jannas's eyes left him open-mouthed.

Four young girls lay naked and shackled on the ground. Sitting on a wooden chest was a fat, fair-haired woman, who laughed periodically as a man branded his victims with bronze tools heated in a fire. He was clearly enjoying his work.

And that man was not just anybody.

'Can it be you . . . the High Treasurer?' gasped Jannas.

Khamudi did not seem in the least troubled. 'It can indeed. And this is my wife, the lady Yima.'

The woman bobbed her head and smiled coyly at Jannas as if trying to seduce him.

'You are interrogating suspects, I suppose?' he asked.

'Suspects?' echoed Khamudi. 'Not at all, Commander. My wife and I are amusing ourselves with these slave-girls who have come up from the country. My steward found some old bronze branding-irons shaped like a goose, the sacred bird of Amon, and a lion's head. I wanted to see if they still worked and I'm trying them out on the skin of these idiot girls. They scream a lot, but that's the fun of the game.'

'Is the emperor aware of these practices?'

'Send your men away, Commander.'

At a sign from Jannas, they vanished.

'Our beloved Apophis knows everything I do,' sneered Khamudi.

'Torture is vital to make rebels talk,' conceded Jannas, 'but, as you said yourself, these girls—'

'I take my pleasure as I choose, Jannas. Is that clear?'

'Very clear, High Treasurer.'

'I don't care if you're shocked. But don't try to use this situation against me, or you will get your fingers burnt. Is that also clear?'

Jannas nodded.

'Yima, my darling, continue to amuse yourself. I am going to hear the commander's report.'

Yima applied the lioness-head brand to the buttocks of the youngest peasant-girl; her screams almost burst Jannas's eardrums.

'Let's go out on to the quayside,' he suggested.

Khamudi unhurriedly put on his robes. 'How are things with our rearward base in Canaan?'

'The city of Sharuhen is fully fortified. It stands at the mouth of the rivers and wadis, and controls the region, which has submitted completely to the emperor. The garrison consists of elite soldiers and I have had a vast port constructed for our warships, which are always ready to sail at a moment's notice. If you will give me the necessary authorization, the ship-building yard I am about to set up will build many more.'

'You have it,' said Khamudi. 'Are you on good terms with the garrison commander?'

'Very good. He's a Canaanite, a very able man, and his loyalty is absolute.'

'Whom have you appointed to command the local fleet?'

'One of my assistants. He'll do nothing without an explicit order from me – from you, too, of course.'

'Then you guarantee that Sharuhen will stand firm?'

'That town is one of the indestructible pillars of the empire,' Jannas assured him.

'Let us move on to Memphis.'

'Ah, there I have some reservations.'

'Why?'

'We built Sharuhen ourselves, and the Canaanites are ancestral enemies of the Egyptians. Memphis is the pharaohs' ancient capital, and' – Jannas hesitated – 'things are very different there.'

'Are you criticizing the measures I've taken?'

'Indeed not, High Treasurer. They are most effective. The government has been solidly established, guards patrol every district of the city, the workshops are producing first-rate weapons and my fleet controls the movements of even the smallest boat.'

'What more could one ask?'

'What worries me are the results obtained by our informants. Not a day passes without our making one or two arrests.'

'Rebels?' asked Khamudi.

'No, simple folk who refuse to accept the reality of the situation and still dare to protest against what they call "the occupation".'

'Why do these imbeciles refuse to understand?'

'Nothing can persuade them that their Egypt is dead and that from now on they are subjects of Pharaoh Apophis.'

'You have them executed, I hope?'

'The executions are held in public and the army forces the citizens to watch. Unfortunately, though, the fire has not yet been put out.'

Khamudi took Jannas's report very seriously. He had discussed the matter at length with the emperor, and was not entirely surprised. Memphis's capacity for resistance was proving greater than foreseen and – as he had suspected – they would have to resort to more radical action.

'Things cannot continue like that, Commander. In his wisdom, the emperor foresaw that certain Egyptians might be mad enough to go on believing in their past glory, so you are to return to Memphis immediately with the following instructions . . .'

Jannas showed no emotion as he listened to the orders. What the High Treasurer was demanding was monstrous, but a Hyksos – and the supreme commander of the navy, to boot – could not worry about that kind of thing.

With a spring in his step, Khamudi went back into the warehouse, from which screams were still issuing. Without a doubt his darling Yima would have kept a branding-iron on the fire for him so that he could put the finishing touches to their handiwork.

## 24

'I'm pregnant,' announced Ahhotep.

'Already? How can you be sure?' asked Teti. 'You must take the tests and—'

'The tests confirm it: I'm expecting a child, and it's a boy.'

'Good, good. Now, you must eat red meat, and take plenty of rest, and—'

'Red meat, yes; rest, no. You know the enormous task facing me, and my son must get used to hard work. Rebuilding the House of the Queen won't be easy – particularly as we must do it in secret.'

'You mustn't upset yourself, Ahhotep. You ought to—'

'Am I or am I not Queen of Egypt?'

Teti saw a new flame burn in her daughter's eyes.

'My first decision is that we must re-establish the link with our ancestors' traditions, and if I am to be a true queen I have an important duty to perform.'

Teti thought she had misheard. 'Surely you don't mean . . . ?'

'Ah, but I do: exactly what you're thinking.'

Watched placidly by Long-Ears, Seqen was busy practising the military exercises that would transform him into an able soldier within a few weeks.

Although a tendency to excitability made Seqen a poor archer, his instructor was gradually teaching him to overcome it; moreover, Seqen had an instinctive feel for the axe and the club. He was nimble enough to dodge even the most vicious strokes and often caught his opponents unawares with swift counter-blows.

The young man was gaining strength at an astonishing rate. Lifting weights, running, swimming: nothing daunted him. And every evening he savoured the blissful moment when Ahhotep massaged his body with a truly magical ointment. Not only did it remove all traces of fatigue, but it gave him all the ardour he needed for new and passionate games. Seqen was madly in love with the young queen, and thanked the gods each morning for the happiness they had bestowed upon him.

'Could you make me a new weapon?' he asked his instructor.

'What sort of weapon?'

'A club with an oval head, longer than the average and with a knife-blade securely fixed to the handle.'

'That's not a bad idea. You could break heads and slit throats as well. I'll make you a wooden one, for you to try out against a peasant who wants to enrol in the Theban army. Don't damage him too much, though – new recruits are in short supply.'

When the new club was ready, Seqen tried it for balance. He liked it. He carried it down to the little barracks courtyard, where he found his opponent, a sturdy fellow with broad shoulders and a low forehead.

'Greetings, friend,' said Seqen. 'Do you want to learn to fight?'

'Yes, I do. Are you really Prince Seqen?'

'I am.'

'And you want to fight the Hyksos?'

'Don't you?'

'Not exactly, Prince.'

The man unsheathed a short-sword.

'During training,' Seqen reminded him, 'we use wooden weapons.'

'This isn't an exercise, Prince, this is your first and last battle.'

Seqen turned to ask his instructor for help, but he had vanished. Running away would mean climbing a high wall. Anyway, there was no time.

His opponent smiled grimly. 'Are you afraid, Prince? Quite right. It's no joke dying so young.' He came slowly closer.

Seqen took a step back. 'Who are you?'

'A good soldier paid to kill you.'

'If you spare my life and tell me who paid you, I'll make you a rich man.'

'The Hyksos wouldn't give me time to enjoy my riches – and in any case you've got no money to give me. You should have stayed a peasant, Prince, and not got mixed up in what doesn't concern you.'

Seqen stopped backing away. 'Kneel before your superior, soldier.'

The attacker was astounded. 'Have you lost your mind?'

'Since you belong to the Theban army and I am assuming command of it, you owe me respect and obedience. I will agree to forget this act of insurbordination, but only if you hand over your weapon to me immediately.'

'I'm going to hand this sword into your belly!'

The attacker rushed at Seqen, but he dodged aside. As he did so, he brought his wooden club down on the back of the man's neck. Scarcely had the soldier turned round when the furious young man broke his nose with a well-placed punch, before slitting his throat with the knife on the handle of his club.

'You should have listened to your prince, you worthless scum.'

Seqen was fast on his feet, and succeeded in catching his instructor, who had been spotted running out of the barracks. With a well-timed sword-thrust, he wounded the man in the thigh, bringing him down.

Faced with Seqen's rage and threats of instant death, the instructor talked a great deal: yes, he had paid a soldier to kill him; no, he was not in the pay of the Hyksos, but several Theban nobles were advocating collaboration with the occupiers and were taking care to nip any sign of resistance in the bud.

With the queen's agreement, Seqen arrested the traitors himself, and a detachment of soldiers loyal to the royal family took them into the Western desert at nightfall. Without weapons or food, the miserable creatures would make fine prey for the bloodthirsty monsters that haunted those fearsome parts.

'Your second victory!' exclaimed Ahhotep. 'And you won it single-handed, with no help at all from anyone else.'

'There's a cancer in Thebes,' said Seqen. 'Before we do anything else, we must be sure of the people who surround us and those who want to fight at our side.'

'You're right. And that will be our second decision.'

'What's the first one?'

'We're going to the temple.'

'To the temple? Aren't you going to tell me why?'

'There's no time for that now.'

Intrigued, Seqen followed the queen to Karnak.

The only other people present in the shrine of Mut were Teti the Small and the High Priest of Amon. A lamp lit the shrine.

'As Queen of the Two Lands,' declared Ahhotep, 'I see Horus and Set made one again. For the reconciliation to take place, it must become flesh in the person of Pharaoh. That is why I recognize you as such: you, Seqen-en-Ra, "Valiant One of the Divine Light". Your second name shall be "Great Bread", which also means "Great Earth", both of which you shall give back to us. You shall become at once "He Who Belongs to the Bee", who knows the mysteries of fire and air, and "He Who Belongs to the Reed", who knows the mysteries of water and earth.'

Ahhotep crowned her husband with the *names* headdress, one of the most ancient royal diadems. It enabled Pharaoh's thoughts to travel across the heavens and bring about the reunification of life and death, sunlight and moonlight, Ra and Osiris.

Seqen was so dumbfounded that he could not even find the words
to protest. Clearly he was not really here in the shrine, and would soon
emerge from this incredible dream.

'This ritual has been cut to its barest bones,' said Ahhotep, 'and your
coronation will remain secret for as long as necessary, but that will not
alter the great scope of your office, O King of Upper and Lower Egypt.
Be at once builder, law-maker, and warrior. Render the earth fertile.
Send forth the creative fire that gives us life, and the destructive fire
that brings death to our enemies. Be the protecting dyke and the rampart,
the hall that is cool in summer, warm in winter. Enable Ma'at to reign,
and drive away injustice and tyranny.'

The High Priest unrolled the papyrus that, in accordance with the
writings of the god Thoth, proclaimed the start of a new reign.

Teti the Small and Ahhotep then spoke the incantation that would
give the young pharaoh the magical energy to carry out his programme
of government – a programme contained in the name Seqen, meaning
valour and the power to overcome.

'Pharaoh is reborn,' declared Teti, 'but the secret must be closely
guarded until Thebes is safe again.'

'Everything is changed,' said the High Priest, moved almost to tears.
'Everything has changed, for Egypt once again has a royal couple.
They will give us the strength to hold our heads high at last.'

## 25

It was not cause enough for celebration, but the events of recent weeks had encouraged even the most demoralized of the rebels.

At Avaris, no more of them had been arrested. Those who had remained in the capital to glean information had to take endless precautions in order to pass it on safely, but the network established by the wily Moustache had proved sound. Untrustworthy people had been eliminated, and passwords and codes were changed frequently.

At Memphis, too, the prospects were improving. Several Hyksos spies had been identified, and the small groups of rebels were at last proving impenetrable. They still had no weapons, strategy or leader, but they talked about the future and had come to believe that freedom was not entirely dead.

The Afghan continued to use his favourite tactic: depriving the emperor of as many eyes and ears as possible. As soon as a Hyksos informant was identified, the Afghan organized an ambush with two or three comrades, and cut out the cancer. He was cautious, took as much time as he needed, and never hesitated to postpone an operation if there was the slightest element of doubt. At first Moustache had been impatient, but he had come to recognize the effectiveness of this meticulous work.

Thanks to the progress they had made, the rebels had been able to set up their headquarters in the heart of the city, near the great Temple of Ptah. The Afghan, Moustache, and their men lived there, in an old, two-storey house surrounded by carpenters' workshops.

Whenever the Hyksos guards inspected the district, the rebels were immediately alerted by a lookout posted on the terrace of the house at the corner of the street, or by an old man sitting opposite, who raised his walking-stick. As a final security measure, a dog had been trained to bark in a particular way.

Despite the Hyksos's vigilance, the rebels were succeeding in weaving their web. Increasingly oppressed, the population of Memphis hated the Hyksos. The majority were too afraid to take action, but they were all ready to help those who were determined to win back freedom. People of all ages were putting themselves forward: but which of them would turn out to be reliable?

'Afghan, the priest of Ptah wants to see you,' said Moustache.

'Who sent him?'

'A temple baker, a very reliable contact.'

'Did you have the priest followed?'

'Of course.'

'Have the baker tell him to go to the first alleyway north of the temple. I will walk towards him, and you will be in hiding with two of our men. At the slightest sign of trouble, kill the priest. If there are too many Hyksos, run for it.'

'I won't leave you.'

'If this is an ambush, you must.'

Although he had not seen anything out of the ordinary, the Afghan was on his guard. He retraced his steps, pretended to walk away, then returned to the man sitting on a stool, with his eyes closed.

'Are you the priest of Ptah?' he asked.

'All three are gods. Do you know the desert?'

'I love only the black earth.'

The passwords had been correctly spoken. The Afghan sat down to the left of the Egyptian, who handed him some onions to munch.

'What have you to offer, priest?'

'An uprising in the northern district of Memphis, involving the majority of the dock-workers. We shall break into the weapons store, steal a lot of weapons, and then seize several Hyksos boats.'

'That's a very dangerous plan – even if you succeed it will be a bloodbath.'

'I know.'

'Who will be in command?'

'The High Priest of Ptah himself. He needs your men to kill the Hyksos sentries who guard the weapons store, and also to create diversions in the south of the city. The Hyksos will head there in force, and then we can attack the port.'

'We may well be slaughtered.'

'We shall be slaughtered anyway – if not tomorrow, some other day. We have only one chance in a thousand of retaking Memphis, but it's better to try than to do nothing.'

'You're right, priest,' said the Afghan. 'When do you intend to make your move?'

'In three days' time, at dusk.'

'This very evening, I shall call a meeting of the rebel leaders. You and I will meet here again at dawn tomorrow, and I'll tell you our plan in detail.'

In the rebels' house, the night was long and filled with enthusiasm. Despite warnings from the Afghan and Moustache, their comrades were eager to take on the Hyksos and inflict a stinging defeat upon them. The High Priest of Ptah's decision was of prime importance: the other Servants of God would follow suit, and the uprising would soon spread throughout the land.

Trying to keep a cool head, Moustache went in minute detail over his diversionary tactics and his plan for killing the sentries. He had to calm a few hotheads who could already see themselves killing Apophis himself, but everyone eventually accepted strict orders. At dawn the meeting broke up, and they parted company with their hearts full of hope.

'Let's go and get some air on the terrace,' suggested the Afghan.

There was a pink glow in the eastern sky, and a few clouds were dclaying the new triumph of the reborn sun.

'The watchman at the corner isn't at his post,' said the Afghan.

Moustache leant over the balustrade. 'Nor is the old man. They must have gone home to bed.'

'Both of them? That's strictly against the rules.'

The sound of barking disturbed the silence, and then came the agonized moans of a dog being beaten to death.

'They've killed the dog,' said the Afghan urgently, 'and the watchmen, too. We must get away from here – we've been betrayed. No, not the street. The only way is across the roofs.'

Jannas had decided to launch the attack at dawn, just as the priests were celebrating the first rites, calling upon the presence of a pharaoh who was not Apophis. Since the priests were entrenching themselves in this spiritual dissidence and providing material help to the rebels, the best solution was to break their back.

Jannas was of the opinion that arrests and the closure of the temples would suffice, but Khamudi had demanded a great deal more: that the priests be put to death and the sacred buildings of the old capital be destroyed.

Without understanding why, Jannas had been somewhat shocked by this order, even though he, a Hyksos warrior, was used to sowing terror and desolation. Perhaps, he thought, too many easy victories and too much comfortable Egyptian living had made him soft. And he should not have been bothered by Khamudi's behaviour towards female slaves, either. Bringing proud Memphis to heel would put an end to these misgivings.

'Commander, how do we tell the high priests from the others?' asked an officer.

'You don't. You kill everyone you find in the temples and burn the bodies.'

'Is looting permitted?'

'Of course. I don't want to see a single temple left standing in Memphis.'

'And ... what about the women?'

'The soldiers may use them. At sunset, all officers are to report to me.'

Moustache was covered in sweat and having difficulty getting his breath back.

Spotted by Hyksos soldiers, he and the Afghan had had to leap from roof to roof, at the risk of breaking their necks. An arrow had even grazed Moustache's temple, but the two rebels had proved more agile than their pursuers and had managed to throw them off.

'Down there,' panted Moustache. 'Afghan, look down there. Flames, huge flames!'

'It's the Temple of Ptah – they're burning it.'

The Egyptian had tears in his eyes. 'The Temple of Ptah? It can't be. They wouldn't dare.'

'A lot of Egyptians are going to die today, and Memphis will be broken. We shall have to find another base as soon as we've made contact with any others who escape.'

'Three days' time,' said Moustache. 'But how did that devil Apophis know he had to launch a preventive attack?'

'Precisely because he is a devil.'

'Then there's no point in going on.'

'Even devils have their weaknesses, my friend. In the mountains of my homeland, we're used to fighting them. Believe me, they don't always win.'

## 26

Sheltered from the sun by a canopy supported by two small pillars in the form of lotus-stems, King Apophis and High Treasurer Khamudi were feasting on dishes prepared by the emperor's personal cook, an Egyptian who was forced to taste every dish in the king's presence. Apophis had demanded antelope cooked in sauce, accompanied by lentils and split peas. Three slaves wielded fans with acacia-wood handles and ostrich feathers, so that the king and his guest would not be troubled by heat or flies.

'This red wine is excellent,' remarked Apophis, sprinkling cumin on his food to aid his digestion.

Khamudi preferred juniper, which was a combined stimulant, laxative and diuretic.

He said, 'This jar comes from the High Priest of Ptah's cellar, Majesty. His fine wines are now in your cellar instead.'

'A satisfactory expedition, wouldn't you say?'

'A total success,' agreed Khamudi. 'Memphis is on her knees at last. The temples have been burnt and destroyed, and the priests and their accomplices executed. Everyone knows what punishment the rebels suffered.'

'Jannas has done well. Have the stone blocks from the temples sent to Avaris; we'll use them to build quays. I want Memphis to be a dead city, whose trade and financial activities are transferred to my capital.'

The cook served the dessert, dates pounded in honey.

'Taste it,' ordered the emperor.

The Egyptian looked unwell.

'Is it sour?' asked Apophis sarcastically.

'Not at all, Majesty. I did not sleep well and I am tired. The dessert is excellent, I assure you.' His colour returned.

'The emperor must not run risks. Have this idiot executed, Khamudi, and replace him.'

At a sign from the High Treasurer, two Cyprian pirates dragged the unfortunate man away, ignoring his pleas for mercy.

'These Egyptians never stop whining,' said the emperor, 'which is why they are useless soldiers. But tell me, what news of our new Information secretariat?'

Khamudi ran a hand through his well-oiled black hair. 'I've made great progress, Majesty. The traditional methods of correspondence are under control, of course, but I have invented a new one which ought to please you. Before I describe it, permit me to give you this gift.'

Khamudi handed Apophis a magnificent amethyst scarab mounted on a gold ring. The emperor slipped it on to the little finger of his left hand.

'A pretty piece,' he said. 'Now tell me about your invention.'

'For the Egyptians, this scarab is a symbol of happiness. It embodies continual rebirth, both on earth and in the otherworld. It is also a hieroglyph meaning "to be born", "to become", or "to be transformed". The one you are wearing belonged to an illustrious pharaoh – though of course his glory was a mere illusion compared to yours. With this jewel, you will confirm yourself as the king who brings happiness to his subjects. At the very sight of this symbol, many prominent Egyptians will be persuaded that you are the sole embodiment of the future. Hence my idea: we shall produce thousands of scarabs and re-use old ones on which we shall write our official messages.'

Khamudi opened a small bag and took out five scarabs of different sizes and made of materials ranging from limestone to fine porcelain.

'On the flat side,' he continued, 'my scribes will write the texts I dictate. These little things are easy to transport, and will soon flood the empire with the information we wish to disseminate. And the Egyptians will regard the messages on our scarabs as signs of good fortune.'

'Brilliant, Khamudi, quite brilliant. But I want to read each and every one of these messages. Not one is to be sent out without my explicit agreement.'

'I understand entirely, Majesty.'

'Indoctrination is as effective a weapon as war-chariots, my friend. With war-chariots we kill bodies; with indoctrination we kill souls.' Apophis paused and scowled. 'Have the fan-bearers replaced. These good-for-nothings are weakening – I can scarcely breathe.'

Only too happy to have escaped with their lives, the slaves yielded their places to a new team.

Apophis stroked his wine-flask; it was the one on which a map of Egypt was drawn. 'Despite the destruction of the temples in Memphis a few small groups of rebels still exist, and they're all the more dangerous because they can move around easily. If they've been driven to despair, they may commit acts of terrorism which would annoy me exceedingly.

They will not surrender and they are very difficult to identify, so we must put so much pressure on them that they have to leave their lairs and regroup.'

'How, Majesty?'

'By providing them with misleading information. We are going to make them believe that Thebes represents a real hope and that they must go there as soon as possible. You will therefore write a letter to this effect and entrust it to a special messenger who will go from tavern to tavern proclaiming – under the influence of drink – that he is the bearer of a very important message to the fortress at Per-Hathor.'

'Where shall I begin?'

Apophis gazed at the flask, deep in thought. 'The one to the south of Memphis – that's where they're hiding. And a little further south, around the old town of Henen-Nesut, elite soldiers will await the rebels as they travel to Thebes. I have the feeling that there is someone dangerous among them.'

Khamudi was astonished. 'But there's no one left capable of challenging us.'

'You must realize that sometimes one man can be more formidable than an entire army. This man must be killed as soon as possible.'

Seqen had been so shaken by his coronation, and the news that he was to become a father, that Ahhotep had granted him a few hours' rest in the Theban countryside. Protected by Laughter, the couple had enjoyed a long walk through the fields, ending by a canal bordered by tall willows.

'You shouldn't have done it, Ahhotep. You shouldn't have—'

'Of course I should. How could I have spent my life with a second-rate man? A queen's first duty is to give birth to a pharaoh, so that's what I did. And Pharaoh will be the father of my son.'

'But you know perfectly well that—'

'If you couldn't shoulder these responsibilities, I'd have given up the idea; but you can. However, I agree that you need a little time to develop your powers, so we shan't rush things – well, not too much.'

She kissed him passionately, and desire kindled within him.

'Let's lie down in the shade of the willows,' she said.

This quiet corner was a little paradise, well suited to the games of love. Seqen took off his kilt and laid it out on the riverbank. This improvised bed pleased Ahhotep, who received her eager lover's caresses with delight. Like her, Seqen was a creature of great enthusiasm, to whom tepid emotions were foreign. And a man like that had the qualities of a king.

\*

'Why don't you catch some fish?' Ahhotep suggested later.

Seqen put together a rudimentary fishing-rod from reeds and used a nice fat earthworm as bait.

'According to my mother,' she said as she watched him, 'the only strong man left in Thebes is the minister for agriculture. He is the descendant of an old, rich family; he owns a great deal of land and the only thing he wants is to keep his wealth intact, so he orders his peasants to go on working for him instead of joining the army. My mother has tried several times to convince him that such lack of action is condemning Thebes to death, and him with it, but he doesn't believe a word of it and has become entrenched in his position. Almost all the nobles listen to him, so nothing changes; and we're behaving like faithful subjects of the emperor.'

'And what are you planning to do about him?'

'Either he obeys me or I shall dismiss him from his offices.'

'But this fellow seems as haughty as he is stubborn – he'll never obey a woman.'

'He's an obstacle which must be removed. As long as he's in office, we shall be powerless.'

Although Laughter seemed fast asleep, his head resting on his crossed front paws, he suddenly made a powerful leap at Seqen. Under the impact, the young man was knocked several paces away from where he had been standing. And the crocodile's jaws snapped shut on empty air instead of on the king's legs.

Thwarted, the creature prepared to attack again, but the giant dog's barking and the stones Ahhotep threw drove it away.

'You've caught the biggest fish of all,' commented Ahhotep.

'The scribes in charge of the canals aren't doing their job any more,' grumbled Seqen. 'In the old days, no crocodile would have been able to venture into them.'

'That's true, but there's something else, something much more serious. The crocodile's attack is a sign that someone has put the evil eye on us. We must fight back against it straight away.'

## 27

'You're right, Ahhotep,' said Teti. 'The evil eye is upon us, particularly upon our new king.'

'How can we save him?'

'You and he must acquire the *heka*, the magical power that deflects harmful influences. Without it success is impossible, but the evil eye is denying you access to it. Fortunately, the way it manifested itself betrays its origins. The willow is the sacred tree of the temple at Dendera. Probably the tree has been badly damaged, and the gods hold Pharaoh responsible.'

'We must repair the damage,' decided the young queen.

'But Dendera is in Hyksos territory!'

'A peasant couple and their donkey won't arouse the Hyksos's suspicions.'

The royal couple travelling without protection on roads controlled by the invader? Their plan was madness, but Teti had no power to oppose it.

Long-Ears did not slow his pace as he approached the guard-post outside Kebet, which meant that the officials would cause the travellers no problems.

In fact, the powerful noonday sun had made them lethargic. They simply made a cursory search of the bags the donkey was carrying, and took two pairs of brand-new sandals as a toll.

The temple at Dendera lay deep in remote countryside. It had been built during the time of the pyramids and was dedicated to Hathor. The overgrown gardens in front of the building were a sure sign that there were no longer enough priests and labourers to care for them.

Long-Ears halted and sniffed the air. Then, reassured, he set off again at a brisker pace.

'No Hyksos around here,' concluded Ahhotep.

An old woman came out on to the temple forecourt and confronted them. 'I am the High Priestess of this temple,' she said. 'It is too poor now to welcome and feed travellers, so I ask you to continue on your way.'

'We shan't trouble you,' replied Ahhotep. 'We've only come to see the sacred willow.'

'It is dying, as is the whole country. Neither you nor I can do anything.'

'I don't agree, High Priestess.'

'And who are you?'

'Ahhotep, Queen of the Two Lands.'

The priestess was taken aback. 'Is Teti the Small dead?'

'My mother is alive, but she has passed on her power to me.'

'Power, Majesty? What power?'

'Perhaps the power to regenerate the Willow of Dendera.'

'Alas, that is impossible! You cannot even get near it.'

'I must,' said Ahhotep firmly.

Wearily, the old woman led her two visitors to the rear of the temple, where there was a small lake. In the middle of it stood a tall willow with withered leaves; it was so bent that it looked as if it might collapse at any moment.

As Ahhotep climbed over the surrounding wall to examine the tree more closely, the water began to bubble and a crocodile's jaws snapped at her, forcing her to beat a hasty retreat.

'Our guardians spirit has turned against us,' explained the High Priestess. 'When the willow falls, the evil eye will have won.'

Seqen had a sudden overwhelming feeling of inner power. 'I shall make it stand straight again,' he vowed.

'Do not risk your life,' urged the High Priestess.

Ahhotep asked her, 'Do you remember the incantations that were spoken when the willow was planted?'

'Of course, but it is a royal rite and has not been practised for a long time.'

'Recite it to me. I shall endow Seqen with magical abilities.'

Ahhotep stood as goddesses were depicted, their hands radiating waves of energy to empower those they protected, while the High Priestess spoke the words of the ancient ritual. They celebrated the moment when the sun had reached its zenith and the sacred tree had stretched up to the heavens, tall and strong.

Banishing his fear, Seqen waded into the lake. If the crocodile attacked, Ahhotep would come to his aid. But the reptile* backed away, its tail thrashing the water in rage. Then it began to grow quieter, and Seqen succeeded in reaching the foot of the willow.

He bent down, plunged his hand into the water and removed a small

---

* The Egyptians classed crocodiles as a kind of fish.

wooden crocodile. 'Look,' he said. 'Now the monster is tamed.'

'And look at the tree!' exclaimed the High Priestess.

The willow was slowly straightening, turning its leaves so that their silvery undersides faced the sun.

'The evil has been defeated,' said Ahhotep.

'How is that possible?' asked the High Priestess in astonishment. 'Only a rightful pharaoh can do that.'

Calm and silent, Ahhotep and Seqen gazed back at her.

'You are Queen of Egypt . . . and you, her husband, are Pharaoh – that's the truth, isn't it? But you have no escort or servants, and you look like two peasants.'

'If we didn't, we wouldn't be able to move around the Hyksos-controlled areas,' explained Ahhotep. 'Now that the evil will has been broken, grant us the *heka*.'

'The most powerful one is in the sacred city of Iunu.'

'Iunu is much too close to Avaris,' replied Ahhotep. 'We'd be caught before we ever got there.'

'In that case, Majesty, you must be content with the *heka* of Hathor. Because of the evil eye and the sacred willow's weakness, the *heka*'s energy has not been reaching the temple. We must hope that straightening the willow has re-established harmony.'

The couple followed the High Priestess into the temple and then to the eastern shrine, which contained an inner shrine of pink granite. As soon as she opened the doors, a gentle light streamed forth from the gold statuette of Hathor the cow.

'Let the *heka* bathe you,' counselled the High Priestess. 'It is the power of the light that the Divine Principle created when it gave order to the universe. With the aid of its power, you shall do worthy deeds and fight off the attacks of destiny.'

Hand in hand, Ahhotep and Seqen forgot time and drank in the goddess's love.

The Afghan and ten of his men were eating dried fish and stale bread at their hiding-place, in the countryside south of Memphis. No Hyksos troop movements had been seen in the area since Jannas's devastating raid.

Moustache came over to them and reported, 'One of the lookouts says a friend is coming.'

They all picked up their weapons.

'It's all right,' said Moustache. 'It's the innkeeper's son.'

The lad was out of breath. 'There's a stranger drinking beer at our inn,' he panted. 'He says he's carrying a special message from Avaris.'

'Well done, my boy,' said the Afghan. 'We'll deal with him.'

*

When the messenger left the inn, the rebels watched closely; he seemed to be alone. He set off down the track that led to the next village.

As soon as the man was far enough from the inn to be out of reach of help. Moustache sprang out and knocked him senseless with a single punch.

Quickly they searched him.

'The boy was right,' said Moustache. 'Here's a sealed letter from Avaris.' He broke the seal and unrolled the papyrus. 'This is most interesting. It's a message from Khamudi to the commander of the fortress at Per-Hathor, telling him that Thebes is still free and that rebels are assembling there. Wonderful! Now we know what we have to do. Let's gather all our men and go to Thebes. If we join forces, we'll be much stronger.'

'We're not moving from here,' said the Afghan firmly.

'But didn't you hear what I said?'

'I certainly did.'

'Then why don't you want to act on it?'

'Because it's a trap. A Hyksos messenger travelling alone, without military protection, and making himself known in a tavern: don't you find that surprising?'

'Well, if you put it that way . . .'

'We've had no news of Thebes, which has probably suffered the same fate as Memphis. The emperor wants to lure those of us who are left to Thebes so that he can ambush us on the way and wipe out every last man of us.'

In rage, Moustache ripped the papyrus into shreds.

## 28

The doctor examined the colour of Ahhotep's eyes, then her skin; finally, he checked that the blood-vessels in her breasts were firm, not flaccid.

'Your pregnancy is continuing perfectly,' he concluded, 'and the birth will be neither early nor late. But you must continue the daily massages.'

'And what about the results of the test?' she asked.

'Your urine made the barley germinate before the wheat, and the wheat before the spelt. So there is no doubt whatsoever: you will have a boy.'

Ahhotep left her bedchamber, ran into the antechamber, and flung herself into Seqen's arms. 'We're going to have a son,' she cried, 'a son who'll fight at your side!'

'I'd have preferred a girl as beautiful as her mother.'

'I decided we're going to have two sons, remember? Because at the moment Thebes needs warriors and leaders. Now, you must go back to the barracks, and I must go to the market.'

'Shouldn't you rest more? You're pregnant and—'

'I am making this child, and he'll be healthy and strong, believe me. Hurry away and train our men.'

The market in Thebes could have been that of a small provincial town. Out of habit people still haggled over prices, but all the cheerful chatter had long since vanished, and their main concern was the rumour of a Hyksos attack. Some people claimed that Memphis had been razed to the ground and that the same fate would soon befall Thebes.

Only a few men selling sacks of wheat and vegetables wore satisfied smiles. They had plenty to sell and, sooner or later, the customers would have to buy their wares, which were the most expensive in the market. They weighed them using a set of limestone cones of graded sizes, enabling them to weigh grain in any quantity from a handful to a whole sackful.

One of the traders, a red-faced man, sensed that Ahhotep was watching him and called to her, 'Come on over, young lady! What would you like?'

'To check your weights.'

The man almost choked. 'What! Who do you think you are?'

'Is it true that you and your colleagues work for the Agriculture secretariat?'

'What's that to you?'

'I have several copper ingots, each of equal weight, and I'm going to check your weights against them.'

'Get out of here this minute, you little hussy!'

A crowd had begun to gather, but it parted hastily as Laughter came thundering through to his mistress's side. Lips drawn back, he bared his teeth and gave a snarl that made the red-faced man's blood run cold.

'Let's . . . er . . . let's not do anything silly, eh?' he said. 'Surely a nice young lady like you wouldn't let that monster attack me.'

Ahhotep promptly laid three copper ingots on one side of the scales, and one of the trader's limestone cones on the other. To the onlookers' surprise, the scales promptly tipped in favour of the ingots.

'Your cone is underweight,' said Ahhotep, 'which means you're stealing from every single one of your customers. Now I shall check all the other traders' weights.'

The men wanted to stop her, but in the face of the angry crowd's demands they had to comply. Not one of the cones was the correct weight.

'I know that girl,' exclaimed one of the onlookers. 'I work at the palace, and I tell you that's Princess Ahhotep. Thanks to her, we shan't be cheated any more.'

Everyone agreed and cheered her.

She turned to an old countrywoman who was selling leeks. 'From now on, you shall be in charge of checking the weights used here. Anyone caught trying to cheat must give his produce away free for one month. If he offends again, he will be expelled from the guild of merchants.'

Heray was regarded as the best baker in Thebes, and loved his work so much that until now he had managed to produce acceptable bread and cakes despite shortages of staff and increasingly erratic payment by his customers. Yet now even he was on the verge of giving up.

This morning had been the final straw. The flour delivered by the Agriculture secretariat was of such poor quality that it was unusable. In despair Heray had gone to see the palace steward, only to receive the usual answer: the agriculture minister had absolute power within his domain, and the palace had to accept the situation.

Heray lowered his considerable bulk on to a stool which was as tired as he was. Today, he would not bother lighting the oven.

As he sat brooding, he heard strange sounds outside in the street. He went to the door and looked out, to be greeted by a giant donkey accompanied by a beautiful brown-haired young woman.

'Are you Heray?' she asked.

'Yes, I am.'

'I am Ahhotep, daughter of Queen Teti, and here is the palace's answer to your complaint: Long-Ears has brought you flour of the finest quality.'

Heray gaped at her. 'Where . . . where did it come from?'

'From the minister for agriculture's granaries. Other donkeys will arrive shortly, and you will have enough for the palace and the barracks. Take on other bakers at once, and train them to take over from you.'

'Take over? But why?'

'Because you have been appointed Overseer of Granaries.'

In a large vat, the brewers mixed together barley loaves, date juice and water; the resulting brew was left to rest until it fermented. That done, they filtered it and then poured it into jars which were lined inside with sedimentary clay so as to keep the beer fresh and cool.

But the brewers were constantly complaining that it was impossible for them to produce good beer when the barley they were given was no good. Moreover, almost all the jars should have been replaced by now. The beer was virtually undrinkable, so nobody wanted to make it any more: after all, they were craftsmen and they had their pride.

The master-brewer was dozing in his brewery when a kick in the side jolted him awake.

'Ouch! What the . . . ? A woman . . . ?'

'I am Princess Ahhotep.'

Suitably impressed, the craftsman got to his feet. 'Forgive me. I was having a little rest, I—'

'There's a lot of work coming your way, so you'll need to employ twice as many brewers. The new Overseer of Granaries, Heray, is going to deliver you top-quality barley, and first thing tomorrow you will get new jars from the Agriculture secretariat. The palace expects to receive some very good beer.'

'It will be a pleasure, my lady!'

The minister for agriculture had a head shaped like a duck-egg. His cook pampered him, so he had been putting on weight. In future, he had decided, he would eat only one dish with a rich sauce in the evening.

In the mornings, he liked to sleep under a sun-shade beside his lotus-pond. In the afternoons, he listened to his stewards' reports. He was perfectly content, since nothing changed from one day to the next and he was still the richest official in Thebes. His policy had not altered since he was appointed: to cling on to all the privileges he had gained. Thanks to the queen's weak government, he had no trouble at all in doing so.

This morning his nap was interrupted: his personal scribe – most unusually – asked to see him before the noon meal.

'My lord, I have to inform you of some extremely serious matters.'

'Let us remain calm and collected.'

'Heray the baker has just been appointed Overseer of Granaries.'

'What does that matter? Honorary titles have to be handed out from time to time.'

'You don't understand,' said the scribe. 'He has become overseer of all the granaries in Thebes – including yours!'

'I trust this is some kind of joke.'

'I'm afraid not. On the palace's orders, large quantities of grain have been removed from your stores and delivered to the main bakery and brewery.'

The minister suddenly lost his taste for sleep. 'Is Teti daring to defy me?'

'No, it's her daughter, Princess Ahhotep.'

## 29

The minister for agriculture paced up and down in front of the door to the queen's audience chamber. Teti would pay dearly for this insult. Not only would she give him back his property, but he would force her to give him arable land as compensation. The fact that her daughter had gone mad was not his concern; but the queen ought to pay more attention to what her first-born was doing.

'Her Majesty will receive you,' announced Qaris very calmly.

'And not before time!'

As he went in, the minister saw that the little audience chamber had been repainted. Then he saw Ahhotep; dressed in white, and with gold bracelets gleaming at her wrists, she was sitting on a gilded wooden throne whose feet were shaped like a bulls' hooves.

'I do not want to see you,' he said. 'I want to see the queen.'

'She sits before you.'

'What is that supposed to mean?'

'Bow before the Queen of the Two Lands.'

The minister's jaw dropped. 'The Queen . . . ?'

'Bow, or I shall have you arrested for insulting the crown.'

Her tone was so stern that the minister took fright. 'I did not know, Majesty, I—'

'Now you do know. Here are my first decisions. I have abolished several posts which have no place in a time of war. Heray, Overseer of Granaries, will take charge of Thebes's agriculture.'

'You mean . . . I am no longer minister?'

'That is correct.'

'But Heray is a nobody, Majesty. He's a simple baker – he'll never be able to manage our province's wealth.'

'Heray is an honest man,' said Ahhotep pointedly. 'In order to support the war effort, your lands and possessions have been requisitioned. I shall leave you just one house: the most modest one. You are to raise poultry there, to feed our soldiers. And try to put your heart into the work, unless you wish to sink lower.'

'Majesty . . .'

'This audience is at an end.'

The ex-minister had gathered together those close to him, with the intention of mounting a vigorous counter-attack. But no one wanted to fall in behind him.

'Why are you all so afraid?' he asked angrily. 'Ahhotep is alone and powerless.'

'Not as powerless as all that,' replied his personal scribe. 'She has the unconditional support of Teti the Small, who as you know is revered by all Thebans, and she is reinvigorating the army – in fact, many of the peasants who worked for you yesterday have just enlisted. True, the army's nothing but a rabble, but they are paid better than on your lands and they're loyal to Ahhotep.'

'I am sorry to leave you so early,' apologized the minister for finance, 'but I have been summoned to the palace before the noon meal, and Ahhotep does not like to be kept waiting.'

The other officials followed suit, each remembering an urgent task.

The ex-minister turned to his personal scribe and said with a sneer, 'What a band of cowards! I'm glad you're still loyal. Together, we shall devise a way of countering these measures.'

'I am dreadfully sorry, but I'm a scribe and I have no taste for poultry-rearing. Heray has offered me a job more in keeping with my skills.'

'Get out of here, you traitor!'

How, the former minister wondered, had that slip of a girl managed to destroy his authority so quickly? And how had she turned against him so many experienced men who owed their careers to him? On the point of breaking down, he drank half a small jar of date wine, which helped him pull himself together. He came to a worrying conclusion: this young queen was really dangerous, and quite capable of going much further than she already had.

He must at once inform his Hyksos friends, whom he had long been supplying with information about everything that happened in Thebes. Thebes was no longer his motherland, and he would watch its destruction with the greatest pleasure.

The minister for finance received the news that his post had been abolished with obvious relief. The old man's only wish was for a peaceful retirement, and he thanked the queen for granting it to him.

In less than a week, Ahhotep had succeeded in dismantling a puppet government and concentrating its powers in the narrow circle made up of her mother, her husband, Qaris and Heray. She had not chosen

Heray by chance: he had always protested against the Hyksos occupation, and Qaris had adopted him as a right-hand man.

She had still to resolve the problem posed by the commander-in-chief of the Theban army. He was much the oldest officer in the army, and was now as frail as the veils of mist on autumn mornings which were quickly dispersed by the sun.

Nevertheless, when she summoned him, he cut a fine figure. He bowed low, and said, 'I am at your service, Majesty.'

'How many men have we at our command?' asked Ahhotep.

'In theory, five hundred; in reality, no more than forty real soldiers. I have not recruited any more, since Thebes is not planning to resist the Hyksos.'

'That is no longer the case.'

'I'm delighted to hear it. Majesty, may I give you a piece of advice?'

'I'm listening.'

'Leave a group of incompetents in plain sight, men who will appear to be the official army. This decoy will keep the Hyksos smiling. Meanwhile, set up a secret camp where real soldiers are trained to handle every kind of weapon. It will take a long time, but it will work. And I can see no other means of preparing a true army of liberation.'

'Will you take on this task?' asked Ahhotep.

'I no longer have the strength, Majesty. Sickness has eaten me away. I fought it for as long as I could, in the insane hope that someone would give back Thebes her lost pride. Now that you are here, I can die in peace.'

That very evening, the old general died and Seqen was appointed commander of the army.

After hesitating for a long time, the former minister for agriculture had taken the only decision left to him: to go to Avaris himself and inform the emperor. The ridiculous Theban revolution would of course come to nothing, but Apophis would be pleased by this demonstration of his full and total allegiance.

Since his fall from power, the ex-minister had been abandoned by everyone and no longer trusted anyone. Entrusting his news to a messenger, however well paid, would be too dangerous. Having to leave Thebes, his lands and his possessions infuriated him, but he would soon return with the Hyksos army and exact his revenge with a cruelty beyond anything the arrogant Ahhotep could imagine.

'Guard-post in sight,' announced one of the bearers.

'Halt,' ordered the former minister. He got down from his carrying-chair and went alone towards the soldiers. This close to Kebet, they were probably pro-Hyksos forces; if they weren't, he would retrace his steps and take a different route.

'Emperor's men,' declared a sturdy fellow armed with a javelin.

'I am the Theban minister for agriculture and I must go as quickly as possible to Avaris to see our sovereign.'

'You, a Theban, recognize the authority of Apophis?'

'I have worked for him for a long time. I am his eyes and ears in Thebes. If you escort me to the capital, you will be well rewarded.'

Then he heard Seqen's grave voice behind him: 'So Ahhotep was right: you are indeed a traitor.'

## 30

The ex-minister almost fainted.

'We are not Hyksos,' said Seqen, 'but faithful servants of the queen. We have been following you since you left, to find out where you were going and intercept you before you reached the enemy.'

The traitor fell to his knees. 'Don't hurt me, I beg you! I am sorry, so very sorry—'

'Tell me who your accomplices are.'

'I . . . I haven't got any.'

'You're still lying.'

'No, I swear I'm not. I was the only one. I did inform the emperor – but only about small things, very small things, and it was in the interests of Thebes.'

Seqen and his men dragged him to the bank of the Nile, and the pharaoh threw a wax model of a crocodile into the water. Less than a minute later, the water began to bubble and swirl, and the gaping jaws of a huge, and very real, crocodile emerged.

'If you don't talk,' said Seqen, 'he will be your torturer.'

Trembling with fear, the traitor denounced all his accomplices, among them a washerman at the palace and an officer who had acted as a messenger.

'May the god Sobek decide your fate.'

The Thebans seized the traitor by the ankles and threw him into the river, which was soon red with his blood.

Seqen took Ahhotep in his arms. 'You were right,' he said. 'The Hyksos traitors in Thebes have all been arrested and executed. From now on, the emperor will be blind and deaf.'

'Only if he believes the minister is still alive and working for him. So we must send him regular messages informing him that Thebes is still declining and has lost the will to resist.'

Teti interrupted them. 'An official letter has come from Avaris. Apophis is demanding that Thebes send him a stele confirming that she recognizes him as pharaoh of Upper and Lower Egypt.'

'Never!' cried Seqen. 'We'll send him a declaration of war.'

'We can't,' said Ahhotep sadly. 'We are still far, far from ready. If he wants a stele, he shall have one. But the stone-cutter must alter most of the hieroglyphs – though with such skill that only someone who knows the secret will notice. He must break the wings of the birds, fix the serpents to the ground and prevent the suns from shining. No one will open the mouth of this stele, no one will bring it to life. The emperor will receive a dead stone.'

Apophis contemplated the stele with a disdainful sneer.

'The art of Senusret's day is indeed dead – Theban sculptors no longer have any talent at all. What do you think, Tany?'

She was munching a greasy cake. 'I loathe Egyptian art in all its forms. It really is the art of a race of slaves.'

'But you're Egyptian yourself,' pointed out Windswept, Apophis's younger sister. She was a magnificent creature, very tall and slim, and with something exotic about her appearance. Since Apophis's rise to power, she had busied herself furnishing the palace at Avaris with masterpieces from the towns of the Delta. Goblets of blue porcelain decorated with lotus-flowers, incense-burners, lamps shaped like lilies, beds decorated with the gods who protected sleep, matchlessly elegant chairs made from sycamore wood. Although he was indifferent to these marvels, Apophis could regard himself as a true pharaoh.

'I'm a Hyksos now,' protested Tany. 'Thanks to me, a lot of rich, arrogant Egyptian women have become slaves – those pretentious bitches have to prostrate themselves before me now.'

Windswept shrugged. She felt only contempt for Apophis's dreadful wife.

'Egyptian women were perverted by their freedom,' said Apophis. 'Our law requires all women to submit to men, for only men are capable of making rational decisions.'

'But,' said Windswept, 'it's the lioness who hunts and brings back the food.'

'Don't contradict me, my dear sister. Surely you aren't defending our slaves?'

'I'm not interested in politics. All I care about is beauty.'

'That's perfect. Continue that way.'

Casting a disdainful look at fat Tany, Windswept went out, leaving a scent of lotus-flowers behind her.

'Your sister hates me,' complained Tany. 'You ought to send her back to Asia.'

'She's useful,' said Apophis.

'Is she? How?'

'Windswept loves love, and no man can resist her. She enjoys being in Egypt, so I have set conditions she must comply with in order to stay. She must sleep with the most senior dignitaries of the empire and obtain their confidences in bed. In this way, I know all their vices and their ambitions. If anyone dares criticize me, he dies.'

'So she's going to stay in Avaris for a long time?'

'As long as she does as I wish.'

'My work is just as important.'

'I know, Tany, I know. Whatever you do, don't slacken your efforts.'

She gave a cruel smile. 'Yesterday my great friend Aberia arrested the widow of the mayor of Sais, who was disguised as a serving-woman. We'd been hunting that rebel for months – in the end she was denounced by one of her former maids.'

'Did she belong to an organized group?'

'No. Aberia tortured her with her own hands before strangling her, and the slut hid nothing from her, you can be sure. I have a list of Egyptian noblewomen who are still in hiding in the foolish belief that they can evade us. But Aberia will find them.'

The stele from Thebes had been set up in the Temple of Set, where the Great Council met. Today every council member brought good news. The Hyksos Empire was continuing to expand without its armies even having to fight; the new trading practices were making greedy men wealthy and keeping the common people in a state of submission from which they would never emerge. The Information secretariat was producing impressive numbers of scarabs, which would carry the emperor's thoughts into even the remotest places.

The world was becoming Hyksos.

And the conquerors owed this victory to Apophis, who inspired mortal fear in everyone who met him. Those who displeased him found their careers cut short; and sometimes their lives. Even the bravest men could not help trembling when they heard the emperor's harsh voice announcing his decisions which no one dared challenge.

As for Khamudi, he hung on his master's every word and did everything he could to turn Apophis's wishes into reality. The High Treasurer grew richer by the day, thanks to the papyrus and scarab-making industries, and he was delighted to discover the power of wealth. He could buy anyone he wanted, whenever he wanted.

'Did our ambush succeed?' Apophis asked him.

'A number of rebels were caught and beheaded at Henen-Nesut, Majesty. They were indeed trying to reach Thebes.'

'Keep the trap in place,' ordered the emperor. 'I am not entirely sure that the most dangerous man has yet been caught in our net.'

'The stele from Thebes shows that the will to rebel has been eradicated,' said Khamudi with relish. 'In addition, the latest letter from the minister for agriculture confirms that Teti the Small can do nothing to change that fact.'

'Let us go and check the tax revenues, High Treasurer. I have the feeling certain provinces are in arrears.'

31

It took Moustache and the Afghan several long weeks to regroup the few rebels who had escaped the massacre in Memphis. They had all lost heart, and most wanted to go home and submit to the Hyksos. Eventually, however, Moustache managed to convince them that if they did they would be signing their own death-warrants, because they were bound to be put to death after lengthy torture. Little by little, the old spirit of comradeship re-emerged. The Afghan gave them no rest, but subjected his band to intensive training, particularly in unarmed fighting.

The rebels were sheltered mainly by peasants, who, exploited and mistreated by the invaders, were happy to welcome men who still believed in freedom. So once again the Afghan began to weave the web that had been torn apart in Memphis, all the time making sure that every place they ate or slept was completely safe – and that they spent no more than a week at any one farm. He stressed the essential difference between sympathizers and true rebels. The former were growing in number by the minute, but there was no point counting on them if it came to a fight; and it would take several months to train the latter.

Moustache was just as wary as the Afghan. He subjected would-be recruits to exhaustive tests before accepting them into the group. He also took care to fence off the network to prevent it being wiped out if one of Apophis's spies managed to infiltrate it.

Then news arrived that the Hyksos had indeed organized an ambush near Henen-Nesut. All those rebels who had tried to reach Thebes had been caught and executed.

'And we are trapped between Hyksos in the north and Hyksos in the south,' complained Moustache. 'We are going to die like wild beasts, crouching in our den.'

'Not at all, my friend,' said the Afghan. 'We are making our den bigger. And if we do die, it will be in battle.'

'You still believe that?'

'So do you, deep in your heart. Today the enemy is a thousand times more powerful than we are, and it would be madness to face him openly. But it won't always be like this. Learn patience – that's the one virtue you lack.'

One of Moustache's men interrupted them. He said, 'There's something going on in a village not far away. Hyksos soldiers arrested a traveller and are preparing to torture him in the forge. Perhaps we ought to do something?'

'Too risky,' said the Afghan.

'But supposing the poor man's a member of a rebel group which is trying to contact us?'

'He's right,' said Moustache. 'I'm going to take a look.'

'Not without me,' retorted the Afghan.

The six Hyksos soldiers were specialists in interrogation. While keeping watch on the path that ran along the edge of the desert, they had spotted the stranger approaching from the south.

Although he looked rather frail, the fellow had proved to be made of sterner stuff than expected. Despite beating and flogging him cruelly, they had still got nothing out of him. However, the commanding officer knew a method which would make even a dumb man talk.

'See the furnace, you dirty spy? It has hot coals ... If you keep silent, you'll have a taste of them, and after that you won't have a face left.'

The prisoner lifted terrified eyes to his torturer. 'I know nothing – nothing at all!'

'Too bad for you.'

The smell of burning flesh was accompanied by such unbearable screams that a Hyksos smashed the tortured man's skull with a stone.

'You've killed him, you imbecile,' snarled the officer. 'How are you going to make him talk now?'

Before the torturer could reply, an arrow plunged into his chest.

The Afghan killed two more Hyksos, while Moustache sank his javelin into the back of a fourth, and then gave vent to his fury by strangling a fifth.

The only survivor, the officer found himself gazing into the Afghan's terrifying eyes.

'I am an officer in the emperor's service. If you lay a hand on me, you'll be condemned to death.'

'Leave him to me,' demanded Moustache.

The officer tried to run away, but the Egyptian was too swift for him. He caught him and dragged him by his hair to the forge.

'Now it's your turn to taste the fire.'

The officer struggled in vain. His face was plunged into the coals. He opened his mouth to scream, only for his tongue to be burned away.

Indifferent to his horrible death-throes, the Afghan examined the Egyptian's corpse. 'Come and see, Moustache. There's a piece of linen sewn inside his tunic, and someone has drawn a strange sign in red ink.'

'It looks like the moon-disc, in its ship.'

'It must be a message. This poor fellow can't tell us what it means, but it must be important – at any rate, he took enormous risks in order to pass it on.'

'Who was it meant for?'

'Certainly not the Hyksos.'

'Then he was looking for rebels,' ventured Moustache. 'He might even be a messenger from Thebes.'

'Don't raise your hopes too high,' said the Afghan. 'But we'll memorize the sign.'

He tore away the scrap of linen and burned it. If, by chance, it was indeed a coded message to rally the rebels, it must remain secret for as long as possible.

'What if there's another messenger?' said Moustache anxiously. 'Perhaps Thebes was sending out a last appeal for help.'

'Is the moon its symbol?'

'Not as far as I know.'

'Then we must forget Thebes and think in terms of a small band of rebels who'll try to make themselves known.'

'How can we join up with them?'

'There's only one solution,' said the Afghan. 'We must head further south.'

'But we'll walk straight into Hyksos patrols.'

'If we do, at least we'll know where they are.'

Although her belly was growing rounder by the day, Ahhotep was as active as ever. By reviving traditional trade practices in Thebes and driving out the fraudsters, she had re-established trust. The Thebans no longer spent their time spying on one another or withdrawing into themselves for fear of what tomorrow might bring. Bonds of friendship were being renewed and people sang the praise of Ahhotep, who visited the sick and found food for those in greatest need. Aware that the time for fine words had passed, the young queen had decided to attend to the basics of daily life.

Not that she neglected larger matters. 'Is there any news of our messengers?' she asked Qaris.

The steward's face darkened. 'I'm afraid not, Majesty. They must all have been killed. I fear it may be impossible to get through all the barriers put in place by the Hyksos. And there are probably no rebels left north of Kebet.'

'I'm sure that is not so,' said Ahhotep. 'Cowards, collaborators and the timid may be in the majority, I grant you, but there are still some, even among the oppressed and the persecuted, who will never bend the knee. Those are the people we must contact.'

Qaris bowed, but said, 'I do not think we should send out more men to certain death, Majesty.'

'We must break out of our isolation and find out whom we can count on. If she has no contact with the outside world, Thebes will wither.'

Qaris wavered. 'One of our few remaining allies may perhaps be able to help us, if he is still alive – but I do not wish to raise your hopes too high.'

'Whom are you thinking of?'

'Babay, the old sage of Nekhen. He used to have excellent messengers at his disposal, and if they can still carry messages they would be very useful.'

'I shall go to Nekhen at once.'

'Majesty, in your condition—'

'There's only one condition which interests me,' said Ahhotep. 'The condition of my country.'

## 32

To reach Nekhen, which lay some four days' journey to the south of Thebes, Ahhotep and Seqen followed a track which ran along the edge of the fields. They were escorted by ten young soldiers ready to give their lives to save the queen. When she grew tired, she let herself be carried in a sycamore-wood travelling-chair.

Nothing untoward happened during the journey. The little group met only a few frightened peasants, who were careful not to ask questions and who hid in their miserable mud huts. It was clear that Waset was almost totally deserted, and that the Hyksos regarded it with such contempt that they had not left a single occupying unit there.

The outskirts of the old city of Nekhen, though, were an unpleasant surprise. Everywhere they saw fallen trees, abandoned pastures, dead cows. Happiness seemed to have abandoned the place for ever.

'Let's turn back,' said Seqen. 'The town will be nothing but ruins.'

'No. We must check,' insisted Ahhotep.

'Looters may have taken over the town, and there are only a few of us . . .'

'I want to know if Babay is still alive.'

Seqen was the first to step through the great open gate in the outer wall. The doors had been torn down, and the guard-post laid waste. In the middle of the main street lay a dead dog.

'Two lookouts,' ordered Seqen, 'one to the left, the other to the right.'

Here and there were burnt-out houses. Everywhere lay broken pottery, fragments of furniture smashed by axe-blows, tattered remnants of clothing. But not a living soul. Even the age-old temple of the goddess Nekhbet had not been spared. Smashed statues and fallen pillars bore witness to its suffering.

'There's someone over there,' shouted one of the lookouts.

He pointed to a very old man who was sitting on the threshold of the roofed temple, reading a papyrus. He did not even look up when the visitors approached, so indifferent was he to the fate that awaited him.

'Are you Babay the sage?' asked Ahhotep.

He did not answer.

'Move further back,' she ordered the soldiers.

As soon as they were a good distance away, the young woman played her trump card.

'Pharaoh Seqen and Queen Ahhotep need your help in order to save Egypt.'

With almost unbearable slowness, the old man began rolling up his papyrus.

When he had finished, he looked at her for the first time, nodded, and said, 'The Divine Light placed the pharaoh upon the earth to bring harmony in place of disorder, to win the gods' favour, to enact justice and drive away injustice. He is not above Ma'at, but must be her servant and protect those who practise her way. It was so once, before the invasion. Today there is no pharaoh upon Egyptian soil.'

'You are wrong,' said Ahhotep. 'Seqen has been crowned at Karnak.'

The old sage looked at the young couple doubtfully. 'The Hyksos have destroyed Karnak.'

'I can assure you they have not,' said Ahhotep. 'Teti the Small has preserved Thebes's freedom and the temple is unharmed. The Hyksos believe us to be submissive and therefore no threat to them, but in fact we are working secretly to prepare for re-conquest.'

'Queen Ahhotep . . . The moon-god protects you and gives you an aptitude for battle. So you are the new royal couple – with neither army nor country.'

'We are training soldiers little by little,' promised Seqen.

The old man tore up the papyrus. 'Help me up.'

Despite his great age, Babay was stocky and heavy.

'Pharaoh Seqen and Queen Ahhotep,' he said when he was on his feet. 'Before I die, I shall have had the most beautiful dream imaginable.'

'What happened here?' asked Ahhotep.

'Three Hyksos warships dropped anchor here two months ago. The invaders ravaged the countryside and the town, killed those few who resisted, and forced the people to march to the North to be made into slaves. They spared me so that I might write an account of the punishment inflicted on any city or person who dares oppose the emperor. I have just destroyed that account. Come, let us go to my house.'

Babay led the royal couple to his home, a small, two-storey house near the temple. On the threshold, he paused and gazed out at his devastated city. 'If you are truly king and queen, never negotiate with the barbarians who destroyed this city and enslaved its citizens.'

Almost everything in the house had been looted; the only things left were a single mat and a worn-out scribe's palette.

Babay sat down. 'I'm tired, too tired to take up arms.'

'Qaris, our steward, thinks you may be able to help us,' ventured Ahhotep. 'He says you have excellent messengers at your command.'

Babay smiled. 'Excellent and very effective – that's true enough. But they have probably all been killed.'

'But you aren't certain?'

'I haven't seen them for a long time. Let us go on to the terrace, and I'll summon their leader.'

Once outside, Babay whistled a rhythmic tune, accentuating the high and low notes. Soon a handsome beige and white pigeon appeared, and alighted at his feet.

'Rascal, you are still alive! Bring me the others.'

The bird flew off. A little while later, he returned with six other pigeons.

'You're all safe!' exclaimed Babay, with tears in his eyes. 'So the gods haven't altogether abandoned us. I spent more than a year training them, Majesty, and I must teach you how to give them clear instructions. When your mind communicates with theirs, they will go where you tell them, and then return to the place from which they left.'

From the very first experiments, Ahhotep saw that the birds were exceptionally intelligent. They quickly grasped the fact that she was taking Babay's place and that from now on they must carry out her orders.

'Grant me one week, Majesty,' said Babay, 'and they will become faithful messengers who will never betray you.'

The birds could travel long distances in a single flight, flying at great speed and never losing sight of north, thanks to their innate sense of direction. The fact that there were so few of them was only a temporary handicap, for one female laid two eggs ten days after mating, and only a month after fledging, the young pigeons were ready to begin work.

'What splendid recruits!' exclaimed Seqen. 'They'll make a mockery of the Hyksos barriers.'

'You cannot stay here, Babay,' said Ahhotep. 'We'll take you to Thebes.'

'That's out of the question, Majesty. I was born here and have spent all my life here. For me, this is the most beautiful place in Egypt. One day, if you respect the law of Ma'at and if you are strong enough to overcome the obstacles, defeats and betrayals, you will return to Nekhen and give her back her past splendour.'

'We cannot simply abandon you,' insisted Seqen.

'Will you give me a little wine, Majesty?'

The old man drank deeply from the jar Seqen handed him, then lay down and rested his head on some cushions.

And then Babay serenely passed away.

## 33

Fat, Thin, Long-Beard, Jovial, Impatient and their colleagues had one thing in common: they all cursed Ahhotep, who had dragged them away from their routine and given them jobs as washermen. They had to soak clothes, lengths of cloth and assorted fabrics in large cauldrons, rinse them in clean water, wring them out, hit them with wooden beaters, hang them up to dry, fold them impeccably and sometimes even perfume them. Theban housewives had recovered their taste for cleanliness, and little by little the entire city was becoming spick and span again, including the districts where the humblest folk lived.

The work was so back-breaking that the washermen forgot all about the Hyksos threat and thought only of their own working conditions, which they planned to improve by complaining to their overseer.

'We're stopping work,' declared Jovial.

'I'm not taking a risk like that,' said Thin. 'The princess is quite capable of having us arrested.'

'We're stopping because we've run out of soap. So we can't do the washing properly, can we?'

'He has a point,' agreed Fat.

Impatient abandoned his pile of soiled women's linen, and they all went to see the overseer. As spokesman for the group, Impatient voiced their vehement protests.

The overseer listened carefully. 'Provision has been made for this,' he said when Impatient had finished.

'Provision? For our justifiable complaints?'

'No, for a shortage of soap.'

'Well, as we've run out, we aren't going back to work.'

'You may rest until the delivery,' said the overseer. 'Ah, here it is now.'

Long-Ears plodded serenely up, bearing a large consignment of soap cakes made from limestone and vegetable fats. He was not alone: just behind him was Ahhotep, resplendent in a pale-yellow dress.

At the sight of her, even Impatient was lost for words.

'By all the gods, she's beautiful!' whispered Jovial.

Ahhotep took a jar from the bags the donkey was carrying.

'Here is some good beer for you to have with your noon meal. The palace is pleased with your work, so you shall all receive an increase in your wages. Also, the overseer may take on apprentices, so that your burden of work becomes less heavy.'

Everyone lost the urge to protest.

'We shall drink to your health, Majesty,' promised Fat, 'and to the health of the child you are carrying.'

Ahhotep had re-established strict rules of cleanliness, which, as far as she was concerned, lay at very heart of the struggle for freedom. When dirt won, morale waned and fear and laziness invaded people's souls. From one day to the next, each Theban must win back his dignity, and he could only do so if his body, his clothes and his home were clean. Teams of street-cleaners complemented the work done by individuals, and the transformation was soon noticeable. Once again, Thebans were living in a charming and spotless city.

This modest victory over despair gave their lives new meaning. Instead of withdrawing into themselves, they started talking and encouraging one another.

'The women have started wearing face-paint again,' observed Teti.

'I am delighted to hear it,' said Ahhotep. 'Their beauty, too, will help rebuild our will to be free.'

'Unfortunately, we shall soon have run out of what they need. The palace reserves are almost exhausted, and the makers of face-paints have all moved to Edfu.'

Edfu, several days' travel to the south, was in the occupied lands.

'Governor Emheb,' said Qaris, 'was one of our most loyal supporters. How can we find out if he is still alive and, if he is, what freedom of action he has? We cannot use the pigeons without contacting him first.'

'There is only one solution: we must go there and see for ourselves.'

'Not you, Ahhotep,' protested Teti.

'No one will look twice at a poor fisherman and his pregnant wife.'

The boat was a humble one, with a patched sail and creaking oars, but the north wind blew steadily, enabling Seqen and Ahhotep to make good progress towards Edfu.

The young king had changed a great deal. Through training and intensive exercise, the thin lad had acquired the stature of an athlete.

'Do you feel ready to become a father?' asked Ahhotep.

'Thanks to you, I feel ready to win any and every battle.'

The young couple spent an enchanting night in the uncomfortable boat, hidden in a papyrus thicket. Alone in the world for a few hours, they knew that their love, fierce as a storm and tender as autumn sunlight, gave them a strength no ordeal could erode.

At daybreak, they set off again.

Near Edfu, a Hyksos war-boat ordered them to stop. Seqen lowered the sail and bowed like an obedient slave.

'Who are you and where are you from?' demanded an officer with hooded eyes.

'I'm a fisherman from Edfu and I'm on my way home.'

'Is this woman yours?'

'Yes, my lord, and she's expecting our child.'

'Show me your catch.'

Seqen opened a willow basket containing three average-sized perch.

'You must pay the toll,' said the officer.

'But, my lord—'

'Don't argue. Just give me those fish.'

'But we're going to have a child and I need to sell them to—'

'I said: don't argue. In future, stay closer to the town.'

The little boat berthed between two skiffs moored to wooden stakes with papyrus ropes, and Seqen helped Ahhotep step out on to dry land.

A rough-looking fellow hailed them. 'Who do you think you are?'

'A fisherman.'

'No you aren't. I'm one myself, and I know all the fishermen around here. You're not from these parts.'

Something she glimpsed in the man's eyes prompted Ahhotep to reveal part of the truth. 'We've come from Thebes.'

'Thebes? But it's been destroyed.'

'The Hyksos have lied about it. Thebes is unharmed, and is resisting the oppressors.'

'Thebes unharmed . . . then Egypt's still alive.'

'Is Edfu occupied?' asked Ahhotep.

'Jannas's army killed all our soldiers and stole all our money and goods, then went back to the North, leaving only guards here. But I'm so afraid of being arrested that it's three months since I dared set foot in the town.'

'Is Governor Emheb still alive?'

'I don't know. But whatever you do, don't try to enter Edfu. You'd never get out alive.'

'Which entrance is the least closely guarded?'

'The eastern gate. But don't do it – it's insane.'

Ahhotep merely smiled. 'Will you help us?'

'I can't myself. Life may not be happy, but I'm getting by. My brother might go with you, as if you're fisher-folk going to sell your fish in the market. He bribes the guards to let him work.'

The brother agreed.

As he watched the couple walking towards the town with his brother, the rough-looking man shook his head in disbelief. Why were this young fellow and his pretty, pregnant wife walking straight into the lion's jaws?

## 34

The outskirts of Edfu were almost silent. People exchanged goods with hardly any haggling, and kept a permanent eye on the Hyksos guards who patrolled the streets and squares at all times. People were often arrested for no apparent reason, and no one emerged unharmed from interrogations. At best, suspects had broken limbs; at worst, they were deported to the copper mines.

The fisherman's brother left Ahhotep and Seqen near the Temple of Horus. The entrance was sealed, for the emperor had forbidden anyone to celebrate the cult of the divine falcon, protector of Pharaoh. That role was now reserved for Set of Avaris.

An amulet-seller flourished his wares, which were as ugly as they were ineffective, at the couple. 'They aren't expensive,' he said, 'and they'll protect your child. I'll give you four for the price of two.'

'We're looking for Governor Emheb,' said Seqen.

The seller hurried away.

'Why do they all refuse to talk about the governor,' wondered Ahhotep, 'unless he has sold himself to the Hyksos?'

'We've got the answer we came for,' agreed Seqen. 'Let's leave.'

They walked along the southern wall of the temple, then set off towards the outskirts.

But this time the eastern gate was guarded by Hyksos armed with swords and clubs; it would have been pointless to try and run away.

Some peasants were leaving the town without being questioned. Seqen and Ahhotep fell into step behind them.

'You two,' said a guard, 'where are you going?'

'To our boat, sir,' replied Seqen. 'We're fisher-folk.'

'You've been heard asking questions about the governor.'

'We'd have liked to meet him,' agreed Ahhotep.

'Why?'

'To ask him to give us a new boat. Ours is rotting away.'

'That story doesn't hold water. Come with us.' The guard beckoned to two of his colleagues, and the three of them marched the young pair towards the centre of town.

Seqen thought he might be able to kill the guards, but he was afraid Ahhotep might be injured in the fight. So he decided on a different plan: once he was in Emheb's presence, he'd take him hostage. For the king had sworn that he and the queen would leave this town unharmed.

The governor's palace was similar in appearance to Titi's at Kebet. Scribes were writing away in their shabby offices, soldiers were apathetically cleaning their weapons, and stray cats were scavenging for the smallest scrap of food.

'Go in there,' said the guards' leader.

It was a dark, dirty outhouse.

'When will we see the governor, sir?' asked Seqen.

'You're a stubborn one! Don't worry, you'll see him.'

The door closed behind them.

The earthen floor was piled with worn-out sandals and dirty rags.

Seqen looked around and spotted a hole in the back wall. 'I can make it bigger, and we can escape through it.'

'No, we mustn't do that,' replied Ahhotep. 'We must see Emheb.'

'But what if they only let us out of here to execute us?'

'The governor will see us, I'm sure of it. I shall kneel before him, then I shall seize his sword and threaten to slit his throat if he doesn't give us a boat to take the three of us back to Thebes. That traitor doesn't know it yet, but he's already our prisoner.'

Seqen took his wife in his arms. Her soft, scented skin made him forget their foul-smelling prison.

When the door opened, they were still in each other's arms.

'Follow me, lovebirds,' ordered a palace guard.

'Are we going to see the governor at last, sir?' asked Seqen in a small, timid voice.

'Move! Quickly now!'

At the centre of the courtyard stood a wooden block, with an axe planted in it. Would Seqen have time to grab the axe and kill the headsman?

'This way.'

They moved away from the place of execution and were pushed into a pillared audience chamber with faded wall-paintings.

An astonishingly big man came forward to observe them. Everything about him was outsize: his eyes, his nose, his shoulders, even his ears. Judging by his huge belly, he was a man who enjoyed the good life, but this impression was belied by the hard glint in his eyes.

'Are you looking for me, young folk?' he asked.

'If you are Governor Emheb, yes indeed,' replied Seqen.

'You, girl, show me your hands.'

Ahhotep did so.

'They are delicate and pretty, and they don't smell of fish.'

'It's my husband who does the fishing.'

With surprising speed for a man of his bulk, Emheb tore off a piece of Seqen's tunic and sniffed it. 'This doesn't smell of fish, either. Who are you really?'

The governor was unarmed, and the guards were too far from Seqen for him to seize their weapons without a fight. They would have time to warn their colleagues, and the king would be overwhelmed by force of numbers. Besides, from the look of Emheb's enormous neck, it would be impossible to strangle him.

'Why have you betrayed your country?' Ahhotep demanded, staring so intensely at the governor that he felt quite uneasy.

'You're Thebans, aren't you?' he said.

'This is your day of glory, Emheb. You and your Hyksos are about to murder Queen Ahhotep, Lady of the Two Lands. I ask only one favour. Spare this peasant: I forced him to accompany me.'

She hoped she could save Seqen; while Seqen swore a silent oath not to let the Hyksos soldiers lay a hand on his wife.

The governor of Edfu knelt. 'I am your servant, Majesty. Command, and I shall obey.'

The guards followed suit.

'These men aren't Hyksos,' Emheb explained, 'they are Egyptians. I had the Hyksos men killed one by one, and replaced them with my own men, while letting the emperor believe that the town had submitted completely to him. I declared myself his ally, and he has entrusted me with the task of bleeding the region dry with higher and higher taxes. My only hope has been to find a way of launching an attack. It would undoubtedly fail, but at least it would allow us to die with dignity.'

'You may rise, Governor.'

Emheb was visibly moved. 'Am I to understand, Majesty, that Thebes still lives and is ready to fight?'

'Forget about your attack. To create a real army, we shall need patience and the utmost secrecy.'

'I am your servant, Majesty.'

'Not only mine, Emheb. You are in the presence of my husband, Pharaoh Seqen.'

Ahhotep thought the governor was going to faint.

'A king? We have a king? Majesty, you are telling me of true wonders!'

'At the moment we are greatly in need of ointments, face-paints and skilled workers who can make them.'

Emheb's face lit up with a broad smile. 'In spite of all their searches, the Hyksos have never found my secret stores of incense and styrax. I also have plenty of ointments of different qualities, so you can supply both the temple and individuals. As for skilled workers, the finest in Egypt do indeed live in Edfu. Several of them will go with you when you leave for Thebes. But now, Majesty, come and see my treasures – all this time they have been waiting for a new royal couple.'

With infectious enthusiasm, the governor showed his guests the underground chambers below the temple, where censers, vases and pots of ointments had been kept hidden.

'We shall change nothing,' decided Ahhotep. 'The Hyksos must continue to believe that Nekhen is dead and Edfu is dying.'

## 35

Seqen paced up and down outside the room where his wife was in labour.

'Are the midwives really skilled enough?' he asked Qaris, who was almost as nervous as he was.

'Have no fear, Majesty. They are the best in Thebes.'

'But Ahhotep was in such pain! She ought to have been resting these last few weeks. The journey to Edfu exhausted her.'

'With respect, Majesty, it was crowned with such success that the future suddenly looks much brighter.'

'I know, Qaris, I know. But the queen ought to take more care of herself.'

'A Queen of Egypt is a Queen of Egypt,' Qaris reminded him fatalistically. 'And when her name is Ahhotep . . .'

'Surely having a baby shouldn't take this long?'

'Our specialists can deal with even the most difficult births.'

'In the time of the pyramids I'm sure they could, but can the specialists we have in Thebes today? If something serious happens, neither Ahhotep nor the child will survive.'

The steward did not have the courage to contradict him. Seqen took to pacing up and down again.

Just as the sun was reaching its zenith, Teti emerged from the delivery room, a baby in her arms.

'It's a splendid boy,' she said, smiling.

Seqen did not dare touch him. 'And how is Ahhotep?'

'She is radiant with happiness.'


There were three of them, a brunette, a redhead and one with chestnut hair. Three widows, whose husbands had owned large estates in the Delta but had been deported by the Hyksos. The women could easily, as so many others had done, have sunk into despair. Instead, to honour the memory of the dead, they had decided to conduct themselves like true Egyptian women.

First, they had acted as funerary princesses, so that their husbands' kas could continue to live. Next they had pooled their skills, to manage their possessions more efficiently. Despite the increases in taxes, they had succeeded in retaining all their workers and ensuring that they had a decent life. Their reputation had spread right across Lower Egypt, until eventually it reached the ears of the emperor's wife.

The gate-keeper of the house where the three widows lived was most impressed when the statuesque Aberia arrived at the entrance.

'Are your mistresses at home?' she asked.

'Of course. Are you looking for work?'

'You no longer have any.'

Lady Aberia's huge hands closed round the gate-keeper's throat and crushed his larynx.

Several peasant farmers saw her drop the body like a discarded puppet. 'We saw everything – you are a murderer,' they cried.

Fifty Hyksos soldiers poured on to the estate, slaughtered those who tried to flee and whipped the others.

Completely at ease, Aberia went to the office, where she found the three terrified widows clutching their tax papyri to their breasts.

'So here you are – the last businesswomen in the land of the vanquished. Don't you know that your practices are against our laws? Females like you should be under the control of a man, not making decisions for yourselves. As of today, your estates and possessions are confiscated.'

'We pay our taxes regularly,' protested the redhead, 'and we—'

Aberia dealt her such a violent slap that she fell to the ground, dazed.

'Pick that whore up,' she ordered the two other widows, 'and follow the soldiers. The emperor has a different kind of work for you.'

Apophis had greeted his wife's idea with great amusement. Beautiful, once-wealthy Egyptian women were to be brought to Avaris, locked in a prison composed of bedrooms with superficial comforts, and offered to any official who wished to enjoy a woman for an hour or a day. The right of entry to the imperial harem would henceforth be one of the most sought-after favours.

The lady Tany had made the selection herself, eliminating those who were too old – Aberia had the pleasure of strangling them before their bodies were burnt.

The harem was run on simple lines: aristocratic Egyptian women must satisfy all the desires of the ruling caste. Any woman who wept, protested or fell ill would be handed over to Aberia for execution.

And Tany, who was still searching for face-paint which would make her look less ugly, took great pleasure in watching as these women – whose servant she would once have been – had their youth and beauty defiled.

Apophis was having problems with his liver, and his thick ankles had a tendency to swell. These unpleasant symptoms were the result of acute irritation, caused by Khamudi's report on Nubia. True, the black warriors were his vassals and had rejoiced at the fall of Egypt, which they loathed. But the tribes had just chosen a young king, Nedjeh, whose reputation for vanity and cruelty was almost the equal of Apophis's.

Taking this disagreeable news seriously, the emperor had summoned his envoy to Nubia, who sent him regular information about his black allies. The envoy was a first-rate spy and, despite having only one eye, knew everything that happened in the far-away South. A former army general, he had so much blood on his hands that no act of brutality repelled him.

It was not an enemy who had rendered him one-eyed, but a little bitch of a Nubian girl whom he had beaten to death for not pleasing him enough. Before she died, she had had just enough strength to drive a bone needle into his left eye.

Apophis found One-Eye awaiting him in the reception hall; the man was already finishing his second jar of white wine.

'Majesty, the harem is a wonderful idea,' said One-Eye. 'I didn't leave it for three days, and enjoyed I don't know how many magnificent Egyptian women – they were so refined I thought I was dreaming: it's a real change from the ordinary. Majesty, you are a genius.'

Apophis did not dislike flattery, but at present he was too worried to appreciate it. 'Don't you think Khamudi's report is too pessimistic?' he asked.

'It simply repeats what I have told you, Majesty. The High Treasurer is efficient and ruthless – we get on wonderfully well.'

'So much the better, One-Eye, so much the better. But you aren't usually nervous in the face of the Nubian tribes.'

'I have a principle: never attack unless you're sure of winning. To exterminate those wild beasts I would need a larger, more battle-hardened army than theirs. Today, that is not the case.'

'You have allowed the enemy to gain the upper hand?'

'In a way, yes, Majesty. I did not foresee the rise of this man Nedjeh, and in any case my informants told me he had no future – I ran one of them through in front of his colleagues, to demonstrate my extreme displeasure. When I came here, I knew that you would, quite rightly, condemn me to death, which is why I took my pleasure in the harem until I was utterly exhausted.'

Apophis thought for a moment. On one hand, his subordinates were not permitted to fail in any way. On the other, One-Eye would not be easy to replace; besides, he would be careful to make not one more mistake. So Apophis decided that the official account would be an adaptation of reality: if Nedjeh had been appointed leader of the Nubians, it was with the emperor's blessing.

'You will leave here alive,' he announced. 'As Hyksos envoy, you will deliver my personal congratulations to the man who has united the tribes.'

One-Eye could hardly believe his ears. 'Will you send me an army to annihilate him, Majesty?'

'Fighting the Nubians on their own ground would be extremely difficult – you know that better than I. And I still have no grounds for declaring war on my subjects in the Great South.'

'To the north of his territory, Nedjeh controls only Elephantine, but he will not stop there, Majesty.'

'Is he a fool?'

'I think not.'

'In that case, he knows that provoking the anger of the Hyksos would be disastrous. No doubt he will seek to strengthen his power in Nubia. One day, we shall use his talents. If he becomes inconvenient, we shall take action. Go back there, flatter him with words of friendship, and inform me of everything he says and does. And this time,' said Apophis menacingly, 'there are to be no mistakes.'

Astounded at having emerged from the interview unscathed, the envoy promised himself a night in the harem before departing for the South on his boat.

## 36

Pharaoh Seqen was close to despair. There would be no joyous celebrations of the new year, for the Hyksos were demanding even heavier taxes than the previous year. The emperor would not be content with another stele proclaiming his glory, and his tax-collectors would count every sack of grain with sadistic pleasure, knowing they were condemning the people of Thebes to starvation.

Fortunately, Seqen's agricultural reforms meant that Thebes would be able to meet the invader's demands. But all his efforts seemed doomed to failure, for the people of the last free city of Egypt were beginning to lose hope.

For more than two years, Queen Ahhotep had been slowly dying of a sickness which the Theban doctors could not cure. She slept for fifteen hours a day, and whenever she tried to stand up she felt so ill that she had to lie down again. She found it difficult to think clearly for more than a few minutes, and a deadly apathy was gradually taking hold of her exhausted body.

All that kept despair at bay was their cheerful little son, Kames, who brought a flicker of joy to the palace. Ahhotep had chosen his name carefully, for it meant 'He Who is Born of the Power of Life', and the child was growing stronger by the minute. Seqen sometimes thought that his wife's health had passed into the body of her son, but of course he could not reproach her for that. There had been such happiness at Kames's birth, such hopes for the future!

Qaris and Seqen were looking at the model of Egypt. Almost the entire country had become Hyksos, and the existence of small groups of rebels in the North remained no more than an unconfirmed rumour.

'My son probably won't celebrate his next birthday in this palace,' said Seqen. 'But where can we go? We can't go to the North, but neither can we go to the South, because Emheb says the Nubians are torturing and executing any Egyptians who refuse to collaborate. They have taken over our former fortresses, and their king, Nedjeh, is planning to expand his borders.'

'Apophis will stop him.'

'Now I understand why he has not razed our city to the ground: Thebes is the bait he has set for Nedjeh. If the Nubians attack the city, the Hyksos army will annihilate them.'

Teti hurried in, and said urgently, 'Come quickly, Seqen. Ahhotep is asking for you.'

Deathly pale, the pharaoh rushed to his wife's bed-chamber. He saw at once that Ahhotep was near death, and he squeezed her hand so tightly that a little light came back into her eyes.

'It is that demon who is stealing my life,' she whispered, 'Apophis, emperor of darkness.'

'I shall attack Avaris and kill him!'

'Take me to Karnak. Tomorrow is the new year, is it not?'

'Yes, but—'

'Draw the sign of the moon on my heart and entrust me to the One who has the power to save me.'


The Nile was turbulent, the annual flood was rising with alarming speed, and the merciless July sun had forced both men and beasts to take shelter.

At noon, Seqen carried his wife slowly up the stairs to the roof of the Temple of Osiris, master of death and resurrection. He laid the Queen's naked body upon the flagstones, exposing her to the light of Ra, the only power that could defeat darkness.

Ahhotep had given so much of herself that every channel in her body had been completely drained of energy. The queen's hope was that she might be regenerated, like the ritual objects that priests recharged at the beginning of each new year. She, the daughter of the moon, was imploring the sun to create the impossible marriage from which new life could emerge.

Seqen felt a terrible anguish. Surely it was madness to expose his wife to such cruel, intense sunlight? And he was nothing: a king without a crown, who could not continue the fight without her. Ahhotep was the soul of that fight.

As the sun's energy entered the queen's body, it became radiant with light.

Fearing that his eyes would be burnt, Seqen turned away. Then, revolted by his own cowardice, he ran to Ahhotep to end her torment.

Her skin was burning hot.

'You must not stay here,' he told her.

'Have faith, Seqen.'

The implacable sun continued to beat down until every channel in the young woman's body was filled with its sap.

At last, Ahhotep got to her feet. 'The emperor of darkness has failed to kill me. This is the first wound I have inflicted upon him.'

Apophis let out a little cry of pain. His barber had just cut the emperor while shaving him.

In terror, the man fell to his knees. 'A thousand pardons, Majesty. It is not serious, I promise you.'

'Work done at the palace must be perfect.'

'This will never happen again, I swear!'

'Oaths are nothing but lies,' said the emperor. 'A dog which has bitten will bite again, and an incompetent fool will always be incompetent. My copper mines consume a great deal of labour. You shall end your days there.'

Two guards took away the barber, whose snivelling exasperated Apophis.

The unfortunate man's assistant dabbed the slight wound with linen and covered it with a honey compress. 'It will heal very quickly, Majesty.'

'Find me a new barber immediately.'

The day had started badly. Impatiently, the emperor awaited news of the army he had sent to Syria to burn down a village which had dared to protest against excessive taxes. As for his war-fleet, it was pursuing some Cyprian pirates who had been mad enough to attack Hyksos trading-ships.

Khamudi requested an audience. He, at least, was in high spirits. 'Total triumph, Majesty,' he announced. 'The Syrian rebels and Cyprian pirates have been wiped out – once again, Jannas has proved remarkably efficient. I have ordered the Syrians' bodies to be displayed in neighbouring villages to deter any future disturbance.'

The emperor was pleased with his High Treasurer. Rich, depraved and hated, Khamudi revered his all-powerful master and obeyed him unflinchingly. As long as he remained in power, Apophis would cover up his worst atrocities.

The empire was continuing to grow, but extreme vigilance was essential. Here and there madmen were setting up rebel movements, which Khamudi put down with extreme cruelty. In every land Apophis controlled, the funeral pyres of men, women, children and animals were growing more numerous every day. Even when a province seemed to have been pacified, Khamudi carried out preventive raids. The sight of local nobles being tortured and an entire town disappearing in flames cooled the fervour of any would-be dissidents.

'We must keep a strict watch on the Minoans, Majesty. I have no proof, but they may have ordered the attacks on our boats. All my informants are on the alert.'

'Tell Jannas to make ready his fleet.'

Khamudi beamed. He was already picturing the destruction of the Great Island.

'Have you heard anything from One-Eye?' asked Apophis.

'Yes, Majesty. He says the Nubian princeling seems to be behaving himself, but I'm convinced that he will eventually attack Thebes. The lure is too tempting for him to resist.'

'First, he'll have to kill the soldiers who control Edfu.'

'That's precisely why I am sending them no reinforcements,' said Khamudi. 'Edfu is the last barrier before Thebes. If he destroys it, Nedjeh will think he's stronger than the Hyksos he has thereby declared war upon. We shall annihilate him during the battle of Thebes, which will be erased from the map; and we can then take control of Nubia at our leisure.'

## 37

'I'm afraid,' admitted Mouse-Face.

'So am I,' said Wry-Nose, 'but there's no danger. You know we have friends in high places. Queen Teti is weak, and her daughter is dying – and so is Thebes. We shall simply make ourselves rich and then leave. There's really nothing to fear.'

'If you say so, but all the same . . . robbing a tomb. I'm afraid.'

'I told you, there's nothing to worry about. Here, on the west bank of Thebes, there are only a few starving peasants left, and plenty of well-hidden tombs full of treasure. Just think what we could buy!'

'Yes, but what if we're caught?'

'We won't be. Come on, let's not waste time.'

Path-Finder was waiting for them at the bottom of the hill. 'The best tomb is over there,' he said, pointing. 'Have you got what you need?'

'Don't worry about that. Just show us.'

The first steps of the stairway leading down to a noble's tomb were easy to find.

'I uncovered them,' explained Path-Finder. 'My father knew where the tomb is. He promised the dead man he'd never reveal the location to anyone. But times are so hard . . .'

'The times are the way they are. Let's go to it.'

With copper crowbars, Mouse-Face and Wry-Nose demolished a protecting wall, entered a passageway and lit a torch. The door of the tomb did not resist for long, and they entered the burial chamber.

Beside the sarcophagus lay chairs and chests containing jewels, clothing, sandals and toilet items which Wry-Nose stuffed into bags.

'Let's get out of here quickly,' urged Mouse-Face. 'I'm sure the dead man's soul is watching us.'

'But,' protested Wry-Nose, 'we haven't yet even touched the most important thing: the sarcophagus.'

'No, not that!'

'There must be a gold collar and some beautiful amulets in there.

We're going to be rich!' He smashed the lid of the sarcophagus.

The mummy was perfectly preserved. On its chest lay a garland of dried flowers.

Wry-Nose attacked the bandages. Horrified, his accomplice returned to the corridor, so as not to be present at this sacrilege. But, when he heard shouts of joy, his remorse evaporated.

'Gold amulets,' gloated Wry-Nose, 'a big lapis-lazuli scarab and rings! Help me fill these bags.'

Although he dared not look at the desecrated mummy, Mouse-Face nevertheless lent a hand.

When they emerged from the tomb, Path-Finder was waiting for them.

'There you are at last. A good haul?' he asked.

'Wonderful,' said Wry-Nose. 'Shall we share it out now?'

'Of course.'

As Wry-Nose was showing him an amulet shaped like a leg, Path-Finder plunged a dagger into his belly and tried to do the same to his companion. But Mouse-Face had dodged quickly aside and was only wounded on the hip.

Although he was bleeding profusely, he managed to run away, hoping that his attacker would not catch him.


'The man is dead,' said Qaris. 'He was called Mouse-Face and, despite the seriousness of his wound, he managed to cross the Nile and reach the palace to tell us everything.'

'Tomb-robbers!' exclaimed Ahhotep. 'How can people be so vile? Do these criminals not realize that the dead man's soul will punish them?'

'Their lust for gold is so strong that nothing stops them. And that isn't all.'

'The queen is still weak,' Seqen reminded him. 'We shouldn't give her any more shocks.'

'Don't hide anything from me,' ordered the queen.

'Then I must tell you that Mouse-Face gave me the name of the man who guaranteed them immunity. The criminal is none other than the officer in charge of the barracks, a man I trusted completely.'

This caused great consternation.

'Still more serious,' Qaris went on, 'is the fact that those who advocate collaboration with the Hyksos have not given up. In fact, the news of your impending death strenghtened them.'

'In other words,' concluded Seqen, 'all my efforts to create a true Theban army have come to nothing. We shall never be able to fight the emperor.'

'Of course we shall!' protested Ahhotep. 'We simply need to change our strategy. The old general gave us the solution shortly before he died: we must set up a secret training-camp.'

'Here, in Thebes? In a population this size, it would not stay secret for long,' said Seqen.

'Now that the energy is flowing once more in my veins,' said Ahhotep, 'I shall pretend to busy myself with the citizens' well-being. The barracks will remain in place, but from now on it is to house only guards, who will ensure public order. The supporters of collaboration will think that our very modest ambitions are no threat to them. Meanwhile you, Seqen, will have your hands free to recruit and train our future soldiers.'

'Yes, but where?'

'On the west bank, of course. We shall make it known that thieves tried to loot the tombs of our ancestors, and that we have therefore posted guards around the burial-ground and forbidden anyone to go there. Only the souls of the dead, which are protected by magic, will have the right to dwell there.'

The queen bent over Qaris's model of Egypt. 'For caution's sake, we shall establish our secret camp here, in the desert to the north of Thebes. If any curious people venture into the area, our lookouts will kill them.'

'Majesty,' objected Qaris, 'this will be a long and arduous business.'

'It will take us several years, I am aware of that. But, if we succeed, we shall at last be in a position to fight.'

In half a day's time, the caravan from the oasis at Bahariya would emerge from the desert and reach the green outskirts of the Fayum oasis, a little paradise where men and beasts could rest before setting off again for Avaris.

The leader of the caravan, Adafi the Thief, had been in the Hyksos's pay for years. A sworn enemy of the Egyptians, who had humiliated his people since the dawn of time, he grew happier by the day as he enjoyed all the benefits of the occupation. Little by little, the land of the pharaohs was bleeding to death, to become merely one more of the emperor's provinces.

Adafi the Thief admired Apophis and, like him, believed solely in the use of force. After all, it was only by murdering three other caravan-owners that he had been able to seize their donkeys, thus becoming one of the richest traders in Libya.

There was an additional source of pleasure. He had recently captured an Egyptian from the South, and had himself cut off his ears and tongue. Like a noble, he had made the wretch carry his sandals and his fan, which must be waved constantly to keep his master cool.

Adafi was delivering jars of good wine, salt and the finest dates to Avaris. The entire consignment was destined for Grand Treasurer Khamudi, who never paid for anything but had authorized the Libyan to take part of the production of the oases for himself.

Despite the early hour, the heat was already becoming uncomfortable.

'More air, you idle blockhead!' The Egyptian slave approached the donkey on which his master was sitting, so as to fan him more easily. He worked hard, in the hope that his heart would soon give out and death put an end to his torment.

Suddenly, the caravan halted. Angrily, Adafi the Thief dismounted.

His second in command soon came hurrying up. 'The lead donkey has stopped,' he explained. 'There's a corpse lying across the road.'

'What does that matter? We'll just trample it underfoot and go on our way.'

'But the corpse is wearing a necklace and bracelets, and the kilt and sandals look of good quality.'

'I'll see to this.'

Followed by his fan-bearer, the Libyan walked to the head of the caravan. Booty was a serious business, and he would help himself first.

The dead man lay on his back. He seemed young, and had a fine moustache and – more importantly – beautiful jewellery. Drooling with anticipation, Adafi the Thief bent down to tear off the necklace.

Coming abruptly back to life, Moustache seized the dagger he had hidden in the sand and slit the corpse-robber's throat.

'Attack!' he yelled, leaping to his feet.

## 38

In accordance with their orders, the rebels gave no quarter.

For more than two years they had been attacking small caravans, sometimes in the Western desert, sometimes in the east. These operations were not easy to mount, for the group had first to obtain reliable information in order to minimize the risks. If the convoy turned out to be too large, or was protected by Hyksos soldiers, the Afghan and Moustache preferred to let it pass unmolested.

Nevertheless, they had won some fine plunder and had amassed large stores of food, together with clothes and various objects which they could barter if necessary. This caravan was their largest prize to date.

'The rebel movement is getting rich,' commented Moustache. 'Why are you pulling that face, Afghan?'

'Because we've hit too close to home. On the looter you killed, I found a scarab signed by Khamudi. This caravan was destined for him, and he will order an investigation.'

Moustache's joy evaporated. 'Whatever happens, he must not learn that we exist. But perhaps he'll think it was a raid by sand-travellers?'

'The sand-travellers are allies of the Hyksos, and they'd never dare attack an official caravan. In the case of a mistake, their first reaction would be to take their booty to Avaris to beg the authorities for forgiveness.'

'We've got ourselves into a fine mess,' said Moustache.

'There's only one thing to do,' decided the Afghan. 'We must make it look as though the merchants killed each other. So we shall leave most of the goods here, and just take a few donkeys.'

The rebels arranged the bodies to make it look as if there had been a general set-to.

'Look at that one,' said Moustache to the Afghan. 'They've cut off his ears and his tongue. But there is something more interesting: he is circumcised like an Egyptian, and under his left arm he bears a tattoo of the moon in its ship.'

'It's a secret sign – that much is becoming clear. This poor fellow was a prisoner. We should have spared him.'

'How were we to know?'

'There must be another group of rebels somewhere,' said the Afghan.

'Thebes is in its death-throes. Edfu is in the hands of the Hyksos, and Elephantine is under the Nubian yoke. Whether we like it or not, we're alone.'

'All the same, that sign exists, and this is the second time we've seen it.'

Moustache blinked. 'Do you mean you want to break through the blockade at Henen-Nesut and head south?'

'We aren't at that stage yet, although things don't look too bad. Our network is growing stronger by the month, we have several reliable bases, the peasants support us and supply us with information, we have a forge to make weapons, and we have enough to eat. Our domain may be a small one, but within it we're safe. When we're ready, we'll take care of Henen-Nesut, I promise you.'

'Come here, my darling,' begged the lady Yima, who had bleached her hair in order to look even more blonde. Bare-breasted and dressed only in a shawl, she lay simpering on her bed.

Khamudi slapped her. 'You are nothing but a bitch in heat. The emperor is waiting for me.'

Yima snivelled. She knew very well that her man was captivated by her charms and could not deprive himself of them for long. Tomorrow night, she would give him a young Canaanite girl, who would experience ecstasy and then become food for the crocodiles. Yima would take part in any kind of entertainment, so long as she was the one to organize it.

Khamudi walked heavily towards the small room in the fortress where he could speak with Apophis without anyone overhearing them. It was not this ridiculous matter of the caravan that was vexing him; those idiotic thieves had killed each other, no doubt because of Adafi's greed, but the goods had reached him in the end. Much more serious was the situation regarding Minoa.

According to one of his spies, the Minoans had indeed engaged the Cyprian pirates, with the firm intention of seizing several Hyksos trading-ships. Admittedly there was no hard proof, but nevertheless Apophis ought to act with all possible speed.

Jannas's war-fleet was within sight of the Great Island, ready to attack. Vessels carrying troops would join it before the assault.

Khamudi hated the Minoans. Arrogant, and steeped in their own past and culture, they did not behave like true vassals. On one occasion, he had thought of arranging for Jannas to be murdered, and attributing the blame to them, but the plan would have required the involvement of too many people, and the High Treasurer could not afford mistakes.

It was the Minoans themselves who had made the mistake this time. Knowing Apophis as he did, Khamudi was certain that the emperor's cold anger would be terrible and that only the destruction of the island would appease him.

Apophis was being shaved by his new barber, who had difficulty in suppressing a slight tremor as he slid the blade of the razor across the master of the world's cheek.

'Good news, Khamudi?' asked the emperor.

'The situation is delicate, Majesty.'

'Hurry up and finish, barber.'

The barber hurried nervously, terrified of making a mistake. Fortunately he shaved the emperor perfectly, without cutting him, and then he vanished with his equipment.

'Jannas must attack Minoa,' said Khamudi. 'That arrogant island deserves to be punished.'

'So you are certain at the Minoans are a threat to our ships?'

'There's no doubt about it.'

'Then we must take action.'

'I shall pass on your orders to Jannas at once.'

'First wait to hear what they are. The Minoans are seasoned warriors, not easy to defeat.'

Khamudi was astonished. 'They will be crushed by sheer weight of numbers.'

'Of course, and they know it. So it is in their interests to satisfy my demands. They are to double their tributes and provide me with two thousand soldiers and fifty ships; and their finest painters are to come to Avaris to decorate my palace. If even one of these conditions is not satisfied, I shall consider myself insulted and Jannas will take action.'

Khamudi was delighted. The Minoans would never accept such humiliation.

Heray, the Overseer of Granaries, was a pleasant and affable man who knew everyone in Thebes and, on Ahhotep's instructions, provided free bread and beer to the poorest families. Thanks to his vigilance, no one went hungry. His officials loved him because he treated them with respect, so they did excellent work. The Theban granaries had never been better managed.

Who would ever suspect Heray of spying for the king and queen? He calmed people's worries, defused conflicts and had a fund of amusing stories to raise the lowest spirits. Affluent families were honoured to have him as a guest, and people went gladly to dine at his house. Consequently he had gained the trust of men and women, young and old, gullible and sceptical alike.

He and Ahhotep were walking in the palace gardens, watched by Laughter.

'I have the impression that this town no longer has any secrets from you,' said Ahhotep.

'Majesty, I have identified the main supporters of collaboration with the Hyksos. They are weak men, true, but I confess that I'm disappointed and worried, because there are many more of them than I thought. Thebes has been undermined by fear, selfishness and cowardice.'

'Anything else would have surprised me. Now, we know that the secret camp is essential if we are to build an army. I am relying on you to persuade the collaborators that we have given up all thought of dangerous ideas. Explain to them clearly that my only ambition is to have a second child and to live peacefully at the palace, enjoying the few privileges I have left.'

'I shall put them off their guard, Majesty.'

Laughter sniffed the air, fully alert, then flopped down on the ground, his front paws stretched out, ready to play. He gave yelps of joy when little Kames ran towards him.

When the dog licked his forehead, the child burst out laughing, then pretended to be afraid. 'Mother, Mother, save me!'

Ahhotep took the child in her arms and swung him up above her head. 'One day, my son, we shall be free.'

## 39

Ahhotep emerged from a byre where a cow was gently licking her new-born calf. The queen was inspecting land which had been abandoned by its owners for several years, but which was now being reclaimed. Encouraged first by the queen and then by Heray, farmers had started rearing stock again, while water-carriers came regularly to irrigate the gardens. Thanks to the fertile silt deposited by the Nile flood, the peasants reaped excellent harvests.

Ahhotep also ensured that dykes were properly maintained and new reservoirs created, so that even in the dry season Waset would not go short of water.

'All is ready, Majesty,' said Heray.

As the wine-growers had worked hard and the wine promised to be excellent, Ahhotep had decided to celebrate a festival in the heart of the countryside, in the presence of the city's leading citizens. Although the Hyksos threat was ever present, people were glad of the chance to forget their worries for a while, and everyone sampled the new wine with gusto. How exhilarating it was to give thanks to the god of the winepress, to chatter about nothing in particular and to believe in the future, even if only for a moment.

Qaris called for silence. When all was quiet, he said, 'Many of you will be surprised not to see Her Majesty Teti the Small here. Our sovereign is with us in spirit, but her frail health does not permit her to leave the palace. She has instructed me to announce that she is officially abdicating and that henceforth her daughter, Ahhotep, will take on all the duties of the Queen of Egypt.'

The news was greeted with cheers.

A dignitary spoke up. 'We are delighted with Her Majesty's choice, but what will Pharaoh Apophis think of it?'

'In the official letter she has just sent him, his very respectful servant Ahhotep asks for his approval and begs him to continue to protect his obedient city of Thebes.'

The dignitary was one of those who advocated collaboration, and he smiled with pleasure at these words.

Many peasants, on the other hand, were not at all happy. The young queen wished she could tell them the truth, but the people of Thebes must be convinced that their new sovereign had given up all thought of fighting the Hyksos.

As for would-be rebels, they were contacted by Heray and his men. If they came through the rigorous selection procedure, they would be advised to announce loudly that they were leaving the miserable city of Thebes to try their luck elsewhere. And they would join the secret camp on the west bank, where they were put to the test by means of ruthless training.

It was with sadness that the revellers dispersed when the festivities were over.

Qaris could plainly see the queen's frustration. 'Have patience, Majesty,' he urged.

'Has the other letter been sent?'

'It has been delivered to the guard-post at Kebet, which will ensure it reaches the emperor. As usual, I imitated the late minister for agriculture's writing and placed his seal upon the letter. The traitor informs Apophis that you, like your mother, are a mere figurehead, the representative of an outmoded tradition which amuses the common folk. Given your youth, your inexperience, your love of children and your lack of interest in public life, there is nothing to fear from you.'

Apophis would not have missed this for worlds. A woman . . . Thebes had chosen a woman as ruler and, what was more, a slip of a girl. But what was there to rule? A mere rabble, terrified at the thought that the Hyksos army might appear at any moment. How surprised they would be when Nubian warriors were unleashed upon them!

For the time being, Apophis would simply mock the ridiculous city of Thebes. The prospect of a confrontation with Minoa wholly occupied his thoughts. If he decided to strike, the blow must be decisive, demonstrating to all his present and future subjects that no one could challenge his authority. So he had encircled the Great Island with three concentric rings of ships: first, those containing elite archers and giant catapults; then ships transporting footsoldiers; and lastly cargo-vessels with supplies. According to Jannas's estimates, there were five times as many Hyksos soldiers as there were Minoans.

Yet the emperor was less sanguine than Khamudi. The battle would be fierce, and after the soldiers had disembarked they would have to capture the well-fortified Minoan capital. So Apophis was already preparing a second wave of attack, which he himself would command.

Nothing would be left of the rebel island. Not one human being, not one animal, not one tree.

'Here you are at last, Khamudi. What is the news?'

'Jannas has passed on your demands to the Minoans. They asked to negotiate, and he of course refused and gave them one day to respond.'

'Jannas is sometimes too conciliatory,' said the emperor. 'Is the second wave of attack ready to leave?'

'It is at your command, Majesty.'

The Afghan was still sceptical. 'According to a message from Avaris, almost the entire war-fleet is preparing to leave port.'

'Where is it going?' asked Moustache, intrigued.

'Rumour has it the Hyksos are planning to invade Minoa.'

'That doesn't make sense. The Great Island is their ally.'

'Our informant stated clearly that the emperor himself is to lead the expedition.'

'Is your man sure?'

'You know him better than I do: he works at the weapons store in Avaris, and you recruited him yourself. He risks his life and his messenger's to send us this kind of information.'

Moustache munched a fresh onion. 'Who's going to rule Egypt while the emperor's away?'

'Probably his faithful Khamudi.'

'Suppose we tried to kill him? With him out of the way, we could cause a peasants' uprising in the Delta.'

'It's a tempting thought, I grant you,' said the Afghan. 'But it's too good to be true, don't you think? Even if the emperor really is away, he won't have left his capital unprotected. A fine trap, no?'

Moustache could have wept, but he had to face facts. A handful of rebels was not going to seize control of Avaris.

Leaning on her daughter's arm, Teti the Small was delightedly exploring her city. She was astonished by the cleanliness of the streets and the large quantities of fine vegetables on display in the market. Everyone was happy to see their new queen's mother, who took great pleasure in talking to people and admiring the cooking-pots produced in the newly reopened workshops. After kneading and shaping clay soaked in water, the craftsmen left the pots to dry in the sun and then fired them at a low temperature. Besides pots, they made ladles, bowls and cups, which they glazed to make them impermeable.

Teti was also interested in the simple baskets woven from flexible reeds and coloured red, blue or yellow. Those designed to carry heavy objects had their bases reinforced with two wooden battens and laid across each other.

'If you like this red basket, Majesty,' one of the craftsmen said to her, 'permit me to give it to you.'

'In exchange, you shall receive a pot of ointment.'

Teti did not open her gift until she reached the palace. Fortunately, the basket was empty. According to the code agreed with Seqen and Heray, that meant that the security of the secret camp was intact and that there was no immediate danger from collaborators. Otherwise, a small papyrus would have told Teti and Ahhotep what they must do.

'I shall drink a little white wine with my midday meal,' said Teti. 'That walk has made me feel young again.'

## 40

From his vantage-point high on the walls of the citadel, Apophis watched Jannas's flagship returning to port, followed by the rest of the war-fleet and a heavily laden cargo-ship.

Guards were stationed on the quayside, to prevent any popular demonstration; for the emperor had forbidden the revelry that used to accompany the sailors' return. Hyksos soldiers must be disciplined and ready for combat at all times.

Apophis received Jannas in the great audience chamber at the palace, in the presence of Khamudi and members of the ruling elite.

'Did the Minoans see reason, Commander?'

'To be certain of winning your favour, they have trebled their tributes and in a few weeks' time they will send you the ships and soldiers you demand. The king of the Great Island sends you his apologies, and promises that there will be no repetition of the unfortunate incident that obliged us to take action. He greatly regrets the fact that he was misled by incompetent advisers – who have since been thrown to the wild beasts.'

'And what about the artists?'

'The finest Minoan painters are at your disposal. They travelled here on the cargo-boat, which is the Great Island's first gift to you. Minoa is determined to prove that she is your loyal and devoted vassal.'

'Bring them in.'

There were ten of them. All had curly hair and wore brightly coloured tunics. The oldest was around fifty, the youngest twenty-five.

'Kneel before the emperor and lower your eyes,' ordered Khamudi.

With the aid of these men, Apophis intended to erase all traces of Egyptian culture from Avaris.

He told them, 'You are to decorate my palace in the Minoan style. I wish it to be even more beautiful than the palace at Knossos, and every painting must be breathtaking. If you succeed, your lives will be spared. If not, I shall consider your failure a personal insult.'

*

'As yet it is only the beginnings of an army,' Seqen told Ahhotep, 'but little by little my first soldiers are becoming true warriors, capable of defeating any enemy in hand-to-hand combat. Their living conditions are very harsh, but it is good that they are, for what awaits them is harsher still.'

Lying naked in the gentle shade of a sycamore tree, the two young people had made passionate love. And yet sadness clouded the queen's eyes.

'I don't understand,' she confessed. 'Although my mother gave me a sea-shell to ward off sterility and the evil eye, I have still not become pregnant. Are you eating enough celery?'

Seqen smiled. 'Do you think I need it to prove my desire for you? Even a single day away from you is too much to bear.'

'I want another son.'

'That would be a great blessing, but we must accept the will of the gods.'

'Kames will have a brother, I know he will.'

Seqen dared not raise the slightest objection. In any case, his wife's caresses made him forget everything except her perfect body, so gifted in the ways of love.

Little Kames enjoyed learning the rudiments of wrestling from his father, walking with Laughter, and being cuddled by his mother while she told him fine stories in which justice always triumphed. But what he liked best was playing with his grandmother. When he played tricks on her, Teti did not scold him; she tried to catch him out in return, and the hilarious battle ended with peals of laughter and wonderful cakes which Teti had baked herself.

Spending time with this lively little rascal had given Teti a new lease of life. Her appetite astonished the palace cook, one of Heray's men, particularly since she never gained any weight at all but remained as slender and elegant as ever.

Teti visited the market without fail at least once a month, to the great pleasure of the people, who were at last beginning to think that their town might escape destruction.

The baskets she was given were always empty.

Heray's lookouts were extremely effective within Thebes itself, and Teti was careful to remind everyone that they must show respect towards the souls of the dead who rested in the burial-ground on the west bank. She and Qaris spread terrifying stories of ghosts and demons which devoured anyone foolish enough to venture into the realm of the dead.

Only the royal household knew about Seqen's frequent absences, and they were all members of the rebel movement. Teti and Qaris had firmly established Seqen's reputation as a hunter and fisherman who could not bear to stay in one place for long.

Those who advocated collaboration understood the situation perfectly: the ruling family had no appetite for war and accepted Hyksos control without question. Better still, since Ahhotep had taken power she had succeeded in improving the daily lives of all Thebans.

Despite this, Chomu the vase-seller was not happy. The son of an Egyptian father and a Canaanite mother, he had had great difficulty in gaining the respect of his fellow citizens, who were rather suspicious and reserved towards him. The death of his most influential enemy, the minister for agriculture, had enabled Chomu to forge links with other traders who believed, as he did, that the Theban dynasty had no future and the province ought to be governed far more directly by the emperor. For who but Apophis could make the city prosperous again?

Ahhotep's behaviour had surprised Chomu and his friends. He had been convinced that the headstrong girl would provoke the emperor's fury, but events had proved him wrong. Starting a family seemed to have given her a taste for the virtues of submission.

Consequently, those who refused to accept the all-powerful Hyksos preferred to leave Thebes, where no one had even been punished for favouring collaboration. And neither the ageing Teti nor the elusive Seqen would push Thebes into war. There was nothing to suggest that a fire still smouldered beneath the ashes.

Nevertheless, Chomu was uneasy. True, thanks to the small increase in trade he was not living quite so poorly; but why had the emperor not driven out Teti and her daughter? His friends said it was because Teti and Ahhotep were governing the enclave to the new pharaoh's satisfaction. After all, Thebes was only a provincial town, far from Avaris, and did not figure among the emperor's main interests. Everyone had enough to eat, so why, they asked, could Chomu not be content with the goodwill of the Hyksos, who seemed to have forgotten all about this small, moribund city?

Chomu rubbed his red beard. The emperor ought to be made aware of a man like him, so that he could entrust Chomu with responsibilities commensurate with his loyalty. But how was he to establish contact with Apophis? Leaving Thebes would mean running grave risks, and Chomu had no taste for danger.

For the time being, he must simply persuade more Thebans to join the side of the collaborators.

'Are you absolutely sure?' Emheb asked the lookout.

'Absolutely. There were definitely two Nubian warriors. They shifted their positions several times, so as to study Edfu from many angles.'

So it was about to happen: the event Emheb had most feared. The Nubians had decided to push northwards and extend their boundaries beyond Elephantine.

Edfu, Nekhen, Thebes . . . so many easy targets.

Easy, but poisoned. Taking Edfu meant attacking the Hyksos. As soon as Apophis heard that the town had fallen, he would send Jannas south with orders to crush the Nubians and lay waste their whole country.

To prevent the Nubians attacking, Emheb would have to ask the emperor for help. But that would also result in Jannas's arrival, and the commander would be bound to unmask Emheb and the rebels, slaughter the inhabitants of Edfu and put to fire and sword the entire region, including Thebes.

Whether to be massacred by the Nubians or by the Hyksos: that was Emheb's only choice.

## 41

'Look, Mother, Look! It's Rascal.' Kames had made friends with the pigeon, which often carried messages between Edfu and Thebes.

Its errand accomplished, the bird fluttered down into the palace garden and allowed him to stroke it. The little boy had learnt how to untie the thread that bound a roll of papyrus to the pigeon's right leg. If it were ever on the left leg, Ahhotep would know instantly that the message had not been written by Governor Emheb.

Of course, the text was written in code and included the sign by which the rebels recognized each other, written three times and hidden among a jumble of meaningless words.

What the queen read turned her blood to ice.

Seqen, Teti, Qaris and Heray listened attentively as Ahhotep read them the terrible message from Emheb.

'We were right,' said Seqen. 'The emperor was sparing Thebes only so that he could use it as bait.'

'Can we withstand the Nubians?' asked Heray, without much hope.

'I have only a hundred fully trained soldiers at my disposal. Even if we joined forces with Emheb's men, we would be destroyed in the first attack.'

'The Nubians' reputation for cruelty is justified,' said Qaris. 'We must prepare the royal family's escape.'

'And what about the people of Thebes?' asked Ahhotep indignantly.

'Even if we tried to move them, they would be spotted and killed, by the Hyksos or the Nubians or both.'

'Then they must take up arms and fight under our command.'

'The civilians cannot do that,' argued Heray. 'Do not forget, Majesty, that the Hyksos's supporters will refuse to fight and will try to persuade their fellow citizens to do the same by promising their lives will be spared.'

'Qaris is right,' agreed Seqen. 'Ahhotep, Teti and Kames must leave Thebes. I and my soldiers will go to Edfu and fight at Emheb's side.'

'I am too old and tired to leave the town of my birth,' declared Teti. 'I shall stay here and try to negotiate with the attackers.'

'I will not leave my husband,' said Ahhotep.

'You and Kames are the future. With an escort, you will hide in the desert and—'

'And die like cowards, far from those we love? Never! Go back to the training-camp, Seqen, and prepare your soldiers to die like warriors. I shall write to Governor Emheb, informing him that we shall join him as soon as he needs us.'

Beautiful Windswept had set her sights on Minos, the most talented of the Minoan painters and the leader of the artists who had been forced to adorn Apophis's palace.

'May I watch you working, Minos?' she asked.

'I hate that.'

The tall, slender woman slid a delicate finger over her sensual lips. 'You know you have to obey the emperor, and the emperor is my brother. He won't refuse me anything – not even the head of a Minoan painter.'

'Without me, this palace will remain what it is: a hideous prison.'

'Do you think you are irreplaceable?'

'I know I am. And as soon as I've finished, I'm going home with my companions.'

'How naïve you are!'

The artist turned to look at the magnificent princess with a teasing voice. 'Why do you say that?'

'Because you will never return to Minoa. Don't you understand that you have become the emperor's property?'

Minos dropped his brush.

Windswept ran her fingers gently through the painter's curly hair and kissed him on the neck. 'It isn't so terrible, if you know how to behave. Egypt is a pleasant country, and you can make this palace more attractive. Besides, you dare not fail, remember?'

Minos did not move.

'I hope you aren't a lover of boys,' said Windswept anxiously as she untied his kilt; when she saw the effect of her caresses, she was reassured.

Unable to resist any longer, Minos took her hungrily in his arms and they lay down on the stone floor.

'There are more comfortable places to get to know each other,' she suggested.

'You seem to doubt my abilities as a lover, so I want to prove you wrong right now.'

*

The tribal ceremonies consecrated Emperor-Pharaoh Apophis's absolute power for a second time. His vassals bowed low before him, presenting him with the wealth of their respective countries, in even larger quantities than the previous year.

Particularly noteworthy was the Minoan envoy's speech. In well-chosen words, he hailed Apophis's greatness and emphasized how proud the Great Island was that its finest artists were decorating the palace at Avaris. Henceforth, Apophis's palace would be considered the centre of the world.

Commander Jannas had been summoned to represent the Hyksos armed forces of both land and sea, and to make it very clear to any aspiring rebels that they were heading for certain death. During Jannas's speech, the emperor watched the Nubian envoy closely, but his face remained untroubled.

Finally, High Treasurer Khamudi announced, as he did each year, that there was to be an increase in levies and taxes. This was vital if the Hyksos state was to ensure the well-being and safety of its subjects. Any delays or attempts at fraud would carry heavy penalties. If a vassal failed to honour his obligations, the army would swiftly remind him of them.

No envoy liked spending time in Avaris, where there were guards everywhere and the atmosphere was suffocating. And everyone knew that the emperor could make anyone disappear if the fancy took him.

The most relieved person at the ceremony was the Minoan envoy, who, despite his country's total submission, still feared reprisals. Knowing Apophis, Khamudi and Jannas, he had persuaded his king never again to attempt any kind of attack on the Hyksos, and to satisfy all the conditions the emperor had imposed upon the Great Island.

As his ship sailed away from Avaris, he spared a sympathetic thought for his Nubian colleague, who had just been summoned by Apophis. He would probably never see him again.

'You were very quiet,' remarked Apophis.

Despite his long experience, the Nubian envoy felt a lump in his throat and butterflies in his stomach.

'The ceremony was perfect, Majesty, and everything was made absolutely clear.'

'As the empire is at peace, I have decided to pay a little more attention to Egypt and Nubia. So I am entrusting Commander Jannas and High Treasurer Khamudi with a new mission.'

The envoy quailed, convinced that the emperor's harsh voice had just announced the extermination of the Nubian people.

'Do not misunderstand me,' Apophis went on. 'My friend and faithful subject Nedjeh is conducting himself loyally and has committed no serious mistakes, so why should I punish him?'

By now the envoy was sweating profusely. In less than one month, Nedjeh intended to attack Edfu, then seize Thebes and present the emperor with a given situation. Apophis would rule the North, and the Nubians the South.

'Public finance is a difficult art,' went on Apophis. 'Despite the local rulers' goodwill, there are still areas of uncertainty, even annoying omissions'. Khamudi is so devoted to the good of the state that he can no longer bear these imperfections. So a census must be carried out.'

'A census . . . ?' stammered the envoy.

'Commander Jannas's troops will leave tomorrow for Elephantine, where they will count men and animals, head by head. Then they will carry out the same process in Nubia, while other soldiers will attend to the Southern provinces. Of course, I am counting on the full and active collaboration of my servant Nedjeh.'

'Of course,' repeated the envoy.

## 42

'A Hyksos boat is coming, Governor,' said the guard.

Emheb was astonished. 'Only one?'

'Yes, and not even a very big one. One officer and a dozen men have disembarked and are heading this way. When shall we kill them?'

'We shan't touch them until we know what they want. If a boat is reported missing, Jannas will react violently.'

Emheb was puzzled. Evidently the Hyksos had been alerted to the Nubians' intentions. Why had they sent only modest reinforcements? But perhaps this was just an advance detachment.

He might perhaps manage to convince them that Edfu was completely under control and could serve as a Hyksos base to bar the way to the Nubians, but that would be only a temporary measure. These emissaries undoubtedly heralded the arrival of Jannas.

'The officer wants to see you, Governor.'

'Bring him to me.'

More than twenty warships laden with Hyksos had sailed up the Nile past Thebes.

The streets of the city were deserted. At the palace, no one could hide their anxiety. Teti still played with Kames, but without her usual gaiety. Even Laughter was nervous.

'The emperor always strikes the first blow,' said Qaris. 'The Nubians were wrong to defy him.'

'And Thebes will pay the price for their folly,' said Ahhotep angrily.

'Take shelter, Majesty,' begged the steward. 'Join the king on the west bank.'

'As soon as Seqen and his men can cross the Nile, they will come to defend us.'

Heray rushed breathlessly into the audience chamber. 'Hyksos are disembarking. They'll soon be here.'

'I shall receive them,' announced Teti, holding Kames in her arms. 'They will not dare touch a grandmother and her grandson.'

'No, Mother,' said Ahhotep. 'Confronting them is my responsibility.' The young queen left the palace to meet the Hyksos.

She would ask their leader to spare Thebes. What could she offer in return, except herself? No doubt the emperor would be delighted to make a slave of her. Once she was in his presence, she would find the right words to tell him what a monster and a coward he was. That would be her last battle.

The soldiers advanced inexorably. Ahhotep stood stock still in the sunshine, refusing to let herself be afraid.

Suddenly, she wondered if her eyes were deceiving her. No, it really was him.

'Governor Emheb!' she said.

'You have nothing to fear, Majesty,' he whispered. 'Neither the Nubians nor the Hyksos will attack you. The emperor has decided to carry out a census of the whole country, even Nubia. Jannas himself is in charge there, at the head of his troops, so it is impossible for Nedjeh to disobey. He is pinned down in his capital and must conduct himself like a loyal subject of the emperor. There is no question now of him seizing Edfu and Thebes, because his plans for conquest have been nipped in the bud. Apophis will know the exact number of Nubian warriors and will tax their king accordingly. As for the small, unimportant town of Thebes, I, the perfect collaborator, am to deal with her most severely.'

Ahhotep would gladly have flung her arms round Emheb's neck, but dozens of eyes must be watching them.

'My city is independent!' she shouted. 'How can you, an Egyptian, betray your country by becoming a tool of the emperor?'

'Apophis is our pharaoh, Majesty, and we all owe him obedience,' replied Emheb loudly. 'I am here with only a few soldiers, who will undertake a census of the inhabitants of Thebes. If you do not cooperate, an entire regiment will undertake this task, after arresting and deporting those who refuse to comply.'

Ahhotep turned her back on him. 'The royal family consists of four people,' she said disdainfully, 'my mother, Teti the Small, my husband, Seqen, my son, Kames, and myself. As to the palace staff, see Qaris, the steward. And you can take care of the rest of the population yourself.'

Hidden behind a half-closed shutter, Chomu had missed nothing of the altercation. As soon as the queen had disappeared, he ran to the governor.

'Welcome, O glorious Hyksos! My name is Chomu. I'm a trader and I represent the many Thebans who revere the emperor. We are ready to assist your soldiers in their task.'

Overcoming his nausea, Emheb managed a faint smile. 'I hereby appoint you local census enumerator. You are to set up an office with two Hyksos scribes, collect the declarations and file them. Be sure to inform me if you find any cases of fraud.'

'You shall have the exact number of inhabitants, Governor.' His lips wet with excitement, Chomu dared to ask the all-important question: 'Have I your permission to sign the final report, stressing my utter devotion to the emperor?'

'If I am satisfied with your work, why not?'

Never had Chomu tasted such a moment of ecstasy. He was the official census enumerator, working on behalf of the emperor! At last he was on the first rung of the ladder that led to the mayor's office. From there he would drive out the royal family and turn Thebes into a real Hyksos city.

The peasants of the Delta barely recognized their region any more. Military posts had sprung up everywhere, replacing shepherds' huts, and breeds of sheep unknown to the Egyptians had been widely introduced for their wool. The Hyksos required large flocks of sheep, for they refused to eat the pork so prized by Egyptians, and, unlike them, preferred woollen clothing to linen.

Each day, noted Moustache, the gulf between occupier and occupied was deepening. Although the number of collaborators might be growing, few of them truly believed in the virtues of the Hyksos order. The majority were trying to save their own lives by pretending to revere a tyrant whose might could not be challenged by any power on earth.

In this climate of desperation, it was not easy to recruit new rebels. On the other hand, those who chose to fight Apophis were ready to sacrifice themselves and would not balk at any danger.

Today Moustache had to admit failure. After working for a month with a group of pig-farmers, without any payment save a little food, he had revealed himself in the hope of signing up at least one. But although the five men were sympathetic, they did not feel able to embark on such a mad venture.

As they were passing the abandoned store-shed where the Afghan was hiding, waiting for the results of his friend's efforts, one of the farmers stopped in his tracks.

'There are Hyksos in our home!'

Ten footsoldiers clad in black breastplates emerged from the farm where the pig-farmers and their families lived.

Moustache could neither run away nor warn the Afghan. The soldiers had spotted the peasants and were coming towards them. His only hope was that the pig-farmers would not betray him.

'Official census,' announced the officer, a sturdy Anatolian. 'Your names and the exact number of your animals. Ah yes, and I must inform you that the selling price of your pigs has been halved and taxes increased by the same amount.'

'You're ruining us!' protested a young farmer.

'That's not my problem, my lad. All you have to do is be like us and not eat pigs. So . . . I don't suppose you've hidden a few in that old shed over there?'

'No, it's abandoned.'

'All the same, we'll take a look, if only to check that you're not lying. And if you are, my lad, you'll be in serious trouble.'

'Defend yourselves – they want to kill you!' roared Moustache, breaking the neck of one of the soldiers, then seizing his sword and plunging it into the chest of the solder next to him.

Enraged, the Anatolian sank his spear into the belly of a pig-farmer who was trying to calm him. With no weapons but their fists, the peasants were no match for the Hyksos, but they held them off just long enough for a wild beast to leap out of the store-shed brandishing a pitchfork which he drove into the Anatolian's back.

The soldiers were too stunned to fight. The two rebels, highly skilled in close combat, left them no chance.

Moustache's blood-stained hands were shaking. The Afghan was trying to get his breath back. Not one of the pig-farmers was left alive.

The Afghan finished off the wounded Hyksos. In fury, Moustache trampled on their corpses until not a single face was recognizable.

## 43

High Treasurer Khamudi was sitting in his luxurious office in Avaris, receiving reports from the census enumerators. The man his underlings secretly nicknamed 'His Royal Self-Importance' and 'Lord Greed' had become exceedingly rich. Controlling the production of scarabs and papyrus, and creaming off a portion of the tax revenues with Apophis's agreement, gave free rein to his greed – he had put on a lot of weight – not to mention his rapacity.

After three years' work, the census was drawing to an end. In accordance with Khamudi's instructions, Hyksos soldiers had explored every far-flung corner of Egypt and Nubia, returning several times to the most densely populated areas, so that not a single human being or head of livestock should escape them. And the result was remarkable: not one person would avoid paying the many taxes decreed by the emperor.

Although somewhat disappointed during the early days of the enterprise, Khamudi had had an amusing idea: to entrust the first declaration to local scribes. If there were any mistakes when the Hyksos officials checked their work, they were burnt alive in a public place. The measure had had the desired effect: the Egyptian scribes had proved excellent collaborators, tracking down the very last peasant lurking on his tiny patch of land in the remotest province.

Khamudi therefore felt justifiably proud when he appeared before his master, who was busy calculating new rates of pay for Hyksos soldiers and state officials. The procedure was as simple as it was effective: their increases in their pay were paid for by taking more from his subjects, who were in no position to protest.

'Majesty, the census is a dazzling success.'

'How much have our revenues increased?'

'By nearly a third. Even the Nubians have been brought to heel. I cannot say for sure that Nedjeh is not hiding one or two family treasures which he forgot to declare, but can we not pardon him that small error?'

'In return, you are to increase the price of the wheat we sell him. Any incidents worth noting?'

'We lost one patrol, which was foolish enough to go swimming at a place where the Nile is infested with crocodiles – all we found were a few fragments of flesh stuck to their uniforms. There's nothing else to report, for who would dare rebel against our army? Even the wild Nubians have realized that it's as well to obey Commander Jannas without question. And there is another reason to be pleased: we have completely destroyed the rebel movement, and the number of our Egyptian collaborators is on the increase. Emheb, the governor of Edfu, has been an active census enumerator. The Waset countryside had twice as many animals as we thought, and he even unmasked the owners of a single pig.'

'Did he do nothing to protect his own town?'

'Nothing at all, Majesty. Giving him an official mission has turned him into a true predator. With his help, we shall bleed Edfu dry.'

'Appoint him Overseer of Taxes for Waset, and ensure that his tax revenues continue to rise. His attitude is sure to inspire other leading Egyptian citizens, and speed up their people's decline.'

Even the Afghan was exhausted. Since the start of the census, the small group of rebels had had to keep constantly on the move, for fear of being intercepted by one of the many Hyksos patrols that criss-crossed Middle Egypt, not to mention the isolated farms.

Several times, the desert had provided them with temporary shelter, but lack of provisions meant they had to return to the countryside, where the peasants had proved hostile. Their concern was no longer recruitment but survival.

'We can't hold out much longer,' confessed Moustache. 'Our men's nerves are stretched to breaking-point. Having to live like hunted animals is tearing them apart with fear. Some of them even want to go home.'

'If they do, they'll be executed,' said the Afghan.

'They'd prefer that to being on the run all the time.'

'I'll try to make them change their minds. But if I can't . . .'

'Surely you won't kill them if they've lost faith?'

'Can you suggest a better solution?'

Moustache knew the Afghan was right; but how could this terrible situation be resolved?

'If we let them leave,' pointed out the Afghan, 'they'll betray us, and everything we've gone through in the past few years will have been for nothing.'

'But they're our comrades, not our enemies.'

'If they lose faith, they become enemies.'

One of the rebels warned them, 'There's a farmer coming this way.'

'Do we know him?'

'He's given us shelter before now.'

'See if he's being followed by any Hyksos.'

The peasant was alone. Protected by the Afghan, who hid behind a tamarisk-tree, Moustache agreed to talk to him.

'What do you want, farmer?' he asked.

'It's over – the census is over! The special patrols have left for Avaris, and so has the war-fleet. There are only the usual occupation troops left. This very night, you can sleep at my house.'

Thebes had been bled dry. Ahhotep did not regret approving Emheb's strategy, but it had brought the inhabitants of the little city close to ruin. The new taxes on harvests would leave them scarcely enough to eat, and it took all Ahhotep's powers of persuasion to preserve their will to live.

Teti assisted her ably. On her frequent visits to the market, she explained to the housewives that the royal family ate neither more nor better than they did. And little Kames declared loud and long that Thebes would overcome all her enemies.

Chomu the vase-seller was deeply depressed. He had hoped the Hyksos soldiers would stay in Thebes and grant him the post of mayor as a reward for denouncing people who owned goods they had not declared to the tax-collectors. But, although he had congratulated Chomu warmly, Emheb had returned to Edfu without dethroning Queen Ahhotep.

How could the popularity of the young queen and her mother be combated? Bogged down in his disappointment, Chomu had hardly any arguments to offer the supporters of occupation, for Ahhotep was meeting all the emperor's demands.

Heray had comforted him a little by promising that he would certainly have an important part to play in the future. Chomu's devotion towards the new master of the country would not pass unnoticed, particularly since Governor Emheb had given glowing reports of this exceedingly diligent collaborator.

In fact, Emheb had been careful to make no mention at all of the little rat. Heray was watching Chomu like a hawk, because sooner or later he would recover from his depression and start doing more harm.

In Waset, the census was by no means at an end. Wary of attracting suspicion, Emheb had not been able to prevent a Hyksos detachment from going to the west bank of Thebes, to inspect the burial-ground and the surrounding areas.

These were reputed to be uninhabited, but not even the tenth part of a cubit of ground must escape the census officials. And if they did their work properly, they would find the secret training-camp.

## 44

Rascal landed on Seqen's shoulder. He stroked the pigeon, then read the message it had brought.

'The Hyksos are inspecting the burial-ground,' he told his men. 'After that, they'll have only the Northern desert left to check.'

'We'll fight them and kill them,' vowed a young soldier.

'That would be a pointless victory,' said Seqen. 'Their disappearance would be reported to headquarters, which would send out an entire army, and we would be powerless against it.'

'But we can't just let ourselves be slaughtered without a fight.'

'We must face up to the urgency of the situation – and quickly.'

At the entrance to the burial-ground, the Hyksos commander recoiled. Governor Emheb had confided to him that no Egyptian would dare venture into this place, which was haunted by vulture-headed monsters with lions' claws. They attacked their victims from behind, put out their eyes, pierced their skulls, drank their blood and ate the marrow of the their bones.

The officer was a former pirate, who had killed enough enemies not to fear that kind of creature. But his soldiers, although well armed, did not share his views. And, despite his determination, the eerie atmosphere and heavy silence of the place made even the commander uneasy.

A dog barked, making the soldiers jump. Straight away, one of the soldiers fired an arrow. It hit a stele cursing unbelievers, and the burial-ground's last guard took to its heels.

'Surely we're not going to count the dead?' said a soldier.

'Why don't we see if there are any valuables in the tombs?' suggested one of his comrades.

'All right – but you go first.'

'Surely you don't believe those stories about monsters?'

'Of course not. But go first anyway.'

The Hyksos commander had a keen eye for booty, but all he could see was small tombs, some of them abandoned, some of them gutted. No, they didn't look at all promising.

'No one to count around here,' he said. 'We'll go and check the last white area on the map.'

'But, sir, that way's the desert.'

'Are you afraid, soldier?'

'Some people say it's dangerous, what with all the monsters out there.'

'No monster can resist three hundred Hyksos soldiers. Forward march.'

Seqen had removed all visible traces of the camp. His men were well hidden, some behind hills deeper in the desert, others in underground tunnels close to the camp. The king and two of his best soldiers had taken refuge in a cave, from where they could watch the area unseen.

Seqen saw the Hyksos scouts arrive. Soon they were followed by the advance guard, then the main body of the troops. They marched along briskly, as though eager to leave hostile territory.

Suddenly their leader halted and gazed down at the ground.

'I hope he hasn't found the entrance to a tunnel,' said one of Seqen's men worriedly.

'There aren't any there,' the king assured him.

The officer picked something up and held it high.

'It's one of the wooden swords we use during exercises,' Seqen cursed under his breath, furious at such carelessness – it might cost them their lives.

'It's a toy,' said a junior officer.

'Maybe. It's seen a lot of use.'

'Those are probably the only weapons the Egyptians have to fight us with,' said a soldier, and everyone laughed.

Turning slowly round, the commander scrutinized his surroundings. 'Search the whole area,' he ordered.

For more than three hours, the Hyksos searched for other objects which would indicate that the place had been or still was inhabited. They found nothing. The toy sword must have been carried there by a sandstorm, or else a brat belonging to a nomadic tribe had left it behind.

'We've covered the whole area, sir,' said a scout. 'Not a living soul.'

'There's still that cave over there, and it interests me. Let's take a look at it.'

*

'They're coming this way, Majesty!' whispered one of Seqen's men.

'Keep calm, soldier.'

'If they come into the cave, we're done for.'

'Have a little faith.'

'We ought to run away,' said the other soldier.

'Too late,' said Seqen. 'Go right to the back, flatten yourselves to the ground, and don't make another sound.'

At the entrance to the cave, Seqen had arranged some animal bones, some still bearing tatters of flesh.

'There's a monster in there,' said a Hyksos.

'Not a monster,' disagreed the commander, 'but certainly a meat-eater.'

'If it's still in there, it'll attack us.'

'There's a simple way of finding out. Archers, take up position.'

A dozen arrows flew to the back of the cave. One hit one of Seqen's soldiers in the arm, but Seqen immediately clamped his right hand over the man's mouth to stop him crying out. The other arrows flew over their heads and broke against the back wall.

'The creature isn't in its lair,' said one of the archers. 'Shall we wait until it comes back?'

'It would smell us and keep away. Besides, we aren't here to count the wild animals of the desert. We'll go back to camp.'

Much relieved, the Hyksos detachment left the forbidding place. Not even the most determined of rebels would want to live there.

Arm in arm, Ahhotep and Seqen watched the soldiers of the new Egyptian army putting up their tents and setting up camp again.

The queen herself had treated the wounded man. All his comrades had cheered her short speech praising their courage, which promised victories to come.

'The desert gives us the strength of Set,' said Ahhotep. 'There could be no better place for our secret camp. Now we must develop it.'

'How?' asked Seqen.

'Our soldiers deserve better than mere tents. We are going to build a fortress, barracks, houses and even a palace.'

'Ahhotep, you—'

'The Hyksos won't check these isolated places again. As we build, we shall have a single watchword: freedom. In Thebes, there are too many collaborators. We must go on deceiving them until we're ready to act. Then we'll kill them to ensure our unity.'

Seqen could not argue with what she had said. This was exactly the mad plan he had been going to suggest.

'Why did you take the risk of hiding in that cave, instead of in one of the tunnels?'

'Because I wanted to see the Hyksos arrive and leave, so that my men wouldn't be in danger.'

Ahhotep led her husband to the cave where death had come so close to him. 'You have become a true leader,' she said, 'and I'm proud of you.'

She took off her dress, dropped it to the ground, and lay down on this improvised bed. 'Give me another son, my love.'

## 45

There were only three scribes in the secret camp. Once they had settled in, they worked hard all day long and a good part of the night administering the small settlement, which now consisted of a fort, a barracks, several houses and a modest palace.

The rebels' enthusiasm increased their strength tenfold. They had absolute faith in the royal couple, whose unfailing resolution was the best encouragement they could have had to continue their impossible task.

Bricks were made at the camp, and water-carriers continually went back and forth between the river and the desert. With the aid of the water, gardeners had managed to create fertile plots around the camp dwellings. Fishermen provided the soldiers with fresh fish, while the brewery and bakery produced basic food and drink. On moonless nights, a detachment crossed the Nile to collect consignments of dried meat from the east bank.

But filling bellies was not enough, Ahhotep knew. So she had ordered the scribes to set up a school where the rebels could learn to read and write. In the future, when Egypt was free, some of them would occupy positions of responsibility.

The queen had only one bodyguard, Laughter, who was not only strong but as fast as a hunting-dog. He had a sense of humour, and loved to sneak up behind the carpenters and put an enormous paw on their shoulders. Most of them sweated profusely until the sound of Ahhotep's voice rescued them.

Craftsmen played a vital part in the preparations for war. While the soldiers trained under Seqen's command, they made arrows, bows, spears, swords and breastplates. But all this would be useless without a means of transport: they must have boats.

So the queen had engaged carpenters one by one, and they had been sworn to secrecy like all the other inhabitants of the camp. Emheb had sent highly skilled men to her from Edfu, which the Hyksos still regarded as a dependable town led by a devoted collaborator, a ruthless collector of taxes. Emheb, too, was secretly rearming, and his recruits had their base on the devastated site of Nekhen, which he was bringing back to life.

Thebes, Edfu and Nekhen: Qaris's model of Egypt now showed three cities free of Hyksos domination.

Promoted to head donkey, Long-Ears proudly led his fellow beasts of burden as they brought boat-building materials to the rebels' boatyard. They carried wood, papyrus and tools and never failed in their task, as if they knew they were taking part in something vitally important.

Everything was going too slowly for Ahhotep's taste, but she bore the waiting patiently. The creation of the boatyard was an all-important step: when the rebels at last had a war-fleet, they would be mobile and could launch their first attack.

The craftsmen worked in the open air, to the rhythm of songs whose words were not always fit for refined ears. The queen did not mind; she loved to linger and watch the craftsmen building the first boat, the bearer of so much hope.

The trunks of acacia trees were sawn into small planks, which the boat-builders fitted together like bricks to form the hull of the boat. They were fixed in place with long nails, or bound together with stout ropes passed through holes made with a drill. With an adze, the head boat-builder shaped the sternpost, which served as a support for the tiller, while his assistants took charge of the stern and the keel.

The queen herself inspected the hull, both inside and out. The work was far from finished, for the planks had still to be smoothed, then caulked to make them watertight.

'Are you satisfied, Majesty?' asked the head boat-builder.

'Can't you go any faster?'

'We are going as fast as we can. If we hurried we'd spoil the materials, and we need strong boats to transport our troops. Unfortunately I haven't enough skilled workers, and training apprentices takes time – a lot of time.'

'We shall succeed,' promised the queen.

Ahhotep's smile was the most beautiful reward the boat-builders could have wished for. It made them happy to be alive and determined to see this through.

One of the craftsmen, however, did not share these sentiments. When he was recruited, he had simply wanted to earn more, and he had never imagined that a camp like this could exist. By creating it, Ahhotep had proved that she had gone mad and was leading Thebes to its downfall. Sooner or later, the Hyksos would discover this rebel band, and the reprisals would be terrible.

He was an apprentice boat-builder only twenty years old, and he had no wish to be killed in a fight which was lost before it began. For some time, he had been trying to persuade himself that Ahhotep's idealism would simply wear itself out. But the camp was working for good or ill, weapons were being made there, soldiers were being trained, and they were even building a warship.

It was pointless to talk to his superiors, because they all supported the queen's cause. It was up to him to act on his own, and to do something radical in order to prevent a catastrophe.

The heart and soul of this crazy plan was Ahhotep. Once she was dead, even Seqen – although undoubtedly a fine leader – would be a broken man. The rebels would leave their base, return to Thebes and recognize the Hyksos's sovereignty.

So he would have to kill her.

Next time she visited the boatyard, he went over to her when there was no one else near, bowed and said, 'Majesty, may I show you something unusual?'

The queen was intrigued.

'It's at the far end of the site,' he went on. 'I think you will be surprised.'

Ahhotep followed him. They walked between rows of carefully stacked planks and entered a narrow space between trunks which had not yet been squared off.

'What is this surprising thing?' she asked.

The apprentice brandished a heavy wooden mallet and a well-honed chisel. 'You are a danger to all Thebans. Only your death will save them from chaos.' His eyes were filled with a murderous resolve.

'You're wrong,' said Ahhotep. 'Fighting is our only chance of survival.'

'You cannot fight the Hyksos – everyone knows that.'

'Are you a coward?'

The apprentice's eyes narrowed. 'We have no choice but to submit to the emperor. The power you seek is only an illusion.'

'If we truly want our freedom, we shall win it back.'

'That isn't true.'

'You're afraid, and I can understand that. But one day fear will change sides.'

'The Hyksos have won. Why won't you admit it?'

'Because the love of freedom must remain stronger than anything else, whatever the circumstances.'

'So much the worse for you, Majesty. You shall die with your illusions.'

He planned to smash the queen's skull with his mallet and stab her through the heart with his chisel; she would have no time to feel pain.

Then he would flee and make for Kebet, where he would enlist in the Hyksos militia.

Just as he was raising his arm to strike, a heavy paw came down upon his shoulder.

He spun round. Laughter was crouching on the top of a pile of tree-trunks, just above his head. Enraged to see Ahhotep threatened, the massive dog turned his head and sank his teeth into the attacker's throat. Then he lifted him off the ground, paying no heed to his screams, which were soon lost in the rattle of his dying breath.

## 46

The report from the small group of rebels in Avaris, who risked their lives every time they passed on information, gave no cause for joy. The emperor's power was absolute. The Hyksos had the whole area in thrall, and the slightest attempt at sedition was repressed with extreme ferocity. The capital was like a gigantic barracks; the Egypt of the gods and the pharaohs was nearing its last gasp.

With the aid of the census, Khamudi had managed to tax even the poorest peasants, and the ruling elite continued to grow wealthier, as well as acquiring more and more Egyptian slaves.

'All we can do is attack the garrison at Henen-Nesut, kill as many Hyksos as possible and then die a worthy death,' said Moustache.

'At least read the message through to the end,' advised the Afghan. 'It mentions Thebes.'

'Thebes no longer exists.'

'It certainly does. Look: Queen Ahhotep has succeeded her mother, with the agreement of the Hyksos and under their control.'

'What does that matter? It's just a puppet dynasty. I'm going to speak to our men.' Suddenly, Moustache had a mad idea. 'Did you say Ahhotep?'

'That's her name, yes,' agreed the Afghan.

'Ahhotep . . . That means "the Moon is Full", and the moon is the secret sign we've been trying to decipher all the time.'

'You think Queen Ahhotep heads a band of Theban rebels? She's only a woman, my friend. How could she even begin to think of fighting the mighty Hyksos army?'

'Thebes may not be dead,' argued Moustache. 'Perhaps Ahhotep has gathered around her a few supporters who are as determined as we are. We must forget about attacking here, and leave for the South.'

'Cross the Hyksos lines? That's impossible.'

'It would be for our whole force, yes; but not for the two of us. And if I'm not mistaken, we'll establish a link with our Theban allies.'

*

First an inadequate Nile flood, and now the negligence of the Hyksos government, which had neither attended to the upkeep of the reservoirs nor filled the emergency grain-stores to feed the inhabitants of Upper Egypt.

Thanks to the measures Ahhotep had taken, Thebes would just escape the famine. But if fate continued hostile and brought another poor flood, many would die of hunger.

In mid-July, many wheat-fields had been stricken by crop disease and the harvest spoiled by unusually wet weather. Only the late November plantings had been spared this fresh misfortune. On the queen's orders, the soldiers and craftsmen at the secret camp were given the largest rations, so that they could continue training and working almost normally.

Now recovered from his depression, Chomu arrived at the palace, and asked to see Heray.

'You've demanded another milch-cow from me,' complained Chomu. 'I shall soon be ruined.'

'It was not my demand, but Governor Emheb's. He collects the Hyksos taxes from all of us, and everyone, even the royal family, is in the same plight.'

'The emperor wants us to be prosperous, not poverty-stricken.'

'Indeed he does, but the law is the law. Thebes cannot disobey it.'

'You must write to Apophis and explain our difficulties.'

'The queen is doing so, rest assured. The main thing is to obey his orders.'

And Chomu could only agree. But, although disarmed, he simply could not understand why the emperor was plunging his faithful Theban subjects into poverty.

He said, 'I hope the queen won't write in insolent terms.'

'On the contrary, Chomu, on the contrary. She has long since given up that attitude, which was as futile as it was childish. We are going through a difficult period, no doubt because we are a distant province, far from Avaris and the centre of the empire. But I'm sure our submission will eventually be rewarded.'

'So am I, Heray,' said the vase-seller. Then, after a pause, he went on, 'We haven't seen much of Seqen lately.'

'He spends his time hunting and running about the countryside. He's restless, and can't stay in one place for long. We don't complain at the palace, because he brings back game. Now, what about that milch-cow?'

'I'm happy to pay my taxes to the emperor and thus contribute to the greatness of the Hyksos,' declared Chomu proudly. 'It's a sacrifice, but it's necessary.'

Heray laid a hand on the Canaanite's shoulder. 'You are an example to all Thebans.'

The trader blushed.

As he left the palace, he was thinking about Seqen. True, Heray's explanations were plausible, but all the same . . . When the occasion arose, he would have that restless fellow followed. So as to be sure he was not fomenting some laughable plot with a few peasants.

Ahhotep, Heray and Qaris were in council in Qaris's model-room.

'Majesty, I have the feeling Chomu's becoming dangerous again,' warned Heray.

'Have you any specific evidence?'

'No, but he seems himself again, and once again determined to do you harm.'

'Have him watched day and night.'

'He always has been, Majesty. All the supporters of collaboration have been identified. When the time comes, they'll be arrested in a matter of minutes.'

'Is there still no news from the North?' Ahhotep asked Qaris.

'No, Majesty. There are probably no rebels left there.'

'Since we are alone, we shall fight alone. King Seqen's hard work is beginning to bear fruit. We now have a small army at our disposal, and our soldiers are a match for any enemy.'

'What of the boats?' asked Qaris.

'The first has left the boatyard, and they have started building the second. The team of boat-builders is also becoming battle-hardened, and will work faster.'

'According to the last message from Governor Emheb, Majesty, the rebels gathered at Edfu and Nekhen form quite a sizeable group. There is no more to fear from the Nubians. They're content with the lands granted them by the emperor, and they have no wish to have Jannas's forces unleashed upon them. And Emheb is still regarded as the very model of a collaborator, who fills the Hyksos coffers by bleeding the region dry.'

Teti rushed into the model-room. 'Come quickly, Ahhotep! Kames has been hurt.'

The little boy had cut his right hand deeply with a razor he had taken from his father's bathing-room. His cries of pain must have been heard all over the city; but there was something more serious about the wound.

'It is not normal,' said Ahhotep as she tried to calm her son.

'The evil eye!' exclaimed Teti. 'The only way to ward it off is with alum.'

'If we have any left . . .'

While her mother went off to find the precious substance, Ahhotep spoke gently and firmly to Kames. 'You are in a lot of pain and you are expressing that – nothing could be more normal. But you must also fight against it and try to overcome it. If you don't, you will never become a man.'

Kames swallowed his tears and dared to look at his hand.

'You and I,' the queen went on, 'hate the bad spirit that hurt you. We're going to deprive it of a voice. The remedy your grandmother is bringing will make it leave your flesh. Then the blood will stop flowing, and your hand will be stronger than before.'

With all the strength of his nine years, Kames talked of his future life. The future of a proud man, determined to fight and conquer.

The alum Teti applied to the wound was remarkably effective: it drove out the evil eye and quickly healed the first wound inflicted upon the pharaoh's son.

## 47

As far as Kebet, all went well. By making lengthy detours, the Afghan and Moustache evaded Hyksos fortresses and patrols. They drank from canals, and ate small animals they killed. And all the time they moved onward, painfully slowly but without incident.

Sheltering at a farm would have been too dangerous. In this region, they could trust no one. On each road there were soldiers and guards. Even the desert tracks were under Hyksos control.

'We'll never get there,' lamented Moustache.

'We still have the Nile.'

'Only Hyksos boats use the Nile. If we steal one, they'll intercept us.'

'I've seen cargo-vessels passing by,' the Afghan reminded him.

'Yes, carrying wheat for the emperor's Nubian allies.'

'We'll hide in a consignment and disembark when we get to Thebes.'

'Supposing the crew spot us?'

'Too bad for them.'

They had one chance in ten of succeeding, Moustache thought. It was a lot better than nothing.


The morning was beautifully warm and the sky incomparably blue. Kames was playing ball with his friends, Teti was making pastries, and Thebes was continuing to measure out its tranquil days as though the sun's dazzling presence had postponed the threat of destruction.

Ahhotep picked up a female figurine her mother had made, following an old magical text, and placed it on a face-paint spoon. The statue had no arms or legs, but had a huge pubic triangle marked by pin-pricks. The spoon was shaped like a naked swimmer, pushing a duck before her. The swimmer was the sky-goddess Nut, swimming in the primordial ocean. She held up the earth-god, Geb, represented by the duck. Together the primordial couple had given birth to many forms of life. Surely bringing these two together would guarantee Ahhotep's fertility?

The queen left the palace and went to find Seqen. He was asleep under a calotrope, an imposing tree with five-petalled pink flowers. Because its fruit was shaped like a testicle, the tree was believed to have aphrodisiac qualities.

The queen knelt and gently stroked Seqen's forehead.

He awoke and blinked up at her. 'Ahhotep, you look radiant.'

'Sometimes I think of the timid young man who was too afraid to talk to me. You have become a true warrior, worthy of leading your men into battle.'

'The reality is not so bright. Soon we shall have been working for ten years, and we still have only a tiny army.'

'What matters is its desire for victory. Can't you feel mine?'

Seqen took her in his arms and drew her down to him. Entwined, they lay together and became one.

'At last,' she told him afterwards, 'At last I'm pregnant again.'

High Treasurer Khamudi had become even fatter and was having more and more difficulty in squeezing into his old clothes. He loathed wasting money, so he wanted to wait until the very last minute before having new ones made by the finest weaver in the capital, who would be given ample incentive not to divulge his illustrious customer's measurements.

Nevertheless, as he looked over his scrolls, Khamudi gulped down a fried pastry spiced with cumin, for today was a festival for the ruling elite in Avaris. The emperor had promised to stage an unrivalled celebration. The army would acclaim him, and Khamudi had only excellent news for him. Nubia and Egypt were prostrating themselves before their sovereign, and all resistance had been wiped out. As the Theban minister for agriculture regularly confirmed, the dying city had but one ambition, and a laudable one at that: to pay its taxes and levies to Apophis.

Only one minor problem remained, but it was a difficult one to resolve: attacks on caravans by small but very mobile robber bands. However, on the road to Wadi Tumilat, between the eastern Delta and the Red Sea, Khamudi had just had a notable success. A detachment of soldiers had ambushed twenty sand-travellers, and killed them with particular relish. Their fate would serve as an example.

'Leave your scrolls,' Yima warned him. 'The emperor is ready.'

Abandoning his work, and paying not the slightest attention to his plump wife, the High Treasurer hurried to join his master, whom he found surrounded by his special bodyguards; they would protect him as he passed through the streets of Avaris.

Partly as a security measure and partly because he loathed the common people, the emperor rarely left the citadel. So his appearance in public unleashed the enthusiasm of a jubilant crowd, carefully organized by Khamudi. Anyone caught failing to cheer Apophis would be deported to the copper mines.

The emperor halted before the garden of an Egyptian collaborator. It was positively magical, with its cornflowers, iris, mallow, chrysanthemums and larkspur.

'Destroy all this,' he order Khamudi.

'Now, Majesty?'

'I do not like repeating myself, my friend.'

The High Treasurer summoned his own men, who trampled on the flowers and tore up the young shoots.

'I do not wish to see a single garden in my capital,' decreed Apophis, 'because the sight of flowers softens men's hearts. The sole exception is to be the garden in the citadel, which I grant to my wife as a special favour.'

'If your Majesty would be so good as to enter.'

With the approval of 'empress' Tany, the lady Yima had organized a reception at the harem in Apophis's honour. Although she loathed the fat, ugly, vulgar Tany, Yima continually heaped flattery upon her, to ward off her rages. Without asking her husband's permission, Tany had all those who displeased her killed by Aberia, who still took great delight in strangling her victims.

Fortunately, Yima's husband and the emperor remained on good terms, and she felt protected. Nevertheless, she was careful to congratulate the appalling Tany on everything and nothing, in order to remain in her good graces.

Yima and Khamudi continued to indulge themselves in the vilest perversions, knowing that Apophis would not reprimand them, particularly since they liked to amuse themselves with Egyptian women, who never emerged alive from their sadistic games.

Apophis gazed round the large reception hall, with its covered pool and comfortable chairs.

'We have a beautiful harem here, Lady Yima,' he said.

'All the credit should go to your wife, Majesty.'

'What have you to show me that is so exceptional?'

'A dance, Majesty. A lascivious dance which used to be performed by women of ill-repute in ale-houses. Today it will be performed for you and you alone, by the last surviving heiress of the richest family in Memphis. If you are dissatisfied with her performance, the lady Aberia will strangle her.'

'Entertaining, indeed,' said Apophis. 'Let her begin.'

She was eighteen years old and beautiful. Aberia tore off the girl's wrap and pushed her, naked, to the centre of the room.

'Show us what you can do,' ordered Yima, 'or else . . .'

Not trying to hide either her genitals or her breasts, the young girl stood as upright and as still as the statue of a goddess.

'Dance!' Yima screeched hysterically.

She grabbed the girl's arm and shook her; the girl slapped her.

'No one is more miserable than you,' said the prisoner with impressive calm. 'When you are all judged in the after life, the Soul-Eater will feast on your rotten souls.'

'The arrogance of these Egyptians is really exasperating,' said the emperor. 'Have the rebel put to death.'

## 48

Although Ahhotep was massaged every day and took preparations designed to prevent bleeding, the palace doctor was anxious. The prospects for the birth were still unclear, and the progress of the pregnancy was causing him concern. Ahhotep ought to have been resting in bed, but she always answered the doctor's advice with 'Everything will go well because everything has to go well. And I shall have a second son.'

Even Teti could not reason with her daughter, who had undertaken the onerous task of reopening the weavers' workshops, which had been closed for too long. Officially, this was because the young queen could not long bear to see Theban women poorly dressed, but in reality clothes were needed for the army.

The resumption of work had attracted Chomu's attention, so the weaving-women made dresses, underclothing and shawls for all to see, while at night tunics and kilts left for the training-camp. The need to deceive slowed both production and delivery, but extreme caution was essential.

Ahhotep herself had recruited four experienced female weavers who dreamt constantly of seeing the Hyksos defeated. They alone knew the truth, while their apprentices busied themselves reclothing the population. Chomu had profited nicely from the work, by hiring out some empty premises at a good rate.

One day, while the queen was visiting the workshops to check that they were properly ventilated and that the workers had suitable materials, Heray came hurrying in.

'Majesty, your presence is required at the palace.'

'Is it urgent?'

'I believe so.'

'Thebes! We're in Thebes. Do you realize, Afghan? We've done it!' To hide the fact that he was almost in tears, Moustache bent his head lower over the moon hieroglyph he was drawing on the palm of his left hand.

'It's much smaller than Memphis.'

'It will grow, you can be sure of that. Nothing is more nourishing than freedom.'

'Provided it still exists. Don't forget, the region is under Hyksos control.'

'And *you* mustn't forget that the sign of Ahhotep proclaims the opposite.'

'Don't get too excited, my friend. We've avoided soldiers, guards and crocodiles, but we must stay on the alert.'

'Let's go to the palace and tell them who we are.'

'Supposing Queen Ahhotep is in league with the Hyksos?'

Moustache was so intoxicated with excitement that he could hardly bring himself to accept the possibility. But it would have been childish to discount it.

'I'll go to the palace,' decided the Afghan. 'I'll explain myself awkwardly, like a foreigner. If all goes well, I'll emerge free and come and fetch you. If I don't, escape and rejoin our men.'

'I won't let you take such a risk.'

Moustache did not have time to develop his argument, for ten sturdy fellows armed with spears suddenly leapt out of the reeds and surrounded them.

In his heart, the Afghan admired the men's skill: although thoroughly accustomed to danger, he had not realized they were there. Their swift, decisive action was worthy of professional soldiers.

Moustache was thinking the same thing.

It was pointless to resist.

'Who are you?' demanded one of the Thebans.

Moustache held out his left hand so that the moon hieroglyph showed clearly. 'We want to see Queen Ahhotep – because of this sign.'

The soldier was unmoved. 'Why?'

'We have important information for her.'

'Your hands will be bound and you will follow us. One false move, and you will be killed.'

She was the most beautiful woman the Afghan had ever seen. Her eyes burned with a fire that would conquer any man in an instant, mingling power, tenderness and intelligence.

'I am from Afghanistan, and Moustache is Egyptian. We are the leaders of a rebel band based in Middle Egypt and we have a few contacts in Avaris.'

Teti and Qaris gasped, and Heray was astonished, but Ahhotep did not turn a hair.

She said, 'Give us good reasons to believe that you are not Hyksos spies.'

'Majesty,' said Moustache, 'we will tell you the names of our men, the places where they are hiding, and the locations of Hyksos fortresses and garrisons. We have trained many fighters, made our own weapons, and created a network of sympathizers. We cannot launch a direct attack, but we raid caravans and kill the emperor's spies one by one, so that he is far less well informed than he thinks he is.'

As the Afghan and Moustache talked, Qaris took notes. Using this priceless information, he would be able to complete his model. And he was already dreaming up plans to attack specific places.

'How can we be sure all this is not lies?' asked Ahhotep.

'We have no other way of convincing you, Majesty,' said Moustache.

'In that case, I am going to hand you over to the emperor's soldiers.'

'You can't be on their side,' he exclaimed, 'not you, Majesty. That's impossible. In the name of Pharaoh – even if there's no one alive to fill that office – I swear to you that we're telling the truth. May my soul be destroyed if I am lying.'

Ahhotep and Seqen gazed out at one of the Theban mountains' matchless sunsets. Before the apparent triumph of night, the sky took on pink and orange tints, while the river acquired a sparkling silver mantle.

'When are you ever going to rest?' asked Seqen.

'The day after the birth, if necessary.'

'The doctor has his misgivings, as you know very well.'

'Let him say what he will,' said the queen. 'I shall trust in the gods. Is the boat-building going well?'

'Too slowly – much too slowly. The carpenters have had serious problems because the wood is of poor quality. There are times when I—'

Ahhotep laid her fingers on her husband's lips. 'Several useless words – for instance "doubt" and "downhearted" – have been struck out of our language. They convey feelings which are luxuries and which only free people can allow themselves. Go on strengthening our training-camp, and don't worry yourself about futile things.'

Seqen kissed her passionately.

'For a little while,' she smiled, 'you must contain your ardour. But when you see our child, you won't regret the sacrifice.'

He stroked his wife's dark hair. 'Do you think Moustache and the Afghan are telling the truth?'

'We'll put them to the test, and if they're spies they're bound to make a mistake. On the other hand, if there really is a rebel group in the North, it will be very useful when we are fighting to reconquer our land.'

'We're still short of weapons,' said Seqen, 'and clothing is reaching us only sporadically.'

'I shall sort things out,' promised Ahhotep. 'And I fervently hope our new guests will prove effective allies.'

Seqen smiled at her. Then his face suddenly darkened. 'Someone's been following me. I managed to lose the man in the desert, but I'm sure the collaborators are beginning to find my behaviour strange.'

'I'll find out who it is,' Ahhotep assured him. 'If he gets too close to the camp, the agreed security measures will be taken.'

## 49

The Afghan and Moustache were collecting flints, some light, some dark, which were harder even than metal. Although they did not balk at the task, the days sometimes seemed very long.

'We've been sentenced to forced labour,' said the Afghan.

'Don't you believe that,' replied Moustache. 'On the contrary, we've been shown the greatest trust.'

Hands on hips, the Afghan threw his companion a quizzical look. 'Would you care to explain that?'

'In our country, we use flint for razors and for doctors' instruments – and for weapons, too. Arrow- and spear-heads, blades for daggers and axes. It's an old-fashioned way, but it's cheap and effective. Everyone must think we are picking up pebbles, whereas in fact we're gathering weapons for the Theban army.'

'Why didn't Queen Ahhotep tell us that?'

'Because she wants to see if we're intelligent enough to realize it for ourselves.'

Chomu drank a cup of goat's milk. Finding it sour, he spat it out again. For a while now, he had been having stomach trouble; and he found it difficult to sleep because he kept asking himself the same question over and over again. Why had the emperor forgotten his faithful Theban subjects? After all, they were carrying out their duties punctually, and Governor Emheb had no cause for complaint.

Queen Ahhotep seemed harmless. Seqen, on the other hand, intrigued him. So Chomu had told one of his cousins, a fellow supporter of the Hyksos, to follow him.

'Well?' Chomu asked irritably when his cousin returned.

'Seqen goes hunting and fishing,' said his cousin. 'I don't follow him absolutely everywhere, so as to avoid being spotted. And the gods may bear witness that his energy seems inexhaustible.'

'In other words, he's leading you a merry dance.'

'Let's not exaggerate. But he certainly knows the desert well.'

What a fool, thought Chomu. He can't even follow someone properly. Aloud, he said, 'You must continue, cousin. I want to know more.'

'It's very tiring.'

'I will pay you more.'

'In that case . . .'

The cousin, Chomu decided, would be simply a very visible decoy. Another, more skilful, man would take over the real job of following Seqen, just when the king thought he was safe.

'Aren't you tired of picking up flints?' asked Seqen.

'We'll collect as many as are needed,' replied Moustache. 'Providing more weapons is vital, isn't it?'

The Afghan nodded his agreement.

The pharaoh surveyed the two men: Moustache, enthusiastic, strong-willed, capable of seeing things through to the end; the Afghan, cold, determined, savage. They made a formidable pair, clearly endowed with several years' experience, and Seqen had the feeling that their mutual understanding would make them unbeatable in a fight.

'Are you good hunters?' he asked.

'If you want to survive in occupied territory, you have to be,' replied the Afghan.

'Then come with me.'

Some distance from the trio as they walked into the eastern desert were ten archers, ready to act if the Afghan and Moustache tried to harm the king.

For some time, the pair had been asking him incessant questions, as if they suspected him of being more than just a high-spirited young man whose only interests were catching big fish and taking game back to the palace for food.

Seqen led them to a reed hut at the edge of the desert. 'Go in and look.'

Warily, the two men hesitated.

'What's inside?' asked Moustache.

'The answer to your questions.'

'We don't like surprises,' said the Afghan. 'As a general rule they have nothing good to offer people like us.'

'And yet your curiosity deserves to be satisfied.'

With a suspicious look, Moustache went into the hut, ready to defend himself if he were attacked. The Afghan, he knew, would not hesitate to pounce on Seqen, although the king was both taller and more heavily built.

He saw animal intestines; dozens of them, of different sizes and lengths.

'This is the main product of the hunt,' said Seqen. 'You understand why, I suppose?'

The pharaoh and the Afghan looked defiantly into each other's eyes. 'What are animal guts used for?' asked the Afghan slowly. 'They can be turned into strings for musical instruments, or ... for bows. Flints, animal gut – Thebes is re-arming, isn't she? And you are the commander-in-chief.'

The Afghan faced Seqen, and Moustache stood behind him. If they attacked at the same time, the king would have to be swift indeed to escape unharmed; he had repeated the exercise a hundred times.

Moustache got down on one knee, and the Afghan followed suit. 'We are at your command.'

Seqen ignored the splendour of the stars shining in a sky the colour of lapis-lazuli. Mad with worry, he paced up and down the passage outside the bedchamber where Ahhotep was struggling to give birth to their second child.

The doctor had not hidden his concern. And the three midwives, although experienced, had also been nervous. 'It will be the mother or the child,' one of them had predicted.

At the thought of losing Ahhotep, the king felt a terrible pang of despair. Their love was the fire that gave him life, the air that gave him breath, the water that allowed him to survive, the earth on which he built. Without her, he could never carry on the fight. The queen was the soul of the battle, embodying the alliance of magic and will. With her, nothing was impossible.

But if their child died, she would be utterly broken.

Qaris gazed at his model with fierce concentration; Heray drank beer, even though he was not thirsty; Teti watched over little Kames as he slept. Everyone knew that Egypt's fate was being played out in that bedchamber, where the god of destiny was juggling with life and death.

It was not only that Seqen was deeply in love with Ahhotep. Each day, he found more to admire in her. In her, the pride of the queens of the golden age lived on, as if, although Egypt had been occupied and trampled underfoot, its greatness refused to be extinguished.

Ahhotep had the strength to crush the life out of misfortune; but misfortune had, like a dragon, seen the danger and was trying to stifle its adversary. Seqen was powerless to help the wife he loved and revered. He wanted to shout, to roar his indignation against this injustice, to call upon the gods not to abandon a woman who heard their voices and tried, at the risk of her own life, to pass on their words.

Looking fragile and anxious, Teti came down the passage towards him.

'Whatever happens,' he promised her, 'I shall attack. At least Thebes will die with dignity.'

The door of the bedchamber opened and one of the midwives appeared, her face haggard with exhaustion.

Seqen seized her by the shoulders. 'Tell me the truth!' he demanded.

'You have a second son. The queen is alive, but very weak.'

## 50

The limestone figure of Senusret I sat on his throne, gazing up at the heavens.

'Now!' ordered the emperor in his harsh voice.

With one mighty swing of his club, Khamudi decapitated the majestic statue that had so exasperated his master.

This was the tenth ancient statue he had destroyed on the forecourt of the Temple of Set. The watching Hyksos dignitaries were delighted to be present at the death of these witnesses to an extinct culture.

Apophis surveyed a sphinx which wore the face of Amenemhat III. 'Have a sculptor replace the name of this worthless monarch with my own,' he ordered. 'The same is to be done with all the few monuments I agree to retain. From now on, they will proclaim my glory.'

A select few of Apophis's servants would have the right to a crudely sculpted statue, its skin painted yellow, created by a sculptor ignorant of the ancient rites.

'Windswept, why are you smiling so scornfully?' the emperor asked.

'Because at least two of the senior officials who have just prostrated themselves before you are complete hypocrites. In public, they heap praise upon you. According to their confidences in the bedchamber, they hate you.'

'You work very well, little sister. Give their names to Khamudi.'

'No, not to him. I find him distasteful.'

'Then tell me.'

'I can refuse you nothing.' Without hesitation, she condemned to torture and death two of the men she had seduced.

'I hear,' said Apophis, 'that you have fallen in love with Minos, my Minoan painter.'

'He is an inventive and ardent lover.'

'Has he criticized me at all?'

'No. All he thinks of is his art – and my body.'

'This evening, send him to me.'

'You're not going to deprive me of my favourite toy, I hope?'
'Not yet. Don't worry.'

The emperor was not displeased with the way his palace had been redecorated. It no longer had any Egyptian features, and faithfully reproduced the main themes from the Minoan royal palace at Knossos. One of them particularly pleased him: a wall-painting of an acrobat jumping off a charging bull in full flight. The man leapt over the animal's head, sprang off its neck with arms and legs outstretched, and landed behind its tail; if the dangerous leap was successful.

One detail intrigued him. The painter's identity could not be readily guessed from his style, which was why he had summoned Minos.

The Minoan was trembling with fear.

'Are you enjoying your stay with us?' asked Apophis.

'Of course, Majesty.'

'And what about your companions?'

'We have all lost desire to return to Minoa.'

'That's fortunate, because it's out of the question. Your work here is far from finished: next you are to decorate my palaces in the main towns of the Delta.'

Minos bowed. 'You do us too much honour, Majesty.'

'Of course, you must not disappoint me.' Apophis turned to the wall-painting. 'Tell me, what is the function of this strange garden, under the bull?'

'That is the labyrinth, Majesty. It has only one entrance and one exit, and it houses a monster with a bull's head. Inside, there are many twists and turns, and the unwary visitor strays so far that he loses his mind, or else falls victim to the monster. Only the hero bearing Ariadne's thread has a chance of coming out alive.'

'How amusing. I want a more detailed painting.'

'As it pleases you, Majesty.'

Seqen held Ahhotep so tightly that she could hardly breathe. 'You are out of danger, my love. But you cannot bear any more children.'

'I wanted two sons, and I have them. What do you think of the second?'

He loosened his hold and gazed in wonder at the chubby-cheeked baby sleeping in its cradle. 'He's magnificent.'

'His name is to be Ahmose, "He Who was Born of the Moon-God", because he saw the light at the moment when the moon became full. Like his father and his elder brother, he will have only one goal: the freedom and sovereignty of Egypt.' She nestled against Seqen again. 'I thought I was going to die as I gave birth to him, and I never stopped thinking of you. If I had died, you'd have gone on fighting, wouldn't you?'

'Without you, what chance would we have had of victory? I command brave soldiers, and they're ready to die for their country, because you are its soul and its magic.'

'You must go back to the camp,' said Ahhotep. 'There is still so much to do.'

'I will, but on one condition: that you take the rest you need.'

'My mother will watch over me.'

'She can't make you do anything against your will. I want you to give me your word, Queen of Egypt, otherwise I'm not leaving this room.'

'You have it – but it's only the word of a hostage.'

The Thebans rejoiced at the happy news: both mother and child were doing well. An attentive grandmother, a queen whose confinements had not diminished her beauty, two fine boys and a father who continued to adore his wife: that was the peaceful picture the royal family presented to Thebes.

The picture did not in the least reassure Chomu, because he was still worried about Seqen. A man could be passionate about hunting and fishing, but really! To leave early on the morning after his son's difficult birth, to cross the Nile, lose himself in the lonely places on the west bank, and take goodness knows how many risks to return with one paltry hare.

Chomu was now sure that Seqen was involved in secret activities. He must be followed properly this time, and the truth revealed.

After spotting Chomu's cousin, who had been used as a decoy, Seqen had pretended to head into a wadi. Then he had retraced his steps and made for the secret camp.

The Canaanite following Seqen was generously paid, because he knew how to make himself almost invisible. The king took many precautions: he stopped frequently, turned round, looked in all directions, wiped away every trace of his footprints. But the man following him avoided all the traps, and knew when to crouch or lie down flat.

So Seqen had not thrown him off the scent.

Lying flat on his belly on top of a small hillock deep in the desert, the Canaanite at last saw Seqen's goal: a camp, full of soldiers at exercise. And it was no temporary camp, either, for it contained a fort, a barracks, houses and even a small palace. So Ahhotep and Seqen were training an army, which sooner or later would commit the fatal error of attacking the Hyksos. Chomu must be warned immediately.

But as he got to his feet, the Canaanite felt a weight on the back of his neck. The weight suddenly became irresistible, and he toppled forwards. His face was plunged into the sand, muffling his shouts of terror.

Laughter sank his teeth into the back of the spy's neck. Security measures were security measures, and the giant dog carried them out most conscientiously.

51

The Persian officer, a man who specialized in lightning raids and summary executions, was in a foul temper. For more than five years, that pig Khamudi had been blocking his promotion and taking all the credit in the emperor's eyes for the bloody raids that had kept the Hyksos Empire free of rebellion.

Khamudi had devised a remarkably effective system: anyone who wished to keep his reputation spotless must go through him and pay for his services. Moreover, Khamudi claimed to have devised every new trade practice, and awarded himself exclusive rights for an unlimited time. Anyone who dared protest saw his enterprise wither, and anyone who continued to protest met with a fatal accident.

With the support of about thirty officers from his own country, the Persian had decided to get rid of Khamudi, taking care to ensure that the emperor did not suspect them. They had devised an infallible plan: to use one of the Egyptian women from the harem as soon as an opportunity arose.

And it had just done so. In order to heap more humiliation upon the daughter of some Egyptian nobles he had himself beheaded, Khamudi had had the girl brought from the harem to attend to his feet. Although they were small and fat, the High Treasurer was very proud of them and made sure that his slave treated them with the utmost respect, before forcing her to satisfy his most depraved whims.

The Persian had not found it difficult to transform the young Egyptian girl into an instrument of vengeance. Although she well knew that she would never emerge alive from Khamudi's villa, she had nevertheless agreed to carry out a mission which would give her terrible life some meaning.

The High Treasurer was in ecstasies as he read the papyrus: in less than a year, his fortune had doubled. And he had no intention of stopping there. Since no important transaction could take place without his authorization, he would increase the compulsory levies and share them out between himself and the emperor.

'The slave has arrived to attend to your feet, my lord,' announced his steward.

'Send her in.'

The young woman prostrated herself before the master of the house.

'Undress little one, and lick my feet.'

Her spirit broken, the slave did so without protest.

'Now cut my nails. If you hurt me, you will be whipped.'

Khamudi derived nearly as much pleasure from being obeyed as from torturing young girls who, after being with him, could never love another man.

The young Egyptian opened the wooden box containing her equipment. She picked up the flint knife the Persian had given her, and thought of her parents, whom she was about to avenge. One blow to the heart, and the torturer's life would be at an end. She had rehearsed the murder a hundred times with the Persian officer, so as to be certain of success.

'Hurry up, little one. I don't like being kept waiting.'

No, she wouldn't stab him in the heart. She would strike lower – much lower. Before dying, her torturer would lose his manhood.

The young girl knelt and raised her eyes, to engrave the monster's face in her memory before she punished him. It was a mistake. Never before had the High Treasurer seen such a flame of hate in his slave's eyes. When she raised her arm to plunge the knife into his penis, he had time to parry the blow and felt only a burning sensation as the knife glanced off his thigh.

He punched her viciously in the face. Stunned, and with blood dripping from her nose, she dropped her knife.

Khamudi seized her by the hair. 'You wanted to kill me – me, Khamudi! You weren't acting alone, I am sure of that. I'm going to torture you myself and you'll give me the names of your accomplices. And I mean *all* your accomplices.'

The Canaanite's mutilated body was exhibited before the palace at Thebes. A large part of the population had gathered there to gaze upon his terrible wounds.

Seqen said, 'I found him in the desert. Does anyone recognize him, despite the state he's in?'

Chomu recognized a large mole on what remained of the man's left hip, but said nothing. For this was the man he had paid to follow Seqen.

'What happened to him?' asked Qaris.

'I expect he ventured too far and suffered the fate of the unwary. Monsters must have attacked him and torn him limb from limb.'

Horrified and shocked, the Thebans began returning to their homes.

'Never again ask me to follow Seqen when he's out hunting,' Chomu's cousin whispered in his ear. 'I don't want to be eaten by desert monsters.'

Even Chomu was shaken. Evidently the unfortunate man had indeed fallen victim to the gryphons and dragons that haunted the inhospitable wastes bordering the Nile. Some day, it would be Seqen's turn.

Aberia's enormous hands closed round the Persian soldier's neck. He was her fifteenth victim of the day, and she had been careful to make him suffer for a long time before allowing him to die.

The reprisals carried out by the High Treasurer, with the emperor's permission, were terrifying. All the plotters against Khamudi, their wives, their children and their animals had been executed in front of the Temple of Set. Some had been burnt alive, some beheaded, others stoned or put to the sword.

Khamudi, still complaining loudly of pain from his wound, watched from his place of honour beside Apophis, who had special treatment in store for the two main culprits, the Persian officer and the Egyptian slave-girl.

'Let us begin with this depraved young slut,' decreed the emperor. 'Come, my faithful friend, marvel at my new creations below the fortress. They will make you forget your pain.'

Obediently, Khamudi looked. He saw an arena and a circular wooden construction, open to the air.

'Bring the criminal forward,' ordered the emperor.

The Egyptian girl had been tortured with such savagery that she could scarcely walk. Leaning against one of the walls of the arena, she nevertheless had the strength to cast a look of hatred at her torturers, who were seated on a raised balcony to get the best view.

Apophis clicked his fingers.

A fighting bull charged into the enclosure, steam rising from its nostrils, hooves thundering.

'Jump over its horns,' advised the emperor in his harsh voice. 'If you succeed, I will spare your life.'

The creature charged. Utterly exhausted, the young girl could do nothing but close her eyes.

The Persian officer did not understand. Why had he been thrown into this circular structure, containing a winding path interrupted by walls which formed double bends?

'Walk through my labyrinth,' the emperor ordered from the balcony above, 'and try to find the way out. That is your only chance of obtaining my pardon.'

The torture that had made him give up the names of his accomplices, one by one, had left the Persian maimed and with almost no strength. He had been given a crutch, which enabled him to walk if he put his weight mostly on his left leg, which was less badly injured.

He took a few steps forward. An axe sprang up out of the ground, cutting off three of his toes. Roaring with pain, the Persian flattened himself against a circling wall, then tried to walk round it. But as he passed, two blades sprang out simultaneously.

The first pierced his flank, the second his neck. And the man who had wanted to kill Khamudi bled to death before the eyes of the emperor and his faithful High Treasurer.

'Those two useless creatures were too damaged to give us pleasure for long,' commented Apophis. 'We shall make sure the next ones are in good condition, so that the spectacle is more compelling.'

## 52

The annual flood had been so slight that there would not be enough silt for all the fields in Waset. Moreover, when next spring came all the reservoirs would be empty. It was pointless to look for help to the emperor, who would not lower taxes even when severe drought threatened.

The only consolation was an abundant harvest of cucumbers; but most of those would have to be handed over to Governor Emheb, who would send them to Avaris.

This evening, Seqen was in low spirits.

'We can cope with this,' Ahhotep promised him. 'Heray's excellent management means we have good food reserves. If we ration food and water, we shall survive this difficult year.'

'That won't be enough.'

'Has something happened at the camp?'

'The soldiers want an increase in their pay. If they don't get it, they'll lay down their arms and return to Thebes.'

'Have they lost the will to fight?'

'It's been too long,' said Seqen. 'They're convinced that we'll never dare attack the Hyksos. If they're to continue such intensive training, they want better pay.'

'Have you tried to reason with them?'

'Usually I succeed, but this time I failed.'

'Don't they know their efforts will soon be crowned with success?'

'Qaris has just told me that the garrisons at Edfu and Nekhen have made the same demands. It's over. We no longer have the means to continue the fight. In a few days' time, we shall abandon the secret camp.'

Ahhotep left the palace in the middle of the night, slipping past her own guards. Crossing the sleeping town, she hurried to the limit of the cultivated lands.

At the point where the kingdom of the desert began, she hesitated.

Set was the master there, and at any moment he could unleash forces so savage that no human could resist them. Monsters did indeed exist, and no sensible Egyptian would risk venturing into this hostile territory without the protection of the sun, which alone had the power to drive away malevolent creatures.

But Egypt was ruled by the empire of darkness, and Ahhotep must confront that darkness if she was to undertake it and steal away a part of its power.

The young queen left the world of humans and entered the desert, reminding herself of the words of the sages. Yes, this was the place of all dangers, but it was also the place of mountains, whose bellies contained gold and precious stones. At the heart of each misfortune, there was hidden happiness.

Ahhotep headed along the bed of a dried-up river and walked at a brisk but comfortable pace. Leather sandals protected her feet, and the moon's light enabled her to make out the undulations of the landscape.

All around her were crackling and hissing noises. A rock shattered, and the scree tumbled down the slope of a hill. The laughter of hyenas mingled with the hooting of owls, while a big snake zig-zagged across the intruder's path.

Ahhotep followed her instinct, which told her to go further, and yet further. She felt as though she were walking in the air, and all her tiredness disappeared. She reached the narrow entrance to a valley framed by menacing rock-faces. If she stepped through the constricted opening, would she be cut off for ever?

The queen walked on. This time she was walking in deepest darkness, for the gentle light of her guiding moon could not reach into the depths of this ravine.

A tall man loomed up before her, a man with an ugly face and a jutting nose. He was bright red, armed with a yellow dagger which shone with evil light, and he was coming towards her, ready to attack.

Emperor Apophis . . . Yes, it was he, the coward who was persecuting the Egyptian people, the tyrant whom Ahhotep had sworn to oppose.

She did not flinch. Although unarmed, she would fight. Picking up a stone, she threw it at her enemy, but it seemed she missed. Twice more she threw. Although certain she had hit her target, she could not prevent the emperor moving forward and he did not even cry out.

A ghost . . . It was a ghost, which had risen from the empire of darkness to devour her.

Running away was impossible. Since the stones had passed right through the ghost, Ahhotep would, too. When it was scarcely more than an arm's length away, Ahhotep rushed at it, head down.

She felt as though she had been plunged into a furnace whose flames licked cruelly at her flesh. Just as she was on the point of fainting, she saw a gleam of light and concentrated all her will on it. The light grew bigger, and as it did so the pain grew less. An orange ball began to form and swelled so quickly that the night was vanquished. A new day had just been born, and the dawn lit up hundreds of trees with long, slender branches, decorated with sweetly scented green flowers.

Balanites: a real treasure-store, providing wood for making tools, oil and even a substance which purified water. Ahhotep ate a few of the yellow fruits; they were sweet and flavoursome.

Where this desert forest ended, the soil changed. In certain places water-courses seemed to flow.

The young woman knelt down to touch this new miracle, and found not water but several veins of pure silver! It had been born of the marriage between the moon-god and the desert-goddess, under the protection of Set the fiery, whose fire had made it grow in the heart of the rock. Seqen could pay his soldiers – the rebels were rich!

Intoxicated with joy, Ahhotep retraced her steps, taking care to remember every detail of her journey.

As she emerged from the desert valley she was confronted by a leopard, which stared intently at its prey. Ahhotep had nowhere to hide. Suddenly a gazelle appeared, its horns shaped like a lyre. To the queen's great surprise, the leopard showed no interest. Nor did it pay the slightest heed to a magnificent lynx, whose hieroglyph represented the word 'dignity'.

Advancing very slowly, Ahhotep saw that other animals had gathered there: a white oryx, an ostrich, a large-eared hare, a fox, a jackal, a badger, a hedgehog and a weasel. On the rocks perched a falcon and a vulture. These inhabitants of the desert gazed at the queen. But what were they waiting for? She knew that, if she did not give them what they wanted, they would not let her pass.

Ahhotep thought for a moment, and realized that she must give some proof of her magic. By confronting the darkness that surrounded the emperor's ghost, she had touched evil. In the full light of day, she must show that her soul was unharmed and that she remained, as the traditional expression had it, 'of just voice'.

So she sang. A hymn to the rebirth of the light, to the emergence of the scarab beyond death, to the mysterious form of the first sun. And all the animals – from the most ferocious to the most gentle – began to dance, forming a circle around Queen Freedom. They were enchanted by her golden voice, and she was nourished by their strength, which flowed directly from the great God. Unlike mankind, no animal had ever betrayed its celestial origins.

To concentrate on singing the words of power, Ahhotep had closed her eyes. When she opened them again, the animals had disappeared. But their footprints in the sand showed that she had not been dreaming.

And her thoughts rose, full of thankfulness and reverence, towards the Divine Light.

## 53

As the palace messenger was walking past a field belonging to Chomu, several of the vase-seller's men barred his way.

Behind him stood their master. 'Where are you going, friend?'

'The same place I always go. I'm carrying official messages to Governor Emheb's patrol, for forwarding to Avaris.'

'I want to see those messages.'

The messenger was outraged. 'That's impossible, absolutely impossible.'

'Give them to me at once, or we'll break your bones.'

Chomu did not look as though he was joking. The messenger had no option but to obey.

There was only one letter. Chomu broke the royal seal and read it. It consisted of a long eulogy to Apophis's infinite virtues, followed by a paragraph in which the writer stated that Thebes was sinking deeper and deeper into its torpor.

The signature gave Chomu a shock. It belonged to the former minister of agriculture – who had been dead for several years! So the palace had not stopped plotting and lying ... With proof like this, he should have little difficulty in rallying the supporters of collaboration.

'Where is Seqen?' he asked.

'Gone hunting in the desert,' replied one of his men.

'What about Ahhotep?'

'At the temple in Karnak,' replied another.

'Perfect. Now I know what we must do.'

'What about the messenger?'

'He must be in league with the rebels. Kill him.'

Greatly heartened by Ahhotep's extraordinary discovery, Seqen had left for the training-camp to tell the soldiers the good news.

As for the queen, she knew that she must do something very important, something that would protect the future army of liberation.

So she had gone to the temple at Karnak, where she ordered the priests to deck all the altars with flowers.

'We are going to honour the memory of our ancestors,' she declared, 'and the pharaohs in particular.'

'But, Majesty, the Hyksos have forbidden such things throughout the land,' gasped a Pure Priest.

'If you are afraid to carry out your duties, leave this temple immediately. If not, obey me.'

The priest bowed.

'Bring the ancient offertory tables up from the vaults.'

The officiating priests unearthed masterpieces made from diorite, granite and alabaster. On the stone, the sculptors had engraved different kinds of bread, sides and haunches of beef, pomegranates, dates, grapes, figs, cakes, vases of wine and milk. The flavours from this eternal banquet would rise instantly to nourish the souls of the dead.

Each image was a hieroglyph which could be read and spoken. It was the priests' task to bring them to life, so that they might have an independent existence, and ensure that the magical incantations would remain effective for ever.

'Majesty, look!' called a priest. 'There's smoke down there. A building's on fire.'

'Down there' was the centre of Thebes.

Moustache had so much sleep to catch up on that he slept for a good part of each day. The Afghan preferred to invent new strategies for *senet*, the Egyptians' favourite board game.

When not out hunting, the two men lodged in a small house not far from the palace. After so many nights in the open air, they appreciated the comfort of their beds and the good food which a woman neighbour cooked for them.

Deep down, mused Moustache, routine was not all bad.

'I'm thirsty, Afghan,' he said.

'You drink too much beer.'

'It helps me believe freedom isn't an illusion. If we're making weapons we will end by using them one day, won't we?'

'Neither Ahhotep nor her husband is an idle dreamer,' agreed the Afghan. 'But we cannot attack the Hyksos with nothing more than the palace guard.'

'That's strange, I was thinking the same thing. So . . .'

'So the queen hasn't told us everything because she doesn't fully trust us.'

'In her position, I'd do the same,' said Moustache.

'So would I. Ahhotep is as intelligent as she is beautiful. Moreover, a woman like that can be trusted completely. Even in my own country, I've never met anyone like her.'

'Don't forget she's married – you'd better not fall in love.'

Suddenly the Afghan stiffened, like a wild animal pricking up its ears.

Knowing how reliable his companion's instinct was, Moustache snapped out of his lethargy. 'What is it?'

'People are running through the streets. Something bad is happening.'

'The local guards will take care of it.'

'Perhaps not. I don't suppose you'd care to stretch your legs?'

'It wouldn't do us any harm.'

The first group of people was joined by a second, then a third, led by Chomu. They were all heading for the palace.

'These people aren't brigands,' reasoned Moustache. 'Surely they're not going to—'

'Oh yes they are!'

The Afghan and Moustache took a short cut, running as fast as their legs would carry them, and reached the palace before the collaborators.

Sitting on the doorstep was an old guard, fast asleep with his spear lying beside him.

'To arms!' roared Moustache. 'The palace is under attack!'

Chomu had set fire to Heray's official residence, and had only one regret: that its owner was not inside.

The neighbours were so horror-stricken that they had not dared intervene. When Ahhotep arrived on the scene, they were still petrified.

'Is Heray safe?' she asked anxiously.

'Yes,' replied a widow, trembling from head to foot. 'It was the vase-seller, Chomu, who lit the fire.'

'What did he do then?'

'He swore that he and his friends would destroy the palace.'

Her sons, her mother, Qaris . . . Ahhotep almost fainted. If she could not save those she loved, she would kill Chomu with her bare hands. But she quickly pulled herself together, and said in a ringing voice, 'Those people are traitors. Come with me, all of you. They must be arrested.' She rushed off, followed by a motley band of old men, women and children.

When they reached the palace, they found a furious struggle taking place outside. Urged on by Moustache and the Afghan, the guards had managed to contain the attack. Heray and some of the peasants had lent their assistance, and evened up the odds.

'The Queen!' shouted one of the collaborators. 'Quick, run!'

But they hesitated for a few moments, and that was their undoing.

Heray and Moustache seized the opportunity to kill the ringleaders, while the Afghan threw Chomu to the ground.

'Don't touch me!' whined the vase-seller, seeing that his fate was sealed.

Ahhotep's gaze was even more frightening than Heray's sword, whose tip was touching his chest.

'You have murdered Thebans,' said the queen in a sombre voice, 'and you have tried to murder the royal family. Have you any other, more serious, crimes to confess?'

'You are rebels who refuse to recognize the emperor's authority – that's the biggest crime of all,' exclaimed Chomu. 'If you surrender now, I will plead your cause to our only sovereign, and beg him to spare Thebes.'

'You will be tried for high treason,' said Ahhotep, 'and as an enemy of Egypt, which adopted you as its son.'

'Don't you understand? You and your rebels are doomed, I've sent a message to the emperor. He will be here soon and will give me my just reward.'

## 54

Ahhotep took Kames in her arms and hugged him for a very long time, then cuddled little Ahmose; fortunately, the children had not had time to feel afraid. If the rioters had succeeded in entering the palace, Qaris would have fled with the two boys, while Teti held back the attackers with her last few loyal supporters.

'You must show no clemency,' Teti urged Ahhotep. 'This time, Chomu and his supporters have gone too far.'

'Much further than you think: he has warned the emperor.'

Teti blanched. 'Then the Hyksos will attack at once. Is our army ready?'

'It will be.'

Shouts made the two women jump. Were other collaborators launching a new attack?

'It is the king,' Qaris reassured them.

Warned by a carrier-pigeon message, Seqen had immediately left the training-camp with a hundred men. Although afraid at first, the people of Thebes had rallied when they recognized Ahhotep's husband and many fellow citizens they thought had left for the North long ago.

The pharaoh hurried into the palace. 'Ahhotep!'

They fell into each other's arms.

'Don't worry,' said Ahhotep. 'Our family is safe and sound. But several of the guards are dead, and, had it not been for prompt action by Moustache and the Afghan, Apophis's supporters would have won.'

'Have the traitors been properly punished?'

'Heray is making sure that they can do no further harm. But Chomu sent a message to the emperor.'

'I shall prepare lines of defence immediately. They will enable us to beat off the first Hyksos attack and then counterattack.'

'There's something vital we must do first. Mother, will you attend to it?'

'With great joy,' said Teti. 'This will be one of the most wonderful days of my life.'

*

'Those fellows are real soldiers,' commented Moustache as he watched Seqen's men, who had gathered at the front of the palace.

'Indeed,' nodded the Afghan. 'They're well trained and disciplined. So this is what the king and queen were hiding from us: an armed force prepared to fight the Hyksos. It is the best news I've had in a long time.'

Heray came across to the two men. 'Her Majesty wishes to see you.'

Moustache led the way, feeling rather intimidated. Neither he nor the Afghan dared lift their eyes to look at the queen, who had put on a magnificent ceremonial robe.

She said, 'I wish to thank you and congratulate you on your courageous deeds. You are both hereby appointed officers in the army of liberation.'

The two rebels exchanged looks of amazement.

'Today,' continued the queen, 'you will learn more about that army.'

The people of Thebes had assembled in front of the main entrance to the temple at Karnak. So that everyone could understand what was being said, heralds relayed the words of Teti the Small, who spoke with an assurance that surprised more than a few townspeople.

'Thanks to the gods, Thebes is once again governed by a Pharaoh and a Great Royal Wife. I can now reveal to you that Seqen has been ritually crowned King of Upper and Lower Egypt, and that Queen Ahhotep has recognized him as such. The line of dynasties is therefore preserved, and the king and queen's rightful power has been consolidated.'

After a moment of stunned silence, the citizens of Thebes cheered their king and queen, whose names were engraved on a stele which would be placed in the temple, under Amon's protection.

When the cheering died down, it was Pharaoh Seqen's turn to speak.

'Those who advocated collaboration with the enemy have been arrested. They will be tried and sentenced. Now we must all face up to the real test of war. Our army is ready to fight, but every citizen must play his or her part. Blood, tears and savage battles are what I promise you. There is only one path open to us. Either we shall be victorious, or we shall be destroyed. And victory depends upon this: all Theban hearts must beat as one.'

This announcement was followed by a long silence. Everyone realized that the long period of false peace was coming to an end and that a terrifying war was about to begin.

Heray struck his chest with his clenched fist. 'I promise to serve Pharaoh, my country and my people, to the death.'

With one voice, the Thebans repeated his oath.

Ahhotep's heart swelled with pride. At last true hope had been born.

The emperor's new game amused him greatly, and it had become a great mark of favour to be invited to sit next to him on his balcony. Below, selected unfortunates perished one after another in the arena and the labyrinth. Watching their death agonies was a source of never-ending pleasure.

Fortunately, there was no shortage of potential victims. There were ambitious men who had annoyed the emperor, lovers who had been careless enough to criticize him in Windswept's bed, foolhardy people who refused to accept Khamudi's extortion, all the beautiful women Tany had taken a dislike to, and even a few innocent folk – strong, healthy individuals chosen at random from among the Egyptian population.

Apophis was well aware that he must soon resume the process of conquest, notably by colonizing Minoa and the surrounding islands, then destroying a clutch of small Asian kingdoms which had been unwilling or unable to form themselves into an alliance. Commander Jannas's troops needed the practice; besides, the emperor's fame must continue to spread.

Now the city of Avaris lived up to his dream: it had become an immense military base, a paradise for all the soldiers, who made full use of the Egyptian slave-girls. And the same was true of the principal cities of the Delta, Canaan and Phoenicia, wherever Hyksos order reigned.

He, Apophis, had succeeded in breaking the back of the civilization that had built the pyramids. One day he would destroy even them, stone by stone, and have a more grandiose monument built to his own glory.

The moment Khamudi stepped into his office, the emperor noticed that the High Treasurer's complexion had a greenish tinge.

'What is the matter with you?' he asked.

'My wife and I amused ourselves with some Lebanese girls yesterday evening, and we made the mistake of sampling some wine from their country.'

'Was it an attempt to poison you?'

'I don't think so, but the girls will make pretty victims for the bull. Majesty, I have to inform you of a serious incident.'

Apophis frowned. 'Serious . . . I trust that is an exaggeration.'

'You alone must judge. I have just received a message from Thebes, consisting of these simple words: "The hippopotamus is preventing the emperor sleeping. The noise it makes offends the ears of the people of Avaris."'

'What does that nonsense mean?'

'It is a code established with our informant, the minister for agriculture. It means that there have been disturbances.'

'An insurrection in Thebes? That's highly unlikely, is it not?'

'One would think so, but the message is quite clear.'

'Is this insignificant minister simply trying to get himself noticed?'

'That is not impossible, Majesty, but let us suppose that he is right. Hasn't the time come to crush Thebes once and for all?'

'I'd completely forgotten that moribund little town. Probably a handful of ruffians tried to steal some wheat, and your little minister wants to get into our good graces by denouncing them. But you're right: we had better check.'

'Shall I send Jannas?'

The emperor smeared pomade over his nose and ankles, which had been swelling up for several days. 'No, we'll be more subtle than that. We'll send an envoy there. If a revolt is indeed brewing, the Thebans will kill him, and our response will be instant and decisive. If they don't kill him, we'll know the minister was making up stories and we'll choose another informant. It is pointless to tire our best soldiers for nothing, when new conquests are in store for them.'

## 55

'Only one boat?' Seqen was astonished. 'It must be a decoy.'

'It seems not, Majesty,' said Heray. 'The lookouts say it's an unescorted civilian boat.'

'If it drops anchor here, we must destroy it.'

'May I advise patience? Even if there are Hyksos hiding on board, there can only be a few of them, and we'll make short work of them.'

'But why should the emperor's response be so restrained?'

'Perhaps he's sending us an ultimatum,' suggested Ahhotep.

'Demanding that we destroy Thebes ourselves and then surrender? Oh yes, of course, you're right.'

'There is one simple way to find out, Majesty,' ventured Moustache. 'I could go aboard.'

'But you'd be risking your life,' said Seqen.

'With the Afghan and fifty men behind me, I shall feel quite safe.'

The envoy was the most important wine-trader in Avaris. Khamudi had entrusted this mission to him in the hope that he would not return alive. Even if he did, his fate would be scarcely enviable. During his absence, in fact, the High Treasurer would seize his accounts and falsify them with all kinds of irregularities which would lead the fraudster to the labyrinth. And his business would fall into Khamudi's lap.

The merchant was a man of sixty, who loathed travelling, especially by boat. But one did not refuse a mission imposed on one by the emperor. The new envoy had been ill all the way down the Nile and had had to lie down in his cabin; as a result, he had seen nothing of the beauties of the countryside.

Knowing that he was in Thebes, a lost city in a far-off province, gave him no satisfaction apart from the knowledge that he had reached his destination. He managed to get up, drank a little water, and went on deck.

'An emissary from the Queen of Thebes wishes to see you,' the captain informed him.

'Show him into my cabin.'

'Am I to search him?'

'There's no need. No one would dare attack a Hyksos envoy.'

As Moustache went aboard, he made sure that no soldiers were hiding ready to attack.

From the look of the envoy, it was clear that he would be unlikely to survive another journey.

'I am the envoy of Emperor-Pharaoh Apophis, our all-powerful sovereign, and I bring your queen a message from him. Take me to the palace immediately.'

An entire squadron of soldiers was assembled at the foot of the gangplank. The envoy stared at them in astonishment.

'Merely a security precaution,' explained the Afghan.

'Is there trouble here?'

'No, but one cannot be too careful.'

There was no risk of the envoy meeting any collaborators, for Chomu and his henchmen had been executed two days before, following a trial during which no extenuating circumstances had come to light.

The envoy thought Thebes looked rather poor, but it was clean. There were no soldiers on the streets, merely old men sitting on the doorsteps of their houses, children playing, women returning from the market, dogs fighting over a rag while a cat watched from the safety of a nearby rooftop. He saw nothing to suggest that the modest city posed a threat to the emperor.

Seeing how shabby the palace was strengthened that first impression. As for the two elderly guards who bowed as he passed, they were armed with spears so ancient that they would snap at the first blow.

Holding her two sons by the hand, Ahhotep greeted the diplomat at the entrance to her small audience chamber, which the envoy thought was positively decrepit.

'Welcome to Thebes,' she said. 'Your visit is a great honour for us, an honour we had never dared hope for. Unfortunately we have little in the way of comforts to offer you, but you may be sure that my husband and I will do everything in our power to satisfy you.'

Ahhotep seemed so fragile that the envoy was quite moved. Forgetting the manly words that every good Hyksos should address to a defeated Egyptian woman, he stammered a few words of thanks.

'How long are you planning to stay among us?' she asked.

'Just long enough to deliver the emperor's message to you.'

'My husband, Prince Seqen, will be delighted to hear it. Children, go back to your grandmother. I must attend to our guest.'

Dressed in a tunic which had seen better days, Seqen had the greatest difficulty in respectfully greeting his enemy, whom he would rather have strangled. But he accepted Ahhotep's advice, and was determined to deceive the envoy in order to gain a little time.

The envoy said, 'I will be brief and precise. The emperor is disturbed by the noise your hippopotamus is making. Do you follow what I am saying?'

Ahhotep had no difficulty in decoding Chomu's message.

'To the east of Thebes,' she said, 'there is indeed a pool where the hippos like to play. But how could their cries have reached the ears of Apophis?'

'Enough riddles, Princess. There are rebels in Thebes, are there not?'

The queen assumed an expression of consternation. 'There were, that's true. A small group of troublemakers led by a vase-seller named Chomu.'

'I order you to hand over these rebels to me.'

'We executed them, on the advice of our minister for agriculture.'

'Ah, that's excellent. May I congratulate him?'

'Unfortunately, he has just died. He will be very difficult to replace – his loyalty to the emperor was an example to all Thebans.'

'Good, good. And are you sure there are no rebels left in Waset?'

'The public executions will have served as a lesson,' said Seqen.

'Our cook has prepared you a good meal, with meat and cakes,' smiled Ahhotep. 'We hope that you will do us the honour.'

'Certainly, certainly. Will there be wine?'

'We have reserved the very best for you.'


Having a Hyksos in their grasp and letting him leave unharmed . . . As he stood on the banks of the Nile, watching the envoy's boat disappear round a bend, Seqen seethed. But he had to admit that Ahhotep was right. Convinced that Thebes was utterly harmless, the envoy would not recommend the emperor to take immediate action. So the carpenters would have time to finish the last boat they were working on.

'I'm glad the envoy is safely on his way, Majesty,' said Qaris. 'He seemed delighted with his brief stay among us.'

'And there was no trouble in the city?'

'No, Majesty. No one tried to approach the Hyksos, and the entire population is with us.'

The Theban army's two newest officers joined the pharaoh.

'You saved my sons,' he told them, 'and I shall be grateful to you for ever. During the war, many men will die. Do you want to leave with the army or stay in Thebes and command the palace guards?'

Moustache scratched his ear. 'We've had a good rest here, but I was born in the North and I'd very much like to go back there.'

'I'm a foreigner, Majesty,' said the Afghan, 'and when we have defeated the Hyksos I want to return to my home.'

'Very well. You shall each command a forward detachment.'

Moustache looked discomfited. 'If we add up the palace guards and the real soldiers you've brought to Thebes, Majesty, that still doesn't amount to an army. Even if we add the Northern rebels, whose numbers have scarcely increased according to our information, we still won't have a big enough force to pierce the Hyksos breastplate.'

'You have still not seen everything.'

A secret training-camp, with permanent buildings and a real army of well-trained men eager to fight. The Afghan and Moustache could hide neither their astonishment nor their pleasure.

'Wonderful!' gasped Moustache. 'So we didn't collect all those flints for nothing.'

'I'm going to introduce you to the other officers,' Seqen told them. 'A perfect spirit of comradeship must unite us.'

'First, Majesty, the Afghan and I would beg a favour of you: let us train with your footsoldiers, so that we can teach them a few cunning blows they can use in close combat.'

## 56

Grey clouds had drifted in off the sea. Now they hung in the sky above the fortress at Avaris, making it look even more sinister than usual. The envoy did not even glance up at them; he felt queasy and suffocated at the prospect of reporting to Apophis.

'Were you well received?' the emperor asked him.

'I could not have been treated better, Majesty. Thebes is a poverty-stricken, defenceless town, which poses no danger. Princess Ahhotep and Prince Seqen are concerned only with their little family and have no wish to do us harm.'

'Did you speak to the minister for agriculture?'

'He has just died. But you may be assured that the sound of the hippopotamus will no longer disturb you. The region is perfectly calm.'

Apophis stroked his blue porcelain flask on which the map of Egypt was drawn. His index finger touched the province of Waset, which shone with a reassuring red glow, proving its submission.

But he had an unfamiliar twinge of anxiety, so he pressed harder. And the light faltered.

'You imbecile, you let yourself be deceived.'

'Majesty, I can assure you that—'

In view of the envoy's age, the trial of the bull would offer no amusement. So it would have to be the labyrinth.

High Treasurer Khamudi and Commander Jannas had been summoned urgently to the secret room in the citadel, where no indiscreet ears could overhear their conversation.

'Something out of the ordinary is happening in Thebes,' said the emperor. 'Our envoy noticed nothing, but I am convinced that rebels are plotting secretly.'

'My informants have not seen anything, either, Majesty,' said Jannas. 'Waset is one of the wealthiest provinces in Egypt, but most of its produce is delivered to us. Perhaps a palace revolution is brewing, but does it really matter in the slightest if Queen Ahhotep is replaced by someone else?'

'This uncertainty annoys me. Thebes annoys me. Hyksos sovereignty must not be contested anywhere, to even the slightest degree – particularly not in Egypt.'

'Do you wish my troops to occupy the town?' suggested Jannas.

'Thebes must be destroyed,' decided Apophis. 'And close by, fortunately, we have just the man we need. Give Governor Emheb the order to raze that insufferable city to the ground.'

'That's impossible, Majesty,' said the High Priest of Karnak.

'Why?' asked Ahhotep angrily.

'Because the gates of the four directions are closed. Until they open, any attack will be doomed to total failure.'

The queen could not ignore the gods' warnings. 'How can we induce them to open?'

'According to tradition, the royal couple do not truly reign until they have crossed the papyrus forest to the north of Thebes. But it must be infested with snakes and crocodiles – to go there would be to risk your lives.'

'The gods' will must be done, no matter what it is.'

Teti was strongly opposed to their going, but Seqen agreed without a moment's hesitation: his soldiers' nerves were on a knife-edge, and the strain of waiting was eating away at their resolve. Ahhotep entrusted her sons to their grandmother's keeping, and the queen and the pharaoh left the palace. Unarmed and alone, although the papyrus forest was so dangerous that not even the most experienced huntsmen would go there, they took a light boat and set sail.

As the boat slowly approached the forest, dozens of birds, the companions of Set, fluttered up into the sky. Ahhotep rubbed several papyrus stems together. The sound made the heavy silence fertile, and calmed the hostile powers that were eager to devour the intruders' souls.

The couple entered the forest, where darkness reigned even on the sunniest day. The small, quivering sounds of a different world brought fear to their bellies.

Suddenly it was there, huge and burning bright: a female royal cobra, called in sacred writings 'the Slaughteress', 'the Goddess of Stability', 'She Who Streams with Light', 'the First Mother Who was at the Beginning and Knows the Borders of the Universe'.

Ahhotep looked into the snake's eyes. 'You may kill me, but I do not fear you, and you are the lady of the heart's blossoming. Give me your flame, so that I may destroy in order to create.'

The cobra swayed back and forth, and from left to right, then wound itself round a papyrus stem before vanishing.

Ahhotep found that she was alone in the boat. 'Seqen, where are you? Answer me!'

The fragile boat had hit an islet in the heart of the forest and, thinking they had found safe refuge on dry land, he had disembarked.

Before he could answer his wife, he saw two enormous crocodiles coming towards him; he had no chance of escape.

'Lie down, Seqen, and don't move.'

The king did as she said, but the crocodiles kept coming.

Certain he was about to be eaten, Seqen thought of Ahhotep's face and closed his eyes. The two monstrous creatures stood on either side of the king, their heads against his. They placed their forefeet on his shoulders and their back feet on his ankles, thus recognizing the King of Egypt as one of their own: a being who could rise from the depths in an instant and close its jaws upon an enemy.

'Three of the four gates, East, West and South, are open,' said the High Priest of Karnak. 'But the North gate is still closed.'

'What new ordeal are you setting us?' asked Ahhotep.

'The texts are silent, Majesty. The decision must be yours alone.'

'We must attack,' declared Seqen.

'Our army is moving northwards,' objected Ahhotep, 'but the people of the North are refusing to support us.'

'Then what more do the gods ask?'

'That is for us to discover. As long as we are deaf and blind, how can we hope for victory?'

'My men are pawing the ground with impatience. If we stretch the rope too far, it will break.'

When they returned to the palace, they found Emheb waiting for them. Though usually so calm, today he was in a state of great agitation.

'Majesties,' he said, 'I have just received an order from Commander Jannas: Thebes is to be razed to the ground.'

'So Apophis did not believe his envoy,' said Ahhotep. 'Are your troops ready to fight, Emheb?'

'They're eager to do so.'

Heray came hurrying in and said, 'Majesties, come quickly. Come and see!' His voice was so authoritative that without protest the royal couple and Emheb at once followed him to the riverside.

'Look at these eggs,' said Qaris.

'The teal have started to lay,' said Emheb. 'They're at least three weeks early, which means the annual flood will begin much earlier than usual, and we shan't be able to launch our boats until its ferocity abates.'

'In other words,' said Seqen, 'we can't possibly attack immediately.'

'No, but perhaps we can turn these unusual events to our advantage,' said Ahhotep. 'We must find out why the North is still hostile. Emheb, you must write a report for the emperor, saying that you have carried out your mission with great zeal, that Thebes has been destroyed, and its prince and princess are dead.'

'Will he believe me?'

'Yes, if you send him my crown, my robe and Seqen's tunic, soaked in blood.'

## 57

'A worthless crown,' sneered Apophis, 'a pauper's dress and a heathen's tunic. The relics of dead Thebes aren't worth keeping.'

'Governor Emheb's report is cause for celebration,' said Khamudi. 'His soldiers destroyed a town full of people too cowardly to fight. Everything, including the corpses, has been burnt. On the site where the city of Amon used to stand, the governor suggests building a barracks.'

'An excellent idea. All the same, send an observer to confirm the report. And tell him to bring this man Emheb back with him when he returns. I want to meet him and congratulate him.'

'We shall need a little patience, Majesty. The flood is particularly strong this year, and river travel will be impossible for some time.'

'By the way, I have a new candidate for the labyrinth,' said Apophis.

He was smiling. A consultation with his blue flask had reassured him that pitiful Thebes had indeed been burnt to the ground.

The royal palace and several houses actually had been burnt, watched in horror by the people of Thebes.

'Why did you decide to do it?' asked Seqen in astonishment.

'Because an enemy as formidable as Apophis has senses more acute than those of ordinary people,' replied Ahhotep. 'He had to have some proof, even at a distance, that our city had truly been destroyed.'

That very morning, Teti, Kames and Ahmose had left for the training-camp where they would live from now on.

Ahhotep and Seqen went to the temple at Karnak, where the High Priest greeted them.

He said, 'I have gazed once more at the corners of the sky. Three of the four gates are open and favourable. But the North remains stubbornly closed, and no incantation can unlock it.'

'Is it true that there is a closed shrine within this temple?' asked the queen.

'Yes, the central shrine of Amon. But, as you know, it will not be opened until the day Egypt wins back her freedom.'

'Amon is the god of the life-giving wind, the north wind. It is Amon who is demanding that we break through this prohibition.'

'You must do no such thing, Majesty,' said the High Priest, horrified. 'That would be an insult to destiny.'

'I am convinced the opposite is true. It is because we have stayed passive that Egypt is still enslaved. Only Amon can open the road to the North for us.'

'The master of Karnak will strike you down!'

'I am not his enemy.'

With the greatest reluctance, the High Priest led Ahhotep to the closed shrine. She meditated for some time before the door, then drew back the gilded wooden bolt, imploring Amon, 'the Hidden God', 'the Unchanging One', upon whom all creation rested, to come to her aid.

Half opening the door, the queen slipped inside the little shrine. A single ray of light entered it, just sufficient to make out the statue of Amon seated on his throne. In his right hand, he held a curved bronze sword coated with silver and encrusted with electrum. On its hilt it bore a gold lotus.

'We have need of your sword, O Lord Amon. It will give us the power to defeat the emperor of darkness.'

Ahhotep laid her hand on the stone hand, though she knew she might not be able to withdraw it again. The granite was not cold. An ageless energy flowed within it. She waited.

After what seemed an age, Amon consented to entrust the sword to her: from it there began to flow an intense light which illuminated the shrine.

Ahhotep withdrew, walking backwards with her head bowed.

When she emerged and held up the sword of light, as dazzling as the midday sun, Seqen and the priests covered their faces.

'The door of the shrine is to remain closed until we have won total victory,' said Ahhotep. 'Henceforth, Pharaoh, you have a weapon, and the road to the North lies open.'

In front of the palace at the training-camp a small garden had been planted, and it was beginning to look lovely, with tamarisks and palm-trees growing around an arbour.

In the shade of the trees, briefly oblivious to the frantic activity raging around them, Ahhotep and Seqen shared a moment of happiness which was all the more intense because they must soon part.

Both knew how much was at stake. But it was the pharaoh's task to lead his troops into battle, and the queen's to govern Thebes in his absence.

'I want so much to live,' he told her as he caressed her wonderful body. 'I want so much to love you until old age carries us away to the other side, to become so completely one with you that even death cannot separate us.'

'Death can never separate us,' she promised him. 'If you die fighting the darkness, my hand will pick up your sword, and your strength will dwell within me. You shall be the only man in my life, Seqen. I swear it upon the name of Pharaoh.'

Their bodies entwined, they gazed up at the immense sky and into the far distance. Why had the gods chosen them to carry out this superhuman task?

They could hear people in the camp calling out to one another, and officers trying to impose order on their excited men.

'I think I'm needed,' said Seqen.

Seqen had appointed a captain named Baba to lead the troops from Nekhen. Emheb would command his Edfu men.

'May I present my young son, Majesty?' asked Baba.

'My name is Ahmes, son of the lady Abana,' the boy said proudly, 'and I'm going to kill hundreds of Hyksos.'

'Aren't you a bit too young?'

'I already know how to use all the weapons, Majesty, and I'm not afraid to fight in the vanguard.'

'Egypt needs men like you, Ahmes son of Abana.'

Seqen took the time to say a few words to each soldier. Their faces were sombre, often full of anxiety. No one underestimated the Hyksos, who moreover had the advantage of numbers. Anyone who thought about it came to the conclusion that the little Egyptian army would be wiped out. But the queen's presence had dispelled many men's fears, and there had been no desertions.

A small hand slipped into the pharaoh's. 'I want to go to war, too.'

'Ahmose!' Seqen picked up his four-year-old son.

'He's right,' said Kames with all the confidence of his fourteen years, 'and so do I. Since we came here, we've trained every day with the soldiers.'

The king set Ahmose down and embraced both his sons. 'This is how the two crocodiles gave me their power; and I am giving you mine. If I don't come back from the battle, it is up to you to continue the struggle under the authority of the Queen of Egypt. Do you understand?'

Kames and Ahmose gave their solemn oath.

'But you will come back, won't you?' asked the latter.

In the middle of a most delightful evening, Khamudi was dragged away by Jannas himself. The commander had forced the door of the villa where the High Treasurer and his wife were teaching perverted games to terrified young girls.

Jannas was disgusted but chose not to say anything, since the emperor tolerated these obscene practices.

Khamudi was sweating profusely and ordered a servant-girl to mop his brow. 'What is so urgent, Commander?'

'Our trading-ships have been attacked by pirates based in the Thera islands.'

'Thera's in the southern Cyclades, isn't it?'

'Yes.'

'We ought to have cleaned up that part of the world long ago.'

'I thought it would be unwise to wake the emperor at this late hour, but I felt I must alert you at once.'

'You were right. I thought those damned pirates had been dealt with, but their greed was too much for them. They won't survive this mistake. And if the Minoans have helped them in any way at all, they will pay very dearly for it. We must go to the palace quickly. But first, wouldn't you like to try one of these little beauties?'

'Certainly not,' said Jannas.

'But they're so delicious. You don't know what you're missing.'

The emperor's icy rage made even Jannas afraid. He was ordered to leave Avaris immediately with several warships and to exterminate every last one of the pirates.

As for Khamudi, he was instructed to send troops into Syria, Canaan and Phoenicia, to show that no one could attack the Hyksos order and live.

## 58

Rascal and the other carrier-pigeons left for the North, bearing messages to the rebels who were to link up with Seqen's army. Aboard their transport vessels, the soldiers watched the birds fly off towards Lower Egypt. That land was so near yet so distant, and only the sacrifice of many lives would win it back.

In the palace, in great secrecy, Ahhotep had made Seqen touch the sceptre with which she hoped one day to measure out their country. Now, on the flagship, in the presence of all the officers, she crowned him with a diadem bearing a gold uraeus. The female cobra would spit fire, lighting the pharaoh's way and burning his enemies.

Admittedly this was only a lesser substitute for the traditional Red Crown of Lower Egypt and White Crown of Upper Egypt, which the emperor had stolen and seemingly destroyed.

Qaris and Heray placed the model of Egypt in the king's cabin, in the hope that day by day he would extend the boundaries of freedom.

And now it was time for the last kiss and the last embrace. Ahhotep wished that she could be simply a loving wife, mother of two fine boys and an ordinary Theban woman; but the empire of darkness had decided otherwise.

'Sail northwards, Pharaoh, break through the blockade at Kebet and travel as far as you can. As your victories are proclaimed, hope will be reborn throughout the land.'

'There are boats coming,' a river-guards officer at Kebet told his colleague, who was dozing under a palm-tree.

'It'll be a merchant fleet from the north. Nobody bothered to tell us.'

'No, they're coming from the south.'

'You've drunk too much date wine.'

'Get up and see for yourself. There are several of them.'

The man snapped out of his doze, and gaped at the incredible sight. 'Quickly, man, the boats!'

The guards hastily created a floating barricade. Its very presence would be enough to deter the culprits from continuing on their way. They were probably Nubians, or perhaps traders from the Great South who were trying to evade taxes.

'Halt in the name of Emperor Apophis!' shouted the officer.

Those were the last words he spoke. Seqen's arrow embedded itself in his throat – the pharaoh had been determined to kill the first Hyksos who tried to bar the way.

Within a few minutes, the Egyptian archers had wiped out their opponents, then they broke through the blockade with ease.

'Aren't we halting at Kebet?' asked Emheb.

'No,' said Seqen, 'because we don't entirely trust Titi, the town's mayor. He'll ally himself with the stronger side.'

At Dendera, the pharaoh's fleet encountered two Hyksos war-boats. Caught off guard by this surprise attack, their crews had no time to organize themselves and put up only feeble resistance.

'Our second victory, Majesty,' said Captain Baba.

At Abydos, there were five Hyksos boats. One of them sacrificed itself in order to slow the Egyptian advance boats, while the other four turned broadside on.

This time, the fight was a real test for the army of liberation. But the Hyksos, too confident of their own superiority, made the mistake of firing their arrows without taking cover, while the Egyptian archers protected themselves with shields.

Emheb's ship ploughed into the side of an enemy boat, and his soldiers from Edfu rushed to board her, while those from Nekhen seized the Hyksos captain. His capture disheartened his sailors, who suddenly had no one to give them clear orders.

'Give no quarter!' shouted Baba, spearing an Asian officer who was trying to regroup his men.

From that moment, the outcome of the fight was in no doubt. The soldiers trained by Seqen completely overran the enemy.

'Four more boats for our fleet, and plenty of weapons we can put to good use,' noted the Afghan, wiping enemy blood off his arm. 'We are becoming a proper army.'

Rascal alighted on Qaris's shoulder.

'It's a message from Pharaoh Seqen, Majesty.'

'You read it first,' said Ahhotep, 'and tell me only the good news.'

Dry-mouthed, Qaris deciphered the coded text, which Seqen himself had written. 'Our army has broken through at Abydos – it's our third victory. The fighting is fierce, but our soldiers acquitted themselves admirably.'

'What about our losses?' asked Ahhotep anxiously.

'Very light. A boat is bringing the wounded home.'

'Make sure everything is ready to treat them.'

'You can rely on me, Majesty.'

Ahhotep herself had taken command of the soldiers who had remained at the training-camp. At first they had been furious at not being allowed to leave with their comrades, but they soon stopped complaining. After all, serving the queen and protecting the royal family was a noble duty.

Without sacrificing any of her grace or femininity, Ahhotep was proving adept at handling the sword and the bow. Many strong fellows, confident that they would easily defeat her, had found themselves unexpectedly floored, for Ahhotep was adept both at dodging blows and at devising unusual holds.

Kames had become a young man. He took part in exercises with such fervour that he had already hurt himself several times; but he bore the pain with great fortitude. Little Ahmose always watched his brother, occasionally with great alarm; his grandmother tried in vain to make him look away.

'This is not a proper way to bring the boy up,' she scolded Ahhotep.

'Can you suggest a better one in time of war?' her daughter asked.

'Of course not, but it is still not a proper upbringing. The sons of a king must know the great classical texts and have a good general education. Kames is backward in his reading, so I want him to work with me for at least an hour every evening.'

'Granted, Majesty.'


Khamudi was ill. His skin was covered with a rash and he had dreadful pains in his belly. But he could no longer put off telling Apophis about the message from his new Theban informant, the agriculture minister's replacement.

At first, he had thought the spy had simply fabricated the story from some minor incident at the Kebet frontier, to curry favour in Avaris. But now the spy said that Hyksos crews had also been killed at Dendera and Abydos. He couldn't possibly give the emperor such news. And yet urgent measures must be taken to halt the rebels.

Alas, Jannas was away hunting pirates in the Cyclades and the best troops were sowing terror in Canaan and Phoenicia. Still, there were enough regiments left in Egypt to crush the vermin who dared to nibble away at the Hyksos Empire.

A burning sun was beating down on the citadel, and the heat made Khamudi feel even worse. Although it was still morning, it was already unbearably hot. Climbing up the palace steps was torture.

When the emperor received him, Khamudi swallowed hard several times.

'There is nothing more hateful than summer,' said Apophis. 'Fortunately, these thick walls hold in a little coolness. You should slow your pace, my friend. From the look of you, you are having too many busy nights.'

Khamudi took the plunge. 'We have been attacked in Upper Egypt.'

The emperor's eyes were as piercing as a knife-blade. 'Where exactly?'

'At Kebet, Dendera and Abydos.'

'By whom?'

'The Thebans.'

'Who is commanding them?'

'Seqen, Queen Ahhotep's husband. He claims to be' – Khamudi swallowed again – 'the pharaoh.'

'Is he still moving north?'

'I don't yet know, but it seems likely.'

'The rebellion is to be crushed, and this man Seqen is to be brought here to me, dead or alive.'

## 59

Since Abydos, Seqen's army had travelled for several days without meeting any resistance. It was almost as if the Hyksos had retreated as soon as they heard of the Thebans' first victories.

'I don't like it,' said Emheb.

'Perhaps our surprise attack was such a shock that the enemy doesn't know what to do?' suggested Baba.

'No,' said Seqen. 'So far we've faced only small forces, which were used to keep order in the provinces. I think they're now massing their troops somewhere, with the aim of halting us in our tracks.'

From nowhere a storm blew up, as violent as it was sudden. A furious wind snapped branches, twisted the palm-trees, blew desert sand over the fields and whipped the waters of the Nile into rough waves.

'Drop anchor,' ordered the king.

The storm lasted for several hours, during which the soldiers sheltered as best they could, their heads resting on their knees. It seemed that Set, Apophis's protector, was angry and had a terrible fate in store for them.

As soon as the sky and the river began to grow calmer, Moustache ventured on to the bridge of his ship to check that it had not suffered too badly.

And then he saw them: about twenty Hyksos warships, anchored off the town of Qis.

'This time,' he told the Afghan, 'it'll be a bloodbath. We aren't going to take these fellows by surprise.'

'That depends, my friend. They are probably expecting us to mount a frontal attack, so we shall advise the king to do something else.'

The best Egyptian archers, including young Ahmes, son of Abana, fired hundreds of burning arrows at a speed which only well-trained men could have sustained. Most reached their target: the Hyksos sails, which the crews had omitted to lower. They soon caught fire and, aided by the wind, the fire spread to the masts, despite the sailors' efforts to put out the blaze. Not a single ship escaped unscathed.

'They are jumping on to the riverbank and running away,' said Baba excitedly. 'Let's chase them and kill them.'

Seqen gave his assent, and the Egyptians disembarked. This was a fine opportunity to destroy one of Apophis's war-bands. Led by Baba, the Thebans cut down many sailors with their axes, spears and swords. Victory was in sight.

Suddenly they halted in their tracks, and the shouts of triumph died in their throats.

'What is it?' asked Seqen, hurrying back to the bow of the ship.

'We've fallen into a trap,' said, Emheb.

The Thebans were now faced with a very different army.

'I have never seen anything like this,' confessed Baba. 'I've never seen contraptions like that or animals like those.'

They were chariots, drawn by horses.

Nor was that all. The Hyksos had bronze swords, much stronger than the Egyptians', more powerful bows, better armour and helmets. The enemy was superior in every respect.

'This is a bad time to die,' said Moustache.

'At least,' said the Afghan, 'This way we shan't feel so badly about this old land.'

Seqen's soldiers were terrified.

'We must retreat, Majesty,' urged Emheb.

'No. We'd be slaughtered like cowards.' The king turned to his men. 'We have dreamt of this battle for many years. Apophis is the one who is afraid. He thinks we're going to scatter like sparrows, because up to now no one has dared take on his elite troops. So we shall be the first – and we shall prove that the Hyksos are not invincible.'

All the soldiers brandished their swords in agreement.

The sound of chariot-wheels and horses' hooves striking the stony ground raised a deafening clamour.

'Attack!' ordered Seqen, pointing the Sword of Amon at the chariots.

The first Egyptian line was cut down. The Hyksos archers and javelin-throwers decimated the second line, and only the energy of despair enabled Seqen to prevent a rout.

Cutting off a charioteer's arm and slitting the throat of the archer who stood beside hum, the pharaoh managed to overturn the chariot. This unexpected success inspired Baba and the soldiers from Elkab, who succeeded in immobilizing several others, though at the cost of many men.

When they saw Hyksos breastplates spattered with blood, the Egyptians realized that the enemy was indeed not invincible, and the two sides began to be more evenly matched.

'Look, there on the enemy's left flank!' shouted Moustache as he disembowelled a Persian. 'Those are our men.'

Alerted by the carrier-pigeons' messages, other rebels had come to join the battle. Their attack took the Hyksos by surprise and disrupted their advance.

'The king!' roared Emheb, who had just killed two Anatolians. 'The king is alone!'

Seqen had fought with such fury that his bodyguards could not follow him. Trapped in a circle of chariots and foot-soldiers, he was trying to parry attacks from all directions.

Sliding under his guard, a short Canaanite caught him a blow below the left eye with an axe.

Ignoring the pain, Seqen plunged his sword into his enemy's chest. But another Canaanite sank his dagger into the king's forehead. Blinded by the blood pouring down his face, the king swung his sword at empty air.

Baba eventually broke through the circle, killed the second Canaanite and, for a moment, thought he would succeed in rescuing Seqen. But a spear caught him in the back, while an Asian officer smashed his heavy axe down on the king's head.

Dying, the pharaoh sank down on to his right side. A Syrian crushed his nose with club and finished him off with a final blow to the base of the skull.

Enraged by the deaths of his father and his king, young Ahmes fired arrow after arrow. One by one, he killed their killers, while the Afghan and Moustache mounted a furious charge and at last managed to reach Seqen.*

In Thebes, Ahhotep searched the sky in vain for carrier-pigeons. She no longer dared to count the days since the birds had last brought news from the front.

This evening, after reassuring her mother, her children and the soldiers, she was exhausted. This lack of news gnawed at her soul, but she was the queen and she had no choice but to bear it.

The sun had not yet set, and the soldiers were attending to their usual duties in spite of the heat. Kames was teaching his little brother how to handle a wooden sword, Teti was reading prayers to Amon, and Qaris was watching over the wounded, whom the queen visited every morning and evening.

---

* The mummy of Pharaoh Seqen-en-Ra has survived, and can be seen in Cairo museum.

'There's a boat coming, Majesty,' said Heray. 'I'll go and ask for news.'

'No, I want to be the first to know.'

They hurried down to the quay, the soldiers from the camp close behind the young queen.

It took an age for the boat to reach the quay and moor. The first person to walk down the gangplank was Emheb, who looked haggard and drawn; he had aged ten years.

He bore the Sword of Amon and the royal crown, both spattered with blood.

The queen went towards him.

'We reached Qis, Majesty,' said Emheb, 'and there we met an elite regiment of Hyksos. Thanks to the pharaoh's courage, we were not defeated.'

'Seqen . . . ?'

'The pharaoh is dead, Majesty. We have brought his body back so that it may be mummified. The wounds are such that it would be better—'

'I want to see him. And the embalmers are to leave the wounds for all to see, so that future generations will know how this hero died, fighting the first battles in the war of liberation. May his name be honoured for ever, as the name of a true pharaoh.'

Emheb had a lump in his throat as he watched her. 'Forgive this pitiless question, Majesty,' he said with difficulty, 'but thousands of men await your answer. Are we to surrender to the emperor, or are you resolved to take command of our army and continue the fight?'

Ahhotep went on board the ship and gazed down for a long time at the disfigured body of the man she had loved so much and whom she would love beyond death. Soon she would have to explain to her sons why they would never see their father again.

She kissed his forehead, then went to the prow of the boat. All eyes were upon her.

'Give me the Sword of Amon and the king's diadem,' she ordered Emheb.

She put on the bloodstained crown and pointed the sword northward.

'As soon as he is old enough, Kames shall succeed his father and become our new pharaoh. Until that moment, I shall act as regent and we shall continue the fight against the empire of darkness. May Seqen's soul shine among the stars and guide us on to the path of light.'

# The War of the Crowns

I dedicate this book to all those men and women who have devoted their lives to freedom, by fighting against occupation, totalitarian regimes and inquisitions of every kind.

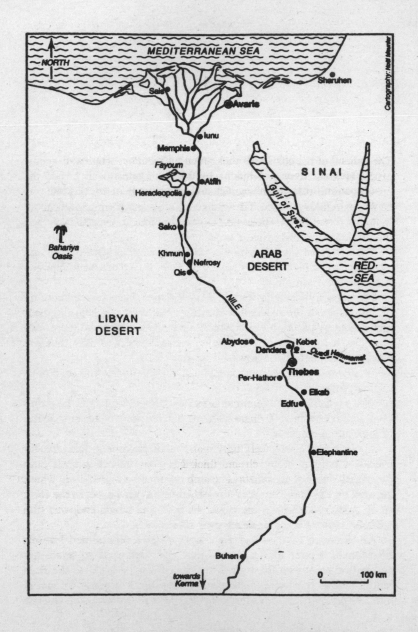

# 1

The general of the charioteers sat at the left hand of Apophis, Emperor of the Hyksos. It was a much-sought-after honour to sit beside the most powerful ruler in the world and watch the ordeal of the bull, yet he was extremely worried. The inhabitants of Avaris, the imperial capital in the Egyptian Delta, spoke of this ordeal with fear, even though they did not know exactly what it was.

The two men were sitting on a platform, overlooking an arena and a circular structure called the 'labyrinth'. It was said that no one emerged from the labyrinth alive.

The general looked down at it. At first glance, there seemed nothing dangerous about the place. It was made up of a twisting, turning path marked out by partition walls, which were covered here and there with greenery. It looked impossible to go wrong: there was only that one winding path, and it led towards the way out.

'You seem rather tense,' commented Apophis in his hoarse, blood-chilling voice.

'Yes, I am, Majesty. Your invitation to the palace, here to the labyrinth . . . I don't know how to thank you,' stammered the general, not daring to look at the emperor.

Apophis was a tall, very ugly man, with a prominent nose, flaccid cheeks, a bulging stomach and thick legs. He allowed himself only two small vanities: an amethyst scarab mounted on a gold ring, which he wore on the little finger of his left hand, and an amulet in the form of an ankh,* which he wore round his neck and which endowed him with the right of life and death over his subjects.

As 'Beloved of the God Set', Apophis had proclaimed himself Pharaoh of Upper and Lower Egypt and had tried to write his coronation names on the sacred tree in the city of Iunu, as the rites required. But the leaves had proved unwilling, refusing to accept him. So Apophis had murdered the High Priest, ordered the closure

---

*The looped cross that is the hieroglyphic sign meaning 'life'.

of the temple, and announced that the ritual had been carried out correctly.

For some time now, the emperor had been dissatisfied.

Much was going well. In the islands off the coast of Mycenae, Jannas, the impressive and ruthless commander of the Hyksos war-fleet, was hunting down pirates who had dared to attack the empire's trading-fleet. Several small Asian princedoms had displayed a wish for independence, but elite troops were putting an end to such wishes by massacring the rebels, burning their towns and villages and bringing back droves of slaves to Egypt.

These episodes had served Apophis's grand design: to increase still further the size of his empire, which was already the largest ever known: Nubia, Canaan, Syria, Lebanon, Anatolia, Cyprus, the Mycenaean islands, Minoa and the Asian steppes had all bowed their heads before him, and feared his military might. But this was only a stage in the process, and the Hyksos invaders, who included soldiers of many diverse races, must continue their conquest of the world.

The centre of that world was Egypt, the Egypt of the pharaohs. The Hyksos had invaded and overrun the country with surprising ease, putting an end to long centuries of civilization based on the rule of the goddess Ma'at: justice, righteousness and unity. The Egyptians had proved feeble soldiers, and their resistance to the invaders' brute force and new weapons had been pitiful. Now he, Apophis, was Pharaoh.

He had set up his capital at the small town of Avaris, which was dedicated to the cult of Set, the god of storms and violence who had rendered him invincible. The town was now the principal city in Middle Egypt. Over it loomed an impregnable citadel, from whose walls the emperor liked to gaze down upon the port, which was always filled with hundreds of warships and trading-vessels. Inland from the port, the town itself had, in accordance with Apophis's wishes, assumed the appearance of one gigantic barracks, a paradise for his soldiers, who were waited upon by Egyptians forced into slavery.

The pharaoh should have been wholly content. But, incredibly, in the south of this defeated, destroyed Egypt, a rebellion was taking shape. At the insignificant and moribund town of Thebes, an equally insignificant prince named Seqen and his wife, Ahhotep, had dared to take up arms against the emperor.

Apophis scowled at the general. 'What, precisely, is happening?' he demanded.

'The situation is under control, Majesty.'

'Where is the battlefront now?'

'At the town of Qis, Majesty.'

'Qis? That's seven days' march north of Thebes, isn't it?'

'Approximately, Majesty.'

'That means Seqen's ridiculous army has conquered a huge amount of territory – far too much.'

'Oh no, Majesty!' said the general hastily. 'The rebels sailed down the Nile surprisingly quickly, and they tried to break through our lines with a lightning strike, but they have not established their rule over the provinces they passed through. In reality, their actions were more spectacular than dangerous.'

'All the same, we have suffered several setbacks.'

'The rebels took a few detachments by surprise, but I took rapid action and halted their advance.'

'At the cost of heavy losses, it would seem.'

'Their weapons may be archaic, but these Egyptians fight like wild animals. Fortunately, our chariots and horses give us enormous superiority. And also, Majesty, do not forget that we killed Seqen.'

Apophis kept his expression unreadable as he thought, 'Only because we have a spy at the heart of the enemy's organization.' Aloud, he asked, 'Where is Seqen's body?'

'The Egyptians managed to recover it, Majesty.'

'A pity. I'd have liked to hang it from the tallest tower in Avaris. What about Queen Ahhotep? Is she still at liberty?'

'Unfortunately, yes. But she's only a woman, after all. Now that her husband's dead, all she can do is surrender. The tatters of the Egyptian army will soon disperse, and we shall destroy them.'

'Ah!' exclaimed the emperor, turning to look down into the circular arena. 'The entertainment is beginning.'

An enormous bull with blazing eyes and pounding hooves came thundering into the arena, into which a naked, defenceless man was immediately flung.

The general went pale. The unfortunate victim was his own second-in-command, who had fought courageously at Qis.

'The game is as simple as it is amusing,' said Apophis. 'The bull charges at its adversary, whose only means of survival is to seize its horns and execute a perilous leap over its back. A Minoan painter, Minos, is decorating my palace, and he says it is a very fashionable sport in his country. A clever man, Minos. Thanks to him, my paintings are more beautiful than the ones at Knossos, don't you think?'

'Oh yes, Majesty.'

'Look at that bull. He's a real giant, and he has a thoroughly vicious temper.'

He was right. The bull instantly charged its victim, who made the mistake of turning and trying to run away. The monstrous horns sank into his back. Snorting, the bull tossed the dying man through the air, trampled on him and gored him again.

Apophis grimaced in disgust. 'That worthless creature was as disappointing in the arena as he was in battle. Running away – that's all he was good for. But the responsibility for our defeats rests with his superior, does it not?'

The general began to sweat profusely. 'Nobody could have done better, Majesty, I assure you, I—'

'You are a fool, General. First, because you failed to foresee that attack; second, because your soldiers were defeated several times on Egyptian soil, and did not conduct themselves like true Hyksos; lastly, because you think that the enemy has been beaten. Stand up.'

Dumb with horror, the general obeyed.

The emperor unsheathed the golden-hilted dagger he always wore. 'Go down into the labyrinth, or I shall slit your throat. This is your only chance of winning my pardon.'

Apophis's murderous gaze banished all hesitation from the general's mind, and he leapt down into the labyrinth, landing on his hands and knees on the twisting path.

When he reached the first partition, he saw a blood-stain on the ground. After a moment's thought, he decided to leap over it, as though over an invisible obstacle. It was just as well he did, for two blades shot out, one from either side, brushing the soles of his feet.

The emperor was highly entertained. Since he had improved the layout of the labyrinth, few candidates had succeeded in getting past this first stage.

The general did the same thing as he emerged from the second bend, and that was his mistake. As he landed, the ground disappeared beneath his feet and he was flung into a pool where a hungry crocodile was waiting. The man's cries troubled neither the crocodile nor the emperor. A servant hurried to bring Apophis a bronze finger-bowl, and while the crocodile devoured its prey he washed his hands of the matter.

## 2

Ahhotep, Queen of Egypt, was in her husband's tomb, meditating beside his body. Since the flagship had brought back the body back from the front, she had not left it for a moment.

Seqen's body was disfigured by several mortal wounds. On Ahhotep's orders, they had not been disguised during mummification: she did not want the signs of Seqen's courage to be wiped away. He had fought fiercely against the Hyksos hordes until he was eventually overwhelmed, and his bravery had given new heart to his soldiers, who had been terrified by the horse-drawn war-chariots, a new and formidable weapon.

Seqen had fallen passionately in love with Ahhotep, who admired him for his purity and nobility, his thirst for freedom and his readiness to sacrifice his life to restore Egypt's former greatness. Hand in hand, Seqen and Ahhotep had faced many ordeals before they were able to attack the enemy positions north of Thebes and thus begin to break out of the Hyksos encirclement.

Ahhotep had had the idea of creating a secret desert camp where the soldiers of the army of liberation could be trained for war. She had entrusted this project to Seqen, and as Queen of Egypt had recognized him as Pharaoh. The office was an onerous one but, though born of a humble family, he had proved himself fully worthy of it, right up to his last breath.

The empire of darkness might have turned the royal couple's life into a wasteland of tears and blood, but there had also been a few shared moments of intense happiness. In Ahhotep's heart, Seqen would always represent youth, strength and love.

Footsteps sounded in the passageway outside, and the queen's mother, Teti the Small, came into the tomb. Although the old lady looked incredibly fragile, she was always impeccably dressed and made-up, and fought stubbornly against the dull exhaustion that forced her to sleep in the afternoons and retire early to bed. Devastated herself by Seqen's death, she was afraid Ahhotep might no longer have the energy she needed if she was to emerge from her suffering.

'You must eat,' she advised her daughter.

'Seqen's very handsome, isn't he? We must forget these ugly wounds, and think only of our king's proud, resolute face.'

'Ahhotep, you are now the sole ruler of the country. Everyone is awaiting your decisions.'

'I shall stay at my husband's side.'

'You have kept vigil according to our rites, and the period of mummification is over.'

'No, Mother, I—'

'Yes, Ahhotep. And I must say the words you are afraid to hear: the time has come to carry out the funeral ceremonies and seal the tomb.'

'I won't do it.'

Frail though she was compared to her magnificent daughter, Teti was unyielding. 'By behaving like a mere grieving widow, you're betraying Pharaoh and making his sacrifice pointless. He must now journey to the stars and we must continue the struggle. The soldiers call you "the Queen of Freedom", don't they? Then act like one. Go to Karnak, where the priests will transform you into the incarnation of Victorious Thebes.'

The authoritative tone and words pierced Ahhotep's heart like a dagger-blade. But she knew Teti was right.

Closely guarded, and accompanied by her two sons, Kames and Ahmose, Ahhotep set out for the Temple of Amon at Karnak, where the priests chanted incantations day and night for the immortality of the royal soul.

Since the beginning of the Hyksos occupation, no work had been done to enlarge or adorn Karnak. Protected by an encircling wall, the temple was composed of two main shrines, one with square pillars and the other with pillars carved in the form of Osiris, proclaiming the resurrection of the god murdered by his brother Set. There was a prediction that the door of the shrine containing the statue of Amon, 'the Hidden One', would open of its own accord if the Egyptians succeeded in defeating the Hyksos.

When the royal party arrived, the High Priest came to greet them. Fourteen-year-old Kames stood up very straight, but Ahmose, who was only four, clutched his mother's hand tightly.

The High Priest bowed low before the queen, who was wearing her mother's gold crown. 'Majesty, are you ready to embody the conquering fire of Thebes?'

'I am ready. Kames, take good care of your brother.'

Ahmose began to cry. 'I want to stay with you – and I want my daddy.'

Ahhotep kissed the little boy tenderly. 'Your father is in the heavens with the other pharaohs, and we must honour him by finishing his work. To do so, I need the support of everyone, especially our two sons. Do you understand that?'

Gulping back his tears, Ahmose went to his brother, who took him reassuringly by the shoulders.

The High Priest led Ahhotep to the shrine of the goddess Mut, whose name meant both 'Mother' and 'Death'. It was she who had given the young queen the strength to carry on a near-impossible fight, and it was she who would transform the modest city of Thebes into the heart of the war to liberate Egypt.

The High Priest attached a gold uraeus to Ahhotep's crown, then handed her a bow and four arrows. 'Majesty, do you swear to fight the darkness?'

'I swear.'

'Then may your arrows reach the four corners of the earth.'

Ahhotep shot an arrow to the east, then one to the north, the south and lastly the west. Her noble bearing impressed all the priests.

'Since the heavens look favourably upon you, Majesty, here are the life you must preserve and the magic you must use.'

The High Priest took an ankh and a sceptre, whose head was shaped like the beast of Set, and held them up before the queen's eyes.

Strong vibrations passed through Ahhotep's whole body. Henceforth, she would be the incarnation of an entire people's hopes.

After the soldiers from the training-camp had paid final homage to the dead pharaoh, the funeral procession set off for the cemetery. Four oxen drew the sarcophagus,* which lay on a wooden sledge. At regular intervals, priests poured milk on to the ground in front of the sledge, to make the runners glide more smoothly.

In this time of war, traditional craftsmanship had been reduced to its most crude and basic form, so Seqen's funerary furniture was very modest, utterly unworthy of a royal tomb: a scribe's palette, a bow, sandals, a ceremonial kilt and a crown. Thebes no longer had a single great stone-cutter or sculptor: every one had long since been executed by the Hyksos.

Ahhotep was accompanied in the procession by her sons and her mother, by Qaris, head steward of the palace, and by Heray, who, though his official title was Overseer of Granaries, was also responsible for Thebes's safety and for catching collaborators with the enemy. There was one notable absence from the ceremonies: Emheb, governor

---

*It is preserved in Cairo Museum (CG 61001).

of the town of Edfu, had had to go to Qis to maintain the morale of the troops at the front.

Outside the entrance to the little tomb, which was derisory compared to the pyramids of the Golden Age, Qaris and Heray stood the sarcophagus upright. Before it was entrusted to the Goddess of the West, who would absorb Seqen into her breast where he would be reborn, his mouth, eyes and ears must be reopened.

The funerary priest handed the queen a wooden adze. As soon as she touched it, it broke.

'We haven't another one,' he lamented. 'That was the last one dedicated when Pharaoh ruled Egypt.'

'The sarcophagus cannot remain lifeless!' protested Ahhotep.

'Then, Majesty, we must use the adze called "Way-Opener".'

'But it is in Asyut,' said Qaris in alarm, 'and Asyut is far from safe.'

'Nevertheless, we must go there at once,' said the queen.

'Majesty, I beg you not to,' said Qaris. 'You have no right to run such a risk.'

'My foremost duty is to ensure that Pharaoh has a peaceful journey to the paradise lands of the afterlife. If I were to fail in that duty, we would be doomed to failure.'

## 3

The ancient town of Asyut – known as 'Way-Opener' because of its association with 'the Opener of the Ways', the jackal-god Wepwawet – lay six days to the north of Thebes. Asyut was in enemy-held territory, and was virtually in its death-throes, but a few brave people still fought on. Two battle-hardened officers in Ahhotep's army, the Afghan and Moustache, had contacts among them.

Moustache was an Egyptian from the Delta, who had joined the rebel movement almost in spite of himself, though it had since become his reason for living. The Afghan's livelihood had been destroyed by the invaders. His prime concern was to restore the trade in lapis-lazuli with an Egypt which once again respected the laws of commerce. Together, the two men had braved many dangers. They were wholehearted admirers of Queen Ahhotep, the most beautiful and intelligent woman they had ever met, and would fight with her to the end, whatever might happen.

Ahhotep consulted the two officers, and it was decided to send a message by carrier-pigeon, to find out how things stood in Asyut. The message was entrusted to a bird called Rascal, the fastest and toughest of the flock. The mission was dangerous and, besides, if Rascal did not return Ahhotep would have lost one of her best soldiers. The white and brown pigeon seemed to listen attentively when Ahhotep warned it of the danger: its head was erect and its eyes sparkled as if confident of success.

Two days went by, while the queen searched the sky in vain. Then, at dusk on the second day, she made out her messenger in the distance. The bird was flying more slowly and awkwardly than usual, but it was definitely Rascal. When he alighted on Ahhotep's shoulder she saw why: his right flank was drenched in blood.

He proudly presented his right leg, to which a small, sealed papyrus was attached. The queen praised him and stroked him gently, then removed the message and entrusted the brave messenger to Teti the Small.

'He must have been wounded by an arrow,' she said. 'Take good care of him.'

'It's only a superficial wound,' said Teti, examining it closely. 'Rascal will be fit and well again in a few days.'

Much relieved, Ahhotep unrolled the papyrus and read the brief message. It said that Asyut had been almost completely destroyed, with the exception of the ancient tombs. It now housed only a small Hyksos garrison, which received supplies from the oases at Khargeh and Dakhla.

'We must leave at once,' decided Ahhotep. 'Have a boat prepared for the voyage. And we'll take my dog, Laughter, and my late husband's donkey, Long-Ears, because they both have a keen instinct for danger.'

Sailing at night was dangerous – there was a risk of running aground on a sandbank or disturbing a herd of hippopotamus, whose anger could be terrifyingly destructive. But in daylight the Nile was even less safe, because here and there the Hyksos were always on the prowl.

It was nearly dawn when the boat reached its destination. The moon, Ahhotep's ally, lit up the countryside and the town. Once a thriving, bustling port, Asyut was now virtually abandoned. Old boats and a leaking barge were rotting at their moorings. The town was sheltered by a cliff-face, in which tombs had been excavated. One of them, that of a High Priest of Wepwawet, contained the adze needed to give life back to Seqen's mummy.

Laughter and Long-Ears sniffed the air, and could detect no danger, so they led the little party off the boat. Besides the huge dog and the donkey, Ahhotep's guards were the Afghan, Moustache and ten young archers, all on the alert for the slightest sign of trouble.

The Afghan looked around warily. 'If I were the Hyksos commander,' he said, 'the burial-ground cliff is where I'd post my sentries. It's an ideal lookout point.'

'Then we'd better check,' said Moustache. 'If you're right, it'll mean one or two fewer Hyksos.'

The two men climbed the cliff with the speed and ease of seasoned fighters. Less than half an hour later, they returned.

'Four sentries, all fast asleep,' said Moustache. 'The way is clear.'

Ahhotep had undergone the same training as her soldiers, so she had no difficulty in scaling the cliff. Several tombs had been defiled, and unfortunately they included the High Priest of Wepwawet's, which the Hyksos were using to store weapons and food. With fury in her heart, the queen explored the ravaged tomb by the light of a torch.

Eventually she reached the small chamber near the back of the tomb where the ritualists generally placed the most precious objects. On the ground lay fragments of storage-chests and statues. She searched through the chaotic jumble and at last, underneath the wreck of a basket containing mummified food, she found the adze of sky-metal that was used in resurrection rituals.

The door of Seqen's tomb was closed once more, and Kames, aided by Qaris, placed the funerary seal upon it. Now that Ahhotep had opened the mummy's eyes, mouth and ears, Pharaoh's soul was no longer chained to the earth.

'Majesty,' ventured Qaris as they walked away, 'we must discuss the military situation.'

'Later.'

'You must stop the attack at once.'

'Governor Emheb will hold the front. All I want is to share my husband's death.'

'Majesty, I hardly dare believe—'

'I must enter the House of the Acacia, and no one shall stop me.'

There were only three of them left: three old priestesses who made up the reclusive community of the House of the Acacia. They would have starved to death if Queen Ahhotep had not granted them accommodation and provisions so that they might pass on their knowledge.

Ahhotep sat with them at the foot of an acacia-tree armed with fearsome thorns.

'Life and death are contained within it,' said the oldest priestess. 'Osiris gives it its green foliage, and inside the mound of Osiris the sarcophagus becomes a ship capable of sailing across the universe. If the acacia dies, life leaves the living, until the father is reborn in his sons. Isis creates a new pharaoh, healed of the wounds inflicted by Set, and the acacia is once again bedecked in leaves.'

The prophesy was clear: Kames was to become king.

But Ahhotep needed more. 'I wish my spirit to remain eternally linked with Seqen's, beyond death.'

'Since death is born,' replied the priestess, 'it will itself die. But what existed before creation does not undergo death. In the celestial paradise, neither fear nor violence exists. The righteous and the ancestors commune with the gods.'

'How can I enter into contact with Seqen?'

'Send him a message from your heart.'

'But what if he doesn't reply?'

'May the god of destiny watch over the Queen of Egypt.'

*

Ahhotep's most valuable possession was a pillar-shaped wooden box, elaborately gilded and encrusted with semiprecious stones. It bore an inscription, '*The queen is beloved of Thoth, master of the divine words*', and in it she kept her writing-brushes and inks. She needed it now.

On a pristine sheet of papyrus, she wrote a love-letter to Seqen in beautiful hieroglyphs, begging him to drive away evil spirits and to help Egypt regain its freedom. She implored him to give her an answer, to prove that he had indeed been reborn.

Ahhotep attached the message to an acacia branch. Then she made a clay statuette of Osiris lying upon his deathbed and laid it at the foot of the tree. Finally, she sang and played the harp, so that the harmonious chords would ensure Seqen a serene journey to the afterlife.

But would she receive an answer from the husband she loved so much?

# 4

Although Jannas was still fighting the pirates in the Mycenaean islands and trying to put down the Theban rebellion, the customary ceremony of paying tributes was taking place in Avaris. Apophis enjoyed this moment, when envoys from every province of the empire grovelled before him and gave him impressive amounts of money and valuables. Unlike former pharaohs, he kept the greater part for himself, instead of putting it back into the cycle of trade.

Khamudi, the emperor's ruthless right-hand man, always made ample use of it, with the blessing of his master, whose safety he ensured. He took for himself a proportion of all sizeable trading operations, and had gained control of papyrus cultivation in the Delta. He was a corpulent man, with jet-black hair plastered to his round head, slightly protuberant eyes, and plump hands and feet – he had grown fatter and fatter since his appointment as High Treasurer. His nickname among his slaves was 'His Royal Self-Importance'.

His interest outside his work was indulging in depraved sexual practices together with his voluptuous blonde wife, Yima, who came originally from Canaan. Here, too, Apophis, who liked to think of himself as austere and moralistic, turned a blind eye. He would keep it turned as long as Khamudi remained in his proper place – in other words, second in rank to himself.

As they did every year, the storehouses of Avaris were filling with gold, precious stones, bronze, copper, rare kinds of valuable timber, fabrics, jars of oil and wine, ointments and countless other riches which ensured the imperial capital's unequalled prosperity.

When the Minoan envoy approached the emperor, dressed in a tunic patterned with red diamonds, Khamudi touched the hilt of his dagger and gestured to his archers. At the slightest suspicious sign from the diplomat, they had orders to kill him. But the Minoan bowed as low as the others, before launching into a long speech in which he praised the greatness and power of the Hyksos emperor, whose faithful vassal he was. (During this boring eulogy, Apophis's sister, Windswept, a magnificent woman, took the opportunity to caress her lover Minos, the Minoan painter who was adorning the palace. The young man blushed but did not resist.) The envoy's servants laid swords, silver vases and intricate items of furniture at the emperor's feet. Minoa was proving equal to its reputation.

'Jannas is cleansing the Mycenaean islands,' declared the emperor in his harsh voice, which made the listening throng shiver, 'and the campaign is costing me dear. As Minoa is close to the battle zone, she shall pay me an additional tribute.'

The envoy bit his lip and bowed again.

Apophis was very pleased with the Minoan decoration of his fortified palace and the furniture he had gathered there. It included a royal bed stolen from Memphis, incense-burners and silver basins placed on alabaster tables in his bath-chamber, which had a red limestone floor, and in particular some splendid lamps comprising a limestone base and a sycamore-wood stem topped with a bronze dish. After washing, the emperor donned a fringed brown tunic and went to the apartments occupied by his wife, Tany. He had refused to grant her the title of Empress, so as not to concede even the smallest crumb of power.

'Aren't you ready yet?' he demanded.

Short, fat Tany was probably the ugliest woman in Avaris. She was forever trying new ointments and lotions in the hope of improving her looks, but the results were disastrous. She made up for it by taking daily revenge on the once-wealthy Egyptian women who had been forced into slavery and now served her, who had herself once been a servant. The emperor was indifferent to his wife's ugliness, but he thoroughly approved of her hatred of Egypt, which had inspired him to some excellent ideas.

Tany held out a necklace whose beads looked like pearls but were made of a strange material. 'Look at this, Apophis. Isn't it strange?'

'What is it?'

'According to my new slave, who comes from Memphis, it's called glass. It's made by melting quartz with natron or ashes, and you can make it whatever colour you want.'

'Pearls made of glass? These are a bit opaque, but I'm sure we'll be able to improve the process. But come on. I'm in a hurry to see our two plans take shape – yours and mine.'

'I'm just finishing my make-up.'

Tany plastered her forehead and cheeks with a thick layer of kohl, and squeezed herself into a brown and white striped dress. Head held high, she followed her husband out of the palace, always one pace behind him.

Khamudi and the imperial guard were waiting for them. 'All is ready, Majesty.'

The procession made its way to the last Egyptian burial-ground in Avaris, where the ancestors who had lived there before the invasion were buried. Hundreds of Egyptian slaves had been herded together there, on the orders of the guards. All of them feared a mass execution.

'All traces of the vile past must disappear,' decreed Apophis. 'This old burial-ground takes up too much space, so we're going to build houses here for army officers.'

An old woman managed to push her way out of the crowd and knelt before him, imploringly. 'No, my lord, do not attack our ancestors. Let them sleep in peace, I beg of you.'

With one violent blow of his hand, Khamudi broke the insolent woman's neck. 'Get rid of that,' he ordered the guards, 'and kill anyone else who dares interrupt the emperor.' He turned back to the crowd. 'Henceforth, you will bury your dead in front of your houses or even inside them. They must not take up space in my city. There will be no more offerings or prayers for the dead. The dead no longer exist, there is no "Beautiful West", or "Eternal East", or "Light of Resurrection". Anyone caught performing the duties of a funerary priest will be executed immediately.'

Lady Tany was delighted: with his usual genius, Apophis had not only made use of her idea but had even improved upon it.

Nothing could have plunged the Egyptians more effectively into despair. To be deprived of all contact with their ancestors would at last make them recognize that a new world had been born.

To reach the small island on which the Temple of Set had been built, the imperial retinue took the royal barge. The brick-built shrine, now the main temple in Avaris, was also dedicated to the Syrian storm-god, Hadad. A rectangular altar stood in front of the entrance, surrounded by oak trees and by ditches filled with the bleached bones of sacrificed animals, mainly donkeys.

The priests bowed very low before the emperor, who had come to consecrate a shrine to his own glory. It was entirely decorated in gold leaf and bore witness to the empire's wealth and its master's divine status. The ceremony ought to have been the signal for rejoicing, but many people were casting anxious eyes at the sky. Threatening clouds were gathering right over Avaris.

Looking perfectly serene, Apophis entered his shrine and pronounced the craftsmen's work satisfactory. All the provinces of the empire would be informed that he was the son and equal of Set.

When he emerged from the temple, lightning was zigzagging across the clouds. Large raindrops began to fall on to the altar, where a Hyksos priest had just killed a fine white donkey, its hooves tightly bound together.

'Majesty, the anger of Set is warning us of a great danger! We must—'

The priest's words died in his throat as Apophis slit it with his dagger.

'Do you not understand, imbecile? The Lord of Storms hails me as master of the empire, and has rendered me invincible.'

# 5

High Treasurer Khamudi had established a gigantic taxation centre at the heart of Avaris, guarded by the army. From this base, he kept tight control of the taxes received from the various provinces of the empire. As the years went by they kept on growing, demanding an equal growth in the number of officials.

Apophis wielded absolute power, and himself commanded the army, but he delegated management of the empire's wealth to his High Treasurer, who would pay with his life if he concealed anything from him. Khamudi was too enamoured of his position to play that game. So he told the emperor about everything he appropriated for himself in order to increase his personal fortune.

The Egyptians and vassals were bled white, but Khamudi kept dreaming up new taxes, or lowered one tax the better to raise another. Convinced there were no limits to the extent to which the empire's subjects could be exploited, he was determined to improve his results. As for the senior officials, who had themselves accumulated considerable wealth since the start of Apophis's reign, they had come to an arrangement with Khamudi.

The High Treasurer's secretary burst into his office, a look of terror on his face. 'My lord, it's the emperor – he's here!'

An unexpected visit from Apophis? Khamudi had a sudden need to scratch his left leg. Problems set off a skin-rash which even the strongest salves had difficulty in soothing. Thousands of figures ran through his head. What mistake had he made?

'Majesty, what a great honour to welcome you.'

His shoulders stooped, the emperor threw him a chilling sidelong glance. 'You have made yourself very comfortable here, haven't you? The luxury is rather ostentatious, with this modern furniture, this army of scribes, these vast archives and your bustling papyrus factory. Still, you have one invaluable quality: efficiency untainted by conscience. Thanks to you, the empire grows richer by the day.'

Khamudi felt somewhat relieved.

The emperor flung his heavy frame into an armchair decorated with wild bulls. 'The Egyptians are mere cattle,' he said in a tired voice, 'but most of our soldiers have gone soft and must be constantly harassed to prevent them resting on past glories. Our generals' incompetence is infuriating.'

'Do you wish them to be . . . cleansed?'

'Their replacements would be no better. We have lost ground in the South of Egypt, and that is something I will not tolerate.'

'And neither will I, Majesty. But this is only a temporary situation. The rebels have been halted at Qis, and they won't get any further. As soon as Commander Jannas returns from the Mycenaean islands he will smash their front.'

'Yes, but that affair is much more serious than I thought,' grumbled Apophis. 'Jannas isn't dealing with simple pirates; he's facing a well-organized enemy war-fleet.'

'Our troops will be back from Asia – the rebels there have been virtually crushed.'

'No, they must stay there a while longer, to ensure that the flame has been properly extinguished.'

'In that case, Majesty, let us send our garrisons from the Delta.'

'Absolutely not, my friend. While we are waiting for Jannas, we shall make use of another weapon at our disposal: false information. You are to have two series of scarabs engraved. The first will be for our vassals, announcing that the Hyksos empire continues to grow. The other will be for the Egyptians who have taken up arms against us. I shall dictate the message to you; take great care in transcribing it into hieroglyphs.'


'Take cover!' roared Governor Emheb. 'They're using their catapults!'

The soldiers of the army of liberation threw themselves belly-down on the ground, or sheltered behind the reed huts that had been built on the front line. The volleys of missiles continued for some minutes, but were not followed by an attack. When they were able to move again, the soldiers investigated, and were surprised to discover hundreds of limestone scarabs, all bearing the same inscription.

They brought them to Emheb.

As he deciphered the text, the governor realized the danger. 'Destroy every one of them,' he ordered.

Emheb copied the message on to a slip of papyrus, which he entrusted to Rascal so that the queen would be alerted quickly.


Ahhotep was hoping for a sign which would prove that Seqen's soul had been reborn, but nothing came, even though all the rites had been carried out correctly. She could think of no other way to make contact with her husband.

As the days wore on, the beautiful young woman seemed to begin fading away, and no one could comfort her. However, she was still very attentive to her sons, who had been very shocked by their father's death. Kames tried to forget his pain through weapons training with his instructors, while little Ahmose spent most of his time playing with his grandmother.

Thebes was sinking into sorrow. How long it seemed since the first days of the campaign to free Egypt!

Qaris, the head steward, steeled himself to approach the queen, who was sitting at the foot of the acacia-tree where she had placed her letter to Seqen.

'Majesty, may I speak with you?'

'From now on, silence is my country,' said Ahhotep sadly.

'It is serious, Majesty, very serious.'

'What could be more serious than the death of Pharaoh? Without him, we have lost our strength.'

'Apophis has had scarabs engraved, announcing your death. If this false information spreads everywhere, the rebels will soon lay down their arms and the emperor will have won without a fight.'

Ahhotep looked even sadder. 'Apophis is right. I am dead – to this world.'

The usually imperturbable Qaris lost his temper. 'That is not true, Majesty, and you have no right to say it! You are Regent Queen of the Two Lands, of Upper and Lower Egypt, and you have sworn to carry on the work of Pharaoh Seqen.'

The queen smiled faintly. 'An implacable enemy occupies the Two Lands. When he killed Seqen, he killed me, too.'

Suddenly Qaris gasped. 'Majesty, your letter . . . It's gone!'

Ahhotep stood up and looked at the branch to which she had attached the papyrus. Sure enough, the scroll was no longer there.

Qaris's face lit up. 'Pharaoh Seqen has received your message, Majesty. Isn't this the sign you have been waiting for?'

'Yes, but I need more than just that.'

She bent down to look at the clay statue of Osiris lying on his death-bed that she had laid at the foot of the tree. Ears of wheat had sprung forth from it. The sight of them took Ahhotep's breath away and she almost fainted.

Qaris smiled even more broadly. 'Pharaoh Seqen has been reborn, Majesty. He lives for ever among the gods, and he will guide you in all you do.'

*

In Thebes itself, the rumours were spreading like wildfire. Some said that Queen Ahhotep was dead, others that she had lost her mind and from now on would live as a recluse within the temple at Karnak. Governor Emheb prepared himself to surrender and beg the emperor for mercy.

And then the good news was announced by Heray, Overseer of Granaries. Ahhotep was alive and in good health, and she would address her troops the following day, at dawn.

Many soldiers were sceptical, but when the sun rose in the east the queen emerged from the palace, crowned with a slender gold diadem and dressed in a long white robe. Her beauty and nobility were greeted with respectful silence.

'Like this reborn sun, the soul of Pharaoh has been born again in the light. As regent queen, I shall continue the fight until Kames is able to command the army. I intend to remain absolutely faithful to the dead king. Therefore today, at Karnak, I have created the office of "Wife of God", which I shall be the first to hold. I shall never remarry, and my only companion shall remain my husband, who rests in the secret heart of Amon. When Egypt is once again free, if I am still in this world I shall withdraw into the temple.'

## 6

Rascal and his small flock of carrier-pigeons had left Thebes in the early morning, bearing messages for the front. They announced that Queen Ahhotep was in perfect health and that the fight against the Hyksos was continuing. The order was given to destroy the scarabs spreading the Hyksos's lies.

From now on, the military camp to the north of the City of Amon was no longer to be a secret. It was to become the official headquarters of the army of freedom, with its palace, its forts, its school for scribes, its barracks, its weapons workshops and stores, and its dwellings. A special detachment of soldiers protected Thebes, where no one now had any thoughts of collaborating with the Hyksos. Seqen's sacrifice, his first victories and Queen Ahhotep's bearing had restored the entire population's taste for battle.

Using the silver mined from a rich seam she had discovered in the desert, and with her mother's help, Ahhotep had set about bringing back royal dignity to the House of the Queen. The old institution was still a long way from its past splendour, but the official buildings in Thebes and at the military base were no longer decrepit and neglected. Under Qaris's direction, skilled artists were working there again, scribes and craftsmen competing to see who could work most zealously.

The queen, her mother and Heray were standing before Qaris's model of Egypt, which represented the whole country from the mouth of the Delta in the north to Elephantine in the south. When Ahhotep had seen it for the first time, only one place had been free of the occupying forces: Thebes. Today, although the situation was still far from good, it had improved a great deal.

'Thebes, Elkab and Edfu,' said Qaris, pointing to them on the model, 'are the three towns we can rely on. Further south, Elephantine is under the control of the Nubians, allies of the Hyksos, and we must not forget the great Hyksos fortress of Per-Hathor, between Thebes and Edfu. To the north, very close to Thebes, Kebet is still not completely free. Titi, its governor, assures us that his network of rebels will be sufficient, but we'll probably have to send him reinforcements. Much further north, Khmun is still the main Hyksos barrier. And then, of course, there's the Delta, which is entirely under the emperor's control.'

'What is the latest news from the front?' asked Ahhotep.

'Thanks to our carrier-pigeons, we are in constant contact with Emheb, who has set up his front-line camp outside Qis. The Hyksos in the town can do little more than fire sporadic volleys of arrows, because the way our troops are deployed and occupy the terrain prevents them from launching a mass attack using chariots.'

'But why doesn't Apophis attack us?' asked the queen in astonishment.

'If we wish to be optimistic,' said Heray, 'we must suppose that he has enough other problems to postpone until later dealing with the small one we present.'

'Each day,' added Qaris, 'Emheb strengthens our hold on the front.'

'What about supplies?'

'They are secure, Majesty, because the peasants in the area have rallied to our cause. The networks of rebels set up by the Afghan and Moustache have proved extremely effective.'

The queen thought for a moment. 'Our weak point is still weapons, isn't it?'

Qaris sighed. 'I'm afraid so. We have neither chariots nor those strange animals called horses, which pull them at an incredible speed.'

'That doesn't mean we must be satisfied with our ancient weapons,' replied Ahhotep. 'Summon all the craftsmen.'

In her left hand, the Regent Queen of the Two Lands held a wooden sceptre bearing the head of Set. In her right, she held the sacred Sword of Amon, a curved bronze blade covered with silver and inlaid with an alloy of gold and silver. Beside her, his face proud and solemn, stood her elder son. During his childhood he had been called Kames, but he now used his true name, Kamose.

'With this sceptre,' Ahhotep declared to the many assembled craftsmen, 'I shall measure Egypt when she is free. But, before we can carry out that peaceful task, we must use the sword the god of Thebes has given us. With it, I consecrate my elder son as war-commander, not for death but for life. May this ray of light illuminate his thoughts and give him his father's courage.'

Ahhotep touched Kamose's forehead with the point of the Sword of Amon. The light that flashed from the blade was so dazzling that those watching had to close their eyes.

The look in the boy's eyes suddenly changed, as though his consciousness had been opened to realities whose existence he had never suspected before. 'In the names of Pharaoh and of the Queen of Freedom,' he vowed, so solemnly that a shiver ran around the watching throng, 'I swear to fight to my last breath so that Egypt may become herself again and joy may once more fill the hearts of her people. Until I have accomplished my task, I shall not allow myself a single moment's rest.'

Kamose kissed the Sword of Amon and prostrated himself before the queen. Childhood had just died within him. Ahhotep raised him to his feet and he again took his place at her side.

Turning back to the craftsmen, the queen said, 'Everyone knows the enemy's weapons are much better than ours. It is up to you, the craftsmen of Thebes, to redress the balance. You are to make new spears, longer and with sharper bronze heads, and new wooden shields, also strengthened with bronze. In future, the footsoldiers' heads are to be protected by helmets and their chests by thick copper breastplates. Axes, clubs and daggers must be of better quality. And our best troops will be equipped with curved swords similar to the Sword of Amon. In hand-to-hand fighting, with these weapons and our will to win, we shall be better than the Hyksos. Now, craftsmen, to work!'

Her words were greeted with resounding cheers.

'What an amazing woman,' commented Moustache, who had hung on her every word.

'She has that power you call magic,' said the Afghan. 'And those eyes . . . With them she could conquer anyone.'

'I've already told you: whatever you do, don't fall in love.'

'Why not?'

'You had no chance before, Afghan, but you have even less now that Queen Ahhotep has become the Wife of God. From now on, no man can go near her.'

The Afghan frowned. 'She's far too beautiful to accept a fate like that.'

'She herself chose it. As you can see, she does not lack character or determination.'

'All the same . . . Remember when we first became rebels? You thought defeating the Hyksos was impossible, too.'

'To be frank, I still do. Ahhotep makes our heads spin, and sometimes we almost forget the imbalance in our forces. But that doesn't matter. She gives meaning both to our lives and to our deaths.'

To strengthen the front, Ahhotep had decided to use the *heka*, the magic, light-born power whose guardian she had become when she travelled to Dendera with Seqen. The most intense *heka* was that of the sacred city of Iunu, which was in Hyksos hands, but the one she had would serve to keep the enemy pinned down, at least for a little while.

In the shrine of Mut, at Karnak, a priestess made wax figures representing Hyksos soldiers, tied up and unable to do any harm. On red bowls, Ahhotep wrote the name of Apophis and ancient incantations ordering the serpent of destruction to spit its venom and attack him. Then the figures were put into the bowls, which were held over a brazier.

'May breath enter these figures,' she chanted, 'and may it burn them. May the wax, born of the bee, symbol of the royalty of Lower Egypt and the Delta, become our ally.'

The flames crackled, the hideous faces of the Hyksos melted out of shape, and Ahhotep smashed the red bowls.

'May I speak with you privately, Majesty?' asked Qaris as the queen was leaving the temple.

'You look worried. Is there bad news from the front?'

'No, it's nothing like that. But I have done a great deal of thinking, and there are certain conclusions I cannot keep to myself. You alone must hear them.'

Qaris was a plump fellow, with round cheeks and a calm temperament, who usually managed to radiate good humour, even at the most difficult times. Ahhotep had never seen him so anxious.

'May we walk a little further away, Majesty? No one must hear what I am about to tell you.'

They went on to the landing-stage outside the temple, and walked along to the end.

'The enemy without is formidable,' declared Qaris, 'but the enemy within is no less so. Fortunately, Heray has rid us of collaborators, and the people are now devoted to you. Moreover, Thebes now realizes that there is no going back and that we must see the adventure through to its conclusion: destruction or freedom.'

'I know all this. Are you worried that support for collaboration will re-emerge?'

Qaris shook his head. 'No. Heray is too vigilant, and Thebes will not take a backward step, I am convinced of that. This is about something else, something equally serious.' The steward's mouth was dry. 'For many years, my main task has been to collect information and to extract what is important. Of course, I have closely studied the reports concerning the tragic death of Pharaoh Seqen.'

Ahhotep halted in her tracks. 'Have you found something amiss?'

'Majesty, I am convinced that your husband fell into a trap. The Hyksos were waiting for him at that place. They knew how to isolate him and were able to murder him because they had received information from someone very well informed.'

'You mean . . . Are you saying there is a traitor among us?'

'I have no absolute proof, but that is indeed what I believe.'

Ahhotep raised her eyes to the heavens. This was one treacherous blow she had not foreseen. 'Have you anything more solid than suspicion, Qaris?'

'No, Majesty, and I hope I am wrong.'

'If you are right, all my principal decisions must be kept secret.'

'As secret as possible, yes. And I would advise you not to trust anyone.'

'Not even you?'

'I have nothing to offer you but my word, Majesty.'

## 7

The destruction of the last Egyptian burial-ground in Avaris provoked an unexpected revolt – by elderly widows and widowers.

In desperation, they gathered together to march on the citadel and protest against the emperor's decision. The stunned guards watched open-mouthed as this tide of harmless folk poured in, many walking with difficulty. A few spears were enough to halt them.

'Go home at once,' an Anatolian officer ordered them.

'We want to keep our burial-ground,' protested an old man in his eighties, leaning on his stick. 'My wife, my parents, my grandparents and my great-grandparents are all buried there, and it's the same for most of us Egyptians. Our dead pose no threat to the security of the empire, as far as I know.'

'Orders are orders.'

With silent determination, the protestors sat down. Killing them all would be no problem, but the officer decided to consult his superior.

'Old men?' exclaimed Khamudi.

'They refuse to go home, my lord, and they want the emperor to see them.'

'Haven't these imbeciles realized yet that times have changed? Are they noisy?'

'No, not at all. How would you like me to execute them?'

'Execute them? I have a better idea. Go and fetch the lady Aberia. I am going to ask for the emperor's permission.'

Aberia was using her enormous hands to indulge in her favourite pastime: strangling people. For the moment, she had to content herself with a gazelle, whose finest cuts would be served at Apophis's table. But it was much less entertaining than wringing the neck of an enslaved Egyptian noblewoman. Thanks to the emperor's wife, Lady Aberia had no lack of prey, some terrified, others fighting back. Her thirst for vengeance was unquenchable, and Apophis approved of this policy of terror, which deterred the defeated from resisting him.

'My lady,' said the officer, 'the High Treasurer wishes to see you urgently.'

Aberia felt a frisson of pleasure. Knowing Khamudi, there must be exciting work in store. She hurried to Khamudi's office.

'Who are they, this herd of old men?' she asked as soon as she arrived.

'Dangerous rebels,' replied Khamudi.

'Dangerous? Them?' scoffed Aberia.

'Much more dangerous than you think. Those old men and women embody harmful traditions and are passing them on to younger generations. They cannot stay in Avaris, because they're setting a bad example. Their place is somewhere else, far away from here.'

The lady Aberia's interest was beginning to stir. 'And it would be my task to . . . see to it?'

'Near our rearward base in Palestine, at Sharuhen, there are marshy areas where a prison camp could be set up.'

'An ordinary prison camp, or a place of killing?'

'Whichever you wish,' said Khamudi.

The strangler now regarded her prisoners in a quite different light. 'You are right, High Treasurer. They are indeed dangerous rebels, and I shall treat them as such.'

The procession took the path that ran eastwards along the lakes. Seated comfortably in a chair carried by bearers, Aberia forced her team of slaves to march as fast as possible, and granted them only a short halt and a little water every five hours.

The stamina of these old Egyptians astonished her. Only a few had collapsed since the beginning of the journey, and Aberia had not allowed anyone else to take care of wringing their necks. Their remains would be feasted on by vultures and other scavengers. Only one prisoner had tried to run away, and he had been instantly killed by a Hyksos guard. The others kept on walking, step after step, under a burning sun.

If anyone weakened, the strongest supported him as best they could and helped him along. From time to time, someone's heart gave out. The corpse was abandoned beside the road, unburied and unmourned. The first man who asked for more water was whipped to death, so the old people kept on walking without complaint, watched delightedly by Aberia, who was already thinking of organizing other journeys like this.

'You must not lose hope,' said a seventy-year-old to one of his companions in misfortune. 'My son belongs to a network of rebels, and he told me that Queen Ahhotep is in command of an army of liberation.'

'She has no chance.'

'She has already defeated the Hyksos several times.'

'No one has said anything about that in Avaris,' retorted the woman.

'No one would dare – the emperor's soldiers and guards are everywhere. But the news will eventually get around, all the same. The Theban army has reached Qis and obviously intends to attack the Delta.'

'The Hyksos are too powerful, and the gods have abandoned us.'

'No, they haven't. I'm certain they haven't.'

Despite her reservations, the woman whispered in the ear of her neighbour, who passed on the information to the woman next to him. Little by little, all the prisoners learnt that Thebes had lifted her head once more and that battle had been joined. Even the most exhausted prisoners found new strength, and the way seemed less agonizing, despite the heat, the thirst and the mosquitoes.

After Avaris, Sharuhen was the most impressive fortress in the empire. High towers enabled lookouts to keep a close watch on the surrounding area and the port. The garrison town housed highly trained troops who could take rapid action in Syria and Palestine at any moment and nip in the bud the smallest attempt at sedition.

In accordance with Apophis's orders, the Hyksos carried out regular raids to remind the civilian population that the emperor's law was inviolable. A village would be burnt and looted, and the women raped and then used as slaves, together with their strongest children. It was the favourite pastime of the garrison at Sharuhen, whose port housed cargo-boats groaning with food supplies.

The fortress commander was surprised by the arrival of the pitiful procession and impressed by the lady Aberia's muscular frame.

'I am on an official mission,' she declared haughtily. 'The emperor wishes me to set up a prison camp near the fortress. He has decided to deport as many rebels as possible, so that they do not trouble the Hyksos order.'

'But these are old men!'

'They have been spreading dangerous ideas, liable to unsettle people's minds.'

'Very well, very well,' said the commander. 'You would do best to travel further into the interior, because it is very marshy around here, and—'

'That suits me perfectly. I want these prisoners to be within bowshot of your archers on the towers. If one of these bandits tries to break through the barriers we build, they are to kill him.'

Aberia chose the worst place she could find: a waterlogged area, infested with insects and buffeted by the wind. She ordered the prisoners to build themselves reed huts. From now on they would live there, hoping for the mercy of the emperor, who, in his great goodness, had granted them a daily food ration.

One week later, half of the old people were dead. Their companions buried the bodies in the mud, digging the graves with their bare hands. They themselves would not survive much longer.

Thoroughly satisfied, Lady Aberia set off again for Avaris. She would thank Khamudi warmly for his initiative. She would also prepare for the next deportation of rebels, who would cause the emperor no further trouble once they had sampled the delights of Sharuhen.

## 8

Although he was almost twenty years old, Long-Ears was still head of all the donkeys in Thebes. He guided them along the tracks and oversaw the carriage of goods. He never balked at any task, so long as the humans did likewise and did not look down upon him. Without Long-Ears and the other donkeys, the military camp could not have seen the light of day. And the donkey continued working, with the same constancy and the same sense of a job well done.

And yet for Ahhotep this beautiful spring morning was touched with sorrow. At dawn Laughter, her unfailing guard and friend, had died. The huge old dog, his body worn out, had laid his enormous head upon the young woman's feet and gazed lovingly at her for the last time. Then he had given one final long, deep sigh.

Fortunately six-month-old Young Laughter not only had the same sandy pelt, black muzzle and amber eyes, but promised to be as strong and intelligent as his father. He could already detect his mistress's every intention.

Old Laughter was mummified and buried close to Pharaoh Seqen. Beneath the bandages was laid a papyrus bearing the magical incantations needed to pass through the gates of the other world.

Long-Ears shared the queen's sorrow, and nuzzled her shoulder gently. She stroked his neck and asked him to grant his friendship to the young dog, who still had a great deal to learn.

The donkey shook his long ears, signifying his agreement.

Aberia's report delighted the emperor, who was in a foul temper after the failure of the lies about Ahhotep's death. He only wished he had thought earlier of deporting rebels to a camp where they would die. Khamudi's new idea was an excellent one, and Sharuhen was a total success. Little by little, Avaris would be emptied of possible opponents, even potential troublemakers, and the Hyksos would keep only the slaves needed to carry out the lowliest tasks.

'Majesty,' said Khamudi smugly, 'I have here a list of rebels whose actions or words merit imprisonment.'

'Keep back a few for the bull and the labyrinth.'

'Of course, Majesty. But I must warn you: there are others beside Egyptians.'

Apophis raised an eyebrow.

'A Hyksos scribe showed a lack of respect for me,' explained Khamudi, 'and there's an Anatolian gardener my wife dislikes. Don't they deserve to be shown the error of their ways?'

'Definitely,' replied the emperor. 'And I shall add a palace guard who made the mistake of sleeping with my loving sister, Windswept, and complaining of inconvenient working-hours. Such criticism cannot go unpunished. The camp at Sharuhen will correct his way of thinking. The lady Aberia shall take charge of this new consignment.'

The deportation of the widows and widowers had spread terror throughout the Egyptian population of the Delta. No one felt safe from the arbitrary decisions taken by the emperor and Khamudi. The rebel networks no longer dared take any action at all, and confined themselves to gathering snippets of information from the front, in the hope that it was true. But hardly anyone yet knew that the army of liberation had reached Qis.

Off the coast of Mycenae, Jannas had won victory after victory, but finding and pursuing the pirates' ships took a great deal of time. Moreover, he had to keep part of his fleet within sight of Minoa, which he suspected might otherwise intervene.

In Asia, Hyksos troops were imposing a bloody occupation, punctuated by summary executions. Despite this brutality, the tribal chiefs still persisted in taking up arms. None resisted for very long, and they and their families all ended up dead, but the irritating unrest meant that Apophis could not bring his regiments home and use them to attack Upper Egypt.

'Queen Ahhotep won't be able to make any further progress,' observed Khamudi. 'Her miserable war-band will soon wear itself out. I shouldn't be surprised if she soon surrendered. Choosing a woman as a war-chief! What a ludicrous mistake! These Egyptians will never make real fighters.'

'Very true,' agreed the emperor. 'We know, of course, that the Thebans are just about capable of controlling a few distant provinces. Nevertheless, we can attack the root of the evil and eliminate the cause of this stupid rebellion without even resorting to battle. One of our good friends will take care of it.'

As he had vowed, Prince Kamose allowed himself no rest. He trained so intensively in handling weapons that his body became that of an athlete, and it took all the queen's authority to make him lie down for a few hours to prevent exhaustion. But Kamose hardly slept, for he was haunted by the face of his father, whom he so badly wanted to emulate.

From his mother, he was learning the art of governing. Together with his little brother, who was thoughtful and attentive, he read the texts of wisdom passed on by the pharaohs of the golden age. From time to time, he caught himself dreaming that Egypt was really free, that it was possible to move from one province to another and to travel peacefully along the Nile. But then reality hit home, and with renewed fire in his belly he continued his apprenticeship to become Pharaoh.

One morning, as Ahhotep was addressing the members of a detachment setting out for Kebet, Qaris informed her that an unexpected visitor was requesting an audience: an envoy from Titi, the governor of Kebet. He showed in a short, fat, bearded man.

The man bowed before the regent queen and said, 'Majesty, I have good news. Governor Titi has at last succeeded in liberating Kebet. The last Hyksos have fled, and we have seized a cargo-boat containing many jars of food. Here are a few of them, in advance of other prizes.'

They were indeed Hyksos jars, pot-bellied and painted brown.

'I and two soldiers from Titi's personal bodyguard brought them here along country tracks,' explained the envoy. 'The region is quiet, and the peasants are regaining confidence. The inhabitants of Kebet await you, Majesty.'

'Is the governor sure of his success?'

'If not, Majesty, he would not have sent me to Thebes. Titi has suffered greatly from the occupation, and he is a cautious man.'

Ahhotep remembered her brief stay in Kebet with Seqen. During their meeting, the governor had told her that he was organizing resistance with the greatest caution, while all the time pretending to be an ally of the Hyksos who controlled his town.

Qaris beckoned to a servant and told him, 'Take these jars to the kitchens.'

'You will dine with us, envoy,' said the queen, 'and tell us all about the liberation of Kebet.'

The hungriest of all was Young Laughter. Had it not been for Ahhotep's stern looks, he would gladly have leapt at the dishes that the servants were laying on the royal table. The dog played for sympathy, as though he had not been fed for several days, and always managed to prompt some gullible person into giving him a titbit or two.

'Do the Hyksos still control the caravan routes?' the queen asked Governor Titi's envoy.

'No, Majesty, not for a long time now. But we shall have to dismantle the forts they set up in the desert, reaching as far as the Red Sea.'

'Has the governor a detailed map?'

'Yes, thanks to the caravan leaders, who are delighted to have escaped the Hyksos yoke at last. By using their information, we shall be able to mount surprise attacks on the enemy and dismantle his installations one by one.'

By using this strategy, Ahhotep could free more of the Theban province, which would once again be able to receive the goods it had been deprived of for so many long years.

'How many men has the governor at his disposal?'

While the little bearded man launched into rather involved explanations, the queen ate mechanically from a dish of beans and braised beef.

Suddenly, Young Laughter nudged her wrist with his nose.

'Laughter! You really are a bad—'

The dog knocked over the dish with his paw, and started barking at the envoy from Kebet.

The queen understood: her best bodyguard had saved her.

'Arrest that man,' she ordered.

The envoy jumped to his feet and ran towards the door of the dining-hall. Two guards barred his way.

'This food is poisoned,' said Ahhotep, 'and I have eaten some of it.'

## 9

Queen Ahhotep had begun to feel ill, and was lying down on a low bed while her mother wiped her forehead with perfumed linen.

Heray, who had been interrogating the 'envoy' came in and bowed. 'The man has talked,' he said. 'He poisoned your food with castor-oil seeds and scorpion's venom. If it hadn't been for Young Laughter, Majesty, you would be dead.'

The huge dog lay at the foot of the bed. He had made up his mind never again to leave his mistress's side.

'Did he really come from Kebet?' asked Ahhotep.

'Yes, Majesty.'

'Then he must have been acting on Titi's orders.'

'He was. It was indeed the governor who sent the assassin, probably at Apophis's behest.'

'We must take Kebet as quickly as possible,' said Ahhotep. She tried to stand up, but her stomach pains were so fierce that she could not.

'We must go to the Temple of Hathor at once,' advised Teti anxiously. 'The priestesses will know how to cure you.'

Despite taking a curative mixture of onion, carob, linen extract and a plant called 'serpent's wood', Ahhotep was seriously ill on the way to Deir el-Bahari. By the time they arrived she was unconscious, and Heray had to carry her to the temple.

Built by Pharaoh Montuhotep II,* the temple was truly remarkable. The vast tree-lined forecourt gave access to a portico. Its pillars were fronted by statues depicting the king wearing the Red Crown and the close-fitting white robe he wore during the Festival of Regeneration. The king's black face, hands and enormous legs made him almost frightening.

*The Montuhoteps were one of the principal lines of the XIth dynasty (c2060–1991 BC).

The pharaoh bore the three colours of the magic of resurrection, and was thus multiplied into the same number of guardians. These watched over the central monument: a representation of the primordial mound, the island that had appeared on the first morning of the world, and on which light had taken corporeal form.

Beside the shrine, priestesses of the goddess Sekhmet were worshipping a very ancient statue which stood before a vast stone-lined pool where, in cases of serious illness, certain patients were allowed to bathe.

Teti and Heray, the latter still carrying Ahhotep, went over to the priestesses.

'I am Teti the Small and I entrust the Queen of Egypt to your care. She has been poisoned.'

'Please read aloud the text written upon the statue,' said the most senior priestess.

'"Come to me, you whose name is hidden, even from the gods, you who created the heaven and the earth, and brought all beings into the world. No evil shall be done against you, for you are water, sky, earth and air. May healing be granted unto me."'

The water first rippled, and then began to bubble.

'The spirit of the statue accepts the patient,' said the priestess. 'Undress her and place her in the pool.'

While Teti and the other priestesses were doing this, the senior priestess poured water on to the hieroglyphs. One of her colleagues collected up the precious liquid, which was now imbued with a magical energy.

As soon as the unconscious Ahhotep was laid in the pool, the servant of Sekhmet sprinkled her throat with healing water. When she had performed this act seven times, she asked all those present to leave.

'Is my daughter going to live?' asked her anguished mother.

The priestess did not reply.

Kebet was celebrating. In return for his services to the Hyksos, Titi had been given permission to celebrate the Festival of Min. Of course, certain elements of the ceremonies were omitted, such as the procession of the statues representing the royal ancestors. The only pharaoh was Apophis.

By obeying orders, Titi had just ended a futile war which would have seen thousands of Egyptians die needlessly. For a long time now, the governor had realized that the invaders' power was going to continue growing and that his country had become a Hyksos province. By playing a subtle double game, he had preserved a few of his prerogatives and enabled his favourites to live reasonably well under the occupation.

Basically, all one needed to do was renounce the old values and adapt to the emperor's demands. Consequently, this old festival of the god of spiritual and material fertility was to lose its sacred character altogether, and become a popular celebration accompanied by a glorification of Apophis, the benefactor of Egypt.

If it had not been for that madwoman Ahhotep and her insane husband, the Theban province would have continued to live peacefully. Fortunately, Seqen had been killed and his army was rotting at Qis.

The last danger was the queen. Having met her at Kebet, many years before, Titi knew that she would never give up the fight. She was too stubborn to face up to reality. Because of her, the South was in danger of falling victim to terrible repression.

However, thanks to its governor, Kebet would be spared. By sending one of his most trusted men to Thebes to poison Ahhotep, Titi had become a hero of the empire. The queen's death would mean the end of the fighting. This was the excellent news Titi was going to announce to the people, who were so happy to be celebrating.

'Is everything ready?' he asked his steward.

'Yes, but the Hyksos guards insist on surrounding the procession.'

'That is quite natural: I would not wish there to be any unruly behaviour.'

Titi hurried to greet the commander of the local guards, a coarse-faced Syrian.

'At the first sign of trouble,' said the commander, 'I shall throw the rioters into prison and have half of them executed.'

'Don't worry, the inhabitants of Kebet are reasonable people. They will be content with enjoying themselves and will thank the emperor for these festivities.'

Priests carried in procession the astonishing statue of Min, wrapped in the white shroud of resurrection. With his eternally erect phallus, he embodied the creative power that enabled life to carry on in all its forms and that, in particular, gave life to wheat.

Desert prospectors, miners and caravan-traders were moved to see the statue pass by, for the god possessed the secret of the stones that were born in the belly of the mountains. With his arm raised, forming a secret angle known to temple-builders, and holding the three-skinned sceptre symbolizing the three births, celestial, earthly and underground, Min reigned over distant roads and guided adventurers.

A magnificent white bull walked placidly behind the statue. According to tradition, it was the queen who mastered its natural violence and transformed it into fertile power. But the last queen was dead, and Apophis forbade women to attend rituals.

Already a huge climbing-pole was being raised and stayed with ropes. The most agile men would try to be first to climb to the top and unhook the sought-after gifts. The competition never took place without incident, and there would be countless falls.

'There are too many temples in Kebet, Governor,' said the Syrian. 'You may keep one – that will be quite enough – and the others will be turned into barracks and weapons stores.'

Titi yielded. The emperor hated obvious displays of the former culture, and Kebet already enjoyed preferential treatment.

'Are you absolutely sure Ahhotep is dead?' asked the Syrian.

'Absolutely. The man who poisoned her has been executed, and Thebes is in mourning. Before long, all the rebels will lay down their arms. Ahhotep was their heart and soul, and without her they will have neither the strength nor the courage to continue. I know the Egyptians well: they will believe that their queen was punished by the gods because she acted wrongly. Shouldn't we encourage the spread of that idea?'

'I'll see to it, Governor.'

Most unusually, two taverns had been opened. Under close watch by the guards, they were selling bad beer which the revellers would have to be content with. At the first sign of drunkenness, troublemakers would be arrested and deported. The emperor would not tolerate any breach of public order, and Aberia would be delighted to increase the number of prisoners destined for the camp at Sharuhen.

'This beer is rubbish,' said the Afghan.

'Just like this pathetic so-called festival,' agreed Moustache.

'In other words, we've been robbed. I think we deserve compensation.'

'Shall we call the innkeeper over?'

'That coward? He's scared to death. What we need is someone with real authority. That armed guard, for example.'

Moustache went over to him. 'My man, my friend and I are thoroughly dissatisfied. The procession is mediocre, the beer is undrinkable and the atmosphere is depressing, all of which is absolutely unacceptable, don't you think?'

The guard was struck dumb with astonishment, but soon got his voice back. 'You're both drunk! Follow me and don't argue.'

'We can't,' said Moustache.

'What the devil do you mean?'

'He's right,' said the Afghan, 'we can't. First, we're not drunk. Second, we're not here to have fun – still less to see the inside of one of your prisons.'

'And who the devil do you think you are?'

'A rebel who's going to kill a Hyksos guard, burn down this pathetic tavern – and so give the signal for the army of liberation to attack.'

# 10

As soon as the flames roared up, Ahhotep's soldiers – half of whom had mingled with the crowd – charged at the Hyksos guards in charge of keeping public order. Well trained in close combat by the Afghan and Moustache, they had the advantage of surprise, and in a few moments they had killed most of their enemies.

The astounded Syrian commander told Governor Titi, 'Go to the palace, quickly! Order your men to join forces with mine.'

The terrified priests had taken refuge in the temple with the statue of Min. From the top of the climbing-pole, two youths were throwing pots at the Hyksos guards. Urged on by Moustache, the revellers turned on their oppressors. Several Hyksos were trampled underfoot by the inhabitants of Kebet, who were only too happy to express the hatred they had held in for so long.

The Syrian and Titi did not get far. Suddenly, there before them stood Ahhotep, at the head of Titi's personal bodyguard.

'These men now belong to the army of liberation,' declared the queen.

'Majesty, you . . . you aren't dead! No, it's a ghost – it must be a ghost. We must run to the Temple of Geb. They won't dare touch us there.'

Ahhotep prevented an archer from firing.

The two fugitives managed to force their way through the skirmish, which was turning definitively in favour of the Egyptians, and reach the forecourt of the Temple of Geb. The door was closed, and Titi hammered on it with his fists.

'Open up! It's the governor, and I demand safe haven!'

The door remained closed.

All at once, a heavy silence fell over the town: no more shouts of victory or cries of pain, no more voices, not even the bark of a dog.

Alone on the temple forecourt, Titi and the Syrian were gradually surrounded by the people of Kebet and by the soldiers of Ahhotep's army.

Ahhotep stepped forward. 'Hear these words, which are spoken in this place each time judgment is pronounced: "May the liar fear Geb, the creative power which loves truth. He detests falsehood. It is for him to decide."'

'Majesty, don't let there be a misunderstanding about me!' implored Titi. 'I pretended to be an ally of the Hyksos so that I could better protect my fellow citizens – without me, many would have been executed or tortured. In fact, I have been loyal to you ever since the beginning of your campaign. You remember our meeting, don't you? I realize now that I should have confided in you. Here are two proofs of my righteousness: first, the names of the sailors, caravan-owners and merchants who betrayed Egypt to the Hyksos – I'll tell you them all, I swear it! And the second proof is even more convincing.'

Titi plunged his dagger into the Syrian's back, rolled the wounded man over and finished him off.

Then he knelt down. 'I am your humble servant, Majesty.'

Ahhotep's eyes flamed. 'You are nothing but a coward, and you have violated this sacred place. This is my decree, which will be kept in our archives. Your title of governor is withdrawn, and it will not be conferred upon any of your descendants. Your goods will be given to the temples of Kebet, your writings will be destroyed, your name is to be accursed and forgotten for ever. Any pharaoh who granted you pardon would be unworthy of wearing the Double Crown and would at once be abandoned by the gods.'

At the trade-tax post outside Kebet, a guard said to his superior officer, 'Sir, I can see smoke.'

'Where?'

'It looks as if it's coming from the town.'

'Probably just some old building burning down. It's not our concern. We're here to collect taxes from anyone who passes through Kebet, charge them the maximum fee and keep the emperor happy. Nothing else matters.'

'Sir?'

'What is it now?'

'There are people coming.'

'You deal with it. My arm's aching from stamping my seal on all those documents, and I need a nap.'

'There are an awful lot of them, sir.'

'Merchants, do you mean?'

'No, sir. I think they're soldiers.'

The officer was jolted out of his apathy. He looked out of the tax-post and his jaw dropped. On the Nile, there were ten warships carrying many archers. On the road, there were hundreds of Egyptian soldiers, commanded by Moustache.

The soldiers soon reached the tax-post.

'This,' announced Moustache, 'is the choice I offer you: you can either surrender or be killed.'

Hollow-cheeked and sad-eyed, Heray bowed before the queen.

'Majesty, I offer you my resignation as Overseer of Granaries and of Thebes's security. I can only hope that you may one day be able to forgive my incompetence and lack of foresight. No one could have been more at fault, and I know it. The only favour I beg is not to be expelled from Thebes, but if you decide I must be I will accept your decision.'

Ahhotep smiled warmly at him. 'I have no reproaches for you, Heray.'

'Majesty! I let an assassin get near you – he poisoned your food and you almost died. Because of me, the battle for freedom could have been lost. Dismissal is the very least I deserve.'

'No, Heray, because every single day you demonstrate the greatest of all virtues: faithfulness. Thanks to that, we shall remain united and we shall win.'

'But, M-Majesty . . .' stammered Heray.

'Do me the honour of continuing in office, my friend, and carry out your duties with the greatest vigilance. I myself have made serious mistakes, and I fear I shall make more in the future. Our enemies will continue to attack us in the most cunning ways they can think of, so there must be no weak points in our armour.'

The big man was moved to tears. He prostrated himself before the Wife of God, whom he admired more each day.

Ahhotep raised him to his feet. 'You have a great deal of work to do,' she said. 'Before he was executed, Titi supplied us with an impressive list of collaborators. But he mixed truth and lies, hoping that we will kill people who really are allies. So you must check each case with great care, to make sure that doesn't happen.'

'You can rely on me, Majesty.'

'Now, let us go and look at Qaris's model.'

Qaris had already, with profound joy, added Kebet and its surroundings to the liberated area on the model. No more Hyksos occupation, no more arbitrary arrests, no more torture: the people were beginning to breathe more freely again.

'How happy Seqen must be,' murmured the queen. 'When we succeed in reopening the caravan routes, many of our difficulties will be solved.'

'Tomorrow,' enthused Qaris, 'we shall celebrate the true Festival of Min! And the Queen of Egypt will lead the ritual, paying homage to the ancestors' memory.'

Ahhotep's beautiful face was sombre. 'This is only a modest victory. It will lead nowhere unless we redouble our efforts.'

'Our weapons have improved a great deal, Majesty,' said Qaris. 'They'll soon be soon as good as you wish them to be.'

'If we are to extend the liberated area northwards, we need more boats. The Hyksos have chariots and horses, and know how to use them; we know how to make use of the Nile. We must open new boatyards straight away, and put as many craftsmen as possible to work.'

## 11

Emheb, governor of Edfu, was a huge man. Everything about him was huge: his head, his nose, his shoulders and his girth. At first sight he looked like a man who enjoyed the good life, but his bull's neck and hard eyes gave the lie to that impression.

He was a staunch ally of Queen Ahhotep, and had been in the thick of the early battles of the war for freedom. He had pretended to submit to the Hyksos occupiers of Edfu, while quietly killing them one by one and replacing them with men from his own rebel network, until eventually he regained control of his city.

Seqen's death had affected him deeply, and he had never imagined that the young woman could withstand such a shock. And yet, with a courage that even hardened sceptics admired, she had decided to carry on the work her dead husband had begun. As the dawn sun rose, vanquishing the dragon of darkness, Emheb pictured Ahhotep's success. To have reached Qis was in itself an achievement, one which had restored a little of his countrymen's lost pride; and they owed that happy fact to a queen who was bold enough to attempt the impossible. Then the cold light of day had come to the front, which had not moved in months, and he had to face facts: Apophis, for whatever reason, was allowing the situation to stagnate. Either the emperor was convinced that the Egyptians would eventually give up, or he was preparing for a massive offensive.

Emheb knew very well that, even if he strengthened his positions, he would not be able to hold out for long against the full might of the Hyksos regiments. But Ahhotep trusted him completely, and he would not withdraw. He no longer asked questions. Ahhotep had ordered him to hold the line, and he would hold it.

His personal scribe showed in Ahmes, son of Abana, a young and extraordinarily brave soldier.

For once, Ahmes looked worried. 'Governor,' he said, 'we must reassure our men. Many of them still believe that Queen Ahhotep is dead and that it would be better to surrender before we're slaughtered.'

'I have just received messages signed by the queen herself. Not only is she alive but she has retaken Kebet. As for those who wish to surrender, have they considered what their fate would be?'

'That's precisely what I told them, sir, but rumours are like poison. We—'

Ahmes broke off as a lookout shouted, 'They're attacking! The Hyksos are attacking!'

They both rushed out to take up their battle positions.

As soon as he was in position, Emheb dispatched carrier-pigeons to Thebes with an urgent request for help. If reinforcements did not arrive in time, the front line would collapse and the enemy armies would overrun the South.


The port at Thebes had become a vast boatyard, where even the soldiers were set to work by the carpenters, so that as many boats as possible could be built in record time without sacrificing quality.

Several teams went off to find timber, mainly acacia and sycamore. Trunks and branches were trimmed with an axe, and split into planks. Hammers and chisels were used to cut out mortises, heavy mallets to force in the tenons, and a short-handled adze for finishing. No one counted the hours, for everyone knew their work was vital and that Egypt's future depended on it. Every time a boat neared completion, the men who varnished the planks with cedar-oil and beeswax rejoiced in the fact that they would soon see a new vessel launched on the Nile.

Ahhotep had set the weaving-women of Thebes to work making linen sails. Some consisted of one large sheet, others were made from strips of varying widths sewn together with great care. With these new sails, the Egyptian war-fleet would be much faster.

Always accompanied by Young Laughter, who watched over his mistress as vigilantly as his predecessor, Ahhotep made constant inspections of the boatyard and encouraged the craftsmen. If a man seemed so exhausted that he was at risk of having an accident, she ordered him to take a rest. She made sure to check the oars, too. The steering-oar enabled an experienced helmsman to manoeuvre his boat with relative ease on a river which could be capricious, while the rowing-oars enabled the sailors to give of their best when the boat was travelling upstream or if there was no wind.

The queen had ordered the construction of several cargo-vessels, each capable of carrying enormous quantities of weapons, raw materials and foodstuffs. These would ensure that the Egyptian army was self-sufficient if it succeeded in breaking through into enemy territory. Even milch-cows would be taken on board, after prayers had been offered to Hathor to calm these precious animals. Calves and oxen would be tethered to rings fixed to the deck, but the cows that were good sailors could wander about freely.

The sound of running feet alerted Laughter, who bared his teeth but then, when he saw that it was Qaris coming, sat down in front of his mistress.

'Majesty,' panted the steward, 'we've had an alarming message from Emheb. The Hyksos are trying to break through the front, and he asks urgently for reinforcements.'

'Are enough boats ready to leave?'

'No, Majesty. If we take those that are, they'd be so overloaded that they'd probably capsize. Besides, would it not be dangerous to leave Thebes unprotected?'

It was not the exhausted Rascal who made the return flight to the front but another pigeon, almost as experienced as its leader.

The traitor who had infiltrated the Thebans had at first thought of killing the bird, but soon thought better of it. Even an excellent archer could not be certain of success, unless he shot as the bird was taking off, and in that case someone was bound to see him.

He decided on a more reliable course of action: in the pigeon's food he'd put a poison which would not take effect until the bird was halfway through its flight. It would never reach Qis, Emheb would think he had been abandoned, and the emperor's army would smash the barrier that blocked its way to the South.

'Still no message?' Emheb asked Ahmes.

'No, sir, nothing.'

'The queen cannot just abandon us!'

'Either our birds have been killed or Thebes can't send any reinforcements. Either way, sir, we must manage alone. Our men are putting up strong resistance, and the Hyksos haven't yet launched an all-out attack. I think they may be testing our mettle before sending in their main body of troops.'

'We must lay more booby-traps,' decided Emheb. 'It's vital that the enemy waste a great deal of time dealing with them. And we must set up more concealed firing positions. The Hyksos may have a larger, stronger army, but they do not know this terrain. Despite our difficulties, all is not lost yet.'

'Indeed it isn't, sir,' agreed Ahmes.

The two men knew that they were lying to themselves, the better to overcome their fear and fight courageously to the end.

'I must go back to our forward positions,' said Ahmes, whose young face betrayed not a trace of emotion.

'As soon as you feel you're in difficulty, send me a footsoldier and I'll hurry to your aid.'

'May the gods preserve you, Governor.'

'May they also protect you, my boy.'

Emheb had no regrets. From the very beginning of this mad adventure, he had known that the Egyptian army was not strong enough to take on the Hyksos monster. And yet that was the only road they could have followed, even if it ended in the death of Ahhotep and the destruction of Thebes. At least these years of rebellion had wiped away the shame and bitterness of the past. The Egyptians had at last stopped behaving like cowards, and could appear before the court of the afterlife in the proud knowledge that they had done their duty.

A young officer came running up. 'Governor, there are two Hyksos war-boats coming,' he said with a cheerful smile.

Emheb thought he must be having a bad dream. 'And you're actually pleased about that?'

'Oh yes, sir, because they've chosen their moment very badly.'

'What do you mean?'

'They're about to meet the most beautiful war-fleet I've ever seen: about twenty Egyptian boats from the south – with Queen Ahhotep at their head!'

## 12

Wearing her mother's gold crown, and holding up the Sword of Amon before her, the Queen of Freedom stood at the prow of the flagship as the oarsmen rowed swiftly along.

The Hyksos boats reacted immediately. After hurriedly lowering their sails, they turned tail and retreated as fast as they could.

On the banks, the Egyptian footsoldiers gave shouts of victory. At last, the reinforcements they had awaited so long!

Emheb was amazed to see a few archers and hordes of peasants disembarking. They looked nothing like soldiers.

'Majesty,' he said, 'what joy to see you again! But ... who are these people?'

'Citizens of Kebet and farmers from the liberated provinces. You shall train them, Governor, and they will help you to consolidate the front. I could not leave Thebes unguarded, but neither could I abandon you, as my message explained.'

Emheb's expression darkened. 'I have received no message, Majesty.'

The smile faded from Ahhotep's face. 'We sent you one of our best pigeons. The poor thing must have been killed on the way here.'

'No doubt by a bird of prey,' said Emheb.

'No doubt,' repeated the queen, though she did not believe it.

'The important thing is that you have come – and at just the right moment. Despite the denials, some of the men still believed you were dead.'

'I shall not leave here until I have met each and every one of your soldiers. You are to keep almost all the boats, three-quarters of which have brought supplies of weapons and equipment for you. If necessary, the others will enable you to travel back to Thebes. Thanks to their new sails, they are faster than the Hyksos boats.'

To see the queen, speak with her, celebrate with her the birth of the sun, hear her beseeching the gods not to leave the land of Egypt but to dwell in the soldiers' hearts: such things swept away all fears for the future.

Ahhotep gave a great banquet for the heroes who were holding back the Hyksos, and promised them future evenings of celebration once Egypt was liberated. She showed them the gift she was going to send to the emperor, and it made everyone burst out laughing.

The emperor dropped the limestone scarab on to the stone floor, as though it were a burning coal. 'Who received this abomination?' he demanded. 'And who dared send it to me?'

'An Egyptian archer fired it over our front line at Qis, Majesty,' replied Khamudi. 'An officer picked it up and gave it to the army messenger.'

'Have those imbeciles executed! Have you read this text, Khamudi? Have you read the loathsome message that loathsome female dares send me?'

The High Treasurer picked up the scarab, which bore a clear inscription in beautiful hieroglyphs: '*Greetings to the vile Hyksos Apophis, who occupies my country. Queen Ahhotep is very much alive, and every Egyptian knows it. They also know that you are not invulnerable.*'

'It must be a forgery, Majesty.'

'Of course it isn't!' snapped Apophis. 'Now that damned woman is going to flood the country with scarabs like this, and wreck our campaign of false information. And the frontier at Qis is now firmly established.'

'Our surprise attacks have not been very effective, I admit, but they have shown us that that's where the Egyptians have massed the main body of their troops, and that they cannot advance any further. Also, the news from Asia is good: the local rulers are becoming less troublesome, and Hyksos order has been re-established. As for Jannas, he is pursuing the last of the pirates in the Mycenaean islands, where they think they are safe. Killing that scum was vital. All that remains is for you to say, Majesty, whether you wish him to destroy Minoa.'

'I'll think about it,' said the emperor, his voice even harsher than usual. 'Now tell me, doesn't one bit of this contemptible message surprise you?'

Khamudi read it again. '"*Every Egyptian knows it*": does that mean there are still rebels in the Delta, who might spread information from the South?'

The semblance of a smile added an extra touch of ugliness to the emperor's face. 'That vainglorious queen has made a grave mistake by trying to insult me. We have been too lenient with the the natives, Khamudi, much too lenient. I require interrogations to be made far more rigorous, and there are to be as many deportations as necessary. No town or village is to be spared.'

Her mother had been raped and beheaded, her father disembowelled by the emperor's bull. Because of her beauty, the young Egyptian woman had had the honour of being chosen to become one of the courtesans in the official harem at Avaris. These courtesans had to be ready, at any hour of the day or night, to satisfy the lust of Hyksos dignitaries.

It was barely survival, and each hour weighed more heavily than the last, but the young woman put everything out of her mind in order to fight in her own way.

By offering herself to one of her guards, who was not permitted to touch these beautiful girls, she had succeeded in convincing him that she loved him. The rough fellow was absolutely besotted with her and would do anything not to lose her.

One night, after enchanting the brute once again, she had begged an immense favour: a meeting with her brother, who was working as a carpenter on the outskirts of Avaris. The guard could contact him via a groom. Just to see him for a few moments, to embrace him, that was all she wanted.

The guard had hesitated for a long time. But then he wondered how his beautiful girl would react if he said no. She might refuse him her charms – and he would never find another woman like her.

The first meeting had been arranged for the middle of the night, at the entrance to the harem kitchens, which the girl had described in detail to her 'brother', a rebel friend of her parents who had contacts in the South. Unfortunately, she could do no more for him.

What he had told her was extraordinary: the army of liberation really did exist, and a queen called Ahhotep was leading the fight! Soon the news would spread throughout the Delta, and new rebels would swell the present meagre ranks.

She had passed on to him an idea which had been haunting her: to get a raiding-party into the harem, kill the guards and take hostage the high-ranking Hyksos who would be found there. Her 'brother' agreed, and had promised he would not not come to the second meeting alone.

Now the moment she had so longed for had at last arrived.

After lavishing sensual delights upon the commander of the imperial guard, the young woman left the room and slipped down a poorly lit servants' passageway. She was barefoot, and hardly dared breathe in case someone heard her.

At this hour of the night, the kitchens were deserted. Here, she would have to give herself one last time to the guard before he would open the door.

'Here I am,' she whispered. 'Are you there?'

There was no answer. Surprised, she let her eyes grow accustomed to the darkness, avoided bumping into a large spit on which geese were roasted, and crept past one of the ovens.

'I'm here. Where are you hiding, my love?'

Her throat dry, she stumbled over something on the floor. She crouched down and felt around. Her hand touched hair, a nose, teeth, and they were sticky . . . She cried out in fear.

Suddenly, a torch lit up the kitchen.

'I slit that guard's throat myself,' said the lady Aberia. 'I knew he was sniffing round you, even though it's strictly forbidden.' She ripped open the girl's dress. 'You have pretty breasts, and the rest isn't unattractive, either. Before he died, that pig told me that he had allowed you to see your brother, which is also forbidden. He has just been arrested outside, with two of his friends. You were going to let them in here, weren't you?'

'I . . . I have nothing to say to you!'

'Come, come, little one. The emperor has ordered us to identify all the rebels, and I think I have sniffed one out. You will tell me everything, otherwise your pretty body will feel the kiss of this torch.'

The young woman leapt forward and threw herself on to the roasting-spit, which pierced her throat. When Aberia dragged the body off the spike, she thought she saw a gleam of victory in the dead Egyptian's eyes.

# 13

All day long, under the cruel sun, Queen Ahhotep herself brought water and food to the carpenters, who were working without a break. In spite of the heat, Long-Ears never balked at carrying heavy loads. Sure-footed and even-tempered, he was constantly alert as he followed her and Laughter.

Only the bustling presence of the queen prevented the Thebans from lapsing into gloom. True, they were free again, but for how long? The Hyksos' power had been barely scratched; sooner or later the dragon would react – and that reaction would be terrifying. But there was Ahhotep, with her beauty, her smile and her determination, which nothing could weaken. Seqen's soul lived in her and endowed her with his strength.

Only Teti the Small sensed that her daughter was beginning to have doubts.

'Should we not pull back the front line and be content with Thebes?' she suggested, as they ate their evening meal on the palace terrace.

'That would certainly be the sensible thing to do.'

'In other words, you don't think it appropriate.'

'It is not appropriate for Egypt, Mother. Partial freedom would simply consign us to an even worse prison than the one we have broken out of. By falling back to our little piece of ground, we would become easy prey for the emperor.'

'Then you are refusing to face reality, Ahhotep.'

'I shall never accept the reality imposed by Apophis, because it is against the Rule of Ma'at. If we accept the supremacy of violence and injustice, this world will no longer be fit to live in.'

'Then what do you plan to do?'

'We have only a few statues of the gods left, and we don't honour them enough, even though without their support we can never succeed. For ten days, I shall offer them the finest food and beg the ancestors to inspire my actions. I shall then consult the moon-god.'

Teti the Small looked long and hard at her daughter. 'Ahhotep, you have become a true Queen of Egypt.'

*

Once again, the ritual upon which the balance of the universe depended was being enacted: caught in a fishing-net, then reassembled by the gods Thoth and Horus, the full moon's silver eye shone with such intense brilliance that the spirits of seers were opened.

'You who know yesterday, today and tomorrow,' declared Ahhotep, 'also know that I will not surrender. My life no longer belongs to me: I have offered it to my people. To live in slavery is worse than death. Trace out a path for me in the heavens, and I will follow it.'

Hieroglyphs appeared on the silver disc, spelling out a name.

When she read it, Ahhotep realized that her heart must continue to bleed, for the gods had left her no choice.

'Don't flatter him, Heray, and don't hide anything from me,' ordered the queen. 'Is he ready, yes or no?'

'Majesty, your son is a true soldier, well capable of fighting in the vanguard.'

'What are his weaknesses?'

'He is as good as our very best archers, wins every bout of hand-to-hand combat and wields a sword better than anyone. And all this with virtually no sleep.'

'Do the soldiers respect him?'

Heray lowered his eyes. 'Majesty, I hardly dare tell you—'

'I want the truth.'

'The transformation has been astonishing. He grows more and more like his father. I have never seen such a young man show such qualities of leadership. He doesn't realize it himself, but all he has to do is make an appearance and he is obeyed.'

So the moon-god had spoken truly when he revealed Kamose's name to her: the hour of his coronation had arrived.

'I don't wish to offend you, Mother, but is it really urgent?' asked Kamose. 'I was planning to practise with my bow this afternoon, and then—'

'I am speaking to you as Regent Queen of Egypt.'

Ahhotep's solemnity made a deep impression on the young man. Together, they walked slowly beside the sacred lake at Karnak. The light was intense, the place peaceful.

'Everyone reveres you,' said Kamose, 'but I have one criticism: why do you insist on being only a regent? Why don't you become Pharaoh?'

'Because that office falls upon you, my son.'

'On me?' Kamose was astounded. 'But I have neither your authority nor your experience.'

'The moon-god has decided that my period as regent is coming to an end, and that your reign is beginning. You are only seventeen, Kamose, but you must succeed your father.'

His face fell. 'He is still my ideal. How can I possibly equal him?'

'If you want to show yourself worthy of him, by achieving more than he did.'

'May I refuse this burden?'

'You know the answer to that question.'

Kamose halted and gazed deep into the blue waters of the sacred lake. 'How far away the war seems,' he said quietly. 'Yet as soon as I am crowned it will be my prime duty. And I must not only deal with the present situation, but go further – much further. Do you think I can do it?'

'The gods demand that you do.'

'You're the incarnation of the goddess of Thebes, aren't you, Mother? You're the true pharaoh, and I shall be merely your strong arm.'

'I shall fight tirelessly at your side, and I'll never fail to support you. But you must reign in your own way, Kamose, and according to your own abilities.'

'There's a fire burning inside me, and it won't let me sleep. It frightens me sometimes. Because of it, I can neither wait on events nor withdraw from them. If power is given to me, this fire will force me to attack all the obstacles I face, even if they're impossible to break down.'

Ahhotep kissed him on the forehead. 'You are my son and I love you.'

Moustache wished he could have thousands more nights like this one. The shopkeeper's daughter was as beautiful as Hathor. With her high, round breasts, her deliciously flat stomach and her slender legs, who would not have been seduced by her? And it was him, a soldier, and not exactly a handsome one, whom she had chosen – at least for a few hours.

The war was not wholly bad. In ordinary times, this young beauty would have thought only of starting a family. Today, who could be sure of living long enough for that? Brief liaisons came and went; people enjoyed ecstasy and forgot their anguish in intense moments of pleasure.

Moustache was caressing his sleeping mistress when out of the corner of his eye he caught sight of a ray of sunshine.

The new recruits! They must have been waiting for him for ages. It was his duty, as senior officer, to greet them – and the queen did not look at all kindly on lapses in discipline. Not even taking the time to shave, he tied on his leather kilt and rushed out on to the training-ground.

It was empty. In fact, the whole base was deserted and silent, save for the sentries at their posts atop the watch-towers.

Moustache walked back to the officers' houses and went into the Afghan's.

He found his friend fighting a rather more amorous battle than usual, with a pretty brown-haired girl with heavily made-up eyes. It appeared that the shopkeeper's elder daughter was no more shy than the younger.

Moustache coughed. 'Ahem, it's me.'

'I can see that,' said the Afghan. 'Did you fall out of bed?'

'I don't understand. There isn't a single soldier on the parade-ground.'

'You were really drunk last night, but I told you quite clearly that the army was enjoying a week's rest in honour of Kamose's coronation.'

Moustache rapped his forehead with his fist. 'It's coming back to me now.'

'Would it bother you if I asked you to leave?'

'No, not at all. I've got some urgent business to finish, too.'

# 14

At Seqen's coronation, the pharaoh had had to be content with a simple crown, because the priests at Karnak had neither the Red Crown of Lower Egypt nor the White Crown of Upper Egypt.

The latter was widely thought to have been destroyed by the Hyksos, but after consulting the archives the High Priest of Karnak had reached a different conclusion.

'Formerly, Majesty,' he told Ahhotep, 'the Red Crown was kept in a temple at Memphis and the White in the ancient city of Nekhen, on whose site Elkab was built, and unfortunately Elkab was looted and destroyed by the invaders. It would probably be no use for you to go there, but ...'

'I shall go there at once,' decided the queen.

Since Emheb had liberated the region, Elkab had changed greatly. Life had returned to the narrow streets, and the little white houses had been rebuilt in the traditional manner, even though the town and its people faced an uncertain future. Like Edfu, Elkab housed a regiment of reserve troops, who could be mobilized at a moment's notice to beat off a Nubian attempt at invasion or a Hyksos attack.

Ahhotep's only companions on her journey were Laughter and the twenty men who made up her personal bodyguard, all carefully chosen by Heray. As soon as they arrived, she made her way to the ancient fort, whose imposing walls were still standing. Inside the curtain wall, the temple of the vulture-goddess, 'Holder of the Royal Title',* lay in ruins.

'Majesty, I beg you not to go any further,' said the town's mayor anxiously. 'This place is haunted – looters who dared go inside were found dead. We must wait until the goddess's anger is appeased.'

'I have no time. I cannot wait.'

'Majesty, I implore you!'

---

*The royal title, *nekhbet*, derives from the goddess's name, Nekhbet.

'Stand aside.'

When Ahhotep set foot on the stone pavement, several black scorpions scuttled away. Dark forces had indeed taken possession of the ruined shrine, where the King of Upper Egypt had formerly received the supreme insignia of his office. No, Nekhen was not yet free. And it fell to Ahhotep to appease the goddess, for the new pharaoh's future depended upon it.

When a vulture flew above the building, tracing wide circles in the blue sky, the queen knew what was killing intruders and what she must confront. The crowns were protected by both a celestial creature, the vulture, which was the supreme incarnation of the Mother, and an earthly being, the snake, which embodied the flame that destroyed the king's enemies.

Darting out of a ruined inner shrine, a female cobra reared up in front of the queen.

Ahhotep raised her hands in a gesture of worship.

'I have come here not to steal,' she declared, 'but to have my son declared the rightful King of Upper Egypt. I bow before you, the great ancestor who existed at the very beginning of all things. You who touch the limits of the universe and cause the sun to be born, you who are at once god and goddess, wipe away impurity and misfortune, and rise once again on Pharaoh's brow.'

For a few moments, the cobra hesitated. Ahhotep was so close that it could have struck at her throat, but the queen's gaze remained steady.

The cobra stretched out on the flagstones, then darted down between them, like a bolt of lightning entering the ground. Where it had disappeared, the stone was burnt, and on it lay the royal cobra's legacy: a gold uraeus which would be attached to the royal crown.

Ahhotep knelt down and picked it up reverently. Without fear, she continued on her way towards the furthermost part of the shrine, which the snake-goddess had guarded so vigilantly.

Despite the fire that had ravaged the temple, one of the stones was still intact, and it shone with a strange light, as though it were lit from the inside.

Ahhotep laid her hand upon the granite. The stone pivoted, revealing a hiding-place which contained an acacia-wood box. Inside it lay the White Crown of Upper Egypt.

After being purified in the sacred lake, Kamose meditated before one of the statues of Pharaoh Osiris, the symbol of the twofold nature of the royal office, which belonged both to this world and to the world beyond.

Then the young man went through the same ceremonies his father had, with one notable difference: whereas Seqen's coronation had been kept secret for a long time, in order to prevent collaborators informing the emperor, that of his elder son would be celebrated openly and would mark a new stage in the liberation of Egypt.

As the new pharaoh had no wife, it was the Wife of God who must recognize in him the presence of Horus and Set, the two brothers who shared the universe and reigned, the first over Lower Egypt and the second over Upper Egypt. Indivisible and constantly in conflict, they could not be reconciled or appeased except within the symbolic person of Pharaoh, who alone was capable of forging solid bonds between the two gods and the Two Lands.

Ahhotep gave her son his coronation names: 'Horus Who is Complete and Makes the Two Lands Bow the Knee', 'He Who Nurtures the Two Lands', 'He Who Restores That Which Endures', 'He Who Appears in Glory upon His Throne', 'The Transformation of the Light Is Accomplished'.

At last his name, Kamose, had taken on its full meaning, 'Power is born'. That power, the *ka*, was displayed in the fighting-bull, nourished by the strength of the moon-god.

'May you make these names complete and may they guide you along the path to victory,' proclaimed the queen, placing the White Crown with its uraeus upon the head of her son. 'May your father's spirit live in you and may his courage strengthen your arm.'

The Hyksos would never understand that Egyptian society was not made up solely of human beings, but consisted also of gods and ancestors, who were present in every facet of daily life. Apophis believed Seqen was dead, but he was wrong. Brought back to life by the rites and the words of knowledge, his radiant spirit travelled between the stars and the earth, and he lived on in the souls of those who remained faithful to him. Thanks to the power of the Word contained in the hieroglyphs, Ahhotep had made the invisible presence of her dead husband real and effective.

'Mother, I would like . . .'

'I know, Kamose. You would like to stay a while in the temple and enjoy its inexpressible peace. But Egypt's peace has not yet been won, and you will have to fight unceasingly to conquer it and give it to our people.'

All trace of hesitation had vanished from the young king's eyes. Pharaoh Kamose went out of the Temple of Amon, that realm of light where war, evil and injustice did not exist. After experiencing unimaginable happiness, he must now confront Apophis and try to re-establish the Rule of Ma'at.

Both soldiers and civilians were gathered in front of the temple to hail their new pharaoh. When he appeared, the White Crown shone so brightly that it dazzled them.

Queen Ahhotep presented her son with the sacred curved bronze sword, covered with silver and inlaid with an alloy of gold and silver; its hilt was decorated with a golden lotus, the symbol of the rebirth of the divine sun at the end of its nightly ordeals.

'As your father did before you, receive the Sword of Amon, with which you will rend the darkness asunder. May you, Pharaoh Kamose, overthrow its empire and be victorious in the war of the Crowns.'

## 15

By the light of an exquisite lamp dating from the days of Pharaoh Menuhotep II, Apophis drew magical signs on a new sheet of papyrus, to stifle Thebes by attacking it from all four directions. To the east and west, the fire of Set made the deserts uninhabitable. To the south, the Hyksos' Nubian allies would be only too happy to massacre any Egyptian fugitives. And what rose up from the north would be as formidable as any army. Without his raising a finger, the emperor's spirit would kill huge numbers of his enemies.

Those Theban madmen had dared to send him a little limestone scarab, announcing the coronation of Pharaoh Kamose. Behind that puppet king, he knew, stood the inexhaustibly stubborn Queen Ahhotep. This time, she would pay very dearly for her insolence. No matter how skilful she might be, she would have no recourse against the misfortune that was about to descend upon Thebes.

Struck by a sudden doubt, the emperor took the secret passageway leading to the Treasury of the citadel. He alone knew how to unlock the door of the strong-room, which contained huge piles of stolen Egyptian ritual objects. The most precious was the Red Crown of Lower Egypt, characterized by its spiral shape, symbol of the harmonious growth of vital forces.

Apophis had worried needlessly. The crown was safe. Without it, Ahhotep would never manage to reconquer Egypt. She was nothing but a little rebel adventuress, lost in a dream that would soon be transformed into a nightmare.

Windswept had wrapped herself in a wonderfully soft bed-sheet which Asiatic merchants had just delivered to the palace. It was made of a material called silk, which was unknown in the land of the pharaohs. Tany, the emperor's wife, considered it coarse and uninteresting, so Windswept had acquired the whole consignment.

'Come,' she said to her companion.

He was the head groom at the palace, a stocky, coarse-faced man of fifty who smelt of the stable. There was nothing seductive about him, but his strength had caught Windswept's attention. She was sure that in his arms she would experience new pleasures.

Fascinated by the luxury of the bedchamber, he dared not take another step forward. 'Is that me?' he gasped in astonishment, catching sight of himself in a mirror whose glass was less cloudy than usual.

'Shouldn't you be looking at me?' Windswept suggested, taking off her wrap and lying down on the bed.

The groom recoiled, sure he must be seeing a mirage.

'Don't be afraid,' she said softly. 'Come closer.'

Her voice was so alluring that he obeyed.

The temptress slowly untied his kilt. 'How strong you are,' she murmured greedily. 'Let me prepare you.'

She picked up a hollowed-out bull's horn containing perfumed oil. Slowly she let oil drip on to her lover's muscular chest, then smoothed it over his flesh so caressingly that his nervousness vanished and he flung himself on her.

Although delighted by her new conquest's hunger for her, Windswept was soon disappointed; the brute had no stamina at all, and even seemed to have difficulty getting his breath back.

'You have an exciting job, haven't you?' she said when he had recovered somewhat.

'That's true. I love horses – and I hate people who mistreat them.'

'Is someone doing so?'

'I can't say anything about it.'

'I am the emperor's sister. And I can help you.'

'You would do that?'

Windswept gave a convincing smile. 'Since we are lovers, what could be more natural?'

The groom sat up and perched on the side of the bed. 'It's that monster Khamudi and his she-devil of a wife. They brought some young women into my stable and did the most horrible things. He is far, far beyond my reach. However, if the emperor knew . . .'

'He will know.'

The groom gazed at Windswept as though she had been sent from heaven. 'Then Khamudi will be punished and will never set foot in my stable again?'

'You can be sure of it. The emperor demands very high standards of morality.'

'Then I shan't have to do anything, after all.'

'What were you planning to do?'

'Lure Khamudi and his wife into an ambush. As she likes stallions so much, I was going to show her one who has a dangerous little trick:

if anyone comes up behind him, he kicks viciously. That madwoman wouldn't have escaped a second time, and her vile husband would have been spitted on my pitchfork.'

'The emperor's justice will solve all your problems,' promised Windswept.

In view of the circumstances, she would save the life of the High Treasurer and his wife, whose peccadilloes Apophis knew and approved of. The groom, though, was destined for the labyrinth.

As for Windswept, she now had useful new information about the unsavoury couple, whom she hated and would attack when the right moment came.

'Get dressed and leave now,' she ordered the groom.

'Thank you,' he said, his voice shaking. 'Thank you for everything you have granted me.'

Scarcely had he left when Minos came in. Still naked, Windswept threw her arms round his neck and kissed him so passionately that she took his breath away. The Minoan artist was her true love, the only one she had not yet sent to his death. Strangely, Minos was not fomenting even the tiniest plot against Apophis, even though the emperor had condemned him to perpetual exile.

With surprising constancy, the Minoan devoted himself only to his art. Thanks to his talent, the palace at Avaris was now fully the equal of the palace at Knossos. Large painted murals depicted Minoan landscapes, acrobats leaping over fierce bulls and labyrinths in which only the souls of the righteous could find their way.

Despite his mistress's innumerable infidelities, Minos never complained. Being loved by the most beautiful woman in Avaris filled him with joy, and he did not see the dangers he ran in sharing her bed.

'That brute of a groom has left me unsatisfied,' she complained. 'Will you console me?'

Her gentle caress of his perfumed skin aroused his desire at once. Not once had their amorous exploits disappointed her. Minos was not like any other man, and knew how to give pleasure with the spontaneity of an adolescent boy.

But after they had made love, she saw that he was troubled.

'Is something wrong?' she asked.

'It's to do with Minoa. Rumour has it that the emperor has decided to destroy the island.'

Windswept curled up against him, moulding her body to his. 'Don't worry, my love. Jannas hasn't yet finished cleansing the islands and eradicating support for Minoan independence. When he has finished, the Great Island will find itself alone again and with no choice but to give absolute obedience to Apophis. Of course, it will have to increase the quantities of tributes it pays, because it didn't do enough to help Jannas, but that will be only a minor inconvenience.'

'Then Minoa will be spared?'

'The emperor will turn it into a submissive and devoted province.'

'Do you think I'll be able to go home one day?'

'On two conditions: that I persuade the emperor your work is finished, and that I go with you.'

The painter's blue eyes were like a child's. 'Those are just dreams, aren't they?'

Windswept ran her fingers tenderly through his curly hair. 'It will take time to turn them into reality, but don't give up hope.'

'You and I, in Minoa . . . Nothing could be more wonderful.'

'Make love to me again, Minos. And never stop.'

## 16

The year was drawing to a close, and Thebes was celebrating its new pharaoh, the completion of a large consignment of new weapons, and the launch of some new war-boats. Ahhotep's reputation was such that the inhabitants of Thebes, Kebet, Edfu and Dendera no longer cast doubt on her beliefs. Yes, victory really was possible – hadn't there been several miracles already? And, since a pharaoh now reigned, the gods would come to his aid.

The army of liberation was about to embark for the North, strengthened by many young soldiers who had enlisted over the last few months. After so many months of intensive training, the troops had only one wish: to leave for the front and kill some Hyksos.

'I'm going too,' little Ahmose informed his mother, as they watched weapons and stores being loaded aboard the war-fleet.

'You're only seven,' Ahhotep reminded him, 'and that's too young to fight.'

'My brother is Pharaoh, and he needs me. If I don't help him, he'll lose the war. I know how to handle the wooden sword.'

'And the small bow, too, I know – I've seen you. But surely a good strategist understands the importance of having a strong rear base? While your brother is at the front, you will watch over Thebes.'

Ahmose did not take these words lightly. 'Does that mean preparing the second wave of attack and making all the necessary equipment?'

'Exactly.'

The boy's face grew intensely serious. 'And I would be responsible for all that?'

'Yes, with me, if you think you can do it.'

'I can, Mother.'

Heray came hurrying up to them and said, 'I must speak with you alone, Majesty.'

Ahhotep entrusted Ahmose to the officer in charge of his weapons training. She hoped Heray was going to say he had identified and arrested the spy responsible for Seqen's death, but he broached an entirely different subject.

'We must postpone the embarkation, Majesty.'

'Whatever for?'

'Some of our best captains and many of the oarsmen are ill.'

'Is there an epidemic of something?'

'I don't think so, because they're suffering from different illnesses. But all the men are seriously ill.'

There was a sudden violent gust of wind, which nearly blew the queen's headdress off.

'What a disgusting smell,' she said. 'It's just like the stink of rotting corpses.'

Fear tightened Heray's throat. 'It's a plague sent by the emissaries of Sekhmet, who is enraged with humanity and determined to destroy it.'

'That ought not to happen except in the five last days of the year,' Ahhotep reminded him, 'during that terrible period when the old time is dead and the new has not yet taken form. There's still more than a week to go before the period of danger.'

'Then it must be a curse sent by Apophis,' said Heray. 'It makes it impossible for us to strike north.'

The plague wind caused panic. How, asked townspeople and soldiers alike, could they protect themselves against the appalling stench, except by shutting themselves away in their houses and barracks, or huddling in the holds of the ships?'

'Summon all the officers,' Ahhotep ordered Heray. 'Tell them to assmble their men and put an immediate end to this disorder. Next, incense is to be burnt in every building.'

'We haven't very much, Majesty. We'll soon run out.'

'Send a boat to Edfu to fetch a large quantity of terebinth resin, and ensure that the infirmary is constantly purified with its smoke.'

Kamose came ashore from the flagship, looking anxious. 'Shouldn't we move everyone out of the base, Mother?'

'It would be no use – this wind will blow over the whole of the Theban province. The emperor is trying to suffocate us.'

It was Teti the Small who reminded them of the first precaution to take when Sekhmet showed her anger like this: the left eye must be closed, to prevent the disease-causing air from entering the body, and the navel must be carefully cleaned, because that was the point of exit.

For both soldiers and civilians, there was one vital instruction: strict cleanliness. Even Long-Ears and Laughter were washed and brushed, in order to prevent the stench entering their flesh. But the evil wind doubled in strength during the last five days of the year, and despite constant care several people died.

If the emperor's curse triumphed, there would be no further rebirth of the light, no more procession of priests and priestesses carrying the ritual objects up to the temple roof to celebrate their union with the sun-disc, no more rites bringing the statues to life, and the army of liberation would die with the dying year.

Kamose and Ahhotep were everywhere, urging everyone not to give up hope but to fight the plague. Little Ahmose's courage greatly impressed everyone. Sprinkling himself with a scented essence at regular intervals, he calmed those who, in his opinion, were panicking needlessly.

On the fifth day, the wind became even stronger, and the number of deaths rose.

According to the ancient texts, there were only two remedies left. The first was to write 'These curses will not attack us' on a strip of fine linen, then tie twelve knots in the cloth, offer it bread and beer, and apply it to one's throat. The second was to light as many torches as possible, in order to illuminate the darkness.

During this terrible ordeal, which threatened to put an end to his reign almost before it had begun, Kamose was able to master his fears and behaved with a composure worthy of a mature man. It was the pharaoh himself who lit most of the torches, watched by the Afghan and Moustache.

'That lad has real spirit,' said the Afghan admiringly. 'In my country, he would be considered worthy to fight.'

'A barbarian like you has no idea of what a pharaoh can be.'

'You've known a lot of pharaohs, have you?'

'With Seqen and Kamose, at least two. Instead of criticizing, why can't you admire what's being done?'

'If this damned wind doesn't drop, there'll soon be no one left to admire.'

'You're too much of a sceptic, Afghan. How can you imagine for a second that a true pharaoh could be struck down by adversity?'

The smoke from the torches rose up and attacked the plague-ridden air. The sky was transformed into an immense battlefield, deserted by the birds. Tortured spirals were drawn there, shot through with the immense red arrows fired by Sekhmet's emissaries.

Ahmose held his mother's hand tightly. 'You aren't afraid, are you?' he asked.

'Of course I am, but what does that matter? We have acted in accordance with the rites and used all our weapons. Now it is for the moon-god to decide. Up there, he fights a never-ending war, and sometimes he seems to be on the point of death, but he always succeeds in regaining the upper hand.'

'Do you think he'll succeed again?'

'I am absolutely certain of it.'

Ahmose never doubted his mother's word. And when the silver disc of the full moon pierced the clouds, he knew that that word was the truth.

As the first dawn of the new year broke, the wind dropped at last and the plague ebbed away. Exhausted, the Thebans fell into one another's arms, aware that they had escaped from mortal danger. Many dived into the Nile to purify themselves of the last traces of sickness; others prepared a celebratory meal.

Young Laughter barked with joy and Long-Ears shook his long ears, while Ahmose fell asleep in the queen's arms.

## 17

The emperor thoroughly enjoyed his meal of a leg of goose cooked in sauce. The report Khamudi had just given him, based on information provided by the spy in Thebes, contained much to rejoice about. Many enemy soldiers had died of the plague, and the morale of Ahhotep's army was shattered. Only the troops at Qis still had to be isolated, made vulnerable to a determined attack.

Apophis had devised a new, rather entertaining plan which would allow him to swell the coffers of Avaris still further. Wholeheartedly enthusiastic about this plan, Khamudi had been instructed to put the emperor's thoughts into practice, on the one hand by sending out hundreds of scarabs into Middle Egypt, and on the other by sending officials charged with spreading the good news.

The stinking cloud had killed many animals and depopulated vast areas of farmland. People were so afraid that the peasants were cowering in their reed huts beside the fields, as if that pathetic shelter could protect them from the arrows of Sekhmet's invisible minions.

Many people, in the first days of the new year, all but despaired as they tried to resume their normal lives. But not Big-Feet. He was one of those who cared more about their milch-cows than about themselves. Plague wind or not, he had gone on feeding and milking his animals, while at the same time grumbling about the poor quality of the grass.

When the first boat arrived, Big-Feet did not run away. He had to defend his cows, even against a Hyksos regiment.

A civilian came towards him. 'I am one of the officials in charge of the floodplains and pastures of the Delta,' he said in a friendly manner. 'Up there, in the North, thanks to Apophis's magic, we haven't suffered any evil winds.'

'That's all very for you,' grunted Big-Feet.

'We benefit from the emperor's generosity, which extends to all his subjects, including you.'

'Oh yes? How?'

'Dozens of boats will take your animals and the other herds – there's plenty of fodder aboard – up north to the area around Avaris. They'll be well fed there, and will soon get their health back. Then you can come home again.'

This ancient practice had been abandoned since the beginning of the Hyksos occupation. To see it revived was something of a cause for celebration. But there was one serious problem.

'How much is this going to cost me?'

'Nothing at all, my friend – the emperor's only concern is the well-being of his people. I tell you, the Delta pastures are incredibly lush, and its stables are well-built and welcoming. Go and tell your village about it, and tell them that our boats are here. But tell them to hurry. Although the Hyksos have sent a huge fleet, there may not be room for everyone.'

After long, noisy discussions, most people opted to go. The emperor's generosity was an unexpected windfall – those who accused the Hyksos of cruelty were wrong. True, the occupation had had its difficult periods, but this decision marked a major turning-point. Apophis was behaving like a true pharaoh, concerned for the welfare of his people. He had realized that this was the only policy that would win the Egyptians' trust.

So the villagers herded their half-starved cows and oxen towards the boats, forgetting that, not far away, the rebels still held the front at Qis. A few peasants regretted not being able to provide them with food any more, but the Thebans had surely been wrong to stand up against their true sovereign. In any case, cow-herds and farmers were not soldiers.

Like his companions, Big-Feet found the journey very agreeable. They had all the beer, bread and dried fish they wanted, and they were able to enjoy long rests, something they were not used to. The further north they travelled, the more luxuriant the countryside became. The cultivated areas grew wider, and there were more and more waterways. It was a veritable paradise for cow-men and their herds.

At last they arrived.

Big-Feet stroked his cows, which had coped well with the long journey. 'Come along, my beauties, you're going to have a lovely time.'

A heavy hand landed on his shoulder, and a black-helmeted Hyksos officer said harshly, 'You, peasant, come with me.'

'I'm not leaving my cows.'

'*Your* cows? That's rubbish. Don't tell me you didn't realize . . . ? These animals are on a boat belonging to the emperor, so they belong to him, too.'

'What are you talking about? They're just going to graze here for a while, and then I'm taking them back home.'

The officer laughed loudly. 'That's the funniest thing I've heard in all my life! Now, stop talking, fellow, and follow me – now.'

'I'm a cow-herd, and I'm not leaving my cows.'

The Hyksos slapped him hard across the face.

Although peaceable by nature, Big-Feet hated being hit. He punched the Hyksos, and knocked him out.

The officer's men were enraged, and reacted at once. The odds were one against ten, and Big-Feet's resistance didn't last long. His head bloody, his wrists shackled, he was chained to another peasant and forced to join a never-ending procession of prisoners.

'Where are we being taken?' he asked his companion in misfortune.

'I don't know anything.'

'My cows ... What will become of them? And the people from my village?'

'The Hyksos killed anyone who tried to run away. The others are chained up, like us.'

A tall woman with enormous hands hailed them. 'You're good sturdy fellows,' exclaimed the lady Aberia. 'That's much better. The journey will be more entertaining. Usually I have too many old men, females and city-dwellers. They're used to a soft life and don't last the distance. You aren't afraid of the sun or the dust or hard work, I'm sure. Whatever you do, don't disappoint me.'

Still thinking of his cows, and the fact that he was the only person who could milk them properly, Big-Feet walked on. Beside the track he saw the corpses of some old women and children.

'I'm thirsty,' said his companion.

'We'll ask them for water. They can't refuse.'

Big-Feet hailed two soldiers who were passing in a chariot drawn by two horses. 'We need water.'

'You'll get it when we stop, all except those who are insolent – like you.'

The chariot moved back up the column, in a cloud of dust.

'I thought the emperor was a good, just man,' confessed Big-Feet, 'because he was looking after my animals. Why has he done this? We haven't done him any harm.'

'He wants to remove all the Egyptians from Egypt and replace them with Hyksos – only Hyksos. Being Egyptian is a crime now.'

Big-Feet still did not understand, but he kept on walking, even when his companion died of thirst.

When they reached the marshes that surrounded Sharuhen, he flung himself into the reeds and drank muddy water. A Hyksos guard hauled him up by his hair and clubbed him, and he had not the strength to fight back.

The guard took off the chains attaching Big-Feet to the corpse he had dragged for so long, then pushed him into a large enclosed courtyard, watched over by archers posted on wooden towers.

The first person he saw there was a young, naked girl with mad eyes, her body covered with sores. She threw herself repeatedly against a stake and managed to break her skull.

Sitting on a mound of filth, an old man held his wife's hand, not noticing that she had stopped breathing. Exhausted men with empty eyes walked past one another without exchanging a single word. Others were digging in the waterlogged earth for any kind of food.

Who could have dreamt up and imposed such atrocities, if not the Emperor of Darkness, that liar who had not hesitated to trick simple peasants? Big-Feet would never forgive him for stealing his cows.

'Cow-herd, get down on your face.'

A guard set his foot on the prisoner's neck, while another branded a number on his buttock with a red-hot bronze rod. The surviving inmates of Sharuhen did not turn a hair as Big-Feet, prisoner number 1790, screamed in pain.

## 18

'I can do that, too,' Ahmose told Kamose. 'I can hit the centre of a target.'

'I have the feeling you're boasting a little bit.'

'Try me!'

'All right.'

Kamose took Ahmose to an archery practice area reserved for beginners. It was surrounded by palisades, so that stray arrows would not injure anyone.

'Do you draw your bow yourself?' asked Kamose.

'Of course!'

'I'll check that the target is fixed firmly in place.'

There was complete understanding between the brothers. The king regretted that Ahmose was too young to fight at his side, but he knew that, if the worst happened, his brother would take up his sword.

Just as Kamose reached the target, he heard a familiar whistling sound.

'Get down, quickly!' yelled Ahmose at the top of his voice.

'It isn't serious,' said Teti. 'The arrow only grazed your neck. And with honey compresses there won't even be a scar.'

'You saved my life,' Kamose told Ahmose, who was still shaking.

'Did you see who fired?' Ahhotep asked him.

'No,' said the child. 'I ran straight to Kamose and didn't think to look around. When I saw blood on his neck I was afraid – so afraid!'

'Come and wash,' his grandmother ordered. 'You really don't look like a prince.' The two of them left the infirmary.

'There's a spy in the camp,' said Ahhotep, 'and he tried to kill you.'

'I don't think so, Mother. Despite Ahmose's warning, I didn't have time to duck. If the archer had really wanted to kill me, he wouldn't have missed. This wound is a warning: either I content myself with ruling Thebes or else I shall die.'

Ahhotep considered his words. 'In other words, your future depends on the outcome of today's council of war.'

Queen Ahhotep, Pharaoh Kamose, Heray, Qaris, the generals and principal government scribes had assembled in the twin-pillared hall of the palace at the military camp. They were all aware that they were participating in a momentous decision, and the atmosphere was tense.

'The current situation is a stalemate,' said the pharaoh. 'The little kingdom of Thebes may have its freedom, but it's an illusory freedom because we're imprisoned by the Hyksos tyrant in the north and the Nubian tyrant in the south. We have no access to caravan or mining routes, and our isolation is becoming more and more intolerable, and even dangerous. The Pharaoh of Egypt wears only the White Crown. He cannot allow the Emperor of Darkness to usurp his right to wear the Red Crown.'

'Indeed, Majesty, indeed,' agreed the oldest general, 'but, all the same, is it wise to hurl ourselves into an all-out war which we will undoubtedly lose?'

'How can we know that unless we try?' asked a scribe called Neshi, a thin, bald man with piecing eyes.

The general, who cordially disliked the scholar, stiffened and retorted, 'In his own sphere, Neshi the Archivist's skills are indisputable, but I do not think he is qualified to suggest military tactics. Unless I am much mistaken, he is only here because of the need to take notes and produce a report.'

Kamose intervened. 'If I understand you correctly, General, you are in favour of maintaining the current situation.'

'To be absolutely frank, Majesty, I believe that is the best solution. I am well aware that the Hyksos are occupying a large part of our country, but is that not a reality we shall eventually have to accept? The enemy army is at least ten times more powerful than our own: it would be madness to attack it. We should be content with what Queen Ahhotep's courage has brought us. Thebes is free, and we can live here in peace. Why ask for more and destroy this fragile balance?'

'So fragile that it is no balance at all,' countered Neshi. 'Stagnation leads to death: that is what Queen Ahhotep has taught us. In believing we are safe, we make ourselves easy prey for the emperor.'

The general grew angrier. 'This is intolerable, Majesty. Neshi ought to hold his tongue.'

'It is I who give the orders, General,' said Kamose coldly, 'and I say that each member of this council may speak his mind.'

The soldier moderated his tone a little, but went on trying to persuade the king. 'Do you realize, Majesty, that the Hyksos are not opposed to peace? They have just given us a shining example of their good will by allowing livestock belonging to peasants from Middle Egypt to graze in the floodplains of the Delta. And that isn't all: they have also given grain to our pig-farmers. Hasn't the time come to lay down our arms and start negotiating about trade?'

'How can you believe such lies?' said Neshi furiously. 'The Hyksos are past masters at spreading false information, and people who let themselves be taken in by it always come to a bad end. Apophis will never agree to yield a single cubit of his empire. The peasants who go to the Delta will be made slaves, and their animals will be confiscated.'

'This really is too much!' exclaimed the general. 'On the basis of what information does this scribe dare contradict me?'

'Neshi is right,' confirmed Qaris. 'The Hyksos have indeed enslaved the peasants they pretended to be helping.'

Another senior officer leapt to the aid of his colleague. 'If the Hyksos are indeed still ruthless and unified, Majesty, surely that is another reason not to provoke them. It is clear that the emperor accepts the present situation, because he is allowing our northern border to exist at Qis. Let us take advantage of his indulgence and keep what we have gained.'

Ahhotep rose to her feet and gazed sternly at the two generals. 'Do you believe that Pharaoh Seqen died merely to enlarge the Theban enclave, and that he would be content with this gain? The whole of Egypt must be liberated, not just part of it. Anyone who forgets that sacred duty is unworthy to serve under Pharaoh Kamose.'

'You are no longer members of my war council,' the king informed the two officers. 'But I trust you will prove yourselves worthy on the field of battle, at the head of your regiments.'

The two generals withdrew sheepishly from the audience chamber.

The king turned to Neshi. 'You are hereby appointed Bearer of the Royal Seal and Overseer of the Treasury. I also charge you with stewardship of the army: ensure that every man is well armed and properly fed.

Neshi rose and bowed deeply to Pharaoh. When he was seated again, he said, 'Although our troops are ready to leave, Majesty, my first advice to you is to wait.'

Kamose was surprised. 'Surely you don't agree that it would be better to negotiate with Apophis?'

'Absolutely not, since the empire of darkness will not change. But you told me to ensure that our soldiers are properly fed, and if we wage war at this time of year there is a risk that we shall run out of food. Late spring would be better, because by then the harvest will be in.'

Heray and Qaris agreed.

'Before launching the offensive, Majesty,' added Neshi, 'it would be a good idea to bring home some of the soldiers from the front and replace them with fresh men. Between now and the offensive, strengthening the front should be our main priority.'

Kamose was convinced his new adviser was right. 'Then that is what we shall do.'

'I believe we should consider another course of action,' said Ahhotep.

The king and his council looked at her attentively.

'Engaging all our forces on the northern front would carry a risk we are too apt to forget: an attack from the Nubians, who would dearly like to capture Thebes. Apophis is waiting for us at Qis, not at Elephantine or in Nubia. The real priority is to reconquer the southern part of our country and to make the Nubians realize that if they attack they will be heavily defeated. For that reason, when spring comes the major part of our army will march not north but south.'

# 19

Yima, Khamudi's wife, was a fat woman with dyed blond hair, who considered herself a ravishing beauty. Knowing how possessive her husband was, she was careful not to be too blatant about taking lovers, and when she tired of her fleeting conquests she instantly got rid of them with the aid of her confidante, Aberia, who was only too happy to kill Egyptian slaves. Aberia could strangle a strong man with one hand, and every day she exercised to strengthen her muscles and amused herself by killing any Hyksos soldiers who dared defy her.

Yima lived in perfect happiness with Khamudi. She could enjoy his fortune, torture as many servants as she liked, and satisfy her perverted urges in the company of a husband who was as depraved as herself. But a lurking shadow threatened this happiness: Tany, the 'empress', always treated her with contempt.

Perhaps Aberia would be able to help her, thought Yima. So she went to the barracks where Aberia lived. She found her wolfing a huge plateful of red meat and washing it down with wine.

'Would you like to to share my meal?' asked Aberia.

'Oh, no; thank you,' replied Yima. 'I'm watching my weight at the moment.'

'Then stop eating pastries. They're food for little girls, anyway.'

'I am worried, very worried.'

'Is someone upsetting you, my poor darling?'

'Yes, but not someone you can get rid of for me.'

'Can't I? Who can it possibly be?' Intrigued, Aberia stopped chewing. 'Tell me the answer to this puzzle.'

'It's Tany – I think she hates me.'

Aberia burst out laughing. 'Tany's too ugly to have any feelings!'

'Don't joke. I really am upset. I don't understand why she dislikes me so much, and I don't know what she has against me. Do you know?'

'I haven't the faintest idea, my poor dear – well, actually, yes, I have. That little barrel contains nothing but venom. She hates absolutely everyone: the only person she loves is herself. She has no intention of letting anyone else share the benefits of being Apophis's woman, so she drives away anyone who might get a little too close to him.'

'But I wouldn't do that, I promise!' protested Yima.

'Your reputation suggests otherwise, my little one. But I believe I can solve the problem for you.'

'Really? How?'

'Myself, I have no taste for men. They're insipid and they tire too quickly. Women, on the other hand . . . what a delight! If the empress thinks you, too, love women, you'll no longer be in danger.'

Yima looked like a frightened child. 'What you're asking of me . . . I'd never dare, I—'

'Yes, you would. In fact, being so perverse, you'll enjoy it, and afterwards you won't be able to get enough of it. Come, let's go to my bedchamber. It's even better after a good meal.'

'But the soldiers will know, and—'

'That's exactly what we want, little one. We want our liaison to be notorious. Who would ever dare lay a finger on my darling?'

A young Egyptian woman, the daughter of a scribe who had been deported, was massaging Khamudi's toes, one of the parts of his body he considered perfect. After he had tried her out, she would end up either in the harem or in Sharuhen, depending on his whim of the moment.

Yima was lying on a comfortable mat beside her husband, her face smeared with regenerative clay.

'You've done the right thing,' he told her. 'The emperor thinks a lot of Aberia, and your being on good terms with her will be very useful for both of us. The more deportations there are, the more important Aberia becomes. As soon as she returns from Sharuhen, the emperor will appoint her head of the guards.'

'Has he decided to kill all the Egyptians?'

'If we want to govern this country in our own way, it's the only answer. At the moment we still need them as slaves, but foreigners brought up in the Hyksos ways will gradually replace them.'

'What a wonderful world the emperor is creating for us,' said Yima. 'A single way of thinking, a single direction, a single policy, a single dominant class wielding all the power, and faithful subjects who will obey because the law of Apophis is the law of Apophis! But when is he going to get rid of the Theban troublemakers?'

'He wishes to leave that pleasure to Jannas, and I think he is right. What splendid slaughter there will be! The Thebans are so afraid that they no longer even dare leave their rear camp. At the front, they will eventually tear each other to pieces. Either they will surrender, and

Aberia will have many, many prisoners to transport, or else Jannas will have a good many heads to cut off. That's what happens to fools who put their trust in a woman like Ahhotep.'

The pirate captain at last got his breath back. When Jannas's ship had rammed his own, he had thought he was hallucinating: the Hyksos couldn't possibly be faster and more cunning than he was.

With incredible stubbornness, the commander had grimly pursued each last one of the Mycenaean, Cyprian and Minoan pirates who, with Minoa's tacit support, were attacking the emperor's trading-fleet. They had hoped to sink so many Hyksos ships that Jannas would be forced to retreat, but he was a formidable sailor and had had an answer to every single one of his adversaries' tricks: little by little, they had become hunted animals.

They had been sure they would find refuge in the Mycenaean islands – only to be disillusioned again. Even there, Jannas pursued them without falling into any of their many ambushes. Patient and meticulous, he isolated each enemy boat before capturing it with his more heavily armed sailors.

The captain and ten of his pirates were good swimmers, and reached the coast of Thera. The island was dominated by a volcano, but its eruptions did not frighten them. They would hide their booty there and then withdraw, their fortunes made.

'They're following us, Captain,' said a pirate.

Five boats full of Hyksos archers were heading for the island.

'We'll climb up higher,' said the captain. 'They won't dare follow.'

The smoking mountain did indeed make a strong impression on Jannas's men.

'Need we really bother with these miserable fugitives, Commander?' asked one officer.

'Every task must be fully completed. The emperor has ordered us to exterminate the pirates, and exterminate them we shall. If we don't, this handful of rebels will only get another ship and begin all over again.'

'Isn't this mountain . . . dangerous?'

'Not as dangerous as my sword,' replied Jannas menacingly.

The officer did not press the point. One more word, and he would be dead.

Slowly, the Hyksos climbed the slopes of the volcano.

'They're coming after us,' warned one of the pirates. 'We must go faster.'

As soon as they were within range, the Hyksos archers felled almost all the pirates. But, hampered by the plumes of smoke, they missed the captain, who skirted the edge of the crater, hoping to run down the opposite side and so escape his pursuers.

An arrow plunged into his thigh. Despite the pain, he dragged himself onwards across the rocks until a Hyksos caught him and kicked him to the ground.

'Don't kill him yet,' ordered Jannas. He had just discovered a strange lake. It contained not water but bright-red fire, which constantly boiled and bubbled.

'Listen to me,' begged the pirate. 'I've got a lot of treasure hidden up here in a cave.'

'Where?'

'I'll tell you if you spare my life.'

'Why not?'

'Do you give me your word?'

'Take your chance, pirate. And don't risk annoying me any more.'

'It's halfway up this slope, opposite a rock with a circle drawn on it. You will see, it's a real hoard! Thanks to me, you'll be a rich man.'

'It is the Hyksos emperor whose coffers you will fill. I'm here only to destroy the bandits who've been attacking us.'

'And you'll spare my life?'

'A promise is a promise,' said Jannas. 'But before that, a quick bath will do you the world of good. You're dirty and you stink.'

'A bath? But . . .'

'That red lake looks suitable.'

'No!' howled the pirate. No! It's the mouth of hell!'

'Get him out of my sight,' ordered the commander.

Four Hyksos picked up the wounded man and threw him into the lake of molten lava.

## 20

The military camp at Thebes was buzzing with activity. After a mild winter, during which many new boats had been built, Neshi presented his report to Pharaoh Kamose and Queen Ahhotep.

'Food supplies have been sent to the front, and it has been reinforced with eager young recruits,' he said. 'The experienced soldiers await your order to embark.'

'In your opinion, how good is the troops' morale?' asked Ahhotep.

Neshi hesitated. 'Our men are brave and determined, certainly, but . . .'

'But they are afraid of the Nubians, aren't they?'

'Indeed, Majesty. The Nubians' reputation for ferocity frightens more than a few of our men. The generals and I have tried to explain that we now have effective weapons and that our combat training is excellent, but we are a long way from banishing their fears.'

'Anyone guilty of cowardice will be executed in front of his comrades,' decreed Kamose.

'There may be other ways of calming this ancestral and understandable fear,' suggested the queen.

Goose-livers stuffed with figs, roast duck, grilled sides of beef, puréed onions, lentils and courgettes, strong celebration beer of a beautiful amber hue, a thousand and one honey-cakes: these were among the elaborate dishes the palace had prepared for the army of liberation.

In addition, each soldier had received two comfortable new mats, and ointments based on terebinth resin to relax the muscles, maintain the proper bodily energies and repel insects.

'The queen is a mother to us,' declared Moustache through a mouthful of fresh bread spread with goose-liver. 'I've never eaten so well in my life.'

'When your country reaches heights like these,' admitted the Afghan, 'I almost forget my own.'

A man at the next table, a veteran soldier, flung away the stripped carcass of a duck. 'Instead of marvelling like stupid children, you'd do better to think. This is the last good meal you'll ever eat. On the boats you'll have to make do with rations, and then you'll be killed by the Nubians.'

'Well, I have no intention of dying,' retorted the Afghan.

'You ignorant fool, it's obvious you don't know where you're going.'

'And you do?'

'I've never set foot in Nubia, it's true, but no one can beat those tall black soldiers – they're ten times stronger than we are.'

'Yet they don't dare attack the Hyksos,' pointed out Moustache.

The footsoldier was silenced, but only for a moment. 'They will one day. The Nubians were born to fight, not like us. Not a single Egyptian soldier will come back alive from this expedition.'

'If you're so sure of that, resign and go home,' advised the Afghan. 'A man who's beaten before he even sets off is as good as dead.'

'Are you accusing me of cowardice, foreigner?'

'I'm telling you to think clearly, that's all.'

'No, you aren't. You're trying to make me look a fool!'

Moustache was about to intervene when silence fell.

Queen Ahhotep began to speak. 'The ordeal we are all about to undergo is likely to be very dangerous, for we shall face formidable enemies. Before we even encounter the Nubians, who are rightly feared as warriors, we must first capture one of the Hyksos' largest fortresses, Per-Hathor. If the garrison manages to alert the Nubians, we shall have lost our chance of defeating them, which is why our first objective is to take Per-Hathor. The Hyksos occupy our country, steal its wealth and make our people their slaves. The time has come to make them realize that Egypt will never submit to tyranny. The will to be free is our finest weapon. Eat and drink well, and may courage fill your hearts!'

The soldier helped himself to another duck and gulped down another cup of strong beer. The queen's speech had reassured him. Capturing Per-Hathor was impossible, so the army would simply make a very brief excursion south and then come home, abandoning all thoughts of Nubia.

Ahhotep kissed her mother's hand; Teti had been confined to bed for several days.

'Mother, I shan't leave with Kamose, I shall stay with you.'

'No,' said Teti. 'Your place is beside the king, your son. He is young and inexperienced. Without you, he might make fatal mistakes.'

'Without you, my beloved mother, our adventure could never have become reality. Now, when you are ill, my duty is to care for you.'

'An old woman must not prevent you leading your troops to victory, Ahhotep. Leave me to face this trial alone, and think only of the future.'

'A daughter who abandons her mother is unworthy to be queen.'

Teti smiled. 'I'm beginning to wonder which of us is the more stubborn. Help me up.'

'The doctors say you must rest.'

'You have entrusted me with a task, and I shall carry it out. Thebes must be governed in your absence, and every single man in the province mobilized in the event of a Hyksos attack. So my death will have to wait – at least until you return.'

Teti left her bedchamber. She was so frail that Ahhotep was sure she would be unable even to stand up for very long, but the old lady welcomed the warmth of the sun and summoned her household.

'Lying in bed is doing me no good,' she said. 'Go to Per-Hathor with a quiet heart, Ahhotep. Ahmose will help me, won't he?'

Moustache attached handles firmly to the knives and daggers, using resin; mixed with powdered limestone, it made an excellent adhesive. The Afghan was sharpening the blades and checking the arrowheads.

Qaris was rushing all over the place, anxious to leave nothing to chance. He spoke with each captain, visited each ship, and inspected each storage-chest and each jar. It was the eve of their departure for the south, and no detail must be neglected.

Heray, however, had other things on his mind.

'Majesty,' he confessed to Ahhotep, 'my investigation has had no results. No one saw the archer who fired at the king. Of course, I have doubled the size of his personal bodyguard and am imposing even stricter security measures.'

'My son thinks it was merely an attempt at intimidation.'

'Whether he is right or wrong, the important thing is to ensure his safety. If the Hyksos spy remains in Thebes, the king will be in no danger, at least for the moment. On the other hand, if the spy is a member of the expeditionary force, his only thought will be to make another attempt on the king's life.'

'Don't worry, Heray. I'll watch over the pharaoh.'

Long-Ears was the first to board the flagship, where he had been allocated a new mat, in the shade of an awning, which he would share with Young Laughter. Then came a long procession, led by King Kamose proudly bearing the Sword of Amon.

The Afghan began to beat a strong, regular rhythm on a strange instrument.

Moustache had never seen anything like it before. 'What's that?' he asked. 'Did you make it yourself?'

'It's a drum. Its music will give the men courage – you'll see.'

The Afghan was right. The stirring rhythm calmed many fears, especially among the youngest soldiers.

After kissing little Ahmose and telling him to help his grandmother, Ahhotep gazed upon her brave men, all of them ready to sacrifice their lives to liberate Egypt. Many would not return from this journey, and she would be responsible for their deaths.

The Wife of God thought of her dead husband, whose absence weighed a little more heavily upon her with each day that passed. In uttering the 'words of glorification' that had brought his name and his spirit to life, the queen had created an energy which was essential if she was to pursue her mad adventure. Seqen was there, close beside her, giving her his strength.

Up in the sky, the moon began to shine.

## 21

'By all the gods!' exclaimed Moustache. 'How beautiful my country is!'

'There is some truth in what you say,' acknowledged the Afghan. 'Your land may not have high, snow-covered mountains, but it does have charm.'

'What is snow?'

'Water from the sky, which hardens as it falls to earth and turns a beautiful pure white.'

'You mean . . . cold water?'

'Very cold. It burns your hands when you touch it.'

'How horrible. Put that ugly thought out of your mind and look at the Nile and its green banks instead.'

On board the flagship, which had just set off for the south, the two men were experiencing a moment of perfect happiness. There was no more war, no more danger, no more Hyksos, simply a boat gliding along the river, while ibis and pelicans soared overhead.

In the bows, a tall, wiry man was sounding the depth of the water with a long forked stick. His role was vital: he decided, according to the depth, how the boat should be handled.

'What is your name?' Ahhotep asked him.

'Moon, Majesty.'

'Moon? Then you and I are protected by the same god.'

'If you only knew, Majesty, how I have longed for this. I was afraid I would die before I could fight the Hyksos and their allies. Thanks to you, my life has finally gained meaning. I swear to you that I shall guide this ship safely to its destination.'

The young helmsman's open smile lifted the queen's heart. 'For the moment, Moon, we shall pause in our journey.'

Their sails furled, the boats of the war-fleet hove to in perfect order.

While the soldiers were eating, Ahhotep and Kamose gathered together the men who had volunteered for the attack on Per-Hathor.

'We have nearly reached the fortress,' said the queen, 'and their lookouts must not see our boats.'

'Faced with such a massive attack,' said an officer, 'they might surrender.'

'I have seen the fortress,' Ahhotep told him, 'and it looks impregnable. Besides, the Hyksos are far more afraid of the emperor than of an Egyptian fleet. Per-Hathor is the gateway to Upper Egypt.'

'What if we just sailed past it as quickly as possible?'

'Their archers would shoot fire-arrows, and most of our boats would be set alight. The Nubian and Hyksos troops at Elephantine would be warned by visual signals and would slaughter our men, and then they'd go on to destroy Thebes. If we are to be able to use the Nile, it is vital that we capture Per-Hathor and do not give its garrison time to ask for help. Do not forget that from the tops of the towers lookouts can see further than a day's march to the south.'

'In other words,' concluded the king, 'we can't attack using our footsoldiers, and we can't lay siege to the fortress. What other option is there?'

'Before taking a decision,' said Ahhotep, 'we must send scouts to observe Per-Hathor.'

'I shall take ten men and do it myself,' said Kamose.

'No, you must remain here to lead our troops. I shall undertake this mission.'

'Mother, it's much too dangerous.'

'The Afghan and I are used to this kind of expedition,' said Moustache. 'If Her Majesty will agree to have us at her side, she will be safe.'

'Then we shall set off at once,' decided Ahhotep.

'I must admit, it's very strongly built and damnably well positioned,' said Moustache grudgingly.

Lying flat in the long grass, the queen and her two companions gazed at Per-Hathor. Thick walls, square towers, ramparts, a vast gateway, protective ditches: the monstrous fort looked invincible.

'You're always an optimist,' said Moustache to the Afghan. 'What would you do?'

'This time, I don't feel optimistic.'

The morale of the two rebels had reached a low ebb, but Ahhotep did not despair. She told them, 'Watch closely. There must be a weak point somewhere.'

Ahhotep had first seen Per-Hathor when she and Seqen had stumbled on it; they had almost been caught by soldiers foraging for food. This time, too, Hyksos soldiers emerged from the fortress to patrol the area, and Ahhotep would again have been caught unawares if the Afghan and Moustache, who were experienced fighters, had not warned her to take cover. The patrol passed very close to the trio, but did not see them.

'Killing them would serve no purpose,' said the Afghan.

'We could get inside when they open the great gate a little way,' suggested Moustache.

'A few of our men might get beyond the outer wall,' replied the queen, 'but they would be massacred.'

A boat appeared, sailing up from the south. As soon as it docked, Hyksos soldiers surrounded the Egyptian slaves who began to unload it, struggling under their heavy loads. One slave stumbled on the gangplank and dropped the jar he was carrying. It shattered on the quayside, and a great lake of beer spilt out.

A soldier plunged his spear into the neck of the clumsy slave, who made no attempt to defend himself or run away. The murderer kicked the man's corpse into the Nile.

Ahhotep tried to leap forward, but the Afghan's strong arms held her where she was.

'With all due respect, Majesty, don't try to do anything. Moustache and I have seen many things like that. If we'd acted in anger, we'd be dead.'

The unloading proceeded without further incident, then the boat left again for the south.

'Couldn't we set the fortress on fire?' suggested Moustache.

'It would take a very, very long time for our soldiers to lay enough wood at the foot of the walls,' replied Ahhotep, 'and they'd be shot down by the Hyksos archers. And I'm not certain that fire would do much damage to such strong walls.'

'Per-Hathor really is impregnable,' muttered the Afghan angrily.

'I've never seen you like this before,' commented Moustache.

'Nothing has ever seemed impossible before. But this time . . .'

Night was falling, and the moon-god was beginning to shine with all his brilliance.

'He will give us the solution,' promised the queen. 'We must go on watching.'

Nothing of note happened the following day, just three patrols at the same times as before. The day after that, the supply boat arrived with an even larger cargo and even larger jars.

One of the slaves, a worn-out old man, buckled under the weight and put one knee to the ground. Unable to go on, he laid down his burden and looked straight into the eyes of the Hyksos soldier who slit his throat with his dagger. A youth managed to carry the jar to the fortress.

Watched by the emperor's soldiers, the gate was opened just long enough to allow food and drink to enter the fortress. Then the boat left again, and it was time for the last patrol before dusk.

Night and day, archers were stationed on the tops of the watchtowers. There were so many torches burning that they lit up the whole area around the fortifications, ensuring that there could be no surprise attacks by night.

At dawn, the trio left their hiding-place. Neither Moustache nor the Afghan had come up with any way, not even a risky one, to take Per-Hathor, so they weren't surprised when the queen ordered, 'We must return to the flagship.'

## 22

Jannas, who was of Asiatic origin, always wore a pleated headdress shaped like a mushroom, closely fitted to his pointed head. His appearance was distinctly misleading. Of average height and almost sickly-looking, slow of speech and gesture, he gave the impression of an honest fellow in whom one might readily confide.

In reality, he was a ruthless warlord who, throughout his brilliant career, had carried out the emperor's orders to the letter and without question. Like Apophis, he was convinced that military might was the only key to power and that all those who opposed Hyksos domination must be exterminated.

Wiping out the pirates hiding in the Mycenaean islands had taken him several years, but Jannas never yielded to impatience. All that mattered was ultimate success. And that was precisely what was annoying him: the leader of the pirates could only be from Minoa, and the emperor – for reasons which eluded Jannas – was refusing to destroy it. Tomorrow, thought Jannas, the Minoans would arm other pirates, and they would immediately start attacking Hyksos trading-ships again.

However, there was one last opportunity to inflict on the Great Island punishment from which it would not recover, if it could be shown to be guilty of harbouring criminals. To this end, Jannas's ships had driven the last active pirate boat back towards Minoa, but had not intercepted it. They saw it enter a narrow creek, where the crew disembarked. Jannas's duty was therefore clear.

The Hyksos war-fleet was drawn up ready for a massive assault. This time, Minoa would not escape. Its towns and villages would be burnt, the countryside laid waste, and its wealth would revert to the emperor.

'An envoy is asking to speak with you, sir,' a junior officer told him. 'He has come by small boat, and he's alone and unarmed.'

The Minoan was around fifty years old, and his hair and beard were meticulously groomed. His face bore the marks of anxiety.

Jannas received him on deck, facing the Great Island.

'May I remind you, Commander,' said the envoy, 'that the Minoans are the emperor's faithful subjects?'

'Subjects who shelter and support our enemies! Do you take me for a fool?'

'If you are referring to those pirates, who thought they could hide among us, you are wrong. We have arrested and executed them. Their corpses are at your disposal.'

Jannas sneered. 'I don't believe a word of it. You've simply killed a few peasants to deceive me, while the real culprits dine at your king's table. Without your help, they'd never have eluded me for so long.'

'Commander, I swear to you that you are quite wrong. Minoa is a province of the Hyksos Empire, and I go each year to Avaris to present the emperor with ever-greater tributes. Apophis is our beloved sovereign, whose authority no Minoan would dream of disputing.'

'What fine, diplomatic words – you lie more fluently than a sand-traveller.'

'Commander, I cannot allow you to—'

'I allow myself!' cut in Jannas furiously. 'I have hunted the pirates down, one by one. Before killing them I tortured them, and they talked. All of them said the same thing: they were attacking our ships on behalf of Minoa, to recover the goods given to the emperor. I took many, many statements, and they leave absolutely no doubt of the Great Island's guilt.'

'They lied to try to save their lives – that's obvious! Why should my country have acted so irresponsibly?'

'I've just explained that to you, Envoy. Are you deaf?'

'The emperor must hear me. Let me sail for Avaris.'

'That's out of the question. Minoa is a refuge for pirates and I must destroy it.'

'Do not do that, I beg of you! We will double our tributes.'

'It's too late, Envoy. For once, your tricks are useless. Go back to your island and tell your countrymen to prepare to defend themselves. I don't like winning without meeting at least a little resistance.'

'Is there no argument which could change your mind?'

'Not one.'

Jannas sat in his cabin, brooding. The destruction of Minoa would mark the summit of his career, proving to Apophis that the Hyksos Empire must continue to extend its borders as ruthlessly as ever. During the invasion of Egypt, it was strength and strength alone that had overcome. There had been no question of diplomacy, or concessions to the vanquished.

In believing that they could strike at the empire by using pirates and without suffering the consequences of their crime, the Minoans had made a fatal mistake. Once their army was wiped out, the Great Island would become the starting-point for other conquests.

Conquest: Jannas's life had no other meaning. Winning demanded sacrifices, courage and a sense of strategy. Failure would be worse than death.

From time to time, he wondered about the emperor's attitude. Was Apophis becoming too cautious as he grew older? True, the army was still everywhere in Avaris, but within the palace luxurious living seemed to hold sway. Egypt was a land of magical charms, where one might easily lose the taste for fighting. In Apophis's place, Jannas would have taken up residence in a much less comfortable country, like Syria, so as never to forget that any land not forcibly integrated into the empire remained a potential enemy.

But Jannas reproached himself for criticisms like these. Apophis saw further than he did, and certainly had good reasons for acting as he did. The High Treasurer, however, was definitely a bad influence on the emperor. Jannas loathed Khamudi, who was utterly corrupt, interested in nothing but his own personal gain. But in this matter, too, how could he oppose the will of the emperor, who had made Khamudi his right-hand man?

Jannas stood at the emperor's other hand, and would not allow him to be manipulated by the High Treasurer. Once back in Avaris, he decided, he must take measures to restrict Khamudi's influence, because Khamudi was extremely prompt in killing anyone he thought might become a rival.

The morning was fine, the sea calm. Ideal weather for attacking the Great Island, which was experiencing its last moments of freedom before paying the price for its hypocrisy.

Jannas's second-in-command, who was in charge of coordinating the attack troops, knocked on the cabin door.

'Commander, all the officers are in their fighting positions.'

'Any problems?'

'No, sir. The weapons have been checked, the boats arranged according to your orders.'

Jannas went on deck and looked towards the coast, to which the Hyksos fleet was very close.

'Not one Minoan soldier,' he noted. 'Anyone would think they were leaving the field wide open for us.'

'Might it not be a trap, sir?' asked his second-in-command.

'Of course it might, and for that very reason we're going to use our catapults to set fire to the vegetation. A lot of Minoans will be burnt to a crisp, and the others will run away. Any who try to resist will be killed by our archers. Next, we shall sweep the entire island, with one single instruction: no survivors.'

The men in charge of the catapults were waiting for his signal.

But at that moment something unexpected happened: a fast, light Hyksos boat was spotted, heading towards the flagship.

Curious, Jannas told his men to wait. What did this intruder want?

An officer climbed aboard and handed Jannas a large limestone scarab. 'Commander,' he said, 'new orders from the emperor.'

Jannas read the words engraved on the scarab. Because of a serious uprising in Anatolia, Apophis ordered him to ignore the last few pirates, leave the islands immediately, and sail east at full speed to put down the rebellion.

'I did not think I would find you so easily,' said the officer. 'It's lucky you're so close to Minoa.'

Jannas smiled enigmatically. 'Lucky? I never rely on luck.'

Before giving the signal to leave, he directed a last, furious glare at the Great Island. Still, he thought, there was nothing to lose by waiting.

## 23

The commander of Per-Hathor was a sixty year-old Canaanite who owed everything to the emperor. In his youth, he had burnt many villages in Palestine and the Delta, raped a fine tally of women and slaughtered plenty of old men. Particularly pleased with his services. Apophis had crowned the end of his career by giving him command of this magnificent fortress, the gateway to the south of Egypt.

He was not worried about the Theban rebels. The fact that they had succeeded in massing troops at Qis had intoxicated them, but that derisory achievement would lead nowhere. Unable to make progress to either the north or the south, they would stay trapped in their little enclave, which the emperor could destroy whenever he chose.

The only danger was Nubia. But the chief who had united the tribes to form the kingdom of Kerma was a reasonable man. He knew very well that being the unconditional ally of the Hyksos was much better than defying them.

So all that remained was routine. To prevent the garrison becoming complacent, the commander imposed an iron discipline, with rigorous standards in all military and domestic activities. Per-Hathor was ready at any time to contain an attack, which would inevitably fail, anyway. And if a Theban boat appeared, a rain of fire-arrows would send it to the bottom.

The only delicate operations were the morning and afternoon patrols, which might encounter a raiding-party. But Queen Ahhotep had never dared send one, knowing only too well that it had no chance of success. Hyksos archers atop the towers kept permanent watch on the surrounding area, and would kill anyone who tried to get near the walls.

Moreover, in the event of an attack Per-Hathor would signal to a watchtower a day's march to the south, which would in turn pass the signal on. The troops at Elephantine would soon be mobilized and would hurry down the Nile to Per-Hathor. They might even join forces with the Nubian soldiers stationed upstream of the First Cataract. Massacring a band of Egyptian rebels would be a welcome distraction.

'Commander, the supply-boat's coming,' an officer informed him.

It would be bringing fresh water, meat, dried fish, vegetables, fruit, good-quality beer: the garrison lacked for nothing.

'Is it the usual one?'

'Yes, sir.'

From his post high on the ramparts, the commander watched big two-handled, egg-shaped jars of Canaanite design being unloaded.

'It is the day when honey, olive oil and wine are delivered,' said the officer greedily. 'I also ordered some boxes of fabric to replace clothes and bedsheets. If the supply-officer has done his work properly, it will all be here.'

The commander never tired of seeing the Egyptians humiliated. His sturdy soldiers in their black helmets never missed an opportunity to beat them and make them well aware of their inferiority. Any slave who showed the slightest sign of resistance was executed on the spot.

The gate of the fortress opened to allow the heavily laden slaves to enter. Forced to hurry, most of them were on the point of collapse. The moment they had deposited their burdens in the storehouses, they had to run back to the gate, heads bowed, to get out of the fortress as quickly as possible.

Twenty archers stood in position on the ramparts and aimed at the slaves. Others aimed at the area immediately around the main entrance, in case madmen thought they could take advantage of the delivery to enter the great courtyard.

As usual, the security instructions were observed to the letter.

'I sense that we shall soon receive a message from the emperor,' prophesied the commander. 'When the front at Qis has been strengthened, he will order us to attack Thebes, together with the troops from Elephantine.'

The crew were raising the sail on the cargo-boat, which was to leave again for the south.

'Shall we sample the wine this evening?' suggested the officer.

'Certainly not. The men must have an early night, because tomorrow they have cleaning duties at dawn and an inspection at noon. If I find the fortress spotlessly clean, we might organize a small celebration.'

Although disappointed, the officer resolved to take this blow patiently. With the aid of a sentry, he would gladly have uncorked a jar for his personal use. But if the commander found out, he would receive thirty days in prison and a transfer to somewhere much less agreeable. So at dinner he would be content with ordinary rations.

Per-Hathor was asleep. Only a few sentries were on lookout, and some of them were having difficulty keeping their eyes open. It was just one more peaceful night in this stronghold, where nothing could harm them.

The silence of the storehouse was almost imperceptibly broken by a small, dry sound: the side of a jar being broken. Slowly, Moustache emerged from his uncomfortable mode of transport. Beside him, the Afghan followed suit. And so did the fifteen other members of the raiding-party.

The first part of Queen Ahhotep's daring plan had succeeded: to seize the supply-boat, replace the Hyksos soldiers with Thebans, persuade the slaves to act out the charade before they were freed, and find volunteers who were mad enough to hide in the largest jars. If the Hyksos had checked the contents before storing them, the raiders would not have stood a chance. But habit and the soldiers' belief in their security had prevailed.

The Afghan and Moustache looked at each other, surprised still to be alive. Their comrades joined them, daggers in hand.

Moustache told them, 'The Afghan and I are going to scout around. As soon as we've located the sentries, we'll return for you, and then we'll kill them all. While one of us opens the great gate, the others are to kill as many Hyksos as possible in their beds. We must move fast and in absolute silence.'

'What if one of the sentries manages to sound the alert?' asked a Theban.

'Then we're all dead, so make sure it doesn't happen.'

Barefoot, as always when moving soundlessly in enemy territory, the Afghan and Moustache ventured out into the fortress. Their fear gave way to intense concentration and economy of movement.

The two first sentries, who were stationed in the inner courtyard, had their throats cut before they could make a sound. Their corpses were dragged into an outbuilding and stripped, and the two rebels put on their tunics, breastplates and black helmets.

The Afghan signalled to his companion that he was going to climb the main stairway to the battlements and that Moustache should take the other one. They reached the two main lookout posts simultaneously; each was occupied by two archers.

With odds of two against one, the operation would be a tricky one.

'What are you doing here?' asked one of the Hyksos when he saw the Afghan. 'You know the commander has forbidden us to leave our posts.'

The Afghan slit his throat, in the hope that his companion's first thought would be to defend himself rather than shout for help. Indeed the man did, and that was his fatal mistake.

Once his two sentries were dead, the Afghan turned to see if Moustache had had the same success. He saw only the silhouette of a Hyksos soldier, but was reassured when the soldier removed his helmet.

Moustache went back down into the courtyard to fetch the Thebans. He showed them where the other lookouts were posted and allocated each man a target.

'These young fellows aren't quite as clumsy as I thought,' he mused as he watched them move into action.

Eager and determined, they did not set a foot wrong. Less than half an hour after they emerged from the jars, the raiding-party had killed all the Hyksos sentries.

'Now for the gate,' ordered Moustache.

Two Thebans opened it while the Afghan set fire to the top of one of the towers. At this signal, Kamose's first attack regiment would know it could move towards Per-Hathor without fear.

'Let's hope he gets here soon,' whispered the Afghan, 'or we may have problems.'

'We must get to the sleeping-quarters,' Moustache whispered back, 'and kill as many Hyksos as possible.'

'No, wait a moment. Look there, at the bottom of the main tower. Do you think that's the commander's quarters?'

'Let's go and find out.'

Protected by the friendly darkness, they pounced on the commander, who was sound asleep – at first.

'Order your men to surrender,' advised the Afghan.

'A Hyksos does not surrender.'

'I know you,' said Moustache. 'You were stationed in the Delta a few years ago, and you tortured several of our comrades.'

'Per-Hathor is impregnable,' said the commander. 'Lay down your weapons immediately.'

'You Hyksos bore me,' said the Afghan. 'It's impossible to have a discussion with you.'

He pushed the commander outside, forced him to climb up on to the ramparts and, seizing his ankles, threw him over the edge.

'Now,' he said, 'we'll go to the sleeping-quarters.'

Fortune continued to smile on them. The Thebans managed to break down the doors of two of the chambers, using heavy beams as battering-rams. The soldiers in the third, awakened by the noise, came rushing out; they were killed one by one as they emerged.

Just as the members of the raiding-party were beginning to tire, the vanguard of the army of liberation poured into the fortress, with Pharaoh Kamose at its head.

Queen Ahhotep stood at the prow of the flagship, watching the impregnable fortress burn.

## 24

As Hyksos envoy and a master spy, One-Eye knew everything that happened in Nubia. It was a vast region, populated by warlike tribes which had recently been united by King Nedjeh, a natural leader of men, and one whose methods were brutal.

One-Eye was a former infantry general and expert killer. Officially, he had lost his left eye during a heroic fight from which he had emerged victorious. Actually, it had been put out by a Nubian girl he was trying to rape.

For a long time, he had worried that Nedjeh might be so full of his own importance that he would dare to attack Elephantine. But the Nubian had contented himself with his rich domain of Kerma, and declared himself a faithful vassal of Apophis, to whom he sent regular tributes.

This sensible behaviour had made One-Eye suspicious. Was Nedjeh secretly preparing to capture Elephantine, the great city that lay at the southern tip of Egypt, beside the First Cataract? Fortunately, the information provided by his spies gave no cause for concern. Several of them indicated that Nedjeh was growing fat and was interested only in consolidating his position locally. After travelling the length and breadth of Nubia to reassure himself that no trouble was brewing, One-Eye had come to Elephantine for a few weeks' rest.

The Hyksos garrison here led a peaceful life. They had a perfect understanding with the few Nubian soldiers stationed upstream of the cataract, and, being so far from Avaris, some of the officers were beginning to forget their people's warlike vocation. Anyone could see that discipline was growing less and less strict, and that the main barracks housed more and more women, whose presence had previously been forbidden. Little by little, the mild winters and hot summers had softened even the hardiest souls, and the men were more interested in having good food and comfortable living-quarters than in keeping their weapons in proper order.

The garrison had neither chariots nor horses, which were reserved for the army of the North. Its boats were ancient and in need of major repair. As for the fortress itself, though it looked as impressive as Per-Hathor it suffered from faults in its construction. Moreover, its great gate was often left open, and the sentries were not as vigilant as they might be.

'But who would ever dare attack Elephantine?' the town's governor asked One-eye, whose initial anger had been softened by the Nubian girl he had found in his bed and the excellent meal he and the governor had just finished.

'Are there any problems with the Nubians?' asked One-Eye.

'Not a single one, dear friend. As allies they are a little hot-tempered, but they're perfectly loyal. The mere name of the emperor brings them to heel, and so it should. Between ourselves, I hope I shall not be recalled to Avaris. Leaving this little paradise would be a wrench.'

A cup-bearer hurried up to the table and handed the governor a shard of limestone. 'An urgent message, my lord, very urgent!'

'What is it now? I'll wager the officers are complaining about the quality of the local beer. All the same, we mustn't—' The governor stopped dead as he read the message, which was written in a sailor's clumsy hand. '"Per-Hathor has fallen." What's that supposed to mean, *"Per-Hathor has fallen"?*'

'Someone has captured it,' said One-Eye.

'But who on earth could do that?'

As the two men looked at each other, stunned, they heard shouts rising up from the Nile.

'We may not have to wait long to find out,' said One-Eye grimly.

They hurried up to the top of the fortress's highest tower. From this vantage-point, they saw the Theban war-fleet, its sails bellying out in a strong north wind.

Taken by surprise, the Hyksos boats were already sinking. In a few minutes, the army of Kamose and Ahhotep would reach land and attack the citadel. Panic overtook the Hyksos soldiers, contradictory orders flying about in all directions.

'The gate . . . the archers . . . the barracks . . . Quickly – we must act quickly!' exclaimed the governor, rushing down the stairway.

In his hurry, he missed a step and fell. On the long way down, his head hit the wall several times. By the time he reached the bottom of the stairway, he was dead.

One-Eye had only one objective: to get out of Elephantine and reach Kerma, to warn King Nedjeh.

For the first time, Moustache and the Afghan did not have to join battle themselves during the final, victorious attack. Although disorganized after their commander's death, the Hyksos defended themselves fiercely, but the Thebans' zeal was so great that it swept away the enemy within a few hours.

'Our young lads gave a good account of themselves,' observed Moustache.

'Hard work always pays off,' replied the Afghan. 'Today they're reaping the benefits of the training the queen demanded of them.'

As he spoke, Ahhotep emerged into the square before the Temple of Khnum, the patron god of Elephantine; beside her was Pharaoh Kamose, who wore the White Crown. Holding a bow in her left hand and an ankh, the sign of life, in her right, she embodied Thebes the liberator.

Kamose had never felt so happy. Thanks to Ahhotep's plan, which had been executed with breathtaking speed, all the land between Thebes and Elephantine was now free of Hyksos. In the streets and squares, the people were honouring the soldiers of the army of liberation, and already banquets were being prepared which would last late into the night.

A very old priest emerged from the temple. He walked with difficulty, leaning on a stick. 'I wish I could bow before Your Majesties, but my back is too stiff. What happiness to welcome you here! I was right to resist death, in the impossible hope that I would see this town set free.'

'Take my arm,' said the queen.

'Majesty, I . . .'

'Please. You are the guardian of the potter's wheel, are you not?'

The old man's lined face lit up. 'In spite of all their searching, the Hyksos did not find it. In this temple, the first steering-oar was made, enabling the ship of state to be guided. Also here, the god Khnum fashioned all living beings on his potter's wheel. I shall reveal these mysteries to you, and then I shall be able to die in peace.'

Dozens of gazelles had come out of the desert, to invade the gardens of Elephantine and play with the children. Once again, the people could celebrate the festival of their patron goddess, Anukis, represented by a very pretty woman wearing a white crown decorated with the slender horns of a gazelle.

While the town was expressing its joy, the old priest reopened the entrance to the the temple's vaults, which lay under the paved floor of the inner shrine. A hundred times the Hyksos soldiers had profaned this place, never suspecting that the treasures they coveted lay beneath their feet.

The acacia-wood steering-oar was so heavy that Kamose had to summon several men to lift it out of the depths. From this day on, it would steer the flagship.

Then the young pharaoh took in his hands the potter's wheel with which Khnum had positioned the celestial vault, raised up the firmament and shaped the cosmos so that light might shine through every part of it. One by one, the gods, animals and men had emerged from this matrix.

The old priest, the queen and the king climbed up to the temple roof. There, they would expose the wheel to the sun so that it would be able to function once more.

'Life begins again,' intoned the priest, 'and breath brings matter to life.'

When the night sky was unveiled, the old scholar showed his guests how to use the sighting-instruments that had helped the ancients to understand the movements of the sun, the moon and the stars. They had known that the so-called 'fixed' stars in fact moved, and that the centre around which they seemed to move also changed position because of the precession of the world's axis.

Kamose was fascinated and could have listened enraptured for nights on end as the old man happily passed on his knowledge.

'First thing tomorrow,' promised the pharaoh, 'you shall begin training your successors. Many priests, servants and craftsmen will be appointed so that this temple may regain its former activity and splendour.'

The priest smiled. 'Then my death will have to wait a little longer, Majesty.'

Ahhotep gazed out at the First Cataract, which marked the border with Nubia. She shared her son's joy at the taking of Elephantine, but it was only a stage in the war and their victory, though dazzling, was very fragile. Beyond the barrier of rocks illuminated by the moon-god lay the enemy. An enemy quite capable of wiping out the army of liberation.

## 25

Queen Ahhotep and King Kamose spent a long time meditating on the isle of Biga where, according to tradition, both the body of Osiris and the sources of the Nile were located. The waters of the river divided as they sprang forth from a cavern, one branch flowing north while the other flowed south. The source of the spring lay so deep that no one had ever reached it.

There was absolute silence on the island. Even the birds forbore to sing there, so as not to disturb the rest of the reborn god whom Isis had snatched back from death. By and in Osiris the souls of the righteous were reborn, the beings of light among whom Pharaoh Seqen now dwelt.

Aboard the boat taking them back to Elephantine, the young king could not hide his profound emotion. 'This town is the head of the country, the capital of the first province of Upper Egypt, and it safeguards the sacred origins of the Nile. By controlling it again, we make the river our invincible ally. Like Osiris, the land of the pharaohs is reborn. Shouldn't we forget the Nubians and leave immediately for the North?'

Ahhotep shook her head. 'No, because we must slacken the noose once and for all by making sure that King Nedjeh will never again wish to attack us. And there is only one way to do that: we must reconquer Buhen and so cordon off the whole of Nubia.'

Kamose unrolled a papyrus on which a simple map was drawn. 'So we must sail almost as far as the Second Cataract. On such a long journey, isn't there a risk that the Nubians will ambush us long before we reach Buhen?'

'It is a possibility,' agreed Ahhotep, 'but I believe he has blind confidence in Buhen's ability to repulse any attack. It is as powerful as Per-Hathor and Elephantine put together. If its Egyptian governor had not betrayed us to the Hyksos, the Nubians would certainly not have succeeded in taking it.'

'Are you planning to use the trick with the jars again?'

'I'm afraid that's impossible.'

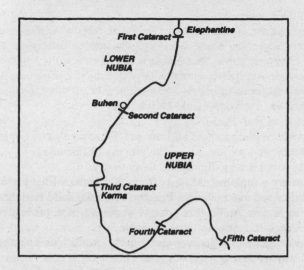

'Then we must expect a long and painful siege, with an uncertain outcome. And during that time, there is a risk that the front at Qis will collapse.'

'That is another possibility,' admitted the queen. 'If you think my plan is wrong, you are free to reject it.'

'I'd never dare oppose you, Mother. You're the liberator of Egypt.'

'And you are Pharaoh. I shall always obey your orders.'

Kamose gazed out over the Nile. 'By becoming the Wife of God, by giving all your love to this country, which you rightly revere, you are following an earthly path which was born in the heavens. I am only a young king and I do not yet have your clarity of thought and vision. Sometimes, I wonder if you are completely of this world or if part of you dwells beyond the visible, leading this army safely to its goal. I shall never give you an order, Mother, and I shall follow wherever you lead.'

The festival was over, the town silent, and the gazelles had returned to the desert. Although most of the soldiers had dreadful headaches, all those who were to leave for Nubia had gathered on the quayside. They envied their comrades who were to form the new garrison at Elephantine.

Neshi went up to the pharaoh and bowed. 'All is ready, Majesty. We have taken on large supplies of foodstuffs and weapons. I checked each consignment myself.'

'You look worried.'

'Our men are afraid, Majesty. The inhabitants of Elephantine have told them about the black warriors, who are as dangerous as wild beasts. Everyone knows that Nubia is full of evil spells which no one can eradicate. After all, the creator's eye fled into those burning deserts, to destroy all forms of life. If you were to give up this expedition into the unknown, everyone would be relieved.'

'Including you, Neshi?'

'I would be disappointed and anxious. Disappointed by our leaders' inconstancy, and anxious about the process of liberation.'

'That is not a very diplomatic thing to say.'

'I am not a diplomat, Majesty. I am the Bearer of the Royal Seal, who ratifies and makes known Pharaoh's decisions. If I find them bad, I must be honest. And if that honesty displeases you, dismiss me and replace me with someone more tractable.'

Kamose smiled. 'Whatever else you do, Neshi, don't change.'

'Our troops' fear is a setback, and I don't know how to counter it.'

'My mother has asked the craftsmen of Elephantine to make some unusual weapons which should reassure them.'

Dazzlingly beautiful in a long green gown and floral headdress, Queen Ahhotep went out into the square to address the army. She was followed by several craftsmen carrying heavy baskets.

'We are about to face formidable enemies,' she acknowledged. 'Before we even reach Buhen, we shall have to defeat Nubian warriors who will fight ferociously. But there is a magical means of weakening them: using these objects covered with powerful symbols.'

She reached into one of the baskets and took out a curved throwing-stick engraved with an eye, a rearing cobra, a gryphon and the head of a jackal.

'The eye will enable us to see danger,' she explained, 'and the cobra to dispel it. The gryphon and the jackal will ward off the destructive forces of the desert. Officers and their deputies will be equipped with these weapons in order to protect the men under their command. And one made of ivory, bearing the same signs, will ensure that our voyage is peaceful.'

The queen had never lied to them, so the men were persuaded that, once again, she would succeed in protecting them from evil. With enthusiasm, the sailors hoisted the sails and yards with the aid of halyards on which they heaved with all their strength. The manoeuvre was a difficult one, even for professionals. But nothing went wrong, and the sails fluttered free, watched attentively by the captains.

On the flagship, seven sturdy fellows hoisted the topsail using two halyards, while an eighth climbed to the top of the mast to help them.

His clambering amused a young monkey, which proved swifter than he and teased the crew with little cries.

Laughter barked, warning the monkey to behave itself. Perched on the top of the mainsail, the animal did not have to be told a second time.

Pharaoh himself took charge of the steering-oar when the boat headed into a channel which would enable it to avoid the rocks of the First Cataract and rejoin the Nile.

Using his long forked stick, Moon measured the depth of the water; there was no scope for error. And slowly the boat continued on its way. Moon had an uncommon capacity for concentration; he was one with his craft. With all his being, with all his senses, he experienced each movement of the water and detected all its many snares.

Ahhotep saw that Moon's brow was deeply furrowed, as if the dangers were growing greater by the moment. She looked down into the channel, which sparkled in the sunshine, and offered a prayer to Hapy, the life-energy of the river, asking him not to hinder the war-fleet's progress.

On the poop of the flagship, Moustache noticed that the Afghan looked ill at ease: his face was taking on a strange green tinge. Moustache grinned and said, 'I have a feeling you don't much like sailing.'

'Turn away. That'll make me feel better.'

'Be sick in peace, Afghan. We only have a few weeks' travelling ahead of us, interspersed with murderous battles. Let's hope for your sake that some of them will be on dry land.'

The Afghan's stomach was heaving so much that he couldn't reply.

'Don't worry,' said Moustache. 'I hear the river is rather calm in Nubia. That's better for delicate constitutions like yours, isn't it? Oh, watch out! We're going over some rapids, and that might shake us up a bit. Just don't look. I'm not even sure if our boat can withstand the shock.'

Little by little, the lines on Moon's brow relaxed and disappeared. Although watchful as ever, he handled his measuring-staff less apprehensively.

Queen Ahhotep stopped gazing at the water and instead looked at some clumps of palm-trees sparkling in the sun.

'Good news, Afghan!' exclaimed Moustache. 'We've just entered Nubia.'

## 26

The riverbed was narrower than in Egypt, and lined with palm-trees which had their roots in the water and their crowns in the sunshine. Most of them lived for a hundred years, and the best gave up to thirty clusters of dates. Ripening with the flood, between July and September, they were a useful source of food during the hot season. The doum-palms were as tall as ten men and had one special feature: their trunk forked twice or more, and each branch ended in a sort of crown. Apart from their red-brown fruit, with its soft, sweet flesh, they provided welcome shade, and their kernels contained a refreshing liquid which Moustache was fond of.

'Are you feeling better, Afghan? I think the boat is pitching a bit less.'

The Afghan was still greenish, and hardly eating anything. 'One day,' he said firmly, 'I shall take you into my mountains in the middle of winter. We'll see how proud you are when you have your feet in the snow. From what I know of you, you'll have an attack of vertigo and won't be able to climb up or down. And don't rely on me to help you.'

'At the moment we're in Nubia, and you'd do better to look straight ahead. We have visitors.'

They were very black-skinned, very tall, very strongly built, and were armed with spears and bows. They wore only a simple kilt, while their faces and torsos were painted with warlike insignia.

Ahhotep gave orders for the flagship to halt and for the gangplank to be put out.

'Mother,' said Kamose anxiously, 'don't leave the boat.'

'These are warlike men, but they have a sense of honour. They will not kill a woman who comes to meet them alone and unarmed.'

Moustache was not so sure.

The Afghan laid a hand on his shoulder. 'Don't threaten them, and let her do as she wishes. She knows what she's doing.'

'Those brutes will slaughter her.'

'People don't kill a woman like her. Look at them. It wouldn't take much to make them prostrate themselves before the Queen of Egypt.'

Surprised by Ahhotep's actions, a tall man wearing gold bracelets pushed through the ranks of his soldiers to confront this unexpected adversary.

'I am Ahhotep, Queen of the Two Lands, and I am travelling with Pharaoh Kamose, at the head of his army.'

'I am the chief of the Medjai tribe and I thought the only pharaoh was Apophis. What do you seek to do on my land, Queen of Egypt?'

'To fight the allies of the Hyksos, who are occupying my country, and to retake the fortress of Buhen, which was handed over to the enemy by traitors and collaborators.'

'Have you decided to wage war against the King of Kerma?'

'Since he is the faithful friend of the Emperor of Darkness, I shall destroy him.'

'King Nedjeh is invincible.'

'Pharaoh will vanquish him.'

The chief looked troubled.

'What do you Medjai desire?' asked Ahhotep, whose serene beauty fascinated the Nubian.

'The Medjai inhabit a large part of this land, between the First and Second Cataracts. For a while, we thought that Nedjeh would be our liberator. In reality, he is nothing but a tyrant, and he wanted to turn us into slaves. When we resisted, with the aid of the Hyksos he killed many of us and destroyed many of our villages. We took refuge in the desert and only re-emerged a few days ago, when we learnt that a fleet from Thebes had liberated Elephantine and entered Nubia. We killed the soldiers of King Nedjeh who were preparing to attack you. We want to fight at the side of the Pharaoh of Egypt.'

While Kamose, Moustache and the Egyptian soldiers looked on in astonishment, the Medjai prostrated themselves before Queen Ahhotep.

The Afghan was only modestly triumphant, for he had not really believed his own prediction. 'That woman is a miracle in herself,' he murmured.

Soped, the Egyptian commander of Buhen fortress, listened attentively to One-Eye. The Hyksos knew Nubia better than anyone, and scaremongering was anathema to him, so his warning was not to be taken lightly.

'So, One-Eye, an army from Thebes has taken Elephantine. A serious blow to the Hyksos, I agree, but it's only a temporary reverse. You know as well as I do that the emperor's reaction will be terrifying. He will raze Thebes and Elephantine to the ground and station garrisons there to prevent any future unrest. Now, I am a loyal servant of the King of Kerma. I have washed my feet in my master's water,* and I belong to his entourage, so I am safe and sound.'

'I'm sure you're right, Commander, but nevertheless you should strengthen your defences.'

'Buhen is impregnable.'

'So was Per-Hathor,' said One-Eye drily.

'The comparison does not hold water. Buhen is a small town, and I have a large enough garrison to resist an attack. Besides, the troops of King Nedjeh and the Medjai tribe must already have sunk most of the ships belonging to that ridiculous pharaoh Kamose. Believe me, my friend, no enemy boat will reach Buhen.'

'Probably not,' conceded One-Eye, 'but Queen Ahhotep is a formidable force.'

'A woman! Are you joking?'

'This woman seems to be in league with the gods.'

'The gods didn't protect Egypt during the Hyksos invasion, and they won't protect her today.'

'I shall go to Kerma to alert King Nedjeh and ask him to send you reinforcements.'

'He will simply laugh in your face.'

'I think it advisable to take every precaution,' said One-Eye.

'Why are you so worried? These are just the last efforts of a Theban faction which is mad enough still to believe in Egyptian freedom.'

'I shall feel less worried when that woman Ahhotep is dead.'

'She's probably dead already, even as we speak. Take your time in Kerma and give King Nedjeh my greetings. It seems his palace grows more beautiful by the day and that his court will soon shine more brightly than that of the pharaohs.'

With some relief, the commander watched the Hyksos leave for the south. One-Eye was beginning to fall prey to an old man's fears, and was no longer capable of dealing with new situations. The emperor would not leave him in office for much longer, and would replace him with a younger, more dynamic man who was not afraid of his own shadow.

One-Eye's advice had not pleased Soped in the least. Nobody knew the fortress's capacity for resistance better than its commander! That very evening, he would write a highly critical report about One-Eye's behaviour and send it urgently to Kerma, so that the king could demand that the emperor dismiss him.

Commander Soped could be proud of his achievements. As a junior

---

*An Egyptian expression denoting absolute loyalty.

officer, he had quickly realized that the Hyksos were the new masters of Egypt and that their work must be facilitated as much as possible. So he had denounced all his superiors as accomplices of the Thebans.

The emperor had proved not ungrateful: in exchange for this spontaneous collaboration, he had appointed Soped commander of Buhen fortress, charged with turning it into an impregnable bastion and beheading anyone suspected of opposing the Hyksos, even in thought. Soped had taken advantage of this to kill everyone he disliked, in full agreement with his assistant, who had come from Kerma to keep watch on him. From time to time, the Nubian was obliged to restrain the commander, whose thirst for executions seemed never-ending.

Today, Commander Soped was the unchallenged ruler of the stronghold, which provided shelter for caravans, acted as a tax-post for goods, a workshop for washing gold and a postal centre. Obeying orders from both the emperor and the King of Kerma, Soped succeeded in annoying neither. And if things were quiet for too long he could always torture a civilian, who would duly be forced to confess that he was conspiring against Apophis.

By appropriating small amounts of gold during each washing operation, the commander was, little by little, amassing a modest fortune. His only worry was the possible emergence of a rival who might try to oust him; but he was so vigilant that it was a very small worry indeed.

'Dinner is served,' announced his cup-bearer.

Another quiet evening lay ahead.

## 27

Nedjeh, all-powerful King of Kerma, was being massaged with oil of shea made from the fruit of the 'butter tree', which contained an oily nut. In the last two years, the handsome, athletic Nubian had gained a lot of weight and he was becoming almost fat. But he could never resist the sauces and desserts prepared by his cooks.

When he seized power in the fertile region of Dongola, just above the Third Cataract, Nedjeh had been a warrior hungry for conquests. Ruler of an extensive river basin where cereal crops grew in abundance and livestock thrived, Nedjeh had thought he would be able to take Elephantine, then Thebes, and so conquer Upper Egypt. But Emperor Apophis's clear-sightedness had decided matters otherwise, and the Nubian felt it preferable not to go to war with the Hyksos.

By remaining their faithful ally and sending tributes to Avaris, Nedjeh ensured his lands were left in peace, and he was able to rule despotically and mercilessly.

He had made spectacular improvements to his capital by having a fortified brick temple built in the very centre, as tall as twenty men. A monumental staircase led to its summit, which looked out over the whole city. To the south-west of the city a vast circular hut served as an audience chamber; to the east there was a burial-ground, whose principal tombs were decorated with bulls' heads. Defensive earthworks, watchtowers and heavy gates ensured the security of Kerma, where slaves were sacrificed as readily as rams.

Nedjeh's latest whim was glazed porcelain tiles and friezes depicting lions. Thanks to the gold mines, the king's wealth continued to grow, and he took advantage of it to make Kerma magnificent, in accordance with his taste. Apophis, with whom he communicated via inscribed scarabs borne by the imperial messengers, had sent him some undeniably talented carpenters. So his palace was filled with refined furniture in the Egyptian style.

The inhabitants of the new capital lacked for nothing. Trading-relations with the Hyksos were good, and consignments of Minoan and Cyprian jars arrived regularly at Kerma, where the tribal chiefs came to pay allegiance to Nedjeh.

Other people, too, had noticed that the king had put on weight, but no one complained. Good food and luxury made him forget his warlike ambitions in favour of comfort. The price to be paid was only an unconditional alliance with the Hyksos, but would those predators be content with exterminating the Egyptians? Nubia's gold was so tempting . . .

Nedjeh reassured himself by increasing, each year, the quantity of gold he presented to the emperor. In this way Apophis kept a tight rein on far-off Kerma, which did not threaten him in any way.

When the king's steward announced the arrival of One-Eye, Nedjeh frowned. The Hyksos was a master of trickery and manipulation, and it would not be easy to lie to him. He had probably come to demand more gold, so the king would have to persuade him that the miners had already produced all they could.

'You look very well, One-Eye,' he said.

'Appearances are sometimes deceptive, my lord.'

'Come, come. Surely you aren't the bearer of bad news?'

'The Theban army has taken Per-Hathor and Elephantine.'

'I know; I received your messages. It's annoying, of course, but they'll both soon be retaken by the emperor's soldiers, won't they?'

'That is a certainty.'

'Then why worry?'

'Because Ahhotep and Pharaoh Kamose have entered Nubia.'

Nedjeh burst out laughing. 'A woman and a boy! Their folly has condemned them to death.'

One-Eye seemed depressed. 'I am not so sure.'

'But how can you doubt it? I have troops stationed close to the First Cataract, and they and the Medjai tribe will make short work of your Thebans.'

'Lately, the Medjai have seemed less and less reliable. Your men have bullied them, and I know they are resentful.'

'They would never dare disobey me. You can be sure that the Theban army has been wiped out.'

'But what if it hasn't? Wouldn't it be sensible to strengthen the defences at Buhen?'

'Buhen cannot be taken. If Soped hadn't betrayed his own kind, I'd have had to besiege it for an eternity – and even then I might not have taken it.'

'I believe we would be making a grave mistake by underestimating the Thebans. Ahhotep is a true war-leader. For an army regarded as of no account, is it not a remarkable achievement to take Per-Hathor and then Elephantine?'

'Don't exaggerate,' said Nedjeh scornfully. 'They took advantage of favourable circumstances, that's all.'

'My lord, I strongly advise you to send reinforcements to Buhen.'

'To be frank, that seems pointless.'

'I very much regret it but, as representative of the Hyksos emperor, I find myself obliged to order you to do so.'

Hiding his anger, Nedjeh bowed. 'As you wish. But I think you're being very alarmist.'

'If the Medjai have turned against your troops, Ahhotep and Kamose have had free rein. Their main objective can only be Buhen. If they retake it, they will pin you down in Kerma.'

'This is all merely conjecture.'

'My instinct rarely deceives me. I know that that woman Ahhotep is dangerous and that you must take action.'

'You need say no more. The emperor's orders shall be carried out, as usual. Has Apophis ever had cause to complain about me?'

'Never,' agreed One-Eye, satisfied with the outcome of the interview. 'And you, the King of Kerma, shall have the privilege of crushing the Theban rebellion. Of course, you will acquire important privileges by doing so. In the report that Apophis will demand, I shall write about you in glowing terms.'

'You will always be welcome in my town, One-Eye. Do you think the emperor will be satisfied if his envoy takes him the heads of Ahhotep and Kamose on the ends of spears?'

'He would certainly appreciate that kind of homage.'

'Then it is agreed, my friend. Now, shall we go and amuse ourselves a little?'

Nedjeh's favourite entertainment, after lavish banquets, was women. And in that respect One-Eye felt capable of rivalling him, especially since Kerma housed some splendid, hot-blooded creatures.

One of the vast bedchambers at the palace was reserved for the king's new conquests; despite his plumpness, he remained a vigorous lover. There were four of them, all young, pretty and smiling.

'I shall leave the choice to you, One-Eye.'

'My lord, you are too generous!'

'Please: it is a gift to celebrate our perfect understanding.'

What the Hyksos liked best about Nubia was its girls. At once challenging and docile, disturbing she-panthers and languorous cats, they fascinated him. If he had an attachment to this rough, sun-scorched land, he owed it to them.

And One-Eye took great delight in the King of Kerma's sumptuous gift.

Night was falling when Nedjeh shook One-Eye awake. 'You have had a good sleep, my friend. Before we dine, I should like to show you my latest project.'

One-Eye stretched. Two Nubian girls had drained every last drop of moisture from his body, and he would gladly have lapsed back into restorative sleep. But he could not displease the king.

Accompanied by two bodyguards, Nedjeh led the envoy to the burial-ground, where vast tombs reserved for officials were hollowed out.

'I am going to grant you a new privilege, One-Eye: to visit my tomb, which will be worthy of a great pharaoh. You, the Hyksos, attach little importance to your final dwelling; here, it is different. I have a palace in my lifetime, and I want another for my death.'

The two men set off along a long, sloping corridor which ended in an antechamber. Beyond it was a vault filled with statues, vases and furniture looted from Elephantine. But the most impressive item was the carpet of human skulls covering the beaten-earth floor.

'I don't like being annoyed,' confessed Nedjeh. 'Anger takes hold of me and makes me kill anyone who contests my power. And you have annoyed me a great deal, One-Eye.'

The Hyksos retreated a pace or two, crushing the bones beneath his feet. There was no way out.

'Listen to me, my lord—'

'Anyone who angers me does not deserve my pardon. But I shall grant you one favour: your skull will remain in this tomb with those of the slaves I killed with my own hands.'

One-Eye tried to force his way out, but he was not strong enough to fight the Nubian, who hurled him to the ground, then broke his neck with a violent blow from his heel. Officially, the envoy would have met a peaceful death in the good city of Kerma.

The emperor would not easily find a Hyksos who knew the region as well as that unbearable lesson-giver. How could vain One-Eye have thought that Nedjeh would tolerate being told how to behave?

## 28

A violent hammering on his door awoke Commander Soped in the middle of the night. Irritably, he got up and opened the door. Outside stood the officer in charge of the night watch.

'What is it?' demanded Soped.

'A patrol has just found a curse not far from the main gate.'

'A curse?'

'An ivory throwing-stick with magical signs. Two soldiers tried to pick it up, but it burnt their fingers. The men are very anxious, Commander. They are waiting for you to do something.'

Soped dressed in haste. In the heart of Nubia this kind of event could not be dismissed lightly, because the black sorcerers had real powers. For reasons as yet unknown, one of them had decided to harm the fortress. The urgent thing was to destroy the basis of the curse.

Soped strode across the courtyard and left the fortress by the great gate. He found dozens of Nubian and Hyksos soldiers gathered around the throwing-stick.

'Stand aside,' he ordered.

The moonlight lit up the ivory, on which signs had been drawn – signs which terrified the soldiers of Buhen, especially the rearing cobra and the gryphon with its menacing beak.'

'This is nothing,' declared Soped, who was shaking like a wind-tossed palm-tree.

'If it's really nothing,' objected a Nubian, 'pick it up and break it.'

'I'm told it burns. I don't intend to burn myself in order to dispel this magic.'

Everyone realized that he was afraid. The sentries had left their posts and joined their comrades, who could not take their eyes off the mysterious object.

'The cobra's eyes . . . they're glowing red!' one of them exclaimed.

'And so are the eyes of Anubis,' gasped his neighbour.

'Bring me a hammer,' ordered Soped. 'I'll smash the ivory.'

The man who went to fetch the hammer did not return. He was

strangled by one of the Medjai who had just entered the fortress through the great gate, which had been left open and unguarded. The attackers would have taken the risk of scaling the walls, but Ahhotep's magic spared them this perilous climb. Swift and agile, they slaughtered the guards in the courtyard, then climbed to the tops of the watchtowers, where they soon dispatched the archers.

'Where is that hammer?' demanded Soped impatiently. He was standing at a respectful distance from the magical ivory, which was still lit by the rays of the moon-god.

The sound of the great gate slamming shut made them all jump, and they swung round in shock.

'The imbecile who did that will be thrown into irons,' promised Soped.

From the tops of the towers volleys of arrows rained down, most of them finding their targets. Soped saw many of his garrison falling around him.

'The Medjai!' roared a Hyksos. 'It's the Medjai – they'll slaughter us to the last man.'

'To the river!' shouted Soped. 'We'll get away on the rescue-boats.'

The survivors ran to the riverbank, but there they were halted in their tracks by a detachment of the army of liberation, commanded by Kamose himself.

Abandoning his men, Soped turned on one of his own officers and killed him, to make it look as if he was fighting for the Egyptians. Then he slunk off towards the Nile. He planned to swim with the current, reach a boat and distance himself from Buhen as swiftly as possible.

The plan would have succeeded had Moustache not foreseen it. He threw himself into the water at the same time as Soped and grabbed him round the neck. 'You're in a big hurry, my friend.'

'I am the commander of the fortress and I have gold, well hidden. Spare my life and you'll be rich.'

'Where is it hidden, this gold?'

'Over there.' Half choking, Soped managed to point to a reedbed. 'In a boat moored in the reeds.'

'We shall go there. But no tricks, or I'll rip out your throat.'

Soped checked that he still had a dagger hidden in a fold of his kilt. That precaution had saved his life more than once. Pretending to be defeated, he swam slowly to the boat.

'There are several bags of gold tied to the hull,' he said. 'All you have to do is dive down and untie them.'

'Well, go on, then.'

The commander dived down into the water, but almost immediately darted up again behind Moustache and tried to stab him in the back. Used to hand-to-hand fighting and this kind of trickery, the rebel seized his attacker's wrist and turned his weapon against him.

'You traitor and coward! It gives me real pleasure to kill you.'

As the blade ripped open his flesh, from belly to heart, the commander's eyes grew glassy.

He was already dead when Moustache cried out in pain. The jaws of a crocodile had closed on his left leg. As the great reptile dragged him towards the bottom, the Afghan jumped on to its back and plunged his dagger into its eye. Maddened with pain, the crocodile let go of its prey and swam away.

With the aid of two Egyptian soldiers, the Afghan got the wounded man back to the riverbank.

'Luckily for you, it was a young crocodile. All the same, the wound is not a pretty sight. We'd better get you back to the fortress straight away.'

On the first day, the military doctor applied meat to the wound. On the second, he used a poultice of bull's fat and mouldy barley-bread, whose medicinal qualities were well known. A drug made from extracts of mandragora, jujube and opium ensured that Moustache felt no pain. Honey and myrrh, used to prevent infection, would eventually heal him.

'Be honest, Afghan. Will I be able to walk again?'

'With no problems at all, and you'll have only a minor scar – it won't even enable you to show off to the girls. Getting yourself bitten by a crocodile is hardly a daring exploit.'

'Without me, that filthy Hyksos would have escaped.'

'Pharaoh Kamose has decided to decorate you for that; and he's decorating me, too, for saving you. What's more, we're being promoted and we're going to lead two attack regiments. Because of your exploits, we're destined for the front line.'

'That's the only thing that interests you, isn't it?'

'Stop thinking for me. It wears me out.'

'Who'd have thought that damned traitor could lure me into a trap with his lies about gold hidden under a boat?'

'But it wasn't lies,' said the Afghan. 'There really was a fine haul of it there, and a share of it will come to you when the war is over.'

'If it ever is over . . .'

A young Nubian girl with a slender body entered the bedchamber where Moustache was being treated.

'This is your nurse,' explained the Afghan. 'She belongs to the Medjai tribe, and knows wonderful herbs which will speed your recovery. Right, I shall leave you now. Looking at sick people depresses me.'

When he saw the girl take off her tiny kilt before preparing a potion for him, Moustache thought he must have a fever.

'It's hot here,' she whispered in a luscious voice, 'and I love being naked. Let me take care of you, brave warrior. You won't be disappointed.'

Queen Ahhotep and Pharaoh Kamose stood at the top of the main watchtower and gazed out over Nubia. The reconquest of Buhen meant that all river traffic was now barred to King Nedjeh. Moreover, the goods transported by the caravans that halted near the fortress now came within the scope of the Thebans, not to mention part of the gold production, which was washed on-site.

'Mother,' said Kamose, 'by persuading the Medjai to become our allies and using that magic ivory, you enabled us to win a great victory, and without losing a single man.'

'It won't always be so.' Ahhotep was silent for a moment, then went on, 'You must appoint a new fortress commander, and administrators who will manage the wealth of the region, and then choose a governor for Nubia.'

'Does that mean that we're turning round and going back to the northern front?'

'Not yet. Even when he learns that we have recaptured Buhen, King Nedjeh will think he is perfectly safe, because he thinks we'll never be able to get past the Second Cataract. He is wrong.'

## 29

Even the Medjai did not venture into the Miu region, between the Second and Third Cataracts. Proud that they now belonged to the army of liberation, they were placed under the authority of the new governor of Nubia, and would take on all guard duties in the reconquered territories.

The general opinion was that it would be best to be content with what had been won, and not to provoke the anger of King Nedjeh, who up to now had been silent. By violating his shrine, the Thebans would provoke a ferocious response.

And yet, when the council of war met, Neshi strongly opposed those senior officers who recommended a strategic withdrawal.

'When are you going to stop behaving like frightened women?' he said. 'And how many victories will it take for you to believe at last in our troops' abilities? Our enemies' magic has proved ineffective in the face of Queen Ahhotep's, hasn't it? To make Buhen our new southern frontier would be a grave mistake, because sooner or later Nedjeh would attack it. So let us create a barrier across our enemy's domain and isolate him, as the pharaoh and the queen recommend.'

'But what if nearly all our men are killed?' asked the oldest general, worriedly.

'We are at war,' King Kamose reminded him, 'and we cannot always make progress without losses. Queen Ahhotep's plan is the only feasible one. Tomorrow we shall cross the Second Cataract.'

The two new commanders of the attack regiments were proudly wearing their decorations, a little gold gryphon attached to their linen tunics. They met at the foot of the flagship's gangplank.

'All the wounded are to stay here, in the infirmary,' said the Afghan firmly.

'I'm all right,' retorted Moustache. 'But as a precautionary measure I'm bringing my nurse with me. The moment my scar starts hurting, she knows just how to soothe it.'

It was the first time Moustache had spent so much time with a woman. At first, he was afraid he'd be lulled into a tranquil state of mind and forget about the war. But he underestimated the fighting abilities of his young mistress, who practised the games of love as though they were themselves a contest. With her, there was no question of wasting time on endless preliminaries or pointless debate. So the patient had not been allowed very much rest, particularly since the plant remedies prescribed by this sorceress markedly increased his vigour.

From time to time, Moustache shivered. If the crocodile had been a little larger, or the Afghan had acted a little more slowly, he would now have only one leg. If he hadn't been able to fight any longer, he'd have killed himself.

'Stop thinking dark thoughts,' advised the Afghan.

'And you stop reading my mind. You mountain folk are really unbearable! By the way, how did you occupy your time while I was convalescing?'

'Do you think you're the only man who knows how to seduce Nubian girls?'

On the prow of each boat large eyes had been painted, enabling the Egyptian warships to see both the visible and the invisible. Moon appreciated this magical assistance, because he had to stay alert for hours on end in order to ensure that the fleet travelled safely. Ahhotep often stood beside him. She had ordered ivory throwing-sticks to be fixed to the ships' rails, so that their signs of power could drive away evil spirits.

The queen's presence both intimidated and reassured the helmsman. Without her, the army of liberation would long since have dispersed, for fear was strong within their bellies. The simple fact of seeing the Queen of Freedom, feeling her so close and yet inaccessible, gave courage to the most timid.

Moreover, young Pharaoh Kamose was gaining more confidence by the day. Like his father, he had an innate sense of leadership, and during attacks he always fought in the vanguard of his men, refusing to heed his mother's orders to be careful.

In accordance with the pharaoh's orders, Neshi ensured that rigorous cleanliness was practised on board the boats. The decks were washed several times a day, the cabins were carefully cleaned, and everyone smeared their skin with ointment to repel insects. To combat eye irritations, they used the froth from good-quality beer, which was also effective against stomach upsets. Each soldier had two mats wound round with a red leather cord, which he assembled to form a comfortable sleeping-bag. Each meal included onions, which were to be chewed, so that the smell would drive away snakes and scorpions.

'Majesty, we are coming to a village,' said Moon. 'Shall I slow down?'

'Not yet,' replied Ahhotep.

The queen wanted to observe the first reactions of the inhabitants of Miu who were under King Nedjeh's yoke.

At first stunned, the villagers hurriedly grabbed their bows and slingshots. The first arrows fell into the water, but the stones almost hit the prow.

'Take shelter, Majesty,' begged Moon.

'Stop the boat,' ordered Ahhotep.

Already, several soldiers were jumping on to the riverbank, at the risk of broken limbs. But the months of training proved their worth, and the young Egyptians were able to position themselves so as to strike down their opponents. As soon as the gangplank was put down, Kamose joined them and led them to the village, whose resistance was soon overcome.

A lone Nubian had succeeded in escaping by diving into the Nile, just in front of the flagship. He scaled the prow, furiously intent on killing the sorceress who had opened up the way to the Egyptian army. He leapt on to the deck and rushed at Ahhotep.

Pushing past the queen, Moon shattered the attacker's skull with his long stick. Ahhotep had not moved, trusting to the helmsman's skilled and steady hand.

Moon knelt. 'Forgive me, Majesty. I might have hurt you.'

Ahhotep raised him to his feet. 'I appoint you to command our naval forces. From now on, Commander Moon, you shall take all decisions regarding our ships and boats, and all the other captains will obey you.'

On dry land, the brief battle was ending. Not a single Nubian warrior had agreed to surrender, and two Egyptians were dead. On Kamose's order, the women and children were allowed to leave.

The conquest of Miu province had begun.

After slitting the throats of a ram and a slave, whose bones would join those of the Hyksos envoy, Nedjeh was preparing for a celebratory feast. There were no fewer than ten dishes, including poultry and an enormous Nile perch. While he was eating, two serving-girls fanned him. As soon as he had finished a dish, one of them washed his hands while the other anointed him with perfume. Nedjeh hated having greasy fingers and liked to smell nice.

The white wine came from the great Khargeh oasis, in the Western desert, and was excellent. Nedjeh never drank less than two large jugfuls with every meal.

'More,' he ordered his cup-bearer. 'Can you not see my cup is empty?'

How pleasant life was at Kerma! Thanks to the region's agricultural wealth, one could live as well there as in the most beautiful Egyptian provinces.

The king's personal scribe arrived at the threshold of the dining-chamber. 'My lord, may I interrupt your meal?'

'What can possibly be so urgent?'

'The Thebans have crossed the Second Cataract and are invading Miu.'

Nedjeh's appetite abruptly vanished. 'Is this information reliable?'

'Unfortunately, yes, my lord. And that is not all.'

'What else?'

'The Thebans have destroyed only one village, but—'

'That's excellent news! So the others have resisted successfully.'

'No, my lord. Queen Ahhotep has spoken to each village chief and persuaded them all to change sides. From now on they are to be under the protection of the Egyptian troops stationed at Buhen and of Medjai guards. We thought we had subjugated these tribes once and for all, but they now form the first line of defence against us. And also . . .'

'Also what?'

The scribe bowed his head. 'And also there is no reason for the enemy army to stop when it is making such good progress.'

'Do you mean that this woman Ahhotep and her damned pharaoh might dare attack Kerma? That would be a fatal mistake.'

Maddened as a fighting-bull, Nedjeh abandoned several very tempting dishes and ordered the city's officials to be summoned to the vast round council-hut, abandoning their daily business.

Nedjeh did not hide the gravity of the situation from them. This time, it was no longer possible to regard the Theban army as of no importance.

'Ahhotep will establish herself in Miu,' he said, 'and consolidate her position in the hope that we will leave our territory to attack her. But we shall not fall into that trap. On the contrary, we shall lay one for her. The best strategy is to strengthen our town's defences and to mass our troops north of the Third Cataract. The Egyptians will eventually become impatient and advance towards us. Thanks to our knowledge of the terrain, we shall easily wipe them out.'

Appealing to the Hyksos was out of the question. If they intervened, they would use the opportunity to seize Kerma. So Nedjeh must resolve the situation himself. He was beginning to realize what it was that prompted Queen Ahhotep to take so many risks: the taste for conquest.

Seeing that Nedjeh was not reacting, she would think he was at bay and attack his capital like a famished beast. A beast which would fall into a deadly trap.

## 30

The sound of drums thundered throughout Miu, but they were not the drums of war. Nubians from every village in the region had laid down their weapons before Pharaoh Kamose and Queen Ahhotep.

The reputation of the great, invulnerable sorceress had spread quickly, and the tribal chiefs had chosen submission in preference to annihilation, particularly since the pharaoh had promised to pardon them, so long as they became faithful allies of Egypt. And every tribe had suffered great cruelty at the hands of Nedjeh, that unscrupulous predator.

Long days of debate proved necessary to establish a clear hierarchy, acceptable to everyone. Several times, Ahhotep's skilful diplomacy averted a split between rival factions, and they were eventually happy to stand together beneath the banner of the young king who would ensure their safety.

'The queen is truly an extraordinary woman,' said the Afghan to Moustache as they gazed at incredible scenes of Egyptian soldiers and Nubian warriors fraternizing: instead of killing each other, they were celebrating, drinking beer and date-wine.

'The only problem,' Moustache pointed out, putting an arm round the nurse who took such good care of him, 'is that the conquest of Nubia isn't our goal. They're waiting for us up there in the North.'

'You are never happy about anything! Take your time, because no one knows what tomorrow will bring. Or rather they do: we shall have to face Nedjeh.'

'You're right. Let's not talk about that tonight. Let's have another drink.'

'What is the situation?' Nedjeh asked the official in charge of defences.

'You should be pleased, my lord. We have dug many ditches, which are perfectly hidden. At the bottom, we have placed well-sharpened stakes. Hundreds of Egyptian foot-soldiers will be impaled upon them.'

There was still much to be done, but the work was going well. The Egyptian army would meet only feeble resistance on the outskirts of

Kerma and, blinded by its successes, would think that the great Nubian city was defeated in advance. Nedjeh would sacrifice a few men who would fight to the death to defend the main road.

At the head of his troops, Pharaoh Kamose would charge towards a new triumph, and all the Nubian traps would be sprung simultaneously. The Egyptian advance guard would fall into the ditches, and the rear guard would be wiped out by Nubian archers hidden in the trees and fields. As for the main body of the army, it would be trapped by Nedjeh's foot-soldiers. Terrified by this ferocious attack, the Thebans would seek salvation in flight and would be wiped out to the last man.

The skulls of Kamose and Ahhotep would end up in the prince's tomb, and Apophis was certain to congratulate him.

At the thought of the joyful times ahead, the fat man moved with more ease than usual. Ahhotep was wrong if she thought her magic was stronger than his. If he had the good fortune to take her alive, he would make her suffer unspeakable tortures before granting her the mercy of death.

The celebrations were still under way. The Nubians rivalled each other in magnificence, wearing red wigs which contrasted with their black skin, gold earrings and kilts decorated with floral patterns. With their necklaces of many-coloured pearls, and bracelets at their wrists and ankles, the Nubian women were irresistibly seductive.

Only Moon and Neshi did not yield to the intoxicating atmosphere. Moon inspected boat after boat, while Neshi was permanently preoccupied with supply matters. Both were perfectionists and thought only of the next battle, which was bound to be terrifying.

This was not the case with Moustache, who had fallen in love with the province of Miu and almost forgotten the Delta of his birth.

'You should settle here and start a family,' suggested the Afghan.

'Me, have children? Are you serious? Live idly here while the Hyksos occupy my country? Sometimes you don't know what you're talking about.'

'Enjoy the rest of the evening and try to have a clear head tomorrow morning. The senior officers have been summoned to the flagship.'

Kamose and Ahhotep listened attentively to the detailed reports given by Moon and Neshi. Moon's appointment had been well received by all the troops, who were also delighted with Neshi's efficiency. Neither man had any problems to report. The war-fleet was ready to set sail for Kerma and attack its ruler, the Hyksos's ally.

This time, most of the soldiers had no fear of the coming battle. Per-Hathor, Elephantine, Buhen, Miu . . . the growing list of their victories gave rise to a solid feeling of comradeship, sustained by Queen Ahhotep's magic.

Kamose himself dreamt of coming face to face with Nedjeh and killing him in his own palace. All that remained was to gain the agreement of the queen, who had consulted the moon-god for a large part of the night.

All eyes turned towards the Wife of God.

'We are retracing our steps,' she declared.

'But, Mother, why not deliver the decisive blow?' asked the king in astonishment.

'Because Nedjeh has set a trap for us and we would not escape unharmed. We would be wrong to think he will not fight back, and that he is resigned to submitting to us. On the contrary, he thinks only of destroying us by means of trickery. We have achieved our objective: Nedjeh is isolated in Kerma. If he tries to leave it, he will come up against our forces in Miu, together with the Medjai and Buhen. What matters most is to make him believe we do indeed intend to capture his kingdom.'

Kamose could not oppose her argument. And he was burning to drive north at last.

'However,' added Ahhotep, 'there is one last thing we must accomplish in Nubia.'

The fleet halted near Aniba, to the north of Buhen. Immediately a caravan was formed and it set off into the western desert, to a quarry begun by Pharaoh Khafra, builder of one of the great pyramids on the Giza plateau. The queen had asked her son to remain on the flagship, and she was accompanied only by fifty men guided by Long-Ears.

As they neared the quarry they saw grey and green stones lying here and there; they also saw unfinished stelae and statues. Warned of the Hyksos invasion, the sculptors had abandoned the quarry, which had lapsed into sleep beneath the burning sun of the Great South.

Seeing that their goal had been reached, Long-Ears halted. Ahhotep gave him and Laughter water to drink. His thirst slaked, the giant dog ran around in all directions, then returned to his mistress.

Ahhotep had obeyed the moon-god and come here, but she did not yet know why. She looked wonderingly upon the unfinished masterpieces and promised that she would reopen this quarry as soon as Egypt was liberated. One day, Nubia must be covered with splendid temples so that the gods might dwell in this proud, burning land.

Alone with her dog at the heart of this overheated stone world, the queen gazed at the seams that had been so carefully cut. They reminded her of the necessary steps that separated her from the final triumph, which was still so far away and unattainable. She would surely need the patience and solidity of stone to wear down the emperor's terrifying strength.

Young Laughter growled. A royal cobra had slithered out of a crack in the rock and was coming towards Ahhotep. The dog was well aware of the danger, so, despite his courage, he kept his distance while he looked for an angle of attack.

'Stay away, Young Laughter,' said Ahhotep. 'This is the lord of the quarry. I have come to meet him, so I have nothing to fear.'

Only half convinced, the dog remained wary.

The cobra did not rear up as if to strike. On the contrary, it stretched itself out flat on the ground.

Ahhotep seized it firmly behind the head.

'Look, Young Laughter! The power that runs through the earth agrees to become my weapon.'

The snake had been transformed into a staff of cornelian, stiff and light.

The dog sniffed it for a long time. Then, satisfied with his examination, he led the queen back to the encampment.

## 31

After a night disturbed by his itching skin and one of his wife's bouts of hysteria, which he had cured with a slap, High Treasurer Khamudi got up much earlier than usual.

It was the time of day when one of his Egyptian slave-girls cleaned the rooms, making not a sound so as to avoid disturbing the couple.

What Khamudi saw took his breath away. Unaware that he was there, the slave slipped into a cloth bag a valuable mirror the emperor's wife had recently given him. The slave was actually daring to steal from him in his own home!

'Curse you, what do you think you're doing?'

The girl was so frightened that she dropped the bag. As it hit the stone floor, the precious mirror shattered.

'Forgive me, Master, forgive me! I wanted to sell it so that I could take care of my parents. Believe me, I beg of you!'

Khamudi grabbed a wooden stool and smashed it down on the girl's head. She collapsed to the floor. Maddened with rage, he trampled her underfoot, shouting so loudly that the whole household was aroused. The other servants watched, powerless, as he killed a young woman born of an excellent family in Sais. She had escaped deportation only to die by the hand of an enraged torturer.

'Stop, Khamudi, stop!' shouted Yima, trying to pull him back. 'She's dead!'

Eventually he emerged from his frenzy and calmed down. 'Have hot branding-irons brought to me and summon all my staff.'

Terror-stricken, the slaves were herded into a corner of the room by Hyksos guards.

'The thief who tried to steal my mirror has been suitably punished,' declared Khamudi emphatically. 'So that no one else will try the same thing, I am going to brand everything that belongs to me, whether slaves or objects. You, come here.'

The assistant cook Khamudi pointed at tried to run away, but two guards pinned him to the ground. As Khamudi branded him on the back, the young man let out a heart-rending cry of pain.

Although he usually had a hearty appetite, Khamudi merely toyed with his food.

'Are you ill, my darling?' asked Yima.

'No, of course not.'

'But . . . you're all yellow.'

'Don't talk nonsense.'

'Look at yourself in a mirror, I beg of you.'

Khamudi had to face facts: he did indeed have jaundice.

Emperor Apophis was eager to examine an interesting discovery made in the library at the temple in Sais: papyri devoted to geometry, mathematics and medicine. He enjoyed nothing more than the world of figures and calculations, which excluded all human considerations. A thousand deportees, a hundred executions . . . It was so simple and so entertaining to write these quantities on a papyrus, which took on the force of law without his having to listen to cries or protestations. Reducing people to numbers, and manipulating them in the tranquillity of his palace: that was surely the summit of power.

Life, divided up geometrically; the state, directed by mathematics; the economy, subject to equations: that was the goal the emperor had attained. Egypt, the supreme land of the gods, was his own private workshop, where he could experiment as he wished.

The festering stalemate at Qis amused him. Little by little, the army of liberation was rotting on its feet, wondering when the Hyksos troops would at last launch a major offensive. Without the support of Queen Ahhotep and Pharaoh Kamose, the rebels would eventually turn on their leaders.

Apophis's only real concern was the rebellion by the Anatolians, tough fighters whom Jannas was tracking in their mountains, where they had innumerable hideouts. As ever, Jannas was proceeding patiently and methodically: he was quartering the terrain and advancing step by step, avoiding the ambushes the enemy laid. In view of the difficulty of the operation, Apophis had sent him reinforcements taken from the regiments stationed in Palestine. Just like the pirates in the Mycenaean islands, the Anatolians would be wiped out to the last man.

As he was preparing to attend his Great Council, the emperor was informed that the High Treasurer was suffering from severe jaundice. He was vomiting and unable to take any food.

Was this the moment to rid himself of Khamudi and replace him?

Carefully doctored medicine would send him discreetly to the tomb before his charming wife was entrusted to the tender care of the lady Aberia. But whom could he find who would be more servile and more skilful? No one knew more secrets than the High Treasurer, who managed the empire's interests – and therefore the emperor's – supremely well. Khamudi had no wish to take the place of Apophis, who allowed him to indulge his corruption and depraved vices and never censured him for them.

No, the emperor could not find a better right-hand man. So he consulted an old treatise on Egyptian medicine.

Lukewarm water and oil injected into the anus with an ivory horn: these were the only remedies Yima would allow, fearing her husband would be poisoned. But Khamudi was fading away under her very eyes and complaining of pains all over.

'Lady Yima,' a frightened servant informed her, 'it is the emperor!'

'You don't mean . . . The emperor is here, in my house?'

'Yes, my lady. He has just arrived.'

The servants rushed to open all the doors to Apophis, whose dragging gait seemed to embody heavy threats. Whenever she saw him, Yima could not prevent her stomach gurgling ridiculously.

'Majesty, I am deeply honoured.'

'Your husband is fond of luxury,' said Apophis in the harsh voice that froze the blood of even the bravest man. 'But that is normal – my High Treasurer should be a rich man. Khamudi must be cured quickly, so I have brought him a remedy prepared at the palace. It is composed of wine, powdered sisyphus, figs, lotus-leaves, juniper-leaves, fresh incense and sweet beer. The proportions recommended by the doctors of the Old Kingdom have been strictly adhered to. Have him drink it immediately.'

As she took the phial, Yima was rooted to the spot. It was impossible to oppose the emperor's will, but she could not help but realize that he was forcing her to kill her own husband.

Up to that moment, she had believed that Khamudi was so vital to the smooth running of the empire that Apophis would not move against him. But a plotter must have sprung up in the shadows, like a poisonous plant, and it was too good an occasion not to get rid of the current High Treasurer.

'What are you waiting for, Yima? The sooner Khamudi drinks that remedy, the sooner he will recover.'

'Must he drink all of it?'

'Of course. According to the old papyrus, four days' treatment are necessary. The three other phials will be delivered to you tomorrow.'

Yima was covered in gooseflesh. Not only would there be no other phials but she would be accused of murder and executed.

'Now hurry up, and come back and tell me what the effects are. You know very well that I have no time to lose.'

Biting her lip, Yima entered Khamudi's chamber, where he lay almost unconscious. With a trembling hand, she opened his mouth and poured in the reddish, odourless liquid.

Supporting himself on the shoulder of a servant, Khamudi entered the vast reception chamber. The emperor, who disliked the light, stood in the darkest corner.

Yima walked behind her husband, still not believing her good fortune. Khamudi had drunk the potion, and not only was he not dead but he had immediately felt so much better that he had insisted on getting up to greet his illustrious guest.

'I am still rather weak,' he said, 'but I have my appetite back. Majesty, you saved my life.'

Apophis's satisfied smile did not reassure Yima at all.

## 32

Nedjeh was putting the finishing touches to his pitfalls. Soon, the Theban army would advance on Kerma, confident of an easy victory and never suspecting that they would scarcely have time to fight at all. After killing Ahhotep and Kamose, Nedjeh would take back Miu and Buhen. Should he then continue north and recapture Elephantine? Yes, but only to give it straight back to the emperor, in order to win his good graces and prove to him that his faithful ally was content with his own kingdom.

The whole city was on a war footing, and everyone was certain that the enemy would be struck a fatal blow, thanks to Nedjeh's strategic skill.

A scout came in and bowed. 'Majesty, I have just returned from Miu. All the tribes in the province have submitted to Ahhotep, and several times I was almost caught by Egyptian patrols.'

'I should have slaughtered the tribes!' roared the fat man. 'Because of me they have all the food they can eat, yet they betray me in favour of those damned Thebans! When are they going to attack?'

'Soon, or so it would seem. They are strengthening their positions and fortifying the villages while preparing for the attack. It will not be easy to get more detailed information, but Kerma must be their next objective.'

'Let them come,' murmured Nedjeh hungrily. 'Let them come, and we shall give them the welcome they deserve.'

The young man was proud to be a member of the army of liberation which, although pinned down in one place, was managing to hold off the Hyksos. Despite a few fierce attacks, the enemy had not succeeded in breaking the Theban line.

Born in Qis, the son of peasants, and a peasant himself, the lad had learnt how to fight where he stood, beside Ahmes, son of Abana, who had taught him to dodge aside before crushing an enemy's skull with a heavy wooden club. True, Hyksos helmets were strong, but the young peasant's arm was even more so. Together with his comrades from his village, he could boast of having halted a murderous assault.

'Duck down,' advised Ahmes, who was crouched at the foot of the earthwork he had just built.

'I'm not afraid of anything.'

'The Hyksos are excellent archers. And they handle the slingshot very well, too.'

'No better than we do,' protested the young man, sending a large stone whistling on its way towards the enemy camp.

'Get down!'

It was the last order Ahmes gave the young recruit. Hit on the forehead by a pointed flint, the peasant died instantly.

A deluge of missiles rained down on the earthworks protecting the main entrance to the Egyptian camp. From time to time the Hyksos unleashed an onslaught like this, pursuing a war of position which went on for ever. But did they know how the Theban forces were dwindling? It was a miracle that they had held out for so long. The messages brought by the carrier-pigeons gave the rebels some comfort, but they were no substitute for fresh troops.

When the slingshots fell silent Ahmes went to the army's headquarters, where Emheb was slowly recovering from a wound in his thigh.

'The pressure is increasing, Governor. We need reinforcements.'

'Every young man from Qis and the surrounding countryside has already joined us. We have no more reserves.'

'Should we not fall back on Thebes with the survivors, before it is too late?'

'And abandon Qis? That would be the start of defeat.'

'It would be a tactical retreat, Governor, nothing more.'

'You know that is not so.'

Ahmes sprinkled his brow with tepid water. 'You're right, I know it isn't. But victories in Nubia are no use to us. It is here that we must fight.'

'You are very young, my boy, and you do not yet see far into the distance. Queen Ahhotep's decisions are vital for our future, but you won't understand them until later.'

'Later? When we are dead? Our men are exhausted – they have given everything. Leave me here with the bravest, Governor, and go. We'll hold back the Hyksos for as long as we can.'

Emheb got to his feet with difficulty. 'My old leg will soon be better, and I shall hold our position myself.'

'Queen Ahhotep doesn't want us all to die, does she? So let us do what is necessary.'

'The queen is much more remarkable than you could ever imagine,' declared Emheb with feeling. 'Since she embarked upon the liberation of Egypt, she has not made a single mistake. Soon, I am sure, a new message will come from the gods.'

Ahmes wondered if the governor had not also been wounded in the head: whether he liked it or not, Qis was on the point of collapse. 'Let us both try to put on a brave face,' he advised, 'and boost our troops' morale.'

As they left the governor's tent, the sound of fluttering wings made them look up.

'Rascal!' exclaimed Emheb. 'Come here quickly.'

The pigeon alighted gently on the governor's shoulder. A tiny papyrus bearing the royal seal was attached to his left leg.

The message was short and to the point: '*Hold fast. We are coming.*'

The Great Council of the Hyksos was held in the Temple of Set. The emperor was last to arrive. As he passed, everyone bowed low, including the High Treasurer, who had recovered completely, much to everyone's surprise. He must indeed be an important man for Apophis to have treated him instead of killing him.

Swathed in a brown cloak, the emperor was even more sinister than usual. If his eyes lingered too long on an official, death was certain. Today, though, he seemed content to listen to Khamudi's financial reports, without glaring at anyone in particular.

The empire's wealth was continuing to grow, and the temporary loss of Anatolian tributes was not going to reverse that growth. Commander Jannas, at the head of a powerful army, was even now crushing the rebellion, which would undoubtedly be the last.

'We have just received a long message from the King of Kerma by ... by the usual route,' said Khamudi; he would not reveal the secret means of communication used. 'He pays homage to Emperor Apophis, thanks him for his goodness, and rejoices in the calm that reigns in Nubia. The tribes are obedient, the country is prosperous, and gold will continue to be delivered to Avaris.'

The emperor deigned to smile faintly.

This demonstration of good temper prompted one of the officials to ask the question that was on everybody's lips: 'Majesty, when will the rebels at Qis be wiped out? Their very existence is an insult to Hyksos greatness.'

Apophis's expression hardened. 'You miserable imbecile, don't you realize that it is only by my consent that the front at Qis exists? The Theban puppets are exhausting themselves there for nothing, and the survivors will soon be forced to retreat to Thebes. We shall pursue them and reduce that rebel city to ashes.'

'Do you not fear, Majesty, that Queen Ahhotep may eventually decide to help them?'

Apophis's eyes burnt with an evil flame. 'The emperor of the Hyksos fears no one. That woman Ahhotep is nothing but an upstart whose horrible death will serve as an example to anyone who might think of trying to imitate her.'

As Apophis had received no alarming messages from his spy, whom even Ahhotep could not identify, he knew that the last rebels at the front would obtain no more help.

'I should add,' said Khamudi, 'that Qis has no economic importance. Trade continues as normal through the great control-post at Khmun, which is beyond the rebels' reach.'

The emperor rose, signifying the end of the meeting. With an irritated wave of the hand, he indicated to Khamudi that the insolent man who had dared doubt his omnipotence was to be killed. The man was rather portly, so he would probably be a poor performer in the labyrinth, but he would amuse Apophis for a few minutes.

As he left the Temple of Set, the emperor felt his legs grow so heavy that he gladly sat down on a chair borne by slaves – a chair which the pharaohs of the Middle Kingdom had used before him.

Apophis shut himself away in his secret room at the heart of the citadel. Then he laid his hands delicately upon his blue-glazed flask, on which a map of Egypt had been drawn. When he placed his index finger on Avaris, then on Memphis and Khmun, each glowed bright red.

Reassured, he touched Elephantine. At first the red glow appeared. But very soon it flickered, and in its place appeared strange images: an eye, a rearing cobra, a gryphon with a pointed beak, and a jackal's head. By using every bit of his magic, the emperor managed to make the vile things disappear, but Elephantine remained a blue dot on the map. That meant Apophis could no longer win back control: the Thebans had seized the great city and neither Nedjeh nor the Hyksos spy had been able to warn him.

Nedjeh was playing his own game, the spy had been caught and killed, and Ahhotep had won back all the land between Thebes and Elephantine. That was the new reality. There was no longer any question of waiting for Jannas to return before breaking through the front at Qis.

## 33

Ahhotep had fixed the ivory throwing-stick bearing the signs of power to one of the highest battlements of the fortress at Elephantine. The eye would blind the emperor, the cobra would extinguish his destructive fire, the gryphon would confuse his perception, and the jackal's head would fill his mind with anxiety. At least, that was what the queen hoped. She was convinced that Apophis had cast many spells on Egypt in order to hold it in a prison of curses, whose bars must be broken one by one.

Several boats and crews had remained in Miu, others at Buhen and the rest at Elephantine. Of the army that had originally set sail to conquer the South, barely half remained.

'Is it wise to lose so many soldiers?' asked Kamose worriedly.

'Holding the South is vital,' said Ahhotep. 'But it is true that we shall be short of men to attack the North.'

'In other words, Mother, our attack is bound to fail.'

'Certainly not, my son. Since the beginning of this war, the situation has always been the same: we are fewer in number and our weapons are inferior, but we are endowed with the energy of the royal cobra that adorns Pharaoh's crown. You must make yourself many, breathe courage into those who lack it, and act with the strength of Horus – but also with that of Set.'

'You can rely on me, Majesty.'

With a pang of nostalgia, Moustache thought of the pretty Nubian girl to whom he had had to bid farewell. Her jet-black, enchantingly soft skin, her breasts, so firm and yet so soft to the touch, her legs, as long as a gazelle's . . . He never stopped reliving the charms of that sorceress, with whom he had almost fallen in love. But he was a warrior, who had no right to become attached to a woman.

Depressed, he headed for the stern of the boat to drink a jar of beer.

Suddenly he stopped in his tracks. A heap of baskets next to the jars had moved. Dagger in hand, Moustache crept closer: there must be a stowaway on board.

'Come out of there!' he ordered.

The baskets moved again, and the Nubian girl's face appeared. Moustache gaped. 'You, here?'

'I didn't want to leave you, so I hid. I want to go with you, wherever you're going.' She wriggled free and threw her arms round his neck.

'You are just like a panther, a she-cat.'

'She-cat . . . I like that very much. From now on, that is what you must call me.'

'Listen, you have no right to travel on a war-boat and—'

'You're a war-hero, aren't you? Besides, I can fight. All you have to say is that I am your Nubian soldier.'

Moustache sensed that he would not win this particular fight. And as he really had fallen in love, he went to see Moon, who with his usual skill was guiding the fleet towards Thebes.

As they neared Thebes, Ahhotep's heart skipped a beat. This was where she had been born, where she had loved and where the desire for freedom had lit up her life. No other landscape could ever replace the splendour of the Nile, the great Peak of the West, the peaceful fields interspersed with palm-groves. Normally dedicated to peace, this enchanting place had nevertheless been transformed into the home of war, since that was the only language that could be used when dealing with the Hyksos.

She relived the Nubian expedition in her thoughts. It was evident that the Hyksos spy had not harmed it in any way. The conclusion was inevitable: he had stayed in Thebes. The names she was compelled to think of were those of people beyond suspicion. And yet Seqen had indeed been betrayed.

Hailed by cheering crowds, the boat reached its moorings. In accordance with tradition, the queen presented Hathor, patron of boat travel, with an offering of incense to thank her for her protection.

The first to rush up the gangplank was little Ahmose, who leapt into his mother's arms.

'Have you worked hard?' she asked.

'Grandmother and I never stopped. You shall see how beautiful and clean the houses are. We've cleaned everything, even the weapons.'

Teti the Small looked ten years younger. Anyone who had forgotten that the fragile old lady was the queen's mother, charged with watching over Thebes in the absence of Ahhotep and the pharaoh, had been forcibly reminded. Angered by the Thebans' easygoing attitude, Teti had re-established strict rules of cleanliness and, with Qaris and Heray, had seen that they were obeyed. Not a single home or storehouse had escaped being cleansed and purified. Each house was now equipped with jugs and basins for washing thoroughly in the morning, and with a supply of natron, the best of all mouthwashes. The weaving-workshops had produced many tunics for both men and women, who were delighted to renew their clothing.

In the shade of fabric canopies stretched between four stakes, barbers shaved the soldiers each morning and washed their hair, while the ladies' hairdressers worked hard to make them as pretty as possible, not forgetting to anoint them with perfume – it was admittedly still rather basic but it spoke of better days to come. By means of curling-tongs and spatulas for spreading wax, wigs were put back to work. The craftsmen were still a long way from achieving the masterpieces of yore, but they were once again making model wooden heads and slowly regaining their forgotten skills.

Even the most modest of houses was now furnished with mats, storage chests, cooking-pots, ladles, grain-bins, jars for oil and beer, and an amulet representing the god Bes, whose hearty laughter drove away evil spirits. Sturdy brooms, made from long, stiff palm-fibres, enabled housewives to banish dust, while teams of washermen ensured that linens were kept clean.

The military base had become an attractive small town. Each morning it was filled with the scent of fresh bread. Young Ahmose had not exaggerated: Teti the Small really had been busy.

The most surprised person of all was She-Cat, who marvelled at the sight of the pretty white houses and their well-kept gardens. 'This is not a place to make war,' she said. 'Are we going to live here?'

Moustache smiled. 'You are. I have to leave again.'

'I've told you I won't leave you, and I'm very stubborn.'

'She-Cat, I—'

'Take me into one of those houses and give me a fine tunic. Then we shall make love.'


The closed council meeting took place on the terrace of the royal palace, bathed by the setting sun. The evening was so delightful that, for a few moments, Ahhotep wished she could forget past and future battles, persuade herself that the goal had been attained and there was no need to go any further.

But to yield to that illusion would have been the worst kind of desertion. Besides, she had to hear Qaris's report.

'Majesties, Rascal has returned from Qis. Emheb received your message and awaits you with impatience. Unfortunately, there is a danger of another front being opened up at Kebet. Our lookouts fear a counter-attack by the last supporters of the Hyksos in the region, aided by the garrisons in the forts on the desert road.'

'The safety of Thebes must be guaranteed,' said Kamose. 'Before leaving for the North, we must resolve the problem of Kebet.'

'Emheb and his men must be at the point of exhaustion,' objected Ahhotep. 'We cannot make them wait any longer. You, the wearer of the White Crown, must sail quickly to their aid. I and two attack regiments will take care of Kebet.'

'Mother, that's madness.'

'With respect, Majesty,' put in Heray, 'I agree with Pharaoh.'

'Perhaps, my son, acts of madness are all we have left.'

## 34

After embracing his mother, whom he feared he might never see again, Kamose set off for Qis at the head of a reduced fleet, his heart in turmoil.

It took Ahhotep some time to console Ahmose, who was furious at not being allowed to accompany his brother. At last he stopped sulking and agreed to continue training, particularly since Teti had promised not to give him preferential treatment.

'Mother,' asked Ahhotep, 'did you notice anything unusual in Thebes during my absence?'

Teti thought, then shook her head.

'Nothing about Qaris's or Heray's behaviour caught your attention?'

'No. But you can't mean you suspect them of—'

'Be very watchful, I beg you.'

'You aren't really going to venture on the road to Kebet, are you? You said that to reassure Kamose, but you mean to stay in Thebes, don't you?'

Ahhotep smiled. 'You know me so well. Why ask?'

The queen had chosen the two regiments commanded by Moustache and the Afghan for a specific reason: their experience of quick, effective raids; she did not have enough men for a frontal assault on the enemy. The little troop would have almost no time to rest and would have to summon their last reserves of strength, especially if they suffered heavy losses.

Ahhotep addressed the soldiers, hiding nothing of the hardships they were about to endure. Not a single man withdrew.

'It's fear, not courage,' explained Moustache. 'They know that the Afghan and I break the backs of deserters. Grant me one favour, Majesty: She-Cat wants to carry my water-skins.'

'Does she know the dangers she'll be facing?'

'A Nubian girl fears neither snakes nor wild beasts. And this one is more stubborn than all other women put together! Oh forgive me, Majesty, I did not mean to say that—'

'We leave in an hour.'

The leading citizens of Kebet gathered in the forecourt of the temple to discuss the future. They dreaded the Hyksos so much that they were planning to change their allegiance, turning their backs on young Pharaoh Kamose, who would never be able to consolidate his power. True, Thebes was holding its head high again, but for how long? It was no good thinking about it: this rebellion would not last long, and only those who collaborated with the emperor would escape his vengeance. Voices in favour of rallying officially to the Hyksos cause were beginning to ring out when the Queen of Egypt made her appearance.

Attired in a gold diadem and a simple white dress, Ahhotep was more beautiful than ever. The crowd fell silent and bowed.

'The wounds of the occupation are still far from healed,' she said, 'and Kebet needs many repairs. Instead of debating idly, you should be at work.'

'Majesty,' said the High Priest of Min, 'we are your faithful servants and—'

'I know that you were preparing to betray me because you do not believe in Thebes's final victory. You are wrong.'

'You must understand, Majesty, the Hyksos are threatening us.'

'I am here to liberate the desert road for ever, and to guarantee Kebet's safety. If you show any more signs of cowardice, you will have me for an enemy.'

The queen's actions gave Kebet renewed life. She set out a programme of urgent works and appointed new administrators who would be responsible directly to her. The common people could approach and speak to her, and that simple contact brought hope to life again.

As always, the Afghan and Moustache looked on admiringly.

'She really is extraordinary,' said the Afghan yet again.

'Be content with obeying her,' advised Moustache, 'and don't waste time on crazy dreams. Every man in Egypt is in love with her, except me, now that I've got my Nubian girl – and even that's not certain.'

'There isn't a woman like her in the world. Even the most battle-hardened war-leader would have lost heart long ago, but she hasn't. The fire in her is not of this world.'

'But we are. This may be our last night on this earth, Afghan, so let's make the best of it.'

The queen had granted leave to all her men, and the taverns of Kebet welcomed them warmly. Everyone preferred not to think of the coming day.

While talking to a caravan-owner, the Afghan, although he was tipsy, had an idea which might save many Theban lives.

'Come on, Moustache, we must speak to the queen.'

'She'll be asleep.'

'Never mind. We'll wake her up.'

Heavy-footed, the two men headed for the governor's palace, where Ahhotep was staying. Not only was she not asleep, but she was actually implementing the plan – which she had thought of long before the Afghan did.

The first Hyksos fort stood about two hours to the east of Kebet and held absolute control of the road. No caravans could reach the city, because the emperor's soldiers intercepted them and stripped them of their goods.

This plunder made the difficult desert living-conditions bearable, but the Hyksos had not given up the idea of retaking Kebet. Soon the garrisons of the five forts between the town and the Red Sea would unite to attack the city. It had been sent an ultimatum: either it recognized the emperor's supremacy, or its entire population would be slaughtered.

'Caravan in sight!'shouted a lookout.

The commander of the fort joined him at his observation post. It was indeed a caravan, and a sizeable one, but it was not coming from the desert.

'It's coming from Kebet,' said the commander, 'and they must be important people. They're surrendering! Look at them, all those frightened people, and all the riches they're going to lay at our feet. Let's run the mayor through and decapitate the others.'

'I'd like to keep the donkey,' said the lookout. 'I've never seen such a fine one.'

'I'm the commander here, and I'll decide who gets what from the booty. Forget that donkey and think of the Kebet girls – they'll lick your feet and beg for mercy.'

Laughing heartily, the Hyksos let the donkeys approach, with the dignitaries and their servants. The governor of Kebet and his retinue were trembling, afraid they would be shot by the archers before they had even reached the gate of the fort. But they were so pitiful that the emperor's men didn't bother to waste their arrows. Torture would be much more amusing.

'Lie face down in the dust,' ordered the commander.

The dignitaries did so, looking more and more terrified.

Long-Ears gave the signal for the attack, by charging the officer and butting him hard. The Theban soldiers stopped pretending to be servants and threw their double-bladed daggers with deadly precision.

Meanwhile, Moustache, the Afghan and ten men arrived by means of a minor road shown on a map which had belonged to the traitor Titi. Taking advantage of the enemy's slackness, they scaled the watchtower and killed the archers.

In less than a quarter of an hour, the Hyksos garrison was wiped out. The Egyptians had suffered only two casualties, and they were minor wounds which She-Cat was already treating.

'You played your part well, Governor,' said Ahhotep, 'and so did your people.'

The governor was still shaking. 'Majesty,' he begged, 'may we go home now?'

'We still have four more forts to capture,' replied the queen with a broad smile.

## 35

The last Hyksos attack had been murderous. With a courage bordering on foolhardiness, Ahmes, son of Abana, had managed to whip up the bravery of a hundred terrified youths and they had fought off a raiding-party of black-helmeted footsoldiers, the very sight of whom scared them out of their wits.

Once the attack had been repulsed, only ten exhausted survivors were left. Covered in enemy blood, Ahmes did not even take the time to wash before speaking to Emheb.

'It is finished, Governor. We can no longer hold the line.'

'The message Rascal brought was perfectly clear,' Emheb reminded him.

'The Thebans have been delayed or killed – either way, they won't come. If we don't fall back, we'll be wiped out.'

The governor did not protest: Ahmes was right. 'Give me one more day.'

'If the Hyksos launch another attack, we won't be able to hold. It would be playing with fire.'

'As a general rule, they take their time – sometimes a lot of time – before they attack again.'

'As a general rule, yes. But this time they saw that the front was no thicker than a sycamore leaf. In their place, I'd attack in the next few hours.'

'We'll organize our defence as best we can, and prepare to retreat.'

Emheb had spent the night burying corpses in simple, hastily dug trenches. There were no sarcophagi, no papyri bearing the words of resurrection, not even an ordinary protective amulet. The governor could do nothing but speak an ancient invocation to Osiris, beseeching him to welcome into paradise these young men, who had not hesitated to give their lives in an attempt to vanquish the empire of darkness.

And then dawn rose over an Egyptian camp which had no strength left. Two seriously wounded men died before the first rays of the sun were seen. Emheb buried them, too.

'You must get some sleep,' urged Ahmes.

'Have you slept?'

'I haven't had time. We strengthened an earth bank, positioned defensive stakes and rebuilt low brick walls behind which our last archers will shelter. But it's all useless . . .'

'The boats are ready to leave. See that the wounded are embarked.'

It was more than a dream crumbling, much more. Once the front at Qis had given way, the Hyksos would pour south and put Thebes to fire and the sword. After Ahhotep, no one would take up the torch. The invaders' barbarity would become the common law, and the empire of darkness would grow ever larger.

On the Hyksos side, all seemed quiet, and that was even more worrying. The enemy was probably awaiting the order from Avaris to launch the final attack and sweep away the rebels.

Emheb ordered most of the soldiers to leave their posts and board the boats. Only the front line, made up entirely of volunteers, would remain in position.

'Your cabin has been cleaned, Governor,' said Ahmes. 'You can go aboard.'

'No, I'm staying here. You are to take command until you reach Thebes.'

'But, sir, you'll be needed there.'

'Our world is on the point of death, my boy, and "there" no longer exists. I'd rather fight to the end with these lads. They're half dead with fear, but they refuse to give in.'

'Then I shall stay as well. I'm the best archer in the Egyptian army, and I shall slow the Hyksos down a bit.'

The two men embraced.

'Take the left flank,' ordered Emheb, 'and I'll take the right. When we can no longer hold the line, the survivors will regroup on the hill.'

Ahmes knew only too well that they would not have time.

Emheb had one final fear: that the Hyksos attack would begin before the boats left and that the whole flotilla would be sunk before they could get away. So they were cast off quickly, at the risk of causing an accident. Fortunately nothing untoward happened. The north wind swelled the sails and the voyage to Thebes began.

Without a word, Emheb and Ahmes moved to their combat positions.

'Sir,' said Ahmes disbelievingly, 'they're coming back.'

He stood up, but with a firm hand Emheb forced him down on to his belly again.

'The boats – I swear to you, they're coming back!'

Emheb crawled up to a small hillock from which he could see the Nile but was out of range of Hyksos arrows.

The youth had good eyesight. But why were those who could escape death returning to Qis? There could be only one explanation: enemy vessels had forced them to turn back.

Nothing. Emheb could do nothing more to save them. He and the front line were caught like rats in a trap. He decided to order the footsoldiers to disperse. But one thing puzzled him: on the decks of the boats, there was not a single sign of commotion. He even thought he saw sailors dancing for joy.

A light shone from the powerful warship that seemed to be pursuing them.

At first Emheb was dazzled, then he realized that the sun's rays were glinting off the 'Resplendently Bright One', the White Crown of Pharaoh Kamose.

In his last report, the Hyksos general commanding the front at Qis had fully reassured the emperor: the war of attrition had proved effective, and the Egyptians were at their last gasp. It was therefore pointless to move an army from the Delta. One last attack would suffice to destroy the last remnants of the front.

'Is everything ready?' he asked a member of his staff.

'Yes, General. Your orders have been given to the officers.'

'This will be almost too easy,' thought the general.

After this wretched war, which had been at stalemate for so long, the Hyksos would take delight in disembowelling the last rebels. And the general's victory would be in Avaris, where he would certainly receive promotion. His boat would sail proudly up the main canal, with Governor Emheb's severed head at its prow.

Suddenly, a strange noise made him jump. 'What's that?'

'I've never heard it before,' said the assistant, his stomach turning over.

No Hyksos, indeed, had ever heard the maddening beat of the drums. Made in Nubia, they gave out fierce resonance, which put the fear of death into the Hyksos' hearts.

'It's a new curse from Queen Ahhotep,' exclaimed the assistant.

'The Hyksos will never retreat because of some damned music!' swore the general. 'Prepare to attack.'

A lookout ran up, his body dripping with sweat. 'General, the Egyptian front line has been reinforced. There are at least three times as many soldiers there now, and more are still arriving.'

'Where are they coming from?'

'From boats arriving from the south, sir. I've even seen Egyptians congratulating each other, as if they're no longer afraid.'

Shaken, the general decided to check for himself. He followed the lookout up to a promontory from where he could see the enemy front line. What he saw took his breath away.

On the highest hillock fluttered a standard bearing the emblem of Thebes, a bow and arrows. And the man who was holding it firmly in his right hand was young and strong, and wore the White Crown of Upper Egypt, which seemed to give off powerful rays of magical light.

## 36

The din of the Thebans' night-long celebrations, which were accompanied by drums, plunged the Hyksos into uncertainty.

Roasted lamb, bean paste, soft cheeses . . . With their bellies and hearts full of the joy of the feast, the Egyptians had the strength to believe in victory again. Now that supply-boats could get through, they were regaining the strength they would need to fight the emperor's troops.

Kamose was less optimistic. He did not hide the reality of the situation from Emheb. 'The messages brought by the carrier-pigeons inform me that my mother has taken the Hyksos forts on the road from Kebet to the Red Sea. But she has had to station Egyptian soldiers there as garrisons, and we have left many others in Nubia and at Elephantine, to hold our positions. I hope that she will soon join us, but with how big an army?'

'In other words, Majesty, we need more men.'

'We cannot mass all our forces at Qis. The Nubians would counter-attack from the south, and Thebes would be in danger.'

'Then we shall resort once again to a war of trenches and attrition. If the Hyksos repeat their savage attacks, how often will we be able to repel them?'

'I don't know,' confessed the pharaoh, 'but we shall not withdraw.'

'All is ready, Majesty,' declared the High Priest of the Temple of Set, as the bearers set down the emperor's chair and he stepped out.

Unlike the pharaohs, Apophis did not begin his day by celebrating a ritual. Usually he came to the shrine only to head a Great Council meeting, which often ended with the killing of an official who had become too insipid for his taste. This time, though, he was alone.

'You and your fellow priests, leave us,' he ordered.

There was such menace in the emperor's eyes that the High Priest scuttled away.

Apophis entered the temple. The oil-lamps had been extinguished, but he moved easily through the shadows. On an altar at the far end, the priests had laid a beautiful statuette of Hathor. The face was so finely sculpted that it quivered with life. The curves of the body expressed at once love, nobility and tenderness.

On another altar lay five daggers.

'Obey me, Set,' commanded the emperor. 'Help me to destroy those who oppose my will.'

Thunder rumbled overhead. Thick black clouds massed above the temple, and dogs bayed at the moon. There was only one bolt of lightning, but it was so fierce that it tore open the whole sky. It struck the daggers, whose blades became incandescent.

With the first, Apophis decapitated the statuette and cut off its feet. He plunged two blades into its breasts and two more into its belly.

'Die, accursed Ahhotep!'

After halting beneath a carob-tree with thick foliage, and savouring its honey-sweet fruits, the queen headed for the temple at Dendera, which was surrounded by tall sycamores. By means of raids organized by Moustache and the Afghan, the Thebans had liberated, one by one, the villages still controlled by the Hyksos. The peasants had been swift to lend their aid to the army that had delivered them at last from unbearable tyranny.

Suddenly, Ahhotep felt a sharp pain in her chest. Ignoring it, she walked on towards the Temple of Hathor, which she feared she would find laid waste. But fire flowed into her feet, and she had to stop.

'Are you unwell, Majesty?' asked the Afghan anxiously.

'I'm a little tired – it's nothing serious.'

The next pain, in her stomach, was so bad that she could not breathe, and had to sit down. When her thoughts began to become confused, she realized what had happened.

'It's a curse. The emperor – it must be him. Take me into the temple.'

Moustache and the Afghan ran to fetch a small boat from the canal where it was moored, and laid the queen in it. Twelve men lifted it up, ran to the great, crumbling gateway, and hurried through it.

In the great courtyard lay broken stelae and statues. The likenesses of Hathor framing the entrance to the covered temple had been decapitated and mutilated.

Three frightened priestesses, two young and one very old, greeted them on the threshold.

'Do not violate this sacred place,' said the old one. 'To enter, you will first have to kill us.'

'We are with the army of liberation,' declared Moustache. 'Queen Ahhotep is ill and needs your help.'

The boat was set down upon the flagstones.

Queen Ahhotep! The old priestess remembered her visit to Dendera with her husband, Pharaoh Seqen. She had given them the *heka*, the magical power that conferred the ability to influence the course of destiny. Today, though, its force seemed to have run dry.

'The Emperor of Darkness is trying to seize my soul,' said the queen. 'Only the Golden Goddess can tear me from his grasp.'

The priestess laid her hand on Ahhotep's forehead. 'There is not a second to lose, Majesty. The fire of Set has already invaded most of your energy-channels. One of you men, help the queen to move.'

With Moustache's agreement, the Afghan lifted her in his arms, carrying his precious burden with anguish and reverence. Fortunately, the priestess walked slowly, and he was able to follow her without stumbling.

Despite the Hyksos' threats, the High Priestess of Dendera had not revealed the hiding-place where Hathor's sacred objects were kept; even under torture, she had kept silent. Today she was being rewarded for her courage. She opened the sliding door of the secret room where the crown, sistra, necklaces and water-clock belonging to the Golden Goddess had been hidden. On the walls were painted scenes which She alone might see.

'Lay the queen on the ground,' she told the Afghan, 'and leave.'

When the door closed, a light sprang forth from a strange painting, an oval surrounded by a broken line, the first wave of creation, which had passed through matter and brought it to life. The vibration made the wall and Ahhotep's body tremble.

'The queen's soul is immersed in the *duat*, the starry matrix where the many forms of life are ceaselessly born,' explained the High Priestess. 'She must remain there for seventy hours, in the hope that the energy of Hathor will be more powerful than that of the Emperor of Darkness.'

'Aren't you certain?' asked Moustache worriedly.

'I don't know what kind of forces Apophis has used. If he called upon Set, who causes tumult in the universe, all Hathor's love will not be too much.'

'But surely the queen is in no danger of dying?' whispered the Afghan.

'May the Golden Goddess welcome her into her ship, which cuts through the darkness.'

At the end of the seventieth hour, the High Priestess of Dendera opened the door of the secret room. For what seemed an eternity, there was nothing but silence. Moustache bit his lip, while the Afghan stood still as a stone.

Eventually, Ahhotep appeared on the threshold of the little room that could so easily have been her tomb. Very pale, and walking unsteadily, she emerged from the darkness of the *duat*.

Seeing her sway, the Afghan offered her his arm.

'You must eat, Majesty,' urged Moustache.

'Before she does so, I must ensure that the queen is protected,' decreed the High Priestess. 'Wearing the goddess's necklace, she will be safe from another attack.'

The priestess entered the crypt and emerged with a *menat*. It was a strange object, formed from a necklace of gold beads and turquoises linked by two short cords to a gold counter-weight which ended in a disc, which was to be placed on the nape of the neck.

'With this symbol, the goddess transmits the magical fluid of life, which enables mothers to give birth and sailors to reach port safely. When it is held before the statue of Hathor, sadness and turmoil are dissipated. Harmful waves will break upon it.'

She placed the *menat*-necklace round Ahhotep's neck.

'It is thanks to you, Majesty, that the province of Dendera has been liberated. But how can Egypt be reborn while the temple at Abydos is still under the Hyksos threat?'

## 37

Kamose's passionate speech had reassured the Egyptian soldiers. Apophis, he said, was a 'weak-armed man whose empty heart boasted of false victories'. With such a pharaoh to lead them, the Thebans would never retreat. And when Queen Ahhotep joined forces with them, they would at last strike northwards.

There was another reason for hope: the new weapons with which the front-line troops were now equipped. Strengthened with bronze strips, the wooden shields would protect them much better from Hyksos arrows and spears. Their own spears, which now had longer, sharper bronze heads, would kill the enemy more easily, as would their sharper swords; and their new axes were easier to handle. The new helmets and breastplates, which were covered in bronze plates, would be invaluable in hand-to-hand fighting.

With this new equipment, the soldiers of Kamose and Ahhotep felt almost invulnerable. True, the fear inspired by the black-helmeted warriors was far from gone, but every man felt able to face them.

And yet, out of sight of his men, the young king's expression was sombre.

'The news is good, Majesty,' announced Emheb. 'Rascal has just brought a message saying that Queen Ahhotep has liberated the province of Dendera. She is heading for Abydos.'

'Even if she manages to join us, she'll bring no reinforcements. And if we don't take action, the Hyksos will eventually crush us.' What, he wondered, would Ahhotep have done in this situation? He was determined to prove himself worthy of her, and not merely be content to hold the ground that had been gained. He said, 'Since we're so short of volunteers, we must persuade the reluctant men to fight on our side.'

'Are you thinking of the sailors, caravaneers or mercenaries the Hyksos employ in this region?'

'We must win them over.'

'These are men without faith or honour, Majesty.'
'Then we had better give them some.'

The caravaneers unloaded the donkeys under the protection of mercenaries paid by the Hyksos. So close to the front, this kind of precaution was a necessary one. According to the latest rumours, a young pharaoh wearing the White Crown had even reached Qis. True, there was talk of a forthcoming offensive which would inflict final defeat on the Thebans, but there was still a risk that the rebels would attack convoys of goods. Only the presence of Apophis's armed men would deter them.

As usual, the animals were unloaded without incident.

Just as the Hyksos were leaving, Ahmes, son of Abana, let fly his first arrow, which killed their commander instantly. With his usual calm and precision, he decimated the enemy's ranks, assisted by other elite archers.

Frozen to the spot beside their wares, the traders saw their protectors being massacred but dared not run away. And they were in no way reassured when they saw Kamose, wearing the dazzling White Crown.

'You have been collaborating with Apophis,' he declared, 'and are therefore enemies of Egypt.'

The traders' leader fell to his knees. 'Majesty, we have been oppressed! Understand us and forgive us. Egypt reigns in our hearts.'

Kamose smiled. 'I am happy to hear that. Luckily for you, the time has come for you to prove your allegiance.'

The man's expression changed. 'Majesty, we are peaceful men and—'

'We are at war,' the pharaoh reminded him, 'and every man must choose sides. Either you stand on the side of the Hyksos, in which case you will be executed for treason, or you will fight with us.'

'But, Majesty, we have no experience of fighting.'

'My instructors will assign you tasks within your capabilities.'

Since there was no way out, the merchant tried to gain an important advantage for his fellow traders. 'The trade-tax control-post at Khmun is choking the life out of us, Majesty. The officers are Asiatics and sand-travellers who steal vast quantities of goods. Are you planning to make changes?'

'That tax-post exists only because of the occupation.'

'So if you are victorious, it will be removed?'

'If *we* are victorious, it will.'

A broad smile lit up the man's face. 'We are your loyal subjects, Majesty, and we shall fight to the best of our ability.'

*

When they saw the detachment commanded by Kamose coming towards them, the villagers fled in terror and hid in their adobe houses. Like many tiny villages to the east of Qis, this one was under the thumb of a mercenary called Large-Knees, assisted by twenty rough fellows; they imposed a reign of terror by applying every one of the Hyksos decrees. Every man had his vocation, and Large-Knees had never lived better than he had since he entered the emperor's pay. He bled the population dry, enjoyed women who would otherwise have been out of his reach, and beat anyone who dared show him disrespect.

'Sir,' shouted one of his men, 'we're being attacked!'

Somewhat fuddled by beer, Large-Knees took several moments to realize that the incredible was happening. Of course, the front at Qis existed, and some people even spoke of the army of liberation's determination. But he had never believed in it. And now here was a band of Thebans, daring to attack his domain!

Although sceptical about the Thebans' ability to advance, Large-Knees had nevertheless foreseen this show of strength. If they thought they could make him submit, they were going to have a nasty surprise.

'Have you done what is necessary?'

'Have no fear, sir.'

Large-Knees got a shock when he emerged from his quarters. The attackers' leader was an athletic young man, wearing a crown so white that it hurt the eyes to look at it.

'Lay down your weapons,' ordered Kamose. 'My men outnumber yours, and you have no chance of winning.'

'The King of Thebes is not wanted on my territory,' retorted Large-Knees with a sneer.

'You have betrayed Pharaoh by selling yourself to the Hyksos. Bow before me or you shall die.'

'My only master is Apophis. If you don't withdraw at once, you will be responsible for the deaths of all the children in this village. You see that barn over there? They have all been gathered in there, and my men won't hesitate to cut their throats as soon as I give the order.'

'What kind of person could commit such an atrocity?'

Large-Knees sniggered. 'The Hyksos have schooled me well. You're nothing but a weakling, because you still believe in the existence of Ma'at.'

'Surrender – you still have time.'

'Leave my land, or the children will be executed.'

'Amon is my witness that not a single villager will die,' declared Kamose, turning to Ahmes.

The archer's arrow plunged into Large-Knees' left eye, and he toppled backwards, dead.

Deprived of their leader and cowed by Kamose's resolution, the mercenaries threw down their swords and bows. They had no wish to die.

'The hostages are safe,' said Large-Knees' second-in-command.

'To make amends for your deeds, there is only one thing you can do: obey me and swear to fight the Hyksos. If you break your word, the Soul-Eater will devour you in the afterlife.'

The soldiers took the oath. Only too happy to have emerged unscathed, they were not unhappy to place themselves under the command of a true leader.

'You will go to the neighbouring village with a detachment of my men,' Kamose ordered his new soldiers. 'There, you will urge the leader of the local guards to do as you have done and join our ranks. Otherwise he will suffer the fate of a bandit who subjugated you.'

## 38

Abydos lay north of Dendera and south of Qis, and was consecrated to Osiris, master of eternal life. Although the sacred city had no economic importance, it housed the stelae of those people 'of just voice' who had appeared successfully before the two courts of earth and heaven.

The queen and her soldiers had pitched camp a good distance from the temple, which was plunged in silence. There was no trace of a Hyksos presence in the surrounding area. After several raids, which had enabled them to liberate the villages between Dendera and Abydos, the Thebans were grateful for a few hours' rest.

'There's no one left here,' said Moustache. 'As soon as my men have recovered their strength, shouldn't we head for the front with all due speed?'

'The Hyksos have replaced life with death,' said Ahhotep. 'At Abydos, Osiris transforms death into life, and we must first make sure that only radiant spirits reign there. Once Egypt is free, Abydos will once again become a magnificent, prosperous temple. The stelae of the just will be raised up again, and priests and priestesses will celebrate the cult and the mysteries of the god, as in days gone by.'

Ahhotep's words made happiness seem more than an illusion. And her voice continued to awaken hope, even in those who thought they had lost it for ever.

Like the other soldiers, Long-Ears and Young Laughter forgot the war for a whole day. The donkey feasted on delicious thistles, while the dog sprawled in the shade of a sycamore tree and gnawed a bone.

Towards the middle of the following morning, the party approached the temple, which was partially hidden by wild grasses.

'I could swear I hear someone mourning,' said Moustache.

'So can I,' agreed the Afghan.

On the ancient processional road leading from the shrine to a little wood appeared ten priests, whose funereal chants related the murder of Osiris by his brother Set. They seemed profoundly moved by the drama they were re-enacting, and moved extremely slowly. At their head walked a tall fellow, his head covered by a hood, and the two who brought up the rear carried clubs to strike down the followers of Set, the enemies of Osiris.

So the ancient cults were still being celebrated, even if only in token fashion.

Just as Ahhotep was approaching the priests, Long-Ears charged forward and knocked over the man in the hood, who fell heavily.

Leaping angrily to his feet, he took a dagger from a pocket of his tunic and tried to plunge it into the donkey's chest. But he had not bargained on Young Laughter, who leapt at the attacker and sank sharp teeth into his arm.

The priests armed with clubs ran at Ahhotep, intending to shatter her skull. The queen dodged the first blow, but she would not have escaped the second if the Afghan's powerful hand had not first blocked the assailant's wrist, then broken it. A second attacker could not escape Moustache, who head-butted him, smashing his nose.

'They are Hyksos!' declared one mourner, as he and the other true priests prostrated themselves at the queen's feet. 'They forced us to lay this ambush.'

Before trusting their words, the Thebans interrogated them at length. It emerged that they had indeed been taken hostage by three Hyksos, who were determined to kill the queen, even if they died in the attempt.

With tears in her eyes, Ahhotep wandered through the dirty, dilapidated temple; almost nothing remained of its ancient splendours. After meditating before the defaced scenes depicting the stages of Osiris's resurrection, she ventured into the desert, where houses of eternity had been created, far from the cultivated lands. These simple, long, narrow brick-walled chambers bore witness to the crucial period when which Upper and Lower Egypt had formed a single country for the first time. The Hyksos barbarians had taken no interest in these modest tombs.

Although the place was not imbued with sadness, Ahhotep felt so alone that the force of her will was shaken. True, the Egyptians' successes far exceeded even their wildest hopes. But was it possible to go further? On reflection, the wounds they had inflicted on the monster were only superficial. No doubt the emperor had allowed the queen to rush about like an insect, which would be easily crushed when the time came.

To go beyond Qis was a foolish dream. Beyond Qis began the true territory of the Hyksos, whose weapons were still far superior to those of the Egyptians. The tyrant would never allow Pharaoh Kamose to impinge upon his domain. But not to continue northwards, not to re-unify the Two Lands, meant losing the war and accepting once and for all an occupation which would only grow worse and worse.

Ahhotep halted before a tomb. On the offertory table before the entrance stood a small wine-jar, dedicated to Pharaoh Aha.

Aha's name meant 'the Fighter', so this must be a message from the pharaohs who had ruled at that time. She had to fight. There was no other way. She would fight to the death if necessary, and never give up the supreme goal: reunification.

When Ahhotep walked once again through the Temple of Osiris, all traces of doubt had disappeared. The spirit of the ancient kings had entered her, demanding that she look beyond the horizon of Thebes.

Under the watchful eyes of Moustache and the Afghan, a priest approached her and presented a request.

'Majesty, our High Priest is still alive. He knows the incantations needed to celebrate the rites once again, and bring back life to the names of those judged righteous by Osiris. So that his wisdom is not lost, we have hidden him in a nearby village. Since you have liberated us from the Hyksos, will you bring him back here?'

Moustache frowned. 'It looks like a trap, Majesty.

'A trap?' protested the priest. 'What do you mean? We wish only to bring our High Priest back to his home.'

'It looks more and more like a trap.'

'We shall go to the village,' decided Ahhotep.

'Majesty, at least take one precaution,' advised the Afghan. 'Make this priest walk in front of us and serve as a shield.'

The village nestled on a mound overlooking a canal. The Hyksos guard-post, which lay below, had posed no problem for Moustache, who had needed only two men to destroy it.

A handful of small children ran up, shouting for joy. A little boy jumped into the queen's arms and kissed her on both cheeks. Anxious mothers joined them, watched suspiciously by Moustache. Then the men dared to emerge from their houses, raising their hands high to show that they were unarmed.

'Is our High Priest still here?' asked the priest anxiously.

'He is, and he's safe and well,' replied the village headman.

Despite his advanced age, the High Priest was a vigorous man. Overcome with emotion, he bowed before the queen. 'I cannot believe it, Majesty! Is Abydos truly free?'

'You may return to the temple. Erect a stele in honour of Pharaoh Seqen, who is of just voice, and ensure that it is glorified each day.'

'It shall be done, Majesty. Forgive my curiosity, but have you decided to establish the border at Qis or to reconquer the North?'

'Egypt will survive only if she is reunified.'

'You speak words of gold, Majesty! But to have any hope of

success, you must know the contents of the Jar of Predictions, which reveals good and evil days. Without that list, you will make mistakes and suffer heavy losses.'

'Where is the jar?'

'At Khmun.'

## 39

As labourers unloaded the boxes sent from Asia, guards surrounded the port of Avaris. Khamudi had ordered that no one was to go near the boat, and that its cargo must be brought immediately to the palace.

As soon as it arrived, the High Treasurer abandoned his work to gaze upon the many ceramic vases. Admittedly they were rather vulgar, but their contents were priceless. As soon as he was alone in the huge cellar, he opened one of them.

It contained opium, which would be sold at a very high price to senior Hyksos officers and citizens of Avaris and the Delta cities. With the emperor's agreement, Khamudi had embarked upon the development of this new trade, which promised to be exceptionally profitable. While trying it out on some of his own entourage, he had found that users quickly became addicted to the drug and demanded more of it. Since it was the state's responsibility to ensure the well-being of those it administered, it should also derive the maximum benefits, the major part of which would go – quite rightly – to swell the emperor's fortune.

There was another, not inconsiderable benefit: many people would become dependent upon the supplies provided by Khamudi, and prices would therefore continue to rise. In a few months, the drug would have swamped all the provinces of the empire, and he would reap colossal profits. But he must first ensure that the opium was of high quality.

Taking with him a pretty, slender red vase, he returned to his house, where he found Yima having her body waxed.

'Back already, my darling?' she said.

'I have a nice surprise for you.'

'As soon as my servant has finished, I—'

'Send her away.'

Afraid of being beaten, the servant-girl hurried away.

Khamudi lit an incense-burner and heated some small balls of opium. 'You are going to sample this for me, my sweet.'

'What is it?'

'A delicacy.'

Yima enjoyed the gift. To judge from her reaction, which was of excitement punctuated with moments of apathy, Khamudi's customers were sure to be delighted.

Minos added a touch of pale blue to the pillar in the audience chamber at the palace, one of the details of the great wall-painting he was working at with meticulous care. He was a perfectionist, and painted the same figure several times before he was satisfied with it.

When a hand caressed his shoulder, he laid down his brush slowly. 'Windswept? You must let me work.'

'You've spent hours wearing yourself out, trying to make this dreary room more agreeable. It's time to enjoy yourself, don't you think?'

She pressed herself against the Minoan. The curves of their bodies fitted together perfectly, as if they had been created for each other.

'You're mad,' he said. 'Someone might catch us.'

'How exciting that is,' she whispered, untying her lover's kilt and revealing his obvious arousal.

'Windswept, no—'

'I'm in love with you, Minos, truly in love. Nothing should be forbidden to us.'

Although she was still a formidable carnivore, and still devoured the emperor's enemies by extracting bedroom confessions, she was sincerely in love with the painter, whose innocence had touched her heart. The more bored she grew in the arms of her fleeting lovers, the more intense was the pleasure she felt each time she gave herself to him. She could no longer do without him. She would never allow him to return to Minoa, even if she let him believe otherwise.

'Your paintings grow more and more beautiful,' she murmured, stretching out on top of him.

'I have made a new shade of blue, which gives greater warmth, and I'm planning to improve my other colours.'

'Will you remake your old paintings?'

'I shall have to.'

'The beauty you have created makes this fortress almost pleasant.'

'Please let's not talk about work any more. I'd rather pay attention to the work of art I'm caressing.'

A wave of pleasure flowed through Windswept. Only Minos could make her forget her crimes.

The special reception hosted by the High Treasurer and his wife was an enormous success. Most of the Hyksos senior officers were present, and they thoroughly enjoyed their first experience of opium; they were sure to become loyal customers.

Windswept had set her cap at an official responsible for weapons. He had made a few acid remarks about the front at Qis, which sounded like criticism of the emperor's policy. If that were indeed so, she would draw out his confidences, and there would be a new candidate for the labyrinth.

Yima had made sure to congratulate Minos on the splendour of his sculptures, and Windswept was jealous to see that hussy getting too close to her lover. If she continued to do so, the emperor's sister would find a way to rid herself of her rival.

'Aren't you going to try our latest delicacy?' Khamudi asked Minos.

'Judging by the behaviour of those who have, it would make my hand shake.'

'Wouldn't it give you new ideas?'

'At the moment, I have plenty of those.'

'You'll come to the drug, I'm sure. How can an artist manage without it? You can rely upon me to obtain it for you at the best price.'

'Your concern touches me, High Treasurer.'

'What could be more natural, my young friend? I'm extremely fond of modern art.'

The reception was drawing to an end, and Minos managed to escape. Pretending to be returning to his own quarters, he walked away from the citadel, glancing round several times to see if he was being followed. As he headed towards the district where most of the senior officers lived, he almost walked straight into a patrol. His heart pounding, he slid into an alleyway, hoping that none of the men had noticed him.

He had to wait several minutes until he got his breath back; then he continued on his way. Ten times, the painter halted and looked around him. Reassured, he ran the last hundred paces that separated him from the house of the man he was to meet in such great secrecy.

As agreed, the house and its outbuildings were in darkness. Minos sneaked up to the entrance, and the door opened.

'Are you sure no one followed you?' asked a strained voice.

'Absolutely sure.'

'Come in, quickly.'

The two men sat down and spoke in hushed voices.

'Have you contacted any other dignitaries?' asked Minos.

'Only two, and I took the strictest precautions. But I cannot say that they are really reliable. In my opinion, it would be better to give up your plans. Conspiring against the emperor is much too dangerous. Everyone who has tried has died in agony.'

'If I can't get rid of Apophis, I'll never be able to return to Minoa

– that would cause me agony, too. Overthrowing that tyrant is the only way.'

'The emperor has many networks of informants, not to mention Khamudi's agents. It's almost impossible to plan any kind of action against him.'

'"Almost" – there's hope in that word! We have two allies already. That's a start, isn't it?'

'Frankly, I'm afraid it won't be.'

'Aren't you determined to fight against Apophis, too?'

'I was, but he's grown so powerful that no one can oppose him. If you try, you'll end up in the labyrinth.'

'The emperor needs me,' Minos reminded him. 'Who else could decorate his citadel in the Minoan manner? He thinks I'm submissive and resigned, and I'm the last person he'd suspect. That's a big advantage, and we must exploit it.'

The other man wavered. 'There's some truth in that, but are you really aware of the danger?'

'I'm prepared to do anything at all to regain my freedom and return to my home. In the meantime, you must continue to make contact with future enemies of the emperor.'

Windswept would have liked to spend the night with Minos, but he had seemed in a hurry to leave the opium reception and go to bed. So she was thoroughly surprised to see him emerge from his quarters, taking a thousand precautions as he did.

Curious, she followed her lover, whose behaviour she found strange. When she saw him enter the house belonging to the weapons official suspected of plotting against the emperor, she felt a brutal pain in her heart.

Minos, the only man she had ever truly loved . . . Was he in league with a traitor?

## 40

Each morning, Teti the Small summoned the officers responsible for security at the military base and in the town of Thebes. Lookout posts had been set up north and south of the city, to raise the alarm in the event of a Hyksos attack. Thanks to hard work by Heray, agriculture was flourishing again. Farmers were celebrating the birth of many, many calves, lambs and piglets; it was as if the herds and flocks felt reassured by the establishment of a lasting peace, and had returned to their normal fertility.

In addition, Neshi was proving an excellent Overseer of the Treasury. Having put an end to the black market, he was now applying the ancient rules, which stipulated that powerful people must not live at the expense of the weak. He reported to Teti about the size and nature of commercial exchanges, which were principally regulated by the temple at Karnak.

Although her days were busy, the old lady took time to oversee the upbringing of Prince Ahmose, who had become not only an excellent archer and a good swordsman, but also a scholar able to write in hieroglyphs or the language of government. Teti made him read stories and the teachings of sages like Ptah-hotep. The little boy's seriousness surprised his military instructors: obedient, determined, never balking at additional work, he pushed himself to the limits of his strength. He was gifted with a remarkable memory and a lively intelligence, and had a real thirst for knowledge of all kinds.

Ordinarily, Ahmose rose with the sun and breakfasted with his grandmother. When he did not appear, Teti asked her maid to wake him.

The servant soon came hurrying back. 'Majesty, the prince has a bad fever. His forehead is burning, and he's shaking all over.'

Teti went to him immediately. She felt responsible for him, and there might be a great destiny in store for him. There could be no doubt that his premature death would be a fatal blow to the queen.

Ahhotep had suffered from similar illnesses at that age, so Teti decided to use similar remedies to relieve the heart by unblocking the channels that led to and from it. This would enable the boy's life-energies to circulate properly again. Ignoring the fever, which was merely a symptom, she concentrated on three vital organs, the liver, the spleen and the lungs. She administered a potion whose ingredients – bull's meat, terebinth resin, sweet-clover, juniper leaves, sweet beer and fresh bread – had been carefully measured out.

The little boy held his grandmother's hand tightly. 'Do you think I'm going to die?'

'Certainly not. You still have too much to learn.'

'There are boats coming, Majesty,' announced Emheb.

'From which direction?' asked Kamose.

'The south.'

'Make the agreed signals.'

If it was Ahhotep, she would reply by hoisting a sail on which was painted a boat containing the moon's disc. If it was not, battle must be joined on the river.

The sail ran up slowly; too slowly. Because of the intense midday sun, it was impossible to see if the sign was there. The Thebans' nerves stretched gradually to breaking-point.

'The moon! I can see it!' exclaimed Emheb. 'It is indeed the queen's flotilla.'

The symbol of Ahhotep and the rebel movement shone from the top of her ship's mast. The drums began to beat a joyful rhythm, celebrating the unification of all the Egyptian forces.

While the young king kissed his mother, the soldiers congratulated each other.

Ahhotep said, in some surprise, 'I am bringing you only meagre reinforcements, my son, but you seem to have recruited many more.'

Kamose could not hide his pride. 'They're boatmen, merchants, former mercenaries serving the Hyksos. They had to be persuaded that they had chosen the wrong side. It wasn't always easy, but in the end they realized where their interests lay. Our victory will ensure that their lives are far more pleasant than under the Hyksos.'

Ahhotep smiled joyfully. 'You are becoming a true pharaoh, Kamose.'

The queen's presence had had a consequence no one had dared hope for: it had united the disparate elements of the Egyptian army. In addition, the men's minds were no longer haunted by fear, but were now nourished by the wildest of dreams: defeating the empire of darkness.

A heavy silence lay over the front at Qis. Everyone was waiting for the council of war's decision. Many had wagered that it would be the sensible one of making Qis Thebes's new northern frontier by erecting fortifications there.

'I've sworn to break through the obstacle posed by Khmun,' Kamose told the council. 'The Hyksos control-post must be dismantled.'

'The Jar of Predictions is said to be hidden in the temple,' added Ahhotep. 'We need it if we are to decide our strategy and save many lives.'

'Let us attack Khmun,' proposed Kamose.

Calm and steady as ever, Emheb felt it necessary to bring the young monarch back to reality. 'Majesty, Khmun is out of reach.'

'Why?'

'While we've been holding the front at Qis, we've had time to study the Hyksos positions. At great risk to their lives, two scouts got through the enemy front line and discovered their rear base. It is Nefrusy, capital of the sixteenth province of Upper Egypt, which is governed by a collaborator, Tita, son of Pepi.'

'Is there a fortress like the one at Per-Hathor?' asked Ahhotep.

'No, but Nefrusy is defended by very strong ramparts indeed, and I don't think our army can take it.'

'Has this Tita sold his soul to the emperor?' asked Kamose.

'Unfortunately, yes, Majesty. He was nothing but a simple boatman who made his fortune by transporting the invaders. He denounced the rebels and Apophis gave him the town as a reward. The only thing that matters to him is the empire, which ensures his wealth and power.'

'The perfect example of a coward and a traitor!' roared Kamose.

'Most of the present governors of the Northern provinces are like him,' lamented Emheb. 'They're convinced that the emperor is invincible and that our army will never get beyond Qis. You won't persuade any of them to change sides.'

'Then they shall die!'

'No one wants such vermin exterminated more than I do. But the Hyksos protect them and make them prosper.'

'Then what do you think would be the best strategy?'

'To make the frontier at Qis impregnable,' said Emheb, 'by building fortifications and blocking the Nile with cargo-boats lashed together.'

'What? And give up our goal of reunifying the Two Lands?' asked Ahhotep anxiously.

'By no means, Majesty. We shall merely be adapting to a given situation. At Edfu, at Thebes and at Qis, we analysed the situation correctly, and success smiled upon us. We must not spoil our progress by acting hastily.'

Neshi had always been opposed to caution. But this time he thought Emheb's analysis was sensible. Besides, no one could accuse the governor of lacking courage: without him, the front at Qis could not have held out for long.

Six days of high fever. Six days, during which little Ahmose was often delirious, imploring his dead father and his absent mother not to abandon him to the hungry mouths of the demons of night.

The palace doctor was pessimistic. He had not added anything to the remedies prescribed by Teti, who spent all her time at Ahmose's bedside and left Qaris to deal with pressing matters of government.

During his moments of lucidity, the sick child regretted being so puny and being unable to continue his weapons training. His grandmother reassured him and read him the teachings of sage Imhotep, the genius who had created the first stone pyramid at Saqqara, near the town of Memphis, which was now occupied by the Hyksos.

Twice, Teti thought she had lost her grandson, whose breathing grew fainter and fainter. But the brightness in his eyes refused to yield to the dark, and he drew his last strength from her unshakeable confidence. Not for a moment did he ever sense doubt in her; she kept him firmly anchored to life.

It was this attitude, as much as the remedies, which brought about the prince's recovery. On the seventh day he rose and ate a hearty breakfast on the palace terrace, in the company of a joyful and very relieved grandmother.

## 41

To people who, like the Syrians, had seen a bear, Tita, son of Pepi, looked just like a monstrous one, with his enormous head, bushy eyebrows and snout-shaped nose. He terrorized his underlings and never forgave even the smallest fault. An excellent pupil of the Hyksos, he based his power on violence and cruelty. In the emperor's image, each month Tita executed one of his fellow citizens, chosen at random. The people of Nefrusy were forced to attend the ceremony, which ended with a ritual song praising Apophis's greatness.

The bear was very pleased with his province and his capital, and wanted nothing but to rule there as absolute master. To thank him for his fidelity, the emperor had given him permission to build ramparts, which made Nefrusy look most impressive.

His wife, Anat, was equally notable. A blue-eyed Syrian with a fiery temperament, she constantly infuriated him by criticizing all his decisions, which she considered were as stupid as they were unjust. Fortunately for her, this particular contest was the only one that Tita enjoyed. Besides, the tussles always ended up in the vast sycamore-wood bed, his palace's finest ornament.

Tita expected to enjoy the day, because he was going to cut the throat of a youth guilty of rebellion against the emperor. Next, young girls would process past, singing a warlike poem composed by the bear himself. Anat had called it ridiculous doggerel, but it praised the emperor's genius.

'Aren't you ready yet?' asked Anat in surprise.

'I want to look particularly handsome, my darling,' said Tita. 'My public appearances must delight the common folk.'

'Is it really necessary to kill an innocent boy to cement your appalling reputation?'

'Of course. At the slightest sign of leniency, rebels would spring up like weeds.'

'I doubt if there are any left.'

'Mistrust, suspicion . . . you're wonderful. How does this new tunic look?'

'Too showy.'

'You really are unbearable, my darling.'

Shortly after dawn, Queen Ahhotep convened the Supreme Council, which had pronounced on the future of Egypt. Its members were hoping for firm orders and for the armed forces to be divided between Thebes and Qis.

'Tonight,' revealed the queen, 'Amon appeared to me, his sword in his hand. He was incarnate in the person of Pharaoh Kamose, and his eyes were as intensely bright as the noonday sun. "Did I not order you to destroy the Hyksos, and to carry out this mission whatever the obstacles?" he asked me. It is true that you are sensible and thoughtful men. It is true that the Hyksos are militarily superior to us. The front holds fast, Nefrusy is impregnable, and Khmun even more so. It is true that we have already achieved the impossible, and we have exhausted our reserves of *heka*, the only force capable of altering the cruel fate that has befallen our country. I know the reality. But it is my duty to reject it, not submit to it, because such is the will of Amon.

'The hour has come to go beyond Qis, to cross that frontier and to strike north. That is the only strategy that will make possible the reunification of the Two Lands. If we are defeated, Thebes will be destroyed and there will be no further resistance to barbarism. If we bend, the result will be the same. No doubt you consider my determination senseless and would prefer to take refuge in a false sense of security. That is why I shall take only volunteers with me when I leave for the front.'

Kamose raised his hands, palms turned upwards to the heavens, in a sign of worship. 'The pharaoh appointed by Amon has heard the voice of the Wife of God. His army will follow her. Any council members who disagree with our decision may return to Thebes immediately.'

No one moved.

'What an incredible woman,' murmured the Afghan for the hundredth time, as he watched Ahhotep speak to each soldier, instilling the courage they would all need.

'It's worth dying for her and for Egypt,' said Moustache. 'At least when we appear before the court of the otherworld, we shan't have to hang our heads in shame.'

When Kamose appeared at the prow of the flagship, wearing the

White Crown, the soldiers raised their weapons to the skies and the drums began to beat a frenzied rhythm.

To break through the Hyksos defensive line, the pharaoh decided to launch a three-pronged attack using the river and both banks, thus involving all his forces. He had two pieces of luck: it was the time when the guards were relieved; and the general in charge of the Qis front was bedridden, suffering from intense pain in his kidneys.

Surprised by the scale of the offensive, the Hyksos lost precious minutes organizing themselves as best they could. Several of their boats were already burning when their camp was attacked from both east and west. As soon as Ahmes, son of Abana, had killed the senior officers, who thought they were safe on the mound from which they were observing the battle, the chain of command was broken and the defenders panicked.

Like an all-consuming flame, the Theban army poured into the many breaches in the Hyksos line, their battle-fever controlled and directed by Kamose's precise, efficient orders. Not until the last Hyksos was dead, burnt along with his camp, did the Thebans' passion die down.

Emheb was amazed. How could this motley assortment of raw troops have beaten the Hyksos, who greatly outnumbered them and were much better armed? The attackers' enthusiasm had been the decisive factor, it was true, but young King Kamose's exceptional leadership had also been vital. Trusting to nothing but his own instinct, he had struck in the right places at the right times. Ahhotep's magic must have been guiding him.

'What were our losses?' asked the queen.

'They were light, Majesty.'

'Send the seriously wounded by boat to Thebes. Are there any prisoners?'

'No, none.'

Kamose emerged from the smoke, his sword dripping blood; he looked so gruesome that even his own soldiers were nervous of him. All trace of youth was gone from his face, which for the rest of his life would bear the marks of all the brutal deaths he had inflicted.

'You exposed yourself to too much danger,' Ahhotep chided him.

'If I don't show an example, who will dare defy the darkness?' Wearily, the king sat down on a modest throne of sycamore-wood; Young Laughter licked his hands, as if trying to wipe away all traces of the terrible battle. 'You were right, Mother: we were indeed capable of breaking through the Hyksos front. This victory has strengthened our *heka*, and we have shown qualities we did not know we had. It was like a birth ... We have given birth to formidable forces which Set himself would not deny. Is this really the path we must follow?'

'Answering violence with gentleness, cruelty with diplomacy and forgiveness – is that what you would like, my son? That policy would lead to the triumph of barbarism. We are facing not simple adversaries, with whom we could negotiate, but the Hyksos, invaders who want to destroy our bodies and our souls. It is because only Set can confront the dragon of darkness that he holds the prow of the sun's ship.'

Kamose closed his eyes. 'I had prepared myself to fight, but not for this war.'

'This is only the beginning,' said Ahhotep. 'Today you were reunited with the courage of your father, and you felt what he felt as he died for freedom.'

Kamose got to his feet. 'Like him, I shall fight to the end. A few days' rest, and then we shall take Nefrusy.'

Ahhotep sighed. 'I cannot let you have those few days. We must take advantage of this victory to force our advantage and swoop down like a falcon on our enemy.'

The Afghan and Moustache gulped down a frugal meal, collected their belongings together and climbed back on to their boat. Despite their status and decorations, they still behaved like simple rebel fighters.

'It would have been good to get our breath back,' grumbled a footsoldier.

'Do you really want to die?' asked the Afghan.

'Of course not.'

'Then be glad about your orders. The sooner we reach our next objective, the better chance we shall have of victory – and therefore of survival.'

'Are we going to fight again?'

'That's what you're here for, isn't it?'

The question plunged the soldier into confusion. 'There is some truth in that, Commander.'

'Come on, my lad. We haven't killed all the Hyksos yet.'

'Now that thought I like!' The soldier made his way happily up the gangplank.

Showing exemplary discipline, the soldiers of Theban army embarked in record time. Then it was the oarsmen's turn to show what they could do.

## 42

The ceremony was at its height. Dozens of children were loudly singing Tita's song in praise of Apophis.

Suddenly, shouts shattered the apparent peace. Enraged, Tita signalled to his soldiers to arrest the troublemakers and have them executed immediately. But the shouts grew louder, and soon it was clear that they came from outside the town.

'It's the peasants, my lord,' said a soldier. 'They're begging us to open the great gate.'

Terminating the celebration, Tita climbed up on to the ramparts and looked down. It was an appalling sight: dozens of farm-workers had left their fields and were trying to take refuge in the city. Across the rich fields of the vast plain, the Theban army was advancing. At its head was Pharaoh Kamose.

'We must give the peasants shelter quickly,' urged the commander of the archers.

'No, we can't risk it. Kill them.'

'Kill them? You mean . . . kill our peasants, our own peasants?'

'Opening the gate is out of the question. Obey my orders, then fire on the enemy, so that they cannot get near our walls.'

Watched in horror by the Egyptians, the unarmed peasants were slaughtered by Tita's archers. A young Theban captain and a few footsoldiers were so appalled that they rushed to the peasants' aid, but they, too, were all shot down.

'No one is to try anything similar,' ordered Kamose. 'You can see what the results would be.'

'We must recover back the bodies of our men,' said Emheb.

'Not by sacrificing other lives. First, we must encircle the town.'

The Egyptian forces were deployed out of range of the Hyksos archers. Tents were pitched, and Neshi ensured that the men were fed. On Ahhotep's orders, the elite regiments commanded by the Afghan and Moustache were posted to the north of the town to prevent any reinforcements from breaking the siege.

As soon as the sun went down, Ahmes and ten volunteers climbed up to the place where their comrades had fallen. They succeeded in bringing back the bodies and also three seriously wounded men, whom She-Cat treated before they were sent back to Thebes by boat.

'The walls look very solid,' observed Emheb. 'An effective siege will take a long time.'

'I am going to my cabin,' said Kamose.

Despite the threat posed by the Theban army, Tita had decided to go ahead with the banquet organized in his honour, and was presiding over it with his wife.

'At least pretend to be enjoying yourself, Anat.'

'Have you forgotten that we're under siege?'

The bear sank his teeth into a leg of goose. 'That band of rebels won't threaten us for long.'

'Are you sure about that?'

'Hyksos reinforcements will destroy them first thing tomorrow morning – they'll take those fools by surprise. I'll send any survivors to Avaris, where they will be tortured to entertain the emperor. In return, Apophis will grant me new privileges. In fact, the arrival of these madmen is a stroke of luck: I shall benefit richly from it.'

A troupe of flute- and oboe-players was apathetically playing a droning melody which irritated him. 'Get out, you idiots,' he bellowed.

The musicians fled.

'Have you taken all the necessary measures?' asked Anat anxiously.

'My archers are patrolling the battlements, and no one can get near. Don't worry, my sweet. We aren't in any danger.'

'Are you really sure that the Hyksos are invincible?'

'They are. You can be sure of that.'

Kamose was pacing up and down in his cabin like a caged animal. Unsure which plan to adopt, he repeatedly weighed the lives of his soldiers against the need to conquer Nefrusy. Eventually, still unable to decide, he went out on deck, where Ahhotep was enjoying the last rays of the setting sun.

'Have you made up your mind?' she asked.

'I can't. A long siege would destroy our impetus, and a badly planned attack would incur unacceptably heavy losses.'

'Your conclusions are the same as mine.'

'Then what do you suggest?'

'Tonight I shall consult the moon-god, the interpreter of the skies. He will send us a sign to guide us. Go and rest, my son.'

*

The Afghan and Moustache, with ten experienced soldiers, were travelling warily down the Nile aboard a light boat. They went very slowly, all their senses alert.

'There they are,' whispered Moustache. 'We were right.'

Two Hyksos war-ships lay moored to the bank. The sailors had pitched camp ashore, and the sentries looked very relaxed. Clearly, the reinforcements for Nefrusy believed that in conquered territory they had nothing to fear.

A member of the raiding-party went back to alert the two elite regiments posted not far away. Less than two hours later, they were ready to begin work.

'First we must seize the ships,' said the Afghan. 'Our best swimmers will approach from the stern and climb aboard. The sailors on guard will be killed quickly and silently. When that is done, one man only is to return to us. The others will prepare to cast off.'

If the operation failed, the Hyksos would immediately search the surrounding area. A pitched battle would be inevitable. The minutes seemed to last for ever.

Then a head emerged from the water, and the swimmer reported, 'The enemy sailors are all dead. The ships are ours.'

'We shall divide into three groups,' said Moustache. 'As soon as the Hyksos are asleep, we shall attack.'

Kamose could not sleep. Ever since his coronation, he had managed only one or two hours' sleep a night, though his energy had not been affected. He thought constantly of his father, and sometimes felt sharp pains in the parts of his body where Seqen had been wounded.

There was a knock at his cabin door.

'There are two Hyksos ships coming,' said Emheb.

Kamose rushed to the prow of the flagship, but it was almost too late to take action. How could he have foreseen that warships would risk travelling in the middle of the night?

Waking with a start, the Egyptian sailors ran to their posts.

'Look at the top of the leading mast!' shouted one of them. 'It's Moustache!'

The tension relaxed. The two ships glided gently to their moorings, and their crews gave shouts of victory.

'Majesty,' declared the Afghan, 'our fleet now has two more boats. As for the reinforcements Tita was expecting, they'll never reach him.'

'That's excellent work.'

'We surprised the Hyksos while they were asleep. On our side, there are three dead and fifteen wounded.'

'See that the wounded are cared for, and then go and rest.'

'If you are planning to attack at dawn, Majesty, we have just enough time for a quick bite to eat.'

The king did not reply.

As the first glimmers of light pierced the darkness, Queen Ahhotep came towards him. Despite a sleepless night, she was surprisingly fresh-faced.

'Mother, did the moon-god speak to you?'

A falcon with multicoloured plumage soared up from the east and flew across the sky. Its wings looked immense, as if they had taken possession of the entire space.

'He has just spoken,' said the pharaoh, 'and I have heard him.'

## 43

Like a falcon, Pharaoh Kamose swooped down on Nefrusy at the head
of his army. Hampered by the light of the rising sun in their eyes, the
Hyksos archers fired wide; Ahmes and the Theban archers did not.

Abruptly awoken, Tita responded quickly to this unexpected attack:
Arming himself with a slingshot, he rushed up to the ramparts, from
where he killed a Theban officer marching at the head of his troops.

'Fire! Defend yourselves!' he ordered.

The instinct for survival provoked a response from his men, who,
despite their fear, unleashed a barrage of missiles to prevent the attackers
approaching the walls.

'We need battering-rams,' said Moustache.

'The masts from the Hyksos ships will serve very well,' suggested
Emheb.

'They're retreating,' exclaimed Tita. 'We've driven them back.'

Although he could hardly believe it, he had won. That is, he had
gained the respite he needed in which to escape. The Egyptians would
mount a siege and Nefrusy would eventually fall, but he would not be
among its victims. He would take with him only a few servants, to
carry his most precious possessions. As for his wife, she would be a
useless burden – there was no shortage of women in Avaris.

The Thebans had attacked from the east, so Tita planned to leave
by the western gate. But to his horror he found that the enemy had
massed troops on the nearby low hills, as well as in the southern and
northern plains. Nefrusy was surrounded.

'You weren't going to run away, were you?' asked Anat pointedly.

'No, of course not! I was working out how best to strengthen the
defences.'

'Don't you think it would be wiser to surrender?'

'Surrender? That would be madness.'

'One way or another, you will be killed. If you order your men to
lay down their arms, you would at least spare the people further suffering.'

'I've been their benefactor, haven't I? They must fight beside me and defend me.'

'You are cruel and cowardly. End your life with one generous deed: open the gates of the city and beg the pharaoh's forgiveness.'

Tita glared at his wife. 'You wouldn't be thinking of betraying me, would you, my beauty? Yes, that's it. You think I'm already beaten and you're switching to the Thebans' side.'

'Don't be ridiculous. Face reality.'

'Go to your bedchamber immediately. Two guards will be posted outside your door. When I've finished with the Thebans, I shall deal with you.'

'My lord, they are coming back.'

Standing high on the ramparts, Tita saw the Theban army attacking again, from all four directions. Protected both by archers and by big, thick shields held by auxiliaries, men carrying battering-rams charged at the gates of Nefrusy.

He spotted the White Crown as Kamose reached the eastern gate, and hurled a javelin with all his might, but it missed. The battering-ram stove in the great gate; the noise of wood breaking and splintering struck terror into Tita's troops. A few moments later, the three other gates gave way.

While the footsoldiers poured into the town, the rammers withdrew and then advanced again to attack the brick walls.

Tita ran to his palace. His men would not hold out for long, and he must hide somewhere to wait for the pharaoh and beg his mercy. After all, he, Tita, was a victim of the Hyksos, too, and the Theban army's arrival was a real miracle, which he had been hoping for with all his heart. From now on, he would be a loyal servant of Kamose. All that remained was for him to kill his evil genius, the traitor Anat, who was the cause of all Nefrusy's woes. As proof of his good faith, he had placed her under arrest.

Some thirty women, whose children Tita had had executed, barred his way to the palace.

'Stand aside!' he roared.

'You killed my son,' declared a tall redhead armed with a cauldron.

'You killed my daughter,' said another, who was clutching a pestle.

Each of the women solemnly stated her grievance.

'Let me pass, and go and fight alongside the troops.'

All at once, they threw themselves upon him and beat him to death with their kitchen utensils, while the rams battered down the walls of Nefrusy.

Kamose had single-handedly killed more than thirty of the enemy, including the head of Tita's bodyguard. The man had tried to stab him in the back, but the king, benefiting from his intensive training, seemed to have eyes in the back of his head.

Spurred on by their leader's almost superhuman bravery, his soldiers had fought valiantly, and the enemy, despite showing the courage born of despair, had inflicted only slight losses before succumbing to force of numbers.

Believing the lies put out day after day by Tita, and thinking Hyksos reinforcements would arrive at any moment, many citizens had fought alongside the emperor's men. So by the middle of the afternoon the streets of Nefrusy were strewn with bodies.

A group of mothers pointed out Tita's body, which was almost unrecognizable.

'Have it burnt, and then raze the whole town to the ground,' ordered Kamose.

In the face of such destruction, Ahhotep's heart was in her mouth. This was only Nefrusy, a small town compared with Khmun, which was itself insignificant compared with Avaris. How many dead would the monster of darkness devour before the words of the song to the Creator, 'Awake in peace', could be sung?

She-Cat, who had been appointed by Ahhotep to take charge of treating the troops, was remarkably efficient. With her Nubian remedies, she eased the men's pain, and she gave hope to even the most seriously wounded. Everyone envied Moustache for having such a mistress, who had become one of the heroines of the war.

After entrusting the White Crown to his mother, Kamose washed thoroughly and changed his clothes. It would take the washermen a long time to cleanse his blood-spattered breastplate.

The young king was neither exhilarated nor downcast. Solemnly contemplating the next battle already, he was simply fulfilling his mission.

Supervised by Emheb, the victors took away the survivors, livestock, jars of oil, milk and honey, weapons and anything else useful, before the flames consumed Nefrusy.

'The palace is still standing, Majesty,' said Emheb, 'Do you wish to be the first to enter it?'

Dressed in a white tunic, Kamose stepped through the doorway of a fine, pillared building. The rooms, although quite small, were filled with beautiful furniture. At the end of the private apartments was a door, held shut by a wooden bolt.

Kamose drew it back and opened the door. Sitting on a low chair with ebony arm-rests was a beautiful young woman with blue eyes.

'Has my husband sent you to kill me?' she asked.

'If you are the wife of Tita, son of Pepi, I must tell you that he will give no more orders to anyone.'

Anat stood up. 'So he is dead. Then justice does exist! Whoever you are, you have given me wonderful news. Now I can die in peace.'

'Why did you marry him?'

Her eyes filled with sadness. 'I made the mistake of thinking he loved me. But he thought so little of me that he had decided to kill me.'

'Nefrusy has been utterly destroyed, and those who fought against me have been punished. Do you also wish to fight me?'

Anat stared at him in astonishment. 'Do you mean . . . ? Are you the pharaoh, come from Thebes?'

'Either you become my loyal subject, or you will share the fate of my enemies.'

## 44

Being a trade-control official at Khmun was a coveted privilege. Only Hyksos soldiers with excellent service records and good connections in Avaris could gain appointment to the largest control-post in occupied Egypt.

The Hyksos imposed a toll upon everything and everyone that passed through Khmun: men, women, children, animals, boats, goods . . . Only the emperor's soldiers were exempt and could move around freely. An official tariff decreed the maximum rate that could be levied from prostitutes who entertained the military, but trade-control officials were free to alter other people's conditions of passage according to their own whims, and could swindle travellers as much as they liked.

Always aggressive, they would take exception to even the most innocent remark. The offender was instantly stripped of his clothes and possessions, abused and sentenced. If he continued to protest his good faith or, even worse, his innocence, he was sent to prison where he would be forgotten for as long as the government pleased.

En-Ilusa, the Libyan who ruled the Khmun control-post, had a small moustache and sly eyes. Appointed by his friend Khamudi, to whom he paid a portion of his illicit earnings, he ruled his domain with a rod of iron. He never needed even to raise his voice. All he had to do was issue his orders, which no one dared question.

En-Ilusa behaved like a little emperor, and dreamt of one day leaving Khmun to take up a more important post in Avaris. He specialized in playing a double game, and ruthlessly betrayed anyone who made the mistake of confiding in him, as soon as they were no longer useful. Through Khamudi's good offices, he hoped to obtain promotion in the coming months. Then he would really show what he could do.

He was not worried about the Theban rebellion. The front would remain fixed at Qis until the moment when the emperor decided to kill Ahhotep.

As he did every morning, En-Ilusa inspected the main trade-control building. A pernickety man, he demanded that everything be in its proper place and that nothing ever changed. He was also strict about the cleanliness of uniforms, and anyone who fell short of his standards was fined several days' pay. Above all, En-Ilusa liked to stir up discord among the officers by encouraging informers and the spread of malicious gossip.

One thing was annoying him: in recent weeks business had fallen slightly, indicating that some of his underlings were being lax. As soon as he had identified them, the miscreants would be transferred to some miserable small town.

En-Ilusa was just beginning to read the previous day's reports when a grain inspector entered his office.

'Sir, we're going to have a great deal of work. Three cargo-boats are approaching from the south.'

En-Ilusa smiled avariciously. 'They're going to pay a high price.'

Ahhotep's plan had been enthusiastically received by Pharaoh Kamose and his council of war: the battle for Khmun would take place in three stages. First, three supply-boats would arrive at the control-post; they would be made to look like ordinary trading-vessels, and so would be allowed through the floating barricade of boats that protected Khmun. Next, a raiding-party would attack from the riverbank, taking the troops by surprise. Finally, the war-fleet would come as quickly as possible to join the fight. Co-ordination would be vital: any confusion would lead to a disaster from which the Thebans could never recover.

The three heavy cargo-boats advanced with prudent slowness towards the floating barricade. Many soldiers were hidden aboard, lying flat on the decks, ready to leap into action the moment the order was given.

When Emheb appeared at the prow of the leading ship, En-Ilusa took him for what he seemed to be: a good-hearted, round-bellied fellow with an open smile. Ideal prey.

As soon as the boats were moored, Emheb would send Rascal back to the war-fleet, which was commanded by Moon. Moon would know that the fight was beginning and that he must set off, urging the oarsmen to row with all possible speed.

The first wave of the Egyptian attack would necessarily entail heavy losses, and Emheb himself might be killed. But what about Queen Ahhotep, who was leading the raiding-party on land? No soldier would let himself show less courage than she did.

The boats nudged gently against the bank, watched covetously by En-Ilusa and his men, who were already mentally sharing out the booty they would obtain legally, by levying their myriad taxes. In accordance with instructions, they arranged themselves in a line along the quay.

En-Ilusa stepped forward and spoke the usual words: 'Have you anything to declare?'

'Not very much,' replied Emheb affably. 'You will soon be finished with my cargo.'

A greedy smile lit up En-Ilusa's cold face. 'That would surprise me. I am very scrupulous and I believe that these three boats are crammed full of both authorized and unauthorized goods.'

Emheb scratched his chin. 'To be frank, you are not entirely wrong.'

'So you admit it already? That's very sensible of you. It's always better to co-operate.'

The governor nodded.

'Continue to be sensible,' recommended En-Ilusa. 'What is your most illicit merchandise?'

'I will gladly tell you, but you won't profit from it.'

'Come on, tell me!'

'Be sure to listen carefully. You won't have much time to appreciate its song.'

Unsheathing his dagger, Emheb threw it with force and accuracy. It hissed viciously through the air, and plunged into En-Ilusa's chest. His eyes filled with astonishment, the man died without even understanding what was happening.

At Emheb's signal, all the Egyptian archers stood up and fired on the trade-control officials, who, lined up as they were, made excellent targets.

Although thrown into confusion by the unexpected attack and by their leader's death, the survivors attempted to fight back. But they were caught between the Egyptians firing on them from the decks of the three boats, and the footsoldiers charging at them along the riverbank, led by Pharaoh Kamose.

Emheb and his men exploited the situation expertly. Khmun's soldiers could have prevented the crushing defeat of the trade-control men, but they had to contain the assault by the raiding-party, which had taken them by surprise.

Moustache and the Afghan were particularly skilled at this sort of fighting, and when they had Queen Ahhotep at their side nothing could stop them.

The Hyksos forces made the mistake of dividing, some rushing to the aid of the remaining trade-control officials, the others confronting the enemy footsoldiers. Before long, the survivors realized that the day was lost. They took refuge on some boats in the floating barricade, hoping to be able to cut them free and escape northwards. At that moment, they saw the Theban war-fleet appear. As soon the fleet closed with the barricade, Moon's sailors rushed to the attack. As in the previous battles, no prisoners were taken.

Kamose was greatly surprised by how easily his army had broken through at Khmun, which many had thought was indestructible. Ahhotep's plan had succeeded, as if the Wife of God could see beyond outward appearances.

On a sign from Emheb, the troops raised an enthusiastic cheer for the pharaoh and the queen. Yet Ahhotep seemed anxious.

'What is it, Mother?' asked Kamose. 'Nothing can halt our progress.'

'From Thebes to Khmun, Egypt has been liberated. But this reconquest may only be temporary.'

'What do you mean?'

'The troops we have defeated did not have the heavy weapons that enabled the Hyksos to conquer our country. The emperor must be sneering at our offensive. He is simply luring us deeper and deeper into a trap, and eventually we shall have to face his real army.'

Once again, the queen's clear thinking convinced the young pharaoh. 'But we cannot be content just to establish a new front.'

'Before we go any further, I must decipher the message of Khmun, and find the Jar of Predictions.'

## 45

At first, the people of Khmun refused to believe it. And then they saw that the news was true: there were no Hyksos guards on the streets, and everyone could express their hatred of the emperor without fear of reprisals. Eventually, even the most sceptical allowed themselves to show their joy when Pharaoh Kamose, wearing the White Crown, and Queen Ahhotep, crowned with a fine gold diadem, appeared before the great Temple of Thoth, which stood in the Valley of the Tamarisks.

'People of Khmun,' proclaimed the young king, 'you are free. The Hyksos have been wiped out, and the control-post destroyed. Pharaoh rules once again, as before and for ever. The darkness has been driven back; the righteousness and harmony of Ma'at are our only law. A great feast, to which you are all summoned, shall seal the return of happiness.'

Emheb, Moon, the Afghan and Moustache were borne aloft in triumph. The prettiest girls in the city had eyes only for the archers, particularly Ahmes. The only person who was not happy was Neshi, who, instead of enjoying the feast, was responsible for organizing it and ensuring that it was a success.

While the city was preparing to celebrate its liberation, the queen went to the temple.

When she arrived there, a young man knelt before her. 'I beg you, Majesty, do not go any further.'

'Stand up, my boy, and explain yourself.'

He dared not look at this gloriously beautiful woman, whom everyone called the Queen of Freedom. Already, storytellers were spreading her legend from village to village. To find himself here, so close to her . . . He had never hoped for such an honour.

'Do not enter this temple, Majesty.'

'Is it filled with dangerous creatures?'

'The Hyksos killed the priests, stole the precious objects and turned the shrine into a storehouse. They took stones and filled up the well that led down to the primordial ocean. The gods have departed, and all that remains is the spirit of evil. Do not challenge it, Majesty. We need you too much.' Surprised by his own boldness, the young man prostrated himself again.

'What work did you do under the occupation?'

'I looked after the temple garden, Majesty. It was not easy alone, but I avoided the worst.'

'I appoint you head gardener of the Temple of Thoth. Employ assistants immediately, to return this place to its past splendour, and begin by clearing out the sacred well.'

Ahhotep turned towards the door of the shrine.

'Majesty, you ... you aren't going to enter that den of curses, are you?'

Ahhotep knew Khmun was not yet truly free. The military victory had been won, but the emperor fought with other weapons, too. Once the well was emptied, the energy that came from the primordial ocean would again fill the temple. But she believed Apophis would not have been content with this simple measure. Inside there must be a device capable of preventing the Thebans from making further progress. He would probably have chosen the most famous place: the library where the writings of the god Thoth were kept, his divine words inspired by the Word of Light.

As she walked through the great open-air courtyard, the queen felt an ache in her heart. The Hyksos had stored swords, armour and sacks of wheat there. The first covered hall was an even more distressing sight: the soldiers of darkness had turned it into latrines, and the stench of excrement was unbearable.

Suddenly, she heard a low growl. She headed towards the sound and came to the door of the library. All around were engraved effigies of ibis-headed Thoth and of Seshat, Queen of the House of Books, crowned with a seven-pointed star.

The growling became threatening. On the temple roof stood a she-leopard, the incarnation of the goddess Mafdet. Her role was to tear apart anyone who tried to violate the secrets of Thoth. On the ground lay bones covered in bloody Hyksos uniforms. After trying in vain to kill the divine animal, which no weapon could harm, the invaders had withdrawn, abandoning Mafdet's victims where they lay. Surely the sacred books must be inaccessible for ever.

Moving forward would make the animal attack, but going back was out of the question. Ahhotep absolutely had to go into the library, where the Jar of Predictions was kept. She had only one chance of pacifying the leopardess: to give her the *menat*-necklace of Hathor, in the hope that its power would turn her ferocity into gentleness.

Keeping her eyes fixed on Mafdet, Ahhotep lifted the symbol of love towards her.

At first, the leopard roared with rage, as if her prey were escaping, then she gave a howl of doubt and frustration, and then an incongruous mewling sound. Her terrifying deep voice had been reduced to the shrill sound of an irritated cat.

Holding the magical necklace high, Ahhotep advanced to the threshold of the library. The leopard turned and walked calmly and elegantly away. The queen's way was clear.

She drew back the copper bolt and entered the ancient hall of archives, where rolls of papyrus were carefully arranged on shelves and in wooden chests. Thanks to Mafdet's leopard, the writings of Thoth had escaped the barbarians.

Calm now, the queen examined the treasures of the ancient library, but could not find any jars. She lingered over a text which evoked the creative powers of the universe: the invisible, darkness, infinite space and limitless waters, each of them possessing a masculine and feminine aspect. Contained within the primordial egg, these eight things were the principal secret of the priests of Thoth, through which it was possible to perceive the ultimate reality of life.

For several hours, the queen forgot the war and devoted herself to the study of these inexhaustibly rich texts. While initiating herself into their mysteries and imbuing herself with their words of light, Ahhotep was still fighting. Overcoming Apophis required more than warlike qualities; she must also be the bearer of a spirituality which was powerful enough to dispel the night of tyranny and injustice.

When she left the library, the town was celebrating, under the protection of the moon.

Ten gardeners were working, supervised by their young overseer.

'Majesty, you are alive!' he cried. 'Thoth has guided your feet.'

'Have you ever heard of the Jar of Predictions?'

'Before he died, one of the priests told me that the Hyksos had taken it away to hide it in a tomb at Beni Hasan, from which it would never be recovered. But rumour has it that it was destroyed in the first days of the invasion.'

'Don't you want to join in the rejoicing?'

'My life is here, Majesty, and I shan't rejoice until the temple is as beautiful as it used to be. It will take months to clean everything, but I already have good assistants and we shall work every hour of the day.'

'Can you read?'

'Yes, Majesty. A priest taught me. I can write a little, too.'

Ahhotep was thinking of another gardener, Seqen, who had become her husband and a great pharaoh, and who had died in the name of freedom.

'Appoint one of your assistants to replace you,' she ordered.

The young man trembled. 'Majesty, have I done something wrong?'

'Shut yourself away in the library for as long as you need, in order to assimilate the message of Thoth. Then you shall assume the office of High Priest at the temple of Khmun.'

## 46

Houses of eternity had been excavated in the cliff-face for the dignitaries of Beni Hasan, not far to the north of Khmun. This grand and lofty site looked out over a vast plain filled with palm-groves and villages served by canals. The majestic Nile flowed through it, forming elegant curves.

Despite their fears, the Egyptian army had encountered no resistance. According to the local inhabitants, who were all overjoyed to welcome their liberators, the emperor's soldiers had retreated from their positions two days earlier.

This serenely beautiful place seemed peaceful, far removed from the war. The countryside's tranquil charms were conducive to meditation. Nevertheless, though much preoccupied, Pharaoh Kamose deployed his troops as if they were about to face an immediate counter-offensive, both on land and from the river. No one, from Moon down to the simplest soldier, relaxed their guard for even a moment.

'This is where the emperor has erected a barrier of curses,' said Ahhotep. 'No one must try to cross it.'

'How can we destroy it?' asked Kamose.

'I must examine each tomb and find the one in which the Jar of Predictions has been placed.'

'But supposing the Hyksos have destroyed it?'

'Then we shall be blind and deaf.'

'Let me come with you.'

Ahhotep shook her head. 'Stay here and lead your army. If the enemy attacks, you must be able to respond instantly.'

She began to climb, watched by the soldiers. Some said that she was preparing to challenge a desert demon; others that she would combat evil spirits controlled by the emperor. The best-informed said that the continuation of the war depended on the confrontation between the Queen of Freedom and a dark force which was capable of eating away at the Thebans' souls.

As soon as she reached the rocky platform along which the tombs lay, Ahhotep knew that she had found the place where Apophis's would-be barrier of curses had been erected. Her head felt as though it were caught in a vice, her legs were leaden and her breathing difficult. It was as if she had been plunged into hell, even though a gentle sun was making the green fields and the white limestone shine magnificently.

Holding the *menat*-necklace tightly, Ahhotep managed to breathe almost normally and approached the tombs.

But a stele barred her way. On it were written these terrifying words: '*A curse upon anyone who crosses the threshold of this dwelling. All-consuming fire upon the profaner, everlasting damnation!*'

These words would never normally have been found in a place of profound peace, linked to eternity. Without any doubt, they had been engraved on the orders of Apophis, in order to create an impenetrable barrier. The Emperor of Darkness had corrupted an *akh*, a 'radiant spirit', distorting it and turning it into an aggressive, fearsome ghost.

Ahhotep addressed it, making the offering of the necklace.

A strong wind began to blow. The queen thought she could hear cries of pain, as if a lost soul were in unbearable agony.

Ahhotep tore the bodice of her dress into four strips, which she laid side by side between the stele and the entrance to the tomb.

The wind grew fiercer, and the moaning became louder.

Ahhotep laid her serpent-shaped staff upon the ground. The cornelian quivered and came to life, and a royal cobra reared up. Writhing on the linen strips, it set them alight.

Picking up these torches, the queen used them to make a path of fire. 'May the goddesses hidden in the flames stand guard by day and ensure protection by night,' she prayed. 'May they drive away visible and invisible enemies. May they cause light to enter the darkness.'

The wind dropped, and little by little the fire grew less intense. When Ahhotep looked around, the menacing stele had disappeared, as if it had sunk into the cliff-face.

Staff in hand, Ahhotep entered the house of eternity of a noble called Amenemhat. She crossed a forecourt, passed beneath a pillared portico and meditated on the floor of the huge shrine, whose door stood open.

Had the emperor laid other traps?

Trusting in her own instincts, Ahhotep spoke the name of 'Amenemhat, of Just Voice', asking him to welcome her into his earthly paradise.

The paintings were extraordinarily fresh, and the queen allowed herself to be soothed by the charming depictions of birds, symbols of the metamorphoses of the soul. Suddenly, she sensed danger. Her eyes fixed upon unexpected scenes, devoted to wrestlers who were engaged in unarmed combat. They were using a great number of different holds, each movement clearly broken down to serve as an example.

The wrestlers' faces turned towards the queen, their eyes filled with the will to attack her. Soon, the seemingly immobile figures would come to life, step down from the walls and assail the intruder.

'I am the Queen of Egypt and the Wife of God. You are soldiers in the service of Pharaoh. May the emperor's enchantments leave your bodies and may your fighting skills enter the service of Kamose.' Defiantly, she held up the serpent-shaped staff in her left hand and the *menat*-necklace in her right. 'Obey me, or your images will be deprived of life. May each movement you make favour the light, not the darkness.'

For a few moments, the wrestlers seemed to confer. Then they returned to their original positions. The sense of danger was gone.

Ahhotep made her way to the alcove containing the statues of the tomb's owner and his wife. At their feet lay a jar.

In the jar was a papyrus on which were written the good and bad days of the current year, in accordance with the myths revealed in the different temples of Egypt. Any important action must respect this sacred calendar.

'Try again,' Moustache ordered a strong, thickset man who was most unhappy at having twice bitten the dust.

On the third attempt, the stocky man feinted at Moustache's head but, at the last moment, tried to hit him in the stomach. Not realizing what was happening to him, the fellow lost his balance, was lifted off his feet sideways, and fell heavily on to his back.

'This hold is truly amazing!' exclaimed Moustache delightedly.

Several scribes had made exact copies of the paintings of the wrestlers in Amenemhat's tomb, and the pictures were being used to teach the old techniques to the Theban soldiers. Moustache and the Afghan had proved best at this game. And they made sure that the training was intensive, so as to increase their men's chances of survival. Although the Hyksos had not counter-attacked, the troops were still on permanent alert.

Kamose was pawing the ground with impatience, but the Jar of Predictions had delivered its verdict: the coming days were unsuitable for military action. Obliged to respect the words of the Invisible, he feared that time was against the Thebans.

'You look worried, Majesty,' said beautiful Anat, who had been placed under confinement in the royal tent.

'That would that please you, no doubt.'

'On the contrary, since you freed me from my chains I wish only for your success.'

'You are very seductive, and you know it.'

'Is that a crime which merits punishment?'

'I have more important concerns than a woman's beauty.'

'But surely the war doesn't prevent you from loving? If it does, you will lack a strength which will be essential to your victory. What violence destroys, only love can successfully rebuild.'

'Do you really want to be loved, Anat?'

'By you, yes, provided you are sincere.'

Kamose took the blue-eyed Syrian into his arms and kissed her passionately.

## 47

Jannas had crushed the Anatolian rebellion, but at what a price! Half the Hyksos war-fleet had been wiped out, many of his best soldiers were dead, and an enormous number of wounded men would not be fit to rejoin the army for a long time, if ever. And hostilities would break out again some day, for the mountain-men of Anatolia would never accept Hyksos domination.

Despite these grim facts, when he returned to Avaris Jannas was celebrated as a hero by a huge crowd of officers and men, who had total confidence in the empire's most highly renowned warrior.

As a sign of honour, High Treasurer Khamudi himself greeted Jannas at the entrance to the citadel. 'The emperor has been awaiting your return with impatience, Commander.'

'I acted as fast as I could.'

'Of course, of course. No one doubts that. Are you satisfied with the results?'

'That information is for the emperor's ears alone.'

'Of course. I shall take you to the audience chamber.'

Apophis was in an indescribable rage. That morning, he had secretly tried to put on the Red Crown of Lower Egypt for an appearance before the Temple of Set. But he was immediately attacked by such severe pain that he had had to remove the accursed crown and return it to its hiding-place. No one must ever know that it had rejected him.

From his spy's reports and by consulting his blue flask with its map of Egypt, Apophis knew that the Thebans had reconquered Qis, Nefrusy and Khmun, and were drawn up north of Beni Hasan. So Queen Ahhotep had succeeded in shattering the magic barrier. She was undoubtedly a formidable enemy, who had escaped trap after trap.

This war would be decisive. The queen and her son had thrown all the rebel forces into the battle, and Egypt would be drained dry after their defeat. It was an ideal opportunity to destroy the ancient spirituality of the pharaohs for ever.

*

Jannas bowed before Apophis.

'You have arrived at the right time, Commander. You are no doubt tired after that long campaign, but unfortunately I cannot let you rest.'

'I am yours to command, Majesty.'

'Are we at last done with the Anatolians?'

Jannas hesitated.

'You may speak freely in front of Khamudi.'

The commander could not disobey an order from the emperor. 'I have killed enough rebels to ensure that Anatolia will cause you no concern for several months. But it is impossible to wipe them out completely. In a year, or perhaps two, we shall have to strike at them again.'

Apophis did not seem angry. 'Our army is not made for sleep, Commander. The greatness of the empire will always demand this sort of action. For the moment, you are to deal with Egypt.'

'Egypt? Do you not think a simple frontal operation—'

'The situation has changed. It was necessary that Queen Ahhotep became bold and that her son Kamose, the puppet king, believed in victory. The further north they advance, the closer they come to the terrain which we know best and on which we shall use our heavy weapons. The rebels are overconfident, and will throw all their forces into a head-on clash which they think they can win. Also, I wanted to reorganize the trade-control post at Khmun and rid myself of the petty tyrant at Nefrusy. By killing a few useless individuals, Ahhotep has done me a service.'

'Is our information about the enemy's movements accurate?'

'It could not be more accurate. The spy who enabled me to kill Seqen continues to serve me efficiently.'

'Then I can attack the Thebans at once.'

Apophis gave one of his icy smiles. 'There is something else more urgent, and we shall use another strategy, beginning with Lisht and Per-shaq.'

Jannas was a soldier and a Hyksos, so he would obey his emperor's orders to the letter. However, he considered them beneath his dignity as leader of the empire's forces. Khamudi and his men would have been quite good enough to carry out this task. But the commander forced himself to believe that Apophis saw further than he did, and that these orders were necessary.

As he made his way to his official residence, Jannas saw fifty old men, women and children pass by, laden with bundles and chained together. They were surrounded by a detachment of Hyksos guards, commanded by Aberia.

'My lady, where are you taking these people?' asked Jannas.

'That is a secret matter of state,' replied Aberia.

'It is your duty to tell me.'

'They are convicted criminals – nothing but dangerous criminals.'

'Dangerous, those miserable wretches? Do you take me for a fool?'

'I am merely obeying orders.'

The pitiful procession continued on its way, and Jannas went to Khamudi's house, where the High Treasurer was totting up his receipts from the last sales of drugs to the notables of Avaris.

'I would like to know,' said Jannas coldly, 'how many matters of state are kept secret from the commander of the Hyksos armies.'

Seeing the commander's anger, Khamudi realized that he must tread carefully if he was to avert an explosion of anger.

'How many? Why, none, Commander.'

'That is not the lady Aberia's view.'

'I'm sure it is only a misunderstanding.'

'In that case, tell me where she is taking old men, children and women whom she describes as dangerous.'

Khamudi looked rather uncomfortable. 'The lady Aberia is not entirely wrong. These people may look harmless, but in fact they are a real threat because they spread dangerous ideas. That is why it is necessary to expel them.'

'Only expel them?'

'We intern them in a place where they cannot cause any more trouble.'

'You mean a prison camp. Where is it?'

'At Sharuhen.'

'But Sharuhen's in Palestine. Why there?'

'It is far enough from Avaris, and the rebels receive just punishment there.'

'In that harsh land, many of them must die very quickly.'

'Surely you don't regret the deaths of the emperor's enemies?' said Khamudi. 'He approves both of the camp, which he considers essential, and also of the deportation of troublemakers. By expelling them, we rid Avaris of all undesirable elements. Isn't it a good idea?'

'Very good. Now, what else is there that I ought to know?'

'Nothing, I assure you.'

'I am glad to hear it, High Treasurer.'

Khamudi smiled. 'My wife and I are holding a reception this evening, with a few young girls who are to be deported tomorrow. It should be amusing, so won't you join us?'

'I have already told you I am not interested in amusements like that. Good night, High Treasurer.'

## 48

Minos was as ardent as ever when he made love to Windswept, and she still found matchless happiness in her lover's arms. But she could not forget his secret meeting with an official suspected of conspiring against Apophis.

If Minos really was guilty of that crime, she ought to denounce him to the emperor, who would delight in sending a new victim to the bull or the labyrinth. But Windswept would not let herself believe in his treason, and kept her suspicions to herself.

She caressed the Minoan's chest with her long, slender hands. 'I have the feeling you're hiding something from me, my love.'

'Don't you think you know everything about me?'

'Sometimes I wonder.'

'You're right.'

At last, he was going to confess. 'You can tell me everything, Minos.'

'It's very intimate, very serious . . .'

'Trust me.'

The artist swallowed hard. 'I'm having doubts about my talent. My early paintings seem colourless to me now, but I can't help wondering if they aren't more accomplished than the new ones. I worry about it so much that I can't sleep. My hand should be my only guide, but I'm afraid it's losing its precision. Is this a new stage, which will improve my work, or is my inspiration running dry?'

Windswept kissed him passionately. 'As long as you love me, you'll have all the inspiration you could want.'

After the midday meal, when most people were asleep, Minos left the fortress, bidding good day to the guards. They regarded him with contempt: this dauber was no use to anyone – he couldn't even handle a weapon.

He walked along with no apparent goal in mind, and turned into a street lined with officers' houses. Several times, he halted and looked around. Then he suddenly dived into a blind alley where grain-stores stood. Since they were not due to be filled for another week, there were no guards there.

In fact, there was no one at all there. And yet his accomplice had agreed to meet him here. His absence must mean that he had been arrested and that Minos would soon be caught, too.

'Come closer,' whispered an anxious voice.

Nervously, Minos did so.

The man was there, crouching between two grain-stores.

'Have you made any more contacts?' asked Minos.

'Jannas's return made it impossible – there are guards everywhere.'

'At the palace, people are whispering that Jannas hates Khamudi. Some say that the commander would make a good emperor.'

'He has the army's trust, certainly, but he's absolutely loyal to Apophis and would never support a conspiracy against him.'

'Then is it impossible for us to do what we must?'

'For the moment, yes. But Jannas is leaving to fight the Theban rebels. When he returns, the enmity between him and Khamudi is bound to take a new turn. Perhaps we can profit from it. Until then, we must wait and stay calm.'

Disappointed, Minos set off back to the palace. The man seemed too afraid to do anything, even in favourable circumstances. It was up to Minos to act, together with the other Minoans who were forced to live in this sinister town. Only the emperor's death would give them back their freedom.

Taking ample precautions so that she would not be spotted, Windswept had almost lost Minos. Choosing the right direction, she had finally found him again and had hidden in the corner of the blind alley where, it was clear, the Minoan was making contact with someone.

By climbing on to the roof of a grain-store, she could have eavesdropped on their conversation, but the stores' convex shape would have made that too dangerous. She had had to be content with watching her lover leave, lost in thought and visibly dejected.

The man who mattered was the other one. When she saw that he was the weapons official who was already under suspicion, the terrible reality hit her full in the face.

Minos was indeed a conspirator. He had lied to her, and she must denounce him.

In Jannas's eyes, there could be no exceptions to the rule of obedience. But he had never to carry out a strange mission as strange as the one to Per-shaq, and he felt that it lay well outside the duties of a soldier with his experience. He had therefore not gone himself, delegating one of his subordinates to execute the emperor's orders.

When the officer returned, Jannas summoned him at once, and asked, 'Is it done?

'Yes, Commander.'

'Any problems?'

'No, sir.'

'What is the latest information on the enemy army?'

'According to our scouts, it's moving slowly towards Per-shaq. They say it's a real army, sir, and surprisingly well organized, and the fleet is big. But the Theban scouts are not unskilled, so ours could not observe at close quarters.'

'Ensure that our operation is thoroughly prepared. I will not tolerate any laxity.'

The site of Lisht,* abandoned since the Hyksos invasion, included pyramids built by illustrious pharaohs of ancient times and the tombs of their senior officials. A profound peace reigned there, as if the kings of that bygone age were still passing on their wisdom.

It was precisely that wisdom which Apophis wanted to see disappear.

'Find me the entrances to these monuments,' Jannas ordered his engineers, 'and unblock the ways to the treasure-chambers.'

The pyramid of Amenemhat I, the most northerly, was as tall as thirty men; that of Sesostris I, which was surrounded by ten small pyramids, was even taller. Despite the precautions taken by the builders, the Hyksos succeeded in breaking into them. The mummies were removed from their sarcophagi, their bandages ripped off, their protective amulets scattered. Precious papyri, covered with texts describing the never-ending metamorphoses of the royal soul in the universe, were burnt.

Apophis's will had been done. Deprived of the protection of their glorious ancestors, Ahhotep and Kamose would find their momentum destroyed.

Nevertheless, the desecration of the royal remains was carried out in heavy silence. Jannas's soldiers were unaccustomed to fighting dead men, and the mummies' serene faces disturbed more than one soldier.

'The operation has been completed, sir,' said Jannas's second-in-command.

'Perhaps . . .'

---

*Lisht is about 50km south of Cairo. Its ruined pyramids date from the twentieth century BC.

'Have we forgotten something, sir?'

'Look at those pyramids. You would swear they're alive and defying us, as if violating the tombs had served no use.'

'What do you suggest we do?'

'We ought to destroy them stone by stone, but we haven't the time. I have received new orders.'

## 49

As the Theban army advanced towards Per-shaq, they knew that a head-on clash with Hyksos forces was inevitable. In the ranks, there was talk of monstrous animals which the emperor controlled with his mind, of long spears which could run through three men at once, and unknown weapons against which even Queen Ahhotep had no defence.

At the head of the war-fleet, Moon had taken up his helmsman's staff again to sound the Nile. As alert as a cat, he watched for the slightest sign of danger. At his side were Moustache and the Afghan, who knew the region well.

'We're very near Per-shaq,' said Moustache, who was getting increasingly edgy.

'Still nothing,' said Moon. 'But they may well have laid an ambush for us.'

'The best way of finding out,' suggested the Afghan, 'would be to send out scouts.'

Moon halted the boats. Ahhotep and the pharaoh agreed with the Afghan's reasoning, but refused to let him command the patrol himself.

'You're too senior,' Moustache pointed out, 'and you have too many decorations. I'll go instead.'

'No, you will not,' replied Ahhotep, 'because you hold the same rank and decorations as the Afghan.'

'Majesty, we cannot send a few inexperienced boys out. Without a skilled leader, not one of them will get back alive.'

'Do you consider me a skilled leader?' asked Kamose.

Moustache and the Afghan stared, open-mouthed.

The king bowed to his mother. 'Queen of Egypt, it is my responsibility, and mine alone, to lead my men into battle. Then they will know that I am not afraid, and that the commander of the army of freedom will face all the risks they do. My father and you yourself have always acted in this way.'

The man who stood in front of Ahhotep was neither a braggart nor irresponsible. He was a twenty-year-old pharaoh who was insistent upon carrying out his duties to the full. Although, as a mother, she felt her heart was breaking, the queen could not oppose his decision.

'If I fall,' whispered Kamose, 'I know you will pick me up again.'

The king had disembarked with a hundred men, less than an hour's march from Per-shaq. As soon as the enemy was spotted, he would release Rascal with a brief message outlining the situation.

'Still nothing,' fretted Moustache, pacing up and down the deck of the flagship, 'and they've been gone for ages.'

'It may be a good sign,' said the Afghan.

'Supposing the king's been taken prisoner? Supposing Rascal's been killed? We must do something.'

But only Ahhotep could give the order, and she said nothing.

'There's something wrong,' declared Moustache. 'I can feel it.'

'I am beginning to agree with you,' said the Afghan. 'Let's go and see the queen.'

At that moment, Rascal appeared above them with a flutter of wings, and landed gently on the queen's forearm. His bright eyes shone with the joy of a job well done.

The message, written in the king's hand, was decidedly surprising.

'He says there's nothing to report,' said Ahhotep. 'He is waiting for us at the gates of the town.'

Per-shaq was deserted. There was not a living soul in its narrow streets, not even a stray dog. Profoundly suspicious, Emheb ordered some of his men to inspect all the houses. All had been abandoned. In the cellars food had been left, untouched.

'The Hyksos must be hiding,' said Emheb. 'They're waiting for a large body of our troops to enter the town, and then they'll encircle us.'

Kamose deployed his men. This time, Moustache and the Afghan walked at the head of their regiments, ready to fight. But there was not a single Hyksos to be seen.

Outside the city, Moustache spotted significant tracks in the damp earth. There were footprints, hoofmarks – much larger than those of donkeys – and strange furrows.

'They have left and headed north,' he said after studying the tracks.

'The Hyksos have fled!' declared the pharaoh incredulously.

This bloodless victory unleashed joy in the whole army. So this was all the emperor's terrifying forces amounted to: a band of cowards who ran away at the enemy's approach and did not even try to hold their positions!

Ahhotep, however, did not join in the jubilation. True, the Hyksos had left Per-shaq, but where were its citizens?

Embheb came hurrying up to her. 'Majesty, come quickly!'

He led Ahhotep and Kamose to the area where the granaries stood. There was blood everywhere, and a terrible stench filled the air. Emheb's archers took up their positions, as if the enemy was at last about to emerge from the shadows.

'Open the doors of the granaries,' ordered Ahhotep.

Several young soldiers did so. Instantly, they bent over and vomited. One of them cried out, and beat his fist so hard against his forehead that an officer had to intervene to stop him injuring himself seriously.

The pharaoh and his mother went to the granary doors. What they saw brought them to the brink of fainting. Hollow-eyed, hearts pounding and breath coming in gasps, they could not believe such barbarity.

The bodies of the inhabitants of Per-shaq were heaped on top of each other, together with those of dogs, cats, geese and little monkeys. Not a single human being, not one animal or bird, had been spared. All had had their throats cut. All had been flung on to the piles like rubbish.

The pharaoh picked up the misshapen body of an old man, which lay across a fat man's back. Before murdering him, they had broken his legs.

Kamose could not weep. 'Remove these victims, human and animal, from this charnel-house with respect,' he ordered, 'and bury them in the earth. The Wife of God will conduct a funeral rite so that their souls may be reunited and at peace.'

A slow procession began, while the artificers started digging tombs.

Most of the soldiers were in tears, and even the Afghan, who had seemed to have no chinks in his armour, could not hold back his sobs as he carried the body of a young woman whose belly and breasts had been slashed to ribbons.

Twenty granaries at Per-shaq were emptied. The queen and the pharaoh looked upon each of the victims. Most had been appallingly tortured before being killed.

Ahhotep could sense her son faltering. But she could not hide from him a fact which she alone seemed to have noticed: 'Among these unfortunates, there is not a single child.'

'They must have been taken away to become slaves.'

'There are still three granaries left,' said the queen.

His head reeling, the king himself opened the door of one of them. He gave a sigh of profound relief. 'Jars – nothing but jars.'

For a moment, Ahhotep wanted to believe that the Hyksos had been merciful, but she had to check. She removed the coarse stopper of clay from an oil-jar. Inside lay the body of a three-year-old girl, her skull smashed.

Every single jar contained the body of a child; each child had been tortured before being killed. The Hyksos troops had carried out the emperor's orders to the letter.

## 50

The burial ceremony was conducted with a fervour which united the living and the dead through their shared faith in the justice of Osiris. Afterwards, everyone felt as if they'd plunged into a kind of abyss, from which only the comradeship of battle could offer an escape. The soldiers gathered in groups to talk about their dear ones, and to prove to themselves that, despite the horrors of Per-shaq, a future still existed.

Alone in her cabin with Young Laughter, who was lying in front of the door, Ahhotep called upon Pharaoh Seqen's radiant soul to give her back the strength she had lost by offering all her love to the victims of the Hyksos. After the slaughter of those innocents, after the torture of women, children, men and animals, the face of this war had changed.

If there still was a war. The emperor's intentions were clear: if the Theban army continued to defy him, thousands of Egyptians would be slaughtered with unparalleled cruelty. Could the twenty-year-old king live with the responsibility for that happening? Deeply scarred already, he wanted only to return to Thebes.

The murderers of Per-shaq had not struck at random, and their appalling crime would prove as effective as even their most destructive weapons of war.

So Ahhotep must stand in the path of her own son, and show him that any backward step would lead to defeat.

'Your attitude is unworthy of a pharaoh,' declared Anat.

'If you had seen—'

'I did see. I also saw Tita cut the throats of innocent people to establish his reign of terror. Those are the methods the Hyksos use.'

'If we continue our offensive,' said Kamose, 'the emperor will order more massacres.'

'If you take refuge in the illusory safety of Thebes, first he will order more massacres, and then his army will charge south and destroy you. The more you hesitate, the more Apophis's fury will be unleashed upon innocent people. Once you attack the Emperor of Darkness, you can never go back. That is what Queen Ahhotep thinks, and it is what I think, too.'

'Has my mother confided in you?'

'No, Majesty, but all I needed to do was look into her eyes. Even if she had to continue the fight alone, or with just a handful of supporters, she would not hesitate. Apophis knows now that he will never subjugate the Egyptians, so he has decided to kill them all. Your army's retreat would not save a single life.'

'So our early victories were nothing but illusions,' said Kamose bitterly.

'Illusions? Breaking through the front at Qis, taking Nefrusy and Khmun? Of course they weren't.'

'When the Hyksos use their heavy weapons—'

'They may be too confident in those weapons' power. You must strive to be worthy of wearing the White Crown when the sons of the light confront those of the dark.'

Ahhotep gazed up at the full moon, the symbol of successful rebirth. Once again, the sun of night had vanquished the forces of chaos, to light up the starry sky and become the interpreter of the hidden light. But from this day onward, the Jar of Predictions had no more to say.

Kamose came up to her. 'Mother, I have made my decision. In the voice of Anat, the woman I love, I heard your voice. And you have set out the only possible way.'

'Destiny is asking a great deal of one so young – perhaps too much. A whole lifetime of suffering and drama has been imposed upon you in a few weeks, and you have been given no chance to regroup. But you are the pharaoh, and your age is of no importance. The only thing that matters is your office, for it is the hope of an entire people.'

'At dawn, I shall inform the army that we intend to continue northwards.'

The small town of Sako, where the army next halted, had suffered the same fate as Per-shaq. Their macabre discoveries once again horrified and sickened the soldiers, and it took all Pharaoh's authority to maintain order in the ranks. The Wife of God conducted the funerary rites, and her nobility calmed the men. Everyone realized that they were fighting not only to free Egypt but also to destroy a monster whose cruelty was limitless.

The king and queen were finishing a frugal evening meal when Moustache came in, pushing in front of him a small, frightened-looking man in a black breastplate.

'Look what I found,' said Moustache. 'He was hiding in a cellar. If Your Majesties permit, I shall hand him over to my men.'

The Hyksos fell to his knees, eyes lowered. 'Don't kill me,' he begged. 'I'm only a messenger. I haven't hurt anyone – I've never even carried a weapon.'

'Why did you not leave with the others?' demanded Kamose.

'I hid in a house so as not to see what they were doing, and I fell asleep.'

'Who is in command of these murderers?'

'Commander Jannas himself.'

'And where is he now?'

'I don't know, my lord, truly I don't know. I'm just a messenger and—'

'Deal with him, Moustache.'

'Wait a moment,' cut in Ahhotep. 'It's possible that he might be useful.'

'You wished to see me urgently, little sister?' The emperor was surprised. 'You look upset.'

Face to face with Apophis, who was colder than the north wind in winter, even Windswept felt uneasy. But it was too late to go back now.

'I . . . I have some information.'

'The name of a conspirator?'

'Exactly.'

'You're wonderful, little sister, far more efficient than my spies. Tell me quickly, who dares devise dark plans against my august person?'

Windswept remembered Minos's body, his caresses, his fervour, the hours of pleasure which only he could give her. 'Someone important, someone we'd never have suspected.'

'Come on, don't keep me waiting. The traitor will enter the labyrinth this very evening and you shall sit beside me to watch him die.'

Windswept took a deep breath. 'He is one of the officials in charge of weapons,' she said.

The arrest warrant had scarcely been signed when a furious Khamudi came in and presented the emperor with a papyrus. 'Majesty, it's a letter from Pharaoh Kamose.'

'How did it reach us?'

'It was brought by a messenger the Thebans captured but then released. I tortured the imbecile, of course, but he died without saying anything interesting.'

'Well, read me the message.'

'Majesty, I don't think—'

'Read it.'

Khamudi did so, in an indignant voice.

*I, Pharaoh Kamose, regard Apophis as nothing but a petty warlord who has been driven back, together with his armies. Your speech is miserable. It calls to mind the headsman's block on which you will perish. Terrible rumours are circulating in your city, where your defeat is already being announced. You desire nothing but evil, and by evil you shall fall. The women of Avaris will no longer be able to conceive, for their hearts will no longer open in their bodies when they hear the war-cries of my soldiers. Look behind you as you flee, for the army of Pharaoh Kamose and Queen Ahhotep is advancing towards you.*

Khamudi was quivering with rage. 'Majesty, should Jannas not immediately crush this vermin who dares insult you?'

The emperor was unperturbed. 'This contemptible letter is intended to provoke me and draw me into a trap. The Egyptians would like us to fight at Sako, on their terrain. But we shall not make that mistake, and Jannas shall continue his cleansing. We shall destroy the rebels at the right place and time, just as we have planned.'

# 51

'Nothing to report, Majesty,' said the commander of the scouts; he was as disappointed as the pharaoh and Queen Ahhotep.

Although his vanity must certainly have been wounded, Apophis had not reacted as they had hoped, so all the measures they had taken around Sako had been for nothing.

'Nevertheless, we have learnt something important,' said Ahhotep. 'Apophis has a specific plan, and nothing will divert him from it, not even insufferable insults to his power.'

'Massacring innocent people and pretending to retreat,' said Kamose furiously, 'that's all his vile plan is.'

'There may be more to it than that,' warned the queen.

Her words worried the king. 'What do you suspect?'

'We must not underestimate Apophis, even for a second. Although we are advancing, he is still in control of the situation. There are three vital questions. First, how far back will he withdraw, and where will he finally join battle? Second, do these tactics mask preparations for a surprise attack? Third, we have still not caught the Hyksos spy: what is he plotting?'

'He must have gone back to Avaris, or else be dead. Otherwise he would have done us serious harm.'

Kamose's argument seemed convincing, but the queen was still doubtful.

'This is what I advise,' she said. 'Soon we shall have to face Jannas, and we have no idea what form the confrontation will take. So I propose dividing our troops into two: one half will remain at Sako, while the other makes for Fayum. The carrier-pigeons will enable us to remain in constant contact, and if we need to join forces we shall be able to do so quickly.'

'Then I shall leave for Fayum.'

'No, Kamose, I shall go.'

'Mother, I don't—'

'It must be so.'

*

The governor of Fayum, Joseph, was a Hebrew. After suffering the jealousy and hatred of his brothers, who had tried to kill him, he had found happiness, wealth and respect in Egypt. As he was not suspected of collaborating with the enemies of the Hyksos, Apophis had appointed him to govern the little paradise the pharaohs of old had created by irrigating the area, which was about three days' march south-west of Memphis. Criss-crossed by canals fed by a tributary of the Nile, Fayum was an immense garden and a haven for game and fish.

Joseph was an excellent administrator. He now lived in opulence, in a big house surrounded by gardens and palm-trees, but he had never forgotten the unhappy times, or what it was like to be hungry. He cared about every inhabitant of his province, and intervened personally to help anyone who was in difficulties. His people lived a pleasant life amid the greenery, far from the ferocity of the desert and the ferocity of war.

The governor was therefore very surprised when Jannas arrived at his house.

'Is everything quiet here?' asked Jannas. 'Has there been any trouble with rebels?'

'No, of course not. There's been no unrest in Fayum for a long time.'

'All good things come to an end. The Theban army is heading this way.'

'The Thebans? How can that be?'

'You do not ask questions, you obey the emperor's orders. I am leaving you two hundred soldiers, under the command of Captain Antreb.'

'That's a very small force to defend the whole of Fayum.'

Jannas looked out at the garden. 'Who said anything about defending it? Their mission is to burn all the villages and crops.'

Joseph thought he must be having a nightmare. 'That's impossible! Surely you aren't serious?'

'Those are the orders, and I demand your full cooperation.'

'But . . . what about the people?'

'They will be killed.'

'What have they done wrong?' asked Joseph rebelliously.

'The emperor's will must not be questioned.'

'Surely you aren't going to kill the children?'

'The emperor said everyone. When it's done, Captain Antreb will take you to Avaris, where Apophis will reward you.'

Captain Antreb was a short, stocky, round-faced man who looked rather like Khamudi. He was a particularly brutal man and loved killing, which was why Jannas had appointed him. He and his murderous troops would thoroughly enjoy their work, especially when the victims begged for their lives. As Antreb had a little time to spare, he was planning to extend the period of torture. In a region as pleasant as Fayum, his men would enjoy the extra entertainment.

Antreb was staying at Joseph's villa, and was revelling in the delicious food, fine wines and other benefits. Never had he been so assiduously massaged and shaved.

'Are you satisfied with my hospitality?' Joseph asked him.

'More than satisfied, overwhelmed. But there's work to be done.'

'This province did not grow rich in a day. Why ruin so many years of work? You can see for yourself that the villagers of Fayum are peaceful people, whose only interest is their gardens and fields. The emperor has nothing to fear from them.'

'That's irrelevant. The only thing that matters to me is my orders.'

'Think again, I beg of you! What good will massacring all these innocent people do you?'

'With the villages and crops destroyed, the Thebans will find no support along their way, only corpses.'

'May I go to Avaris and plead Fayum's cause to the emperor?'

'That's out of the question. My work will begin tomorrow morning and will be finished by the evening. Not a single village will be spared. Do you hear me? Not one. And if you drag your feet, you might just have an . . . accident. Do I make myself clear?'

'Very clear.'

'We shall begin with the largest village. You will tell all the people, including the children, to assemble in the main square because you have some good news to announce to them. Then I shall take over.'

Moon had insisted on commanding the fleet on its voyage to Fayum. Aboard were the regiments led by Moustache and the Afghan, and the archers commanded by Ahmes, son of Abana. Emheb had remained in Sako with the pharaoh, as had Neshi.

Everyone was very tense. Ahhotep stood at the prow of the flagship, scanning the riverbanks.

'The Hyksos have destroyed everything in their path,' grieved Moon. 'There's probably not a single villager left alive.'

As they neared Fayum, the air grew fragrant. The province was like one huge oasis, where the very idea of war seemed out of place. Trees as far as the eye could see, gardens in the shade of palm-groves, herds of cattle browsing on juicy grass, and even the sound of a flute playing, as if there was still such a thing as a happy peasant.

'It is a trap!' exclaimed Moon. 'To your combat stations!'

While it was in the middle of the river, the fleet had nothing to fear. And, surprisingly, the lookout at the top of the highest mast did not give the signal that meant enemy vessels were near.

'The Hyksos must be hidden among the trees,' said the Afghan. 'As soon as we disembark, they will attack.'

'There's one,' said Moustache, pointing to the riverbank where a man had just appeared.

Arms raised above his head, the man ran towards the Egyptian ships.

'Do not fire,' ordered the queen. 'He is unarmed.'

The man waded thigh-deep into the river. 'I am Joseph, governor of Fayum,' he shouted, 'and I need your help.'

## 52

'I'll deal with him,' declared Moustache, diving into the Nile.

The Egyptian archers aimed their bows. If this man Joseph was in fact a decoy, he would not live long.

'You must help me,' he repeated. 'The Hyksos want to slaughter all the people of Fayum! Their leader is at my house, and he's about to begin the killing.'

'How many Hyksos are there?' asked Moustache.

'Two hundred – two hundred torturers determined to destroy Fayum! You're the only ones who can stop them.'

Moustache scanned the area suspiciously. There were no Hyksos in sight, so Joseph might not be lying. He beckoned to the war-fleet.

As soon as the ships were moored, Ahhotep was first to descend the gangplank.

At the sight of her, Joseph was overcome. He knew instantly that she was the famous Queen of Freedom, whose legend grew greater every day. This sublimely beautiful woman radiated a light whose intensity made the heart swell. At that moment, he knew he had been right to hope she would come.

'We must act quickly, Majesty,' he said, prostrating himself. 'Please do not abandon my people.'

It was a pitiful Joseph who presented himself before Captain Antreb.

The Hyksos adjusted his black breastplate. 'Here you are at last. If I'd had to wait much longer, I'd have cut your servants' throats to relieve the boredom.'

'Your orders have been carried out, Captain. The villagers have gathered and are waiting for the good news I promised them.'

Antreb put on his black helmet. 'Excellent. Carry on like this, Joseph, and you'll save your skin.'

'Will you at least spare those closest to me?'

'That depends how tired we are when we've finished with the others.'

Antreb had some difficulty gathering his men together, as most of them were drunk. When they entered the main square of the village, which was fringed with palm-trees, they found all the men, women and children huddled together in terror. The soldiers knew they were going to enjoy some fine sport.

'I have two pieces of news, one good and one bad,' announced Antreb jauntily. 'The bad news is that you are all, including your governor, dangerous rebels.' He grabbed Joseph by the shoulder and hurled him into the huddle of villagers. 'I hate Hebrews, so I shan't spare you, after all.

'Now, here's the good news: the emperor has ordered me to prevent you from doing harm. We're going to torture you to make you confess what you are plotting against our sovereign. Those of you who tell us absolutely everything will be allowed to die quickly. For those who are stubborn, death will be very slow and very painful.'

The torturers held up thick clubs studded with metal. There was nothing more effective for interrogating victims.

A man emerged from the mass of villagers. 'You, Hyksos, are you aware that you are a murderer?'

Antreb was so astounded that for a moment he was speechless. Then he said, 'Who the devil are you? Some sort of priest?'

'No, just someone who will no longer tolerate the rule of tyranny and blind violence.'

Antreb turned to his men. 'You see? They really are rebels. As for you, little man, with your fine words, I have a special fate in store for you: you will be roasted alive over a slow fire.'

'That's unbelievable.'

Antreb was amazed again at this peasant's fearlessness. 'You're making a big mistake if you think I won't do it, my lad!'

'The unbelievable thing is that that's exactly what I intend to do to you.'

Antreb's third attack of astonishment proved fatal, for Moustache dived at his legs and, using one of the holds he had learnt from the wrestling scenes at Beni Hasan, hoisted him high before dropping him heavily on the back of his neck.

The Hyksos soldiers were cut down by the Egyptian archers' arrows. Ahhotep had ordered that they were to be shot in the back, so that they would die like the cowards they were. In just a few minutes, all the torturers were dead.

Antreb lay still, his eyes glassy.

'Good grief,' grumbled Moustache, 'even that vermin's neck was weak!'

'You took an unnecessary risk again,' scolded the Afghan.

'No I didn't – you were covering me. Besides, I really wanted to try out that hold.'

The villagers embraced their rescuers.

'Last week,' Joseph told Moustache, 'we received supplies from the North. With those and what we grow here, I can promise you and your men an unforgettable meal.'

The joints of meat cooked in milk were as delicious as anyone could wish. Fayum had been transformed into a gigantic open-air banqueting-hall, where its return to freedom would be joyously celebrated. Kamose was welcomed with shouts of joy, as if he had been sent from another world, where Ma'at still reigned.

Before the celebrations began, the Wife of God had celebrated a ritual in honour of the ancestors and of Amon, lord of Thebes. As she did so, she sensed a presence close by, a gentle warmth, a loving caress, a south wind enveloping her whole body in tenderness. It was he, it was Seqen, intensely present at that moment when a new part of Egypt had been torn from the emperor's clutches. Never before had the late pharaoh manifested himself in such tangible form, as if the queen needed a new kind of energy, sent from the otherworld, before facing terrible ordeals.

'Aren't you hungry, Mother?' asked Kamose.

'We ought to be thinking about the future.'

'I cannot really share the people's happiness, either,' he admitted.

The queen and the pharaoh withdrew into the royal tent, to study Qaris's model of Egypt.

How far they had come since young Ahhotep's rebellion, since the time when only the Theban enclave knew any freedom at all. Many provinces and towns had been reconquered, but there had also been many atrocities and much suffering, and there were still innumerable obstacles between them and true victory.

Ahhotep leant over the model. 'That's where Jannas is waiting for us. That's where he plans to crush us.' She pointed to Memphis.

Memphis, 'the Balance of the Two Lands', had been Egypt's capital at the time of the pyramids, the heart of the country's system of trade, and it was made sacred by the Temple of Ptah. Memphis, gateway to the Delta for the South, and to the Nile valley for the North. Through his policy of destroying villages and crops, the emperor planned to lure in all the Theban forces, which would have no chance of defeating the main Hyksos army.

'Then the battle at Memphis will be decisive,' said Kamose. 'But Apophis must not find out that we know it and that we shan't throw ourselves head-first into his trap. He ought to have launched a surprise attack by now, before we can reach Memphis. He probably has absolute confidence in his own military power, so whatever tactics we adopt will seem ridiculous to him.'

Ahhotep said pensively, 'Do you remember the three questions I posed? We have the answer to the first, but there are still the other two. Memphis is so obvious that it may conceal another trap which is still hidden from us.'

'How can we detect it?'

'Let us pray to Amon, and ask him not to abandon us but to offer us a sign.'

## 53

The Afghan and Moustache were always among the first to rise in the morning. They had acquired this habit in their early days as rebels, at a time when they had feared they might be caught at any moment. It gave them a chance to inspect the camp and see if anything was amiss.

This morning, despite a dreadful headache resulting from the previous night's excesses, the Afghan noticed something unusual.

'What's wrong?' asked Moustache.

'Have we set up enough guard-posts?'

'I saw to it myself. If there'd been even the slightest problem, we'd have been warned immediately.'

The Afghan sniffed the air like a lion on the prowl. Then he delivered his verdict: 'There's someone coming, from the south.'

A moment later, the ground shuddered under the weight of heavy, powerful feet. A colossal ram with spiralling horns emerged from a dense thicket of tamarisks. The majestic animal halted and stared at the humans. A supernatural light shone in its eyes.

'Go and fetch the queen and the pharaoh,' Moustache told the Afghan.

The sovereigns meditated before the incarnation of Amon. Then their eyes began to speak, and the ram moved off, heading due west.

'Judging by the shape of its horns, that was a Nubian ram,' observed the queen.

'Does that mean the Nubians are still a danger?' asked the pharaoh. 'Surely that's impossible – they're much too far from here.'

'I must follow the direction the beast of Amon showed us,' said Ahhotep.

'But, Mother, all you'll find will be the desert and then an oasis.'

'As soon as I have found another sign, I'll send Rascal to you.'

'You know how much the army will need you during the battle for Memphis.'

'We must not attack blindly. Gather together as many fighters as you can and, together with your council, draw up a battle-plan which does not involve any fighting on land. Our best weapon is our fleet. And we have one other ally: the Nile flood.'

Long-Ears guided Ahhotep and her troop of soldiers. For him, following the trail left by Amon's ram was easy, but he set such a fast pace that some of the soldiers had difficulty keeping up. The queen knew he had a good reason for hurrying, so stops were kept to a minimum and everyone remained on the alert at all times.

Suddenly, they saw a white antelope standing on top of a rocky outcrop. Long-Ears halted, and nuzzled the queen's shoulder.

Ahhotep went slowly towards the antelope. It was the incarnation of Satis, wife of the ram-headed potter-god Khnum, and the new sign sent by Amon. And this sign, too, pointed to the Great South and Nubia. The animal licked the queen's hands, and its infinitely gentle eyes told her that it would guide her to her goal.

In the Bahariya oasis, which was ordinarily calm and far removed from the sounds of war that disturbed the Nile valley, the atmosphere had abruptly grown tense. Usually, the governor was content to collaborate limply with the Hyksos, who showed only a cursory interest in this obscure place, a mere staging-post for army messengers.

It was, in fact, by way of the oases of the Western Desert that messages passed between Avaris and Kerma, the capital of Nubia. True, it was a long and difficult route, but the Thebans did not know of it.

This time, the head messenger was accompanied by a hundred particularly savage Hyksos soldiers, and they had joined up with as many Nubians, who were just as menacing. The Bahariyans had to give them all free beer, wine and date alcohol.

'Do not cause any trouble here,' the governor told the messenger.

Backed by so many soldiers, the messenger was openly scornful of the stocky, bearded man who dared admonish him. 'This oasis belongs to the emperor, like the rest of Egypt. Or have you forgotten that?'

'We pay him enormous taxes, and he takes almost everything we have. So let him at least allow us to live in peace. This place is of no strategic importance.'

'That's where you're wrong, my fine friend.'

The governor frowned. 'What does that mean?'

The messenger relished his moment of glory. 'You see, these Nubians are only a forward detachment, whose job it is to collect a very important letter to King Nedjeh. Before long, hundreds of Nubian warriors will be arriving here, and you are to serve them zealously.'

'I won't do it! I—'

'You cannot refuse to help the emperor and his allies – unless, of course, you're a rebel, a supporter of Queen Ahhotep.'

'No, I swear I'm not!' said the governor.

'Now I see what your game is. Still, it doesn't work out too badly for me. I've had enough of being a messenger. I shall enjoy being the new governor of Bahariya.'

The governor panicked and tried to escape. He ran towards the edge of the desert, pursued by two Nubians.

He was almost at his last gasp when all at once, there before him, he saw a magnificent white antelope, which bounded off into the desert. In its place stood a majestic woman, wearing a red band round her hair and a tunic of the same colour. She was so beautiful that he forgot his fear.

The two Nubians thought they could kill their quarry with one blow from their clubs, but they suddenly froze: they were facing a whole army. They heard arrows whistle through the air, and scarcely had time to register the fact that they were about to die.

The governor was shaking from head to foot. 'Majesty, you . . . ? Are you . . . ?'

'How many Nubians are there in the oasis?' asked Ahhotep:

'About a hundred, and the same number of Hyksos, but they're all trying to drink themselves into a stupor. Majesty, they want to turn Bahariya into a military base.'

The matter was quickly resolved. Dead drunk and caught by surprise, the enemy offered only feeble resistance.

The sole survivor was the head messenger, who had taken a little girl hostage.

'Don't touch me,' he yelped, 'or I'll break her neck. If you spare my life, I'll give you an important letter.'

'Give it to me,' ordered Ahhotep.

He handed her an official letter, marked with the emperor's seal. The queen read it and learnt a great deal.

*From Emperor Apophis to King Nedjeh:*
  *Do you know what Egypt has undertaken against me?*
  *Kamose is attacking me in my own domain. He is persecuting the Two Lands, yours and mine, and he is ravaging them. Come to Avaris without fear. I shall hold Kamose until you arrive, and no one can intercept you as you traverse Egypt, because all the enemy forces are in the North. We shall defeat them and share the country between us.*

So that was the answer to Ahhotep's second question: the emperor was indeed planning to entrap the Egyptian army. While it was pinned down by the Hyksos, it would be attacked from the south by the Nubians.

'Will you spare my life?' whined the messenger.

'On two conditions: that you carry a letter to the emperor and that you release that child immediately.'

He obeyed. The little girl ran to hide in the queen's arms and Ahhotep comforted her for a long time.

While the man stood waiting, not daring to move, Ahhotep wrote a biting letter informing Apophis that the route through the oases was now under Egyptian control, that his message would never reach Kerma, and that the Nubians would not leave their province.

# 54

The emperor had ordered Jannas to remain at Memphis and to mass troops there on the plain, to prevent the enemy from advancing. Soon, the Nubians would charge down on the Thebans, whose only option would be to retreat to the north, where Jannas was waiting to wipe them out.

Jannas did not approve of this plan. Never in all his brilliant career had he depended on the actions of third parties like the Nubians, whose lack of discipline worried him. There was something else, too: the annual Nile flood had begun, which made it impossible to leave chariot regiments on the plain. He had had to pull them back to the east of Memphis where, for the moment, they would be of no use whatsoever. Redeploying his forces would take several days.

In Kamose's place, he would have chosen this ideal moment to launch an offensive. But the young pharaoh was inexperienced in war, and his early victories had probably turned his head. As for Queen Ahhotep, she suffered from an incurable fault: being a woman, and therefore incapable of holding a command. In fright, she would persuade her son not to venture too far forward, for fear of losing what had been gained.

The river was rising fast.

'It will be a very fine flood,' predicted Moon.

'All the finer because it has already forced Jannas to withdraw his chariots,' said the Afghan, who had just received the reports from his scouts.

'We should attack immediately,' said Kamose.

'Give us one day, Majesty,' begged Moustache, 'one single day, so that we can try to revive our networks of supporters in Memphis. If we manage to make a large proportion of the population rebel, Jannas will have to face another and unexpected opponent.'

'That is very dangerous.'

'The Afghan and I can pass unnoticed.'

Kamose turned to Ahhotep, who nodded. 'Tomorrow at dawn,' he said, 'our fleet will enter the port of Memphis. Kill as many Hyksos as possible.'

Memphis was Moustache's favourite town. With its white walls, dating from the first dynasties, and its great temples, which had alas been burnt down by the Hyksos, the former capital retained its proud appearance despite the occupation. But this was no time for contemplation, and the two water-carriers were bent double under the weight of heavy jars as they arrived at one of the gates, which was guarded by Hyksos soldiers.

'Who are you?' one of them demanded.

'Conscripted peasants,' replied the Afghan. 'Because of the flood, the river water is no longer fit to drink. We've been told to bring reserves to the barracks.'

'You may enter.'

The town was in upheaval. It was clear that the chariots' forced retreat had obliged the high command to alter its plans. The Afghan and Moustache headed for the poor district around the ruined Temple of Ptah, where they hoped the last members of their rebel network might have gone to ground.

In a deserted alleyway, close to a safe-house, they heard characteristic barking: a rebel dog was sounding the alert, according to the agreed code.

The two men laid down their burdens and took off their tattered tunics to show that they were not carrying any hidden weapons.

'It really is us,' said the Afghan. 'Have we changed so much?'

The heavy silence that followed this question ought to have made them run for safety, but neither man moved.

'We're in rather a hurry, friends. If you want to kill some Hyksos, now is the time.'

The blade of a dagger pressed against the Afghan's back.

'A good move, little one, but a bad final position.' Using one of the wrestling holds from Beni Hasan, the Afghan tripped the youth who was threatening him, disarmed him and twisted his arm behind his back. 'If you want to fight, my lad, you still have a lot to learn.'

Five rebels emerged from the house, among them a priest of Ptah who had escaped the mass arrests. 'I know them,' he said. 'They led our group. Everyone thought they were dead.'

The Afghan smiled. 'Well, we aren't. And – can you believe it? – we've even been decorated by Queen Ahhotep! Tomorrow at dawn, the Egyptian fleet will attack the town. Can an uprising be organized?'

'Too many people would get themselves killed.'

'You don't get anything for nothing,' Moustache reminded him. 'If the townspeople can put the city guards out of action and set fire to the docks, our army will take care of the rest.'

'The whole city is ready to rise up,' declared the youth. 'If we spread the message through every district straight away, we'll succeed.'

Jannas did not sleep well: he had a nightmare in which fire destroyed the Hyksos war-fleet. Thinking about the vital new precautions he must take, he did not fall asleep again until the small hours.

He was awakened by a smell of burning, which made him leap out of bed. From the window of the barracks, he saw that the docks were on fire.

His second-in-command rushed into the room. 'The Egyptians are attacking, sir! Several boats have breached our first line of defence.'

'The queen and her little king aren't as incompetent as I thought,' admitted Jannas. 'Every man to his post.'

'There are several fires, sir, and loud shouting can be heard in most districts – it's as if the whole of Memphis is rebelling.'

'It is. Let's hope the city guards can contain the rioters. I have other priorities.'

Very soon, Jannas realized that the enemy had carried out a masterly manoeuvre. Taking advantage of the flood, war-boats had sailed right up as far as some of the city ramparts, from where Pharaoh's archers were ideally placed to aim at the Hyksos defenders, who retaliated furiously. Kneeling on the roof of a cabin, along with the other elite archers, Ahmes, son of Abana, cut down several officers, causing consternation among the enemy ranks.

As soon as Emheb and his men succeeded in setting foot on the battlements of the citadel, the Hyksos weakened. Galvanized, Egyptian soldiers appeared from everywhere. And in the town, under the command of Moustache and the Afghan, the guards were killed with mattocks, stools, carpenters' mallets and anything else that would serve as a weapon. The Memphites gave full vent to their rage.

Before long, under the onslaught by over seven thousand soldiers, all as reckless as their pharaoh, the Hyksos army began to buckle.

'Is there still no news of the Nubians?' Jannas asked his second-in-command.

'No, sir.'

'That stupid plan has failed. It's impossible to defend Memphis any longer. We must get out of this hornets' nest as fast as possible.'

It was the first time that Jannas had ever been forced to beat a retreat. But circumstances were against him, and he found himself with no choice. To continue to fight in such bad conditions would have been madness. He therefore sacrificed a small part of his troops to ensure that the rest could pull back to the north-east. Soldiers, chariots and horses were loaded on to boats which headed rapidly away from Memphis.

Jannas had prevented the worst. True, he had barely scratched the enemy army and was abandoning a great city to them, but his forces were almost intact, and the fact that the Egyptian victory was spectacular did not mean it was decisive.

Kamose himself shattered the skull of the last Hyksos footsoldier, who had obeyed Jannas's orders by holding his position to the death.

In disbelief, the Egyptians realized that the battle was over. Memphis, capital of Egypt during the time of the pyramids, was free again. In the residential districts, where not a single Hyksos guard had been spared, people were singing and dancing. Old men were weeping, the prison gates had been thrown open, and children were already beginning to play in the streets again, while doctors and nurses, under She-Cat's vigorous direction, were taking care of the many wounded.

In the palace, Ahhotep and Kamose received the homage of the surviving town dignitaries, most of whom had suffered torture and interrogation. Standing in the front row, Anat marvelled at the pharaoh's bearing.

When, a little weary, the Afghan and Moustache went into the palace, they met Emheb, who had been wounded in the arm.

'So you two have survived again,' he commented.

'It would have been a pity to miss this,' replied Moustache. 'You should get that arm seen to.'

'Can you imagine how the queen must feel?' asked the Afghan.

At that moment, Ahhotep had only one thought in her head: the road to Avaris, the Emperor of Darkness's lair, lay wide open.

## 55

Like all the soldiers of the Egyptian army, the Afghan and Moustache were shaved and perfumed, and their skin was rubbed with a pomade made from honey, red natron and sea-salt. This was vital to keep the skin healthy and protect it from insects, which were more numerous in the marshy areas of the Delta than in the Nile valley.

Ahhotep and Kamose had just made known their decision: the Egyptian fleet was to sail for Avaris, taking full advantage of the flood, which had turned the vast stretches of the Northern provinces into one immense lake.

'This time,' enthused Neshi at the final council of war before departure, 'we shall strike the emperor a death-blow!'

'It won't be that easy,' warned Emheb. 'The Hyksos army is almost intact and we don't know the system of defences around Avaris.'

'The emperor is not expecting an attack,' said Ahhotep. 'Logic dictates that we establish our main military base at Memphis and take the time necessary to prepare for a decisive attack.'

'Our boats are ready,' said Kamose. 'We shall leave tomorrow morning.'

A liaison officer asked permission to speak. 'Majesty, we've had a message from Sako. The town has been attacked, and the officer in charge of our detachment requests urgent assistance.'

'Do you know any more details?'

'Unfortunately not. And the carrier-pigeon arrived exhausted and wounded – we couldn't save it.'

'I shall go to Sako immediately,' decided the queen. 'If the Hyksos counter-attack isn't halted, Thebes will be in peril. Nevertheless, we must not delay our attack on Avaris.'

The pharaoh and his counsellors were worried. Without Ahhotep, the Egyptian army would be deprived of its soul.

'The White Crown and the steering-oar of the flagship, with its gold-covered prow, shall guide Pharaoh along the waterways of the Delta,' said Ahhotep. 'He will find the quickest route to Avaris and will swoop down like a falcon upon the tyrant's city.'

The young king rose. 'Commander Moon, prepare to embark.'

The golden ship made good speed, with the war-fleet in her wake. At the helm, Moon was having a strange experience: the steering-oar seemed to have a life of its own, and he was no more than a witness to its movements as it steered the boat in the right direction.

Almost all the soldiers were seeing the Delta for the first time, and it was very different from the Nile valley. Here, the land was flat as far as the eye could see, criss-crossed by canals and tributaries. Alongside the fields grew veritable forests of papyrus and reeds, partly submerged by the flood.

The fleet was not planning to stop anywhere. It had passed by the towns of Iunu, Taremu and Bubastis, all of which it could have attacked, so as not to lose a second on the way to Avaris.

Still elated by the conquest of Memphis, the young soldiers were joking about the Hyksos' cowardice.

'They're good lads,' mumbled Moustache, through a mouthful of dried fish. 'It's better that they don't know the truth.'

'Don't you think we'll succeed in taking Avaris?' asked the Afghan.

'We've had a lot of good luck since the beginning of the war, but this time the queen isn't here to lead us.'

'All the same, we'll have the benefit of surprise.'

'Can you imagine the fortress of Avaris? We shall break our teeth on it.'

The Afghan shook his head.

Emheb came over to them. 'Wouldn't you like something better to eat?'

'Not hungry,' replied Moustache.

'I know Avaris is getting closer,' said Emheb, 'but isn't it pleasanter to fight with a full stomach? In the front line we'll have no chance of coming through alive, but we must make sure that Kamose does. Pass on the order.'

Moustache went to join She-Cat. He wanted to taste the pleasures of love one last time.

Fascinated by the beauty of Lower Egypt, the kingdom of the Red Crown, Kamose retired to his cabin shortly before Avaris came into view. Travelling across provinces which were still beneath the Hyksos yoke gave him an immeasurable desire for victory.

Gently he took Anat's face in his hands. Her blue eyes expressed an increasingly intense passion for the king, whose most intimate life she now shared.

'Do you think what I'm about to do is mad?' he asked.

'It has taken many mad acts to get so close to the monster, in the hope of plunging your sword into his back. By believing himself invincible, the emperor gives you a chance of victory.'

Kamose opened a phial which had been given to him by a perfume-maker in Memphis. Slowly he spread its contents over the young woman's neck and shoulders.

'I am a foreigner and the widow of a traitor,' she said. 'How can you love me?'

'Will you marry me, Anat?'

'That's impossible; you know it is. You are Pharaoh of Egypt, and I—'

'You are the woman I love, and you love me, too. There's no law forbidding our marriage.'

'Please, don't say any more. Not another word.'

Almost everyone was delighted by the flood. Born of Hapy, the vital energy of the Nile, it deposited silt which made the earth black and fertile. It also acted as an immense purifying wave which drowned a vast numbers of rodents, scorpions and even snakes. At the moment, it was disturbing a big herd of hippopotamus, who were accustomed to remaining submerged during the daytime and climbing out on to the banks at night to find food.

The hippopotamus's only enemy was the crocodile, which was apt to seize and carry off calves at the very moment of birth, unless it was fought off by one or more females. Although the hippopotamus looked placid, if disturbed or frightened it sometimes became enraged and very dangerous.

'I've never seen so many,' said Moustache. 'Fortunately, there's room to pass, otherwise they might capsize our boats.'

'It won't be easy,' warned Moon. 'I fear we may incur serious damage.'

'We could spear them,' suggested the Afghan.

'We'd never be able to kill enough of them,' objected Emheb.

'Then let us use them as a weapon,' said Kamose. 'Let us turn the strength of Set within them to our own advantage.'

'How, Majesty?'

'By using a good old method well known in Thebes: to anger a hippopotamus, all you have to do is tickle its nostrils with a reed. We shall gather reeds long enough to keep risks to a minimum, and try to drive the herd northwards. The hippos will be the perfect first attack-wave.'

Several good swimmers volunteered for the task. They were linked to the boats by ropes tied round their waists, but in spite of this precaution two young men died, crushed between the angry animals.

At first it was chaos, as if the creatures' fury were summed up in the deafening din. Amid the turbulent waters, every animal bellowed more loudly than its neighbour. Then, led by the dominant male, some semblance of order was brought to the confusion. At last, the animals began to move in the right direction.

At the prow of the golden ship, Kamose donned the White Crown, which was under the protection of Set. He would need all its power to attack the capital of the Emperor of Darkness.

## 56

Jannas found it difficult to contain his anger. He paced up and down the audience chamber at Avaris, which, infuriatingly, was empty. He had been waiting for the emperor for more than an hour.

At last High Treasurer Khamudi appeared.

'When can I see His Majesty?' demanded Jannas.

'The emperor is ill,' explained Khamudi. 'His ankles have swollen and his kidneys are not working properly. For the moment he is sleeping, and no one may disturb him.'

'Are you serious?'

'Those are his orders, and we must all obey them.'

'You don't understand the gravity of the situation. The Egyptian army is about to attack Avaris.'

The High Treasurer smiled condescendingly. 'You seem perturbed, Commander.'

'That army is a real army, with a real commander and real soldiers! Our Nubian allies never arrived in Memphis, so I had to retreat to save the majority of my troops. Besides, the flood means I cannot use my chariots. In Kamose's position I would immediately attack Avaris, whose defences are laughable.'

'Kamose is nothing but a petty princeling. He has installed himself in Memphis, which you will retake without difficulty as soon as the flood is over. For the moment, in accordance with our emperor's instructions, march your regiments to Sharuhen. The lady Aberia will accompany you with a large convoy of deportees. Make sure none of them escapes.'

'Don't make another mistake, Khamudi. I shall be needed here.'

The High Treasurer's voice hardened. 'Just obey your orders, Commander.'

The emperor had burnt Ahhotep's letter and put the head messenger to death in the labyrinth. Angered by his plan's failure, he had shut himself away in the citadel's strong-room, to gaze upon the Red Crown of Lower Egypt. He handled it lustfully, hoping to see himself crowned with this sacred emblem. The ancient texts considered it to be an eye, which made the pharaoh able to see the invisible.

No one knew what the crown was made of; it was as solid as granite but as light as fabric. Soon Apophis would enclose it within the White Crown of Upper Egypt, taken from Kamose's dead body, thus forming the Double Crown, the total vision that would give him absolute power.

As he was preparing to place the Red Crown upon his head, a burning pain ripped through his side and stopped him. His blue flask was glowing red like molten metal. The emperor cut the string that tied it to his belt.

As the flask fell to the ground, it exploded into fragments. With it vanished the map of Egypt that Apophis had manipulated for so many years.

The herd of hippopotamus surged along the eastern canal, which passed in front of the citadel of Avaris. They caused panic among the fishermen and the river-guards patrolling the area around the city.

Puzzled by the uproar, Tany, the emperor's wife, climbed to the top of the ramparts with her serving-women. Suddenly, a brilliant light blinded them.

'It's coming from the river,' said a frightened serving-woman. 'A golden boat . . . It's coming nearer.'

The powerful voice of Pharaoh Kamose rose into the sky above Avaris.

'Fledglings cowering in your nest, see: I have come, for destiny looks favourably upon me. My cause is just. The liberation of Egypt is in my hands.'

Flattened against the wall like lizards, Tany and her servants could not move.

The Egyptian fleet had no time to be impressed by the gigantic citadel that loomed over Avaris. After sinking the guards' boats, Kamose's soldiers recovered the heavy stones they used as anchors, and turned them into projectiles which they then used against a Hyksos war-boat, sending it straight to the bottom.

Khamudi was aghast. Jannas had left the capital and nobody, not even the High Treasurer, was permitted to enter the strong-room where the emperor had shut himself away.

It was like a dream. The pharaoh with the White Crown was cutting through the enemy defences, thanks to the agility and speed of his warships.

Nevertheless, the ramparts of the citadel were lined with archers, whose accurate aim was bound to cause serious losses in the Egyptian ranks.

'We cannot tackle this monstrous citadel from the river,' said Moon. 'Not even a very high flood would enable us to reach the ramparts.'

'Then we shall go round the other side,' said Kamose, 'and take the western canal.'

Once out of range of the Hyksos arrows, the war-fleet headed along a broad waterway which led directly to the trading-port. There they found three hundred cedarwood boats had just arrived, laden with gold, silver, jars of wine and oil, and other supplies from the provinces. They were about to be unloaded, and the appearance of the Egyptians caused utter chaos.

The dock-workers tried to take refuge in the guards' offices, but the Hyksos killed several of them. In fury, their colleagues attacked the killers, and the quays became the scene of a fierce fight.

Moustache and the Afghan were the first to jump from the prow of the flagship to tread Apophis's domain underfoot. Using light axes and short-swords, they cut a path towards the main building, where the official responsible for checking goods had just been trampled to death by the dock-workers.

'The Egyptians have seized the trading-port,' an officer told the High Treasurer. 'We must send reinforcements immediately, both from inside and along the canal. If we don't, Kamose will invade Avaris.'

Khamudi was wholly unprepared for such incredible news, but he owed it to himself to ensure the safety of the governing authorities. 'The citadel and its surroundings must not be left undefended,' he snapped. 'It must remain impregnable.'

'There are not enough soldiers at the port, High Treasurer. They will be massacred!'

'Tell them to do their duty and resist for as long as possible. The main body of our forces will stay here, in order to preserve the centre of the empire.' But when, he wondered, would Apophis decide to make his appearance?

Another officer rushed in. 'High Treasurer, the enemy is approaching!'

Well shielded behind an arrow-slit, Khamudi saw the White Crown glitter, and heard Kamose's voice ring out again.

'Apophis, vile, fallen tyrant, weak of heart: you still dare to claim, "I am the master; everything as far as Khmun and even Per-Hathor belongs to me." You are nothing but a liar. Know this: I have wiped out those towns, and not one Hyksos remains there. I have burnt your lands, I have transformed them into bloody mounds because of the evil they inflicted upon Egypt by serving you.'

He turned to face the citadel, and raised a goblet. 'See, I am drinking wine from your vineyard! Your peasants, who are now my prisoners, will press the grapes for me. I shall cut down your trees, I shall lay waste your fields, and I shall seize your dwelling-place.'

Already, the Egyptian sailors were steering the boats out of port, laden with riches.

As Khamudi and the soldiers gazed in fascination at the pharaoh, whose bearing was deeply impressive, he felt an icy chill run round the ramparts. Apophis was standing there. Wrapped in a brown cloak, his head hooded, the emperor gazed down upon the disaster from the heights of his citadel.

'Majesty,' stammered Khamudi, 'I thought I was doing the right thing by—'

'Order Jannas back immediately. Tell him to gather together the largest force he can muster.'

## 57

Because there was little or no wind, Ahhotep's journey took longer than planned. At last she sighted Sako, and all the boats in the flotilla were put on the alert.

Was there anything left of the Egyptian garrison? If it had been wiped out, how many Hyksos would still be there and what traps had they laid?

The queen watched Young Laughter constantly and was surprised by his calmness. The huge dog was dozing in the shade of an awning, showing not the slightest sign of anxiety.

'There's someone down there!' shouted the lookout.

The archers drew their bows.

'Don't fire,' ordered the queen. 'It's a child.'

The little boy ran up, waving his arms to greet the ships that bore Ahhotep's colours. Soon he was joined by several of his friends and their mothers, who were visibly enthusiastic. On the quayside, a crowd of civilians and soldiers gathered, waving palm-fronds as a sign of welcome. The boats berthed to the accompaniment of joyful shouts and spontaneous songs, celebrating the queen's return.

Forcing his way through, the commander of the little garrison prostrated himself before her.

She looked at him, puzzled. 'But you were attacked by the Hyksos, were you not?'

'No, Majesty. Everything is quiet here.'

'But Sako sent a message asking for help.'

'I don't understand, Majesty. There really is nothing amiss here.'

It had been a false message, designed to separate Ahhotep and Kamose, in order to weaken the army of liberation. The queen had the answer to her third question: not only was Apophis's spy still alive, but he had chosen a crucial moment to try to strike a fatal blow against his enemy.

Now a new dilemma arose. Should she go to the North and rejoin Kamose or continue southwards to Thebes, which was probably the real target of the coming Hyksos counter-attack?

Ahhotep did not hesitate for long. Kamose had proved his worth. He would know how to weigh up the situation and conduct the siege of Avaris. The thought of Thebes being attacked by barbarians was unbearable. If the Hyksos had the intelligence to hide troops in Middle Egypt, so as to strike at the heart of the rebels and destroy their main base, all that the Thebans had accomplished so far would be wiped out.

'I would like to organize a festival to celebrate your arrival, Majesty,' said the garrison commander.

'It is much too soon to rejoice.'

'But, Majesty, have we not defeated the Hyksos?'

'Certainly not, Commander. Your women and children must leave Sako and take refuge, under close guard, in a neighbouring village. Increase the number of lookout posts. If the enemy attacks in numbers, do not try to resist. You must go to Thebes.'

The Afghan caressed a little piece of lapis-lazuli, which he had been allowed to take from the supply delivered to the Hyksos.

'It must remind you of your homeland,' commented Moustache.

'Only the mountains of Afghanistan produce such beautiful stones. One day the trade will begin again, and I shall be rich again.'

'I don't want to be a pessimist, but we're still a long way from that. Have you seen the size of Avaris's citadel? It makes even *my* stomach turn over. There isn't a ladder in the world long enough to reach the top of the ramparts, and the Hyksos archers seem as good as our own.'

'All the same, we've given them a good shaking, haven't we?'

'We haven't killed very many. There are a lot of them left behind those walls – and tough ones, at that.'

'You really are feeling a bit pessimistic, aren't you?' said the Afghan.

'To be frank, I don't like this place. Even when the sun's hot, I feel cold.'

'Come and drink some of Apophis's wine. That'll cheer you up.'

The cargo-boats were now travelling south; the pharaoh thought of the moment when they would arrive in Thebes and be offered to Amon. Above all, though, he was preoccupied by the strange silence that filled Avaris. Holding the trading-port meant that they could block exchanges between Avaris and the outside world, but had the emperor's power really been diminished?

With his usual energy, Neshi was running around, checking that the men were well fed. Emheb was worried that the troops sheltering in the town and the citadel might try a lightning raid, so he had posted small groups of archers in many different places to give the alert.

'How shall we organize the siege, Majesty?' he asked.

'We must explore the surrounding area and see if it is possible to isolate the city and starve out the emperor.'

'That will take a very, very long time. Meanwhile, do you not find this lack of reaction surprising? Apophis certainly has enough men available to try and break through our blockade.'

'Perhaps he thinks otherwise.'

Emheb shook his head. 'No, Majesty. I think he is waiting for reinforcements, in the belief that they will crush us. Seeing us pinned down, he believes, heralds victory for him.'

'In other words, you advise me to retreat when we are right at the gates of Avaris?'

'I do not wish it any more than you do, Majesty, but I believe it necessary for us to regroup if we are to avert a disaster.'

'You say that because we do not have Queen Ahhotep's magic with us. As soon as she is back among us, our doubts will be swept away and we shall take the citadel.'

There were three of them, three Hyksos guards who, instead of fighting the dock-workers with their comrades, had taken refuge in a guard-post. An officer there had arrested them and handed them over to his superior.

Tied to a stake in the courtyard of the citadel, they had been beaten with clubs. Their ribs broken, they feared a long prison sentence at the end of which they would be condemned to carry out the lowest menial work.

'Why did you behave like cowards?' demanded the icy voice of the emperor, who was accompanied by Aberia.

'Majesty, we thought the battle was lost and we would be more useful alive than dead. The dock-workers were in a blind rage – it was no longer possible to contain them.'

'Those are indeed the words of a coward,' said Apophis, 'and cowards have no place among the Hyksos. Whatever the circumstances, my men must obey orders and remain at their posts. Lady Aberia, carry out my sentence.'

'Have mercy, Majesty, and—'

Aberia's enormous hands choked him into silence. She strangled him slowly, with obvious pleasure, and inflicted the same torture and death on the other two.

The emperor's calmness reassured his troops, who were champing at the bit at the thought of taking their revenge on the Egyptians. But Tany was so distressed that she had taken to her bed. A long procession of serving-women came to bathe her forehead and give her drinks. She was feverish and caught in a delirium of flames, torrents of mud and falling stones.

Yima soothed Tany's anxiety with the drug her husband had procured for her own use. No, the Hyksos Empire was not on the point of crumbling, and Apophis's knife would rid it of the Egyptian cancer.

As for Khamudi, he was not a happy man. The emperor had reproached him for sending Jannas away at the wrong time. But those had been the orders of Apophis himself, who did not wish to see the commander gain too much power.

Only the trading-port was under Kamose's effective control. He dared not attack the outskirts of the town, where Hyksos soldiers were ready to contain an attack.

High on the walls of the citadel, the emperor gazed down on his domain, which had been violated by a spirited young man who believed himself invincible because he was wearing the White Crown.

That illusion would cost him his life.

## 58

Water-bags made from tanned goatskin turned inside out were distributed to the soldiers of the Egyptian army. The supplies were vital, because the river water would not be drinkable for a day or two and the heat was increasing. Balanite fruit and sweet almonds had been dropped into the water to keep it pure.

Neshi handed Kamose his water-skin, which was to be carried by a young footsoldier, proud to serve his king.

'The fleet is ready, Majesty,' announced Emheb.

Kamose had decided to sail down the eastern canal, pass the citadel, where many skilful archers would certainly be posted, and see if it was possible to attack from the north. If not, the war-boats would establish a blockade and, as soon as Ahhotep returned, the king planned to seize Avaris, district by district.

He drank a little water. 'How is the troops' morale, Emheb?'

'They will follow you to the end, Majesty.'

'Unless we take the citadel, all our achievements will have been in vain.'

'Every soldier knows that.'

Emheb's solidity reassured the young king. Through all these hard years of struggle, the governor had never once complained, never once given in to despair.

Just as the pharaoh was climbing the gangplank of the flagship, a lookout's warning shout stopped him in his tracks. Many Hyksos boats were approaching from the north. They were entering both the eastern and the western canals, and would trap the Egyptian fleet in the trading-port.

At last Jannas had received coherent orders: to assemble the regiments stationed in several Delta towns, then reduce Kamose's army to nothing.

Khamudi's insult and the emperor's indifference were forgotten. Jannas was once more fulfilling his role as commander-in-chief of the armed forces, and he would show the young pharaoh what Hyksos military power really meant.

Aboard ship, Jannas had absolute command and would not be hindered by the stupid decisions of a civilian like Khamudi. He would conduct the battle for Avaris as he chose. He was well aware that it would be ferocious, because of the quality of the enemy boats, which were fast and easily manoeuvrable, and the zeal of the Egyptians, who had been hardened in several battles.

The emperor had underestimated the enemy, but Jannas would not make the same foolish mistake. By surprising Kamose's fleet from the east and west simultaneously, he would force it to divide, and thereby weaken itself. If the pharaoh had not thought of evacuating the cargo-vessels as a matter of urgency, he would be trapped in the port.

'Trading-port in sight,' announced the soldier on watch. 'No cargo-vessels.'

'That little king is not a bad leader,' thought Jannas, 'and the fight may be yet more difficult than I thought.'

'They want to ram us,' said Emheb. 'They're much heavier than we are, so it will be a massacre.'

'There is only one solution,' decided Kamose. 'Our ships must head east. We shall concentrate all our forces in the same direction.'

The manoeuvre was carried out with such cohesion and promptness that it took the Hyksos aback, and they had no time to turn side-on so as to form a wall. The flagship with the golden prow slipped between two enemy vessels, and for a few moments Kamose thought he might open up a breach. But the Hyksos threw out grappling-hooks and slowed his ship enough to board her.

The first to set foot on the deck did not enjoy his triumph for long, for Moustache's axe sank into his neck. The two men who followed him were felled by the Afghan's dagger, while the arrows fired by Ahmes and his men soon sapped the attackers' zeal.

Several Egyptian vessels escaped from the Hyksos, but three were boarded and fierce hand-to-hand combat ensued. The flagship could not free herself. The boat carrying archers from Emheb's town of Edfu rushed to her aid and, firing arrow after arrow, held off another Hyksos boat which was trying to join the attack.

In the western canal, Jannas was hindered by his own vessels, which had no room to turn and come back at the Egyptians, some of whom sacrificed themselves to protect the pharaoh.

Kamose fought with incredible courage, and Moon himself took charge of the steering-oar. Seeing him threatened by a gigantic Asiatic, Moustache flung himself between them, and the man's axe-blade slid along his left temple. Despite the pain, he sank his short-sword into the belly of the enemy, who staggered backwards, collided with the ship's rail and fell into the water.

'We've done it! We're free!' roared Moon, and his words gave renewed courage to his crew. The flagship had indeed freed herself at last.

With two precise slashes of her dagger, beautiful Anat hamstrung a veritable wild beast of a Hyksos, who was about to stab the Afghan in the back. As an Egyptian sailor finished him off, she looked up and saw a Hyksos aiming his spear at Kamose, who was standing at the prow.

Shouting would be futile – the pharaoh would not hear. Leaping forward with all her strength, Anat threw herself in front of the spear, which plunged into her chest.

At that moment Kamose turned, and he saw her sacrifice. Maddened with grief, he dashed across the deck, jumping over corpses. Bringing down his sword in fury, he sliced the murderer's skull almost in two.

It was the hardest battle Jannas had ever had to fight. True, the Egyptian losses were severe, but the Hyksos's were even worse, because of Kamose's tactics and the manoeuvrability of his boats.

'Are we going to follow them, sir?' asked his second-in-command.

'They are too fast, and Kamose may have laid traps for us to the south of the city. But the flood will not last for ever and, however skilful the adversary may be, he will one day come up against our chariots. For the moment, let us concentrate on bandaging our wounds and taking effective measures to ensure the safety of our capital.'

Standing on the highest tower of the citadel, Khamudi had watched Jannas achieve victory, hailed by cheers from the Hyksos archers. Already very popular, the commander was now seen as the saviour of the Hyksos and the emperor's true right arm, in place of the High Treasurer, who from now on would have to treat him with the greatest respect.

Khamudi knew he had neglected the army in favour of the city and provincial guards. As soon as possible, he would make good that mistake.

His wife ran to meet him. 'We're saved, aren't we? We're saved!'

'Go and comfort the lady Tany. I must go and give the good news to the emperor.'

Apophis was sitting on his austere throne, in the half-light of the audience chamber.

'Majesty, Commander Jannas has put the Egyptians to flight.'

'Did you ever doubt that he would, my friend?'

'No, of course not! But we have lost a great many boats and sailors. That is no doubt why the commander chose not to pursue the defeated fleet but to ensure the defence of Avaris. Unfortunately, our victory is not complete, because Kamose is unscathed.'

'Are you quite sure of that?' asked the emperor's icy voice.

## 59

She-Cat was horrified to find Moustache's body. She leant closer: he was still breathing. To her relief, most of the wounds were superficial, though his left ear had been almost completely sliced through.

'A remedy for pain, quickly!'

One of her assistants brought her a small round vase, containing a powerful pain-reliever based on opium. Opening Moustache's mouth a little way, she made him take enough to ensure that he would feel no pain for several hours.

With a linen net soaked in sycamore-sap, she cleaned the wound and removed the fragments of tissue that might become septic, then brought together the two parts of the ear. Using bronze needles and linen thread, she sewed it up.

'Do you think it will work?' asked the Afghan.

'When I do something,' retorted She-Cat in annoyance, 'I do it well. Do you want me to take care of your shoulder? At first glance, it doesn't look too good.'

The Afghan's eyes rolled upward. More seriously wounded than he wanted to admit, he fainted.

Kamose held Anat's hands for some time after she died. Then he tenderly wrapped a shroud round her body. He loved her, and she had given her life to save him, but there was no time now to grieve for her.

'About turn!' he ordered.

'The men are exhausted,' objected Emheb, who was himself at the end of his strength.

'We must show the Hyksos that we are capable of taking the offensive again.'

'Majesty . . .'

'Order to all vessels in the fleet: about turn and head for Avaris. Tell the soldiers to wash, change their clothes, and prepare for battle.'

Under Moon's direction, the boats carried out the manoeuvre.

She-Cat emerged from the cabin where the wounded were being treated. 'What is happening?' she asked Emheb, who was sitting on a coil of rope nearby.

'We are turning back to attack Avaris. The Hyksos believe we have been put to flight, and the king thinks the effect of surprise will be decisive because Jannas has not yet had time to organize the city's defence.'

'But our losses were heavy, and the enemy outnumbers us enormously.'

'That's true,' said Emheb.

'And Jannas is an experienced commander, who won't be thrown into confusion even by a surprise attack?'

'That's true, too.'

'So if we launch this attack, we shall all die?'

'And so is that.'

The heat, the sun, the sparkling waters of the Nile: the Hyksos lookout thought he was seeing a mirage. It could not possibly be an enemy boat coming back towards Avaris.

He signalled to his colleagues to alert them, and they relayed the message to Jannas, who with his officers was studying the capital's future system of defence.

'That little king is becoming a serious problem,' said Jannas. 'He wants to take us by the throat even though he has not one chance in a hundred of succeeding. In his place and at his age, I might perhaps have committed the same folly.'

'Are we in any real danger?' asked an officer anxiously.

'Kamose does not know the size of the reinforcements I have not yet committed – they're waiting to the north of the city. He is committing suicide.'

The pharaoh stood at the prow of the flagship, thinking of Ahhotep. If she had been here, she would have done exactly the same. The Hyksos could not possibly have guessed that the Egyptians would find the resources necessary to resume the fight.

The sombre expression of the sailors, including Moon, told Kamose that they thought his decision pure madness. But he knew that none of them would flinch from the challenge.

'A lookout has sighted us,' said Moon. 'Shall we continue at full speed, Majesty?'

Kamose could not reply. The river was becoming confused with the sky, the riverbanks were spinning. Large drops of sweat trickled down his face.

'Majesty, are you ill?'

The sensation of vertigo was so great that Kamose swayed.

Moon helped him sit down. 'Have you been wounded?'

'No. No, I don't think so.' But he could hardly breathe.

'She-Cat must examine you.'

The Nubian could find no wound. 'This is a sickness I don't know,' she confessed. 'The king must drink plenty of water, and rest in his cabin.'

'Am I to order the attack, Majesty?' asked Moon.

Kamose took several seconds to understand the question and to realize what it implied. His brain had slowed down, and he had to make an intense effort to compose his reply.

'No, Commander. We shall stay here for a few hours, then head back towards Thebes.'

'The Egyptian fleet is withdrawing, Commander,' said Jannas's second-in-command.

Jannas frowned.

'Are we to give chase, sir?'

'Absolutely not. Obviously, Kamose wants to lure us after him and into a trap. He has proved that he can attack Avaris again, and he hopes to provoke just that reaction from us. Further south, there are other troops commanded by Ahhotep. If we pursued Kamose, we'd be mauled by the claws of that she-panther.'

'Then what are your orders, sir?'

'Remove the wrecked ships from the trading-port, bury the dead, and strengthen Avaris's defences to the maximum. I am to be alerted as soon as an enemy boat makes a move.'

Jannas had many details to sort out, notably the reorganization of the army and the war-fleet. From now on he intended to be their true commander-in-chief, free from the influence of Khamudi and his henchmen. True, he would have to be careful not to put too much emphasis on Khamudi's incompetence, because the emperor trusted Khamudi completely as regards government and the economy; but Apophis must accept that the Egyptian army was not just a collection of bunglers, and that there was a real war to fight, a war between Lower and Upper Egypt, between the North and the South.

Because of their speed, the Egyptian warships quickly rejoined the cargo-vessels captured from the Hyksos. Throughout the journey to Thebes, liberated towns and villages greeted Kamose's fleet in triumph.

Wonderful news was spreading: the pharaoh had beaten the Hyksos, the White Crown was victorious! Everywhere, feasts and other celebrations were being organized. Everywhere, people were singing and dancing. In the summer sky the sun shone, driving away the darkness.

Despite his exhaustion, the pharaoh stood at the prow of the golden vessel at each principal stopping-place, notably Memphis, Khmun and Qis, the scenes of his great victories. Cheered by the people, Kamose had believed his strength would return. But the dizziness was wearing him out, his legs gave way under him, and he had to stay lying down, even though he could not sleep.

Moustache and the Afghan were leaning on the ship's rail. Moustache's ear was healing well, but the Afghan was still a bit weak from his wound.

'We're nearly at Thebes,' said Moustache. 'I don't understand why Queen Ahhotep withdrew instead of joining us at Avaris.'

'And I don't understand why our system of carrier-pigeons isn't working,' added the Afghan.

'Still, we reached Avaris and stood up to Jannas.'

'Yes, we did, and it was a great achievement. But the emperor and his citadel are untouched, and I doubt if Jannas's troops will stay on the defensive for ever.'

Moustache thought about the next battle, in which Jannas was sure to use his heavy weapons. But he soon shook off the thought, for there ahead of them were the green banks of Thebes and a crowd mad with joy, awaiting the heroes to congratulate them and celebrate their triumph.

## 60

Married soldiers fell into their wives' arms, while the others enjoyed the attentions of enthusiastic young Theban girls who wanted to touch the victors and show their undying admiration.

Already, the cargo-vessels' precious contents were being unloaded, while the people of Thebes watched in awe. Seeing this, they did not doubt for a moment that Kamose had defeated the Hyksos.

Supported by Moon and Emheb, the pharaoh was cheered for a long time. Officially, he was suffering from a leg wound which made it difficult for him to walk. But, as soon as she held him to her heart, Ahhotep realized that her elder son was dying.

Putting on the bravest face she could, so as not to spoil the Thebans' happiness, she saw him helped into his travelling-chair to be borne to the palace, and then climbed into her own.

Teti and Ahmose greeted them, Ahmose rapturously happy to have his elder brother home again.

'You've got very thin,' exclaimed the boy.

'The battles were very hard,' explained Kamose.

'Did you kill all the Hyksos?'

'No, I have left you a few.' He suddenly felt ill again, and had to be helped by Qaris.

'Kamose must rest,' said Ahhotep. 'I shall make the ritual offerings in his place.'

The riches from Avaris were offered to Amon, in his temple at Karnak, before being distributed to the Thebans, with the exception of the gold and lapis-lazuli, which would be used to adorn the temple.

Concealing her anguish, the Wife of God spoke the ancient words that enabled the Invisible One to manifest himself upon earth. This caused the light that had appeared on the world's first morning to shine out, as it had done upon the mound that emerged from the primordial ocean, at the very spot where Karnak had been built.

As soon as the ceremony was at an end, Ahhotep returned to the palace and hurried towards Kamose's bedchamber.

In the passageway outside, she was met by Qaris, who, despite his anxiety about the king, was supervising preparations for the victory banquet. 'Majesty, do you think . . . ?'

'All this noise must stop at once.' The head palace doctor appeared in the doorway of the patient's bedchamber. 'Majesty, my diagnosis is definite: Pharaoh Kamose has been poisoned. It is impossible to cure him, for the heart of his being has been affected. The poison has spread through all his vessels, and the king's life-energy is almost spent.'

Ahhotep entered the room and closed the door behind her.

Kamose was sitting down, his head resting on a cushion, and was gazing at the Peak of the West. She took his hand gently.

'Avaris is intact and the emperor is still alive,' he whispered, 'but we inflicted severe losses on him, and I have shown him that we can strike at any moment. Jannas knows that our army can fight. We must strengthen our positions, then seize Avaris and finally liberate the Delta. But the course of my life is run. It falls to you, my mother, to continue the struggle that you yourself began. Forgive me for leaving you this superhuman task, but my breath is leaving me; I can no longer hold it within me.'

Scalding tears flowed down Ahhotep's cheeks, but her voice was steady. 'It was the Hyksos spy who took me away from you, and it was he who poisoned you, in order to make the attack on Avaris fail.'

Kamose managed a small smile. 'So he believed that I would win victory. A victory which you will achieve in my name and in my father's, won't you?'

'I give you my oath upon it.'

'I have tried to be worthy of him and you. I hope my brother will fight at your side, and I ask one last favour.'

'You are Pharaoh. Speak, and I shall obey you.'

'Will you have stelae engraved, telling of my fight for freedom?'

'Nothing that you have accomplished will be forgotten, my son. These monuments will sing of your exploits and your bravery, and they will be displayed in the temple at Karnak, where your glory will be preserved among the gods.'*

'It is not easy to die so young. But you are beside me, and I have the good fortune to gaze upon the western bank where the soul's peace reigns. For several years I have been unable to sleep. Now I am going to rest.'

---

*Two stelae were indeed found at Karnak. Their texts have provided much valuable information.

Kamose raised his eyes to the heavens and his hand gripped his mother's very tightly.

'The mummy is cold, Majesty,' a priest told the queen. 'That is an excellent sign: it signifies that the deceased has expelled his bad heat, which is made up of passions and resentments, and that his soul has been purified. Henceforth, Pharaoh Kamose possesses the serenity of Osiris.'

A widow, now in mourning for a twenty-year-old son, Ahhotep yet again refused to succumb to the blows of fate. Since Kamose had no son or successor, it was she who must lead the funeral rites. Just as she had done after the death of her husband, she took on the office of regent queen and governed Egypt.

Kamose's sarcophagus was decorated with feathers evoking the travels of the soul-bird in the heavens. Inside, she laid a gold and ebony fan to ensure him eternal breath, axes, and a gold boat, in which his spirit would sail for ever across the universe.

With surprising gravity and composure for a child of ten, Ahmose had followed every stage of the mourning, from the mummification of his elder brother to the interment in the burial-ground on the western bank of Thebes. But, after all, the sages of Egypt considered ten to be the age at which one became fully responsible for one's own actions.

Ahhotep had a threefold mission: to continue the war of liberation, to prepare Ahmose to become pharaoh, and to discover the identity of the Hyksos spy, that person who was so close to her and who had already inflicted so much suffering upon her.

As the funeral procession went towards the riverbank, Emheb approached the queen.

'Majesty, I can no longer keep my thoughts to myself.'

'What is it, Emheb?'

'I saw the citadel of Avaris at close quarters, and it is impregnable. Everyone knows that you have achieved many miracles and that the gods have filled your heart with magical power. But the emperor has built himself an indestructible lair. We can certainly attack it and attack it again, but each time we will lose many men. I believe that is exactly what Apophis is hoping for, and that when we have been weakened enough he in turn will attack us.'

'For the time being, in accordance with the wishes of Pharaoh Kamose, you are to go to Memphis, strengthen its defences and consolidate our positions in the liberated provinces.'

Sorely tried, Teti the Small had not been present at the final stages of the funeral ceremonies. She could not accept that death had spared her, only to strike down a young king of twenty summers. And she knew that little Ahmose would never laugh as he had done before, and that from now on he could no longer enjoy the carefree existence of childhood.

Kamose's death had put a premature end to rejoicing and reality had imposed itself again, with all its cruelty: the war was far from over, Hyksos military power remained almost intact, and even the survival of Thebes was uncertain.

Ahhotep helped her mother to her feet.

'I am so tired,' said Teti. 'Leave me to sleep.'

'Qaris has prepared us an excellent dinner, and you need to regain your strength. Don't forget that Ahmose's education is not complete and that he still needs you.'

'I admire you so much, my daughter. Where do you get so much courage from?'

'From the will to be free.'

To show herself worthy of her rank, Teti joined her family for the meal. And when Ahmose asked her to tell him about the Age of Gold, she realized that she could not slacken her efforts. She had to educate a future pharaoh; that must be the joy of her old age.

Accompanied by Young Laughter, Ahhotep was walking in the palace garden. Suddenly, the dog stopped. Neshi was coming to meet them.

The queen stroked the dog, whose eyes remained fixed on the official.

'Forgive me for disturbing you, Majesty, but I have something important to tell you.'

Was Ahhotep at last about to find out the appalling truth?

'I served Pharaoh Kamose faithfully,' said Neshi, 'and I approved of all his decisions. But now he is dead, and so am I, in a way. For that reason, I wish to resign from my offices, while beseeching you to save this country, which needs you so much.'

'Neither our country nor any other needs a saviour, Neshi. What it does need is righteousness. When Ma'at once again governs the Two Lands, misfortune will disappear. Put aside your devotion to one man, and serve only that righteousness. Then, and then alone, will you deserve to be called a true servant of Egypt.'

Ahhotep walked away, followed by her dog. She needed to be alone with her husband and her elder son, two pharaohs who had given their lives fighting the Emperor of Darkness. And the Queen of Freedom gazed up at the waxing moon, her protector, praying that it would grant her the faith necessary to re-establish the reign of Light.

# The Flaming Sword

I dedicate this book to all those men and women who have devoted their lives to freedom, by fighting against occupation, totalitarian regimes and inquistitions of every kind.

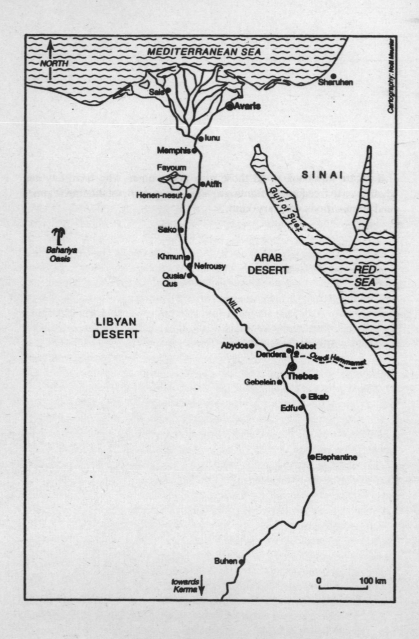

# 1

Prisoner number 1790 collapsed, face down in the mud. Big-Feet had lost the will to live. After all these years in the death-camp at Sharuhen, in Canaan, the last of his strength had finally drained away.

Sharuhen was the rearward base of the Hyksos, who had occupied Egypt for more than a century and who had set up their capital at Avaris, in the Delta. Their supreme commander, Emperor Apophis, was not content merely to use his army and security forces to impose a reign of terror. Approving a tempting idea dreamt up by High Treasurer Khamudi, his faithful right-hand man, he had set up a prison camp at the foot of the fortress of Sharuhen, in a marshy and unhealthy area. In winter the winds were ice-cold, in summer the sun was mercilessly hot, and always the place was infested with mosquitoes and horseflies.

'Get up,' urged Prisoner 2501, a thirty-year-old scribe who had lost a fifth of his body weight in three months.

'I can't go on any longer. Leave me alone.'

'If you give up, Big-Feet, you'll die – and then you'll never see your cows again.'

Big-Feet wanted to die, but he wanted even more to see his herd again. No one knew how to care for his beasts the way he did.

Like many others, he had believed the Hyksos' lies. 'Come and graze your scrawny animals on the lush Northern grasslands,' they had said. 'Once they are in good health again, you shall return home.' In fact, the Hyksos had stolen the herds, killed any herdsmen who protested, and thrown the others into the death-camp at Sharuhen.

Big-Feet would never forgive them for separating him from his cows. He could have borne extra work, forced labour, arduous marches through the flooded lands, a pitiful recompense, but not that.

Prisoner 1790 clambered to his feet.

Like his companions in misfortune, he had suffered the horrible ordeal of being branded with his prison number, all the other prisoners being forced to watch. Anyone who turned away or closed his eyes was executed on the spot.

Big-Feet could still feel the appalling pain of the red-hot copper branding-iron. The louder the victim screamed, the longer the torture lasted. Several of the wounded had died from infection, because at Sharuhen there were neither doctors nor nurses, and no one was given the slightest care. Had he not been strong, naturally lean and accustomed to getting by on little food, the herdsman would have died long ago. At Sharuhen, big eaters lasted only a few months.

'Here, have a little stale bread.'

Big-Feet did not refuse the sumptuous gift offered by his friend, who had been sent to the camp for keeping a hymn to Pharaoh Senusret in his house. Denounced by a neighbour, the scribe had been condemned as a dangerous conspirator and deported immediately. Emperor Apophis, the self-proclaimed pharaoh, did not permit references to Egypt's glorious past.

A frail little girl approached the two men. 'You haven't got anything to eat, have you? I am so hungry.'

Big-Feet was ashamed to have swallowed the scrap of bread so quickly. 'Didn't the guards give you your rations today?' he asked.

'They forgot me.'

'Didn't your mother ask them?'

'She died last night.'

The child turned and went back to her mother's corpse. No one could do anything for her. If someone took her under their wing, she would be snatched away instantly and thrown to the whims of the mercenaries at the fortress.

'There's another convoy arriving,' said the scribe.

The heavy wooden gate of the camp swung open, and the new prisoners straggled in. A tall woman with enormous hands was hitting some of the old men with a club, even though they could scarcely walk. One of them collapsed, his skull fractured. The others tried to hurry, in the hope of escaping the blows, but the Hyksos torturers did not spare a single one.

Eventually, astonished still to be alive, the strongest of the new arrivals got up very slowly, afraid of yet more torments. But their torturers were content to sneer at them.

'Welcome to Sharuhen!' shouted the lady Aberia. 'Here, you will at last learn obedience. The living shall bury the dead and then clean up this camp. It's a real pigsty!' No worse insult could be uttered by a Hyksos, for they never ate pork.

Big-Feet and the scribe hurried to obey. Aberia liked the prisoners to prove their goodwill; any lack of enthusiasm for the task in hand led to torture.

They dug shallow ditches with their bare hands and threw in the bodies, unable to perform even the most perfunctory funerary rite. As always, Big-Feet addressed a silent prayer to the goddess Hathor, who welcomed the souls of the righteous into her bosom and whose incarnation was a cow, the most beautiful of all creatures.

'Tomorrow is the night of the new moon,' announced Aberia with a cruel smile as she left the camp.

An old man who had arrived with the latest convoy came over to Big-Feet and asked, 'May we speak?'

'Now that she has gone, yes.'

'Why is that she-devil so preoccupied with the moon?'

'Because each time it is reborn she chooses a prisoner and slowly strangles him or her in front of the others.'

Shoulders slumping, the old man sat down between prisoners 1790 and 2501. 'What are those numbers on your arms?'

'Our prison numbers,' replied the scribe. 'First thing tomorrow, you and all the new prisoners will be branded.'

'You mean . . . more than two thousand unfortunates have been deported here?'

'Many more,' said Big-Feet. 'A lot of prisoners died or were tortured to death before they could be reduced to a number.'

The old man clenched his fists. 'We must keep hope alive,' he declared with unexpected vigour.

'Why?' asked the scribe in a cynical tone,

'Because the Hyksos are getting more and more worried. In the Delta towns and at Memphis, resistance is being organized.'

'The emperor's security guards will root it out.'

'They have more than enough work on their hands, believe me.'

'There are too many informants,' said the scribe. 'No one slips through the net.'

'With my own hands I killed a papyrus-seller who had denounced a woman to the Hyksos militia because she refused to sleep with him. He was young and much stronger than I am, but I found the strength I needed to kill that monster – and I don't regret it. Little by little, the people of Egypt are coming to understand that bowing the knee to the enemy leads only to slaughter. What the emperor wants is to wipe out all us Egyptians and replace us with Hyksos. They steal our goods, our lands, our houses, and they want to destroy our souls, too.'

'That's what they're trying to do in this camp,' said the scribe, his voice faltering.

'Apophis forgets that Egypt has a real reason to hope,' blazed the old man.

Big-Feet's heart beat a little faster.

'The Queen of Freedom,' went on the old man, 'she's our hope. She will never give up the fight against Apophis.'

'The Theban troops failed to capture Avaris,' the scribe reminded him, 'and Pharaoh Kamose is dead. Queen Ahhotep is in mourning and has gone to ground in her city. Sooner or later, the Hyksos will seize Thebes.'

'You're wrong, I tell you! Queen Ahhotep has already worked a lot of miracles. She'll never give up.'

'That's nothing but a myth. No one will ever defeat the Hyksos – and no one will get us out of this camp alive. The Thebans don't even know it exists.'

'Well, I believe in her,' said Big-Feet. 'The Queen of Freedom will enable me to see my cows again.'

'In the meantime,' advised Prisoner 2501, 'we'd better get on with cleaning the prison, or we'll be flogged.'

Four of the new arrivals died during the night. Big-Feet had just finished burying them the next morning, when Aberia stepped through the gates of the camp.

'Come on, quickly,' he told the old man. 'We must line up.'

'I can't. I have a terrible pain in my chest.'

'If you aren't on your feet, Aberia will beat you to death.'

'I shan't give her the pleasure . . . Whatever else you do, my friend, hold on to hope.' The old man's voice faded, and his death-rattle sounded. His heart had given out.

Big-Feet ran to join the others, who were drawn up in orderly ranks in front of Aberia. She was a good head taller than most of the prisoners.

'The time has come for some entertainment,' she announced, 'and I know you are eager to know the number of the lucky prisoner chosen to be the hero of our little celebration.'

She stared greedily at each prisoner in turn. Here, Aberia held the power of life and death. As if she were not satisfied, she walked back up the rows, then halted before a man who was still young, a man who could not help shaking from head to foot.

'You, Prisoner 2501.'

# 2

Bathed in the bright light of dawn, the beautiful thirty-nine-year-old Queen Ahhotep raised her hands towards the Hidden God in a gesture of worship.

'My heart inclines unto your gaze. Because of you, we are satisfied without food and our thirst is quenched without drink. You are father to those who have no mother, and husband to the widow. How sweet it is to gaze upon your mystery! It tastes of life, it is as a delicate fabric to those who robe themselves in it, it is a fruit swollen with sunshine.'

The queen had gone alone to the east of Karnak, and was celebrating the resurrection of the light, which had defeated the darkness.

That defeat sometimes seemed merely an illusion, when the provinces of upper Egypt still groaned under the Hyksos emperor's yoke. After losing her husband and her elder son, who had fought valiantly against the occupying power, Ahhotep, who held the office of Wife of God, now felt only one love, the love of freedom. Yet freedom seemed out of reach because of the enemy army's superiority.

She was well aware of the courage and determination with which the Theban troops had fought their way to Avaris, the Emperor of Darkness's capital. But their advance had been halted by that impregnable fortress, and they had been forced to beat a retreat.

After the death of Pharaoh Kamose, a worthy successor to his father Seqen, the Regent Queen had withdrawn to Thebes, to regain her strength in silence. Within the enclosure of the beautiful but modest temple, she had meditated under the protection of Amon and Osiris. Amon, the lord of Thebes, the creator of the good wind, the keeper of the secret of the origins of life, whose shrine would not open willingly until the day total victory was won over the Hyksos. Osiris, who had been murdered, then brought back to life, the judge of the afterlife, master of the brotherhood of those who were 'of just voice', a brotherhood which now included Seqen and Kamose.

Seqen had died in battle, lured into an ambush. And Kamose, just when he was preparing to launch a new assault on Avaris, had been poisoned and had come back to Thebes to die, his mother by his side as he gazed upon the Peak of the West. In both cases, one person had been responsible: a Hyksos spy who had infiltrated the Theban headquarters. Twice he had struck a lethal blow.

Yet the men who surrounded Ahhotep were above suspicion, for they had all proved their bravery and risked their lives, each one fighting the Hyksos in his own way. Qaris, the palace's head steward, was a specialist in gathering information, while Heray, officially the Overseer of Granaries, was an excellent minister for the economy. Emheb, the Governor of Edfu, had held the front at Qis during a desperate time, and had been wounded more than once. The scribe Neshi, Bearer of the Royal Seal, was so devoted to Kamose that he had offered his resignation, which the queen had refused; while the superbly skilled archer Ahmes, son of Abana, was a great killer of Hyksos officers. Then there were the Afghan and Moustache, two rebels who had been appointed to lead elite regiments and had been decorated for their deeds; and Moon, commander of the war-fleet, who was exceptionally skilful and whose courage never failed.

How could she imagine, even for a moment, that one of them could be a spy in the pay of the Emperor of Darkness? All the evidence suggested that she must look elsewhere and remain constantly on the alert. Despite his diabolical cunning, the spy would eventually give himself away, and when that happened Ahhotep must strike with all the speed and decisiveness of the royal cobra.

The Wife of God walked alongside the little sacred lake from which, each morning, the pharaoh should have drawn fresh water derived from the Nun, the ocean of energy. This was needed in order to proceed to the purification ceremonies and so create a new dynamic energy, vital for all forms of existence from the star to the stone.

But young Pharaoh Kamose had died at the age of twenty, and his successor, his brother, Ahmose, was only ten. For the second time, Ahhotep had had to become Regent Queen and steer the ship of state. Although still far from defeated, the emperor was not going to triumph. It was for the Queen of Freedom to prove to him that he would never reign over the Two Lands.

Ahhotep's huge dog, Young Laughter, came bounding up and greeted his mistress with obvious joy. Forgetting how heavy he was, he reared up and put his two enormous front paws on the queen's shoulders, almost knocking her over. After licking her cheeks thoroughly, the dog led the way as Ahhotep headed for the palace at the large military base north of Thebes.*

*On the site of Deir el-Ballas.

Here, deep in the desert, young King Seqen had trained the first soldiers of the army of liberation, in notably harsh conditions; later a barracks, houses, a fortress, a small royal palace, a school, an infirmary and shrines had been built. And here the recruits learnt their trade as soldiers, under the command of rigorous instructors who hid nothing of the terrifying battles that awaited them.

At the entrance to the palace, Young Laughter halted and sniffed the air. More than once, just like his father Old Laughter, he had used his keen sense of smell to detect danger and so save Ahhotep, who was careful not to ignore his warnings.

Qaris appeared in the doorway. A plump fellow, with round cheeks and an air of imperturbable calm, he was the very embodiment of good humour. Even at the height of Hyksos oppression, he had unhesitatingly acted as a contact between the few existing rebels and collated all the information, at constant risk of being denounced and condemned to death.

'Majesty, I was not expecting you so soon,' he said. 'The cleaners are still at their work, and I have not had time to supervise the meal.'

With smiling eyes, Laughter calmly licked the steward's hand.

'Summon the officials to the council chamber,' said Ahhotep.

In the centre of the chamber stood Qaris's masterpiece, a model of Egypt showing those parts of the country which had been liberated and those which were still occupied by the Hyksos. When Ahhotep had first seen the model, only Thebes had enjoyed relative autonomy. Today, thanks to the achievements of Seqen and Kamose, the Hyksos controlled only the Delta, and their Nubian ally, the King of Kerma, remained lurking in his far-off realm of the Great South.

It was true that the 'Balance of the Two Lands', Memphis, which acted as a crossing-point and fulcrum between Upper and Lower Egypt, had been liberated, but how long could it stay free? The troops led by the Hyksos commander, Jannas, would not be content to defend Avaris for ever, and would soon launch an offensive.

The officials bowed before the Regent Queen. Their long faces betrayed their anxiety and discouragement.

Neshi, the thin, shaven-headed Bearer of the Royal Seal, whose responsibilities included supplying the army with food and weapons, afforded his colleagues some relief by breaking the silence.

'The news is not good, Majesty. If we wish to defend Memphis, which would be particularly difficult, we shall have to mass the greater part of our troops there. If we are defeated, the road to Thebes will lie wide open.' Ordinarily so incisive, Neshi seemed crushed beneath the weight of reality.

'What do you think, Emheb?' asked the queen.

That big, stout-hearted man had just returned from Memphis; he looked as impressive as ever, with his bullneck, broad shoulders and generous girth. Because he had fought for so long in the front line, he had the authority to speak his mind, and many considered his opinions conclusive.

Emheb expressed himself with his customary candour. 'Either we attack Avaris again, and break Jannas's back, or we must establish a defensive line against which his men will come to grief. The first solution seems much too risky to me, so I would advocate the second. But in that case Memphis would be a very bad choice. Except during the annual flood, the Hyksos could use their heavy weapons, their chariots and horses, and we wouldn't have time to build walls round the city.'

'That means we have no choice but to abandon the city to its fate,' concluded the queen.

The officials hung their heads.

'Have weapons delivered to the Memphis garrison,' ordered Ahhotep, 'and use carrier-pigeons to keep us informed of the situation as it develops. We shall establish our line of defence at Faiyum, three days' march to the south of Memphis, at the place renamed the Port of Kamose in honour of my son. Neshi is to set up a military camp there immediately, and the artificers must build stone platforms. Commander Moon will regroup the majority of our warships there, and Governor Emheb will take whatever measures are necessary to halt a Hyksos chariot attack. And instruct our boatyards to redouble their efforts – we urgently need more warships.'

Everyone agreed with the queen's decisions.

The members of the council were dispersing when an officer of the guard rushed into the chamber. 'Majesty,' he panted, 'something very serious has happened. Hundreds of soldiers have just deserted.'

# 3

In a terrible rage, Emperor Apophis replaced the Red Crown of Lower Egypt in the strongroom of the citadel at Avaris, from which it would never again emerge. Once again, he had tried to put it on; once again, it had caused unbearable pain in his head and burnt his fingers.

Rejecting this emblem of an age of rebellion, the lord of the Hyksos climbed slowly to the top of the citadel's highest tower, which loomed over a capital city which had been transformed into one gigantic military camp.

The seventy-year-old emperor was a tall man, with a prominent nose, flabby cheeks, a pot belly and thick legs. His ugliness was so frightening that he used it as a weapon to intimidate those he addressed.

From round his neck he removed a gold chain on which hung three amulets embodying life, prosperity and health. Gullible people believed they gave him the power to know the secrets of heaven and earth, but now, at a time of total war against the Thebans and their damned queen, he could no longer bear to wear these worthless trinkets. The Emperor of Darkness broke all three amulets and flung the pieces over the battlements.

His nerves soothed, he gazed down upon his realm, mighty Avaris, the greatest city in the world, which he had established in the north-east of the Delta, on the eastern bank of the branch of the Nile that the Egyptians called 'the Waters of Ra'.

Ra, the divine Light. Many years had passed since the Hyksos had replaced the Light with armed force, so perfectly symbolized by the thick walls, battlements and crenellated towers of the seemingly impregnable fortress.

Since the abortive assault by Pharaoh Kamose, who had been poisoned by Apophis's spy, the emperor had left his lair only once, to go to the Temple of Set, lord of storms and cosmic disturbances, and faithful protector of Apophis. He who was nourished by the violence of Set could never be defeated.

Formerly a hive of activity, the trading-port at Avaris now housed only a few cargo-vessels, which were closely guarded by the war-fleet. No one had forgotten the exploits of Kamose's troops, who had seized three hundred boats filled with valuable cargo and carried them off to Thebes.

This slump in trade with the empire's vassals would not last long; as soon as the Theban rebellion had been crushed, enormous quantities of gold, silver, lapis-lazuli, precious woods, oil, wine and other goods would once again reach the Hyksos capital. The wealth of the emperor and his inner circle would continue to grow, even faster than before.

Apophis loathed sunshine and fresh air, so he went back into his palace, which had been built inside the fortress. Small openings allowed only the minimum amount of light to enter.

Using the team of painters he had brought over from Minoa, the emperor had had the walls decorated with frescoes of the kind popular in Knossos, the capital of the Great Isle. Apophis had destroyed numerous masterpieces of the Middle Kingdom, and boasted of having eradicated all traces of Egyptian art from his city. Each day, in his council chamber, he gazed admiringly at the Minoan landscapes, labyrinths, winged griffins, yellow-skinned dancers, or acrobats jumping over the horns of a bull.

Once he had conquered Upper Egypt and razed Thebes to the ground, the emperor would have vast numbers of immigrants brought in, and would wipe out every last vestige of the Egyptian population. The old land of the pharaohs would become a true Hyksos province, from which the very notion of Ma'at, the frail goddess of truth, justice and harmony, would disappear.

Apophis liked to wander around the citadel for hours on end, dreaming of the vast extent of his empire, the largest ever created, which stretched from Nubia to the Mycenean islands, by way of Canaan and Anatolia. Any fools who tried to rebel were ruthlessly massacred. The Hyksos army tortured the ringleaders and their families, and burnt down not just their houses but their villages, too.

And, thus, Hyksos order reigned.

Only Queen Ahhotep still dared defy that order. Though he had initially regarded her as a madwoman and a mere schemer, the emperor had been forced to admit that she was a formidable adversary. Her ridiculous army of peasants had become battle-hardened over the years, and the intrepid Kamose had even succeeded in leading it up to the walls of the citadel of Avaris itself.

Fortunately, that amazing feat had done no more than scratch the surface of Hyksos power. The Thebans had had to withdraw, and were no longer in a position to retake the offensive, but they excelled in the art of laying traps because of their perfect knowledge of the terrain.

So the emperor was taking care not to act hastily, particularly since he must resolve an annoying dispute between his two most senior officials, High Treasurer Khamudi and Commander Jannas.

Khamudi was depraved, cruel, and ready to do anything to increase his own wealth, but faithfully carried out the emperor's decisions. Jannas, the commander-in-chief of the Hyksos forces, was the hero who had saved Avaris, and his popularity continued to grow.

To please his senior officers, Apophis ought to have sacrificed Khamudi; but doing so would have made Jannas far too powerful – many soldiers already regarded him as the future leader of the Hyksos.

Nourished by the strength of Set, Apophis would continue to reign for a long time. Fortunately, Jannas was a true soldier, who scrupulously obeyed orders and would never consider plotting against the emperor. Khamudi must be brought to understand that the commander guaranteed the empire's safety, and that he, Khamudi, would have to be content with his many privileges.

The emperor did not pay a visit to his wife, the lady Tany – he had not granted her the title of Empress, for real power could not be divided. Tany was an Egyptian woman of modest origins, who had sent many prosperous ladies to torture and death by denouncing them as rebels. She had been so terrified by the sight of Egyptian soldiers, during Kamose's attack, that she had taken to her bed.

When Apophis emerged from his apartments, he was greeted by Khamudi, who bowed very low.

The High Treasurer had black hair plastered to his round head, rather bulging eyes, a heavy frame, and plump hands and feet. He was a man of large appetites, a lover of fine wines and of young Egyptian women, upon whom he inflicted the most hideous tortures in the company of his wife, Yima, who was as perverted as himself. He hid none of his perversions or financial misappropriations from the emperor, and did nothing without his master's consent.

'All is ready, Majesty.'

Khamudi was also the commander of Apophis's personal bodyguard. He had selected Cypriot and Libyan pirates who would instantly kill anyone who made the slightest threatening gesture towards the emperor. Dressed in tunics with floral motifs, these dogs of war with their tattooed arms and plaited hair formed an impregnable wall around the lord of the Hyksos whenever he appeared in the streets of his capital. Generously paid, they could afford any woman they wanted. Since his abolition of the courts of law, Apophis was the only judge in Egypt, and he never punished his servants.

The procession crossed the palace burial-ground, where Hyksos officers killed in battle had been laid in makeshift tombs, along with their weapons. Because of the lack of space and the number of bodies to be buried, the emperor had taken a decision which horrified the Egyptians. Instead of creating a new burial-ground, he decreed that the dead were to be buried in gardens and even inside houses – it would have been stupid to waste space on mortal remains which would soon be reduced to bones.

'Have there been any protests against my burial policy?' enquired Apophis, in his hoarse, chilling voice.

'A few,' replied Khamudi, in honeyed tones, 'but I have done what was necessary. Sharuhen is full at the moment, so it was necessary to open another one at Tjaru.* The rebels have been sent there.'

'Excellent, Khamudi.'

Commander Jannas's appearance was deceptive. Of medium height and almost frail-looking, slow of speech and movement, he habitually wore a mushroom-shaped, striped headdress. Those who had thought him no danger, however, were no longer of this world.

After he, too, had bowed before the emperor, the commander attended the brief funeral ceremonies for his men, who had died of the wounds they received during fierce fighting with the Egyptians in the trading-port of Avaris. Jannas could boast of having beaten off Kamose's attack, but Queen Ahhotep remained a real danger.

Amid general indifference, more than a hundred donkeys had their throats slit and were thrown into the ditches with the soldiers' bodies.

Then the emperor inspected the security arrangements put in place by Jannas to prevent a future Theban attack from the river having any chance of success. 'Good work, Commander,' he said.

'Majesty, when are we to go back on the offensive?'

'Just obey my orders, Jannas.'

---

*Tjaru-Sileh, in the Delta, on the isthmus formed between the lakes of Ballah and Menezaleh.

# 4

In less than a day, the rumour had spread all over the military base at Thebes. Queen Ahhotep was going to withdraw once and for all into the temple at Karnak, Pharaoh Ahmose had abdicated, and the army of liberation was to lay down its arms. Before long, the Hyksos hordes would sweep down upon the city of Amon and slaughter anyone who tried to resist.

Flat-Nose was the first to desert, followed immediately by Lively, an officer who had fought at Avaris and who knew the enemy's savagery. Convinced by their explanations, hundreds of footsoldiers had made up their minds to leave the base as quickly as possible. A lone officer tried to remind the men of their duty, but his voice was lost in a chorus of shouts and he had had to step aside to avoid being trampled to death.

'We must warn our comrades at the fortress,' said Lively.

The guards joined the crowd of fleeing soldiers, who were soon followed by the majority of the troops billeted in the building.

'Which way are we going?' asked Flat-Nose

'Not north,' replied Lively. 'We'd come up against the regiments led by the Afghan and Moustache.'

'So what? They may be the best, but they surely don't want to die any more than we do.'

'There'd be bound to be a fight. I'm going to head south.'

In a state of utter confusion, the deserters dispersed. Led by Flat-Nose, a howling mob marched northwards.

Beautifully shaped feet, long, elegant legs, a shapely bottom and a back made for caresses . . . After Queen Ahhotep, She-Cat was the most beautiful woman in the world. And he, Moustache, had the insane good fortune to make love with her! When he met her, during the Nubian campaign, he had fallen for her instantly, but had decided against a lasting relationship, which was incompatible with his life as a soldier. But She-Cat had hidden on the boat as it left for Egypt, and Moustache had not had the courage to resist her.

The beautiful Nubian had not been content simply to become a wonderful wife. A specialist in potions, drugs and talismans, she tended wounded soldiers, had saved many lives, and had been appointed head of the battlefield medical service. She-Cat was regarded as a heroine of the war of liberation.

Moustache kissed her neck tenderly as they reclined on their bed.

'The meeting of the Great Council is taking for ever,' she complained.

'What does that matter? The queen is wasting her time trying to persuade her officials. As usual they'll disagree with her decisions, and as usual she'll implement them anyway. Anyway, shouldn't you be thinking about something else?'

Someone hammered furiously at the bedroom door.

'Oh no!' protested Moustache. 'Surely I'm entitled to just one hour's privacy.'

'Open up, quickly,' demanded the Afghan, his voice filled with urgency.

'What is it now?'

'Some sort of riot,' said the Afghan, a sturdy, bearded man who wore a turban. 'A mass of soldiers are deserting, and they're trying to get our men to join them.'

'They'll never do it!' roared Moustache, suddenly very sober. 'Our fellows won't behave like cowards!'

But Moustache was wrong. Convinced the rumours were the truth, the men of the elite regiments were allowing themselves to be swept away by the tide.

The Afghan tried to stop a man as he fled, but Moustache caught his arm and said warningly, 'They're like madmen. We can't hold them back.'

'What about the ones who are heading for the palace?'

'Surely they won't attack the queen?'

Carried away, Flat-Nose and more than two hundred deserters were marching on the palace at the military base, set on looting it.

'There may only be two of us,' declared the Afghan, 'but we're not going to let them do that.'

'It is vital that you do not go out, Majesty,' urged Neshi. 'Our soldiers have lost their minds! We should leave the palace by the back entrance and take refuge in the desert.'

Qaris agreed. If the queen's personal bodyguard confronted the horde, it would be a massacre, and Ahhotep would not escape the fury of her own troops.

'Leave the camp, all of you, and return to Thebes to protect my mother and my son,' ordered Ahhotep.

'But what about you, Majesty?' asked Neshi anxiously.

'Do not argue.'

'But, Majesty, we cannot simply abandon you!'

'The only thing that matters is Ahmose's safety. Go back to Thebes – you must not waste a single moment.'

The queen's tone was so imperious that her officials and guards could offer no further resistance.

Placing a fine gold diadem atop her brown hair, the green-eyed, majestic queen went out to confront the rioters, who were so astounded to see her that they halted.

Taking advantage of this moment's vacillation, Moustache and the Afghan positioned themselves on either side of the queen. Even with their bare hands, they would kill a good number of attackers.

Flat-Nose stepped forward. 'People said you were withdrawing into the temple, Majesty. But you're here . . . No, you can't be – you must be a ghost!'

'Why did you listen to the rumours?'

'Because the Hyksos are coming and we no longer have a leader.'

'I am Regent Queen, and I am in command of the army. No attack forces have been detected, and if an attack were launched we should halt it.'

'Are you really . . . real?'

'Touch my hand, and you will know I am.'

Flat-Nose hesitated. Fighting the Hyksos frightened him, but he had a minuscule chance of emerging from that alive. On the other hand, touching the Wife of God would be such an insult that he would be struck down dead.

So he bowed lower and lower, until his flat nose touched the ground. All his comrades followed suit.

'You were lied to,' declared Ahhotep, 'and you have behaved like frightened children. I shall therefore overlook this incident. Every man is to return to his post.'

The soldiers got to their feet and cheered the Queen of Freedom. Never again would they give credence to rumours.

But the crisis was not yet over. Full of alarm, Neshi came hurrying up. 'Majesty, deserters led by Lively are trying to seize boats and leave the base.'

Followed by Moustache, the Afghan and the soldiers who had been won back to the cause, the queen hurried to the landing-stage. There, the war-fleet archers commanded by Ahmes were facing Lively's supporters, and the incident was threatening to turn into a major disaster.

'The queen!' shouted a deserter. 'The queen is alive!'

Alone and unarmed, Ahhotep stepped between the two sides.

Lively knew he had committed an unpardonable crime. By spreading false rumours and inciting many soldiers to flee, he had condemned himself to death. He drew his sword.

'I am sorry, Majesty,' he said, 'but I have no choice. I need a boat so I can get away, and I'll kill anyone who tries to stop me.'

'Keep your sword for fighting the enemy and liberating your country.'

Lively gaped at her. 'Majesty, do you mean . . . ? But surely you cannot pardon a deserter?'

'I need you. I need you all if we are to defeat the Emperor of Darkness. If we had started killing one another we would have given him victory, but I have destroyed that curse. Let us once more become one soul, and from now on you must trust no one's word but mine.'

Lively sheathed his sword. Under Ahhotep's bright gaze, her soldiers became brothers once more.

## 5

'Commander Jannas, an unauthorized cargo-boat is coming this way along the northern canal.'

'Intercept it.'

This could hardly be a trick on the part of Ahhotep, but since the attack on Avaris Jannas had taken even the most minor incident seriously. All river access to the capital was guarded day and night, and the smallest vessel strictly controlled. At the slightest hint of danger, the archers were under orders to fire. It was better to make a mistake than to put the capital at risk.

Jannas was a perfectionist, who inspected several warships each day and checked their weapons himself. Each ship had to be permanently ready for combat. Either the Egyptian fleet would try to launch a new offensive, or Jannas would receive orders to leave for the south and destroy the Thebans. Either way, he must ensure that victory was certain.

During his short break at midday, while he was eating a frugal meal of grilled mullet and lentils aboard his flagship, his assistant came in to warn him that High Treasurer Khamudi had arrived.

'He is very upset and demands to see you immediately, sir.'

'Tell him to wait. I am finishing my lunch.'

Jannas took his time. Khamudi had humiliated him before the attack on Avaris, so he would return the favour. Here, on the flagship, the High Treasurer, a mere civilian, could rant and rage as much as he liked. No sailor would let him into the commander's cabin.

Unusually for him, Jannas ate some pomegranates and figs, which he decided were to his taste; in certain circumstances, he appreciated sweetness. Then he washed his hands, put on his striped headdress and stepped out on to the bridge, where Khamudi was pacing up and down.

Red-faced with anger, the High Treasurer rushed towards Jannas, who raised a hand and halted him in his tracks.

'No sudden movements on my ship, Khamudi. Here, everything is regulated and precise.'

'Do you know what you have just done, Commander?'

'After a morning's inspections, I had lunch. Any other questions?'

'You have intercepted a boat which belongs to me!'

'The one on the northern canal? It was not on my list of vessels authorized to enter the trading-port.'

'Shall we go into your cabin? No one must hear us.'

Jannas nodded. Given Khamudi's agitated state, the conversation promised to be interesting.

'I'd like to accept that the boat belongs to you, Khamudi, but why did its Cypriot captain not say so?'

'Because his mission is highly confidential – as is his cargo, which ought to have been delivered directly to me.'

'You seem to have forgotten that we are at war and that I am required to inspect all goods entering Avaris.'

'Not these goods,' said Khamudi. 'Return them to me and we'll say no more about it.'

'I'd like to, but I can't. Supposing you've been tricked? Unknown to you, your vessel might be bringing dangerous goods into the capital, or even weapons for the rebels.'

The High Treasurer turned purple. 'How dare you accuse me of such a thing!'

'I am not accusing you of anything. I am simply afraid someone might have taken advantage of your good faith, which is why I must know the nature of the cargo you were expecting.'

'Do you expect me to believe you haven't examined it?'

Jannas pretended to think. 'I had no choice, I'm afraid, but I was puzzled by what was found. I'd be glad to hear your version of the facts.'

Khamudi was boiling with rage. 'It's a drug, Commander, and all the officials and senior officers use it.'

'I do not.'

'Everyone has his own own form of amusement. In times like this, many people find the drug indispensable, and I have to ensure they have access to that little pleasure. Moreover, I have the full agreement of the emperor, who would be extremely unhappy to learn that you were impinging on my territory.'

'Nothing could be further from my thoughts, High Treasurer.'

'Then have that cargo delivered to me immediately.'

'Since everything is now out in the open, that is indeed what I shall do. To prevent any more incidents like this, kindly see to it that your next delivery conforms with security regulations.'

Khamudi slammed the door of the cabin behind him.

Feeling relaxed, Jannas allowed himself a cup of lukewarm beer.

He had known for a long time about Khamudi's lucrative traffic in drugs, and in fact he thought it an excellent idea, because such things soothed people's anxieties.

The important thing was that the High Treasurer now realized he was not the only master after the emperor. From now on, all trade would have to be approved by Jannas. No detail would escape him, and Khamudi's influence would start to wane.

At the end of a trying day, the sun's burning heat was at last on the wane: soon it would sink swiftly in the west. Indifferent to this magnificent sight, Jannas was angrily reprimanding the commander of a vessel whose crew discipline was poor. There would be no second warning. One more mistake and the culprit would end up in the emperor's labyrinth, from which no one had ever emerged alive.

An officer of the river guards came up and saluted. 'Commander, there is a small problem.'

'What sort of problem?'

'We have arrested a suspect in a storehouse at the trading-port. He claims to have important information for you, and refuses to speak to anyone else.'

'Very well. We'll go and hear what he has to say.'

The drugs had been unloaded and delivered to Khamudi, and the dock-workers were now carrying heavy jars of lamp-oil destined for the palace, where the lamps burned night and day. A cargo-vessel laden with copper could wait until the following day. Mined by forced labourers with a limited life-expectancy, the metal would be used to manufacture weapons.

Jannas had authorized only a single access canal, the others being blocked by floating barrages. If Ahhotep applied the same strategy as her dead son Kamose, she would meet with crushing failure.

But what insane plan could this incredibly stubborn queen come up with now? The death of a husband and a son should have been enough to break any woman, yet she doggedly went on believing in a victory she knew was impossible. Even the summary execution of civilians and the destruction of entire villages had not persuaded her to give up her madness.

'This way, Commander.'

Two guards were on duty in front of the storehouse, which was old and ought to have been demolished. Inside were broken packing-cases and old rags.

Sitting with his back to a wall was an unshaven young man with manacles on his wrists.

'Are you Commander Jannas?' The prisoner spoke haltingly and his eyes were unfocused.

'I am indeed.'

'I want to speak with you alone.'

'Why?'

'It concerns the emperor's safety.'

The commander gestured to the guards to leave. 'Now talk.'

Quick as a cat, the man leapt up, seized Jannas by the throat, and tried to throttle him. He was so much bigger and heavier that Jannas seemed bound to die. But the commander had lost none of his fighter's reflexes. Unsheathing his dagger, he plunged it into his attacker's belly. The man screamed with pain and let go.

After freeing himself, Jannas cut the man's throat.

'Probably drugged,' he concluded. 'A drug-addict sent by Khamudi to kill me.'

# 6

Despite the years of war and the seeming inevitability that it would crumble into ruin, the modest city of Thebes had actually grown. Here and there small white houses had been built for newly married couples. Defying destiny, they gave birth to children who would perhaps be the future of Egypt.

At Ahhotep's insistence, the most beautiful room in the hastily rebuilt royal place was the large bedchamber belonging to her mother, Teti the Small. Teti was very old and increasingly fragile, but she still painted her face and dressed with great care. Although she had been deeply affected by the deaths of her son-in-law and elder grandson, she had taken charge of bringing up the younger boy. Mingling strictness and gentleness, alternating games and teaching, she passed on to ten-year-old Ahmose the honey of ancient wisdom. True, he must learn how to fight, to handle the bow and the sword; but he must also be able to write beautiful hieroglyphs so that he might become an exemplary scribe.

His brother's death had abruptly matured the boy, and in any case ten was the age at which a person became fully responsible for his actions. Far from minimizing the ordeal he faced, his grandmother always spoke to him as to an adult whose path would be strewn with obstacles.

Today, Ahhotep found Teti sitting by the window of her bedchamber, watching the birds flying around in the garden.

'How do you feel today, Mother?'

'A bit more tired than yesterday, but I am so proud of you! I understand that you have put an end to some sort of rebellion by our soldiers.'

'They had been misled by malicious rumours. In future, Neshi will give them official information each week, and I shall take action myself whenever necessary.'

Teti took her daughter's hand tenderly. 'Without you, Ahhotep, Egypt would no longer exist.'

'Without you, I would have been nothing but a feeble would-be rebel. Through the way you conducted yourself, you taught me everything. And you are the one who is preparing Ahmose for the harsh battles that await him.'

'Although he is astonishingly mature, he is still only a child. He is as careful and measured as Kamose was lively and enthusiastic. He needs time to assimilate an idea. It would be best not to overwhelm him and to let him grow at his own pace, but will you be able to do that?'

Ahhotep shared her mother's view. It did indeed depend upon whether the Hyksos precipitated events by unleashing a general offensive.

Qaris brought Teti some honey-cakes and fresh carob juice. 'The doctor would like to examine you, Majesty.'

'There's no need for that,' protested the old lady. 'Just order me a good dinner.'

Seeing Qaris's troubled expression, Ahhotep said goodbye to her mother and left the room with the steward.

Once outside, Qaris said quietly, 'The High Priest of Karnak has just died, Majesty. Your mother is bound to hear about it soon, and, as they liked each other and were the same age, I'm worried that the news may upset her.'

'You may be right, Qaris. What else?'

'The High Priest's assistant, who considers himself the natural successor, is not the man for this situation.'

'Why not?'

'He is ambitious by nature, his heart is not generous, and he has confused the service of the gods with the forging of his own career.'

Ahhotep had rarely known Qaris be so critical: he usually tended to minimize people's faults.

'Majesty,' he went on, 'you must be able to trust the High Priest of Amon implicitly. When you leave to fight again, it is he who will ensure that the link with the Invisible here in Thebes is maintained. This man will not fulfil that vital function, but will think only of ways to increase his own worldly power.'

'Then whom do you suggest as a candidate?'

'I cannot think of anyone, Majesty, and I have faith in the clear-sightedness of the Wife of God.'

'With your experience, Qaris, you yourself would make a perfect High Priest.'

'Oh no, Majesty! My place is here, in the palace.'

'Summon all the priests, scribes and administrators to the open-air courtyard of the Temple of Karnak.'

'Including Heray?'

Ahhotep smiled. 'No, because I shall never find a better minister for the economy.'

When the Wife of God entered the courtyard, all eyes turned towards her.

The High Priest's assistant came forward. 'The inventory of this temple's possessions is at your disposal, Majesty, as are the documents concerning its management.'

'Before consulting them, I must pay homage to the late High Priest.'

'He rests in his official residence. May I escort you there?'

'I know where it is.'

The assistant frowned.

The queen walked slowly past the men Qaris had selected. One of them impressed her: he was contemplative, and had a serious expression, although he could not be much more than thirty years old.

'What is your office?' she asked him.

'I am a bearer of offerings, Majesty.'

'Do you know the words of the gods?'

'Between carrying out my duties, I study the hieroglyphic texts.'

'What do you know of Amon?'

'He is the sculptor who sculpted himself, the creator of eternity whose perfect act was the birth of the Light. He is the One who remains all by creating multiplicity. His true name is secret for ever, for he is life itself. His right eye is the day, his left eye the night. A good shepherd, he is also the ship's pilot. Master of the silent ones, he brings the gods into the world.'

'These words lead us nowhere,' protested the assistant. 'Karnak has need of a serious administrator, not a thinker lost in abstractions.'

'It is for the Wife of God to choose the new High Priest, is it not?

'Indeed, Majesty, but I beg you to think deeply. I worked for many years at my superior's side, and he did not appoint me at random.'

'Then why did he not name you explicitly as his successor?'

The assistant looked embarrassed. 'Illness had weakened him greatly ... but no one could doubt his intention. And Djehuty, the offerings-bearer, is not the man to replace him.'

'Djehuty ... the name of the god Thoth, master of the sacred language on which we base our civilization. Surely that is a sign from heaven.'

The assistant stared, open-mouthed.

'Write your name upon a piece of papyrus and Djehuty shall do the same,' commanded the queen. 'I shall place both in the innermost shrine of the goddess Mut, and she shall take the decision.'

*

As soon as the funeral vigil was over, under the protection of Isis, the High Priest's mummification began. After meditating before the mortal remains of her faithful servant and speaking the words of glorification, Ahhotep entered the shrine of Mut, opened the innermost chamber and withdrew the papyri. Then she returned to the great courtyard.

The assistant's fists were clenched, whereas Djehuty seemed strangely calm.

'One of the papyri was burnt by Mut's fire,' she revealed, throwing the charred fragments to the ground. 'The other is intact.'

'We must accept the will of the Invisible,' said the assistant, who had recognized the piece of papyrus in Ahhotep's hand.

She showed it to him. The name that had been preserved was Djehuty's.

## 7

With his mother, Young Prince Ahmose crossed the threshold of the temple at Karnak. He was tall and thin, with eyes which radiated depth and seriousness. For a long time he gazed at the central gateway, which was built of pink granite, then he went on towards a square-pillared portico whose austere beauty made his heart swell. This accorded with his view that all beings must behave righteously when confronted by the vagaries of destiny. And he marvelled at the second portico, whose pillars were gigantic statues of Osiris standing with his arms crossed over his chest and the sceptres of judgement and resurrection in his hands.

Before each statue stood a priest of Amon.

'Look carefully at the priests, my son,' said Ahhotep, 'and choose the one you believe capable of fulfilling the office of High Priest.'

'What does the office involve?'

'Serving the hidden principle by celebrating the rites daily, so that he will consent not to leave this earth.'

Ahmose looked deep into the eyes of each priest in turn, without arrogance and without haste. He allowed his mother's words to enter his soul and tried to determine whether the man he was looking at matched up to them.

'I choose this one,' said the prince firmly, looking into Djehuty's eyes.

The High Priest's assistant prostrated himself before the queen. 'Forgive my vanity, Majesty. I shall obey Djehuty and do my utmost to accomplish the tasks he entrusts to me.'

After enthroning the new High Priest by handing him the Staff of the Word and slipping a gold ring on to the middle finger of his right hand, the queen took Ahmose to the east of the temple.

On an altar facing the shrine of Amon lay the Sword of Light, which had been borne by Pharaohs Seqen and Kamose.

'The door of this shrine will not consent to open until the Hyksos are defeated once and for all,' Ahhotep told him. 'Until that happens much blood and many tears must be shed, and you must know how to wield this weapon unfalteringly. Do you feel capable of so doing, Ahmose?'

The prince approached the altar, touched the hilt and ran his finger along the blade. 'The Sword of Amon is too heavy for me now. But when my arm is strong enough, I shall wield it.'

'You are only ten years old, and you have lost your father and your brother, who both died to liberate Egypt. Despite their courage, that task is a long way from being achieved. Do you agree to continue it, despite the danger to your life?'

'To live without freedom is worse than death.'

'Egypt cannot survive without the presence of a pharaoh, Ahmose, and destiny has chosen you to hold this supreme office, as you have just proved. Until you are truly capable of fulfilling it, I shall continue my duties as Regent Queen.'

'Why don't you become Pharaoh, Mother? I shall never be able to equal you.'

'When my task is done, when Egypt can breathe freely, she will need a great king, young and steeped in the spirit of Ma'at, to rebuild a world in harmony with the creative powers. So the energy of government must quicken your heart.'

Ahhotep and her son made their way towards the new High Priest, Djehuty.

'Prepare for the coronation ceremonies,' the queen told him.

At the very moment Ahhotep spoke those words, Emperor Apophis was seized with a violent sickness as he rested in his bedchamber, whose many lamps burned day and night. His lips and ankles swelled, his throat tightened, and he could not breathe.

'There will never be any king but me,' he muttered, with such venom that his strength returned.

Seizing his dagger, whose hilt was inlaid with a silver lotus and whose triangular blade was made of copper, he plunged it into the wall, stabbing through a palm-tree the Minoan painter had drawn.

'Everything belongs to me, even this picture.'

The emperor opened the door of his bedchamber. Outside stood two guards.

'Send for the High Treasurer and have the bearers prepare my travelling-chair.'

'How do you feel, Majesty?'

'Send for the High Treasurer, then take me to the Temple of Set. And hurry.'

Khamudi had to abandon his calculations of the profits from drug sales, and run to the palace. As soon as he arrived, he helped Apophis into the magnificent travelling-chair that had been used by the pharaohs of the time of Amenemhat III. Twenty sturdy fellows lifted it and set a quick pace while taking care not to jolt the lord of the Hyksos. Fifty soldiers ensured his safety and Khamudi, who was a lover of the good life, found it difficult to keep up.

As the procession went through the streets, the few passers-by darted aside. Women and children rushed back into their homes. But one little boy dropped his wooden toy, a toy crocodile with moving jaws, right in the procession's path. He let go of his mother's hand to retrieve it.

'Stop!' ordered the emperor.

Wide-eyed with astonishment and curiosity, the child gazed up at the soldiers with their black helmets and breast-plates. If Apophis had not spoken, he would have been trampled underfoot. He hugged his wooden crocodile to his chest.

'Bring him, Khamudi.'

As Khamudi picked the child up, the child's mother rushed towards the soldiers, frantic with worry. 'He is my son! Don't hurt him!'

At a sign from the emperor, the procession recommenced its forward march. The little boy did not see an officer slit his mother's throat.

The priests of Set and of Hadad, the Syrian storm-god, ceaselessly chanted words of conjuration to hold back the heavens' anger. Since early morning, strange clouds had menaced Avaris. A furious wind from the south was shaking the oak trees around the main altar, making them moan. The waters of the nearby canal were whipped up into furious waves.

'The emperor has arrived!' exclaimed a priest.

The chair was gently set down. Apophis got to his feet with difficulty; he was very pale and short of breath.

'This bad weather is abnormal, Majesty, and we are very worried,' confessed the High Priest of Set.

'You and your colleagues are to leave. Continue to recite the incantations.' Apophis's hoarse voice and icy gaze were even more terrifying than usual, and the priests hurried away.

The emperor gazed up at the enraged sky, as if he alone could decipher its message. 'Bring the child here, Khamudi.'

The High Treasurer led the little boy, still holding his toy, to the altar.

'I must regenerate myself,' said Apophis, 'because Ahhotep has just devised a new way of attacking me. Her plans must not come to fruition. To prevent them doing so, Set demands a sacrifice which will give me back my health, a sacrifice which will unleash a monstrous storm against Thebes. Lay the child on the altar.'

The High Treasurer realized what his master intended. 'Majesty, would you like me to do this myself?'

'Since it is I who shall henceforth possess his breath, only I can take it from his body.'

Ignoring the child's screams and tears, Khamudi broke his toy and forced him down upon the altar. The emperor unsheathed his dagger.

# 8

Teti the Small was awoken by a peal of thunder. As if she had regained her youth and energy, the old lady leapt out of bed, donned a dark blue tunic and hurried down the corridor to Ahhotep's bedchamber.

The door opened before she had time to knock, and Ahhotep stood there.

'Did you hear it, Mother?' she asked.

Zigzags of lightning criss-crossed the dawn skies.

'I cannot remember a storm like it,' said Teti.

'This is not normal,' said Ahhotep. 'There is only one possible explanation: the Emperor has unleashed the fury of Set.'

'Then it will be impossible to celebrate the coronation ceremony, won't it?'

'You are right. It will be impossible.'

Even the heaviest sleepers had been jolted out of their sleep. Everyone in the palace was worried, and Qaris could not calm their fears.

Ahhotep hurried to her son's bedchamber. He was standing at a window, gazing out at the furious heavens.

'Are the gods angry with me?' he asked soberly.

'No, it isn't that. The Emperor of Darkness has realized what we intend to do, and wishes to prevent you from ascending the throne of the living.'*

Torrential rain pelted down on Thebes, and darkness hid the sun.

'This is the blackness of hell!' cried one serving-woman, while another, who was even more frightened, ran away, her arms flailing.

'Light all the lamps,' the queen ordered Qaris.

The steward's face fell. 'The oil will not burn, Majesty.'

An enormous crash made the whole household jump. The raging wind had just blown the roof off the nearby barracks, sending it smashing down on to a granary.

---

*These cosmic disturbances are recorded on a limestone stele 1.80 metres tall and 1.10 metres wide, which was exhibited in the temple at Karnak.

In utter panic, the Thebans emerged from their houses and ran about in all directions. The dogs howled, all except Laughter, who did not leave his mistress's side. The walls of a house on the outskirts of the city collapsed, killing the children of the family as they huddled in their bedroom.

'We're all going to die!' predicted a blind man.

Then the Nile's fury was in turn unleashed.

A boat carrying fishermen, who were trying to head south, was lifted up by a wave and capsized. Although they were excellent swimmers, all five men drowned. In the port, the boats disintegrated as they bumped into each other. Even the warship that had brought Ahhotep from the military base to Thebes could not withstand the storm. Her masts fell on to the sailors on guard, and her captain was crushed by the bar of a steering-oar which had become uncontrollable. In less than a quarter of an hour, the ship had sunk.

And still the thunderbolts kept coming. A ball of flame set a carpenter's workshop alight, and the fire spread to the neighbouring houses. The wind fanned the flames, negating the efforts of the water-bearers.

Ahhotep watched the disaster, powerless. Soon, Thebes would be no more than a ruin, as would the military base. By using the power of Set, Apophis was reducing twenty years' work to nothing.

Without a war-fleet, and with only a few hundred soldiers left, all the queen would be able to do was beg for mercy from the tyrant, who would have the survivors of the cataclysm executed. It would be better to die in battle. Ahhotep decided that she would hide her son in the desert with a few faithful followers, and then confront Apophis alone. She would have no weapon save the flint dagger she had wielded as a young girl, when she became the first person to rebel against the invaders.

Twenty years of struggle, suffering and hope, twenty years in which she had known love and times of intense happiness, twenty years fighting oppression, were now ending in a defeat from which Egypt could not recover.

She called her son to her and told him, 'You must prepare to leave Thebes.'

'I want to stay with you.'

'You cannot. Set's fury will not abate until Thebes is destroyed, and you must survive. One day you shall take up the struggle again.'

'What about you, Mother? What will you do?'

'Gather together all the soldiers who can still fight, and attack Avaris.'

The boy was indomitable. 'But that would be suicidal, wouldn't it?'

'Apophis must believe that his victory is total. If I were dead and you had died at Thebes, he would have nothing more to fear. You will have to begin from nothing, Ahmose, as I did myself. Above all, never give up. And if death interrupts your work, may your *ka* inspire another heart.'

Ahmose rushed into his mother's arms, and she hugged him for a long time.

'Think only of righteousness and the respect of Ma'at, my son; those are the only forces the emperor shall never wield.'

The storm grew even more ferocious. Many houses had been destroyed and there were countless deaths and injuries. The wadis had turned into torrents, carrying along stones and debris. On the western bank of the Nile, the ancient burial-grounds had been invaded by rivers of mud.

'Hurry, Qaris,' commanded the queen. 'You must leave with my son for the eastern desert. Heray shall go with you, if you can find him.'

'Majesty, you should—'

'I shall stay here with my mother.'

Ahhotep kissed Ahmose one last time and entrusted him to the steward, in the hope that they would escape from the storm.

When she turned, round, the queen found she had unexpected company: Long-Ears, a huge grey donkey with a white belly and muzzle, large nostrils and enormous ears. He was gazing at the queen with his bright, intelligent eyes.

'What are you trying to tell me?'

The donkey turned and moved away, Ahhotep following closely. When she left the palace, the queen was soaked within seconds. Long-Ears lifted his head and pointed his muzzle at the inky-black clouds which were still zigzagged with lightning.

'Yes, we must try,' she said, stroking him.

She ran to the palace shrine, which housed a gold sceptre whose head was shaped like the beast of Set. The embodiment of power, it had been entrusted to the queen by Mut.

And another creature of Set, the donkey, had just opened up a possible way: since the emperor had petitioned the god of storms, why should she not do the same?

Ahhotep climbed up to the palace roof and raised the gold sceptre to the heavens.

'You who command the lightning, unveil yourself! What have you to fear from me? I wield your symbol. I possess this light, which does not destroy but illuminates the earth. Obey me, Set, or you shall no longer be worshipped. No, the Emperor of Darkness is not your only master. Why do you rise up against your country and against your brother Horus, the Pharaoh of Egypt? Show your true face, and may your energy enter your sceptre.'

The clouds parted, and in the northerly part of the sky appeared the shape of a bull's hoof,* in which resided the mysterious force that humans could never master. And another bolt of lightning, more violent and more intense than the others, flashed out from the depths of the heavens and entered the golden sceptre, which the Queen of Freedom gripped with a firm hand.

---

*The Great Bear, believed to be the seat of Set's power.

## 9

Apophis's howl of rage echoed through the citadel, chilling the blood of all who heard it.

An atrocious pain had just seared through the emperor's flesh: a burning sensation, signifying that the fire of Set was turning against him.

Above Set's temple black clouds were gathering from all four corners of the sky, faster than a galloping horse. Lightning forked from them, striking the priests' houses and the avenue of oak-trees leading to the altar. The branches caught fire, and the wind whipped up the flames.

The rain fell on Avaris in such violent torrents that the soldiers took refuge in their guard-posts and barracks, covering their heads with their hands in an attempt to escape Set's wrath.

'We are cursed!' cried Tany, the emperor's wife, standing on her bed, her lips flecked with foam.

Two serving-women forced her to lie down, but she went on, 'It's the Thebans – they're coming back! I see Queen Ahhotep, with a sword . . . Waves are submerging the capital, fire is destroying the citadel.'

While Tany raved in her delirium, the emperor slowly climbed the stairs to the top of the highest tower.

Ignoring the deluge, he pointed his dagger at the inky sky and bellowed, 'You are my ally. Set, and you must strike down my enemies!'

There was an even more blinding flash than before and, with an ear-splitting roar, lightning struck the tower.

Since his narrow escape from the assassination attempt, Jannas had ensured that he was guarded closely night and day. Khamudi would not get another chance of a surprise attack.

The commander had not been surprised to learn that his enemy had taken precisely the same protective measures. Khamudi knew Jannas knew who had been responsible for the attack, and feared that he would be killed. A struggle to the death had begun between the two men.

His assistant came in bowed. 'Commander, the Supreme Council meeting is to go ahead,' he confirmed.

'Is there any news of the emperor?'

'Some say he was killed by a thunderbolt, some say he is on his deathbed, and some claim he has lost the power of speech. Commander . . .'

'What is it now?'

'The majority of the Hyksos are ready to acknowledge you as their leader.'

'You are forgetting Khamudi.'

'He has his supporters, it is true, but they are far fewer than yours. As soon as necessary . . .'

'Let us see what the Supreme Council says,' decided Jannas.

Despite the Minoan paintings, with their brilliant colours, the council chamber was cold and sinister. All the great dignitaries of the empire were present, and Jannas and Khamudi were face to face, next to the emperor's modest pinewood throne.

Everyone was nervous. When the palace doctors officially announced Apophis's death, or his inability to rule, what would happen? Some thought Khamudi would use his position as High Treasurer as an excuse to take temporary power which he could later make permanent, but Jannas, the commander of the armed forces, would never accept that solution. Only a bloodbath could resolve the inevitable conflict between the two claimants to power, and in that game the commander would be the stronger man.

For that reason, Khamudi, who was suffering from an itch that salves could not soothe, did not look as confident as usual. Although he had bought with him as many loyal senior officers as possible, he feared that he might not emerge from the citadel alive.

Suddenly, Apophis appeared. Dressed in a dark brown cloak, he walked heavily to his throne, staring icily at each of the dignitaries, and sat down.

Everyone felt guilty for having doubted him, and Khamudi's smile returned.

'Set has inflicted terrible damage on Thebes,' declared Apophis, in his harsh, chilling voice. 'The city has been half destroyed; Ahhotep's army has been decimated, and her war-fleet wiped out.'

'Majesty,' asked Jannas, 'will you give me the order to attack the rebels in order to deal them a death blow, and bring back their queen to you, dead or alive?'

'All in good time, Commander. First, you should know that my protector, Set, has made me into a new Horus. In official documents,

I am from now on to be called "He who Pacifies the Two Lands". Next, Set has revealed to me the reasons for his anger with Avaris. This city, my capital, is harbouring traitors, plotters and faint-hearts who dare to criticize and disapprove of my decisions. I am therefore going to eliminate this rottenness. And then, Commander Jannas, we shall deal with Ahhotep.'

The harem at Avaris was a hell. The most beautiful young women of the former Egyptian aristocracy were imprisoned there. At any time of the night or day, they must satisfy the lusts of the empire's dignitaries. If one of them tried to kill herself, her family were tortured and deported. Yet some of the women clung to survival, reminding themselves that, a while ago, a plot conceived in the harem had almost succeeded. And people said that the emperor was on his deathbed. Perhaps his successor would be less inhuman.

Dreaming of a less cruel fate, a magnificent brown-haired girl of twenty opened the door of the room where she and her companions put on their face-paint while waiting for visitors.

Her cry of terror stuck in her throat, for the Hyksos officer who stood there smashed her skull with a blow from his club.

'Kill all these vermin,' he ordered his men, who were clad in helmets and breastplates as though about to go into battle. 'The emperor has decided to close this harem, where there are murmurings against him.'

The murderers regretted not being able to enjoy these beautiful girls before killing them, but Apophis's orders had been strict.

The grey donkey with the gentle eyes died without understanding what it was being punished for, its heart pierced by a dagger. This was the hundredth donkey sacrificed to appease the god's fury.

The High Priest of Set hastily changed his blood-spattered robe when he saw Khamudi heading towards him at the head of a squad of men.

'Follow us, High Priest,' ordered Khamudi.

'But I still have animals to kill and—'

'Follow us.'

'Where are you taking me?'

'The emperor wants to see you.'

'The emperor? I must wash, and—'

'That is not necessary. And you know how much the emperor dislikes being kept waiting.'

Apophis was sitting in state on the platform that overlooked his two favourite entertainments: on one side the labyrinth, on the other the arena where a fighting-bull pawed the ground. Since the start of the purge, he had spent several hours each day watching the deaths of the men and women he had condemned. Some were gored and trampled, others were torn to pieces as they fell into one of the labyrinth's many traps.

The High Priest prostrated himself at the emperor's feet. 'We pay continual homage to Set, Majesty. Your orders are being faithfully carried out.'

'I am glad to hear it. But during the storm you began to doubt me, didn't you?'

'Not for one single moment, Majesty.'

'You are a bad liar. Because of your high office, I shall allow you a choice: the labyrinth or the bull.'

'Majesty, my obedience is unswerving, and I assure you that—'

'You doubted me,' cut in Apophis. 'That is treason, a crime which merits death.'

'No, Majesty! Have pity!'

Exasperated by the condemned man's sobs, the emperor kicked him hard and he fell into the arena.

The High Priest ran from the monstrous bull, but it soon caught him and ran him through with a single toss of its horns.

The emperor was more interested in his next victim, a palace cook. The insolent woman had dared to say that Apophis was gravely ill. That one would end her days in the labyrinth. She would be followed by soldiers, traders and government officials who had also doubted Apophis's greatness. As for the Egyptian suspects, they were all to be sent to Tjaru and Sharuhen, the operation being overseen by the remarkably skilled and efficient Aberia.

All this would take time, but eventually Avaris would be purged.

# 10

Crowned with the sun-disc, its eyes aflame, the statue of Mut gazed upon Queen Ahhotep. The queen had just given thanks to her for protecting the Temple of Karnak during the devastating storm, from which Thebes was recovering only with great difficulty.

As soon as the lightning had been imprisoned in the gold sceptre, the clouds had dispersed, it had stopped raining and the wind had dropped. Little by little, the sky became calm again, once more lit by a triumphant sun.

Heray had organized groups of volunteers to clear up the aftermath of the cataclysm. The only effective weapon in the face of misfortune was unity. A daily manifestation of Ma'at, it gave back hope to the victims and increased tenfold the effectiveness of those who helped them.

The legends surrounding the queen, who was already the subject of a thousand tales, was now embellished by her ability to appease the violent Set and capture his fire. Ahhotep herself paid no heed to people's extravagant praise, for she was waiting in desperate anxiety to learn the judgement of Mut. Would the Wife of Amon, who was at once Father and Mother, Life and Death, accept that young Ahmose should become Pharaoh? Without the goddess's assent, even miracles would be useless.

'You, Mut,' she prayed, 'have always shown me the path to follow. Ahmose is not only my son, he is also the future Pharaoh. If it were not so, I would have sought someone else to take on that office. I am convinced that Set's fury was unleashed by the Emperor of Darkness in order to prevent the coronation, not because Ahmose is incapable of reigning over the Two Lands. But perhaps I am wrong ... Your eyes can see through the darkness, and you have never lied to me. Is Ahmose to ascend the throne of the living?'

The statue inclined its head in assent.

Ahhotep was conferring with Heray, Qaris and Neshi about the damage the storm had wreaked.

As Heray lowered his considerable bulk on to a sturdy low chair, she saw that he seemed to have lost his usual cheerfulness.

'Majesty, the damage is extensive,' he said. 'It will take many months to repair everything and build all the houses we need – and then there are all the temporary shelters we must provide straight away.'

'The Treasury will help those who have suffered most,' Ahhotep promised.

'Unfortunately there have been many deaths, including a lot of children.'

'Each is to be ritually buried, and I shall appoint *ka* priests to bring them back to life each day.'

'In addition, Majesty,' said Qaris, 'the military base has been seriously damaged. Despite the sailors' best efforts, more than half the war-fleet was destroyed.'

'The carpenters must begin work at once and take on as many apprentices as possible. Until enough boats have been built, there will be no holidays – but pay will be doubled.'

Neshi said worriedly, 'Majesty, it is pointless to ignore the truth. If the Hyksos attack now, we shall be wiped out.'

'First they must get past the obstacle of the troops we have massed around Faiyum.'

'You know very well, Majesty, that our men could not hold off a mass offensive. And rebuilding our forces will take time – a lot of time.'

'Everything you have all said is true,' said Ahhotep. 'But the most urgent matter of all is the coronation of the new pharaoh.'

For a few days, Thebes decided to forget its wounds, not to think about the probable Hyksos attack, and to devote itself to the coronation ceremonies, the secret part of which would take place within the Temple of Karnak. The new High Priest, Djehuty, and the Wife of God presided over the proper conduct of the rites, which saw Ahmose purified by Horus and Thoth, then proclaimed King of Upper and Lower Egypt by the vulture- and cobra-goddesses.

His first act as pharaoh was to offer a statuette of Ma'at to Amon, the Hidden One, and to swear that all his life he would observe righteousness and justice so that the links between the divine and the human should not be broken.

After being acclaimed king, Ahmose emerged from the temple to go and meet his people. He was preceded by bearers of signs symbolizing all the provinces of Egypt, which he was to unify.

'Ahmose is he who brings together the Twofold Land,' proclaimed Ahhotep, 'the son of Amon-Ra brought forth from his being, the inheritor to whom the Creator has given his throne, his true representative on earth. Courageous, and free of all falsehood, he endows us with the breath of life, radiates royalty, firmly establishes Ma'at and spreads joy. He supports the heavens and steers the ship of state.'

Late that night, while the full moon shone directly above the temple and the city still echoed with the sounds of celebration, the ten-year-old boy thought back over every word his mother had spoken. Caught between fear and pride, he had come to realize that his life would never be like that of other men and that, little by little, the office of king would take over his entire being.

Having destroyed or defaced all the palace's Egyptian stelae and statuettes, Apophis was taking full advantage of Minos's paintings. And he had just summoned the Minoan artist, plunging Windswept into anguish. The empress's beautiful young sister was a formidable seductress and a veritable man-eater, who lured into her bed any dignitaries suspected of not agreeing unreservedly with Apophis's policies. After obtaining their bedroom confidences, Windswept denounced them, and the traitors were condemned to the labyrinth.

But her whole life had been turned upside-down when she fell passionately in love with Minos. Although she continued to play her role as a spy, she was being torn in half, because she knew the Minoan's terrible secret: willing to do absolutely anything in order to return home, he was plotting against the emperor.

Windswept had almost told Apophis the truth, but that would have meant condemning the man she adored to a terrible death. For the first time in her life, she had decided not to obey the emperor.

When Apophis looked at her, she felt as thought she were imprisoned in a spider's web, struggling helplessly. Surely he would eventually realize the truth and then, at the moment of his choosing, devour his prey, both Windswept and Minos.

The young woman paced up and down her bedchamber. At the moment, she knew, the emperor was talking to Minos. In her torment, she feared the worst. Apophis might have her beloved tortured, or deport him, or fling him into the labyrinth ... And then it would be her turn. Her brother, so much older than she, had always frightened her, although she was one of the few people, if not the only one, who could talk to him with a certain lack of respect. But Windswept was under no illusions: the day she ceased to be useful to Apophis, he would throw her to his officers or, worse, to the two women who hated her most, the 'empress' Tany and Yima, the High Treasurer's wife.

Windswept would not be able to justify her silence. As a conspirator, Minos ought to have been executed. And she could not hope to gain the slightest mercy from the emperor by talking to him about love.

It was impossible to imagine life without Minos. In the cruel, perverse world she inhabited, he was the embodiment of innocence and true love, free of dark shadows and calculation. A painter of genius, a sincere lover, he gave her a happiness she had not dared to hope for.

Whatever the consequences, she would protect Minos. But was he still alive?

Windswept disdained the drug that was circulating in the capital and making a fortune for Khamudi, that pretentious upstart whose greed was equalled only by his cruelty. He was just as depraved as his half-mad wife, their favourite form of entertainment being to inflict appalling tortures on young slaves. But he was still the emperor's right-hand man.

The bedchamber door opened.

'Minos,' cried Windswept in passionate relief, 'there you are, at last! But you look so pale. What did Apophis want?'

'Griffins – he wants me to paint griffins on either side of his throne, like the ones in the palace at Knossos. That will make him invulnerable.'

Almost physically sick, the painter could not admit to his mistress that he had thought his last hour had come.

Even in the arms of Windswept, who gave herself to him with such fervour, the Minoan still felt impaled by Apophis's icy stare.

He knew. The emperor knew, and was toying with his prey. The griffins would probably be Minos's last work.

## 11

Minos was working on the griffins, determined to beat all records for slowness. As long as the work remained unfinished, his life would be safe and he might perhaps find a way of killing the emperor. Despite the difference in their ages, he doubted that he would be able to kill Apophis with his bare hands. He would need a dagger, but no one, not even Windswept, could come before the lord of the Hyksos without being searched.

Suddenly, a gust of icy breath sent a shiver down his spine.

'Your work is not going very quickly, Minos, and the months are passing,' commented the emperor in his cruel, rasping voice. As usual, he had appeared like a demon emerging from the shadows. No one ever heard him coming.

'Majesty, if I hurry I might spoil the work.'

'I need these griffins very quickly, my young friend. Above all, they must inspire fear and their gaze must be terrifying.'

Despite Jannas's repeated requests, Apophis would not launch an offensive until the two griffins were in a fit state to defend his throne. The commander was fuming with impatience, and saying that they should not give Ahhotep time to build up her forces again, but that was too short-term a view. The emperor knew it would take several years for the damage inflicted on the Thebans to be put right. As soon as his griffins' eyes blazed forth destruction, as soon as his power was beyond the reach of conspiracy, and the purge was complete, Apophis would settle the matter of the queen and the rebels once and for all.

Minos dared not turn round.

'Do you understand me clearly, my young friend?'

'Yes. Oh yes, Majesty!'

Apophis turned and moved off down the corridor that led to the council chamber.

Khamudi greeted him on the threshold, in a state of great agitation. 'My lord, there's a message, a message from your informant.'

The Hyksos spy had not been in touch for a long time, probably because he had had great difficulty in sending the papyrus, which was written in a code to which only the emperor had the key.

As he read the words, Apophis's face expressed such hatred that even Khamudi was awed by it.

'That damned Ahhotep! She has dared to have her son – a boy of ten – crowned, and has presented him to the people as Pharaoh! Both of them are to be utterly destroyed. But first of all we shall sow discord in their ranks.'

Khamudi suddenly doubled up in pain, his hands clutching his belly. 'Forgive me, Majesty, it is a bladder-stone. I do not think I shall be able to attend the council meeting.'

'Summon the doctor and have it removed. We have a great deal of work ahead of us.'

Khamudi's wife, Yima, paced up and down, biting her nails, while she waited for the doctor. Without her husband, she was lost. If, as some people whispered, his malady was the result of a curse laid on him by Apophis, the unlucky man had no chance. After his death, Yima was sure she would lose most of her wealth, because it would be requisitioned by the palace. True, she could plead her cause to the lady Tany, but Tany was bedridden and cared about nothing but herself.

'The doctor has arrived,' her door-keeper informed her at last.

The doctor was a Canaanite, as Tany was, a skilled man reputed to be able to treat a case like Khamudi's. Meanwhile, the High Treasurer moaned and groaned in agony.

'My husband is a very important man,' said Yima haughtily. 'You must take great care of him.'

'Everyone knows of the High Treasurer's eminent status, my lady. Have faith in my method.'

'Does it really work?'

'Yes. But it will be painful.'

'I have a drug which will kill the pain.'

Yima fed her husband a potion made from poppies. Ordinarily, he took only a little to improve his love-making, but this time the dose sent him into a deep sleep.

The doctor took from his bag a tube made out of cartilage, and slid it up the patient's urethra, as far as the neck of the bladder. Khamudi did not react.

The surgeon slid a finger into the patient's anus, located the stone and pushed it towards the bladder's neck. Then he blew with all his strength into the other end of the tube to dilate it, and breathed in suddenly to make the stone pass through. Attaching another tube to the one he was using, he brought the stone down into the patient's penis and removed it by hand.

Khamudi's mind was still hazy when he entered the emperor's office, where Apophis was putting the finishing touches to a hieroglyphic text.

'Ah, Khamudi. How do you feel, my friend?'

'Better, Majesty, just tired and feeling a bit sick.'

'You'll soon recover. There is no better remedy than hard work, and that is precisely what I am planning to give you.'

Khamudi longed for a few days' rest, but one did not question the emperor's orders – especially not when facing an adversary as alarming as Jannas.

'Have we plenty of scarabs?' asked Apophis.

'We have them in all sizes and several materials, from stone to porcelain.'

'I shall need thousands, and I require them to be inscribed with the utmost speed. Here is the message. It is to be sent out into every single region.'

In Middle Egypt, at the Port of Kamose, which had been renamed thus in honour of the dead pharaoh, Governor Emheb was consolidating his military defences day by day, and the work was going well, thanks to the enthusiasm of his veteran soldiers. Soon he would have to hold the front line again, and he was glad that fighting alongside him again would be the great archer and ship's captain Ahmes, son of Abana. The two of them could always keep their men in good heart, even in the most difficult conditions.

The big man often thought of his home, Edfu, to the south of Thebes; he knew he would probably never see it again. Luck had favoured him during the fighting at Qis, but he had called upon luck so often that it was bound to abandon him eventually. When he learnt that Thebes had been terribly damaged by the storm, he could not help wondering if the age of Ahhotep was in danger of ending in disaster.

Without reinforcements, how could Emheb possibly fight off a major Hyksos offensive? The emperor was taking his time, enabling Jannas to prepare an enormous army whose first action would be to raze Memphis to the ground. Then, as it moved along, it would destroy the pockets of resistance, the largest of which was at the Port of Kamose, before finally thundering down on Thebes, which would be utterly defenceless.

Emheb's musings were interrupted by the arrival of Ahmes, who said, 'Governor, our allies in Memphis have just sent us these messages put out by the emperor.'

He showed Emheb ten porcelain and cornelian scarabs. They all bore the same inscription, written in coarse hieroglyphs and containing mistakes which no experienced scribe would have made.

'We must send them to the Regent Queen at once,' advised Emheb. 'This attack could be our death-blow.'

# 12

*In the name of Emperor Apophis, King of Upper and Lower Egypt, let this be made known to all inhabitants of the Two Lands: the thunderbolt of Set has struck Thebes, the rebel city. Its palace has been destroyed, Queen Ahhotep and her son Ahmose, the puppet pharaoh, have perished in the ruins. The rebel army no longer exists. The survivors have deserted. Let every man submit to Apophis. Anyone who disobeys him will be severely punished.*

'We must make sure no one sees these scarabs,' said Neshi furiously.

'It's too late,' lamented Ahhotep.

'They might cause a general collapse,' agonized Qaris. 'Here, at Thebes, you can easily prove that these are simply more of the emperor's lies and half-truths, but in other places . . . Our soldiers will lay down their arms at Memphis, and perhaps even at the Port of Kamose.'

'We still have a way of fighting back,' said Ahhotep. 'I shall immediately write a short message for our scribes to copy on to small pieces of papyrus. These will be entrusted to Rascal and his fellow carrier-pigeons.'

Rascal, an exceptional and much-honoured bird, was the undisputed leader of the pigeons, and could cover vast distances in a single flight. Wounded during a dangerous mission, he had recovered completely and spent happy evenings with Laughter, telling tales of his adventures as a tireless warrior.

Although able to navigate using the earth's magnetism, the pigeons were at risk from from birds of prey and enemy arrows, but Rascal's flock had learnt to be cunning, making full use of their acute eyesight. There was also another, more treacherous danger. Ahhotep believed that the Hyksos spy had previously poisoned one of the birds to sever communications between her and Kamose. Since then, soldiers had kept a constant watch on the pigeon-loft.

Rascal and his comrades took to the skies in a great flapping of wings, some heading south, the others north, to spread the message from Queen Ahhotep.

'Don't move,' Ahmes warned two soldiers with bundles on their shoulders, who were preparing to desert.

'You can kill only one of us with one arrow,' retorted the younger of them.

'Be careful,' disagreed his comrade. 'He will have fired a second shot before you can get near him.'

'I have no wish to kill Egyptian soldiers,' said Ahmes, 'but I hate cowards. If you take one more step it will be your last, because I'll cripple you and you'll never walk again.'

'Haven't you heard the news? The queen is dead, there is no more pharaoh, no more Thebes, no more army of liberation. We have to get away before the Hyksos arrive.'

'The emperor is a liar.'

'Then why doesn't the queen come?'

Ahmed's attention was caught by the sound of wings, but he kept on aiming at the deserters. The pigeon landed, and he recognized it: Rascal, with a message attached to his leg.

'We're going to wake up Governor Emheb,' he said. 'And you can lead the way.'

The two men took one look at Ahmes's resolute face and decided to obey.

The governor was not sleeping. He, too, recognized Rascal, who greeted him with bright, intelligent eyes. After gently stroking the bird's head, he unrolled the tiny papyrus bearing the royal seal, looked through it quickly, then read it aloud:

*Year two of the reign of Pharaoh Ahmose, the third day of the first month of the second season.*

*The vile Apophis, Emperor of Darkness and usurper, continues to send out scarabs bearing lies and false information. Queen Ahhotep, Wife of God and Regent Queen of the kingdom, is extremely well, as is her loving son, the Pharaoh of Upper and Lower Egypt, Ahmose. At Thebes, the rites are conducted in respect of Amon, god of victories, and the army of liberation continues to prepare to strike down the invaders and re-establish the reign of Ma'at.*

The two deserters listened, open-mouthed.

'I told you so,' said Ahmes.

'All right, we made a stupid mistake,' admitted the older man. 'But we can forget about it, can't we?'

'It is for Governor Emheb to decide what your punishment will be.'

Ahmes's bow remained drawn, the arrow ready to fly. And Emheb had a hard, fiery expression which did not augur well. He went round behind the two soldiers, and kicked them both hard in the backside.

'That will be enough this time,' he decreed. 'But if you ever do anything so stupid again, I shall let Ahmes deal with you.'

The war of words lasted several months. At Memphis, after the initial panic, the senior rebel officers managed to restore and maintain order among their troops.

Everywhere, inundated with Hyksos scarabs contradicting the papyri brought by the carrier-pigeons, the citizens and peasants constantly gathered to discuss them. At the beginning of year three of Ahmose's reign, they came to their conclusion: the emperor was lying. Officers arriving from Thebes confirmed to the leaders of the liberated provinces that Queen Ahhotep was continuing the fight and that young Pharaoh Ahmose was every bit as determined as his father and brother had been.

With a little luck, the news might spread to Avaris and the Delta.

'I've worked all day and I'm exhausted,' complained Minos.

'I'll cure your tiredness,' promised Windswept, as she washed her lover's firm young body with scented water.

Minos quickly forgot the hours spent perfecting every tiny detail of the griffins, in accordance with the emperor's very precise demands, and eagerly caressed the beautiful woman's perfect form.

Together they attained pleasure, a dazzling new height which calmed Windswept's anguish and gave Minos back hope. But, once their ecstasy had passed, reality once more stared them in the face. Never could Windswept confess to her lover that she had spied upon him and that she knew his intentions. Never could Minos admit to his mistress that he wanted to kill the emperor. Convinced that Apophis had unmasked him and was toying with his prey, the painter was afraid he might not survive once he had finished his griffins.

'The palace talks of nothing but your new masterpiece,' said Windswept, 'yet no one has seen it. The throne room has been out of bounds for such a long time.'

'Apophis won't use the monsters until he thinks they're perfect. He's in a terrible hurry, yet he makes me amend my work so that it matches his vision exactly. They're terrifying, Windswept – I hardly dare look at them! All that's needed is a little more intensity in their eyes, and I shall have finished. And then the emperor will bring them to life with his destructive magic.'

'Why are you so afraid, my love?'

'When you see the griffins, you'll understand.'

'Surely you don't think Apophis will choose you as their first victim?'

'He's quite capable of doing that.' The painter stepped away from his mistress. 'Do you know that Avaris is filled with strange rumours claiming Queen Ahhotep and her son are still alive?'

'Don't pay any attention to gossip.'

'I want to return to Minoa with you, Windswept. We could marry there, we could have children and we could live happily and simply.'

'Yes, simply . . .'

'King Minos the Great loves artists – he himself gave me permission to bear his name. We'd have a beautiful house, near Knossos, in a sunny valley. My work's nearly finished, so you must speak to the emperor and ask him to let us leave.'

# 13

Khamudi had to abstain from all sexual activities while he was convalescing, which his wife considered was taking far too long. So Yima simpered in the palace corridors, in search of a man who was both attractive and sufficiently discreet never to reveal their brief liaison.

She stepped out in front of the handsome Minos as he was returning to his apartments. 'Have you finished your masterpiece?' she asked, with a winning smile.

'That is for the emperor to decide.'

'People talk of nothing but you and your extraordinary talent. I should like to know you better.'

'My work takes up all my time, my lady.'

She wiggled her hips, rubbing herself against him.

'One must also know how to enjoy oneself, don't you think? I'm sure you deserve better than the arms of just one woman.'

Cornered in the narrow passageway, the Minoan did not know how to escape this ever-more-demanding blonde.

'Keep away from Minos!' commanded Windswept's icy voice.

Yima's smile did not slip. 'Ah, here is our beautiful princess! So the rumours are true: you still haven't tired of him.'

Windswept slapped Yima, who squealed like a frightened little girl.

'Go back to your husband, and never again set your eyes on Minos – or I'll tear them out.'

The lady Tany could not bear either daylight or the darkness of night. She had had ten lamps arranged around her bed, so that their flames might reassure her.

With the windows covered by heavy curtains, which let not even the smallest ray of sunshine through, the emperor's wife felt safe. Never again would she dare to gaze out at the canals of Avaris, which the Egyptians had used to launch an attack against the city.

Each evening, Tany took a sleeping-draught made from crushed lotus-seeds, hoping not to be awoken by the nightmare that maddened her: an extraordinarily beautiful woman was destroying Apophis's army, burning the emperor with her gaze, dismantling the citadel, and reducing the empress to the status of a slave forced to kiss the feet and hands of her servants.

Tany howled in terror; her night-robe was soaked with sweat. Her maids came running in and soothed her, propping her up with cushions and rubbing soothing ointments into her skin.

'Majesty,' one of them informed her, 'the lady Yima would like to see you.'

'That dear, sweet friend. Send her in.'

Khamudi's wife bowed before Tany. The empress was the ugliest woman in the capital and, despite all the ointments, she stank. But Yima needed her. Although the frightful Tany no longer left her bedchamber, she still exerted a certain influence, and Yima intended to make good use of it.

'Majesty, how are you feeling today?'

'As dreadful as ever, alas! I shall never get better.'

'Do not say that, my lady,' purred Yima. 'I am quite sure you will.'

'How kind you are, my faithful friend. But you look upset. What is the matter?'

'I dare not burden Your Majesty with my petty worries.'

'Dare, I beg you!'

Yima put on the look of a sulky child. 'I have been insulted and dragged lower than the dirt.'

'Who can have done such a thing?'

'Someone very important, Majesty – I cannot reveal that person's name, even to you.'

'Do not annoy me, Yima.'

'I am so embarrassed . . .'

'Tell me what's in your heart, my sweet friend.'

Yima lowered her eyes. 'It was the painter, Minos. He may look like a shy boy, but in fact he's a vile, disgusting goat! Never has a man treated me like that.'

'You mean . . . ?'

Yima nodded.

Tany kissed her on the forehead. 'My poor darling. Tell me all about it.'


Helped by Qaris, Teti the Small made her way determinedly to the council chamber, where Moon, Heray, Neshi, Moustache and the Afghan were assembled. Like young King Ahmose, they looked grave.

Ahhotep helped her mother to sit down.

'The news from the Port of Kamose is bad,' revealed the queen.

'The soldiers are badly demoralized, and even Governor Emheb cannot give them back their courage. At the first Hyksos offensive, there will be a rout. I therefore think it vital to strengthen the front with almost all the weapons at our disposal.'

'The rebuilding of our fleet is far from completed,' warned Neshi. 'If we send all our boats and troops to the Port of Kamose, Thebes will be defenceless.'

'It will only seem to be,' Ahhotep corrected him, 'because if we can strengthen our lines enough the Hyksos will not get through. If they do succeed, it will be because we are all dead. But you have become very cautious, Neshi. There was a time when you would have been the first to approve of this plan.'

'I do approve of it, Majesty, and unreservedly at that. Surrounding Thebes with a wall would achieve nothing. It is indeed vital to take a new initiative and to move the theatre of war as far north as possible, whatever the risks.'

Ill at ease in debate, the Afghan and Moustache were content to go along with this. At the thought of cutting down some Hyksos, they forgot the enemy's obvious superiority.

'Queen Ahhotep is right,' declared Teti. 'We must distance the danger from Thebes and protect the person of Pharaoh, who must grow in wisdom, strength and harmony.'

The queen saw from Ahmose's expression that he had nothing to add.

'Heray and Qaris,' she said, 'you are charged with the pharaoh's safety. You shall have the usual palace guard at your disposal and reinforcements whom I shall choose myself. If we are defeated at the Port of Kamose, a pigeon will bring you the order to leave with the king so that he may continue the struggle.'

The work was so terrifying that Minos dared not look at it. With a superhuman effort, he had succeeded in making the griffins' gaze unbearable. It seemed as if the two monsters flanking the emperor's throne were ready to leap forward and tear apart anyone who tried to approach.

'Just one more small thing,' rasped Apophis, 'and it will be perfect. The left eye lacks the last shade of cruelty that will make my two guardians utterly merciless.'

Swallowing hard, the painter asked the question that had been haunting him. 'What is to be my next task, Majesty?'

'You and your companions shall decorate the palaces in the Delta towns. Thanks to you, the gods of Egypt will disappear one after the other. Everywhere, people will undergo the ordeals of the bull and the labyrinth, and no one will dream of rebelling against me.'

So the emperor was allowing the painter to live in order to continue his propaganda work. Minos would never see Minoa again.

Leaving the artist, Apophis went to the small, secret room hollowed out in the centre of the fortress. No one could hear what was said in there.

The emperor sat down heavily on a sycamore-wood chair.

Soon, two guards announced the arrival of Commander Jannas.

'Come in and close the door, Jannas.'

Although accustomed to battles and death, the commander was impressed by the place and by this man who knew how to use his ugliness as a menacing weapon.

Apophis asked, 'Are you satisfied with our new security arrangements, Commander?'

'Yes, my lord. No Egyptian raid could possibly succeed, Avaris is impregnable.'

'But you don't think that is enough, do you?'

'Indeed, Majesty. I still believe it necessary to attack the enemy front, to break through it and destroy Thebes.'

'The time has come,' said Apophis. 'Launch the first wave of attack.'

# 14

Emheb was dazzled. Dazzled by the nobility of Queen Ahhotep, whose appearance at the prow of the flagship had transformed exhausted, despairing soldiers into tough fighters determined to die for her. Dazzled also by the measures that had turned the Port of Kamose into a true military base, capable of withstanding a Hyksos attack.

With his usual minute attention to detail, Moon had created an imposing barrage of war-boats. On the banks of the river skilled artificers had dug deep ditches which, when hidden by branches covered with grass and earth, would trap the Hyksos chariots. The archers would be drawn up in several lines, to cut down any enemy troops who got past the first obstacles. In addition, at Neshi's suggestion many large tents had been erected in the shade of the sycamores and palm-trees, for the troops to use while the stone-cutters were building the barracks. As for Moustache and the Afghan, they were submitting their troops to intensive training. And the queen had set another grand plan in motion: to dig subsidiary water-channels, which might prove decisive in the coming battle.

When the queen held aloft the Sword of Amon before the calm, confident army, each soldier felt invincible. The blade flamed in the dawn sun. Powerful rays of intense light flashed from it and touched their hearts. And Emheb felt ever more admiration for the queen, whom he had known since she was a passionate, stubborn girl, and whose faith in freedom never ceased to grow.

But one thing bothered him. 'How is Thebes being defended, Majesty?'

'There is not a single boat left there, not a single regiment, and the military base is almost empty. It is here that everything will be played out, Emheb. The Hyksos must not get past the Port of Kamose.'

The role of spy was definitely not an easy one to play, especially in the face of an adversary like Ahhotep. Getting a message to Avaris was extremely difficult anyway, and first a thorny question had to be asked: what information should be sent?

The queen had had the good sense to divide up the preparations for battle, assigning a specific task to each person, but she alone knew the entire plan. Was the abandonment of Thebes merely a bait? Would the Port of Kamose really be the main front, or would it serve as a rearward base for an offensive in the Delta? The spy could not answer these questions, or many others. And why had the emperor not attacked? Was it because he was having difficulties in Avaris which obliged him to remain there?

Watching and waiting patiently for the right moment: applying this strategy had already enabled the spy to kill two pharaohs, Seqen and Kamose. So common sense told him not to change it now.

The condemned man, a chariot officer who had dared criticize the emperor's waiting game, had just got past the third door of the labyrinth: a notable achievement. Evading the deadly traps, he was proving as cunning as he was quick. A gleam of interest flickered in Apophis's eyes.

In front of the fourth door, a privet arch, red earth was spread over the ground. The officer saw that it was studded with pieces of glass which, had he run across them, would have stabbed up into the soles of his feet. Having avoided this trap, he grew bolder and managed to get a grip on the arch. He found his balance, picked up speed and jumped over the danger zone.

That was his mistake.

In the greenery lurked a double-edged blade, which he seized with both hands. As the pain hit him, he let go and fell heavily on his back on the shards of glass. His neck pierced, he bled to death.

'Another useless idiot,' remarked Apophis. 'Did you enjoy it at all, Windswept?'

Sitting at the right hand of the emperor, his sister had watched the spectacle rather distractedly. The officer she had sent to his death had not been a good lover.

'I can't help thinking about my troubles.'

'What are they?'

'Minos has done everything you asked. Why won't you let him go back to Minoa?'

'Because I still need his talent.'

'The other Minoan painters are talented, too.'

'Minos is different – you know that very well.'

'What if I beg the emperor to grant me this favour?'

'The love of your heart will never leave Egypt.'

Moustache could not believe the gods had ever created a more beautiful work of art than She-Cat's body. He was not the only one to appreciate her beauty: she attracted many admiring looks from the soldiers, through they knew her husband's character well and so never overstepped the mark.

Whenever Moustache was with her, as now, he forgot the war, the war that had led him far into the south where he had met this Nubian with her long, golden-brown legs. When he joined the rebel movement, he had sworn that he would never become attached to a woman – given how slim a front-line soldier's chance of survival was, it was better to move from one mistress to another, as the Afghan did. But he hadn't counted on She-Cat's magic and her stubbornness. Once she had chosen Moustache, she had proved as tenacious as a jungle vine. And what a delicious prison that vine was!

Drawing away from him, She-Cat looked at him mockingly. 'What are you thinking about at the moment?'

'About you, of course.'

'But not only about me. Tell me the truth.'

Moustache gazed up at the ceiling. 'There's danger coming.'

She-Cat did not smile. 'You aren't afraid, are you?'

'Of course I am. It won't be easy, fighting one against ten. You could even say the battle is lost before it is begun.'

'Aren't you forgetting Queen Ahhotep?'

'How could I ever do that? Without her, Apophis would have conquered all of Egypt a long time ago. We shall die for the Queen of Freedom and not one of us will regret it.'

Someone knocked at the door. 'It's the Afghan.'

She-Cat wrapped herself in a linen shawl.

'Come in,' said Moustache.

'Sorry to bother you, but things are moving. Jannas and his troops have left Avaris and are heading south. The commander had a nasty surprise in the outskirts of Memphis: the people of the city had wiped out the Hyksos guard-posts.'

'The people will all be slaughtered.'

'Yes, probably, but they succeeded in slowing down Jannas's advance and warning us.'

'Is the queen going to send them reinforcements?'

'Only two regiments: yours and mine.'

'Then we'll be slaughtered as well.'

'That will depend on how quickly we move. The aim of the operation is to lure the Hyksos towards the Port of Kamose. It's tempting to pursue fugitives and kill them, isn't it? But, obviously, if we fail we die.'

Moustache began to dress. 'We must distribute strong beer to the men.'

'That's already been done,' replied the Afghan. 'Now we must explain the situation to them.'

'Explanations won't do any good. They'll have to be content to die as heroes, like their leaders.'

'Don't be so pessimistic.'

'Don't tell me we've known worse situations than this!'

'I won't.'

'I'm coming with you,' declared She-Cat.

'No you aren't,' retorted Moustache. 'And that is an order.'

The couple embraced for a long time, convinced that this would be their last kiss ever.

# 15

Windswept had been wrong to plead with the emperor and reveal her love for the painter. By trying to give Minos the happiness he dreamt of, she had placed him in danger. She decided to tell him she knew his true intentions, so that he would stop plotting against Apophis. Together, they would learn to endure reality.

Night had long since fallen, but the Minoan had still not come to her bedchamber. She lay there alone, lost in thought.

Eventually, unable to rest, she got up and went down the corridor that led to his workshop. It was empty.

Perhaps he was with his fellow painters. She found them in the dining-hall set aside for them, but Minos was not with them.

Anxiously, Windswept ran to his room. It, too, was empty.

In panic, she questioned several guards, but to no avail. Methodically, she searched the citadel. And at last she found him, in a shed where linen chests were stored.

Minos had been hanged from a hook strong enough to take the weight of his body.

Jannas went to see Khamudi. Each man was accompanied by his bodyguards. The commander would have dispensed with this measure, but it was Khamudi who paid the soldiers and, before beginning the conquest of Thebes, the situation must be clearly spelt out.

The two men dispensed with the usual polite formalities.

Jannas said bluntly, 'The Hyksos army consists of two hundred and forty thousand men. I am not planning to withdraw any men from Canaan or the Delta, nor, of course, from the capital. Therefore I shall leave with fifty thousand soldiers, to whom you must immediately pay a special bonus.'

'Has the emperor agreed to this?'

'He has.'

'I must check, Commander. Being responsible for public finances, I cannot make any mistakes.'

'Check, but do it quickly.'

'In your absence, I shall be in charge of the security of Avaris. Issue orders that all forces are to obey me without question.'

'It is the emperor's orders they must obey.'

'That is exactly what I meant.'

When Jannas inspected the army, he was disagreeably surprised to find that a lot of officers and men had become regular users of the drug sold by Khamudi. Some might fight even more fiercely in battle, but most of them had lost a great deal of their energy. Nevertheless, the Hyksos' weapons were so superior that the Egyptians could not possibly hold out for long.

Besides the destruction of the guard-posts, the outlying districts of Memphis held another unpleasant surprise for Jannas: a series of ambushes in which hundreds of Hyksos were killed. The slingshots and bows wielded by the rebels, who were as fast and deadly as hornets, proved formidably effective, and the chariots got stuck in the narrow alleyways so often that using them was pointless. So Jannas decided to take one house after another, then destroy all those harbouring rebels.

Cleansing the area around the great city took him several weeks, so determined were his adversaries. Even when surrounded, they refused to surrender and preferred to die with their weapons in their hands.

'These people are mad,' said his assistant.

'No, they merely hate us. The hope that the Queen of Freedom keeps alive gives them almost supernatural courage. When she dies, they will go back to being sheep.'

'Commander, would it not be a good idea to forget Memphis and head south?'

'No, because the people of Memphis would rush out of the city and attack us from the rear.'

The gates of the 'Balance of the Two Lands' refused to open when Jannas reached them. That meant the rebels believed they could withstand a siege.

Jannas was organizing it when his assistant reported an attack by Egyptian regiments coming from the south.

'They have come to help the rebels, sir, and they are no amateurs: our vanguard has been wiped out.'

Jannas realized that his task would be much less easy than he had expected. Little by little the Egyptians had learnt the art of war, and they were now a far from negligible power. Moreover, they had the will to liberate their country.

'We must stop these regiments entering Memphis,' he decreed.

'Part of our troops will encircle the city and the rest will follow me.'

Moustache and the Afghan were not ordinary generals who conformed to well-established custom, adopted a rigid battle-plan and watched from afar as their men were killed. Their early experience as rebels, used to surviving in even the worst conditions, had taught them to act as promptly and destructively as possible. They therefore divided their troops, so that in case of failure their losses would not be irreparable.

The Hyksos' over-strict discipline had been the rebels' best ally. The Egyptians struck in successive waves, after killing the officers and sinking the lead Hyksos war-boat. Some officers wanted to exploit their advantage by pushing the offensive further, but Moustache gave the order to beat a retreat aboard fast sailing-boats.

'We've only ten dead and twenty wounded,' reported the Afghan, 'and we did them plenty of damage. If all goes well, Jannas should give chase.'

'Our archers will kill the helmsmen,' said Moustache, 'and our strongest swimmers – led by myself – will pierce holes in the boats' hulls.'

'Don't overestimate your strength. And don't forget that you're here first and foremost to command.'

For a few hours, the two men wondered if Jannas would raze Memphis to the ground before pursuing them. But at high noon the first sails of the heavy Hyksos boats appeared.

Not a single word was spoken. Every man knew what he had to do.

The Hyksos scout's job was to detect any suspicious movement on the riverbank and to alert the lead boat immediately. He was getting more and more uneasy, even though there was no one and nothing suspicious to be seen.

Nothing, that is, except a thicket of tamarisks whose branches were moving in the wind; in fact, moving a little too much, as if enemies were trying to hide in them. But why would they conceal themselves so badly? The scout lay down on the path and watched. There was no further sign of life in the tamarisks. It must have been just the wind, after all.

He continued his exploration, turning to look behind him several times. The countryside seemed quiet, and there were no boats on the river. The Egyptians had fled south like rabbits, but they would not escape from Jannas's army. The scout climbed to the top of a palm-tree to signal to his colleague, who was inspecting the other bank, that all was well.

The same message reached the lead boat, which continued its slow progress up the river. Moustache waited until it was well within range before unleashing his archers, while the Afghan and his men killed the scouts.

But the Hyksos reacted so quickly that only by retreating hastily did the Egyptians manage to save themselves. Arrows whistled past the Afghan's ears, and he saw several young soldiers fall nearby.

'Our ambushes inflict nothing but scratches,' grumbled Moustache. 'Jannas doesn't care if he suffers a few losses. He has decided to advance, and we cannot stop him.'

## 16

Encircled and defenceless, Memphis was awaiting its total destruction, which the emperor was delaying so as to cause the citizens greater torture. Jannas's army was forging south, and the purge was proceeding apace . . . Apophis had plenty of reasons to be pleased. As for Minos's murder, that was a minor irritation. The other Minoan painters would do the work the emperor had planned.

Apophis knew the murder had been committed by Aberia on Tany's orders. But, as Minos had been plotting against him in a minor way and would have been sent to the labyrinth sooner or later, the emperor had decided not to punish his wife.

Windswept came in and bowed. 'I should like to ask a favour.'

'Forget that painter. He was unworthy of you.'

'I should like to take his body back to Minoa.'

Apophis was curious. 'What a strange idea. Why should you want to do that?'

'On one hand, to prevent King Minos's being angry, by telling him that his favourite artist died from natural causes. On the other, to seduce him and sleep with him in order to learn his thoughts and make him my slave.'

An evil smile lit up the emperor's face. 'You want to attack a king . . . Well, why not? You are as beautiful as ever, so you have every chance of succeeding. Ridding me of Minos's corpse and using it as a weapon against the Minoans is a fine idea. I shall place a ship at your disposal.'

Rascal landed on the deck of the flagship, just in front of Ahhotep. After congratulating and stroking him, the queen read the message he had brought. Then she convened her council of war.

'The good news,' she said, 'is that, although Memphis is surrounded, it is resisting and delaying part of Jannas's troops. The bad news is that the traps set by the Afghan and Moustache have not worked. A powerful, heavily armed force is heading towards us.'

'If I understand you correctly, Majesty,' ventured Emheb, 'you are not convinced that our front will hold.'

'It must hold.'

'Everything is ready to hold off an attack,' said Neshi. 'Jannas will certainly not expect strong opposition – he thinks we are fleeing towards Thebes.'

Another carrier-pigeon from the south alighted on the deck. It was one of Rascal's flock, and flew back and forth to the royal palace.

The short text made the queen turn pale. 'I must return to Thebes at once. My mother is dying.'

Taking advantage of Jannas's absence, Khamudi was arranging a dinner for the senior officers stationed in the capital, in order to offer them a fine quantity of drugs, houses in the Delta, horses and slaves, in exchange for their unhesitating co-operation.

Jannas would try to crush the enemy as the emperor had ordered – it was obviously necessary. However, the commander must not become enraged, empty the Delta garrisons and disorganize Avaris's defences. Khamudi had to ensure the safety of the emperor and the capital by avoiding any ill-advised ventures. From now on, no order issued by Jannas would be carried out without Khamudi's assent.

None of the senior officers Khamudi approached had rejected his invitation, so he was sure he was winning back all the ground he had lost. By ensuring that he had these men's friendship, Khamudi was sapping Jannas's authority and reducing his support. So the High Treasurer was in an excellent mood when he returned home, and eager to enjoy a lavish meal.

But the sight of Windswept waiting in the antechamber took away his appetite. There was such contempt in her beautiful eyes that it made him shiver.

'I wish to see your wife,' she said calmly.

'She . . . she is at the bedside of the lady Tany.'

'I shall wait for her as long as is necessary.'

'Would you like some refreshment?'

'That will not be necessary.'

'But please, will you not sit down and make yourself comfortable?'

'I prefer to remain standing.'

Khamudi could not meet Windswept's gaze, which was no longer in any way that of a seductress. Luckily, just then his wife made a noisy entrance, calling loudly for her maid.

She, too, was astonished to see the visitor. 'Windswept! What a delightful surprise, but—'

'You ordered Minos's murder.'

'What? How dare you—'

'You wanted the head of the man I loved and you got it. That has made you think you're all-powerful, but you're wrong. You're nothing but a madwoman, and you will die as one.'

Yima ran to her husband. 'Listen to her, my darling. She's threatening me!'

Appalled, Khamudi tried to calm his wife down, while not angering the emperor's sister. 'It must all be a misunderstanding, and I am sure that—'

Windswept's eyes blazed. 'The murderers and their accomplices will be punished,' she promised. 'The fire of heaven will strike down upon them.'

Slowly, she stalked out of the villa, indifferent to the hysterical crying that shook Yima from head to foot.


With a kick, Jannas turned over the body of the Egyptian archer his men had at last managed to kill. Perched in a sycamore tree, the marksman had killed many Hyksos.

'Have the others been dealt with?'

'There is only one left, sir,' replied his assistant. 'And he soon will be.'

Jannas saw the sails of three warships burning; all three had been badly damaged and were in danger of sinking. 'Bring me the captains of those ships.'

The three captains hurried to him and saluted.

'You knew the risks,' snapped Jannas. 'Why did you not take the necessary precautions?'

'The enemy is very skilful, sir,' said the most experienced man. 'We did not make any mistakes.'

'Wrong. You were beaten by someone weaker than yourself, and that is unworthy of a Hyksos. It was your sailors who averted a disaster, so I shall choose the new captains from among them. As for you, your corpses will decorate the prows of your ships and show the enemy how we punish incompetence.'

Turning aside from the condemned men, Jannas proceeded to make the new appointments immediately.

'Both ashore and on the Nile, the way is clear now,' reported his assistant. 'We can move on without fear.'

'That is what the Egyptians want to make us to believe,' Jannas corrected him, 'and they have sacrificed a lot of brave men to do so. They are only pretending to give up, and are playing on our credulity.

Those ambushes and skirmishes were only the prelude to their real trap, which has been in preparation for a long time. We shall therefore moor the fleet here and scour every inch of land until we have discovered the true positions of their forces.'

## 17

The queen's boat had beaten all records for speed. The moment it touched the quayside at Thebes, the gangplank was hastily put in place and Ahhotep disembarked. Bearers carried her quickly by travelling-chair to the palace, where she was greeted by Qaris, who was clearly overwrought.

'Is my mother still alive?'

'She is on her deathbed, Majesty.'

Ahmose came to meet Ahhotep. 'I have been constantly at my grandmother's bedside,' he assured her. 'She spoke to me about my duties and about the loneliness a king must experience, but she promised that she will always be beside me whenever fear enters my heart. Her only worry, Mother, was that she might not see you again.'

Ahhotep quietly opened the door to Teti the Small's bedchamber.

The old lady had had her servants lift her from her bed, and was sitting facing the setting sun. There was so little life left in her that she was scarcely breathing.

'I am here,' whispered Ahhotep, laying her hand on her mother's.

'That makes me very happy. I begged the goddess of the West to wait until your return. Have the Hyksos attacked?'

'Not yet.'

'They are making a big mistake in letting you organize our defence. For you will succeed, Ahhotep. You were born to win Egypt's freedom, and you will win that victory for all of us, for those who are dead and for the generations to come.' Although extremely weak, Teti's voice was clear. 'Do you know what life is, my dear daughter? The sages wrote the answer in the hieroglyphs. Life is a knot on the belt that separates and links our thinking being and our animal being. It is also the thongs on our sandals that enable us to walk and make progress, the mirror in which we can see the sky, the flower that blossoms. Life is the ear that hears the voice of Ma'at and makes us alive, and the eye that gives us the ability to create.

'You possess all these qualities, Ahhotep, and you must use them so that a pharaoh may be truly reborn on the throne of the living. I have never doubted you, for there is nothing low or ignoble in your heart. You have survived adversity; the fire of hope has nourished your soul. I am going to rest in death, Mut, the divine mother. If the court of the afterlife grants me the gift of rebirth, my *ka* will strengthen yours.

'And now, will you put a little cream on my cheeks and red ochre on my lips? I don't want to take my leave looking unkempt.'

'Of course I will, Mother.'

In the few moments it took Ahhotep to fetch Teti's face-paints from the room where they were kept, her mother died. Concerned, as always, for elegance, she had not wished her daughter to hear her last sigh.

Keeping her promise, Ahhotep applied her mother's facepaint with great care.

Ahhotep perfumed the palace as never before. The gods were formed of subtle essences, and the sweet scents would enchant the nose of Teti the Small, whose body had been mummified according to the ancient rules. Djehuty, the High Priest of Amon, directed the funeral vigil during which the dead woman became at once a Hathor and an Osiris, thanks to the words of glorification.

Teti's heart of flesh was replaced by a stone scarab clad in gold, as it was for all great initiates. This would not bear witness against her in the hall of judgment and would guarantee her eternal youth.

As the Wife of God, Ahhotep presided over the funeral ceremonies for her mother, that remarkable woman who had prevented Thebes from dying and had taken part in every stage of the war of liberation. Teti and Ahhotep had very different characters, and had not been in the habit of exchanging fulsome confidences. But they had understood each other with a look, always steering the ship in the same direction.

When the entrance to the house of eternity was sealed, hundreds of swallows flew over the burial-ground on the west bank of Thebes, bearing away the righteous soul of Teti the Small. Tomorrow, at dawn, it would be reborn with the new sun.

Ahhotep suddenly felt so alone that she was tempted to give up an unequal struggle whose outcome was all too easy to predict. But that would be to betray her family and make her unworthy of an entire people whom she had persuaded to fight and never weaken.

Her son came and stood close to her. 'I shall never forget Grandmother,' he promised. 'When we have driven out the invaders, we shall pay her great homage. And, Mother, I haven't been idle while you were away. First, I have been reading a great deal; also, I watch people; lastly, I recruit.'

Ahhotep was astonished. 'Whom do you recruit?'

'New soldiers. I know all our forces must be concentrated on the Port of Kamose, but Thebes cannot do nothing. I carry out regular inspections of the naval boatyard, where our carpenters are building new war-boats, and I travel through the outlying districts and the countryside to recruit volunteers. The officers of the royal guard train them, and Heray sees that they are fed and housed. That's how you and my father created our first regiment, isn't it? Soon Thebes won't be defenceless any more.'

Despite his young age, thought Ahhotep, he was scarcely a boy any more. Within him, the office was already beginning to devour the individual.

'I am proud of you, Ahmose,' she said.

Suddenly, the young pharaoh frowned. 'I have been robbed: someone stole a pair of ceremonial sandals. It was Qaris who noticed, but we can't tell when they were stolen, because I hadn't worn them since the coronation.'

'Do you suspect anyone?'

'No. Dozens of people could have got into the room where they were kept.'

Was it really a simple theft, wondered Ahhotep, or was it something more sinister? Had the spy struck again? Harming the pharaoh, killing him like his predecessors: that must still be the spy's aim.

She asked, 'When you travel about, do you take all the necessary precautions?'

'As far as possible.'

'Is your bedchamber guarded at night?'

'Yes, by men I chose myself.'

'Apart from this theft, has anything else happened?'

'No, nothing.'

When they got back to the palace, Ahhotep and Ahmose had to console Qaris who, for the first time since Teti had appointed him head steward of the palace, felt unable to carry out his duties.

'I am too old, Your Majesties. Replace me with a younger, stronger man.'

'Teti the Small is irreplaceable,' declared the queen, 'and so are you, Qaris. How could I find a successor in the middle of a war? This palace must continue to live, and who but you would have the skill to see that all the daily rituals are properly carried out? You must pass on everything you know to King Ahmose.'

'You may rely upon me, Majesty.'

Mother and son spent the evening beside the sacred lake at the Temple of Karnak. Here, where the gods' spirit reigned, all conflict seemed utterly impossible.

'Come here often,' advised Ahhotep, 'so that you may detach yourself from immediate reality and soar above it, as if you were a bird. Spread out your thoughts as the bird spreads its wings and gaze upon the waters of the *Nun*, where life was born and to which it will return when time is at an end. The moment is your kingdom, Ahmose, eternity your wet-nurse; and yet it is here and now that you must combat the forces of darkness.'

'Are you leaving for the Port of Kamose tomorrow?'

Ahhotep tenderly embraced this young man who was threatened by a thousand deaths. 'First thing tomorrow, yes. Continue with your recruiting, and see there is no slackening of effort at the boatyard.'

'Without Grandmother, everything will be more difficult.'

'This is only the beginning of your trials.'

# 18

Windswept was the only passenger who was not paralysed with fear during the voyage from Egypt to Minoa. The first few days had passed without incident, but a storm transformed the next three into a living hell. Even the captain had been seasick, and three crew-members had been swept overboard.

Indifferent to the raging of the sea, Windswept thought only of Minos, of the intense happiness she had known with him, of the hours of pleasure that filled her thoughts constantly. Her lover seemed so close, yet she would never again hold him in her arms.

The Minoan officer who welcomed the emperor's sister when the ship reached the Great Island confined himself to brief courtesies, and escorted her to King Minos's palace at Knossos. Windswept did not even glance at the countryside as they travelled.

She had no greater interest in the palace – or, indeed, in the King of Minoa, a bearded old man with an imposing presence, who sat on a stone throne flanked by two painted griffins.

The sight of those two fantastical beasts jolted her from her apathy. They were at once splendid and disturbing, but did not bear the mark of her lover's genius. Windswept noticed that the reception hall was filled with dignitaries whose hair was meticulously dressed, either in long, wavy locks or in short curls. They were all fascinated by her beauty.

'Majesty,' she said, 'I have brought you the body of Minos the painter, to whom you granted the honour of bearing your name.'

'How did he die?'

'King of Minoa, I would speak with you alone.'

Murmurs of protest were raised against such insolence.

'Majesty,' said one of his advisers, 'do not take any risks, I beg you.'

Minos smiled. 'If you fear that such a beautiful woman may be driven by evil intentions, search her.'

'No one is to touch me,' ordered Windswept. 'You have my word that I carry no weapons.'

'That will suffice,' said Minos. 'Leave us, all of you.' He got up from his throne. 'Let us go and sit on that bench.'

Windswept gazed blankly into the distance.

'What use is so much beauty when the soul is filled with despair?' asked the king.

'I loved Minos the painter. I wanted to live with him, here in Minoa.'

'Am I to understand that his was not a natural death?'

'He was murdered,' admitted Windswept, her face contorted in pain.

The king let this sink in for a long time. 'Do you know who committed the crime?'

'A female assassin in the pay of the wives of the High Treasurer and Emperor Apophis. But the guiltiest person of all is Apophis himself. Nothing can be done without his agreement. He permitted Minos's murder because Minos was conspiring against him so that he could come back to Minoa. There was nothing I could do to save him.'

'I condemn this vile deed,' said the king, 'but what is the use of protesting?'

'The Hyksos must be destroyed,' declared Windswept solemnly.

'Has your grief robbed you of your reason?'

'I have come to tell you two vital state secrets. The first is that there is bitter enmity between the emperor's right-hand man, High Treasurer Khamudi, and the commander-in-chief of the army and war-fleet, Jannas. Khamudi and Jannas hate each other and dream only of tearing each other apart. Jannas is a skilled and ferocious soldier, but Khamudi will defeat him, even it means doing harm to the empire.'

'But that would make no difference. The Hyksos forces are invincible.'

'Not any longer – and that is the second secret. Thebes has rebelled, and the troops commanded by Queen Ahhotep have proved extraordinarily courageous. Since her young son Ahmose was crowned Pharaoh, Egypt has regained its strength and resolution. Ahhotep has only one aim: to liberate her country.'

'She will never succeed!'

'The army of her elder son, Kamose, actually succeeded in breaking through all the Hyksos lines and seizing three hundred boats in the port of Avaris itself.'

The king was astounded. 'What? Surely you must be exaggerating!'

'Form an alliance with Ahhotep and stop relying on the Hyksos for help. If you do not, sooner or later Minoa will be destroyed.'

'But to cease being the emperor's vassal would be tantamount to signing my own death warrant.'

'Not if your alliance with Ahhotep brings about her victory.'

Minos got to his feet. 'I need to think. My steward will take you to your rooms.'

While a horde of servants attended to Windswept, the king assembled his close advisers and informed them of her revelations.

'She must be mad,' declared the envoy in charge of presenting tributes to Apophis. 'She sleeps with scores of Hyksos dignitaries, encourages them to speak indiscreetly, and then denounces them to the emperor if she suspects them of the slightest reservation about him. How could she possibly be so much in love with Minos the painter that she hates her own people?'

'She appeared sincere to me.'

'It is a trap, Majesty. She is trying to seduce you, too, in order to know your intentions and draw down Appophis's thunderbolts on you. Neither Jannas nor Khamudi will disobey him. As for Queen Ahhotep, she's nothing more than a troublemaker whose rebellion will be punished with the greatest cruelty.'

The other advisers agreed.

The king seemed to hesitate. 'First of all,' he decided, 'we must get rid of her. I shall write to Apophis informing him that her ship was wrecked off our coast and that, in spite of our best efforts, we were unable to retrieve her body. As regards the rest, we shall think upon it.'

The commander of the chariot corps charged with encircling Memphis watched the progress of the tenth assault he had launched against the great white-walled city. True, he had seized most of the suburbs after fierce house-to-house fighting; true, the Egyptians were suffering heavy losses; but they were holding fast.

The entire city had risen up, convinced that the Queen of Freedom would fly to its aid. Memphis would eventually fall, but the siege would last a long time. So the commander had sent messages to Jannas and Khamudi, asking for reinforcements. With a few thousand more soldiers, he could force open the gates of the city.

Jannas's reply had been in the negative: busy with the reconquest of the South, he could not spare a single man. But, he said, there were such large reserves of infantry in the Delta that no doubt the High Treasurer would oblige.

Consequently the officer was astonished when he received the official message, written in the name of the emperor. Since the safety of Avaris was of prime importance, he must resolve the problem of Memphis on his own – the rebels' obstinacy would mean they would starve in the end.

Afraid of angering his superiors, the officer dared not press the point. He would carry out his orders to the letter, as a good Hyksos should, and would take whatever time he needed to knock down the white walls of Memphis and put its inhabitants to death.

## 19

When the flagship docked, all the soldiers in the Port of Kamose shouted for joy. The Queen of Freedom had returned to lead the Egyptian forces, increasing their potential tenfold; and she would first halt the Hyksos in their tracks, then retake the offensive.

Since the town had become a military base, it had changed greatly. Permanent buildings had replaced the tents, stone quays enabled supplies to be unloaded more easily, and a new boatyard ensured that the warboats were properly maintained.

'What progress has been made?' Ahhotep asked Emheb.

'Everything is ready, Majesty.'

'Is Moon satisfied with his defences?'

'As satisfied as he will ever be.'

'We must deploy our men immediately. According to Rascal's last message, Jannas is not far away.'

The last clash with the regiments commanded by the Afghan and Moustache had been particularly violent. Jannas's army was winning victory after victory and continuing its slow southward progress, but it had lost two more warships and its losses were far from insignificant. Everyone praised his wariness. The Egyptians joined battle in the most unexpected places, using small units destined for certain death.

'The enemy does not lack courage,' Jannas admitted to his officers. 'We can be certain that they won't lay down their arms, but will fight to the last man.'

'The worrying thing, sir,' said his assistant, 'is that we still do not know exactly where Ahhotep has massed the main body of her troops. All our scouts have been killed – not one has survived to bring us that information. In my opinion, the queen has doubled back to Thebes, and that's where she will await us.'

'She would be taking an enormous risk,' objected Jannas, 'not only of military defeat but of the destruction of her capital. No, I believe she has established her main line of defence far from Thebes, certainly in Middle Egypt. I sense that we are close to our objective.'

Utterly exhausted, the Afghan and Moustache arrived back at the Port of Kamose with the tattered remnants of their regiments.

She-Cat and her assistants immediately began to tend the wounded, some of whose injuries were fatal. Fortunately, Moustache had suffered only a leg wound and multiple bruises, which would easily be healed by the Nubian's remedies.

Queen Ahhotep received the two men in her little palace, whose main room was a shrine in which she had laid the Sword of Amon.

'I am sorry, Majesty,' said the Afghan, 'but all we could do was to slow Jannas down, and we paid a high price for doing even that much.'

Moustache was as downcast as his companion.

'You carried out your mission perfectly,' said Ahhotep. 'You won us precious time, enough for us to dig channels and divert the water.'

A faint smile lit up the two warriors' tired faces.

'Then our men did not die for nothing,' said Moustache.

'Quite the opposite: they played a vital role. If you had not succeeded in slowing Jannas down, we would have had no chance of victory.'

'We killed many Hyksos and did some damage to their fleet,' said the Afghan, 'but they are still far superior in terms of numbers and weapons.'

'In your opinion, when will Jannas attack?'

'He has become so wary that he is advancing very cautiously,' replied Moustache. 'We must go on killing his scouts so that he does not find the Port of Kamose until the very last moment. I think it will take him three weeks to get here.'

'I agree,' nodded the Afghan.

Three weeks had passed since the last serious clash with the Egyptians. However, the Hyksos continued to advance extremely slowly. There was not a single boat on the Nile, and all the villages on the riverbanks had been abandoned.

'Obviously, the enemy must have retreated,' said Jannas's assistant. 'Should we not speed up our advance towards Thebes?'

Jannas shook his head firmly. 'We still do not know the enemy's exact position. But we can be sure the Egyptians are preparing more ambushes. For us to hurry would be suicide. It is better to gain territory cubit by cubit.'

'But we have not met any opposition for several days, sir.'

'That is precisely what worries me. The Egyptians must be regrouping in an attempt to bar our way.'

As the war-fleet rounded a bend in the Nile, the Hyksos saw the wall of boats created by Moon at the Port of Kamose. Their mouth watered with anticipation: a real battle at last!

Coldly Jannas analysed the situation. On the banks there were palm-trees and tamarisks, where Egyptian archers were no doubt hiding. In front of him was the major part of the enemy fleet, composed of boats which were swifter than his but also lighter.

'Commander, look! It's her!'

At the prow of one of the Egyptian vessels, whose standard was decorated with the sun-disc in its crescent-shaped ship, stood a woman wearing a gold diadem, dressed in a red gown and holding the Sword of Amon, which glittered in the sunlight.

Queen Ahhotep: it could indeed be no one else.

'She is taunting us and trying to lure us on,' said Jannas. 'The centre of the barrage will open, we will enter it and be caught in the trap. Clever – but not clever enough. Ahhotep has underestimated me, and that mistake will be her last.'

'What are your orders, sir?'

'We shall attack across the whole width of the river, and drive right through the barrage. The battle will be hard and there will be fierce hand-to-hand fighting, but the element of surprise will work in our favour.'

'What about our chariots?'

'We shall keep them in reserve to crush Thebes.'

The heavy Hyksos boats moved slowly into position. Surely the Egyptians would soon realize that their plan had not worked, and would disperse, becoming easy prey.

But nothing moved.

The queen is no coward, thought Jannas. She prefers to die rather than withdraw. A brave madness; but madness all the same.

Sheltered behind shields, the Hyksos archers made ready to return the enemy's fire. To their amazement, they did not have to fire a single arrow. The whole fleet, except for the ships transporting chariots, advanced peacefully towards the floating barrage, which it could destroy without difficulty.

Suddenly, the banks of the Nile seemed to be torn apart. Palm-trees sawn through at the base of their trunks were pushed down on to the attackers. Great thickets of tamarisks were dragged aside to unblock subsidiary channels, from which scores of war-boats emerged and rushed at the Hyksos.

It was a ferocious battle. There were archers with flaming arrows, grappling-irons for boarding vessels, furious skirmishing in which many men died. Then Ahhotep's fast, easily manoeuvrable war-boats joined the fighting, and several Hyksos ships were overrun, set alight and sunk.

White-lipped, Jannas ordered the retreat.

## 20

Ahmose was no longer a child. He had become a young man whose presence impressed everyone, and each day he gave yet more proof of his fitness for the office of pharaoh. Although less athletic than Kamose had been, he had the bearing of a resolute king, whose seriousness and ability to work hard astonished those close to him.

With the aid of Qaris, Neshy and Heray, his closest advisers, Ahmose had taken charge of the Theban province and the neighbouring regions, and agriculture there was flourishing. Thanks to the careful government for which he stood, the king could feed not only the civilian population but also the soldiers at the front, and could even build up reserves in case the Nile's annual flood was poor.

The damage caused by the wrath of Set was no more than a bad memory. At Ahmose's instigation, intensive rebuilding had been undertaken: those who had suffered most had been speedily rehoused and their living conditions improved markedly. Within a few months, all Thebans would have a suitable house or other living-quarters. A new city was being born, one which was even more pleasant to live in.

Almost every day the king went to the boatyard, where the carpenters were working hard, well aware that they probably held the key to victory. Egypt would need many war-ships, their main weapons against the Hyksos. Ahmose knew each craftsman, took an interest in his family and his health. Whenever he saw that one was exhausted, he ordered him to rest. But he dealt ruthlessly with idlers and malingerers, who were sentenced to forced labour. In the middle of war, the king would not tolerate cowardice in any form.

As he had promised his mother, Ahmose had also taken charge of the defence of Thebes. Travelling around the countryside and villages, he succeeded in creating a small army of volunteers willing to fight to the death to prevent the Hyksos from destroying Amon's city. He had no illusions about the effectiveness of this modest force, but its existence soothed the Thebans' fears and enabled them still to believe in a better future. Like his father before him, Ahmose trained true soldiers at the Theban military base, with a view to future battles.

The king was in a small town south of Thebes, enlisting new recruits, when he heard someone call for help. Accompanied by his hand-picked guards, Ahmose entered the farm building the shouts were coming from.

Two recruiting-officers were threatening to whip a dazzlingly beautiful young girl.

'What is going on here?' demanded the king.

'This traitor refuses to say where her brother is hiding. You ordered us to check the civilian status of every man in the province, Majesty, and that is what we are doing.'

'Well?' said Ahmose, looking straight into the girl's eyes. 'You had better explain yourself.'

She gave him a look as straight as his own. 'My parents are dead, and my brother and I take care of the farm they left to us. If he is forced to join the army, how am I supposed to manage on my own?'

'No one is forced to join my army. But your brother may be no more than a fugitive. How can I tell if what you say is the truth?'

'In the name of Pharaoh, I swear it is.'

'Leave us,' Ahmose ordered his men. He could not stop gazing at the young woman, who was tall, naturally elegant, and proud, with the bearing of a queen. 'You are in fact standing before Pharaoh. What is your name?'

'Nefertari.'

'Nefertari, "the Beauty of Beauties". The name was well chosen.'

The compliment did not make the young woman blush. She merely said, 'About my brother, Majesty, what is your decision?'

'Since you have given me your word, he shall continue to tend his farm. It is too much work for one man, so I have decided to grant him the assistance of two peasants, who will be paid by my government.'

At last she showed emotion. 'Majesty, how can I ever thank you?'

'By leaving this place and accompanying me to the palace.'

'To the palace? But . . .'

'Your brother no longer needs you, Nefertari, and your place is no longer here.'

'Are you forbidding me to see him again?'

'Of course not. But we are at war, and we must all play our parts to the best of our abilities.'

'And mine is not to help my brother?'

'It is now to help your king.'

'But how?'

'A woman who knows how to manage an estate is undoubtedly

good at organizing. I need someone to supervise the weaving workshops that make sails for our warships, and to help Steward Qaris, whose strength is beginning to fail. It is a heavy responsibility, but I believe you are capable of taking it on.'

An infinitely sweet smile lit up Nefertari's face.

'Then you accept?'

'I know nothing of the court's customs, Majesty, and I—'

'You will learn quickly, I am sure.'

The royal procession was approaching Thebes when the commander of the guard halted. Immediately several soldiers surrounded the pharaoh and Nefertari.

'What is it?' asked Ahmose.

'A sentry was supposed to meet us at this guard-post, Majesty. He is not here, so I would advise you to send out scouts.'

'We ought not to separate,' objected the king.

'Majesty, going any further might be dangerous.'

'I must know what is happening.'

Everyone was thinking about the Hyksos attack, which must have begun, and the sack of Thebes, whose streets would be littered with corpses. Not a single building would escape the flames.

'There's no sign of smoke, Majesty.'

The first guard-post they encountered had also been deserted. Had its soldiers fled, or hurried to the city to help their comrades?

Nefertari listened intently. 'I can hear singing coming from the city.'

They went a little closer. It was indeed singing: joyful singing!

An officer came running towards them, gasping for breath. Ahmose's guards brandished their spears.

'Majesty,' cried the officer, 'we have just had a message from the Port of Kamose: Queen Ahhotep has beaten the Hyksos – they're in full retreat!'

## 21

Wearing his usual striped headdress, Jannas appeared before the emperor, whose face was alarmingly pale.

'I require the truth, Commander.'

'Half my fleet was destroyed at the Port of Kamose, but our chariot corps is intact, and I inflicted severe losses on the enemy. Nevertheless, there may be a counter-attack, so I recommend destroying Memphis.'

'There is a more urgent matter,' said Apophis. 'That damned city's rebellion has led others to follow suit. Several towns in the Delta are rising up against us. You are to take action immediately.'

As he was leaving the fortress, Jannas encountered Khamudi, who looked angry. Surrounded by their bodyguards, the two men glared at each other defiantly.

'Your campaign was hardly brilliant, Commander,' sneered Khamudi. 'You were supposed to destroy all the Egyptians, but Queen Ahhotep is still alive.'

'Why did you not send reinforcements to my troops besieging Memphis?'

'Because the emperor did not wish it.'

'Did you actually speak to him about it?'

'I will not allow you to question my word, Commander.'

'Your word? There is no such thing, Khamudi. Today, the very safety of the empire hangs in the balance, and it is my task to ensure it. Do not obstruct me, or else . . .'

'Or else what?'

Turning aside contemptuously, Jannas continued on his way.

The members of Ahhotep's council of war were all jubilant.

'You have won a magnificent victory, Majesty,' said Moon. 'It is only a pity that Jannas did not order his chariots to disembark, because they would have fallen into our ditchtraps.'

'Victory is an exaggeration,' replied the queen. 'We lost a great many sailors and war-boats, and Jannas himself is unharmed.'

'That is true, Majesty,' observed Emheb, 'but this time the enemy suffered more than just scratches. It was Jannas in person whom you forced to withdraw. Who could have dreamt of a result like that when we began our fight?'

'The latest news from the Delta is quite good,' added Moon. 'Part of Memphis is resisting the Hyksos siege, and several other cities are ready to rise up.'

'It's too soon – much too soon,' said Moustache. 'The rebels will all be slaughtered.'

'Can we not at least help Memphis?' suggested the Afghan.

'It is essential that we do,' said the queen. 'We must send them food and weapons, so that they can find new ways of pinning down the Hyksos.'

'That is our speciality,' nodded the Afghan. 'Moustache and I will mobilize all the rebel networks and poison the attackers' lives. From now on, they will not spend a single peaceful night. Their food and their water will be poisoned, their patrols attacked, their sentries executed.'

It began in the city of Bubastis, on the vast plains of the Delta.

First of all, a few bold young men killed two Hyksos security guards who tried to throw them in prison. Then some women joined in, to fight the soldiers charged with deporting them to Tjaru. Finally, the people of the city, armed with hatchets and sickles, attacked the barracks and trampled its occupants underfoot. Exulting in this unhoped-for triumph, the rebels celebrated by burning the clothing of the torturers they had killed. Tomorrow, the whole city would rise up!

But then, as dawn broke, they heard the neighing of horses, growing louder and louder. Orders rang out like whip-cracks, clear and precise.

'It's Jannas's chariots!' cried a young man fearfully.

On the plains, no one could withstand the Hyksos' deadly weapon. After a brief parley, the Egyptians walked out in front of the hundreds of chariots, which were drawn up in perfectly straight lines; and threw down their weapons.

'We committed an act of madness,' shouted one of them, 'and we beg for pardon!'

They knelt in submission.

'A bloodless victory,' commented Jannas's assistant.

'With or without weapons, rebels are rebels,' replied the commander. 'Sparing their lives would be a sign of weakness and would rebound against us.' He raised his arm and brought it down sharply, ordering the attack.

Indifferent to their victims' screams, the Hyksos charioteers crushed every last one of the rebels beneath their wheels. Jannas used the same methods at Hwt-Heryib, Taremu and all the other towns where madmen had dared to rebel against the emperor.

Surrounded by his bodyguard of Libyan and Cypriot pirates, High Treasurer Khamudi paraded in his new fringed cloak. His profits from the drugs trade were still growing, and so was his immense fortune, but he was concerned that his success might be threatened by Jannas.

The commander's failure at the Port of Kamose had not damaged his popularity at all. It was incomprehensible, as if most of the army's senior officers simply could not admit that this blinkered soldier was leading them to their doom. Moreover, Khamudi had not yet managed to subvert even one of Jannas's general staff or bodyguards. They were all soldiers who had fought under Jannas for many years and believed in him implicitly. But Khamudi would find a weak link eventually.

In accordance with the emperor's orders, Jannas had killed all the rebels in the Delta cities. The whole army spoke glowingly of him, and this very morning he was to be publicly congratulated by Apophis for his services to the empire. There would be no mention of the humiliating defeat at the Port of Kamose – still less of Queen Ahhotep, who was still defying the Hyksos. If everyone else was becoming blind and deaf, who but Khamudi could save the empire? Yet he, the only one aware of the true dangers, was going to be forced to bow the knee to Jannas.

His secretary brought him a confidential and urgent message from the Hyksos fortress which kept watch on the roads leading to the mountains of Anatolia.

When he had read it, Khamudi at once requested an audience with the emperor, whom he found conversing with Jannas.

'Alas, Majesty,' he said, 'there's bad news, very bad.'

'You may speak freely in front of Jannas,' said Apophis.

'The Anatolian mountain peoples have rebelled again and have attacked our principal fortress. Its commander is asking urgently for help.'

'I predicted this, Majesty,' said Jannas. 'Those people will never submit. If we want to be rid of them, we shall have to kill every last one of them.'

'You are to leave immediately for Anatolia, and put down this rebellion,' ordered the emperor.

'But what about Queen Ahhotep?'

'The Delta has been pacified, and Avaris is impregnable. Thanks to my spy, I now know how to barricade the queen and her son in their lair. Today, nothing is more important than re-establishing total control of Anatolia.'

## 22

Contrary to what many soldiers had hoped, Queen Ahhotep did not march on Avaris but confined herself to providing essential help to Memphis, so that the rebels there could continue to hold off the Hyksos.

For several nights now the sky had been turbulent, and energy was no longer circulating normally. The message from the moon-god, Ah, was unambiguous: King Ahmose was under threat. Without the slightest doubt, Apophis had put a curse on him.

'Will you at last permit me to return to Edfu, Majesty?' asked Emheb. Despite his great strength, he was clearly very tired.

'You know I cannot do that,' replied Ahhotep gently. 'Whom else could I rely on to ensure that there is no slackening of effort at the Port of Kamose? But I am convinced that Jannas will not counter-attack immediately, so, although you must stay on the alert, you may be able to rest a little before the next battle.'

The queen's smile was so enchanting that Emheb did not press the point.

'I must return to Thebes,' she said. 'As soon as we are ready, we shall go on to the offensive.'

'I shall be at your side, Majesty.'

Thebes would gladly have marked the victory at the Port of Kamose with a great feast, but how could they celebrate when the king was ill? The doctors could not understand why he could no longer set foot on the ground without unbearable pain. No remedy relieved it, and the doctors' conclusion was deeply worrying: it was an unknown sickness which they could not cure.

Despite this severe handicap, Ahmose kept up his pace of work. Whenever he could not walk his guards supported him, and he continued to travel all over the countryside to recruit new soldiers. Qaris and Heray advised him to take things more slowly, but he paid them no heed although he was growing weaker by the day.

The only thing that comforted him was the presence of Nefertari, who was so tactful yet efficient that she had won the heart of everyone who worked at the palace. Helping this marvellous young woman learn the customs and rituals of the court had made Qaris feel young again.

The steward was smiling as he informed the king, 'Your mother is coming, Majesty.'

'We shall receive her in the great audience chamber,' decided Ahmose.

There was rejoicing on the quayside. As soon as Queen Ahhotep set foot once again on Theban soil, her way was strewn with flowers by the citizens of the capital, eager to acclaim the heroine who had won such an incredible victory over the Hyksos.

At the entrance to the palace, the dignitaries formed a guard of honour. When Ahhotep entered the audience chamber, Pharaoh Ahmose bowed his head as a sign of veneration.

'Homage shall be paid unto you, my mother, for you have come once more to save Egypt. The spirit of Amon is within you and guides you. Through me, the love, respect and trust of the people of the Two Lands are offered to you.'

Moved to tears, Ahhotep prostrated herself before the pharaoh.

'Please stand up. It is we who should bow the knee before the Queen of Freedom.'

After conducting a long and intense ritual at Karnak, during which the Wife of God called upon Amon to become incarnate in the stones of the temple and in the hearts of men, mother and son found themselves alone once more.

Ahmose did not attempt to hide his pain, or the extent to which his health had declined.

'It was Apophis's spy who stole your sandals,' said Ahhotep. 'He sent them to the emperor so that he could curse them and prevent life from flowing through your feet.'

'What can we do?'

'High Priest Djehuty knows the incantations of Thoth that will destroy the curse. So that each part of your body may be protected from now on, I shall lay the amulets of resurrection upon you.'

These incantations dated from the time of the great pyramids, and opened up the paths of the afterlife to the reborn soul, whether those paths were of fire, water, air or earth. On the soles of the king's feet, the High Priest drew the outline of sandals which would permit the wearer to travel across any space. And when Ahhotep laid the amulets on the nape of the king's neck, she ensured that all his vital energy centres were protected.

Being able to walk without pain was like a rebirth to Ahmose. The blood flowed round his body normally, and all his former energy returned.

'I owe you my life for a third time,' he told his mother. 'After giving me birth and crowning me pharaoh, you have now given me back my life-force.'

'The emperor was right, Ahmose. You are indeed the future of Egypt. But now tell me, who is that beautiful young woman who cannot take her eyes off you?'

'So you have noticed her.'

'One would have to be more sightless than a blind man not to.'

'If you consent, Mother, I should like her to become my Great Royal Wife.'

'Did you think long and hard before taking this decision?'

Ahmose hesitated. 'No, I took it in a moment.'

'What is her name?'

'Nefertari. She is the daughter of peasants, but she was born to be a queen.'

Ahhotep saw her son in a new light. So this patient, serious young man with the iron self-control was capable of deep passion.

The queen's long silence worried Ahmose. Of course, she had already judged Nefertari. And if she was opposed to the marriage, what could he do? The thought of life without the woman he loved was impossible, but so was the prospect of losing Queen Ahhotep's support.

'Will you not speak with her, Mother?'

'That will not be necessary.'

'Is it her lowly birth?'

'Your father was a gardener.'

'You think she and I have not taken enough time to think, but—'

'Nefertari has the eyes of a Great Royal Wife, my son. And it is vital that the pharaoh should be personified by a couple.'

Apophis congratulated himself. In sending him Ahmose's sandals, his spy had provided him with an effective way of neutralizing a young warrior who might one day have become a threat. By harming Ahmose, the emperor would break Ahhotep's heart and mother and son would both be made powerless.

Apophis had placed the sandals in a large glass vase filled with scorpions' venom, and was on his way up to the ramparts of the citadel, to expose it to the midday sun. Once heated, the poison would become corrosive, and as the days passed it would eat into the lower limbs of the madman who dared claim to be pharaoh. Little by little, the pain would become unbearable, and Ahmose would eventually kill himself rather than suffer any longer.

As the emperor climbed the steps, his ears were assailed by his wife's screams. Day and night, Tany was tormented by hideous nightmares, and Yima had to give her larger and larger doses of drugs. It was a long time since Apophis had visited his half-crazed wife. He had to admit, though, that her idea of getting rid of Minos had been a good one. The painter's death had led to that of Windswept, who had become far too much of a nuisance – sooner or later, he would have given her to the bull.

Although the rays of sunlight had not yet struck the glass vase, it became burning hot. Apophis set it down on the ramparts. Scarcely had he done so when the vase exploded, and the venom poured all over his feet, burning them as though it were acid.

## 23

In Anatolia the fighting was ferocious, and frequent rebel attacks were preventing Jannas from achieving a final victory. But in Egypt time had stopped in its tracks, and so had the war. Memphis remained divided in two: one part under Hyksos control, the other in the hands of the Thebans, who were supplied with food and equipment by the troops at the Port of Kamose.

Month after month, Queen Ahhotep, who was still dazzlingly beautiful though she was almost fifty, consulted the moon-god, who told her to be patient. With joy, she witnessed the birth of a new royal couple, Ahmose and Nefertari. The profound love that united them was complemented by an increasingly strong sense of their office and their duties.

Each evening, Ahhotep meditated beside the sacred lake while the swallows soared overhead, souls from the afterlife who were regenerated in the sunshine.

Her son, now an austere young man of twenty, came to join her. 'We shall soon celebrate the eleventh year of my reign, Mother, and Egypt is still occupied. In the past, I did not feel I could fight like my father and brother. Now I know I can.'

'That is true, Ahmose, but the omens are still unfavourable.'

'Must we heed them?'

'Haste might be dangerous – even fatal.'

'The Hyksos have not retaken any of the positions they lost, many warships have been launched from our boatyard, and we have mobilized thousands of men. Why put off the battle?'

'It pleases me to hear you talk like that,' said Ahhotep. 'Liberating our country must always be our foremost concern. But only the gods' assent and the breath of Amon will give us the strength we need.'

'Then we must enlarge Karnak and the god's shrine at the military base. I shall attend to the matter first thing tomorrow.'

Apophis's feet and ankles were so painful that he had to be carried everywhere on a pine-wood throne by two Cypriot guards, whose tongues he had had cut out. Although he seemed more and more passive and less and less talkative, the emperor continued to govern without delegating even a scrap of his power.

Jannas was reimposing Hyksos control in Anatolia at the cost of thousands of deaths, while Khamudi did the same in the Delta by means of deportations. And the ruin of Memphis, which was still under siege, favoured the expansion of Avaris as a trading centre.

But there remained Queen Ahhotep and her puny little king. True, they had given up fighting and were pinned down in their positions, but their very lives were an insult to Hyksos greatness. As soon as Jannas returned, he must think up a new way of destroying them.

When the curse of the sandals had turned against him, the emperor had felt an even greater desire to destroy the queen, whose magic rivalled his own. It would be the most satisfying victory of his entire reign.

Beneath a threatening sky, Apophis was carried to the Temple of Set, where he was currently the sole High Priest. Who but himself could really communicate with the thunder?

As he entered the shrine, where animals were being sacrificed to Set, the emperor felt a fierce pain in his feet and he realized at once that something important was about to happen.

Seizing the blood-soaked head of a sacrificed donkey, Apophis gazed deep into the animal's eyes.

And he saw. He saw Thebes, a queen and her son. He saw a pact sealed between them, and knew that this alliance would have all the power of an army.

He called once again upon Set, bidding him to unleash his power against these enemies and separate them for ever.


On the morning of the third day of the first month of the first season of the eleventh year of the reign of Ahmose, the pharaoh left by boat to set in train the building of Amon's shrine at the military base.

On the same morning, Djehuty, High Priest of Karnak, at last managed to reassemble the ancient calendar of favourable and unfavourable times, which had come to him in disjointed fragments. As he put the final touches to this vast puzzle, the learned scribe had a terrible shock. Ordinarily the very model of self-control, he could not prevent himself running full tilt to the palace, where Ahhotep received him immediately.

'Majesty, all royal activities must be halted and the king given extra protection. Today is the day of Set's birth, and if the emperor knows it he will unleash his thunder against us.'

'Pharaoh Ahmose is on his way to the military base. I shall try to join him there.'

'Do not take any risks, I beg of you! You may fall victim to the heavens' fire, too.'

But the queen paid no heed to the High Priest's warning.

Before she embarked, he handed her a strip of linen on which an ancient incantation was written. 'Place this round the pharaoh's neck,' he advised. 'It may perhaps save his life.'

When he had unleashed the terrible storm that had destroyed much of Thebes, Apophis had allied himself with the clouds and the winds. This time, in addition to a storm which raged over the city and the burial-ground on the west bank of the Nile, he let loose the river's fury.

In a few minutes, the water began to boil, and enormous waves attacked both the riverbanks and the hull of Ahmose's boat, which was nearing the military base.

At Karnak, in the palace, at the entrance to the burial-ground and inside each house, the Thebans obeyed Ahhotep's instructions by making offerings to the dead and burning clay figurines on which the name of Apophis had been written. Djehuty took the additional precaution of placing a cornelian eye on the wax effigy of the emperor, so as to destroy the evil eye with which he was seeking to lay waste Thebes.

Aboard a boat sailing north, Ahhotep firmly gripped the gold sceptre with the head of Set. The god of storms was now not her enemy but her ally. Having captured his thunder, the queen no longer feared his violence. Within the sceptre the energies of heaven and earth were united.

Ahhotep thought only of the pharaoh. Even if she died in the attempt, she must save him.

Ahmose helped the crew lower the sails so that the smallest possible surface faced the raging wind, which was spinning the boat spin round and round. Without its rudder, which had snapped off, the captain could not steer towards the bank.

Only the pharaoh's calmness stopped the sailors panicking. When all seemed lost, Ahmose issued an order which the crew obeyed to the best of their ability, and in so doing prevented the vessel from sinking.

Emerging through the torrential rain, the queen's boat reached the pharaoh's. She raised the sceptre towards the mass of clouds, and the rain began to slacken.

The timbers of the royal vessel made a sinister cracking noise. Several holes opened up, letting in water.

Ahhotep intoned the words written on the linen strip: 'The universe of the stars obeys you; the light rests upon you.'

The boat stopped spinning. Just before it sank, its occupants jumped on to Ahhotep's boat and she immediately tied the linen band round her son's neck.

The storm died down, and Thebes emerged from it almost unscathed.

## 24

Never had the security measures around the fortress at Avaris been so spectacular. It was the time of the tribute ceremonies, and in Jannas's absence High Treasurer Khamudi was determined to prevent any untoward incidents. The towers and ramparts bristled with watchful archers, and the pirates who formed the emperor's personal bodyguard had orders to arrest and kill any suspicious persons.

In this oppressive atmosphere, the envoys from the countries that had submitted to the Hyksos, and their gift-bearers, were given permission to enter the fortress through the main gate. Then, under heavy escort, they were ushered into the audience chamber of Apophis's palace.

Seated on his pine-wood throne, flanked by the two griffins, the emperor enjoyed the fear of his guests, who dared not raise their eyes to look at the tyrant, sitting above them swathed in a voluminous dark-brown cloak. Even the beauty of the Minoan-style frescoes had a disturbing aspect, as if the bulls were about to come charging out at the visitors.

In both summer and winter, the place was icy cold. The emperor exuded a chill which prevented the slightest breath of warmth from entering.

The envoys and their entourages lay prostrate before Apophis for a long time. He savoured this moment, which confirmed his omnipotence over the most extensive empire the world had ever known. His right hand caressed the gold pommel of his dagger, with which he could inflict death on anyone he chose, whenever he wished. It was because they had forgotten this aspect of true power that the pharaohs had been defeated.

With a disdainful gesture, Apophis ordered his vassals' representatives to stand up.

'A few Anatolian barbarians have tried to rebel,' he declared in his rasping voice, which made everyone present shiver. 'I have sent Commander Jannas to exterminate them. Anyone who gives them aid, in any way whatsoever, will suffer the same fate. Now I consent to receive your homage.'

Gold and silver ingots, fabrics, costly and elegant vases and pots of priceless ointments were laid before the throne. But Apophis's ugly face did not brighten and the atmosphere remained tense. The Minoan envoy was the last to offer his gifts: gold rings, silver cups and lion-headed vases.

'That is enough!' bellowed the emperor. 'Your tributes are even more ridiculous than your predecessors'. Do you not realize who it is that you dare to mock?'

'My lord,' said the Phoenician envoy nervously, 'we have done everything possible. I beg you to understand that the rumours of war are very harmful to trade. And also long periods of bad weather have prevented our ships from putting out to sea. So the trade in goods has been less good than normal, and we have grown poorer.'

'I understand, I understand. Come here.'

The Phoenician recoiled. 'I, my lord?'

'Since you have given me an explanation, you deserve a reward. Approach my throne.'

Trembling, the envoy obeyed.

Flames darted from the griffins' eyes; flames as intense as they were short-lived. His face ablaze the Phoenician howled with pain and rolled about in the heap of gifts to try and put out the fire consuming him. Dumb with terror, those present witnessed his death-throes.

'That is the punishment reserved for anyone who dares treat me with insufficient respect,' stated the emperor. 'You, the Minoan envoy, what have you to say for yourself?'

Although old and sick, the diplomat managed to contain his fear. 'We could not give any more, my lord. Our island has suffered greatly from rain and gales, which destroyed most of our crops. In addition, the accidental death of some of our best craftsmen in a fire has caused chaos in our workshops. As soon as the situation has returned to normal, King Minos the Great will send you more tributes.'

For a few moments, everyone thought these explanations had calmed the emperor's cold fury. They were wrong.

'You have all insulted me,' he continued. 'These miserable offerings show that you are refusing to pay your taxes and that you are all rebels. First thing tomorrow, regiments will leave for the provinces of my empire, and those responsible for this insurrection will be put to death. As for you, you ridiculous envoys, I shall grant you a fitting end.'

Using the great axe, which she wielded as well as any headsman, Aberia had beheaded all the gift-bearers. As for the two Nubians and the three Syrians who had tried to rush the guards and escape, she had enjoyed cutting off their feet before strangling them.

The rejoicing was not yet at an end: like the other Hyksos dignitaries, she was about to watch the great game Apophis had devised.

Before the citadel a rectangle had been drawn. Inside it were twelve white and twelve black squares, arranged alternately.

Their hands tied behind their backs, the twenty-four envoys from the provinces of the empire were brought forward by guards.

'You will be untied,' announced Apophis, who was seated in a travelling-chair overlooking the gaming-board, 'and you will be given weapons. Twelve of you will form one army, the other twelve the opposing one.'

Speechless, the envoys bowed to Apophis's instructions.

'Whom shall I play against? Ah yes, against you, my faithful Khamudi.'

The High Treasurer would happily have dispensed with this favour. There was only one possible thing to do: let the emperor win.

Appophis turned back to the prisoners. 'Do exactly what I order you to do and respect the rules of the game,' he warned them, 'or the archers will kill you. You are now nothing but pawns, to be moved around by myself and Khamudi.'

From the oldest to the youngest, the envoys trembled.

'Persian, advance one square straight ahead,' ordered Apophis.

Khamudi moved forward the Nubian, who was armed with a spear, to confront him.

'The Persian must try to kill the Nubian,' decided the emperor.

In terror, the two envoys stared at each other.

'Fight,' snapped Apophis. 'The victor will drag the loser's corpse out of the game and take his place.'

The Persian wounded the Nubian on the arm, and the Nubian dropped his spear.

'I have defeated him, my lord!' quavered the Persian.

'Kill him or you are dead.'

The spear came down once, twice, three times. Then the Persian dragged the bloody body out of the rectangle and stood at the head of Apophis's pawns.

'Your turn, Khamudi.'

If he allowed himself to be defeated too easily, the High Treasurer risked displeasing the emperor.

'The Syrian is to attack the Persian,' he announced.

The Persian tried to run, but the archers stopped him by firing arrows into his legs. And the Syrian smashed his skull with his club.

'Do not forget that the victors' lives will be spared,' added Apophis.

From that moment, the 'pawns' killed each other in quick, vicious duels. Khamudi played well, making the game interesting but enabling Apophis to win decisively. At the end, the emperor had only one pawn left, the Minoan envoy.

Numb, not knowing where he had derived such energy, the old man gripped the bloody dagger with which he had killed three of his colleagues.

'As you are a victorious soldier, your life shall be spared,' decreed the emperor.

The Minoan let go of his weapon and staggered out of the gaming-board.

'But as a traitor,' Apophis added, 'you must be punished. Lady Aberia, deal with him.'

## 25

The five men disembarked at a deserted spot on the Egyptian coast, after which their boat immediately put out to sea again. Then, instead of taking the route to Sais, they moved away from the green fringe of the Delta and headed into the desert. Armed with rough maps showing a number of water-holes, they hoped to avoid any confrontations on the long journey that would lead them to the province of Thebes.

Several times they were almost intercepted by Hyksos patrols, by nomads, or by caravans. Halfway to their destination, they began to fear they would die of thirst, for one of the wells on their map had dried out. They had to detour to the edge of the desert, to the cultivated area, to steal fruit and water-skins from a farm.

Two of them did die. The first collapsed, exhausted; the second was bitten by a cobra. If the other three had not been well-trained footsoldiers, used to moving about in hostile terrain, they would not have survived their ordeal – they had never imagined it would be so harsh.

Less than an hour's march from the military base at Thebes, they ran into an Egyptian patrol. At the end of their strength, thin as skeletons, they fell to their knees in the sand.

'We have come from the island of Minoa,' croaked one of them, 'and we have a message for Queen Ahhotep.'

Neshi had interrogated the three men separately; each claimed they had been sent by Minos the Great. As their accounts tallied, he agreed to their request.

Washed, shaved, fed and dressed in new kilts, they were taken under guard to a small room in the Theban palace, where the queen and Pharaoh Ahmose were studying a report by Heray on the army's supply system.

'I am Commander Linas,' declared a bearded, square-faced man, 'and I shall speak to no one but the Queen of Egypt.'

'You and your two companions must bow before Pharaoh,' ordered Ahhotep.

She had such authority that the three Minoans obeyed.

'Why did you undertake this arduous journey?' she asked.

'Majesty, the King of Minoa's message is strictly confidential, and . . .'

'The guards will take your friends back to their rooms. You shall remain here. The pharaoh and I will hear you.'

Linas, who was accustomed to giving orders, not taking them, sensed that it would be as well not to displease this woman.

'Minos the Great has ordered me to invite you to Minoa, Majesty. He wishes to converse with you about plans which are as important for your country as for our own.'

'What plans?'

'I do not know.'

'Have you brought no written message?'

'No, Majesty.'

'Why should I deliver myself into the hands of one of the Hyksos' principal allies?'

'Because of the laws of hospitality that obtain in Minoa, you will be in no danger: in our land, a guest is sacred. King Minos will welcome you in a manner worthy of your rank, and, whatever the outcome of your discussions you shall leave free and unharmed.'

'How can you guarantee that?'

'I am not only a commander in the Minoan war-fleet, but also King Minos's youngest son. Naturally, I shall remain here in Thebes until your return.'

Neshi, Heray and Qaris all agreed that the invitation was a crude trap laid by Apophis to lure Queen Ahhotep into enemy territory and capture her. The only possible response was to send Linas and his companions back to Minoa.

'But supposing the king is sincere?' suggested the queen. 'Minoa finds Hyksos domination hard to bear. Her people are proud, her culture rich and ancient. Her relations with Egypt have always been excellent, because the pharaohs, unlike Apophis, did not try to subjugate her.'

'That is true, Majesty,' said Neshi, 'but in the current situation—'

'Precisely. The current situation is not at all favourable to Minoa. Let us suppose King Minos is afraid that he will be attacked and deposed, that he suspects Apophis of wishing to lay Minoa waste. What can he do, except form an alliance against the Hyksos? Despite all his efforts, Apophis has not succeeded in keeping our victory secret. The news of that victory, however minor it may have been, must have reached Knossos. Minos now knows that the Hyksos are no longer invincible. If Minoa rebels, other conquered lands will follow suit, and the empire will begin to disintegrate. Destiny is offering us an unexpected opportunity, and we must seize it.'

Ahhotep's reasoning was tempting, but old Qaris refused to be swayed. 'If the king is intelligent and shrewd, he probably hopes we take that view – and the trap is all the cleverer. I detect here a new sign of Apophis's cunning. As he has failed to kill you himself, he is using the services of a faithful vassal who offers you a tempting glimmer of mad hope.'

'Qaris's voice is the voice of reason,' agreed Heray.

'To which I have never listened,' said the queen, 'since the moment when I decided to fight the Hyksos. You all know that we cannot win this war without taking risks. This invitation is the sign I was hoping for.'

Qaris turned to Ahmose. 'May I beg Pharaoh to persuade the queen not to do this?'

'If you die, Mother,' said the king sombrely, 'what will become of us?'

'You have been crowned and you rule Egypt, Ahmose. First of all, you should go to the Port of Kamose, and you should continue to support the rebellion in Memphis so that only the Delta remains safe territory for the Hyksos. While you await the results of my discussions with King Minos, you should build more and more war-boats. If the invitation really is a trap, Apophis will be sure to gloat publicly over it, and you must then attack him. If, on the other hand, King Minos agrees to become our ally, we shall be in a much stronger position.'

'Am I to understand, Mother, that you have already made your decision?'

Ahhotep's smile would have charmed the sternest of opponents. 'Yes, because I know you are capable of ruling.'

Ahmose knew that the death of the Queen of Freedom would be far worse than any military reverse. But no one could persuade Ahhotep to change her mind.

'I have always agreed with your plans, Majesty,' said Neshi, 'but I cannot support you in this, for one simple reason: it would be impossible for you to reach Minoa. You would first have to cross Middle Egypt, then get through the Delta – which is entirely in the hands of the Hyksos – and finally find a ship with an experienced crew.'

'There is another way, the one by which Linas and his men reached us.'

'Through the desert? But, Majesty, that is an exhausting, highly dangerous journey.'

'The expedition will include Egyptian sailors and Linas's

companions, who can give us detailed information about which tracks are safe. As for the ship, we shall transport a boat in sections and assemble it on the coast at the point of departure.'

'Majesty,' said Neshi, 'this plan . . . this plan is . . .'

'I know, it makes no sense. But just imagine if I succeed!'

Only one thing worried Ahhotep: that the emperor's spy would discover her plan and bring her journey to an abrupt end by prompting Hyksos intervention.

## 26

The sadness in Long-Ears eyes was matched by the despair on Young Laughter's face. But Ahhotep could not yield to their entreaties. She explained to them that crossing the desert, and then the sea, was much too dangerous for them and that, in any case, they had important work to do. Long-Ears must continue to guide the other donkeys as they delivered equipment to the army, and Laughter must watch over Ahmose. Like his father, Old Laughter, the huge hound had become a formidable guard-dog, ready to fight to the death to save the king. The two faithful servants pretended to be content.

'But I wish I could take you with me to protect me,' she whispered.

As the sun set, the heat of the day began to wane. A gentle breeze wind began to blow from the north, strenuous work in the fields stopped, and all over the countryside the sounds of flutes could be heard. Ahhotep thought of her dead husband and son, and knew that they were sharing the banquet of the gods.

Nefertari came in and bowed. 'Your evening meal is ready, Majesty,' she said. 'Oh, forgive me. I have interrupted your reflections.'

'This is not the time for reflecting on the past. There is too much to do building the future.'

As she looked at the Great Royal Wife, Ahhotep mused that Ahmose, ordinarily so cautious, had been right not to hesitate over his marriage. Although blessed with gifts which could have earned her a life of easy contentment as a prosperous lady, Nefertari had the soul of a queen: conscientious, radiant, caring more about the destiny of her country and her people than she did about her own.

'If I do not return, Nefertari, you must fight at the pharaoh's side. Without your radiance and your magical power, he will lack the energy necessary for victory. It was Isis who brought Osiris back to life, and it is the Great Royal Wife who fills the king's soul with the flame of just deeds. Above all, do not waste your time on unworthy tasks or your words on banalities.'

Nefertari's unflinching gaze belied her delicate appearance. 'I promise, Majesty.'

'Now we can have our meal.'

Ahhotep was extremely pleased to have retaken control of the road to the oases: the Nubians and Hyksos could no longer use it to send each other official messages. In the Great South, which was now under Egyptian control, the King of Kerma seemed content with his wealth and his pampered life, far removed from the war. Ahhotep was still wary, and feared that his warlike nature might be reawakened. But, hoping that she was mistaken, she put such thoughts aside and enjoyed the harsh beauty of the desert, even though it was hostile to humans.

The men were suffering, but they were so proud to have been chosen to accompany Ahhotep that they made light of their difficulties. Only the two Minoans, who had been firmly invited to carry their share of the load, looked unhappy. Eventually the good food and wines cheered them up, and rest periods at the oases put them in a better temper. They consented to answer the queen's questions as she asked them about life in Minoa, where, according to them, there was a pronounced taste for games, celebrations and fashion.

They all had to be constantly on the alert, and Ahhotep slept with one eye open. If the spy had been able to warn the emperor, the Hyksos would travel to the ends of the earth to capture the queen.

The last week of the journey, when they had to cross the coastal marshlands, was particularly arduous; the travellers almost wished they were back in the desert. They had to wade for hours through stagnant standing water, with snakes brushing against their legs and under constant attack from mosquitoes. Much use was made of She-Cat's remedies and ointments, but the Egyptians were convinced that they really owed their lives to the protective magic of the Wife of God, who shared their trials without a word of complaint.

Fortunately, the expedition encountered not a single enemy patrol, and eventually reached the coast safely. To the Egyptians it was a new world: a sandy beach, waves, salt water constantly in motion. At the Minoans' suggestion, they dared to bathe in it. The water felt heavy and sticky, although it made them feel much better after the water of the marshes.

Ahhotep allowed the men to relax, only too happy that they were all alive. Surely, she thought, that must be a sign that she had made the right decision? All the same, she did not lower her guard.

'The demons of the sea are even more formidable than those of the desert,' she warned them as they ate beneath the stars. 'We know the Nile's whims well, but the caprices of this immense ocean may take us by surprise. Nevertheless, we must cross it.'

Watched sceptically by the two Minoans, the Egyptians assembled a boat designed for long journeys. With its double mast, constructed from two oblique shafts joined at the top, its flat-roofed cabin, new sails, oars and sturdy rudder, it looked very fine.

'Are you planning to sail all the way to the Great Island in ... that?' asked one of the Minoans.

'Our ancestors did,' replied Ahhotep.

'But, Majesty, you do not know all the dangers that lie in wait for us. With a good following wind, it takes only three days to cover the distance between Minoa and Egypt,* but going from Egypt to Minoa will take almost twice as long because we shall be sailing into the wind. Besides, the winds are gusty and unpredictable, and the swell is dangerous – and then there are the storms. In short, the boat's hull must be able to withstand tremendous pressure from the wind and waves.'

'It will.'

'Also, if the weather is bad and the clouds hide the stars from us, we shall lose our way.'

'Not with the map I have. Our ancestors, who often sailed to and from Minoa, left us invaluable documents, and you would be wrong to scorn their knowledge. Do you know, for example, why it is stated that the length of the *duat*, the intermediary world between the sky and the underground ocean, is 3,814 *iterus*, to use a map-maker's term? Because it corresponds to the perimeter of the Earth.† The sea may frighten many Egyptians, but our people have included great navigators and we know how to tame it.'

'But, Majesty, this crew certainly does not!'

'Then this will be an opportunity for them to acquire that knowledge.'

When they saw how well the queen's sailors handled their vessel, the Minoans were slightly reassured. But they knew how suddenly the ocean's fierce storms could strike, and were afraid the crew would panic if anything went wrong. The wind veered several times, and at dawn on the third day the sea became very rough. The captain reacted by adjusting the sails and the course of the boat, whose manoeuvrability was a great asset. The crew adapted surprisingly quickly, not once losing their confidence.

And each night Queen Ahhotep conversed with the moon-god, asking him for a peaceful crossing.

---

* About 500 kilometres.

†3,818 *iterus* = 39,894.48 kilometres. This information, provided by the tombs in the Valley of the Kings, was probably known before (see J Zeidler, 'Die Länge der Unterwelt nach ägyptischer Vorstellung', Gttinger Miszellen 156, 1997, pp 101–12).

On the evening of the fourth day, the two Minoans suddenly thought they were seeing things. 'Look over there! It's our island, the Great Island!'

'Let us pay homage to Amon, master of the wind, and to Hathor, queen of the stars and of sailing,' said Ahhotep. 'Without their aid, we would not have reached our destination safely.'

The queen laid bread, wine and a phial of perfume on a small altar, and everyone bowed their heads in meditation.

'Ships in sight,' announced the captain.

Four warships were closing swiftly on the Egyptian boat.

'They think we're an enemy boat, and they're going to ram us,' cried one of the Minoans.

Indeed, the warships' course left no doubt as to their intention. Ahhotep gave the order to lower the sails and went to stand at the prow, presenting an ideal target for Minos the Great's archers.

## 27

Khamudi paced back and forth in his villa like a caged bear. Although he had doubled the number of guards who protected him day and night, he no longer dared go out.

'Why are you so afraid?' asked his wife. 'Surely Jannas isn't going to attack our house?'

'He's quite capable of doing so. There is now only one obstacle between him and imperial power: myself. He and I both know it, believe me.'

'But you're still the emperor's right-hand man, aren't you?'

Khamudi sat down heavily in an armchair and drained a cup of white wine. 'Apophis is getting old. Every day he's a little less lucid.'

Yima was shocked. 'That's the first time I've ever heard you criticize the emperor.'

'It isn't a criticism, it's an observation. If we want to preserve the empire's power, Apophis needs more and better help.'

Yima understood nothing of politics, but her husband's worry made her afraid she might actually lose all her money and possessions. 'Are we in danger?'

'No, because the emperor still trusts me.'

'Would he dare put his trust in anyone else?'

'Jannas is trying to persuade him to, because Jannas and I are enemies and he is determined to reduce my influence on all the leading government officials. In other words, he wants to get rid of me.'

Yima turned pale. 'Is that just rumour, or do you know it for a fact?'

'I have carried out a detailed investigation, and all the evidence points one way. As soon as he returns from Anatolia, Jannas will try to remove me from power.'

Yima sat on Khamudi's knee and covered him with nervous kisses. 'You won't let that happen, will you, my darling? You won't let him steal our fortune?'

'Not if you help me.'

'How?'

'You still have the empress's ear, haven't you?'

'Yes, but she is a crazed old woman, ill and powerless.'

'All the same, she gave the order to kill Minos.'

'Jannas is a much bigger and more dangerous target.'

'Indeed he is. So you must convince Tany that he's leading the empire to ruin. After all, Jannas's incompetence led to the attack on Avaris and to her illness, didn't it? That man is the cause of all our troubles. If we don't kill him, he'll certainly kill us.'

Yima seemed to understand. 'Supposing he has been killed in Anatolia?'

'According to his latest message, he'll be back here in less than a week – no doubt he'll be greeted as a conquering hero.'

His old striped headdress and his clothes, which were scarcely better than those of a simple soldier, reflected Jannas's indifference to the cheering that punctuated his march to the citadel. Soldiers, guards citizens were celebrating a great triumph. Only the emperor must know the truth: that the celebrations were utterly unjustified.

In accordance with custom, it was Khamudi, as head of security, who greeted the commander. 'Did you have a good journey?'

'Can the emperor receive me immediately?'

'He is taking his afternoon rest. I am ordered to hear your report and pass it on to him.'

'That is out of the question.'

'Commander! That is the usual procedure, and—'

'I don't care about procedure. Now that I am back, I shall again take charge of the safety of the capital and of the emperor. Go back to your finances and your drugs-trafficking, and above all do not try to stop me entering the citadel. I shall wait there until Apophis awakes.'

Furious, Khamudi stood aside.

Despite all the cares that weighed him down, Jannas had dozed off. An icy breath jolted him abruptly awake. The emperor was standing right in front of him.

'You have been away a very long time, my friend. Have our troops grown soft?'

'The situation is grave, my lord.'

'Follow me.'

The two men shut themselves away in the little room at the centre of the palace, where no one could hear them.

'Has Asia been pacified, Jannas?'

'I have killed thousands of rebels and their families, burnt hundreds of villages, slaughtered entire herds, and brought terror wherever I went. Everyone knows that to offend the emperor of the Hyksos leads to implacable punishment.'

'You have not answered my question.'

'No one dares face us in pitched battle, because nothing and no one can withstand our chariots, but there are interminable ambushes, minor clashes and skirmishes. Normally, I would simply have wiped the rebels out, but a new class of real warriors has succeeded in uniting the tribes and sweeping away the local rulers to form a new power. They call themselves Hittites.'

'Why did you not simply wipe out the Hittites?' demanded Apophis.

'Because they know every inch of their mountains and can survive in even the most difficult conditions. Even when they are starving and dying of cold, they still fight like wild beasts and lay murderous ambushes for us. I hanged their wives, disembowelled their children, razed their houses to the ground, and still they did not surrender. If I had sent my men into the gorges and the ravines, they would have been slaughtered.'

The emperor's harsh voice grew menacing. 'Then what do you suggest?'

'I have left in position enough men forces to keep the Hittites pinned down in their enclave. In the short term, they are not a serious threat. However, on our homeward march I reflected at length. In Anatolia there are the Hittites, in Egypt there is Queen Ahhotep. The two cases are comparable: pockets of rebellion which must be annihilated if we are not to see them grow stronger or, worse, infect other regions.'

'That is precisely the sort of catastrophe I ordered you to prevent.'

'Majesty, I have done all that was possible with the means at my disposal.'

'That is for me to judge, Commander.'

'Majesty, you can of course send me to the labyrinth or consign me to the bull, but my death would not solve any of the problems facing the empire.'

The emperor did not like Jannas's tone, but he recognized the validity of his arguments. 'What exactly do you want?'

'Full powers.'

Apophis remained rigidly motionless for endless seconds. Then he said, 'And what does that mean?'

'I regret to have to say that the High Treasurer has more than once interfered in military matters and has acted in a way which undermines my authority. By doing so he has weakened us. Let him confine himself to his role as an administrator – and stop trying to suborn my senior officers.

'As for my plan, it is this is: to use almost all our forces, except for a single regiment which will protect Avaris, in order to achieve three things as quickly as possible. The first is to raze the city of Memphis to the ground. The next is to break through the Egyptian front, destroy Thebes and bring you back Queen Ahhotep and her son, dead or alive. The last is to crush the Hittites, by obliterating the whole of Anatolia if necessary. My inability to achieve complete success was due solely to the dispersal of our men to several fronts, which was Khamudi's doing. We must therefore put an end to the dissension between him and myself, and destroy our enemies. There is only one way to do so: at each stage, we must use our full military power. That is how the Hyksos conquered their empire, and that is how you will enlarge it.' Jannas was well aware of the risk he was taking but, as commander-in-chief of the army, he could not bear not to succeed.

'Have you finished?' asked Apophis.

'I have nothing to add, my lord, except that my only concern is for the greatness of the Hyksos Empire.'

## 28

The captains of the Minoan war-boats were preparing to ram the enemy ship and to order their archers to fire, but Ahhotep's appearance halted them where they stood. With her gold diadem and her long red gown, she truly possessed the bearing of a queen. Could this possibly be that Egyptian woman who the storytellers said had driven back the Hyksos? None of the sailors in her crew looked warlike . . .

Then one of the captains recognized the two Minoans, who were waving frantically. Immediately the attack was halted, and the Egyptian ship was guided into port.

The two Minoans were the first to step on to their native soil. They explained to an officer that they were royal envoys returning from a secret and dangerous mission, and that Queen Ahhotep requested an audience with King Minos.

Following a stormy discussion, the situation calmed down. None of the crew was permitted to disembark, and the boat would remain tied up and under permanent guard in the port, where cargo-vessels were unloading jars of oil.

The queen was invited to climb into a large, comfortable chariot drawn by oxen.

'One moment,' she said. She told her ship's captain not to attempt anything, but to await her return calmly. Then she turned to the two Minoan envoys and said, 'I ask you to guarantee the safety of my sailors, and to give me your assurance that they will be well treated and properly fed during my absence. If you do not, I shall leave Minoa this instant.'

While the Minoans discussed what she had said, Ahhotep examined the chariot's massive wheels with great interest. Egypt had made wheels as long ago as the time of Djer, notably to move military towers designed to attack Libyan strongholds across hard terrain. But wheels were useless in soft sand and, in any case, for transporting materials, men or animals, the Nile had no equal. The Hyksos invasion, however, proved that the Egyptians had been wrong to forget the wheel. The queen began to form a plan to be put into action on her return – assuming, of course, that King Minos did not take her prisoner.

The Minoans ended their discussion, and helped Ahhotep mount into the chariot.

As they travelled along, Ahhotep had the chance to see Minoa for the first time. Forests of pine and oak crowned a succession of hills. The road leading to the capital, Knossos, was lined with guard-posts and small inns, and she could see the hills that rose above the valley of Kairatos, where cypress trees grew. In the distance was Mount luktas. How different this land was from her own, and how much she already missed Egypt!

The city of Knossos was open: there were no fortifications, no ramparts, but instead busy, narrow streets filled with workshops and shops. Many people were curious and came out of their homes to marvel at the beautiful stranger, who smiled at them and gave signs of friendship. Very quickly, the atmosphere relaxed; women and children wanted to touch the queen, who, to them, had come from another world, and whose legend held that she was the bearer of good fortune.

Overwhelmed, the guards tried to push the onlookers back, but Ahhotep stepped down from the chariot and went to greet them. Immediately calm returned, soon to be replaced by the cheers of a happy crowd who had taken this beautiful, warmhearted woman to their own hearts.

On foot, crowned with lilies and accompanied by laughing children, the Queen of Freedom made her entrance into the royal palace of Knossos, whose guards dared not bar her way.

The imposing palace was sheltered behind thick walls. From the river, stepped terraces could be seen, hiding a vast courtyard a hundred and twenty cubits long and sixty wide. Each side of this rectangle faced one of the cardinal points. Oblong windows with crosspieces, painted red, opened on to the courtyard, which was a most agreeable place to be when the weather was at its hottest.

An officer led the queen along a corridor whose walls were decorated with axes and bulls' heads. The throne room was less austere. In remarkably delicate and lifelike colours, the painters had created enchanting scenes of crocus-gatherers, young girls with delectable bodies, women carrying precious vases, cats, hoopoes, partridges, dolphins and flying-fish. Spirals and palm-leaves decorated the ceilings.

Every single noble of the Knossos court was present, and their eyes all turned towards Ahhotep.

Clean-shaven, and dressed in short, multicoloured, wrap-around kilts, the men clearly took great care in dressing their hair: some wore it in long, wavy locks alternating with shorter, curled sections, while others had spirals which hung over their foreheads. Some wore leather boots, others long socks.

The women vied with each other in elegance and were evidently eager to seek out the latest fashion. There were long skirts, short skirts and ones with many-coloured panels, transparent bodices, gold jewellery, and agate and cornelian necklaces, showing the Minoan women's taste for luxury.

But Ahhotep outshone them all, although she had opted for simplicity, with her traditional gold diadem and an immaculately white linen dress. Subtle face-paint emphasized her perfect features.

She turned her gaze upon the high-backed gypsum throne, flanked by two griffins. It was occupied by a bearded old man with great presence. In his right hand he held a sceptre, in his left a two-headed axe, the symbol of the thunderbolt he used against his enemies.

Ahhotep bowed. 'Majesty, Pharaoh Ahmose offers you his good wishes for the health of yourself and of Minoa.'

King Minos contemplated her. So she really did exist, and she was here in his palace, alone and without an army, utterly at his mercy. He could have her arrested and sent to the emperor, or execute her himself and send her head to Apophis.

His decision astounded the court. 'Come and sit at my right hand, Queen of Egypt.'

Since the death of his wife, Minos had lost all interest in women. To pay such homage to a foreign queen was certainly not in accordance with custom, and specialists in court ritual were shocked. But when Ahhotep took her place on a gilded wooden throne decorated with geometrical figures, they forgot their criticisms.

'Is this palace worthy of comparison with the one at Thebes?' asked the king.

'It is much larger, better built and more beautifully decorated.'

'And yet the Egyptians are said to be unrivalled builders,' said Minos in surprise.

'Our ancestors were, but compared to them we are mere dwarves. But we are waging a war, and the only thing that matters is the liberation of my country. If destiny favours us, everything will have to be rebuilt and we shall then follow the example of our predecessors. Majesty, I pray that the Great Island may be spared the misfortune that has stricken Egypt.'

For that simple but provocative declaration alone, King Minos, as a vassal of the Hyksos emperor, ought to have thrown the woman in prison.

'What do you think of my court?' he asked.

'It is as beautiful is it is refined. And I see no Hyksos here.'

Most of the Minoan nobles were of the opinion that Ahhotep had far overstepped the mark, but the king seem unconcerned.

'I trust your journey was not too wearisome?'

'Fortunately, the sea was calm.'

'My people love music, dancing and games. So, without further delay, I invite you to a celebratory meal in your honour.'

The king rose, and Ahhotep followed suit. Side by side, the two rulers left the throne room and went out into the garden, where tables had been set out, decked with flowers and groaning with food.

# 29

At the end of the banquet the court headed for the square. Acrobats and dancers performed, before giving way to the most exciting spectacle of all: the trial of the bull. The one that entered the arena was enormous, fully the match of Egyptian wild bulls, which experienced hunters considered the most fearsome animals in all creation.

For the agile, swift-footed performers, the 'trial' consisted of angering the beast so that it charged headlong at them. At the last moment, they seized its horns and, in a perilous leap which made the audience shiver, sprang over its back and landed behind it. The young men were so skilled that not a single mishap marred the game.

'Majesty,' asked Ahhotep, 'what will happen to the bull?'

'We shall set it free. To kill such a noble animal, the embodiment of royal power, would be barbarous.'

'What does that strange design represent, there on the wall of the arena?'

'The labyrinth, a symbol linked to the bull. It was built near Knossos and housed a spirit with terrifying power, the Minotaur. Guided by a thread Ariadne gave him, the hero Theseus entered the labyrinth, killed the monster and escaped with his life.'

'Majesty, do you think Ariadne's thread might link our two countries together?'

Minos rubbed his beard. 'If I understand you correctly, you have tired of the entertainment and would like to discuss more important matters.'

'Egypt is at war, my lord. However impressive your welcome, I cannot tarry here long.'

The king paused; the air was heavy with menace. 'As you wish. Let us leave the court to enjoy themselves and withdraw to my private quarters.'

The old man walked with difficulty, but it was clear that his vital energy was undimmed. Ahhotep was glad to be negotiating with a true king.

He showed the queen into an office decorated with rural scenes. On shelves lay wooden tablets covered with writing.

'How difficult it is to govern a country,' he grumbled. 'One moment's inattention and chaos beckons.'

'But is it not even more exhausting to have to account for everything you to do a tyrant like Apophis?'

The king poured red wine into two silver cups, handed one to Ahhotep and sat down in a sturdy armchair, while the queen sat on a bench covered with multicoloured fabric.

'How is my son, Linas?'

'When I left Thebes, he was extremely well and seemed to like our modest capital very much. I must stress that it was he who decided to stay in Egypt until my return.'

'Those were my orders. If I had not given you a guarantee of that magnitude, would you have come to Minoa?'

'In fact, he is not your son, is he?'

The king avoided her eyes. 'No, he is not.'

'Now may I know the reasons for your invitation?'

'I, a faithful vassal of the Hyksos, receiving their greatest enemy on my island . . . Why did you not refuse when you were invited into such a clumsy trap?'

'Because it is not a trap. You know that the Hyksos want to destroy you, and you cannot fight them alone. That is why you are planning an alliance with Egypt.'

Minos gazed at Ahhotep for a long time. 'What supernatural force enables you to confront the emperor?'

'The desire for freedom.'

'And you will never give up?'

'My husband and my elder son died in battle, and my younger son is now Pharaoh, firmly determined to carry on the fight, even if we are outnumbered ten against one. Thanks to our carpenters' hard work, our war-fleet now rivals that of the Hyksos.'

'But on land their chariots will crush you.'

'We have not yet found a way to defeat them, that is true, but I am convinced that one exists.'

The king sat back in his chair. 'Windswept, the emperor's sister, came to the Great Island to tell me that her lover, a Minoan painter I thought highly of, had been murdered on Apophis's orders. As an act of vengeance, she told me two vital secrets. First, she confirmed your existence and your military successes.'

'My son Kamose led an attack against Avaris, and our men repelled a counter-attack led by Commander Jannas himself. At the moment, we control Upper Egypt, a fact which the emperor is trying desperately to keep hidden.'

'By using our trading-fleet, I can spread the truth across many lands.'

'Then Apophis's vassals will know that he is not invincible, and the rebellion will grow.'

'Do not hope for too much, my lady: not everyone has your courage. Nevertheless, it is possible that such news would shake the empire to its foundations.'

'Have you made up your mind to act?'

'First, I must tell you the other secret Windswept shared with me. There is bitter rivalry between the two men charged with carrying out Apophis's wishes: Commander Jannas and High Treasurer Khamudi. They hate each other, and, although for the moment their enmity is concealed, eventually it will explode into the light of day, weakening the Hyksos regime in the process. Apophis is growing old, and the war of succession is being prepared. Who will win it?'

'That matters little,' said the queen. 'The important thing is to take full advantage of this opportunity. Whichever of them emerges the victor will be no less a tyrant than Apophis at his worst, so we must act before he takes power.'

'Minoa is a very long way from Egypt, and I must think first and foremost of my own country.'

'If you will not fight at my side, may I at least be assured that you will not fight for the Hyksos?'

'Such a promise cannot be given without mature reflection, for the consequences might be fearsome.'

'I believe you have only one course of action, my lord: to recognize my sovereignty over the Mycenean islands, most notably over yours. As Queen of the Distant Shores, I shall offer you protection, and Apophis's anger will be unleashed against me and me alone.'

Minos gave a half-smile. 'Are you sure you will not be more demanding than the emperor?'

'All I ask is your word that you will not betray me. You will remain King of Minoa, your country will remain independent, and we shall exchange envoys and tribute-gifts.'

'There is another course of action. I am a widower, and my country has no queen. You would be safe here, and my people would readily accept you.'

'My lord, I am faithful to one man, Pharaoh Seqen. As the Wife of God, I try constantly to strengthen the King of Egypt's power and to draw Amon's goodwill to him. My place is at the heart of my army – to take refuge with you would be cowardice of the most disgraceful kind. I therefore ask you again to recognize my sovereignty, to spread the truth by means of your trading-fleet, to give the Hyksos no further assistance, and to prepare the Great Island to withstand an attack by Jannas's war-fleet.'

'You ask a very great deal of me, Queen Ahhotep!'

'But I have told you what you wanted to know, have I not?'

Minos did not reply.

Eventually the queen broke the silence. 'What happened to Windswept?' she asked.

'She drowned – a most unfortunate accident. But now, my lady, it is time to go and rest.'

'When shall I have your answer?'

'When the right moment comes.'

The apartments set aside for the Queen of Egypt were luxurious, and included a bathing-room and a lavatory whose wooden seat was right above a water-channel, part of the drainage system underneath the palace. Rainwater flowed down terraces through mortared pipes, and all the various branches ended up at one large collecting pool.

Her bedchamber was provided with beautifully carved and painted wooden furniture. On a porphyry table stood cups decorated with spirals, and conical and lion-headed vases containing water, wine and beer. As for the bed itself, it was most comfortable.

As she lay down, Ahhotep wondered if she would ever emerge from this gilded prison.

## 30

'I am sorry, my lord,' said the guard. 'The emperor is ill and will not receive anyone today.'

'Not even me?' demanded Khamudi in astonishment.

'My orders are strict, High Treasurer: no one.'

It was the first time Khamudi had ever been refused admittance to see Apophis. True, Jannas had also been turned away, but the High Treasurer's privileged position had just been wiped out.

Anxiously, Khamudi questioned those faithful to him to find out how long the conversation between Jannas and the emperor had lasted. More than an hour! Usually, all that happened was that the emperor issued brief orders. This time there must have been long, important discussions.

Jannas himself, Khamudi learnt, was at the main barracks in Avaris, surrounded by his most senior officers. In other words, he was holding a meeting of his general staff – and the High Treasurer had not been invited to attend.

On the verge of nervous exhaustion, Khamudi went home.

'Back already?' simpered Yima. 'You've come because of me, of course! Come, my dear one, I shall—'

'We are in danger.'

Yima's simper vanished. 'Why? What has happened?'

'I am convinced that Jannas has asked the emperor to grant him full powers.'

'But surely Apophis will have refused?'

'I'm afraid he may not have. He refused to receive me, and Jannas is at this moment telling his generals about his plans.'

'Can't you find out what they are?'

'Yes, but by then it will be too late. Anyway, I think I know what he wants: total war, in Egypt as well as in Anatolia, using all our forces. If he gets his way, either my status and authority will be reduced to almost nothing, or else I shall be executed for trying to thwart Jannas's plans. Soon his henchmen will come to arrest us.'

'We must escape at once!'

'It would be useless to try. Jannas will have stationed men on all the routes out of Avaris. And where would we go?'

'You must force your way in to see the emperor!'

'That's impossible.'

'But then . . . what are we going to do?'

'Fight with every weapon we have. Have you convinced Tany that Jannas, the man who failed to defend Avaris, is also responsible for her illness?'

'Yes, oh yes!'

'Go and see her and explain that he has an insane plan to wage war on all fronts at the same time, and that he will leave only the imperial guard in the capital. If the Egyptians attack again, they will have no difficulty in taking the citadel, and Tany will be captured and tortured.'

Without bothering to paint her face or change her dress, Yima ran to the empress's apartments.

Jannas was pleased with the way things had gone. The generals had unreservedly approved of his plans. Neither Anatolian nor Egyptian rebels could continue to defy the Hyksos Empire. They must be attacked and mercilessly destroyed, to show that the emperor's army had lost none of its efficiency. Even the officers bought by Khamudi had rallied to the commander's cause. As for Khamudi himself, he would be arrested within the next few days, then sent to one of the two death-camps he was so proud of.

However, even while contemplating the inevitable sequence of events, Jannas was not fully satisfied. Although in practice he would have sole and absolute command of the Hyksos forces, he had not obtained Apophis's explicit agreement. To a soldier who had always obeyed the emperor's orders, this vagueness was annoying. He still hoped to acquire full powers unequivocally, and decided that he would lay siege to Apophis's apartments until he obtained the necessary official declaration. The emperor knew that he could not refuse.

If the old man refused to face reality and by doing so condemned the Hyksos Empire to death, Jannas owed it to himself to save it. If Apophis persisted, the commander would have to get rid of him.

His assistant interrupted his troubled thoughts. 'Sir, there's a terrible scandal. People are saying you have had your servants beheaded so as to present their corpses to the Temple of Set before setting off on campaign.'

'That is nonsense!'

'An accusation of murder has been lodged against you by High Treasurer Khamudi.'

'We shall go to my house at once and prove the absolute falsity of these allegations.'

When Jannas, accompanied by his bodyguards, arrived at his house, there was no sign of the sentry who should have been guarding the gate. Fully alert, they went into the grounds.

'Split up and surround the house,' Jannas ordered his men; his assistant remained at his side.

The front door was wide open. The admiral called his steward. No reply. Cautiously, he went inside.

The steward lay in the entrance hall, his throat slit. The pool of blood was still warm and wet.

'The murderers must have only just left,' said his assistant.

Although he had both ordered and participated in many massacres, Jannas seemed lost. He had never dreamt that anyone could confront him in his own home and attack his household.

With wary steps, he crossed the hall and entered the reception chamber. On a chair, in a grotesque posture, sat the body of his chambermaid. At her feet lay her severed head. Not far from her were the bodies of the cook and the gardener, their bloody heads laid on their bellies. His assistant vomited.

Stunned, Jannas slowly walked into his office. His secretary had been hacked to death with an axe, and his head lay on a shelf.

'I shall continue to explore this charnel-house,' Jannas told his assistant. 'You must go and see if my men have spotted anyone. If not, tell them to join me here.'

In the commander's bedchamber were the last three serving-women, also decapitated. The bed, chairs and walls were covered in blood. Not a single member of his household had been spared.

Jannas snatched up a jar of fresh water and poured it over his face. Then he left the house and called for his assistant. To his surprise there was no answer.

He went round the corner of the house and almost tripped over the body of one of his guards, an arrow sticking out of the back of his neck. Ten paces away lay his assistant, who had been killed in the same manner. A little further off lay other guards.

Petrified for a moment, Jannas realized that he must flee.

Two enormous hands closed about his throat. He jabbed his elbow into his attacker's stomach to try get free, but the lady Aberia took the blow without batting an eyelid.

'No one is stronger than the emperor,' she told him as she strangled him savagely. 'You dared to defy him, Jannas, and that insolence merits death.'

The commander fought with every last bit of his strength, still clutching at his killer. As he died, his larynx crushed, with his last breath he cursed Apophis.

Khamudi had been watching from a safe distance, surrounded by the Cypriot pirates who had cut down Jannas's staff and guards. Now he came nearer.

'It is done, High Treasurer,' said Aberia.

'Disembowel him with a sickle. Officially, his gardener murdered him in order to steal from him.'

## 31

Ahhotep had just dozed off when her bed shook so violently that she almost fell out of it. The furniture creaked, and a vase fell off a shelf and broke. Calm returned for a few moments, then another tremor, even stronger than the first, made the queen get up. The ceiling of her bedchamber had cracked. Up above, she could hear shouting.

Ahhotep tried to leave the room, but the door was locked from the outside.

'Open this door immediately,' she ordered.

An embarrassed voice replied, 'Majesty, my orders—'

'Open it or I shall break it down.'

The man who let her out was no ordinary guard. He was Minos's private secretary, and – like the king – spoke passable Egyptian.

'Am I a prisoner, then?' asked Ahhotep.

'No, not at all, but your safety—'

'Do not trifle with me: I want the truth.'

The secretary gave in. 'King Minos has gone to the sacred mountain, Majesty, to hear the oracle of the bull in the cave of mysteries. Ordinarily, he goes there only every nine years. Because of the exceptional nature of the question he must ask, he has broken with tradition, which may be very dangerous. Sometimes the reigning king does not emerge from the cave, and has to be replaced. At the court, many believe that King Minos has made a double mistake: inviting you to Knossos, and submitting to this ordeal.'

'Most of the court favour the Hyksos, do they not?'

'Let us say they fear the emperor's anger, Majesty – and with good reason. Your presence has persuaded more than one to change his mind, but there are still some who refuse to do so and who might prove dangerous. In his absence, the king asked me to watch over you, and I believe the best way to do that is to lock you in your room, which will be guarded day and night.'

'How long will it be before King Minos returns to Knossos?'

'His consultation with the oracle will take nine days.'

'And . . . what if he does not return?'

The secretary looked perturbed. 'That would be a tragedy for Minoa. I fear there would be a fierce struggle for the throne and the victor would be a supporter of the Hyksos.'

'Then do not lock me up any longer. I must be free to move about.'

'As you wish, Majesty. But I beg you not to leave this wing of the palace, where every guard can be trusted.'

'I understand.'

'Your food and drinks are tasted by my cook, so you can eat and drink absolutely safely. And may I say, Majesty, that I hope fervently for the king's return and for your plans to come to fruition.'

'Are these earth tremors common?'

'They have happened more and more often in the last two years. Some people claim they express the anger of a volcano whose peace was broken by the Hyksos when they murdered some Cypriot pirates on its slopes. The tremors are impressive but do not cause serious damage. The palace at Knossos is so strongly built that you have nothing to fear.'

'I should like to speak with you each day about how the situation is developing.'

'It shall be as you wish, Majesty.'

Aboard the Egyptian ship, at anchor in the little Minoan port where jars of oil were stored, the mood was not optimistic. There was no contact between them and the natives. Soldiers brought them two meals per day and jars of water. No wine or beer.

They were forbidden to disembark, and the captain's only attempt had ended at the bottom of the gangplank. Threatened by spears, he had had to retrace his steps.

'We'll never come to an understanding with these people,' said the helmsman.

'In the past, before the Hyksos invasion, we used to trade with them,' the captain reminded him.

'That may be so, but they're our enemies now.'

'Perhaps Queen Ahhotep will succeed in making them our allies. It wouldn't be her first miracle.'

'You're dreaming, Captain. Minoa is a vassal of the emperor and will remain so. Otherwise Jannas will turn it into a desert.'

'Let me dream anyway.'

'It would be better to face reality. We have been stuck here for ten days and have had no news of the queen. Wake up, Captain.'

'What do you mean?'

'Ahhotep must be either dead or a prisoner. Soon the Minoans will come aboard and kill us. We must get away as soon as possible.'

'What about the mooring-ropes?'

'We have two good divers, who can cut them during the night. At dawn we can weigh anchor and row out of port.'

'The archers will fire on us,' objected the captain.

'They won't be able to see clearly in the dawn light. And we shall fire back.'

'Minoan ships are bound to give chase.'

'I am not so sure about that. They know we're inexperienced at sea and will expect us to be wrecked – besides, we're faster than they are. With the maps and a little luck, we'll get back to Egypt.'

'I cannot abandon Queen Ahhotep.'

'Her fate is sealed, Captain. At least save your crew.'

It was a bitter thought, but he could not help acknowledging its truth. 'Very well, helmsman. Warn the men. We leave at dawn.'

Ten days had passed, and still King Minos had not returned from the cave of the oracle. He must be dead, thought Ahhotep, which meant a war of succession was about to start. She would be merely a pawn in that vicious fight. Either the new ruler would execute her and dispose of her body, or he would hand her over to Apophis. According to what Minos's secretary had told her, all the claimants believed she was a danger which must be got rid of.

If she did not manage to leave the palace in the next few hours, Ahhotep would never see her country again. But the wing in which she was staying was now guarded by new soldiers, who would never let her pass.

How could she get away? All she could think of was to disguise herself as a maidservant and try to escape with other members of the household. Then she would have to get out of Knossos and make her way to the port – but would her ship still be there? Ahhotep refused to think of the obstacles that would lie in her way. As soon as the maidservant entered the room to change the bedlinen, she would knock her unconscious.

There was a soft knock on the door, and a whisper: 'It is King Minos's secretary, Majesty. Open the door quickly.'

Was he accompanied by a host of soldiers? This time there was no way out.

Ahhotep opened the door. The secretary was alone.

'There can no longer be any doubt: the king has died in the cave of mysteries,' he said. 'The priests are demanding a delay before announcing the succession. This is your only chance of escape, Majesty. Get into my chariot; I will take you to the port.'

'Why should you take such a risk?'

'Because I believe in an alliance between Egypt and Minoa. For my country, as well as yours, there is no other way of escaping from Hyksos tyranny. That is the position I shall defend at court and before the new ruler – even though I have no hope of being listened to.'

Stealthily, they made their way out of the palace and round to the stables. The chariot was waiting, ready, and they set off at once along the road to the port. At every moment, the queen expected to be stopped, but Minos's secretary was known and recognized, and they passed all the guard-posts unhindered.

The Egyptian ship was still at the quayside, guarded by some twenty footsoldiers, who refused to let them pass.

'You were ordered not to let anyone disembark,' said the secretary to an officer. 'Queen Ahhotep is going aboard, not disembarking.'

The officer considered for a moment, then stepped aside.

Though his nerves, like the rest of the crew's, were stretched to breaking-point, the captain dared not show his joy. 'We were sure we would never see you again, Majesty, and we were ready to leave.'

'You would have been right so to do. Weigh anchor, cut the mooring-ropes and hoist the sails. If the Minoan archers fire at us, we shall fire back.'

While the Egyptians ran to carry out these orders, the king's secretary debated hotly with the officer, trying to stop him firing. Eventually, he managed to convince him that King Minos wished Queen Ahhotep to leave, because her stay in Minoa must remain a state secret.

Uncertain about these arguments, which he had no time to refer to a superior, the officer watched the Egyptian ship move out of the harbour. With the aid of a strong following wind, it sailed quickly away from the Minoan coast.

## 32

Under the command of Pharaoh Ahmose, the Egyptian army assembled at the Port of Kamose had taken on a proud appearance. Everyone respected the king's authority, yet he remained close to his men. Besides ordering frequent exercises and manoeuvres, he made sure that supplies were delivered regularly and orders followed to the letter. Strict cleanliness was observed in the camp, and the meals were excellent.

Although conditions were as good as possible, no one could forget that a Hyksos attack would come sooner or later, so there was a permanent state of alert. Day and night, many lookouts were on duty, with instructions to alert the pharaoh at the first sign of danger.

Through Rascal and the other carrier-pigeons, Ahmose kept in contact with Moustache and the Afghan, who were in Memphis, helping the resistance there. The Hyksos were still besieging the city, but had made no attempt to take the part that was not under their control.

Ahmose thought often of Nefertari, who had remained in Thebes to carry out the duties formerly performed by Teti the Small. With the aid of Heray and Qaris, the Great Royal Wife must ensure the prosperity of the provinces of Upper Egypt, which provided the soldiers' food. Each morning, she went to the temple at Karnak, where she celebrated the rising of Amon and implored his protection. The people already loved their new queen, who was both unpretentious and imbued with a sense of responsibility.

Emheb was shown in and bowed to the pharaoh. 'Nothing to report, Majesty,' he said.

'Tell me the truth. Is there anything we can do to improve our warning-system?'

Emheb had regained all his old strength and vigour. 'I cannot see how, Majesty,' he said confidently. 'Every system is fallible, of course, but I have doubled the number of guards at each post. Whether the enemy approaches by river, through the countryside or from the desert, he will be spotted.'

'How is the Minoan behaving?'

'He accepts that he is confined to quarters.'

Ahmose had thought it best to bring Linas to the Port of Kamose, while ensuring that he knew as little possible about the Egyptian army. No doubt he missed Thebes, but he was a guest of a very special kind, and must not be indulged.

'Why do you think Jannas isn't trying to destroy us?' asked Ahmose.

'Because his hands are tied, Majesty. Either the emperor has sent him to spread terror through some far-off country, or else he is in charge of the Delta's security and is preparing an offensive which will sweep away everything in its path. He must have learnt many lessons from his failure last time.'

'But suppose internal disputes are weakening the Hyksos? The emperor is old, and his throne may soon become vacant.'

'I suspect that evil old man will outlive us all!'

Ahmose recognized the characteristic flapping of Rascal's wings as he returned from the oasis at Sekhet-imit, near the border with Libya. The bird landed with his usual neatness; there was a bright gleam in his eyes.

When he read the message, the king realized why Rascal was happy. 'My mother has returned safely,' he told Emheb. 'She and her crew crossed the marshy part of the Delta, followed the desert tracks, and have just reached the oasis.'

'The road is under our control,' said the governor, smiling broadly, 'but even so I shall send some men to meet the queen.'

Young Laughter and Long-Ears gave the queen a noisy welcome. As soon as they permitted the pharaoh to approach her, Ahhotep and her son embraced.

'Are you well, Mother?'

'Very well. The voyage enabled me to rest after our hurried departure from Minoa.'

'So it was a trap!'

'Not exactly. Minos knows the Hyksos will one day invade his country, but he is afraid of their reaction if he allies himself with Egypt. So I suggested that he should place himself under the protection of the Queen of the Distant Shores.'

'And did he accept?'

'He went up to the cave of mysteries, where the kings of Minoa meditate when they have need of new energy, but he did not return and his potential successors have begun to tear each other apart. Without the help of Minos's secretary, who believes in an alliance between our countries, I would have been held prisoner.'

'Your return is another miracle,' said Ahmose earnestly.

'Good luck has not yet deserted me.'

'So we cannot depend upon Minoa.'

'The Great Island is about to undergo violent upheavals, and who knows what the outcome will be? If the next king does not accuse Minos's secretary of treason, perhaps he will listen to him. To be honest, there is not much hope. Yet my journey may not have been in vain, because the king told me that Jannas and Khamudi, the two most important Hyksos after the emperor, are bitter enemies. They are already virtually at war with each other, each one no doubt hoping to succeed Apophis.'

'So that's why Jannas hasn't attacked us!' Ahmose thought for a moment. 'This knowledge gives us an advantage. Now would be a good time to retake Memphis and gain a foothold in the Delta.'

'We must indeed do both things, but first we must solve the problem of the Hyksos chariots.'

'You have a new plan, haven't you?'

'Before we discuss it, summon the Minoan.'

Linas had a hearty appetite for food and drink, and during his enforced inactivity he had put on weight.

'Majesty, how happy I am to see you again!' he exclaimed as he greeted Ahhotep. 'I dare to think that you will give me permission to return to Minoa.'

'Who are you?'

'But . . . Majesty, you know who I am,' Linas stammered 'I am the son of King Minos, his youngest son.'

'He told me himself that he had lied to me, so that I would not be afraid to leave Egypt. A king would not have sacrificed his son, would he? I did not believe your story, Linas, but I went to Minoa anyway.'

He knelt down. 'I was obeying King Minos, Majesty, but even so I am not just anybody. I am considered one of Minoa's finest ship's captains, and in case of war my ship will be in the forefront of the fighting.'

'You may return safely to your home,' said the queen.

'I thank you, but . . . how?'

'Go to a small port under Hyksos control and join the crew of one of their trading-ships leaving for Minoa. If your new king ever wishes to send me a message, tell him to give it to you. We shall be happy to receive you here again.'

Why had the Hyksos spy not stopped Ahhotep going to Minoa? For two reasons. First, because he had hoped that she would not reach the

Great Island, in view of how dangerous the journey was. Second, because he was certain that King Minos would not dare form an alliance with the Egyptians. What he did not know, of course, was that Windswept had turned against Apophis and had betrayed state secrets.

During the queen's absence, there had been no attempts to assassinate Ahmose, and nothing untoward had happened in Thebes. But neither Ahhotep nor the pharaoh could believe the spy had given up.

'Have any senior officers died recently?' asked the queen.

'Yes, an old general of artificers, but he was not the sort of man to be one of Apophis's lickspittles.'

'Surely that is precisely the sort of man Apophis would make use of.'

'But if he really was the lickspittle, Mother, now that he's dead the emperor no longer has a spy here.'

'That is a very fragile theory, Ahmose, and we cannot lay too much weight on it. All the same, it would be a good idea for you to return to Thebes and make detailed inquiries about the general. It will also give you an opportunity to see Nefertari again.'

Ahmose smiled. 'You can still read my thoughts, Mother. As for me, I'm burning to know your plan for fighting against the Hyksos chariots.'

'It involves first of all changing our own methods, and then using the enemy's.'

## 33

Rascal brought Ahhotep's message to the Afghan and Moustache, who were at the rebels' headquarters in Memphis, a half-ruined and apparently abandoned farm. As it had long ceased to interest the Hyksos, this was where they stored food and weapons from the south before sending them into the besieged city.

The Egyptians knew all the enemy's habits and timetables, and made best use of their weak spots. The commander of the chariot corps had stopped attacking, and confined himself to shows of strength, in the form of large-scale manoeuvres designed to impress the rebels, who were condemned to rot where they stood.

Moustache decoded the message. 'We can't do that! It's impossible – we'd be flayed alive.'

'Is the queen ordering us to attack Avaris?'

'You're not far from the truth! No, not that, but—'

'Then what are her orders?' demanded the Afghan.

'We are to capture a Hyksos chariot and several horses.'

The Afghan stared at him. 'We can't do that,' he murmured.

In silence, the two men downed a whole jar of the local red wine to give themselves courage.

'I suppose,' said the Afghan eventually, 'the queen leaves us no choice in the matter?'

'You know what she's like,' agreed Moustache.

'It's a nice idea, but carrying it out will be rather tricky, particularly as we don't know how to handle horses or chariots – we can't just steal one by driving it away.'

'That's true. So some of the raiding-party will take charge of the horses, which are apparently rather like enormous donkeys, while the others seize the chariot, which will have to be pulled as far as the river. And then we'll have to load the whole lot on board a sailing-boat.'

'I like your summary – it has the advantage of missing out all the critical phases of the operation. Do you think we can politely ask a

Hyksos officer to let us examine his chariot? I think your first reaction was the right one: we'll be flayed alive.'

'Orders are orders. And surely we aren't going to disappoint the Queen of Freedom?'

'No, Moustache, you're right about that.'

The two men gathered together their best men to form a raiding-party thirty strong; any larger and they might be spotted. There was no point asking the men if they were volunteering for an impossible mission, because they had done that already. Nevertheless, the plan was heard without enthusiasm. Each man realized he had very little chance of surviving this mad venture.

'I suggest three simultaneous operations,' said the Afghan. 'One: the people of Memphis create a diversion by attacking the Hyksos camp closest to the white wall. Two: twenty-five of us remove as many horses as possible from the stable. Three: the other five steal a chariot.'

A hundred questions were fired off, emphasizing the difficulties of the raid. And the local wine flowed in abundance.

Following in the steps of Teti the Small, to whom she paid homage every day, Nefertari was making Memphis more and more beautiful. She had won everyone's heart, even those of the old priests and the most sour-tempered craftsmen. Qaris had become her devoted colleague, and Heray made it a point of honour to present her with proofs of perfect management.

The young queen did not remain shut away in the palace. She travelled all over the countryside, visited houses in the capital, treated rich and poor with equal consideration, and gave help to the sick and the destitute. Her days were long, and sometimes exhausting, but she did not dream of complaining. How could she, when Ahhotep had for so many years risked her very life in the struggle to free Egypt?

Only Ahmose's absence really weighed upon her. Without his peaceful strength, she felt vulnerable. But now, at long last, he was coming back.

Long before he arrived, Nefertari was at the landing-stage, where the people were already celebrating the pharaoh's return. Neither she nor he heard the cheers. In their eyes there was such profound, intense joy that they were alone amid the merrymaking crowds.

They spent such joyful, passionate nights of love together that Nefertari almost managed to make him forget the war. But Ahmose was the pharaoh, and when morning came he owed it to his people to go about his official duties. To worship Amon at Karnak was the first of these, in order to maintain the link between heaven and earth. Next came a meeting with his counsellors, which Nefertari attended and at which her recommendations carried weight. With her detailed knowledge of the strengths and weaknesses of the region, the Great Royal Wife influenced people towards the right decisions.

'How long are you planning to remain in Thebes?' she asked Ahmose, as they enjoyed the gentle evening warmth on the palace terrace one evening.

'Only for as long as it takes me to investigate the death of an old general and find out if he was the Hyksos spy we have been searching for.'

'The Hyksos spy? But . . .'

'My mother believes he was responsible for the deaths of my father and brother.'

'Then that monster murdered two pharaohs – and you might have been his next victim!'

'Be very careful, Nefertari, and take note of any suspicious behaviour.'

Next morning, the king received Heray in his office. While continuing to oversee the harvests and the stocking of the granaries, a weapon of war as essential as the sword, Heray had extended his domain to include the entire Theban economy. He was a man with lively eyes and an easy manner, who got along with everyone. No one would ever forget the time when he had rooted out the Hyksos supporters in Thebes. Still spritely despite his sizeable frame, he had maintained his network of informers, so that nothing escaped him and the capital's safety was assured.

'Heray, have you studied the general's case?'

'In detail, Majesty. He was a Theban who rose through the ranks, mainly because of his skill at training raw recruits. He spent most of his life at the base in the desert, and always displayed fervent support for the struggle against the Hyksos. On his deathbed, he told those close to him to remain loyal to the Queen of Freedom.'

'And you found nothing lurking behind that fine façade?'

'Nothing at all, Majesty. He was a soldier who lived at the barracks and cared for nothing but his soldiers.'

'Did he ever travel to the North?'

'No, never.'

'And no one in his entourage has voiced suspicions about his conduct?'

'No one, Majesty.

'So he was an honest, respectable officer who served his country well.'

'Exactly.'

'Have your informants suggested any likely suspects among the Theban dignitaries?'

'No, Majesty.'

Ahmed sighed. 'Do not let your guard down, Heray.'

'If one single Hyksos supporter still exists in our good city, I shall find him.'

In accordance with Queen Ahhotep's wishes, the pharaoh went to the military base to prepare a vast enclosed training-area and stables. These were destined to house the Hyksos horses which, if destiny favoured the raiding-party, would soon arrive in Thebes.

## 34

At last the new moon rose, fortunately accompanied by a few clouds.

'Time to go,' decided the Afghan.

'Will you deal with the horses or the chariot?' asked Moustache.

'The horses are more dangerous.'

'Then I'll deal with them.'

'Why you?'

'Because that's how it is.'

'We'll draw lots.'

'There isn't time. I know about donkeys, and the horses are a bit longer and taller, that's all. Just don't fail. Without the chariot, my efforts won't be much use.'

'The chariot without the horses won't be much use, either, remember.'

'It's strange, isn't it? When I joined the rebels I was sure I wouldn't live long. Yet tonight here we are, about to deal the Hyksos invader a terrific blow.'

'You can dream all you like later. Let's go.'

During some highly risky scouting trips, the two men had found a place, away from the main encampment, where some chariots were being repaired. Quite a number of horses were stabled there, too, perhaps because they were sick or tired. The place had the notable advantage of being less well guarded than the other stables.

Now, at about midnight, there were only ten sentries watching the animals and three guarding the shelter where the chariots were awaiting repair. Lying flat on their bellies in the sharp-bladed grass, the Egyptians watched.

'If a sentry gives the alarm,' whispered the Afghan, 'we're done for. We must kill them all at exactly the same time, and without making a sound.'

'I'm worried that their four-legged friends may sound the alarm, too,' said Moustache. 'Before taking them away, we'd better raid the sleeping-quarters and kill all the other Hyksos.'

They both knew that the slightest slip in carrying out their plan would mean death. But there was no time for debate and, daggers in hand, all the men moved towards their designated targets.

One sentry had just time to let out a cry, though it was stifled almost instantly. Their hearts thumping, the members of the raiding-party froze. Endless seconds went by, but no Hyksos appeared.

The Egyptians converged on the sleeping-quarters and, at Moustache's signal, they poured in. Only the two officers who slept at the far end of the room put up any fight, and the raiding-party were swift and determined. Without a word, they proceeded to the next phase of their mission.

On the Afghan's side, there was no difficulty. He chose the only chariot that still had both its wheels, and he and his four men began dragging it towards the river.

Moustache's task turned out to be a good deal harder. The first Egyptian who approached a horse did so from behind. He was kicked square in the chest and fell flat on his back.

Moustache helped him to his feet. 'Can you walk?'

'I've broken half my ribs, but I'll be all right. But be careful with those brutes.'

'We'll put ropes round their necks and lead them.'

Most of the animals accepted this with more or less good grace, but one neighed and tried to bite, and another reared up, rushed out of the stable and galloped away.

'Let's not waste time here,' ordered Moustache, who was worried that the horses might cause more trouble.

In fact, apparently quite pleased at this unexpected exercise, the rest of them calmly let themselves be led down to the river. On the bank, the Egyptians congratulated each other: only one wounded, and their mission a complete success!

'We still have to get them on board,' the Afghan pointed out.

The gangplank was too narrow for the chariot. The emergency one had to be laid across it and the chariot pushed very slowly so that it didn't fall into the river.

'Now the horses,' ordered Moustache.

The first refused to climb the gangplank, and so did the next.

'Jab them in the backside,' suggested the wounded man, who was not feeling kindly towards them.

'Too risky,' objected Moustache.

'But we can't just leave them.'

'I have an idea.'

Moustache picked out the largest, strongest horse, a white stallion with a steady gaze, who seemed less edgy than the others.

'We're taking you to Thebes,' he told the horse, 'and you will be well treated. The only way of getting there is to board this boat. Show an example by climbing this gangplank. Do you understand?'

He stroked the animal's head and let him sniff his human scent. After a long time, the animal accepted the invitation. A mare calmly followed him, and then the others did likewise.

'You know how to speak to horses,' remarked the Afghan.

'I have so many gifts that I shan't live long enough to use them all.'

As dawn broke over Memphis, the guard was changed at the vast Hyksos camp. Another dismal night when nothing had happened, another dismal morning during which attackers and besieged alike would remain fixed in their positions. Perhaps the commander would order a parade of chariots to impress the people of Memphis and remind them who was the stronger.

The sentry yawned, glad to have finished his watch. He would breakfast on milk and fresh bread, and then sleep until noon. Then have lunch and an afternoon nap. Suddenly, he saw what he thought must be a mirage: a horse, wandering around the camp on its own. He immediately alerted his senior officer, whose eyes were still misty with sleep.

'Look over there, sir.'

'Anyone would think . . . No, that's impossible. Who has let a horse escape? I shall tell the commander immediately.'

Abruptly awakened from his sleep, the commander insisted on checking for himself. What he saw sent him into a violent rage.

'Bring me those responsible for this appalling breech of discipline immediately. And have that horse taken back to its stable.'

A good half-hour later, a white-faced groom returned. 'Sir, the soldiers . . . They're all dead, and the stable's empty.'

'What is this nonsense?'

'The western stable and barracks. There's not a single man left alive.'

The commander went straight there, accompanied by his assistant. The groom had not exaggerated.

'The rebels have dared steal our horses!' bristled the assistant. 'We must warn Avaris.'

'In my opinion, that would be a bad mistake.'

'But, Commander, that is the order. An incident as serious as this—'

'I, you and our subordinates will be accused of incompetence and negligence. At best, we'll be sent to prison. At worst, we'll go to the labyrinth and the bull.'

The force of these arguments shook his assistant. 'Then what do you suggest, sir?'

'Absolute silence. We'll bury the bodies and kill the groom. Then we'll forget the entire incident.'

## 35

Proud, strong and tall, the Hyksos horses amazed and fascinated the Egyptians. Long-Ears and Young Laughter watched them attentively, and the donkey soon decided that they would not be able to carry heavy loads. An Egyptian word meaning 'the Beautiful' was chosen for the imposing creatures.

At the secret base at Thebes, Ahhotep and Ahmose called a meeting of their general staff. Those present included Emheb, who had been permitted to come to Thebes from the Port of Kamose, leaving Moon in temporary command. At the first sign of danger, Moon would alert the capital.

As they looked at the horses, everyone was full of praise for the Afghan and Moustache.

'They are truly beautiful,' said Qaris. 'I am happy to have lived long enough to see them at close hand.'

'But do not go near them,' advised Neshi. 'Some of them are easily angered. I have given up trying to understand their character.'

'It is no more difficult than that of donkeys,' said Heray. 'We must simply be patient and thoughtful in order to gain their trust.'

'The most urgent thing is for them to start providing us with foals,' said Emheb. 'Even if we succeed in mastering the horses, we shall need many, many of them in order to rival the Hyksos chariot corps.'

'Work has already begun on that,' Moustache assured him. 'From what I have seen so far, the horse likes authority. As Heray said, their masters must establish a friendly relationship with them, so the rule should be one horse to one man. They will learn to know each other and become inseparable.'

'Have you chosen yours yet?' asked the queen.

'The large white male who is watching us, Majesty. He is the one who enabled us to embark and disembark without too much difficulty.'

'Hyksos horses are used to pulling chariots. Why should we not ride them, too?'

'Moustache shall be the Egyptian army's first cavalry officer,' laughed the Afghan. 'He had better try it here and now.'

'What? You want me to climb up there?'

'You've sat on a donkey before, haven't you?'

'In case you haven't noticed, the horse is bigger and taller.'

'That big male has adopted you. He can guess what you want to do. Surely you aren't going to disappoint Queen Ahhotep?'

Stung, Moustache clambered up on to the horse's rump. Not only did the beast refuse to go forward, but it reared. Moustache slid magnificently off and landed on the sandy training-ground, in front of a multitude of guards.

He leapt to his feet in annoyance. 'Hey, White Giant, we're friends, you and I. You've no cause to play nasty tricks on me.'

'Try to find a better sitting position,' advised Ahhotep.

'Near his neck?'

'No, in the middle of his back.'

This time, Moustache managed to sit down. 'Forward, White Giant!'

The horse neighed and set off at a gallop. Caught unawares, Moustache tried to cling on to the horse's neck. The spectators marvelled at its power and its speed, before watching the Egyptian army's first cavalry officer fly unceremoniously through the air.

'Ow! It really hurts,' groaned Moustache, who was stretched out on his belly.

'Behave like a hero,' She-Cat told him as she massaged him gently. 'This ointment will soon relieve the pain.'

'That damned horse has broken all my ribs.'

'It was your fall, not the horse, and you still have a few unbroken ones. No serious injuries.'

'I'm never getting on that monster again.'

'White Giant is magnificent and he is already getting bored with you. You've scarcely begun your apprenticeship, my darling. In two days, you'll ride round the training-ground again.'

'Do you want me dead, She-Cat?'

The way she caressed him proved otherwise. 'There were one or two small problems, but your experience was very instructive. Queen Ahhotep has thought of some improvements which should please you.'

She-Cat was as gifted at healing as she was in the arts of love. A few days later, virtually recovered, Moustache faced White Giant again. Ahhotep had placed a piece of fabric on the horse's back, and he was now equipped with a leather bridle and reins.

'He has accepted this?' gasped Moustache.

'We talked for a long time,' said the queen, 'and tried to find a way for the rider to guide the horse without hurting him. I think we are on the right track, but you will have to perfect the method.'*

Moustache was delighted to find that he could now easily convey his wishes to his mount. He could make him speed up, slow down, turn to the right or the left. The horse responded quickly and clearly enjoyed the exercise.

'You surprise me,' admitted the Afghan. 'I didn't think you'd be able to master this new weapon.'

'While my ribs were healing, I did some thinking.'

'Oh? What about?'

'One rider won't be enough. Others must do what I've done.'

'No doubt,' agreed the Afghan flatly.

'I've noticed a grey horse eyeing you with interest.'

'I like solid ground. Having my feet in the air would make me very uneasy.'

'Emheb and Heray will lift you up easily.'

The two big men promptly did so.

After falling off a few times, the Afghan became the Egyptian army's second horseman.

As there was no activity around the Port of Kamose, the general staff remained in Thebes where they continued to discover the world of horses.

She-Cat healed a mare's sore eye and saw that her remedies worked well on the animals. Young Laughter gradually grew used to the huge creatures. Ahhotep calmed the nervous ones and reassured those that were anxious. She fed them in turn and had long talks with them.

Moustache and the Afghan, who by now were good riders, had moved on to another stage by persuading White Giant and Grey to jump increasingly high obstacles. Several times they headed out into the desert, where the horses loved to gallop across the empty spaces.

But the two men and their mounts hardly constituted an army able to take on the Hyksos chariots. It remained to be seen if the Egyptian carpenters could make chariots like the one spirited away from Memphis.

*Egyptian horses were not shod, and riders did not use a saddle or stirrups.

## 36

Jannas's body was thrown into a deep ditch, along with those of his assistant, his servants and his bodyguards. Once the house had been hastily cleaned, it became the official residence of the new commander of the war-fleet, an elderly man suggested by Khamudi and duly appointed by the emperor. The man was delighted by his unexpected promotion. He was also a heavy user of drugs, and would cause Khamudi no trouble.

None of the Hyksos officials believed a word of the official story about Jannas's death, but they dared not try to find out the truth. In any case, it was easy to guess: threatened with downfall, Khamudi had got rid of Jannas. Now a single question was being asked: had he or had he not acted on the orders of the emperor?

Apophis had not been seen for several days. Many people thought he must be on his deathbed. Some advocated rallying around Khamudi. Others advised killing him – but then whom would they place on the throne? No one in the army or the war-fleet had a reputation to rival Jannas's. Factions were already forming, ready to tear each other asunder, when news came that all army officers were summoned to the citadel.

One general in the chariot corps, regarded as Jannas's right-hand man, decided to escape. He would leave on a trading-ship – its destination did not matter – would disappear at the first port they came to, and would make sure he was forgotten. But the captain refused to take the unexpected passenger aboard and alerted the port guards, who took him immediately to Khamudi.

'You are a traitor and you deserve to die,' declared the High Treasurer. 'I offer you one choice. If you tell me the names of Jannas's accomplices you will be beheaded, but if you refuse to talk you will be tortured.'

'I refuse to talk.'

'You imbecile, you won't hold out for long.'

Khamudi was right. His face burnt and his limbs lacerated, the general revealed the names of Jannas's supporters in the army. They were arrested in their homes or at the barracks, and were beheaded in front of their soldiers.

The audience chamber at the citadel was as icy cold as ever.

'The purge,' said the emperor in his harsh voice, 'has eliminated many subversives. However, do not think that I have therefore lowered my guard. Any of Jannas's supporters not yet identified will be unmasked and punished. Those who confess here and now will receive my clemency.'

A young captain of footsoldiers stepped forward. 'Majesty, I was wrong to believe what Commander Jannas said. He claimed to have full powers, and I wanted to fight under his command to affirm my belief in the empire's omnipotence.'

'Your honesty has spared you the shame of public beheading. Your throat shall be cut before the Temple of Set.'

'Majesty, I beg you—'

'Cut out the traitor's tongue and take him away.'

Within seconds, the captain's blood poured on to the floor of the audience chamber.

'High Treasurer Khamudi is hereby appointed commander-in-chief of all the Hyksos forces,' announced Apophis. 'He will carry out my orders to the letter. Anyone who refuses to obey him, for any reason whatsoever, will be sentenced to torture.'

Dead drunk, Khamudi stretched out on his bed and tried – with some difficulty – to get his breath back. Never before had he come so close to the edge of the abyss.

If Jannas had been less respectful of the emperor's person, and had taken full powers more quickly, Khamudi would now be languishing in a prison camp. Fortunately, though, Jannas had not been cunning enough. He had made the fatal mistake of revealing his true intentions to the emperor, and Apophis, sensing that he was under threat, had reacted ferociously.

The emperor strongly opposed dividing his forces, and wanted to keep most of his regiments in the Delta and near Avaris. The new commander-in-chief would therefore have to let matters go on much as before, continuing the siege at Memphis and making greater efforts to put down the Hittite rebellion. The Hyksos would burn more Hittite forests, crops and villages, and massacre on the spot any civilians – women, children and old men included – suspected of complicity with the rebels.

There remained Ahhotep and her petty pharaoh. They seemed to be following the same path as the King of Kerma, who was slumbering peacefully in far-off Nubia, content with his harem and his fine food. If Ahhotep was an intelligent woman, she must have realized that she would never enter the Hyksos shrine and that she must be content with the lands she had conquered. The old emperor might endure this state of affairs, weakened as he was by Jannas's downfall, but Khamudi would not put up with it for very long. He wanted to see the rebellious queen helpless at his feet, begging for mercy.

However, there were other priorities, beginning with an expansion of the drugs trade. Khamudi was preparing to offer two new products for sale, one of poor quality and cheap enough for anyone to buy, and the other rare and expensive, reserved for the elite. The profits would ensure that the High Treasurer soon doubled his immense fortune.

With Jannas dead and the emperor growing old, the future lay wide open. But there was still one threat he could not ignore. So Khamudi confided in Yima, his devoted wife.

'What a terrible night!' Tormented by ever-more-terrifying nightmares, the lady Tany had soiled her bed several times, obliging her serving-women to change the linen. Even now she was awake, the empress trembled when she remembered the torrents of flame she had seen engulfing Avaris.

At dawn, she wolfed down some game in sauce and drank some strong beer. She ate and drank so fast that she immediately got stomach cramps, and had to go back to bed.

'The lady Yima would like to see you,' one of her ladies informed her.

'That dear, loving friend. Show her in.'

Yima was made-up to excess and simpering even more than usual. 'You look less tired this morning, Majesty.'

'Alas, I only look it. You were right, Yima. That damned Jannas did put a curse on me. I am so glad he's dead! With your husband in command of the army, Avaris has nothing to fear.'

'You can depend on Khamudi, Majesty. As long as he is alive, the Egyptians will never get near Avaris.'

'That's so reassuring! I hope the emperor has not caused any problems over what happened?'

'He was only too glad to be rid of Jannas and his ridiculous demands.'

'That's good. But we must keep our little secret. No one must know about the part played by our dear Aberia.'

'Have no fear, Majesty. All anyone knows is the official version: that Jannas was murdered by his gardener.'

'Has Aberia received her reward?'

'My husband has been very generous. As for your devoted servant, she would like to provide you with a remedy which might speed your recovery.'

'Go and fetch it quickly.'

The statuesque Aberia entered the empress's bedchamber.

'You, Aberia? You know a potion which will restore my health?'

'It is not a potion, Majesty.'

'Then what is it?'

'Something much more radical.' Aberia held up her enormous hands.

'I . . . I don't understand.'

'The best way of keeping our secret, Majesty, is to silence you once and for all. It seems that you talk in your sleep. That is dangerous.'

Tany tried to struggle to her feet, but Aberia's hands closed round her throat.

Tany was buried in the palace burial-ground. The emperor did not attend the ceremony; he was busy checking the accounts Khamudi had submitted to him.

'Majesty,' said Khamudi, 'permit me to offer you my condolences.'

'No one will miss that old sow, least of all me.'

Thanks to Khamudi, Aberia was rich; and from now only she would work for no one but him. The death of the empress, whose pernicious influence he had feared, took him one step closer to absolute power. But Khamudi did not allow himself that thought in Apophis's presence, for the Emperor of Darkness might have read his mind.

## 37

Emheb gave Ahhotep his verdict. 'Before taking charge of my good city of Edfu, I plied my trade as a carpenter. Since you wished to be sure no information would leak out, I attended to the Hyksos chariot myself. It's a remarkable piece of work, but very heavy – as it needs to be to carry four soldiers.'

'Then let us lighten it and adapt it to use by only two men,' suggested the queen. 'That will give us greater mobility.'

'Indeed, but the problem of stability will be difficult to solve. And then there is the choice of the right wood, which must be both light and strong. Three kinds seem suitable: tamarisk, elm and birch. We have plenty of tamarisk, but the other two are rather rare. I can use all we have in stock, which will be enough for about a hundred wheels, but then we shall have to go obtain more in the Delta or from abroad.'

Ahhotep's disarming smile wiped away his reservations. He showed her how he planned to bend the wood, by moistening it and heating it until it became pliable enough.

Before long the first two wheels were finished. Each was two cubits in diameter, with four spokes.

'I took the Hyksos wheels as a model,' Emheb explained to Ahhotep, 'but improved on them. Their wheel-spokes are made from two pieces of wood, but I have made mine differently. In particular, I have joined together several V-shaped pieces, which makes the spokes extremely strong, and have used glues and coatings to harden them.'

Proudly, he ran his hand along an axle four cubits long, which would support the shell of the chariot, and a five-cubit shaft, whose height could be adjusted according to the size of the horses.

'How do you plan to make the chariot floor?' she asked.

'I shall use well-stretched leather strips on a wooden frame. The floor will be strong, but flexible enough to absorb jolting on bumpy ground.'

At last the moment came to try the chariot for the first time. Two horses were harnessed to it; all that was needed was a crew.

'Where will we find two men mad enough to climb into that thing and drive it off at top speed?' wondered Moustache.

'The queen insists that the trials must be held in absolute secrecy,' replied Emheb. 'Of those who know, Pharaoh Ahmose clearly cannot possibly run such a risk, Neshi is a scholar and not used to such exertion, Qaris is too old, and Heray is too heavy. And I am in charge of manufacture. So . . .'

'The Afghan and me?'

'You've faced bigger dangers than this.'

'I'm not so sure about that,' said the Afghan.

'Come on, now, climb aboard. Moustache will drive and you, Afghan, will act as the archer and fire at a straw target. The goal is simple: to score a direct hit while moving as quickly as possible.'

'The future of the war depends on you,' declared Ahhotep, and the pharaoh nodded.

Moustache and the Afghan took their places in the chariot.

In this kind of situation, both men had the same attitude: full speed ahead. When they went in a straight line, the trial was a great success. But at the first turn, taken without slowing down, the chariot tipped over and the two men were flung out.

'I'm not in pain any more,' said the Afghan. 'She-Cat, you're a real sorceress!'

'My wife is in charge of the battlefield doctors,' said her proud husband, who had also recovered well. 'Anyway, you aren't an emergency any more.'

'When are you going to try again?' asked She-Cat.

'There's no hurry, my darling, and—'

'Yes there is: we have no time to lose. Making a better chariot than the Hyksos ones will take a lot of trials, and you do not have the leisure to be lazy.'

'But we were injured, and—'

'All you had was some bruising, which has already healed. You're both perfectly healthy, so you can certainly take a few more falls.'

She-Cat's prophecy proved accurate.

During the months that followed, Emheb made repeated adjustments to make the chariot as effective a weapon as possible. He used more coatings and adhesives, fixed the rear of the shaft more solidly into the bar under the platform, and made a better harness from a wide strip of fabric covering the horse's withers, another narrower one under its belly and a third, lined with leather, against its chest so that the animal was not hurt. He lightened the shell still further, and left it open at the rear. Its frame consisted of several curved wooden bars and its thin walls were covered with leather. The same material reinforced the parts of the chariot that were exposed to friction and the joins between the different sections.

Each day, Ahhotep feared she would receive bad news from the Port of Kamose. But the pigeons always brought the same message: 'Nothing to report.'

The rebels at Memphis sent an astonishing message. According to rumours from Avaris, Jannas had been murdered by one of his servants, and Khamudi, who had been appointed supreme commander, was to carry out a purge and reorganization of the Hyksos army. If this was true, it meant that a rebel network, however tiny, had been recreated inside the enemy capital and was managing to communicate – no doubt with great difficulty – with the besieged city.

'The death of Jannas would explain why the Hyksos are playing a waiting game,' observed Ahmose.

'It is all the more important that our chariots are a success,' said Ahhotep. 'Horses take a long time to breed, and we have only a few pairs. We shall have to steal more from the enemy, and hope that our chariots work well – which is not always the case!'

'I shall see to it,' promised Emheb.

Moustache and the Afghan had lost count of their attempts, some of which went better than others. A particular success was that they had learnt how best to handle the reins. The driver wrapped them round his waist, so that simply turning his body to right or left made the horses turn in that direction, while leaning back made them slow down or stop, depending on how steeply he leant.

Inside the shell, Moustache had installed leather pockets containing arrows, spears, daggers and leather straps for emergency repairs.

'This time,' he confided to the Afghan, 'I can tell it's going to go right.'

'You've said that lots of times!'

'Gee up, my lads, full speed ahead!'

Given their heads, the horses galloped off. Although the ground was uneven, the chariot did not slacken speed. It safely negotiated the first turn, round a boundary stone, then the second, which was very tight because of a rut. The chariot remained perfectly balanced.

The Afghan fired five arrows at the straw figure of a man. Every one hit the target.

Moustache turned for a second run, which was as successful as the first.

'We have succeeded,' the queen told Emheb, who was almost weeping with happiness. 'Work is to begin immediately on making more chariots and training more drivers.'

# 38

After smoking plenty of opium, the officer in charge of port security at Avaris flung himself on top of the young Egyptian girl he had selected for his pleasure, but he had beaten her so badly that she was unconscious.

'Wake up, you idiot! I can't have any fun with a dead woman.'

He slapped her several times, but there was no response. Too bad for her. She would be thrown into a mass grave with all the other whores.

The Hyksos emerged from his official residence to urinate over the edge of the quay, taking care not to fall in the water. Suddenly, he was surrounded by ten pirates belonging to Khamudi's personal guard. He thought he must be having a bad dream.

'Follow us,' one of them ordered him.

'There must be some mistake.'

'Are you in charge of port security or not?'

'Yes, but—'

'Then follow us. The High Treasurer wants to see you.'

'It's been a hard day, and I . . . I'm very tired.'

'If necessary, we'll help you walk.'

Khamudi had taken up residence in Jannas's office, at the heart of the largest barracks in Avaris. He had changed the furniture and had the walls painted red. On the work-table lay papyri giving the names of men who had supported Jannas, soldiers of all ranks and regiments. Khamudi examined the cases one by one, and set his accusatory official seal upon almost all of them. Only a truly thorough purge of the army would enable him to command the Hyksos troops without fear of betrayal.

When the latest suspect was brought before him, Khamudi said, 'You have a good deal of explaining to do.'

'I do my work well, High Treasurer. For me, the port's security is a sacred duty.'

'You were a friend of Jannas, were you not?

'Me? Oh no, my lord, I hated him.'

'You were often seen with him.'

'He was giving me orders, that's all.'

'That may be true.'

The suspect relaxed a little.

'I have summoned you here for another reason, which is just as serious,' Khamudi went on. 'There was a young Egyptian girl in your bed.'

'That is so, my lord, but—'

'Last night there was a different one, and the night before that yet another.'

'Well, my lord, I am a man of strong appetites and—'

'Where do these girls come from?'

'I meet them, and—'

'Stop lying.'

The accused squirmed. 'Since the harem was closed down, a man has to find ways of getting by. So I . . . I've found ways.'

'You have set up your own little harem and you hire out your girls to others, don't you?'

'Several of us do benefit, but it's because of the closure – I'm sure you understand, my lord? In a way, I'm providing a service.'

'I am the High Treasurer, and no trade can begin on Hyksos soil without my prior knowledge. Defrauding the state is a very serious crime.'

'I will pay any fine, my lord.'

'I want to know how you have organized your operation and the location of all the closed houses in Avaris.'

The officer talked for some time. Khamudi was delighted. Now he could take control of this prostitution and make substantial profits from it.

'You have co-operated fully,' he conceded, 'so you deserve a reward.'

'And I am not a suspect any more?'

'Not at all, now that the facts have been established. Come with me.'

The officer did not really understand the High Treasurer's meaning, but he followed him without hesitation. Khamudi led him to the barracks gate where Aberia dealt with the Hyksos officers and soldiers convicted of conspiring with the criminal Jannas.

'You are now not a mere suspect,' explained Khamudi, 'but guilty of treason and are therefore sentenced to deportation to a prison camp. I wish you a good journey.'

The man tried to run, but Aberia seized him by the hair, making him cry out in pain, then threw him to the ground and broke one of his legs.

'You still have one leg to walk with. And I advise you not to fall behind on the journey.'

This was the third time in a month that the guards had raided the weapons store at Avaris port. Fifty of the workforce had been arrested, and nobody knew what had become of them.

One of the team in charge of making and repairing chariot-wheels was called Arek, a vigorous young man born of a Caucasian father and an Egyptian mother. He had seen his elder brother leave in a convoy of men, women and children, accused of having plotted with Jannas. Rumour had it that those who survived the march were thrown into a camp from which no prisoner ever emerged alive.

Convinced that the emperor's madness would become more and more murderous, Arek had joined the rebel movement, passing on all he knew to a man who delivered sandals. When necessary, the merchant went to Memphis with supplies of sandals for the Hyksos troops, and afterwards, taking a thousand precautions, he contacted the Egyptians.

Although he felt very alone, Arek lived for one hope. According to the sandal-merchant, the Queen of Freedom was no mirage. She had raised an army which had more than once defeated the Hyksos. Thanks to her, one day Egypt would defeat the darkness.

Apart from the scraps of information he could offer the sandal-merchant, Arek devoted himself to an dangerous, delicate task: damaging the chariot-wheels. He made deep cuts in the spokes or the rim so as to weaken them, then disguised the cuts with varnish. When the chariot travelled at high speed, an accident was inevitable.

Suddenly he heard shouts and the sounds of running feet.

'It's the guards,' a colleague warned him.

'Stay where you are and do not try to run away,' ordered the imperious voice of the lady Aberia.

The workers obeyed. The guards herded them together with blows in the back from their staves, and drove them to where Aberia stood. At her feet lay a warehouseman, covered in blood from his appalling wounds.

'This criminal was plotting with Jannas,' she said. 'He must have had an accomplice among you. If you do not denounce him immediately, I shall have all the members of this man's family executed.'

Aberia forced the unfortunate man to his feet.

'He has had his eyes put out!' exclaimed a workman in horror.

A guard knocked the insolent man unconscious and dragged him out of the workshop.

The tortured man staggered towards his colleagues. 'I swear to you . . . I haven't got an accomplice.'

'All you need do is touch the guilty man and your family will be spared,' promised Aberia. In fact, she had already sent them to the camp at Tjaru.

The blind man reached out. His fingers brushed the face of Arek, who dared not breathe. The dying man's fingers closed on the shoulder of the man next to Arek, a Syrian, who cried out in fear.

## 39

Two happy events occurred on the same day. First, Nefertari gave birth to a son, who received the same name as his father, so that the dynasty of the moon-god might continue the fight. Second, Emheb informed Ahhotep that the first regiment of Egyptian chariots was ready for battle.

Ahmose had been training with Moustache and the Afghan, in order to master the new weapon. Obstinate, serious and precise, he was now fully the equal of his teachers. The last trials in the desert had pleased him greatly.

Ahhotep rocked the baby, who would be suckled by his mother for three months before being entrusted to a wet-nurse.

'Majesty,' said Nefertari, 'will you do me the honour of giving my son the secret name he will bear if he proves worthy of it?'

'May he become the founder of a new dynasty, which will witness the reunification of the Two Lands and the re-establishment of the rule of Ma'at over Egypt. May his secret name, the completeness of his being, be Amon-hotep, "Amon is at peace".'

The queen had no time to lavish more affection on her grandson, for Rascal had arrived from Memphis and was awaiting her on the sill of her bedchamber window.

The news he had brought necessitated an immediate meeting of the general staff.

'We now have a source of information within Avaris itself,' said the queen. 'It reaches the rebels in Memphis, who pass it on to us.'

'Are we sure, Majesty, that the information is true?' asked Neshi sceptically. 'We must take care that we are not deceived by lies spread by the emperor.'

'That warning is important,' agreed the queen, 'but I tend to believe what we have been told: confirmation of Jannas's death, the appointment of Khamudi to lead the Hyksos armed forces, and the fear that reigns in Avaris. Jannas's supporters are being ruthlessly pursued, arrested and executed.'

'Is Khamudi planning to attack us? asked Emheb.

'Our informant speaks only of a terrifying purge, in which not even the highest officers are being spared.'

'It's almost as if the invaders are withdrawing,' said Qaris, 'and their barbarity is gnawing away at them from the inside.'

'Surely this is a new sign from destiny?' suggested Heray. 'The time has come for us to go on to the offensive.'

Moustache and the Afghan nodded in agreement.

'Does any of you disagree?' asked Ahhotep.

Each man was conscious of the weight of his own silence.

'Then the Council of Pharaoh is unanimous,' concluded the queen. 'But it is he who must make the decision.'

'Let us make ready to leave Thebes,' declared Ahmose.


Now fully recovered from the birth of her son, Nefertari was walking in the palace gardens with Ahhotep. The Great Royal Wife was both overflowing with happiness and overwhelmed with anguish as she thought about the intensification of the war.

'Once again, Nefertari, you will be solely responsible for Thebes,' said Ahhotep. The battle will be terrible, and no one can predict the outcome. Like his father and his brother before him, Ahmose will fight in the vanguard, for his example will be vital to ensure the unity of his men and stem their fear. We are about to defy the darkness. It is possible that neither I nor my son will return from the front, so I must take measures which affect you directly.'

Nefertari made no futile protests. She had to face reality as clear-headedly as Ahhotep did.

'I scarcely had time to be young,' Ahhotep went on, 'which I hope will not be the case for you. But if destiny proves merciless, you will have no right to show any sign at all of weakness. Come with me.'

In a chariot driven by Ahhotep, the two women went from the palace to the temple at Karnak, where Pharaoh Ahmose and High Priest Djehuty were waiting for them. Despite the seriousness of the moment, Nefertari enjoyed the unexpected ride and the novel sensation of speed.

Once the purification rites had been carried out, the quartet crossed the open courtyard to the shrine where the pharaoh's coronation had been celebrated. Nefertari was surprised to find a stele there.

Ahmose summarized its inscription. 'At the request of Queen Ahhotep, I grant to Great Royal Wife Nefertari the title of Wife of God and the office of Second Servant of Amon. She will govern the Temple of Karnak with the High Priest. To enable her to do this, she will receive gold, silver, clothing, pots of ointment, fertile fields and servants. May this institution endure and prosper, may it enchant the spirit of Amon and maintain his goodwill towards the land beloved of the gods.'

Nefertari bowed to the king. 'You clothed me when I had nothing, you made me rich when I was poor. This fortune belongs to the temple; it is in the service of the creative power that gives the temple life.'

Ahhotep embraced the new Wife of God, who would take her place if she fell to a Hyksos sword.

The next day, at dawn in order to avoid the worst of the heat, Ahhotep led Ahmose, Nefertari and a few soldiers of the Royal Guard across the Nile and into the desert, to test the chariots on the desert tracks. Once again, the chariots proved both stable and manoeuvrable.

Ahhotep halted at the opening to a valley protected by hills. She said, 'The true riches of Egypt are the builders who create it. While my son and I fight the Hyksos, you, Ahmose-Nefertari, shall found a craftsmen's village here, the Place of Truth.* The men must work in secret, far from prying eyes and ears, and create the ritual objects we need. Within them will be written Ma'at, the righteousness of the work. Gather together the men you believe worthy of this work, put them to the test, initiate them according to the ancient rites, and accept no one who is not of good character. The oldest Theban goldsmith shall be your assistant. Here is the offering he has created for Pharaoh.'

The queen hung round Ahmose's neck a pectoral combining gold, cornelian, lapis-lazuli and turquoise. It depicted the king standing in a boat, flanked by Amon and Ra. Both gods were holding vases from which celestial energy was gushing. As this energy impregnated the king's being, it would enable him to carry out his office.†

'And now,' said Ahhotep, 'we may leave for the Port of Kamose.' Qaris came to see the queen. 'Majesty, the man arrived an hour ago. I thought it fitting to give him a room in the palace, but under guard. I have taken him wine and a dish of hare, and he is asking for more.'

'Which man do you mean?'

'The Minoan, Linas. He has returned.'

Ahhotep agreed to see him, and Qaris went and fetched him. Linas had not changed.

'Did you have a good crossing, Commander?' asked Ahhotep.

'No, Majesty, a very bad one. The sea was rough, and the winds chancy. If I were not a good sailor the ship would have sunk, and that would have been a great pity, both for myself and for you.'

---

*In Egyptian *Set Ma'at*; its modern name is Deir el-Medina. We encountered the brotherhood in the four volumes of *The Stone of Light*.

†This pectoral was found in Ahhotep's tomb at Dra Abu el-Naga (western Thebes).

'Does that mean you bring good news?'

'Permit me to give you two presents: this battleaxe, decorated with griffins, and this dagger, depicting a lion racing after its prey. The handle is shaped like a bull's head, the symbol of King Minos.'*

'Are you saying that he is still alive?'

'Indeed, Majesty. He eventually returned from the cave with an answer from the oracle, and he showed no mercy to those who had tried to seize his throne. He wishes you to have the strength of the lion and the magic of the griffins to triumph over your enemies.'

'Am I to understand that it is not a question of *our* enemies?'

'Everywhere Minoans go, they shall declare that the Queen of Freedom is waging war on the emperor, who is incapable of defeating her. Minoa recognizes you as Queen of the Distant Shores, places herself under your protection and will send the Hyksos no further tributes or assistance.'

*They were also found in Ahhotep's tomb.

## 40

He was the last one left. The last senior officer who had fought at Jannas's side in all the provinces of the empire. He had been heaped with honours, but he lived modestly in his official residence, with just two servants.

All his old army comrades had been executed or deported to the prison camps, whose existence he had only just discovered. Horrified, he had shut himself in his house to get drunk.

So the High Treasurer was sending loyal Hyksos warriors to end their days in prison camps! Why was the emperor yielding to the whims of this sick-minded man, who was guided solely by his own rapacity?

He himself must have been forgotten, no doubt because of his age – he was fifty-seven. So should he not try to avenge Jannas and his comrades? He would request an audience with Khamudi, on the pretext of denouncing traitors who were so far undetected. As soon as he was face to face with the monster, he would strike.

Although it was rough and ready, his plan might succeed.

The officer called to his servant, to bring him some flavoured wine. When she did not reply, he left his living-room and found her in the hallway, lying on her back with her tongue lolling out of her mouth. Next to her lay her husband, who had also been strangled.

Aberia emerged from the shadows. 'I have not forgotten you, my friend.'

The old emperor spent most of his time in the secret room, at the centre of the citadel where cold and darkness reigned. It was there that Khamudi came, each morning, to give him his report and the list of appointments.

'Have you wiped out all Jannas's supporters?' asked Apophis.

'The purge is under way, Majesty. We are hunting down the traitors without mercy.'

'That is good, Khamudi. Do not relax your efforts for a moment.

Can you believe it? That man Jannas demanded full powers! He forgot that, like any other Hyksos, he owed me absolute obedience.'

'Thanks to the lady Aberia, we are even arresting conspirators who thought they were safe.'

'That's good. Purge and deport: those are our two priorities. Once Avaris and the Delta contain only faithful servants of Apophis, the Hyksos order will have been re-established.'

'I have some good news from Memphis, Majesty, where your plan is proving its worth. According to the commander besieging the city, the Memphites are at the end of their strength. He asks if you wish him to launch a new attack.'

'No. He must continue to let them rot, I want those rebels to die in their own filth. Then we shall burn the city. Decay, Khamudi, that is the true law of life.'

'The news from Anatolia is satisfactory, too. As you ordered, our army is killing civilians and rebels, and is retaking one village after another. In the mountains, the reconquest is slow but sure. Soon there will be not a living soul left in Anatolia, and the Hittites will have been eradicated.'

'Jannas was wrong to demand an attack on several fronts. In the event of success, our soldiers would have become idle. It is good that they should fight and kill.'

'There is still Ahhotep, Majesty. It appears that she has given up the fight, which is probably why there has been no word from our spy.'

'There has been. Here is his latest message: "Whatever happens, I shall fulfil my mission."' Suddenly, the rasping voice became even more sinister, as if it was rising up out of dark depths to which Apophis alone had access. 'Ahhotep is approaching, I can feel it. She is coming towards us because she thinks she is capable of defeating us. The disasters that have already struck her are not enough to halt her. She will know more despair and suffering. Come, Ahhotep, come closer. I am waiting for you.'


'Majesty, there is information from Elephantine,' Qaris told Ahhotep, whom he found contemplating his model of Egypt. 'The annual flood will be ideal: it will reach about sixteen cubits.'

This was the last, and oh-so-important, detail that Ahhotep needed before giving the signal for departure. Using the strength of the current, the Egyptian fleet, made up of new war-boats launched from the boatyard at Thebes, would soon reach the Port of Kamose, where it would join up with the main body of the troops. Sailing onward with the aid of the Nile, it would make for Hyksos territory.

The queen gazed at the model with emotion. 'This was our first state secret,' she recalled. 'I was nothing but a headstrong little girl and you, the wise, cautious steward of a decrepit little palace, were gathering information on the enemy and trying to believe that a few rebels still existed. You showed me this model, on which the last free space was the city of Amon.'

'You ought to have been discouraged, Majesty, but instead that realization increased your strength tenfold. Thanks to you, we have lived in dignity and hope.'

Ahhotep thought of Seqen, Kamose and Teti the Small. For her, they were not shades but living allies who continued to fight at her side.

'The model has changed a great deal,' observed Qaris. 'You have liberated the South of the country, Majesty, and part of Middle Egypt.'

'You and I both know that that is still not enough. The next battle will be decisive.'

'You have horses and chariots now, Majesty.'

'They are not enough, either, Qaris. And we have no experience of fighting on level ground, army against army.'

'Do not give in, Majesty. Even if you are defeated, even if Thebes is destroyed, even if we all die, you will have been right. Pharaoh must reign over the Two Lands, celebrating the union of Upper and Lower Egypt. Outside that harmony, that brotherhood of Set and Horus, no happiness is possible.'

The steward had rarely spoken so forthrightly, and his words swept away Ahhotep's last traces of hesitation.

The atmosphere at the palace and on the quaysides of Thebes was effervescent. Despite his weight of years, Qaris saw that nothing was forgotten to ensure the comfort of Queen Ahhotep and Pharaoh Ahmose. He checked everything, from the quality of the bedlinen to the sharpness of the razors.

As for Neshi, he refused to place his trust in any of his assistants. Some people called him 'the Star of the Two Lands' because of his exceptional mind, but he showed scant care for his reputation, and threw all his efforts into the preparations for departure. He examined each shield, each spear, each sword; equally carefully, he examined the moringa pods, which were dropped into jars of water to purify it, and were also used to clarify jars of oil. Nor did he overlook a single mat or kilt. Fortunately, She-Cat and her assistants packed and loaded the remedies and ointments themselves.

Far from this bustle, Ahmose and Nefertari gazed at the Nile, which was rising and taking on a reddish tint. After embracing his son for a long time, Ahmose had taken his wife to the riverbank, to savour a last moment of intimacy in the shade of a tamarisk, before launching himself into a venture from which he had little chance of returning alive.

Not far away, hidden in a thicket of papyrus, the Hyksos spy planned to take advantage of this opportunity. The king was unarmed, and his guards were posted a long way off so as not to disturb him.

If he crept along the bank and struck very quickly, the spy would not be seen. With great meticulousness, he went over every move he must make; his victims must have no chance of sounding the alarm. The slightest mistake would be fatal to him. Hesitating, he took one last look around.

Once again, his caution saved him from disaster. Well hidden near the royal couple was a soldier, alert and dangerous. And stretched out under the low branches of the tamarisk, his eyes bright and alert, Young Laughter was protecting the royal couple. The spy instantly abandoned his plan.

## 41

'The stars of Sah* have risen,' declared High Priest Djehuty. 'Osiris is reborn in the celestial light.'

Twenty new war-boats cast off, including *Shining One of Memphis, Offering* and *Fighting Bull*. They were followed by *Septentrion*, which attacted great interest because she was carrying horses. All the vessels flew Ahhotep's standard, showing the full moon's disc in its ship.

At the prow of the *Septentrion*, the queen held the golden Set-headed sceptre. Near her stood Ahmose, dressed in a leather corselet and wearing the White Crown of Upper Egypt and a leather corselet. When he raised aloft the Sword of Amon, the priests of Karnak roared out the sacred song composed in his honour: 'When he appears, Pharaoh is like the moon-god amid the stars. Accomplished in government is his arm, happy are his steps, firm his tread, lively his sandals; he is the sacred symbol upon whom rests the Divine Light.'

After entrusting the sword to the Queen of Freedom, Ahmose took his place at the steering-oar, which had been brought all the way from Elephantine, and the fleet set off towards the Port of Kamose, aided by a strong current.

'We are almost there,' said Emheb.

Housed in vast cage-like structures, each comprising two stalls which were partially open to the air, the horses had shown no distress during the voyage. When the fleet halted at the Port of Kamose, they were able to exercise, watched dubiously by Moon and Ahmes.

'Are you sure you can control them?' Moon asked Moustache and the Afghan.

'We've trained intensively,' replied Moustache. 'There won't be any problems.'

Moon wanted to see the chariots, which were stowed securely on another cargo-boat and guarded by archers.

*The constellation of Orion.

'Will our chariots be as effective as the Hyksos ones?'

'Probably more so,' replied the Afghan. 'Emheb has greatly improved upon the one he used as a model.'

The halt had to be a short one, for they could not let the flood rise too far.

As the fleet was to about leave, a strange wind arose. It was swirling and icy, like a winter gale.

'This will seriously hamper our manoeuvrability,' said Moon worriedly.

'It is the emperor,' said Ahhotep. 'He is trying to delay us by unleashing the evil breath of the dying year.* Let us call upon Amon, the master of the winds, and ask him to protect the fleet.'

On the deck of each vessel they laid dozens of offertory bags containing incense, powdered galenite, dates and bread. Then Ahhotep raised her sceptre towards the sky, which had grown threatening, to win the favours of Set.

The wind dropped, and the clouds dispersed.

In this seventeenth year of his reign, Ahmose gave the order for the army of liberation to depart for the North.

The Theban soldiers who had taken part in the raid on Avaris under Kamose's command were greatly moved when they revisited landscapes that were engraved for ever in their memory. The others were venturing into an unknown world which was, none the less, the land of their ancestors.

Thanks to the strong current, the fleet made swift progress. Ahhotep expected to join battle with the enemy at any moment. But the emperor had abandoned the area between the Egyptian front and the outskirts of Memphis. The only soldiers there were Hyksos mercenaries who terrorized the villagers and stole most of their harvests to send to Avaris.

'Majesty,' ventured Emheb, 'we cannot abandon these unfortunate people. If we do, the mercenaries will kill them all.'

To stop or slow the fleet would be fatal, so Ahhotep entrusted a message to Rascal: the three last vessels were to halt and their footsoldiers were to liberate several villages. Once the Hyksos were wiped out, the peasants would be given weapons and, under the command of a Theban officer, would spread the rebellion throughout Middle Egypt.

Neshi was still checking the weapons: straight and curved swords, in imitation of Hyksos weapons, for hand-to-hand combat, bronze-headed spears, light, stabbing daggers, clubs, easily handled axes,

---

*The new year began with the flood, approximately at the beginning of July.

bows of various sizes, wooden shields strengthened with bronze, breastplates and helmets. The equipment was of better quality than ever before, but would it be as good as the enemy's?

As the fleet approached its first major objective, an acid test for the army, hearts began to beat faster. Even those who, like Emheb and Ahmes, were used to fierce fighting knew that the next battle would be completely different.

If they were defeated, Egypt would not survive.


The Hyksos officer directing the siege of Memphis was in a foul mood. The heat did not agree with him and, worse still, the annual flood had forced him to alter the deployment of his forces. Soon the Nile would flood the land and much of Egypt would turn into a shallow inland sea.

He had already had to move the horses from several stables on low ground. The animals were being held in an enclosure, ready for evacuation to the north. Only a single chariot unit remained operational and, like the others, it would soon take shelter in the fortress of Taremu, near the sacred city of Iunu.

A soldier came up to him and saluted. 'Artificer officer reporting, Commander.'

'What is it now?'

The artificer was excited. 'We could use the flood to take Memphis once and for all. If we station our archers on pontoons, the river will lift them up to the walls, and they will easily wipe out the defenders. My men will destroy a part of the walls, and our footsoldiers will pour into the city through the breach.'

'It would be a delicate operation, and it isn't in accordance with the orders I've received.'

'I know, sir, but the defenders are at the end of their strength. And the emperor will hardly reproach you for capturing Memphis. Our men want to end this siege, and success should be worth promotion for you.'

Pillaging this rat-hole and then razing it to the ground, at last leaving this camp where he was dying of boredom, achieving total victory . . . The commander let himself be tempted. He would explain to Khamudi, the new commander-in-chief, that the desperate Memphites had made a fatal mistake in attempting a mass break-out.

The order was given to deploy boats side by side, so as to form a sort of wall in the canal closest to the white wall. Next, the pontoons would be placed in the water and the river allowed to do its job.

The last strip of land still accessible to chariots would be flooded within the next few days. So the chariots had been gathered together in the widest section, before being loaded on to cargo-vessels destined for Taremu.

The commander summoned his subordinates and revealed his intentions to them.

A sentry interrupted the meeting.

The commander glared at him. 'What is the meaning of this insolence, soldier?'

'Sir, there are chariots in sight.'

'What nonsense is this?'

'It is not nonsense, I assure you, sir.'

So Khamudi had at last sent reinforcements. But what use would they be during the time of the flood? Angrily, the commander left his tent to have frank words with whoever was in charge of this useless regiment.

The sentry had forgotten to say that the chariots were coming not from the north but from the south.

The astounded commander was the first man to die in the battle of Memphis. An arrow fired by Moustache, who was securely balanced on the platform of a chariot driven by the Afghan, lodged square in the middle of the Hyksos' forehead.

## 42

The Egyptians could not have wished for better fighting conditions. The Hyksos' horses were gathered on one side, their chariots on the other, their boats moored and unable to manoeuvre, their soldiers busy with domestic tasks. The men commanded by Moustache and the Afghan took instant advantage of the situation, and their skilled archers killed many Hyksos.

This swift and significant breakthrough eased the task facing Emheb's footsoldiers, while the sailors commanded by Moon and Ahmes attacked the enemy vessels. Once the effect of surprise had passed, the emperor's men attempted to regroup, but their units were too isolated from each other.

At the height of the battle, as the Sword of Amon flamed in the pharaoh's hand, the rebels emerged from Memphis and came to the Thebans' aid. Realizing that none of them would emerge unscathed from the fight, the Hyksos fought ferociously. But the Egyptians sensed imminent victory, and cut them down one after another.

'Memphis is free,' Ahmose told his troops, 'and we have captured a considerable number of chariots and horses. But before we celebrate our success let us think of our dead, of all those who have given their lives for Egypt.'

At the sight of the many corpses strewn across the ground or floating in the canals, Ahhotep felt almost as much grief as if the army had suffered a defeat. War was one of the worst depravities in the world, but what other way was there of defeating the Emperor of Darkness?

Rather than withdrawing into her thoughts, Ahhotep made sure that none of her faithful companions had been wounded or killed. Only Moon was wounded, in the arm. Treated by She-Cat, who hardly knew where to turn, he refused to rest even for a moment, so anxious was he to know the extent of his losses.

Gathering together the least exhausted soldiers and the chariots,

Emheb formed a front line north of Memphis, in case the Hyksos reserve troops counter-attacked. If that happened, the apparent victory would be transformed into a disaster. Moustache, the Afghan, their soldiers and horses got their breath back. They, too, knew that they were in no condition to fight off a Hyksos attack.

Evening fell. An oppressive calm hung over the Memphis plain.

'This place is very difficult to defend,' commented Ahhotep.

'The white wall of Memphis will be a valuable ally,' replied Neshi. 'Let us shelter our chariots and horses inside the old city.'

'No one shall sleep until it has been done,' ordered Ahmose.

The Egyptians consolidated their new positions at the edge of the land the Hyksos considered sacred, at once so close and so inaccessible. Although this breathing-space was welcome, it could not last long. Everyone was already thinking about the next objective: Avaris. That was the battle they must win. If they failed, all their sacrifices would have been in vain.

'Our men are ready,' Ahmose told Ahhotep. 'They are afraid, but nevertheless they are ready to attack Apophis's lair. They are aware of the enormity of the task, and no man will flinch in the face of his duty.'

'Marching on Avaris would be madness,' said Ahhotep.

'Mother, we cannot simply give up!'

'I said nothing about giving up. There is a reason why the emperor did not send reinforcements to Memphis: he wanted to find out what we are really capable of. He has tried for a long time to lure us on to his own ground, in the hope of entrapping and defeating our entire army. No, Ahmose, we are not ready.'

'But we must strike into the Delta!'

'Yes, indeed we must, but only when we decide the time is right. After Kamose's raid, the Hyksos will certainly have taken measures to repel any naval attack, and our chariot corps is still too small. We must adapt the Hyksos chariots we captured, make them lighter, and then train men to drive them. Besides, we cannot defeat the emperor with material weapons alone. You and I must go to Saqqara, so that your royal power may be confirmed.'

Young Laughter greatly enjoyed the chariot ride to Saqqara. As he watched attentively, Ahhotep and Ahmose gazed in wonder at the immense burial-ground, which was dedicated to the ancestors who had been reborn into the Light. Pyramids and houses of eternity bore witness to their presence, and their words continued to be passed on, through the radiance of the hieroglyphs and architectural forms.

Dominating the site and seemingly guarding it was the step pyramid of Djoser, built by the masterbuilder Imhotep, whose fame had endured through time. It was a true staircase to heaven, enabling the pharaoh's soul to commune with the stars, then to come back down to earth as the embodiment of the harmony on high.

The pyramid reigned at the heart of a vast ritual space, surrounded by a curtain wall. The king and his mother saw that there was only one entrance and that it was – to all appearances – eternally open.

'That's strange,' said Ahmose. 'Why have the Hyksos not destroyed this shrine? They must know that the royal soul is regenerated here in mystery, away from human eyes.'

'I am quite sure they do,' nodded the queen, 'but the emperor found himself confronted with such power that his evil magic failed.'

The pharaoh made to step through the narrow gateway, but Ahhotep held him back.

'Apophis is undoubtedly still trying to do us harm. If he has left this monument intact, without even destroying the gateway, he must have discovered a way of blocking its radiance.'

'You mean he has locked the regenerative energy inside?'

'That is what I fear. He must have made this gateway impossible to pass through, by placing a curse upon it. So no pharaoh will now be able to feed upon the ancestors' inheritance.'

The queen prayed for a while, calling upon her dead husband and son.

'The curse must be broken,' she told Ahmose. 'I shall do it, for I think I know the name of this gateway.'

'Mother, I—'

'My death does not matter. It is you who must live, to reunite the White Crown and the Red.'

Ahhotep walked forward very slowly. When she reached the stone gateway, she was halted by a blast of icy breath. Then it seemed to her that the uprights were as hot as burning coals, and that they were crowding in on her, trying to crush her. She could not take another step.

'Gateway, I know your name. You are called "Righteousness Gives Life". Since you are known to me, open.'

An intense light began to shine from the beautiful white stone, and the icy wind disappeared.

Ahhotep told Ahmose to follow her, and walked across the narrow space between the sturdy columns. Laughter lay down on the threshold, in the posture of Anubis, and guarded the gateway to the world of the Invisible.

Guided by the spirits of Seqen and Kamose, the queen sensed that the emperor's curse had not been completely destroyed.

When she emerged from the colonnade, she saw several carved cobras on the top of a wall, ready to rear up and strike from the stone. Were they about to attack Ahmose?

She said to them, 'Your task is to open the way of Pharaoh and to cover his enemies with your fire. Have you forgotten the spirit that devised you and the hand that created you? I know your name, O royal serpents: you are the first flame.'

The queen and the snakes stared fixedly at each other, and then the sculptures returned to stone.

Exhausted but serene, Ahhotep could at last gaze upon the great open-air courtyard before the step pyramid. It symbolized the whole of Egypt, over which her son had been called to reign.

# 43

Apophis now devoted all his time to one of two activities. Either he watched the suffering and death of those he sent to the labyrinth or the bull's arena, or he shut himself away in the secret room and lit a lamp. Its flame glowed with a disturbing greenish light, and in it he witnessed scenes visible only to him.

The High Treasurer had to wait impatiently upon the emperor's pleasure in order to give him the alarming information he had received. 'Majesty, the rebels have retaken Memphis! The regiment besieging the city has been wiped out.'

'I know.'

'Our mercenaries in Middle Egypt have been wiped out, too.'

'I know.'

'Majesty, we must accept that Ahhotep and her son have a formidable army.'

'I know,' said Apophis again. 'The queen has even succeeded in breaking my curse on Saqqara. Now Ahmose is a true war-chief.'

'What are your orders, Majesty?'

'To wait. Although she is still hesitating, Ahhotep will come to us.'

'Should we not attack her before she reaches Avaris?'

'Absolutely not.'

'Forgive me for pressing the point, my lord, but these Egyptians can no longer be taken lightly.'

Apophis's icy gaze stabbed right through Khamudi. 'Do you really think I would make such a foolish mistake? Ahhotep is a fitting adversary for me, because I have allowed her to grow. There is a power in her, *the* power I must destroy. If I had acted sooner, she would not have got beyond the borders of Thebes. Now she thinks she is as strong as I am. The flame tells me that her hope for freedom has never been so intense, and it is that very hope which is leading the Egyptians towards the abyss. I am going to inflict on them a defeat so terrible that they will never recover from it. And it is at Avaris, before my citadel, that they will suffer that defeat. Once

Ahhotep is dead, not a single one of her countrymen will dare take up arms against me.'

Mad with rage, Khamudi smashed a low table and trampled it underfoot.

'Calm yourself, darling,' begged Yima.

He hurled the remains of the table out of the window. 'The emperor is too old to rule,' he declared through clenched teeth.

'Hush, please! Someone might hear.'

'You're the only one who can hear me, and you aren't the sort of woman who'd betray me, are you?'

She simpered. 'Of course not, my love. And I shan't hide my deepest thoughts from you. You are rid of Jannas now, so don't delay any longer.'

Khamudi was surprised. 'What exactly do you mean?'

'You know as well as I do.'

Memphis was coming back to life. Gradually, the survivors were growing used to the fact that there would be no more Hyksos attacks. Now they could leave the city without fear of being killed, had enough to eat and had begun to talk about the future. With the footsoldiers' help, priests and stone-cutters worked to repair the least badly damaged temples.

The soldiers were relieved not to have to march on Avaris immediately. They awaited a decision by the Council of War, which was meeting at the palace, itself badly damaged during the siege.

'The king's power has been confirmed at Saqqara,' Ahhotep told the council, 'but there is still a danger dogging our steps: our lack of *heka*. Without that magical force, which has helped us to overcome so many obstacles, we stand no chance of defeating the Hyksos forces massed in the Delta. So we must gather the *heka* where it shines forth in its purest form, at Iunu.'

'From what the Memphite rebels have told us,' said Neshi, 'I very much fear that Iunu is out of our reach.'

'Why?'

'Because it is in the area controlled by the fortress of Taremu, the largest in the Delta after Avaris.'

'We know how to deal with fortresses,' Ahhotep reminded him.

'This one is different, Majesty: it has thick walls twenty cubits high, and gates too strong to be broken by battering-rams.'

'Are the monuments of Iunu intact?'

'The emperor has written his name upon the leaves of the sacred tree,' said the mayor of Memphis, 'and so has taken his place in the line of pharaohs. That is why the shrine of Atum is still standing – but it is guarded by Hyksos.'

'In a certain way,' said Neshi sadly, 'the tree has made Apophis immortal. Besides that, he has probably destroyed the source of the *heka*.'

'Before we give up hope,' said Ahhotep, 'we must check this for ourselves.'

Mounted on White Giant and Grey, Moustache and the Afghan had gone on a scouting expedition to Taremu. They returned safely, but their news was not good. Built on a promontory beyond reach of the flood, Taremu looked impregnable. Two war-boats blocked the canal linking it to Iunu.

'Our swimmers will damage them so badly that they will eventually sink,' said Moustache.

'And there will be no problems with the Hyksos foot-soldiers at Iunu,' added the Afghan. 'Our chariots will win through.'

'The fortress is bound to send reinforcements to Iunu,' Emheb pointed out. 'Then the emperor will be alerted, thousands of Hyksos will converge on Iunu, and we'll be crushed. We stand no chance of sucess unless we take Taremu.'

'Precisely. So our carpenters must set to work at once,' said Ahhotep. 'Why look elsewhere for the weapon we need when it exists in our own tradition?'

Although he knew of the Egyptian army's victory at Memphis, the commander of Taremu was concerned only with matters of supply. The fortress was temporarily housing a huge number of horses, which had to be fed, and two chariot regiments, which caused a difficult problem of overcrowding. Fortunately, the flood had begun to recede. In a few days' time, his inconvenient guests would be leaving.'

'Commander,' shouted a sentry, 'enemy boats in sight!'

Astonished, the commander climbed to the top of the highest guard-tower.

It was true. Dozens of vessels flying the Queen of Freedom's standard were coming up the canal leading to Taremu's landing-stage. The rebels must have destroyed the guard-boats. Not that that would do them any good. When they reached the high walls, the Egyptians would present perfect targets for the Hyksos archers. Then the great gate would open, and the chariots would charge out and kill all the rebels as they fled.

And the commander of Taremu would have the honour of bearing Queen Ahhotep's head to the emperor.

## 44

The Egyptian boats halted, out of range of the enemy.

To the Hyksos commander's astonishment, the enemy's best archers were armed with large bows, with which they were able to shoot down many of the Hyksos stationed on the ramparts.

The soldiers of the artificer corps disembarked, carrying enormous wooden beams. Under cover from the archers, and with only light losses, they reached the great gate. The commander smiled. No battering-ram would ever break it down.

But the Egyptians did not even try. On the contrary, they used the beams to bar the gate, trapping the Hyksos inside. Then other footsoldiers arrived, bearing very long ladders mounted on wheels. The archers on the boats began to fire more rapidly, enabling their comrades to raise the ladders against the walls.

Alarmed, the commander ordered all his men to the ramparts. But the ramparts were narrow, and the first attackers were already reaching the tops of the wheeled ladders.

Big-Feet, prisoner number 1790, was the longest-surviving inmate of the camp at Sharuhen. The only thing keeping him alive was the will for revenge. Since death would not take him, he would make the Hyksos pay for the theft of his cows.

For several weeks, convoys of deportees had been arriving continuously. They were mostly Egyptians from the Delta, but some were a new category of prisoner, discovering the horrors of the camp for the first time: Hyksos soldiers.

The Hyksos huddled together and avoided the eyes of the women, children and old men who were dying of hunger and suffering at the whims of their torturers. Like them, the former soldiers now had a number branded into their flesh.

One night, an officer approached Big-Feet, who was sleeping on some planks, a vital protection against the mud.

'1790 – you didn't arrive yesterday! What is your secret for surviving in this hell?'

'I will never accept injustice. You, or others like you, stole my cows.'

'Well, my honour and my reason for living were stolen from me.'

'Why are you here?'

'There was a purge. My comrades and I believed that Commander Jannas represented the future. The emperor had him murdered.'

'One Hyksos fewer. Good.'

'There's better news than that, as far as you're concerned. Queen Ahhotep has freed Memphis and captured the fortress of Taremu. Soon she'll attack Avaris.'

Big-Feet wondered if he was dreaming. Then he understood. 'You're lying to torture me, aren't you? You filth! You think it's funny to give me hope again!'

'Don't lose your temper, my friend. It is absolutely true. Now the emperor wants me dead and your queen does, too, so my only chance is to escape.'

Big-Feet was stunned. 'No one can escape from here!'

'I and the other Hyksos will kill the guards. You seem a good fellow, which is why I'm telling you. You can either follow us or rot here in this pigsty.'

Big-Feet wanted to believe the man was telling the truth; but he did not follow when he and his comrades tried to force the gates of the camp, because he was sure they would fail.

He was right. Cut to pieces, the would-be escapers' bodies were thrown to the pigs.

The chariots and horses captured at Taremu meant that the Egyptians boasted twice as many as before. Now the chariots had to be made lighter, and drivers and archers trained so that they would be fit to fight the Hyksos at Avaris.

As the floodwaters receded, a vast plain was uncovered. Training began immediately, while Ahhotep and Ahmose went to Iunu, which was at last free.

Emptied of its priests and the craftsmen who had formerly worked in the temple workshops, the old city seemed almost dead, sleeping in an oppressive calm. How could it possibly provide *heka*?

All his senses on the alert, Laughter led the queen and the pharaoh to the great Temple of Atum and Ra. Its monumental doorway was closed, so they followed the outer wall round to the little gate of purifications, which had been crudely walled up. A soldier removed the bricks, and Ahhotep and Ahmose went inside.

They saw a gold-tipped obelisk, standing on the primordial mound that had emerged from the ocean of energy when the universe was born. Then they found the sacred tree of Iunu, the huge-branched persea on whose leaves were preserved the names of all the pharaohs.

In accordance with ancient ritual, Ahmose went down on his left knee, his right leg stretched out behind him. He offered the Sword of Amon to the persea tree, so that the Invisible might imbue it with power.

The Wife of God examined the leaves. She was so astonished by what she found that she checked again. This time, there could be no doubt.

'Apophis lied,' she said. 'His name is nowhere on the leaves of the sun's tree. The persea refused to preserve the memory of that tyrant, so the *heka* of Iunu has not been defiled.'

As Ahhotep wrote the ritual names of Pharaoh Ahmose on the leaves, the Sword of Amon became a ray of light so intense that the king had to close his eyes.

'Come and stand beside me,' said his mother.

She performed the rite of Sechat, who brought the gods' words to life, and Ahmose performed that of Thoth, who passed on their message. As they did so, the young pharaoh's names began to radiate light.

In his heart, he heard the voice of Atum, the indissoluble bond of being and non-being, totality preceding time and space, the first matter from which everything had originated. And the link was recreated with his predecessors, whose protecting magic entered his breath.

'There is more we must do,' said Ahhotep. 'The temple does not yet vibrate as it should.'

Continuing her exploration, she entered a huge shrine. There lay the pieces of two large acacia-wood boats.

'The ship of day and the ship of night,' she murmured. 'If they no longer sail, the rhythms of the cosmos are disturbed and darkness invades the earth. That is why the emperor was able to impose his law.'

Patiently, Ahmose assembled both boats. At the prow of the ship of day stood an Isis made of gilded wood; while Nephthys stood at the prow of the ship of night. Facing each other, the goddesses stretched out their hands to pass across the gold disc that embodied the regenerated light. But there was no disc: Apophis had stolen it and destroyed it.

However, on the ground lay the Amulet of Knowledge,* which the queen hung round her son's neck.

---

*The *siat*, a word formed from the root *sia*, 'to know intuitively, to be wise'.
'Stand between Isis and Nephthys,' she told him. 'Like every ruler of Egypt, you are the son of the light who returns to the ocean of energy with the evening sun and is reborn in the east with the sun of morning.'

A serene smile lit the goddesses' faces, and they filled the pharaoh's spirit with *heka*.

After Ahhotep and Ahmose had left, a gold disc appeared in the hands of Nephthys, who passed it to Isis in the secrecy of the temple. The ships of day and night had begun to sail again.

## 45

Far, far from Egypt, the Nubian kingdom of Kerma enjoyed a prosperity which its king, Nedjeh, relished more every day. After trying to get the better of the Hyksos in southern Egypt while proclaiming himself their ally, and then waging war against Queen Ahhotep, Nedjeh now contented himself with his golden existence.

The King of Kerma, once so warlike, had given up fighting. He remained within his kingdom with its rich agriculture, and had grown fat on delicious food. He rarely left his palace, which was built in the Egyptian manner, its windows and doors arranged so as to ensure a constant flow of cool air. He ate five meals a day, sweetened with favours dispensed by the magnificent women of his harem. None of the women allowed her disgust to show, for the old despot's anger still made his subjects tremble. Anyone who displeased him died instantly, their skull smashed, and joined the huge pile of bones in Nedjeh's future tomb, which was even bigger than the tomb of a Theban king.

'You again!' growled the fat man when Ata, head of his security guards, approached the soft bed the king was reclining on.

'My lord, we cannot go on like this. Ahhotep's soldiers, in alliance with the Nubian tribes that betrayed us, make it impossible for us to set foot outside Kerma.'

'That is nothing new, so keep calm.'

Ata was tall, thin and edgy. Nedjeh was always reproaching him for not being able to stand still, but he was a good officer and kept good order in the city.

'Kerma is a warrior kingdom and must regain its pride,' he insisted.

'Those are dangerous dreams. Forget them and make the most of life. I am beginning to tire of some of my women, and I shall graciously give them to you. They will calm your nerves.'

'For too long we were cut off from the outside world and knew nothing of events there,' said Ata. 'I have put an end to our isolation.'

The king frowned. 'What have you done?'

'My best men risked their lives to cross Egyptian-controlled territory and reach Avaris by way of the desert.'

'I did not give permission for anyone to do anything so foolhardy!' thundered the king.

'You must approve of what I did, my lord. You were right to play a waiting game, but it is now time to re-establish our links with the Hyksos and take back the territory we lost.'

'You have lost your mind, Ata!'

'My messengers informed the emperor that Kerma is taking up arms against Egypt again.'

Nedjeh was stunned. 'How dare you!'

'You must approve of what I did,' repeated Ata.

'You are very much mistaken!'

'Then too bad for you.' Ata plunged his sword into Nedjeh's belly as he lay there appalled at this crime of insolence.

The king rose to his feet with menacing slowness. 'I shall crush you, you vermin!'

Ignoring the deadly blade, Nedjeh walked towards Ata, who recoiled in disbelief. How could the fat man still move? Snatching up a bronze lamp-stand, he hit him savagely on the head.

Nedjeh stood still for a moment, then began to move forward again, his face dripping blood. Ata struck again, and this time the king fell. Ata could inform the people of Kerma that they had a new ruler.


'Taremu has fallen,' Khamudi told the emperor, who was huddled in a crudely carved armed chair.

'It does not matter.'

His ankles swollen and painful, his jowls more pendulous than usual, his voice tired, Apophis no longer left the secret room at the heart of the citadel. Only Khamudi had access to it.

'Majesty, the fall of Taremu led to the fall of Iunu.'

Now, thought the emperor, Ahhotep knows that the sacred tree refused to accept my name and that I do not belong to the line of pharaohs. She must die.

'We must not remain passive any longer, Majesty. The queen is winning too many victories. I propose to attack her at once. On the Delta plains our chariots will rout the Egyptian army.'

'Allow her to come right up to the capital,' ordered Apophis. 'My plan is unfolding stage by stage, and it is here that Ahhotep will fall into my hands, here and nowhere else. The more vainglorious her futile victories make her, the more vulnerable she will be.'

'Majesty, I—'

'That is enough, Khamudi. I need to rest. Inform me when Ahhotep reaches the city gates.'

Khamudi's rage knew no bounds. How could he make that senile old man see reason, face up to reality? True, at one time Khamudi had himself opposed deploying the Hyksos forces on more than one front, but the situation had changed completely. Ahhotep and Ahmose's army had just seized a fortress reputed to be impregnable, and had violated the Hyksos shrine.

It was clear what they planned to do: destroy all the Hyksos strongholds in the Delta, one by one, and attack Avaris only when it was isolated. To wait for them would be suicidal. Now that they had made the mistake of venturing on to level ground, the Hyksos chariots could attack and annihilate them. But a chariot attack could not be launched without the emperor's explicit order.

While he was pondering what Yima had said, Khamudi was informed that messengers from the Prince of Kerma had arrived. Good, he thought. He would be able to to take out his temper on the Nubians, whom Ahhotep had reduced to the state of sheep.

'My lord,' said a military-looking young man, 'we bring you greetings from the Prince of Kerma.'

'That coward who does nothing but eat and fornicate?'

'Nedjeh is dead, and Prince Ata is not at all like him. Leading the warriors of Kerma, he will break out of the chains that have bound us for so long.'

'Do you mean he intends to fight the Egyptians?'

'To begin with, he will reconquer all Nubia. Then he will seize the South of Egypt, on condition that you agree not to hinder his onward march.'

Khamudi did not have to think for long. 'I agree.'

'Majesty, Egyptian scouts have been spotted,' said Khamudi.

'At last, she is here! Come, Ahhotep, come to me.' The hatred that filled the emperor's eyes made them impossible to look at.

'Should you not go to the Temple of Set to unleash his rage against the enemy?'

'Ahhotep knows how to ward it off. But you are right: we must not neglect that valuable ally. A fierce storm will strike the Egyptians, and lightning will destroy part of their fleet.'

Khamudi helped the emperor to his feet and led him out of the palace. On the threshold, Apophis got into a travelling chair. He did not notice the discreet signal Khamudi gave to the leader of the Cypriot guards.

Obsequiously, Khamudi supported Apophis again when he got into the boat that would take him across to the islet where the Temple of Set stood.

'These oarsmen are not members of my personal bodyguard,' remarked the emperor.

'No, Majesty, they are my men.'

'What does this mean, Khamudi?'

'That I am taking power.'

'You have lost your head, like Jannas!'

'Jannas bided his time too long. I shall not make the same mistake.'

'You are a only little man, my friend, and you always will be, despite your vanity, your wealth and your sordid scheming.'

Apophis's voice and gaze chilled Khamudi's blood, and he felt his limbs becoming paralysed.

Delving deep into his rage, he drove his fist into the emperor's face, breaking his nose and tearing his lip. With loathing, he plunged a dagger into his heart. As the old man collapsed on to his side, Khamudi seized Apophis's dagger and stabbed him in the back.

Wide-eyed, he stepped away from the corpse.

'Keep on rowing,' he ordered the crew.

When the boat reached the islet, he told them, 'Take this corpse to the altar of Set and burn it.'

'He's still moving!' exclaimed a sailor in terror.

Khamudi grabbed an oar and hit the emperor ten, twenty, a hundred times, until he was no more than a bloody, broken puppet.

Apophis's right hand rose slightly. Hysterical now, Khamudi realised that the old man was wearing protection: at his throat the *ankh*, the cross of life, attached to a gold chain, and on the little finger of his left hand an amethyst scarab on a gold ring. The High Treasurer tore them off and trampled on them.

The old man's hand fell back, motionless at last.

'Quickly, take him and burn him!'

The smoke that rose above the Temple of Set smelt of plague.

## 46

'It is done,' Khamudi announced to Yima.

'So are you Emperor of the Hyksos now?'

'I am. From now on, everyone will have to obey me without question.'

'That is wonderful, wonderful! But . . . my love, you're covered in black dust and it smells dreadful. Go and wash, quickly, and I'll pour you some of our best wine. And I . . . I am Empress!'

Leaving Yima to dreams of grandeur which were becoming reality, Khamudi hastily summoned all the senior officers and dignitaries to the citadel's audience chamber.

'Emperor Apophis has died,' he said. 'I had the sad privilege of carrying out his last wishes: that his body should be burnt on the altar of the Temple of Set, and that I should succeed him in order to maintain the greatness of the empire.'

There was no one left capable of opposing his seizure of power. Through his purges of the army and his complete control of the Hyksos economy, he had eliminated all his rivals. Everyone therefore bowed before the new emperor, who felt his chest swell with pride. This was more intoxicating than all his drugs put together!

Walking rather unsteadily, as though he were drunk, Khamudi entered Apophis's private apartments. The former emperor's guards had been killed that very morning by Khamudi's Cypriots, and he had ordered Aberia to send all Apophis's servants to Sharuhen. A clean sweep: that was the watchword, and it also applied to objects. Every memory of the tyrant must disappear, with the exception of the Minoan paintings, whose freshness pleased Khamudi.

Yima ran from one room to another, weeping, laughing, kissing one servant girl and slapping the next, lying down on a bed, getting up, demanding a drink, forgetting her cup, taking quantities of drugs and shrieking as she ripped up her old dresses.

'We have succeeded! I am Empress! Empress, just think of it!'

She threw her arms round her husband's neck, but he pushed her away and said, 'We have work to do. The purge must continue, and you must investigate everyone who works in the citadel. If there is the slightest suspicion about any of them, Aberia must get rid of them.'

Leaving his wife to her own devices, Khamudi summoned the senior officers of the army and war-fleet. He was determined to prepare a counter-attack which would enable him to retake Taremu, Iunu and Memphis, while the new Prince of Kerma's Nubians poured into Upper Egypt. Forced to fall back to Thebes, Ahhotep would be caught in the crossfire.

Khamudi wanted her alive. For her, he would invent hitherto unknown tortures, so that she would die as slowly as possible, in unbearable agony.

Lost in his thoughts, the new emperor bumped into the elderly man he had appointed to command the fleet.

'Egyptians, my lord!'

'What do you mean, "Egyptians"?'

'They are here!'

Why was this imbecile repeating the lie he had told Apophis to induce him to leave the citadel? 'Return to your post immediately.'

'You don't understand, my lord! The Egyptians are attacking Avaris!'

'Don't talk nonsense. Our lookouts would have spotted them long ago.'

'No, because they did not come from the south.'

'That's impossible!'

'We await your orders, my lord.'

The Hyksos would be expecting an attack similar to the one led by Kamose. So Ahhotep had proposed doing something totally different: attacking Avaris in several different ways and places at the same time. It meant first destroying all the lookout posts, then throwing the entirety of the Egyptian forces into the battle.

The Afghan and Moustache saw to that, while the queen strengthened the guard around Ahmose. If the Hyksos spy was still active, he would try to kill the pharaoh in order to halt the forward march. More than ever, Young Laughter was on his guard.

'There is Avaris,' said Emheb with emotion.

At last Ahhotep set eyes upon the capital of the Empire of Darkness!

Like his mother, Pharaoh Ahmose was impressed by the extent of the site, the size of the naval base and trading-port and, above all, by the vastness of the citadel. No fortress could compare with it.

When the Egyptian troops saw the countless Hyksos war-vessels, and the chariots lined up on the eastern bank, they were afraid. Everyone had prepared themselves for this moment, but no one had imagined that the enemy would be so terrifying.

'We are walking into a massacre,' predicted Neshi, white-faced.

'What do our two most intrepid officers think?' asked Ahhotep.

'Neshi is right,' nodded Moustache.

'For once,' admitted the Afghan, 'my colleague here isn't wrong.'

'It would be better to fall back than to suffer a crushing defeat,' advised Emheb. 'I know that you have never retreated, Majesty, but no one will criticize you for it.'

Moon's silence showed that he agreed with his colleagues.

But in her son's eyes the queen saw very different intentions.

'Look at the Hyksos,' said Ahmose. 'They are running about in all directions like frightened animals. Our attacking deployment is excellent, and it will compensate for our shortfall in men and weapons. Every man to his post immediately. When the drums beat, all our units are to act according to the agreed plan.'

Khamudi had not crumbled; quite the contrary. He was so enraged at the prospect of the Egyptians attacking Avaris that he ordered his officers even more fiercely to regain control of their soldiers. Were the Hyksos not superior to their enemies? Was Avaris not impregnable?

The real battle was about to begin, and it absolutely must be won. Fired by their new commander's determination, the Hyksos organized themselves. The chariot-drivers and their crews leapt into their vehicles, the sailors rushed to their positions, and the archers took their places in the citadel's towers.

The Egyptian flagship, the *Golden Falcon*, entered the canal that led to the citadel's landing-stage, followed by several other vessels. It was the fatal mistake Khamudi had been hoping for! Imitating his elder brother, Ahmose was trying to seize the ports – but they would soon become graveyards for the Egyptian boats.

But the *Golden Falcon* halted halfway along the canal, while other ships entered the northern canal to attack the Hyksos vessels from the rear, to the heady beat of the drums.

This unpleasant surprise was followed by a much worse one: out of the flagship came a chariot, drawn by two horses and driven by the pharaoh himself, wearing the White Crown of Upper Egypt. On the vehicle's sides were painted Hyksos, bound and kneeling.

'They have managed to build a chariot!' gasped Khamudi.

'Not one chariot, my lord,' a horrified general corrected him. 'Hundreds of them.'

At top speed, the Egyptian chariots thundered down on the Hyksos.

## 47

Ahhotep firmly believed that only combined and surprise actions would give the Egyptians a chance of victory.

The flagship and her escort vessels acted as a lure for the Hyksos war-fleet, which – wrongly – thought they would be easy prey. A fierce battle commenced, during which other Egyptian vessels approached along the northern canal and cut the enemy fleet in half. Meanwhile the naval footsoldiers commanded by Emheb and Ahmes used fortified barges to attack and board the heavy Hyksos vessels, catching them completely off guard. On both fronts, the Egyptians' enthusiasm and mobility enabled them to fight the opponent on an equal footing.

There remained the main arena, on which the outcome of the battle of Avaris would depend. Whose chariots would gain the upper hand?

At first taken aback by the Egyptian attack on level ground with two-man vehicles, the Hyksos chariot commander sent a regiment up the line to sweep away everything in its path.

On an order from Ahmose, the Egyptians swerved aside and fired on the enemy's flanks. Most shots reached their targets. Horses fell, causing absolute chaos in which many Hyksos were wounded or killed. Like a swarm of hornets, Pharaoh's chariots rushed at their opponents, which were slower and less manoeuvrable. The archers killed the enemy drivers. Uncontrolled, the horses crashed into each other and caused confusion which spread to other driverless teams.

The Egyptians observed the orders to avoid head-on confrontation with the Hyksos, and to attack them from the side and the rear. As expert charioteers, Moustache and the Afghan had a fine hunt in prospect. Surrounded by the chariots that Ahhotep had ordered to protect him, Pharaoh Ahmose fired arrow after arrow.

Amid the appalling cacophony of neighing horses and men screaming in pain, the Hyksos found themselves surrounded. The Egyptians encircled them, and gave no quarter.

Then a new wave of Hyksos chariots began a counterattack. Ahhotep watched anxiously, afraid it might turn the tide of the battle. Would the exhausted Egyptians manage to contain it?

But the new chariots' wheels were those Arek the storeman had weakened, and most gave way as soon as the chariots picked up speed. So those which ought to have changed the the course of the battle added to the rout in their own ranks, which were now unable to defend themselves.

Urged on by Ahmose, the Egyptian chariot troops, both men and horses, redoubled their efforts. Spears and arrows rained down murderously.

Things were not going well on the flagship. After repelling two boarding-parties, the Egyptian sailors were beginning to yielding to weight of numbers. It would take a bold breakthrough by Moon to avert the worst. He pulled back from the northern canal, which enabled several Hyksos boats to regroup and retake control of this route to Avaris.

She-Cat heated a knife in the fire and cauterized a deep sword-cut in the Afghan's flank. Although made of stern stuff, he could not repress a moan of pain.

'You were lucky,' she told him. 'It looks bad but it isn't serious.'

'What about me?' complained Moustache. 'Don't I get any treatment?'

'All you have is scratches.'

'But I'm covered in blood and I almost died a hundred times!'

'First I must treat the serious cases. You and the other survivors must help me.'

There were countless wounded, and She-Cat and her staff were overwhelmed with work, but the Egyptian chariots had just won their first great victory. But there was no celebration in the ranks, because the citadel was still intact, defying them with its massive bulk.

The time came for reports, which Ahhotep and Ahmose listened to attentively in the flagship's cabin.

'A quarter of our chariots have been destroyed,' said Neshi, 'but we have captured a great deal of equipment. Our soldiers acquitted themselves admirably. First thing tomorrow, we must train new drivers to replace the dead. Fortunately, the countryside around here is lush, so the horses will be well fed.'

'I've nothing to add,' said Moustache, and the Afghan nodded.

'How is your wound, Afghan?' asked the queen anxiously.

'It will keep me out of the front line for a few days, Majesty, but I can still train the new charioteers.'

'Ten boats were sunk or badly damaged,' said Moon, 'and there were heavy casualties among the sailors and foot-soldiers aboard them. Fortunately, the Hyksos fleet was hit much harder than our own, but it is still large and has massed in the northern canal. I would advise against renewing battle immediately, because our men are exhausted.'

'I shall need time to organize supplies,' said Neshi, 'and that is not likely to be easy. Our brave men must have proper food and sleeping-quarters.'

'Our mobile ladders cannot be used,' said Emheb. 'The citadel's walls are too high and, unlike at Taremu, the Hyksos archers are perfectly protected by the crenellations. They are out of range, and will kill any soldiers who try to get near the walls.'

Ahhotep agreed that these arguments were valid. Despite their bravery, the Egyptian troops had been only half successful.

'I am very worried,' confessed Neshi. 'There must still be many thousands of Hyksos in the east of the Delta, and yet more in Syria and Canaan. The emperor will summon them to the rescue of Avaris, and we shall be overwhelmed.'

'Withdrawal is out of the question,' said Ahmose. 'We must take Avaris, no matter what the cost.'

'Indeed we must, Majesty,' agreed Emheb, 'but it will be a long siege, very long.'

'We all need to rest and reflect,' said Ahhotep.

What a strange night! Although the starry sky was that of Lower Egypt, the black earth, the canals and the fields still belonged to the Emperor of Darkness.

Ahhotep thought of Kamose who, with only slender resources, had launched the first attack on Avaris and had succeeded in pillaging its trading-port. Had it not been for the Hyksos spy, he would have caused much more serious damage. But he, too, would have been powerless in the face of this citadel, which seemed to scorn Ahmose's army.

Until now, each time the army had encountered an obstacle the queen had found a way to overcome it or to go round it. This time, the obstacle seemed insurmountable. Nevertheless, Ahhotep had known since she was a girl that, when no way through existed, you must create one.

Allowing her thoughts to wander among the stars, the eternal dwelling-place of Pharaohs Seqen and Kamose, she went toward Ahmose's tent, to check that all the guards were on the alert. During the battle the Hyksos spy had been unable to make any move, but he might try now.

All was well. The king's bodyguard was made up of his most loyal men, and ensured that he had the best protection possible. Young

Laughter, lying in the doorway of the tent, slept with one eye open. Moreover, all the king's food and drink was tasted by two volunteer cooks, so the spy could not poison the pharaoh.

The ships of night and day were sailing again. Ahhotep watched the passing of the old sun to the new, and its rebirth in the east, after it had vanquished the serpent of darkness in the lake of flame.

By dawn, the queen's decision was made. Either the army of liberation would take Avaris, or it would be annihilated.

48

Thanks to the drugs Khamudi had had distributed, the Hyksos soldiers were not afraid of the Egyptians. Some felt their anxieties vanish, others felt capable of fighting ten enemies at once. Some of the lower-quality drug had even been distributed among the city's population, so that they would not give way to panic.

It was clear that Ahhotep and Ahmose were interested in only one objective: the citadel. But they had no means of getting inside it. The siege would crumble, and the reinforcements from the Delta and Canaan would inflict a decisive defeat upon them.

From the top of the main watchtower, Khamudi observed the enemy. They were doing something very strange. The archers and ship's soldiers were embarking on the war-boats, which, one by one, were entering the canals and the lake of Avaris. At the prow of the flagship stood Pharaoh Ahmose, easily recognizable because he wore the White Crown.

They want to destroy my fleet, thought the new emperor, the better to encircle Avaris.

'Find me a first-rate archer,' he ordered the officer standing nearest him. 'Have him take a light boat with two good oarsmen to within firing range of that insolent little king.'

The boat commanded by Ahmes, son of Abana, had been renamed 'He Who Appears in Glory at Memphis' since the liberation of that great city. Ahmes and his skilled archers had ravaged the enemy ranks, thus making it easier to board their ships. Already, two Hyksos vessels had fallen into the hands of the Egyptians.

As he looked around, Ahmes spotted a light boat. On board were three bare-chested men, two of them oarsmen rowing fast.

Suddenly the oarsmen slowed their pace. When the third man stood up and took an arrow from his quiver, Ahmes saw that he was looking towards the flagship. The pharaoh! The Hyksos archer wanted to kill the pharaoh, whose White Crown was glinting in the sun!

Ahmes drew his bow and fired; he scarcely had time to aim. The shot grazed the head of the Hyksos, who was so shocked and afraid that he dropped his weapon. Abandoning his comrades, he threw himself into the water.

As a precaution, Ahmes killed the two oarsmen. Then, enraged at the thought that this vermin could have harmed the king, he dived in, too.

Swimming with a powerful, rhythmic overarm stroke,* he soon caught the Hyksos. He punched him hard on the back of the neck before dragging him to the bank and throwing him on to his back like a sack of grain. Although only semi-conscious, the prisoner made a grab for Ahmes's dagger. Ahmes held him down, cut off his hand and then knocked him out properly.

'Commander Ahmes, son of Abana, I award you the gold collar for bravery,' declared Pharaoh Ahmose, hanging a slender collar about the officer's neck.

Ahmes's reputation was steadily growing in the Egyptian army, which had seized several Hyksos boats. Soon the fight would begin again, intense and murderous.

Ahmes bowed. 'May I request a favour, Majesty?'

'Speak.'

'Will you grant me the honour of commanding your personal bodyguard, so that I may be the first to protect you in all circumstances?'

'After what you have just accomplished, I grant your request willingly.'

Queen Ahhotep raised her eyebrows. What if Ahmes was the Hyksos spy? What if his brave deed had been a deception, designed to win the pharaoh's trust? As head of Ahmose's bodyguard, he would always be close to the king, and sooner or later would have the ideal chance to kill him.

She shook her head. These suspicions were absurd. Ahmes had served in the army since he was a youth and had risked his life a hundred times, fighting the Hyksos in an exemplary fashion. Nevertheless, she would warn her son to be on his guard.

'We shall now question the prisoner,' decided Ahmose.

The Hyksos' wounds had been treated but he was terrified, and dared not raise his eyes to look at the king.

'Tell me your rank and station.'

'Leading archer in the regiment of the lower citadel.'

'Describe the interior to us,' ordered Ahhotep.

'I was never allowed inside. All I know is that it houses enough soldiers and supplies to hold out for years.'

---

* This stroke, a form of the crawl, was used as early as the Old Kingdom.

'Who gave you the order to fire on Pharaoh?'

'Khamudi – Emperor Khamudi.'

'Don't you mean Emperor Apophis?'

'No, Apophis is dead – or, rather, the High Treasurer killed him, and his body was burnt. Now Khamudi is the emperor.'

'If you want us to spare your life, go and tell him that the pharaoh has been seriously wounded.'

'Oh no, Majesty!' cried the Hyksos. 'Khamudi would never believe me! I'd be thrown into the labyrinth or the bull arena.' He told them in detail about the ordeals and tortures so beloved of the former and the present emperor alike, and begged, 'Kill me now.'

'When we have won this war,' decreed Ahhotep, 'you shall become the servant of Ahmes, son of Abana.'

All the workers in the weapons storehouses of Avaris had taken cheap drugs and were dreaming dreams in which they were impervious to Egyptian arrows and spears.

All except Arek, who could hardly contain his delight. At last the Egyptians were attacking Avaris! Khamudi might be another fearsome brute, but the death of Apophis had weakened the Hyksos.

After the chariot-wheels, Arek had secretly weakened the bows: when they were drawn, the wood would snap. This was much easier than his work on the wheels, but it was also more dangerous, because he was not authorized to be in that storehouse. So he had to wait until his colleagues were asleep to unbar the door and work through the night.

'What are you doing there, my little man?'

Arek froze.

It was the gravelly voice of his overseer, whose resistance to drugs was unbelievable. 'This evening I noticed that you did not take any drugs, and that interested me. You have no right to be here.'

'I . . . I wanted a bow.'

'That is theft. And the theft of a weapon in wartime is a crime.'

'Forget it, and I'll do the same for you.'

'I haven't anything wrong! You're coming with me to the citadel to explain yourself to our new emperor. If you have anything to hide, he will make you confess it. And he will thank me.'

Arek leapt forward, knocked him down and ran out of the storehouse. The overseer shouted to the guards patrolling the quayside. At once a terrible burning sensation tore through Arek's shoulder as a spear hit him. Ignoring the pain, he threw himself into the canal.

He could not swim, but at least this death was gentler than torture.

## 49

Yima clung to her husband's arm, her eyes unfocused and her gait unsteady. 'Are we really safe, my Emperor?'

'You have taken too much of the drug,' commented Khamudi.

'But we must combat fear. Here, no one is afraid of the Egyptians any more, because you are omnipotent, the country's sole master. And I am helping you. With the aid of my friend Aberia, we shall execute all the traitors.'

'That's an excellent idea. If you have no proof, choose a suspect at random, assemble those close to him and kill him in front of them. Everyone must understand that Khamudi is invulnerable.'

Delighted at the prospect of such fun, the empress went off to join Aberia, while the emperor called a meeting of his generals.

'The battle is beginning to rage on the canals and the lake,' one of them told him. 'Contrary to what we thought, Ahhotep and Ahmose are not interested in the citadel. Their goal seems to be to destroy our fleet. They will not succeed in doing so before our reinforcements arrive. Unfortunately, it is no use sending out raiding-parties to kill the pharaoh, because he is very wary and no longer shows himself in the open.'

'Change the guard every three hours. Fill the watchtowers and battlements with archers,' ordered Khamudi.

While Ahhotep, Emheb and Moon were directing the naval battle and taking care to prolong it as much as possible, Ahmose was far from Avaris, on the road used by supply caravans. Guarded by Laughter and Ahmes, he was carrying out his mother's plan: to cut the trading-route and prevent Hyksos reinforcements from Canaan and the eastern Delta reaching Avaris. He had already captured several consignments of food, which provided his soldiers with a feast.

Now the chariot regiment commanded by Moustache was engaging its Canaanite counterpart, while the Afghan and his men fought the Hyksos from the Delta. Maintaining contact with them through Rascal and the other carrier-pigeons, Ahmose was able to hurry to wherever his troops were in difficulty.

Although outnumbered, the Egyptians made good use of their greater mobility. Under the burning sun, the Sword of Amon flashed out such intense brilliance that every soldier felt filled with inexhaustible energy.

Not the seasons, the months, days, nights, hours or anything else counted now. All that mattered was the battle of Avaris in which, little by little, the Egyptian war-fleet was gaining the upper hand. In She-Cat's absence Ahhotep took charge of the wounded, most of whom demanded to return to the front. Now they were so close to their goal, no one would give in, although the proud citadel still looked down haughtily on the fierce fighting.

'We have sunk their best boats,' announced Emheb. 'At last we have a marked superiority in numbers.'

Rascal chose this moment to perch upon Ahhotep's shoulder. As usual, she lavished caresses upon him before reading the precious message he bore.

The queen thought constantly of her son, fervently hoping that he really was protected; she could never forget the battle in which her husband had been betrayed and murdered. But they had no other choice. Unless Ahmose could block the Hyksos reinforcements' way, the Egyptian army would be crushed.

Emheb could not hide his anxiety. 'Is there any news, Majesty?'

'The reinforcements from Canaan have had to retreat.'

'What about those from the Delta?'

'They have fallen back, too, but our chariot regiments have suffered severe losses. Pharaoh asks us to send him more men and equipment.'

'It would be possible, but we would be very much weakened here. If the Hyksos tried to break out of the citadel, it would be a very close-run thing.'

'Then, Emheb, we must finish off their war-fleet.'

At the sight of Ahhotep's sceptre, which symbolized the power of Thebes, the Egyptians forgot their exhaustion and their wounds. On both the lake and the canals, their vessels rushed to attack the enemy. And despite a bad spear-wound in his leg, Moon cut off the hands of the last Hyksos captain, who had fought to the death.

'Majesty, ought we not to try to break out?' suggested a Hyksos general.

'Absolutely not!' said Khamudi angrily. 'Do you not understand that that is exactly what the Egyptians are waiting for? We no longer have a single boat, Ahhotep has blocked all the canals, and Avaris is surrounded. In other words, our chariots would fall into a trap. We are safe only inside the citadel.'

The general and his fellow officers all wondered what had happened to the thunderbolt of war, which was supposed to ravage everything in its path.

'Is there at least some news of our troops from Canaan and the Delta?' fumed the new emperor.

'No, Majesty, but they will be here soon.'

'Have our links with the North been cut?'

'It would appear so, my lord. No messengers can now get though to Avaris. Nevertheless, you may be certain that our men will swarm down on the Egyptians like locusts.'

To calm his nerves, Khamudi attended a mass execution. With great pleasure, Aberia strangled the supposed traitors one after the other.

Each day, the Queen of Freedom shared her soldiers' meals, which were of dried fish or pork, garlic, onions, bread and grapes, washed down with small beer. After the privilege of spending time with her, every man felt his courage renewed.

'The Hyksos couldn't eat this,' laughed a footsoldier, 'because they are forbidden to eat pork. Me, I'm dreaming of a good meal of roast pork with lentils.'

'Thank you, soldier,' said the queen. 'You have given me an excellent idea for sending a message to Emperor Khamudi.'

The soldier gaped, and his comrades all began to tease him. The queen prepared a pigskin water-bag, into which she slipped an inscribed tablet.

'Boat coming!' shouted a Hyksos lookout.

Immediately, the citadel's archers took up their positions, and a deluge of arrows rained down upon the war-boat, which did not respond.

'Cease fire,' ordered Khamudi.

The boat ran fast to a quay to the north of the citadel, and halted.

'It's one of ours,' said an archer, 'but there's no one aboard.'

'Look, at the top of the mainmast!' urged his neighbour.

From it there hung a wooden effigy of a man dressed in a black breastplate and with a water-skin on its head.

'It must be a message from the enemy,' said an officer.

'Go and fetch it,' commanded the emperor.

'Me, my lord? But—'

'Are you daring to argue?'

Faced with either being tortured to death or else falling beneath a rain of Egyptian arrows, the officer chose the second. Climbing across from the top of the ramparts with the aid of a rope, he was utterly astonished still to be alive when he reached the top of the mast and retrieved the strange effigy.

Safe and sound, he reappeared before Khamudi. 'Do not touch this water-skin, Majesty. It is a horror – it's made of pigskin!'

'Open it.'

The officer took out the tablet, and laid it on a crenellation in disgust. Ahhotep's message informed Khamudi that he could no longer count on getting help, because his troops had been halted by Ahmose.

'Throw that thing away.'

The officer obeyed.

'You stink of pig – you are impure. Bring me a cloth for my hands, quickly!'

Using the cloth so as not so soil his hands, Khamudi grabbed the water-skin, put it over the officer's head and pushed him off the battlements.

# 50

The fighting had ground to a halt again. From the safety of his citadel, Khamudi still sneered down at Ahhotep and her forces. As for Ahmose, he could not continue his offensive. In the months – no, years – to come, he would have to be content with consolidating the new front and barring the road to Khamudi's hoped-for reinforcements.

The queen sat beside Long-Ears, gazing at the magnificent sunset in all its many-coloured splendour. The donkey was tired after a long day carrying weapons and provisions, and was glad of this quiet moment. Suddenly, as she sat there Ahhotep realized the truth.

Once the Egyptian camp was soundly asleep, she summoned Moon, Emheb and Neshi.

'Avaris is impregnable because of Apophis's magic,' she said, 'but until the citadel has been destroyed all our efforts will come to nothing. It is my responsibility to destroy it by honouring the ancestors. Without them, Ahmose will not win the war, and will never unite the Red Crown and the White. I must leave at once.'

Moon was horrified. 'Leave? I don't understand, Majesty.'

'I am going to the Isle of the Flame, where I shall implore the ancestors to come to Pharaoh's aid. Continue to prosecute the siege while I am away.'

'How many soldiers will you need?' asked Neshi.

'Two oarsmen.'

Emheb was outraged. 'It's too dangerous, Majesty,' he protested. Ahhotep simply smiled.

'Are we to tell the king?' asked Neshi anxiously.

'Of course. If I have not returned in twenty-eight days' time, ask him to fall back to Thebes. Amon shall be our final bulwark.'

Using the network of waterways, Ahhotep's boat crossed vast stretches of the Delta populated by goats and sheep kept for their wool. Civets ran away as they approached the landing-stage, watched by wild bulls half hidden in the tall grass. Everyone had to be constantly on the alert for hippopotami, which had to be left undisturbed, or crocodiles, which could be driven off by thrashing the water with oars.

The boat sailed on a shallow lake, bursting with fish such as Nile perch, grey mullet and silurids. The queen and her oarsmen smeared their skin with ointment to avoid being bitten by the swarms of mosquitoes.

Little by little, the papyrus thickets grew thicker until they were impenetrable.

'We cannot go any further in this boat, Majesty,' said one of the oarsmen. 'We must build you a raft.'

The two men laid bundles of papyrus on a frame of interwoven branches, and bound the whole thing up with ropes.

'Wait for me here,' said the queen. She drove a long pole down into the mud, then pushed hard on the pole, thus moving the raft forwards.

Alone, she entered a dark, hostile forest. Hundreds of birds and small predators lived in this perpetually flooded area, where the vegetation was more than three times the height of a man. Ibis, hoopoes, lapwings and woodcock bred here, despite attacks by civets and wild cats.

Suddenly, she saw a net stretched between two posts, and poled the raft to a halt.

Someone was watching her.

'Show yourself,' she commanded.

There were four of them. Four naked, bearded fishermen.

'Well I'll be damned!' exclaimed the oldest. 'It's a woman! A woman, here!'

'She must be a goddess,' said a red-haired fellow, 'unless . . . You wouldn't by any chance be that Queen of Freedom, the one all the Hyksos want to kill?'

'And you wouldn't by any chance be their allies?' asked the queen.

'Absolutely not. It's their fault that we're starving to death.'

'Then take me to Buto.'

The fisherman froze. 'That is a sacred place and no one can enter it. There are monsters there, and they devour the unwary.'

'Then take me near the place, and I shall go in alone.'

'As you wish, but it's very dangerous. The place is infested with crocodiles.'

'My cornelian staff will keep them at a distance.'

Impresssed by the queen's calmness and confidence, the four men helped her into a papyrus boat and skilfully steered it into a maze which could only be negotiated by those who knew it intimately. At the end of the day they stopped by a low mound or bank, and ate an evening meal of grilled fish and bitter-tasting papyrus stems.

'The Hyksos tried to explore these marshes,' said the red-haired man, 'but none of them came out alive. We shall sleep now, and tomorrow we'll set you on your way to Buto.'

When they awoke, one of the fishermen had disappeared.

'It's Loudmouth, an odd, half-crazy fellow,' said the redhead. 'He's stolen fish from us before now – a fine thing to do!'

After several hours of arduous travel, the thickets began to open out. The forest disappeared, giving way to a lake across which ran a narrow strip of land.

'All you have to do is cross it to reach the island of Buto. We shall wait a while for you here. But you must realize that you won't be coming back.'

Armed only with her cornelian staff, Ahhotep hurried towards the resting-place of the spirits of the first kings of Egypt and those of their divine ancestors, the Souls of Pe and Nekhen, the two mythical cities built in their honour on the island of the first morning of the world.

The queen walked with a light step. The birds had fallen silent, and the water was incredibly clear.

Then she saw it. An island, planted with tall palm-trees sheltering two shrines guarded by statues, the first group representing falcon-headed men, the second men with the heads of jackals.

At the instant Ahhotep stepped into this sacred place, a flame flared up from its centre. She stopped, and the flame changed into a cobra crowned with a gold disc.

Ahhotep was in the presence of the Eye of Ra, the Divine Light.

This was where the impossible marriage was accomplished between water and fire, earth and sky, time and eternity.

'I have come to seek the aid of the Souls,' said the queen. 'You who have brought together that which was scattered, you who have accomplished the Great Work, permit Pharaoh Ahmose to wear the Double Crown, upon which the Eye of Ra shall rest to light his way.'

A long silence began. When it was as deep as the *Nun*, the ocean of primordial energy, the voices of the ancestors sounded in Ahhotep's heart. Her cornelian staff was now topped by a rearing gold serpent, wearing the Double Crown.

The queen would have liked to stay on the island and enjoy for a little longer the peace that reigned there, but harsh battles still awaited her.

She retraced her steps across the strip of land. When she came within earshot of the papyrus forest, she heard shouts and the sounds of a struggle. The water was red with the blood of the three fishermen.

Loudmouth appeared, leading a patrol of Hyksos with their black helmets and breastplates. He had guided them through the labyrinth of foliage.

Ahhotep had no chance of escape.

## 51

To run like a terror-stricken animal towards the island, which she had no hope of reaching, and to be felled by an arrow in the back as she fled. That was a fate unworthy of a queen. So Ahhotep turned to face the Hyksos.

'It's her,' shouted Loudmouth, 'it's really her, the Queen of Freedom!'

She gazed at him with such contempt that he took fright and hid behind a soldier.

When they saw the beautiful queen walking composedly towards them, the Hyksos drew back. They felt sure her poise must conceal a curse against which their swords would be powerless.

'She's unarmed,' cried Loudmouth, 'and she's only a woman! Seize her!'

The soldiers pulled themselves together. Taking her prisoner would earn them a fabulous reward.

When they were only a few paces from their prey, a dolphin leapt gracefully nearby and swam towards the strip of land.

Its eyes called to Ahhotep. She dived into the water.

'Catch her! Go on, catch her!' roared Loudmouth.

But the Hyksos soldiers did not dare try, because the weight of their breastplates would have drowned them, so the traitor leapt in and set off alone in pursuit of the queen.

With a movement of supreme elegance, the dolphin ripped open his face with its sharp dorsal fin, which it used to slice open the fragile bellies of crocodiles.

As the Hyksos hurled their swords and daggers at her, the queen clung on to the dolphin, which towed her away to the south. Without a guide, the emperor's soldiers would never find their way out of the papyrus forest alive.

The dolphin was nicknamed 'Sun-Disc', and as if by magic he always saw that the nets of the fishermen who were his friends were well filled. He brought the queen to where the two Egyptian oarsmen were waiting for her.

*

Like Tany, Yima loathed Egyptian art, especially pottery. She refused to allow into the capital anything but egg-shaped Hyksos jars of the Canaanite type, narrow-mouthed and with two handles. Each year, Avaris took delivery of more than eight thousand of them. The most beautiful ones, which were covered with a bright-pink glaze, were reserved for the military aristocracy.

Despite the official ban on making traditional pottery, one old craftsman had dared to use his wheel. Reported by the wife of a Syrian officer, he had just been strangled by Aberia in front of his colleagues. They had become slaves, and realized that the same fate awaited them before long.

'There's to be a meeting tomorrow morning at the lame man's house,' said the dead craftsman's son.

The only people living in most of the Hyksos houses where the enslaved potters worked were the wives and children of officers who were in the citadel or campaigning in Anatolia. 'A meeting at the lame man's house' – the lame man was the father of Arek, the storeman who had killed himself to escape torture – had a special meaning: they would no longer bear the humiliation and intended to rid themselves of their tormentors.

First thing the following morning, the empress once again summoned all the former potters to a small square in Avaris. Behind her stood Aberia and some guards.

'You have not learnt your lesson, you obstinate ruffians! What madman left an old-style pot outside the house of the rebel who was executed yesterday? Unless the culprit confesses, you will all die.'

Intoxicated by her new power, Yima rejoiced. After these, she would kill some more craftsmen.

'I did,' confessed the old man's son.

'Step forward.'

Head lowered, hesitant, the guilty man obeyed.

'You know the fate that lies in store for you.'

'Have pity, Majesty!'

'You sicken me, you band of cowards! Do you think your Queen of Freedom is going to save you? Well, you're very much mistaken. The reinforcements will soon be here, she will be taken prisoner, and I shall torture her with my own hands.'

The potter fell at the empress's feet. 'I am sorry, Majesty. Have pity!'

Yima spat on him. 'You and your accomplices are lower than the beasts.'

The potter suddenly leapt up and slit the empress's throat with a shard of glass hidden in his right hand. Blood instantly soaked the front of her dress. While he finished her off, his colleagues rushed at the guards. Taken by surprise at this violence from men they had regarded as sheep who were incapable of fighting, the guards were slow to react. Since they had nothing left to lose, the craftsmen struck and struck again.

Directed by Aberia, however, the guards soon regained the upper hand and immediately put all the rebels to the sword.

'You look as stupid dead as you did alive,' commented Aberia, looking down at Yima's body.

As soon as Ahhotep returned, to great acclaim from her soldiers, Emheb entrusted a message to Rascal so that he could alert Ahmose. The legend of the Queen of Freedom had just acquired a new chapter.

'The Souls of the ancestors are protecting us,' she declared. 'Ahmose now belongs to their line. So that you shall have no doubts, and so that Emperor Khamudi is aware of the punishment that awaits him, let us approach the citadel.'

Emheb frowned. 'Majesty, what exactly are you planning to do?'

'Have a platform built.'

Artificers carried out the order, but the queen was not satisfied. 'Move it closer to the citadel.'

'We cannot, Majesty. You would be within range of their arrows.'

'Khamudi must understand clearly what I have to say to him.'

To avoid digging a new grave in the palace burial-ground, which was small and overcrowded, Khamudi had Tany's grave reopened. Yima's body, still in the bloodstained dress, was thrown on top of her predecessor's, then they were covered with earth again.

She had been a great help to Khamudi, who had enjoyed the perverse games she had so cunningly devised. But today, as supreme commander of the Hyksos, he was not displeased to be rid of her. A hundred craftsmen had been beheaded as a reprisal, and Aberia would now be at the emperor's side at all times, so as to ensure his safety.

'My lord, the Egyptians are about to attack the citadel,' an officer warned him.

Khamudi ran up the steps to the highest tower, taking them four at a time. The attackers had indeed assembled, but at a good distance from the ramparts. All except Ahhotep, who was standing on a platform not far away, brandishing a staff made of cornelian.

'Look, Khamudi,' she said loudly and clearly, 'look closely at the cobra-goddess of Buto, who wears the Double Crown. You try to deny the truth, but your reign is already at an end. If you have even a little intelligence left, surrender and beg Pharaoh Ahmose for mercy. If you do not, the anger of the Eye of Ra will utterly destroy you.'

'Give me a bow!' demanded the emperor, mad with rage.

Ahhotep's eyes did not leave the killer as he aimed at her.

'Majesty, step back!' begged Emheb.

The queen continued to hold high the cornelian staff. At the moment he drew his bow back to its furthest extent, the wood split and the bow fell apart.

The Hyksos and the Egyptians both understood what it meant: that the Eye of Ra was protecting Ahhotep and the pharaoh.

## 52

The Afghan and Moustache exchanged glances. They were numb with weariness. This was the third attack by Canaanite chariots that they had repulsed in less than ten days.

Utterly exhausted, they and their soldiers wondered how they could still find the strength to fight. As for the horses, they had acquitted themselves admirably, responding to their drivers' smallest instruction. An intimate understanding had developed between man and beast, enabling them to survive in the most desperate situations.

'What are our losses?' asked Pharaoh Ahmose anxiously.

'They're miraculously light,' replied the Afghan. 'Only ten dead – and thirty enemy chariots have been put out of action.'

'With respect, Majesty,' ventured Moustache, 'you should not expose yourself to danger so much.'

'With an archer like Ahmes covering me, I am not afraid of anything. And I must take part in the fighting. Why should my men risk their lives for a coward who merely looked on?'

At sunset, a scout returning from the east of the Delta brought them some good news. Several areas had risen up against the Hyksos, and everywhere rebels were damaging chariots and stealing horses. Fully occupied in trying – and failing – to re-establish order, the enemy was in no position to retake the offensive.

'We must support the rebels,' decided the king. 'Two hundred men are to go to their aid, so that they can continue to cause as much disruption as possible.'

Since Ahhotep had returned unharmed from Buto and ridiculed Khamudi, each soldier in the army of liberation regarded her as a protecting goddess who, with the aid of the Eye of Ra, could extricate them from even the worst danger. But the enemy's resources were still vast and the citadel of Avaris remained impregnable.

'The men are physically exhausted,' said She-Cat, who had herself grown thin through long nights spent caring for the wounded. 'If they do not take some rest, they will collapse where they stand.'

'After the punishment we've just inflicted on the Canaanites,' said Moustache, 'the enemy can't be much fresher than we are.'

Ahhotep received Neshi, who had just returned from the Northern front.

'Tell me what is happening – in plain words,' she said.

'The situation is not wonderful, Majesty. Since we began intercepting the caravans, we have plenty of good food, but our troops are exhausted. The rebellion rumbling on in the east of the Delta looks very promising, and many of the Canaanites' chariots have been destroyed, but time is not on our side, and the fact that the citadel is easily holding out ensures that our enemies remain united.'

Unfortunately, he was right. And the information the queen had just received from Elephantine made things look even worse. The new Prince of Kerma, Ata, had recaptured villages controlled by the Egyptians and was advancing down the Nile. The garrison at the fort of Buhen and the Nubian tribes loyal to Ahhotep were trying to halt him. War was raging between the Second and First Cataracts.

If Ata won, first Elephantine would be threatened, then Edfu and eventually Thebes itself. And not even one regiment could be spared to go to the rescue.

'What do you suggest we do, Emheb?' asked Ahhotep.

'The volunteers who reached the walls of the citadel were killed by archers or by slingshots. A massive attack would be suicidal. There is nothing we can do, Majesty.'

'Then we must wait until their food and water run out.'

'The Northern front may collapse before that happens,' predicted Emheb.

'Then we must find another way.'

The weary governor withdrew into his tent.

The Egyptian scout was dying from wounds to his belly and forehead. Without the drugs administered by She-Cat, he would have been in terrible pain and unable to speak. But his expression was almost peaceful, and he was proud to be able to deliver his report to the King of Egypt.

'The gods protected me, Majesty. I succeeded in crossing the Canaanite lines. Things are serious, very serious . . . Thousands of Hyksos soldiers will soon arrive from Anatolia to join the Canaanites. Horde and hordes of chariots and footsoldiers will thunder down on us.'

The scout's body tensed, his hand gripped the king's, and the light faded from his eyes.

\*

Pharaoh wandered round the camp for a long time, after entrusting Rascal with an urgent message informing Ahhotep of the situation.

So this was the end of the road. All those people dead, all that suffering, all that heroism, would end beneath the chariot-wheels of the invader, whose repression would be terrifying. Nothing whatsoever would remain of Thebes. Khamudi would complete Apophis's destruction.

The pharaoh gathered together those close to him, and told them the truth.

'Do you wish to strike camp first thing tomorrow morning, Majesty?' asked the Afghan.

'No. We shall stay here,' declared Ahmose.

'But, Majesty, not one of us will escape!' protested Moustache.

'It is better to die as warriors than as fugitives.'

Rascal knew that he had brought very bad news, and remained at a distance from Ahhotep, who did not even think to stroke him.

'It is over,' she told Emheb, Neshi and Moon. 'Alongside the Canaanite chariots, the troops from Anatolia will attack first Ahmose, then us. The pharaoh will hold out for as long as possible, to cover our retreat to Thebes.'

'If we retreat, the Hyksos will pursue us and destroy us,' said Moon, 'so why not attack the citadel with all our forces? If we must die, Majesty, I should like to do so without regrets.'

'It is more important to protect Thebes,' said Emheb.

'Could you not persuade the king to combine our forces?' suggested Neshi. 'Together, we would be much stronger.'

'I shall give you my decision tomorrow morning.'

Whatever it did, the Egyptian army would be wiped out. And yet Ahhotep had gone to Buto, had heard the voices of the ancestors and received the Eye of Ra.

The queen raised her eyes to the night sky and begged her protector, the moon-god, Ah, for help. It was the fourteenth day of the waxing moon, when the eye was made complete again, caught, and put back together by the gods Thoth and Horus. It shone forth in his ship, encouraging all forms of growth. No, her celestial companion could not abandon her like this!

Refusing to believe in disaster, the queen spent all night thinking about the deeds of those who had fought for freedom. When dawn came she had still not heard the voices of the ancestors.

Suddenly there was a terrifying roar. The sun, which had only just risen, vanished. The sky became blacker than ink, incredibly strong winds carried away the tents and attacked the walls of the citadel.

And, added to this fury, there was an earthquake.

Several days' voyage away, in the Mycenean islands, the volcano on Thera had erupted.*

*Thera is also known as Santorini.

## 53

'Majesty, it is raining rocks!' exclaimed Neshi.

It was true. Pieces of pumice stone from the volcano, carried along by the wind, were falling on Avaris, and black ash veiled the sky. Terrified, the Egyptians ran about in all directions.

'Calm the horses,' ordered Ahhotep.

For his part, Long-Ears brayed imperiously, urging his fellow donkeys to remain calm.

Little by little, the stones stopped raining down, the wind dropped and the black veil disappeared. With the return of the sun, Ahhotep saw that the Egyptian camp had been laid waste and that there were many wounded. Nevertheless, a broad smile lit up her face. What the Egyptians had suffered was nothing compared to the damage inflicted on the citadel.

Deep cracks had torn through the walls and many of the battlements had collapsed, dragging hundreds of archers down with them. Where the great gate had stood, there was a gaping hole.

'Assemble the footsoldiers and the chariots,' the queen ordered Emheb.

An entire wall swayed and fell, its stones and bricks coming apart with a great crash. The army gazed at the incredible sight. All that stood before them now was a ruin.

'Thanks be to Set for his help,' said Ahhotep. 'He has just placed his fury and his power at the service of freedom. Attack!'

Still covered in ashes, both footsoldiers and archers rushed to attack the disembowelled monster.

Khamudi gazed in shock at the results of the earthquake. Whole rooms had disappeared, roofs and ceilings no longer existed, and countless corpses strewed the great inner courtyard.

'We must organize our defences,' urged Aberia, who had a slight head wound.

'It would be useless. We must escape.'

'And abandon the survivors?'

'They will not hold out for long. Let us go to the strongroom.'

Khamudi hoped to seize Apophis's treasures, above all the Red Crown of Lower Egypt, but blocks of stone barred his way.

He summoned the commander of his personal bodyguard, a Cypriot with a moustache, and told him, 'I shall drive back the attackers to the north of the citadel. You are to gather together the survivors and deal with the south. The Egyptians have not won yet. If we manage to contain their first assault, they will lose heart.'

Bloody hand-to-hand fighting broke out. Determined to hold off the Egyptians, the Hyksos took up station in the intact corners of the citadel and formed pockets of resistance which were difficult to stamp out.

For long hours, Ahhotep urged her soldiers not to weaken. Despite the favourable circumstances, victory was far from won.

'Majesty, the pharaoh is coming,' said Emheb.

How good it was to hear the sound of chariot wheels!

By great good fortune, the earthquake had severely affected the Hyksos' Canaanite and Delta troops, but not the Egyptians. Hoping that the citadel would be shaken by the anger of heaven and earth, Ahmose had headed for Avaris. The result filled him with joy.

Immediately taking command, the king broke down the enemy defences one by one. All that remained for him to conquer was a hall of arms, the least damaged part of the citadel. When he entered it, the king did not see the Cypriot with the moustache step out behind him, ready to bury an axe in his back.

Swift and accurate, an arrow fired by Ahmes, son of Abana, sank into the Cypriot's neck.

After again receiving the gold award for bravery, together with three female prisoners who were to become servants in his household, Ahmes proudly reread the hieroglyphic text written by Neshi on the trophy he held most dear: '*In the name of Pharaoh Ahmose, gifted with life: an arrowhead brought back from defeated Avaris.*'

In the eighteenth year of Ahmose's reign, the capital of the Hyksos Empire had expired.

Several carrier-pigeons left for the South, bearing the wonderful news, while Egyptian scouts were charged with spreading it throughout the cities of the Delta, where the rebellion was intensifying.

'But,' lamented Emheb, 'there is no trace of Khamudi.'

'He has fled, the coward,' said Moon contemptuously.

'As long as he is alive,' said Ahmose, 'the war will continue. Khamudi still has a powerful army, and he will be bent on revenge.'

'His men will soon learn that Avaris has fallen,' said Ahhotep, 'and the defeat will dishearten them. Our most urgent task is to free the Delta completely and to recruit more men. First, though, we must carry out the will of the ancestors. I am convinced that the Red Crown is hidden here. We must take the citadel apart stone by stone if necessary.'

Units of soldiers at once set off on the hunt.

As the men left, Ahhotep heard the Afghan calling from outside the palace. 'Majesties, come and see, I beg you.'

When they found him and Moustache, both men looked shaken and horrified. The place was a strange garden, littered here and there with bricks from the fallen palace walls. Before the first arch, which was covered with climbing plants, stood around fifty large jars.

'I removed the lids,' said the Afghan. 'Inside are the bodies of children and tiny babies. Their throats have been cut.'

Hundreds of other jars were heaped up in the garden. During the siege of Avaris, Khamudi had done away with all those who could not fight.

'Down there, in front of the thicket of tamarisks, is the body of a man almost cut in two,' said Moustache.

'This must be the evil labyrinth,' said the queen. She was certain that the Emperor of Darkness had dreamt of throwing her into this death-trap, with its deceptively pleasant appearance. 'Burn it.'

Not far away, an animal bellowed. Emheb went to investigate, and found a wild bull shut up in an enclosure whose door was blocked by rubble.

'Set it free,' ordered Ahhotep.

'But, Majesty, it is dangerous,' warned Moon.

'The bull is the symbol of Pharaoh's power. Apophis put a spell on this one to turn it into a killer. We must bring it back into the realm of Ma'at.'

As soon as the entrance was unblocked, spears, swords and arrows were pointed at the animal, which fixed its eyes on the queen.

'Do not go any closer, Majesty,' urged Emheb. 'He could easily run you through with one toss of his horns.'

The huge creature pawed the ground.

'Be calm,' Ahhotep told it. 'No one will force you to kill any more. Let me offer you peace.'

The bull was on the point of attacking.

'Lower your weapons,' ordered the queen.

'This is madness, Majesty!' protested Moon.

In one quick movement, the queen laid the Eye of Ra against the bull's forehead. Instantly a look of intense gratitude appeared in its eyes.

'Now,' she told it, 'you are truly free. Go now.'

Immediately, the bull rushed out of the fortress towards the marshes.

'There are still Hyksos at large,' warned Neshi. 'One of our footsoldiers has been seriously wounded in the ruins of the throne room.'

The Afghan and Moustache were the first there, daggers in hand. A flame attacked them from the back of the room, burning the Afghan on the wrist.

'There is an evil being in here,' said Moustache.

'The Eye of Ra will blind it,' promised Ahhotep, who had entered the chamber just behind them. She pointed her cornelian staff at the place from which the flame had sprung.

In the chaos of bricks and rubble, the faces of the two griffins had been spared. They struck down anyone who approached the emperor's throne.

Protected by the Eye of Ra, Ahhotep covered the eyes of the evil spirits with a cloth. Then Emheb coated them with plaster to render them harmless.

'Smash the throne into a thousand pieces and block the noses of all the intact statues,' ordered the queen. 'The emperor must have cast a spell upon them so that they would spread evil vapours.'

'Majesty,' said Neshi excitedly, 'we have found a strongroom.'

Fearing one of Apophis's traps, Ahhotep had a fire lit at the foot of the door. When the metal bolts melted, the door opened with a creak.

In the strongroom lay the Red Crown of Lower Egypt.

## 54

Big-Feet was worried. There had not been a single convoy of new deportees for more than a month.

Around him, people continued to die. Since becoming the camp's official gravedigger, Big-Feet had received an additional weekly food ration. Being clever with his hands, he repaired the guards' sandals, and they were no longer wary of this walking skeleton, whose continued survival amazed everyone.

'I have two children and an old man to bury,' he told the head guard, a bearded Persian. 'Look, my pickaxe is broken. May I take another one?'

'Dig with your hands!'

Big-Feet was trudging away resignedly when the guard called him back.

'All right, all right, get one from the hut.'

Among the tools were several bronze branding-irons, which were used to burn each prisoner's number into their skin. Big-Feet stole one, and hid it in a corner of the camp. If he came out of this hell alive, he would have evidence of his sufferings and would gaze upon it each day while giving thanks to destiny.

After finishing his painful task, he returned the pickaxe to the guard.

'There haven't been any new people for a long time,' he commented.

'Does that bother you, 1790?'

'No, but . . .'

'Clean up this pigsty and get out of my sight.'

From the man's bitter tone, Big-Feet realized that all was not going well for the Hyksos. Had the Queen of Freedom won some significant victories? Was the empire beginning to disintegrate?

Now, more than ever, he must not despair. Today his stale bread would taste better.

Pharaoh Ahmose stood for a moment in the Hyksos' emperor's former throne room, for the first time wearing the Double Crown, the union of the Red Crown of Lower Egypt and the White Crown of Upper Egypt. Then he went out to his troops, so that they could see the two crowns reunited. They cheered loud and long.

Ahhotep stood several paces behind him, trying to hide her tears of joy. But her son made her come forward.

'We owe this great victory to the Queen of Freedom. May the name of Ahhotep become immortal and may she be the benevolent mother of a reborn Egypt.'

The queen thought of Seqen and Kamose. They were here, close beside her, and they were sharing this moment of intense happiness.

But the victors of Avaris had no time to rest, for the citadel must be transformed into an Egyptian military base. The first task for the prisoners they had taken, women included, was to purify the houses that were still standing, by burning herbs and other cleansers. Then the prisoners were placed in the service of Egyptian officers and assured that they would be freed one day if they behaved well.

While the artificers began demolishing the parts of the fortress that were damaged beyond repair and restoring those worth preserving, the queen arranged for the soldiers who had died in combat to be buried. She was outraged to discover that the Hyksos had buried their dead in the courtyards of the houses or in the houses themselves, and that many of the tombs in the palace burial-ground contained nothing but large quantities of drugs. There was no trace of stelae or offerings, nor the inscriptions of eternity that ought to have been recited by a servant of the *ka*. Cut off from their traditions and their rites, the Egyptians of Avaris had lived through terrible times.

Before an army could be created to liberate all the cities of the North, the Temple of Set must be purified. Ahhotep went there by boat with the pharaoh, guarded by Young Laughter and Ahmes. As nothing untoward had happened during the many battles the king had fought in, reason said that he no longer needed to be so closely guarded. But the war was not over, and Ahhotep refused to let him run even the slightest risk, for he must establish a new dynasty.

'According to my latest information,' said Ahmose, 'the Prince of Kerma's advance has stalled, so there is no need to send troops to help Buhen and our Nubian allies.'

The pharaoh and his mother were astonished by the insignificance of the temple, which was a shoddy brick building, utterly unworthy of a divine power.

On the altar, which still stood intact amid the oak trees, lay Apophis's scattered remains, which had been torn apart by vultures. There was also a deep ditch, filled with sacrificed donkeys.

'What a sinister place!' said the pharaoh. 'We must eradicate all traces of this shrine to evil.'

Ahhotep agreed. 'Here we shall build a great temple dedicated to Set, he whom the emperor failed to enslave, he who gave us his strength when we had sore need of it. May Horus and Set unite and be at peace within the being of Pharaoh.'

Scarcely had Aberia driven the chariot into the fortress of Sharuhen when the two horses collapsed, dead from exhaustion. Khamudi was glad to have his feet on the ground again, after a difficult journey during which he had constantly been afraid they would be intercepted.

Everywhere, they had seen the damage done by the earthquake: trees had been uprooted, farms destroyed, huge cracks ran through the fields, and the ground was strewn with the bodies of hundreds of Hyksos who had been killed in the accompanying storm. But, to the emperor's great relief, the fortress of Sharuhen seemed almost intact.

'What is the extent of the damage?' Khamudi asked the commander, who came to greet him.

'Just some cracks in one wall, Majesty, and we are repairing it. But a few horses went mad and trampled some footsoldiers, and several men who were on watch on the ramparts were carried away by the storm.'

Khamudi ordered the commander to set aside the best rooms in the living-quarters for himself, and others for Aberia, and to bring him food and wine. The rooms were far removed from the luxury of the palace at Avaris, but Khamudi knew how to be patient until he once again enjoyed surroundings worthy of him. Famished, he wolfed down some grilled mutton, duck and goose, and drank a jar of white wine.

When he had finished his meal, he summoned the commander again. 'I have decided to bestow a great honour upon Sharuhen,' he said. 'I am making it the capital of my empire. Summon all the officers to my throne room.'

He was still free, he mused, still invincible. He had, after all, succeeded in getting rid of Apophis and seizing supreme power.

'The Egyptians were in no way victorious,' he announced to the officers. 'Faults in its construction meant that the citadel at Avaris could not withstand the earthquake and the storm. All the enemy did was invade a ruin. You may be sure that I shall not make the same mistakes as my predecessor. Our army is still the best, and it will crush the rebels. Ahhotep and the pharaoh do not know that we have an immense reserve of troops in Anatolia, all of whom I shall order to return forthwith. We shall begin by retaking the Delta, then we shall raze Thebes to the ground. My reign will be the greatest in Hyksos history and my fame will exceed that of Apophis. Prepare the men for battle and have no doubt that we shall triumph.'

The officers withdrew, all but five of them.

'What do you want?' demanded Khamudi in surprise.

'We have just arrived from Anatolia,' replied a Syrian general, 'and we bring very bad news. That is why we, the surviving generals, preferred to speak with you in private.'

'Surviving? Surviving what?'

'We no longer control any territory at all in Anatolia. King Hattusil I formed an enormous Hittite army and defeated us. In addition, our bases in the north of Syria have been destroyed, and Aleppo has fallen. The few regiments that still exist are surrounded, and there will be no survivors.'

Khamudi was speechless for a long time. Then he said, 'You must have fought badly, General.'

'All our provinces rebelled, my lord – even the civilians took up arms in the end. The Hittite rebels were very effective fighters, and all they needed was a man like Hattusil to bring them together.'

'A defeated Hyksos is unworthy to obey me. All you incompetent generals shall be taught your place: the prison camp.'

## 55

Left to their own devices by the emperor, the soldiers, mercenaries and security guards in the Delta no longer received clear orders. With their means of communication cut, they were unable to offer coordinated resistance, and were perpetually harried by the rebels and by Ahmose's raiding-parties.

When the Egyptian army entered the eastern Delta, it encountered only weak opposition from a demoralized enemy. The towns of Lower Egypt were liberated one after another, in a climate of inexpressible celebration.

In the ancient city of Sais, where the goddess Neit had spoken the seven words of creation, a wrinkled old woman collapsed not far from Ahhotep, whom everyone was eager to approach. The queen immediately had her carried to a bedchamber in the palace, where She-Cat examined her.

With a glance, the Nubian woman gave the queen to understand that the poor old woman's body was worn out. Nevertheless, she opened her eyes and managed to speak; there was such pain in her voice that Ahhotep was almost overcome.

'The Hyksos took away my husband, my children and my grandchildren to torture them.'

'Where are they?' asked the queen gently.

'In a death-camp at Tjaru. Anyone who dared speak of it was deported as well. Save them, Majesty, if there is still time.'

'You have my word.'

At peace at last, the old woman died a gentle death.

The pharaoh was as deeply moved as his mother. 'A death-camp? What does that mean?'

'Apophis travelled further along the path of evil than any demon of the desert, and I fear we shall find unspeakable horrors. I am leaving for Tjaru at once.'

'But the area around it is still controlled by the Hyksos, Mother.

Khamudi is undoubtedly regrouping large forces in Syria and Canaan, we must prepare for another major battle.'

'You must prepare for it, Ahmose. I gave my word that I would act as quickly as possible.'

'Listen to me for once, I beg you. Do not take any risks. Egypt needs you too much – and your son does, too.'

The pharaoh and the queen embraced.

Ahhotep went on, 'Tjaru is at the very edge of the Hyksos area, and I shall take Moustache and the Afghan, and two chariot regiments. If we cannot take Tjaru ourselves, we will wait for you.'

'Hold out? Hold out? That's wonderful,' said Tjaru's commander furiously. 'Hold out with what and with whom? Khamudi seems to have forgotten that since the fall of Avaris our position is the furthest forward in the whole Hyksos empire.' He had grown used to living comfortably within the shelter of the fortress's walls, and had no wish to undergo the rigours of a siege.

Standing at the end of the trade route from Canaan, and within reach of the many canals that crossed the Delta in the direction of the Nile valley, Tjaru was both a trade-control post and a place where goods were stockpiled. It was built on the isthmus that had formed between Lake Ballah and Lake Menezaleh, at the centre of a landscape which alternated between desert and broad expanses of greenery.

'Let us not give up hope, sir,' urged his second-in-command. 'The emperor is rebuilding his army, and a counter-offensive is bound to come soon.'

'But in the meantime we are in the front line. Is there any news from the Delta?'

'Nothing good. I fear the pharaoh and Queen Ahhotep may have retaken all of it.'

'To be defeated by a woman – what shame for the Hyksos!' The commander stamped in rage, but only hurt his heel on the flagstones.

'The men are to be put on permanent alert,' he ordered. 'Archers on the ramparts, day and night.'

Nervously, the commander reviewed his men and inspected the reserves of weapons and food. He could hold out for several weeks, but what was the point of resisting if he was going to get no help? He was as distrustful of Khamudi as he had been blindly obedient to Apophis, because the new emperor was a dishonest money-maker and drugs-seller with not a scrap of military experience.

'The Egyptians are coming, Commander,' said his second-in-command in a quavering voice.

'Are there many of them?'

'Yes, sir. And they've got chariots – hundreds of chariots – and ladders on wheels.'

'Every man to his post.'

'A fine beast,' commented the Afghan as he gazed at the fortress of Tjaru. 'But compared to Avaris it's almost a toy.'

'Don't fool yourself,' said Moustache. 'That beast is sturdy and knows how to defend itself.'

Ahhotep asked, 'Have any Hyksos troops been seen in the area?'

'No, Majesty. It looks as though Khamudi has abandoned Tjaru to its own devices, in the hope that it will slow down our advance towards the north-east. The fortress probably has enough supplies to withstand a long siege.'

'We must free the prisoners as quickly as possible,' said Ahhotep.

'We could try an assault, but we would lose a lot of men,' said the Afghan. 'Before we do that, let us study the terrain in detail and identify the fortress's weak points.'

'I cannot wait so long,' said the queen.

The plan she outlined made Moustache and the Afghan extremely nervous. But how could they prevent the queen from carrying it out?

'What? Alone?' asked the commander in astonishment.

'Queen Ahhotep stands alone before the great gate of the citadel,' confirmed his assistant, 'and she wishes to speak with you.'

'The woman's mad! Why haven't the archers killed her?'

'A queen, alone and unarmed ... They didn't dare.'

'But she's our worst enemy!'

The men have lost their minds, thought the commander, and he rushed off to chain up this she-demon himself before she could put a spell on the whole garrison.

The great gate had been opened a little way, and Ahhotep was already inside the fortress. A fine gold diadem, a red gown, and eyes filled with intensity, honesty, perception ...

The commander was enchanted. 'Majesty, I—'

'Your only chance of survival is to surrender. Your emperor has abandoned you, and the army of liberation is coming. No fortress has held out against it, in the South or the North.'

The commander could arrest Ahhotep and deliver her up to Khamudi, who would make him a wealthy general. She was here, at his mercy. All he had to do was give the order. But the Queen of Freedom's eyes forced him to acknowledge the truth of what she had said.

'I have been told,' she went on, 'that there is a camp here, containing deportees.'

The commander looked down at his feet. 'The lady Aberia opened it, on Khamudi's orders. It is nothing to do with me.'

'What happens in this camp?'

'I don't know, Majesty. I am a soldier, not a prison guard.'

'The Hyksos soldiers shall become prisoners of war and will be employed in rebuilding Egypt,' decreed Ahhotep, 'but not the torturers. Gather together immediately all the torturers who have worked in the camp. If a single one is left free, I shall regard you as one of them.'

## 56

The queen could not even weep. After so many years of struggle, she had thought she knew everything about suffering, but what she found at Tjaru tore her heart into pieces.

She had managed to rescue only fifty deportees, including ten women and five children, some of whom would not survive their injuries and starvation. One little girl died in her arms. Everywhere on the ground lay corpses, half eaten by rats and birds of prey.

The only two prisoners who could still talk, spoke haltingly, often incoherently, about what Aberia and her henchmen had done to them.

How could human beings, even in the service of a terrifying monster, have behaved like that? Ahhotep would not hear any explanations; only the facts counted. To have forgiven the torturers would have been so terrible a crime against the gods that it would have led inevitably to a repetition of these same horrors. So the queen had them executed on the spot.

As soon as he arrived, Pharaoh Ahmose saw that Tjaru was a fine prize: horses, chariots, weapons, provisions. But he was horrified when he learnt how Ahhotep had taken it.

'Mother, you ought not—'

'The commander says there is another camp, larger than this one, at Sharuhen, a fortified city. That is where Khamudi has taken refuge.'

The war in Canaan had been going on for over two years, and Big-Feet was still holding on. It was no longer Egyptians from the Delta who were being thrown into the camp, but Hyksos soldiers guilty of desertion or of retreating in the face of the enemy. Tortured by Aberia, they died quickly.

At least Prisoner 1790 now had some rumours to be happy about. Step by step, and despite their ferocity in battle, the Egyptian army was finishing off the Syrian and Canaanite troops. The fortified town of Tell Hanor, whose governor enjoyed killing dogs for sport, had surrendered. Sharuhen was now isolated.

Big-Feet went over to a Phoenician youth with only one arm. 'Did you lose your arm in the war, youngster?'

'No. Aberia cut it off because I hid from the Egyptian chariots.'

'Are they still a long way away?'

'They'll be here soon. We can't hold them back any longer.'

Big-Feet breathed deeply, in a way he had not done for a very long time for fear of shattering his fragile body.

'My lord,' said the commander of Sharuhen, 'the war is lost. All our strongholds have been taken, and we have not a single regiment left. If you wish, Sharuhen can still resist for a little longer, but in my opinion it would be better to surrender.'

'A Hyksos dies with his weapons in his hands!' snapped Khamudi.

'As you command.'

The emperor withdrew to his apartments, where Aberia, who was hated by the garrison, had taken refuge. At night, she enjoyed satisfying Khamudi's whims.

'Arrange for our departure, Aberia.'

'Where are we going?'

'To Kerma. Prince Ata will give me a welcome worthy of my rank and he will place himself at my service.'

'You have no great fondness for black men, my lord.'

'They will be better warriors than this rabble of cowards, who have dared let themselves lose the war. The Egyptians will make the fatal mistake of believing that I have been defeated. We shall take a boat to the Libyan coast, then follow the desert tracks. Select a reliable crew, and load the boat with as much gold and drugs as you can.'

'When are we leaving?'

'At dawn, the day after tomorrow.'

'Once the boat is ready, I shall have one small formality left to undertake,' said Aberia greedily. 'I shall close the camp myself.'

Ordinarily, the torture ended at nightfall, just before the prisoners' miserable daily meal, so Big-Feet was astonished to see Aberia and her men enter the camp at dusk. What new torment had she invented now?

'Come here,' she ordered the one-armed Phoenician.

The prisoners looked at the torturer who ruled this hell.

'In a few hours,' she said 'the Egyptians will enter Sharuhen and this camp. We cannot, you will agree, leave it in such a untidy state, which would damage my reputation. You and your laziness are the cause of the untidiness, and I must eliminate that cause.'

She put her arm round the young soldier's neck and snapped it.

While the guards were busy restraining a Libyan who had tried to run away, Big-Feet dug up the branding-iron he had hidden.

With her foot, Aberia forced the Libyan's face into the mud and held it there until her victim had stopped breathing.

Very slowly, Prisoner 1790 went towards her. 'Am I to bury the bodies?'

The idea amused her. 'Dig me a large grave, and do it quickly.'

Aberia was taller than Big-Feet and could easily have killed him with a single blow of her fist. Neither she nor any of the guards would ever have imagined that submissive, broken Big-Feet was capable of rebelling. It was precisely that supposition that enabled him to do what he did.

'This is for my cows,' he said calmly, and he plunged the bronze branding-iron into Aberia's right eye. She roared with pain. Big-Feet struck again, thrusting his weapon into Aberia's mouth so savagely and so deeply that it pierced right through her neck.

Stunned for a moment, the guards raised their swords to kill Prisoner 1790. But the Hyksos prisoners, sensing that this was their one chance to escape, hurled themselves at the guards.

Before leaving the camp, Big-Feet picked up a sword and cut off Aberia's enormous hands. 'Now,' he murmured, 'I have won my war.'

Great Royal Wife Nefertari reread the message brought by Rascal to old Qaris, the steward: Sharuhen, the last pocket of Hyksos resistance, had been conquered.

'Ahhotep is victorious!' exclaimed the old man. He could not help thinking of the young girl who, more than forty years before, had been the only one to believe in the liberation of Egypt.

'I am taking you to the temple,' said Nefertari.

'Of course, Majesty, of course. But the chariots make me a little nervous.'

'Would you prefer a travelling-chair?'

'Majesty! I am only a steward and—'

'You are Thebes's memory, Qaris.'

The good news spread very quickly. Already people were busily preparing an immense celebration for the return of Queen Ahhotep and Pharaoh Ahmose.

High Priest Djehuty stood on the threshold of the temple. His face was grave, showing not a sign of joy. 'The door of the shrine of Amon is still closed, Majesty. This means that the war is not over and that we have not yet won the final victory.'

## 57

After informing King Hattusil I that Egypt had been freed from the Hyksos yoke and that he hoped to develop better relations with Anatolia, Pharaoh Ahmose sent troops to occupy Syria and Canaan, in order to discourage any would-be invaders. A special secretariat would govern the region, and the use of carrier-pigeons would ensure that the king was kept informed of all that happened there.

There was only one dark cloud: the disappearance of Emperor Khamudi, who, according to witnesses, had left Sharuhen by boat.

'He has no hope of finding allies in the north or in the Delta,' said Ahmose. 'Either he has left for the Mycenean islands, hoping to hide there until his death, or he is plotting ways of taking his revenge.'

'To raise the question is to answer it,' said Ahhotep. 'But there is one other possibility. He may have tried to reach Kerma, the last enemy we must confront. Thebes may be filled with celebration, but our work is not yet done.'

While Ahmose was joyfully reunited with his wife and son, Ahhotep consulted the latest reports from Nubia. It was true that Prince Ata was not advancing, but the civil war was continuing unabated. There could be no doubt that this running sore was the reason why Amon had put the Egyptians on their guard.

'Is there no news of Khamudi?' she asked Neshi.

'Nothing,' he replied. 'Perhaps he lost his way in the desert.'

'We should not assume as much. Hatred will have enabled him to find his way again.'

Neshi bowed, then changed the subject. 'Majesty, may we hope to be honoured with your presence at the banquet this evening?'

'I am tired, Neshi.'

Ahhotep spent the night at the Temple of Karnak, communing with the statue of Mut. She had received so much from the Wife of Amon, the mother of the living souls and the keeper of the divine fire, that she owed her the tale of those taxing years of war, at the end of which Ahmose at last wore the Double Crown.

To no one but Mut could Ahhotep confide that she longed for silence and solitude. 'Pharaoh no longer needs me,' she told her. 'He has become an excellent leader in his own right, and inspires respect and trust.'

An angry gleam appeared in the statue's stone eyes.

'If you grant me rest, O Mut, incline your head.'

The statue did not move.

The first contact between Ata, Prince of Kerma, and Khamudi, Emperor of the Hyksos, was icy.

'Your presence honours me, my lord, but I would have preferred to see you at the head of thousands of soldiers.'

'Do not worry, Ata, they exist. Everywhere my reputation holds firm. As for the Egyptians, they tremble at the very thought of speaking my name. As soon as we have reconquered Nubia and destroyed Elephantine, my supporters will rise up and join us. Of course, I shall march at the head of our army.'

'You are not a Nubian, my lord, and my warriors obey only their prince.'

Khamudi took the insult without flinching. 'What is your plan, Prince?'

'To recapture the villages the Egyptians stole from us, then retake Buhen. Otherwise it will be impossible to begin the conquest of southern Egypt.'

'You know nothing of fortresses, Ata. I do.'

'Then your counsel will be invaluable.'

'First we must clear a path to Buhen, and mere attacks by raiding-parties will not be enough for that.'

'What do you suggest, my lord?'

'Give me a map of the region and we shall talk again. For the moment, I wish to rest.'

A tall, strongly built steward showed Khamudi to spacious, comfortable rooms in the palace of Kerma. Khamudi's attention was caught by the look in the steward's eyes: a drugged look.

'What is your name, steward?' he asked.

'Tetian, my lord.'

'You smoke herbs, do you not?

The tall fellow nodded.

'I have brought something better – much better. If you want the finest drugs, listen to me. You have the look of a warrior, not a servant. Ata has ordered you to spy on me, hasn't he?'

'That is so, my lord.'

'Why did you accept such humiliating work?'

'We do not belong to the same tribe. One day, mine will take its revenge and govern Kerma.'

Khamudi smiled. 'Why wait, Tetian? Strike immediately, and we will fight the Egyptians together. You will kill many hundreds of them, and your people will be at your feet.'

'I shall kill many, many hundreds, and I, Tetian, shall be admired by everyone.'

'First, my friend, taste the promised marvels.'

For a whole night, Tetian took the best drugs Khamudi had brought. Next morning, he went to see Ata as arranged, to deliver his report.

'Have you won Khamudi's confidence?' asked Ata.

'Yes, my prince.'

'What are his real plans?'

'To take command of our army and invade Egypt. And also he has entrusted me with a mission.'

'What mission?'

'To kill you.'

Ata had no time to defend himself. The dagger thrown by Tetian pierced his heart. Kerma had a new prince.

In view of Amon's warning, Ahhotep took the Nubian affair very seriously. Some people thought a simple expeditionary force would be enough to put down the rebellion, but the queen disagreed, and had persuaded her son not to treat this last obstacle lightly.

So Ahmose was leaving for the Great South with almost the entire army of liberation. Moon, Emheb, Neshi, Moustache, the Afghan and all the other heroes of the war were in the party, as were Ahmes, son of Abana, and Young Laughter, both of them still charged with protecting the king. Only Long-Ears was to be left behind. The old donkey was at last enjoying a well-deserved retirement.

On the quayside, where the last of the party were embarking, the atmosphere was gloomy.

'So Queen Ahhotep isn't coming?' asked the Afghan.

'No, she needs rest,' replied Moustache, who was as downcast as his friend.

A young sailor summed up the general opinion: 'Without her, we may well be defeated. The Nubians are much more frightening warriors than the Hyksos. The queen would have known how to destroy their magic.'

'There are ten times more of us than of them,' pointed out the Afghan.

'There were ten times as many Hyksos, too,' said the sailor, 'but they weren't commanded by the Queen of Freedom.'

There was a sudden hubbub at the far end of the quay, accompanied by cries of joy.

Ahhotep appeared, carrying her cornelian staff, wearing her fine gold diadem, and dressed in a green gown woven for her by Nefertari. As soon as she was aboard the flagship, the fleet set off with all speed.

## 58

The first halt Ahhotep ordered took the Egyptian fleet by surprise. Why were they stopping at Aniba, which was a long way short of Buhen?

Only a hundred men, twenty of them quarrymen, disembarked, together with donkeys laden with water-skins and provisions. They set off for the diorite quarry that had been opened by Pharaoh Khafra, builder of one of the three pyramids on the plateau of Giza. Solemnly reopening the quarry, Ahhotep inaugurated a long-term programme: once Nubia had been pacified, it would be covered with temples in which the divine powers would come and dwell. By producing Ma'at,* the temples would lessen the risk of conflict.

When the fleet reached Buhen, the fortress's commander, Turi, welcomed Pharaoh's army with immense relief. Forgetting protocol, he spoke to the queen and her son without concealing his anxiety.

'You have arrived just in time, Your Majesties, for there have been dramatic events in Nubia, and the balance of power has changed. Khamudi has allied himself to the new Prince of Kerma, a man named Tetian, who murdered his predecessor and stirred up tribes which had been peaceable until then. Our defensive arrangements have been thrown into disarray. It seems that the warriors of Kerma have never been more ferocious – even when they are mortally wounded, they go on fighting. According to my scouts, they have just crossed the Second Cataract and are charging towards Buhen. My men and I are afraid. Fortunately, a sculptor has fashioned a work which preserves hope.'

He showed them a painted lintel on which were depicted Pharaoh Ahmose, wearing the Blue Crown of war, and Queen Ahhotep, wearing the vulture-shaped wig symbolic of Mut. Mother and son were worshipping Horus, the region's protector.

'To work,' ordered the king. 'We must prepare for a fierce battle.'

---

*In ancient Egyptian it was possible to 'say', 'do' or 'produce' Ma'at.

*

Khamudi congratulated himself on having brought sufficient drugs to turn the warriors of Kerma into veritable killing-machines. Tetian was a madman, but a notable leader of men, with no fear of danger. Handling the slingshot as ably as the bow or spear, he enjoyed only extremely savage battles in which he killed as many as possible of the enemy, most of them too paralysed with fear even to fight.

Urged on by Tetian and Khamudi, the army of Kerma had killed all the Egyptian troops and their Nubian allies, laid waste many villages housing supporters of Pharaoh, and seized trading-boats, which had then been converted into warships.

The next objective was Buhen. If he could force back that bolt, Khamudi would open wide the doorway to Egypt.

'My lord, a messenger wishes to speak with you,' his assistant told him.

'Where is he from?'

'He says he is from Buhen.'

Khamudi smiled. An Egyptian soldier ready to sacrifice his life to kill the Hyksos Emperor? What a clumsy trick!

'Bring him to me.'

The man was a young Nubian, and was clearly afraid.

'So, my lad, you wanted to kill me, did you?'

'No, my lord, I swear I did not. Someone gave me an urgent message to deliver to you. He promised that in exchange you would give me gold, a house and servants.'

'What is his name?'

'I don't know, my lord.'

'Show me this message.'

'Here it is.'

The moment the young Nubian slipped a hand into his kilt, Khamudi's assistant pinned him to the ground, fearing that he was about to draw a dagger. But the only thing he was hiding was a small Hyksos scarab covered with coded writing, whose key Khamudi knew.

So Apophis's spy was still alive! And what he suggested made Khamudi rejoice.

'Am I to have what was promised to me, my lord?' asked the messenger.

'Do you want to know what the writer of this message advises me to do?'

'Oh yes, my lord!'

'To keep the messenger's mouth shut, kill him.'

*

'The Nubians of Kerma have chosen to fight us head-on,' said Ahmose as he watched the enemy boats approaching, laden with warriors in red wigs, gold earrings and thick belts. 'Order our archers to take up their positions.'

An officer ran up. 'Commander Ahmes, son of Abana, is called to the rear.'

'Why?' asked Ahmes in surprise.

'Commander Moon wishes to consult him urgently.'

Ahmose gave his agreement, and Ahmes went off just as the fighting was about to begin.

Only the presence of the Queen of Freedom reassured the Egyptian soldiers, even though they outnumbered the enemy and were better armed, for the roars of the warriors of Kerma chilled their blood. Ahhotep gave the order to beat the drums to drown out the din. And when the first attackers, unaware of the danger, fell beneath the Egyptian arrows, everyone realized that they were only men.

Tetian had only one idea in his head, for it had been drummed into him a thousand times by Khamudi: he must smash Pharaoh Ahmose's skull with his club.

While the battle was unfolding, Tetian swam at top speed. He scaled the prow of the flagship as fast as if it were a palm-tree, determined to kill anyone who got in his way. In his drug-induced fever, he could already see the pharaoh dead, his face covered in blood. Once deprived of its leader, the enemy army would fall apart and Egypt would be defenceless.

His eyes filled with madness, Tetian found himself on the deck of the flagship. But the prow of the *Golden Falcon* was empty.

'Where are you, Pharaoh, where are you? Come and fight with Tetian, the Prince of Kerma!'

'Drop your weapon and surrender,' demanded Ahmes.

Roaring like a wild animal, Tetian charged at the archer, who shot him in the forehead. Despite the wound, the Nubian managed to club Ahmes down.

She-Cat's operation had been perfectly successful. Ahmes was now endowed with a little toe made from wood and painted the colour of flesh, which replaced the one crushed by Tetian's club.

The Prince of Kerma's body had been added to those of his defeated warriors, and thrown on to an immense bonfire. For his latest exploit, Ahmes had received yet another gold award for bravery, plus four servants and a priceless gift: a large arable field at Elkab, his native town, where he would spend his old age.

Not for one moment had he believed that Moon wished to consult him. It was just a trick to get him away from the pharaoh. So he had asked the king to go to the poop of the flagship, while he awaited the inevitable attack by a killer.

Summoned by the king. Moon confirmed emphatically that he had not asked to see Ahmes, but it was impossible to interrogate the officer who had brought the message, because he had been killed during the battle.

'Only one boat managed to escape,' said Moon, 'but Khamudi was aboard it.'

## 59

After Ahhotep had distributed food to the communities hit hardest by the demands of Ata and Tetian, the Egyptian army travelled up the Nile towards Kerma. It met no resistance.

When the fleet reached the rich grain-producing basin of which Kerma was the capital, the soldiers prepared to fight again. Given the Nubians' well-known bravery, there would have to be more fighting before Khamudi could be unearthed from his lair.

The flatness of the terrain would enable the chariot regiments commanded by the Afghan and Moustache to launch the first attack, as soon as the last boats from Kerma had been disabled. But those boats were moored at the quayside; there was not a single sailor aboard.

'Be careful,' advised Moon. 'It is probably a trap.'

An old man came forward, a staff in his hand, and raised his eyes towards the pharaoh and the queen, who were standing at the prow of the *Golden Falcon*.

'I am an envoy from the Council of Ancients,' he declared, 'and I hand you the city of Kerma. Please spare its people, who long for peace after so many years of tyranny. May Egypt govern us without enslaving us.'

Queen Ahhotep was the first to step ashore on to the soil of Kerma.

Emheb looked around suspiciously. Part of the army had disembarked, the archers remaining on full alert. But the old man had not lied, and the anxious inhabitants of Kerma were huddling in their homes, awaiting the pharaoh's decision.

'We shall grant your request,' announced Ahmose, 'on condition that Khamudi is delivered up to us.'

'When he fled here, he ordered us to take up arms and make all the people of Kerma join the fight, women and children included. We refused, and he insulted us. What right had that evil-hearted man to talk to us in that way?'

'Did he run away again?'

'No, he is still here.'

'Take us to him,' ordered Ahmose.

With its monumental gateways, bastions and its cross between a temple and a castle, Kerma looked very fine. The old man slowly climbed the staircase that led to the top of the palace.

The last emperor of the Hyksos would have no further opportunities to attack Egypt. Impaled on a long post, carefully sharpened by a grinning rubbish-collector, Khamudi was transfixed in a final cry of hatred.

The door of Amon's shrine had opened of its own accord.

Pharaoh Ahmose presented to the dawn sun the flaming sword with which he had vanquished the darkness, then he handed it to Queen Ahhotep who, as Wife of God, entered the shrine and laid it on an altar. It was Great Royal Wife Nefertari's responsibility to tend the altar flame so that the unity of the Two Lands would henceforth shelter Egypt from invasion.

'I worship you, O One of many manifestations,' chanted Ahhotep. 'Awake in peace. May your gaze light up the darkness and give us life.'

To Amon, Mut and Khonsu, the Sacred Three of Karnak, the pharaoh made the offering of Ma'at, the righteousness from which Ahhotep had never departed and thanks to which it would be possible to rebuild an Egypt worthy of many happy years.

'I have an important promise to keep,' Ahhotep reminded her son.

The whole court moved on to the place where the young Princess Ahhotep had met a surveyor, now long dead. He had permitted her to touch the Sceptre of Set for the first time without being struck by a thunderbolt, in the hope that the queen would one day give Egypt back her true borders.

The place was deserted, the land registry offices threatening to fall into ruin.

'Why have they not been restored?' Ahhotep asked Qaris.

'I ordered it several times, Majesty, but the workmen would not work here. They say the place is haunted.'

With the sceptre of power in her hand, Ahhotep took a few steps forwards. At once she had a strange sensation, as if the land refused to be conquered.

In one corner of the dilapidated buildings grew a tamarisk tree. Only two of its branches still had flowers on them. At its feet lay a heap of dried wood. Detecting a seat of negative energy, the queen went towards it. Hidden in the wood were torn, bloodstained clothing, tufts of hair and fragments of papyrus covered in magical incantations and words, including the name of Apophis.

Ahhotep placed the end of the sceptre on this cursed construction. A red light shot out of the eyes of the beast of Set, setting fire to the wood. Despite the efforts of his spy, Apophis was at last truly dead.

So the queen was able to survey the stretch of ground reserved for the land registry. Beginning the very next day, an official in charge of fields, an archive-keeper and specialist scribes would work there. The land of Egypt would once again attract the love of the gods.

Then the court moved on, to a vast ploughed field. Nefertari sprinkled powdered gold there, ensuring that seed sown throughout Egypt's provinces would be fertile.

The true order had at last been re-established. At its summit ruled the gods, the goddesses and the glorified spirits whom the king and queen represented on earth; it was their responsibility to appoint a tjaty, judges charged with applying the law of Ma'at, and officials responsible for each sector of the community of the living.

'We shall begin by rebuilding the temples,' said Ahmose. 'The curtain walls will be rebuilt, the sacred objects placed in the shrines, the statues erected in their proper places. The circulation of offerings will be restored and the rituals of the mysteries shall be celebrated once more.'

'Where is this boat taking us?' Ahhotep asked her son curiously.

'It should be you who closes our former secret base, Mother. Also, I have a surprise for you.'

Ahhotep remembered the days of anguish when her husband, Seqen, had gathered together the first soldiers of the army of liberation, to the north of Thebes. Today the barracks was deserted, the palace disused and the temple abandoned. In a few years, the sandstorms would have covered over the whole of this base, where hope had been born. Hundreds of men trained here had lost their lives on the fields of battle; others had suffered serious wounds and could never forget the terrible battles in which they had fought.

But Egypt was free. Future generations would forget the blood and the tears, for Pharaoh was rebuilding happiness.

With her sceptre, the queen closed the mouths of the temple and the palace. This time, the war really was over.

When she returned to the boat, she saw a broad-shouldered man standing on the quayside next to the king and Ahmes, son of Abana. Young Laughter was lying down peacefully.

'This is the Master of the Place of Truth, the craftsmen's village,' said Ahmose. 'He wished to present you with his Brotherhood's first great work, here in this very place where the clash of weapons has faded away.'

The Master laid his precious burden on the ground. It was covered with a white cloth, which he gently removed, revealing a perfectly cut cube of stone.

'We extracted the raw stone from a deep valley, lost in the mountains,' he explained. 'It is a lonely place, dominated by a pyramid-shaped peak in which there dwells a cobra-goddess who demands silence and punishes liars and people who say too much. With copper chisels and wooden mallets, we created this plinth, on which our future works shall rest, on condition that Your Majesty consents to give it life.'

The pharaoh handed his mother the white club, the Illuminator, with which he consecrated offerings. Ahhotep struck the stone, which instantly flamed like the Sword of Amon. Then the rays of light became concentrated inside the stone cube, which the Master covered with its cloth again.

'May this Stone of Light transform matter into spirit,' declared the queen, 'and may it be faithfully passed on from one Master to the next.'

## 60

Although he had murdered two pharaohs, the Hyksos spy had not succeeded in killing the third. But the army of liberation would have achieved its goal even if he had succeeded, for its true heart was Ahhotep.

At first he had been amused by her. He would never have believed her capable of such deeds, and he had wanted to know just how far she could go. At each new stage, he had been convinced that she would go no further. And yet, no matter what blows destiny struck her and what terrible sufferings she had to bear, she continued determinedly, as if nothing could make her turn aside from her path.

He admired her, and probably even more than that. She had benefited from the favour of the gods, with the death of Apophis and the eruption of Thera. Today the Hyksos empire had been annihilated and the Two Lands reunited.

But the spy had promised to carry out his mission. And he would keep his word.

This reborn Egypt was much more fragile than it thought. By killing Ahhotep, he would destroy its foundations. During the coming festivities, he would choose the best opportunity to prove to the people that the Queen of Freedom was not immortal. Deprived of the person who had given it back its life, Egypt would sink into chaos. And the Emperor of Darkness would finally have triumphed.

In the presence of Ahhotep, Pharaoh Ahmose celebrated the start of the twenty-second year of his reign by opening the famous quarries at Tura, where the most beautiful limestone in the land was extracted. Two stelae, carved and placed at the entrance to the galleries, commemorated the event.

Six humped oxen drew a wooden sledge, bearing the first block for the future Temple of Ptah at Memphis. The ox-herd who gently urged the animals along was none other than Big-Feet, who had recovered well. He had become the owner of a farm and an estate where many cows grazed, and he employed prisoners of war who had neither killed nor tortured Egyptians.

Everywhere people were restoring and building. Little by little Memphis, the white-walled city, was regaining its former splendour. Gold and silver were once more arriving from Asia and Nubia, copper and turquoise from Sinai; and from Afghanistan came lapis-lazuli, the symbol of the celestial vault and the primordial waters.

Who but the Afghan – like Moustache, he had been promoted to the rank of general in the reserve forces – could have been appointed overseer of imports?

'Still determined to go back home?' his friend asked him. 'Here you're rich and heaped with honours, the women run after you, the wine is excellent and the climate is wonderful.'

'I miss my mountains.'

'You know, Afghan, I can understand almost everything, but that . . .'

'Don't forget you have to climb a snow-covered slope to prove to me that you're a real man.'

'Instead of that, look at this lapis-lazuli and tell me if it's worthy of being taken to the temple.'

'It's magnificent.'

The ways of trade were picking up again. At Memphis and Thebes, the royal workshops had set to work once more, as had the land registry, weights and measures, waterways and census offices. The principle of the redistribution of wealth was once again applied under the aegis of Ma'at, the guarantor of stability and social cohesion.

The royal fleet sailed towards Abydos.

Despite his great age, Qaris wanted to be present at the ceremony during which the memory of Teti the Small would be honoured. Pampered by Emheb, who was soon to return to his good town of Edfu, and by Neshi, who had grown increasingly careworn since the tasks of government had accumulated on his shoulders, the old man could remember every episode in the war of liberation.

'What an incredible life we have lived!' he said to Emheb. 'Thanks to Ahhotep, we are nourished with hope and we have created a future where once it did not exist.'

Heray brought them some cool wine and cakes.

'Your responsibilities haven't made you lose any weight,' commented Neshi.

'Qaris and I did not have the good fortune to be in the front line, as you were. At Thebes we were often anxious, and anxiety makes you hungry. Look at the Afghan and Moustache: since they stopped cutting Hyksos into pieces, they have put on weight.'

'We have arrived,' Moon informed them.

'You look worried,' said Heray in surprise.

'The journey was not easy. The Nile sometimes has whims which demand extreme watchfulness. I did not even have time to taste that wine.'

'You will catch up,' predicted Emheb.

Nefertari was particularly anxious to venerate her husband's grandmother, whose popularity had never declined. Worshipped in Thebes, she must also be so at Abydos, in the sacred domain of Osiris.

So the king did 'what no king had done before', in the words of the ritual, for Teti the Small. A shrine and a small pyramid were built, surrounded by a garden, and a service of offerings was set up with a staff who would each day nourish the dead woman's *ka*, which was present among the living. Housed, fed, clothed and endowed with lands and animals, the priests would have no other care but to carry out their duties impeccably.

A large stele was raised depicting Ahmose, sometimes wearing the White Crown of Upper Egypt, sometimes the Double Crown, consecrating offerings before Teti the Small.

In the treasury set aside for her mother, Ahhotep laid the fine gold diadem she had so often worn, which had protected her from so many dangers.

For the spy, this ceremony was much too intimate an occasion. He would not strike until they were back at Thebes, so that Ahhotep's brutal death would have the greatest possible impact.

It looked very much as if Heray, Qaris and Neshi were plotting something.

'What are you talking about?' Ahhotep asked.

'Nothing important, Majesty,' replied Neshi.

'Is that true, Qaris?'

The old steward hesitated. 'In a way . . . Well, from a certain point of view . . .'

'You have never been able to lie to me,' said Ahhotep with a smile.

'Permit me to keep the secret, Majesty.'

'Is this plot restricted to the three of you, or do others also know of it?'

'All the most senior officials do,' confessed Heray, 'and the order comes from very, very high up.'

'In that case,' said the queen with amusement, 'it is pointless to question you any further.'

Ahhotep joined her son in the cabin of the flagship, whose door was guarded, as ever, by Ahmes and Young Laughter.

'Surely, Mother, the strict guarding of my person can be relaxed now?'

'The general staff believe that the officer who brought the false message from Moon, and who was killed during the battle, was the Hyksos spy. I disagree.'

'Even supposing that the spy is still alive, surely his sole aim is be forgotten?'

'He murdered your father and your brother. To leave those crimes unpunished would be to bow before the ghost of Apophis. So long as the criminal remains unidentified and still able to do harm, how can we truly know peace?'

# 61

Once again, the Temple of Amon at Karnak was alive with the sound of hammers and chisels. In accordance with his plan for extending and developing the temple, Ahmose was overseeing the installation of new offertory tables, which were copiously laden each morning. The king opened the eyes, mouths and ears of the divine statues with the worshipful staff. Then, using gold ewers and vases, the priests performed the rites with calm solemnity, carefully purifying the food so that its immaterial aspect would recharge the statues with positive energy.

For each member of the Sacred Three, a large cedar-wood boat had been made, covered with gold leaf. The boats would sail on the sacred lake and be borne in procession during festivals.

'I have taken two new decisions,' Ahmose told Ahhotep. 'The first is to build a new temple at Thebes to house the secret form of Amon and to worship his *ka*. The temple is to be called "Inventory-Maker",* in other words the one which reveals the Number, the true nature of the gods.

The second decision concerns you, Mother. It is time that you were honoured as you deserve to be.'

'So that is what the plot was all about!'

'I asked those close to us to keep the secret, it is true, for a great ceremony is being prepared.'

'But this is far, far more than I deserve.'

'No, Mother, it is not. Without you, Egypt would no longer exist. And it is not only your son who sets great store by this celebration. Pharaoh does, too.'

The great day had arrived.

In the open-air courtyard of the Temple of Karnak, all the notables of Thebes and even other Egyptian cities were present at Ahhotep's

*Ipet-sut, the Temple of Luxor.

Christian Jacq

triumph. Outside, a huge crowd was already gathering, eager to cheer the queen, who had never flinched in the face of adversity.

Ahhotep regretted having given in to Ahmose, for she did not seek honours. Like the many, many soldiers who had died for Egypt's freedom, she had only done her duty.

Ahhotep remembered that Teti the Small, in all circumstances, had been immaculately dressed and made-up. To do her honour, the queen therefore placed herself in the hands of two palace maids who handled the combs, alabaster detangling-needles and face-paint sticks with special skill. Using exceptionally fine cosmetics, they made the queen more alluring than a young beauty.

With as much respect as emotion, Qaris crowned Ahhotep with a gold diadem. On the front was a raised braid and the cartouche of Ahmose on a background of lapis-lazuli, flanked by two sphinxes. Round the queen's neck he put a broad collar made up of many rows of small gold pieces, some representing lions, antelopes, ibex and uraei, others geometrical figures such as spirals or discs. It was fastened by a clasp in the form of two falcon's heads.

The old steward added a pendant, made up of a gold chain and a gold and lapis-lazuli scarab which embodied the soul's perpetual regeneration and its never-ending metamorphoses in the celestial paradise. All that was left was for Qaris to adorn the queen's wrists with fine gold, cornelian and lapislazuli bracelets. Far from being simple objects with an aesthetic purpose, they depicted scenes confirming the pharaoh's sovereignty over Upper and Lower Egypt. The earth-god, Geb, enthroned him in the presence of Amon. And the vulture-goddess, Nekhbet, Holder of the Royal Title, recalled the queen's vital role.

Deeply impressed, the old steward stepped back. 'Forgive my forwardness, Majesty, but you are as beautiful as a goddess.'

'My damned back,' complained Moustache. 'It's still hurting! Couldn't you rub it for me, She-Cat?'

'The ceremony starts in less than an hour, I haven't finished dressing, and you've just put on your ceremonial robe. Do you really think we have time for that kind of thing?'

'It really hurts! If I can't stay standing up and be present at Ahhotep's triumph, I shan't ever recover.'

She-Cat sighed. 'Just a moment. I'll fetch you some pills to take the pain away.'

Moustache looked at himself in a mirror. He had never in all his life looked so splendid, what with the golden collars rewarding his exploits, his broad belt and his fine sandals.

'I forgot,' said She-Cat. 'I gave them to the Afghan for the pain in his neck. You two aren't very wonderful for war-heroes!'

The Afghan's house was next door to Moustache and She-Cat's. Moustache rushed round there.

'My master is in the bathing-room,' said the maid.

'Don't disturb him. I'll manage on my own.'

Moustache went into the room where his friend kept weapons, kilts and medicines. After rummaging through a linen chest in vain, he happened on a box containing little pots of ointment and a curious object which he examined in astonishment.

It was a scarab. Not an Egyptian scarab, a Hyksos one, bearing the name of Apophis. Clearly, it had often been used as a seal. On its back were signs written in a coded script.

'Are you looking for something?' asked the Afghan, who appeared in the doorway, still dripping water.

With fury in his eyes, Moustache brandished the scarab. 'What does this mean?'

'Do you really need an explanation?'

'Not you, Afghan. Not you! It's not possible!'

'Everyone has his own battles to fight, my friend. There is one thing you don't know: it was Egypt that ruined my family, by trading with a rival tribe. I swore to take revenge, and the oath of a man of the mountains cannot be retracted. The Hyksos gave me my chance. Apophis ordered me to infiltrate the rebels, and I succeeded beyond my greatest hopes. Two pharaohs to my credit, Seqen and Kamose, do you realize? What other spy could boast as much?'

'But you fought alongside me, you took insane risks, and you killed dozens of Hyksos!'

'That was unavoidable. I had to make sure that I was trusted totally and that no suspicion would ever attach to me. And I haven't finished yet.'

'You mean you're going to try to kill Ahmose?'

'Not him, Ahhotep. She is the one who destroyed the Hyksos Empire, and I'm going to destroy her at the height of her glory, so that Egypt will crumble again.'

'You've gone mad, Afghan!'

'On the contrary, I am at last completing the mission with which I was entrusted – and my dead emperor will be the true victor in this war. I have many regrets, my friend, for I have not stopped admiring Ahhotep. I believe that I even fell in love with her the moment I saw her, and that I still love her now. That is why I have spared her so long; too long. But I am a man of honour, like you, and I cannot return to my country until I have fulfilled all my obligations. I am sorry, but I shall have to kill Ahhotep – after I have killed you, my friend.'

Each as swift as the other, the two men snatched up their daggers. Each knew that he had never faced a more difficult opponent. Moving very slowly, eyes locked, they searched for an opening, each man certain that the first blow would be decisive.

Moustache struck first. His dagger only scratched the Afghan's arm, and the Afghan knocked Moustache off balance and threw him down on his back. As he fell, Moustache dropped his weapon. The traitor's blade was at his throat, and blood was already trickling from it.

'It's a pity,' said the Afghan, 'but you shouldn't have searched my things. I liked you and I've been happy fighting beside you.'

Suddenly, he stiffened and let out a muffled cry, as though trying to contain the terrible pain that was taking his life away. Even mortally wounded by the dagger She-Cat had just plunged into his back, the Afghan could have cut Moustache's throat. But he spared his brother in arms and, his eyes already staring into nothingness, collapsed on to his side.

'I forgot to tell you how many pills to take,' She-Cat explained to Moustache. 'Taking too many would have been dangerous.'

On an altar Pharaoh Ahmose laid a silver boat mounted on wheels not unlike those of the war-chariots. This evoked the power and ability to move of Ahhotep's protector, the moon-god.

Like the others, Moustache – whose wound was concealed by a bandage – could not take his eyes off Queen Ahhotep in all her finery and her great beauty. This sixty-year-old woman outshone all the elegant ladies of the court.

Having heard Moustache's story, Ahhotep was at last truly at peace. No further dangers threatened the pharaoh's life.

'Let us bow before the Queen of Freedom,' ordered Ahmose. 'We owe her our lives, and she has brought life back to this land, which we shall rebuild together.'

In the silence that reigned over the great courtyard at Karnak, love of all her fellow-countrymen filled Ahhotep's heart.

The pharaoh turned to his mother. 'Never, in all the long history of Egypt, has a queen received a military decoration. Majesty, you shall be the first – and, I hope, the last, since peace has succeeded war through the accomplishment of your name. May this symbol of the unceasing struggle you led against the powers of darkness bear witness to the worship of all your subjects.'

Ahmose decorated Ahhotep with a gold pendant, from which hung three beautifully stylised golden flies.

In the front row, Young Laughter, Long-Ears and Rascal all had the same thought: there was no insect as tenacious or as persistent as the fly. Ahhotep had transformed that idiosyncrasy into a warlike virtue in order to defeat the Hyksos.

'Supreme power ought to return to you, Mother,' whispered the king.

'No, Ahmose. It is your task to found a new dynasty, a new kingdom, and to make the Golden Age live again. As for me, I swore an oath: to withdraw into the temple as soon as our country had been liberated. And that happy day has arrived, my son.'

Radiant with joy, the queen walked towards the shrine where, as the Wife of God, she would henceforth dwell in company with Amon, in the secret realm of his Light.